Pulled
Spat
Knocked

The Amra Thetys Omnibus 1

MICHAEL McCLUNG

ISBN: 1546830103
ISBN-13: 978-1546830108

DEDICATION

Always and ever, for my crazy chickens.

CONTENTS

The Thief Who Pulled on Trouble's Braids

CHAPTER 1

When Corbin showed up banging on my door at noon one sweltering summer day, I can't say I was particularly happy to see him. It should come as no surprise that one in my profession tends to sleep during daylight hours. And since I tell no one where I live, I was more than a little annoyed to see him.

"Hello Amra," he said with that boyish smile that tended to get him past doors he wasn't supposed to get past. He stood nonchalantly at the top of the stairs, one hand on the splintered wooden railing. Well, what was left of the railing. Most of it had disintegrated before I moved in. He was looking ragged. Dark bags under his eyes, stubble that had gone beyond enticingly rough to slovenly. The yellow-green shadow of an old, ugly bruise peeked above his sweat-stained linen collar. His honey-colored locks were greasy and limp.

"Corbin. What the hells do you want?"

"To come in?" He kept smiling, but glanced over his shoulder.

"If you bring me trouble, I'll have your balls." But I cracked the door a bit wider, and he slipped past me into the entry hall.

"Take you boots off if you're going to stay, barbarian. You know how much that rug is worth?"

"Depends on who's buying, doesn't it?" He sat down on the bench in my tiny foyer and worked his laces loose. "Nice robe," he said with that silky voice of his, but I could tell his heart wasn't in it. I pulled my wrap tighter, and he chuckled.

"Don't worry, Amra. The knife sort of spoils the effect anyway."

I'd forgotten I was still holding a blade. I don't answer my door without one. Come to think of it, I don't do much of anything without one. I made it disappear and frowned at him.

"You can't stay here, and I'm not lending you any money."

He stretched, wiggled the toes of his stockinged feet. "Money I don't need. A place to stay, maybe, but your garret isn't what I had in mind." He looked at me, and I could tell he had something gnawing at him. This was no social call. "You have anything to drink? I'm parched."

"Yeah. Come into the parlor."

I'm not terribly feminine. I've a scarred face, a figure like a boy, and a mouth like a twenty-year sailor. In the circles that count, I'm recognized as good at what I do, and what I do is not traditionally a woman's profession. I was a few rungs up from pickpocket. Still, in the privacy of my own hovel I enjoy a few of the finer, more delicate things. Silks and velvets. Pastels. Glasswork. When Corbin walked into the parlor he gave a low whistle.

"Amra, this is positively decadent. I expected bare walls and second-hand furniture." He wandered around, peering at paintings, books, the tiny glass figurines I kept in a case.

"Shut up and sit down. You want wine?"

"Have anything else?"

"No."

"Then I'd die for some wine." He sprawled out on the huge Elamner cushion I used for seating. He stretched his legs and smiled. I shook my head, and went to dig around in my sorry excuse for a pantry. I came up with a couple of relatively clean glasses. When you live alone and don't entertain at all, ever, doing the dishes is a relatively low priority. I uncorked a palatable Fel-Radoth that was better than he deserved. But it was too early to punish myself with swill.

I poured a couple, handed him one and leaned against the wall. He took his and put it back in one gulp. I shuddered, snatched up the Fel-Radoth and corked it.

"What?" he said.

I put the bottle back in the pantry and came back out with a jug of Tambor's vile vintage. It was barely fit for cooking with. I dropped it in his lap. "Remind me never to give you anything worth drinking again."

He shrugged and began sipping straight from the jug.

"You don't want to borrow money. You don't want a place to stay. What *do* you want, Corbin?"

He sighed, reached into his voluminous shirt—I'd thought he'd looked a little lumpy—and brought out something smallish, wrapped in raw silk. About the size of my two fists put together. He held it out to me. "I need you to hold this for a while."

I didn't take it. "What is it?"

"Ill-gotten gains, what else? But I earned it, Amra, and a lot more besides. This is all I managed to come away with, though. For now."

I took it from his hands. Reluctantly. I was surprised at the weight. I knew without looking that it was gold. I unwrapped it, discovered I was right. It was a small statuette, one of the ugliest things I'd ever seen.

I held a bloated toad, two legs in the front and a tail in place of hoppers in the back. Pebbly skin. Two evil little emerald eyes, badly cut. It was devouring a tiny gold woman. She wasn't enjoying it. The artist must have been familiar with torment, though, because her small face was the very picture of it despite the crude overall rendering. All but her head and one arm were already in the belly of the beast. Her hand reached out in a disturbing parody of a wave. I don't think that was the effect the artist intended.

"Where did you get this ugly bastard?" I asked him.

"Doesn't matter. The place collapsed around my ears as I was leaving anyway." He leaned forward. "It was part of a commission, Amra. There were a dozen other pieces. I got them all, and it wasn't easy."

"Where are all the rest?" I asked.

He scowled. "The client double-crossed me. He's got the others, but he wants this one bad. Bad enough that I've got him by the balls." His face brightened and he chuckled. "I'm getting my original commission, plus a bad faith penalty. All told, it's three thousand gold marks, and I'll give you a hundred just to look after this thing for a few hours."

I frowned. I'd known Corbin for three years; he was a good thief and a good man. Thin as a blade, with one of those faces that sets girls blushing and whispering to each other behind cupped hands, and prompts women to cast long, speculative glances. He had the longest lashes I've ever seen on a man or a woman. He was an easy drunk, and so drank little, though he was free with rounds. He had fine-boned hands and honey-blond, wavy hair, and when I told him 'no' one night when his hands got too free, I didn't have to back it with a blade and I never had to tell him again. Maybe once or twice I wished I hadn't been so firm, but as regrets go, it was a mild, melancholy one. The 'what if' game isn't much fun to play.

That said, Corbin was not the smartest man I'd ever met. Not stupid; stupid thieves don't live long. But his cunning was situational. When it came to people, he seemed never to really understand what they were capable of. Or perhaps he just didn't want to believe what people were capable of was the rule rather than the exception.

"Amra? It's easy money."

"Too easy," I replied, taking a sip of wine.

"Gods above, woman! I thought you might want a little extra moil, and I need somebody I can trust. But if it's no—" He reached for the statuette, and I slapped his hand away.

"I didn't say no."

Corbin smiled, showing his remarkably straight, remarkably white teeth. It made me want to throw the ugly thing back in his face. But a hundred marks wasn't something I could walk away from. I should have, of course. Just as he should have cut his losses.

"One condition," I said. "Tell me who you're squeezing."

He didn't like that. The customer was supposed to remain anonymous. It's the closest thing to a rule there is in the business. He frowned.

"Oh, come on, Corbin. You said yourself they tried to screw you out of your fee."

"True. Why would you want to know, though?"

"Because if I'm going to stick my toe in the water, I want to know what's swimming around in it."

"And whether it has teeth. All right, fair enough. It's some Elamner by the name of Heirus. All I know is he's rich as sin. He's rented a villa down on the Jacos Road. It backs onto the cliffs. He's got hired blades all around him, and a hunchbacked little flunky named Bosch that does all the dirty work. Bosch is who I dealt with. I never met the Elamner himself."

I'd never heard either name. "Is this Bosch a local?"

"He's Lucernan, but not from the city I don't think. A Southerner by his accent."

"One more thing. Where did the statues come from?"

"I took them from an old, old temple in the Gol-Shen swamps. Like I said, the place doesn't exist anymore. I barely got out with all my limbs and digits. It wasn't the best time I've had." He took another swallow of Tambor's Best and corked the bottle.

"Any other questions?"

"For a hundred marks, I'll watch your back if you want. They tried to stiff you once; why wouldn't they try again?"

"The first time I got sloppy. I still can't figure out how they knew where I stashed the other pieces. I'd swear I wasn't tailed. I brought that one along to the meet, to show the goods. They were supposed to pay out then and I'd tell them where the statues were. When I got there nobody showed up and when I went back the rest of it was gone." He grinned that easy grin of his. "I guess I fouled up their plans a bit by bringing that one along instead of leaving it with the rest. It was just an impulse. A virtuous impulse that paid off. Like I said, I've got them by the balls this time."

I wasn't so sure of that.

"So now you're supposed to bring it and you won't. What's to stop them from trying to beat it out of you?"

"Don't worry about it. I've arranged a nice safe place to conduct business, and a long tour abroad after. For my health."

I grunted. I've been called a pessimist. And a suspicious bitch. And then there were those who weren't interested in compliments. But this wasn't my play, it was Corbin's. I'd back him to whatever extent he wanted me to. A hundred marks and friendship had earned that.

"Whatever you say, Corbin." I hefted the idol in my hand. "When will you come get this?"

He stood and stretched. "Midnight, or a little later."

"And if you don't show up?"

"If I'm not here by dawn, the statue's yours. Melt it down, though. Make sure there's no chance they get it on the open market." He went back to the hall and started lacing his boots.

"What about you?" I asked.

"What about me?"

"If you don't show up."

He shrugged. "Take care of Bone for me. You know where I live."

"I don't like dogs."

"No, you don't like being responsible for anyone but yourself. For the meltdown value of that thing, though, you can put up with Bone. Besides," he said, "he likes you. Oh, and Amra? This one is lovely." He held up a tiny blown-glass hummingbird he'd filched from my cabinet, stuck it in his pocket with an incorrigible smile. And with that he was out the door and clumping down the rickety steps.

I locked the door behind him. Nothing had better go wrong. Bone was a massive brute of a mongrel. Who slobbered. Copiously. I wasn't having that all over my house.

I took another look at the statuette. It was just as ghastly. The gold wasn't particularly pure, and the carving was crude. Ancient grime darkened the creases. There wasn't much polish to it, so I assumed it hadn't been handled very much or very often.

A half-dozen frog-aspected gods, godlings and demons came to mind, but none of them were less than four-legged, and only two were man eaters. I shrugged. It either belonged to some backwater cult nobody'd ever heard of, or it was something from before the Diaspora. If it was the first, it was worth nothing more than the meltdown value. If it was the latter, it could be worth much, much more. To the right person. Given Corbin's experience, I thought the latter was more likely, but I'd melt it down just the same if it came to that.

I put the ugly little statue in my hidey-hole and went back to sleep. I dreamed that I could hear its labored breathing there in the wall, punctuated by the shrieks of its meal. And when I woke just after sunset, it was with a miserable headache and a mouth that tasted like I'd been on a three-day drunk. What, you've never been on a three-day drunk? Take a big bite out of the next dead cat you see lying in the gutter; you'll get the idea.

CHAPTER 2

Feeling restless and out of sorts, and with a handful of hours before midnight, I washed and dressed and went out into the night. My headache was a nasty little needle spearing both temples.

Downstairs, I could hear the swirling and clacking of bone tiles from the gaming tables of the Korani Social Club. Endless rounds of push were played down there by gruff old men far from their island home. Once a month they had a dance, and the peculiar music of a three-piece hurdy-gurdy band moaned and shuddered and wheezed up through the floorboards. Otherwise they were good neighbors.

I walked a bit in lantern light through the Foreigner's Quarter, along streets that looked more dangerous than they really were. Lucernis had grown beyond all thought of being quartered long ago, but the name had stuck. I liked it there. It was close enough to the harbor to catch a breeze in summer, which in Lucernis was worth the rotting fish stench that came with it. And the Foreigner's Quarter was home to all stripes and classes.

I had the least trouble there of anywhere in Lucernis. But a woman walking alone still has to watch herself and her surroundings, and I regularly put up with a nominal amount of abuse and innuendo. I dress like a man and have the figure of a boy, and if someone gets close enough to see my face and figure out my gender, they're also close enough to see a few of my more prominent scars. It's usually enough. If not, I've spent a lot of time working up competence with knives.

I wandered down through the Night Market, past every imaginable type of hawker, and grabbed a meal from Atan. Atan is a burly Camlacher street vendor who smells of the charcoal stove he's habitually bent over, face red and shiny from the heat. He doesn't use any ingredients that are too foul or too rancid. He keeps the gristle quotient to a minimum. I've never gotten sick off it, though I'm never entirely certain what I'm eating.

"What kind of meat tonight, Atan?"

"Edible," he grunted, fanning the charcoal.

"Sounds like something my mother would have said."

His broad, craggy face grew even more morose than was usual. "Yes, compare me to a woman. Why not? I cook, I must not be a man." He shook his head.

I think all Camlachers must have a touch of the morose, as if they'd fallen from some great height and were bitter about having to slog down in the mud with the rest of humanity. Comes of being a defeated warrior race, I suppose. Grey-eyed Atan should have been handling a broadsword, not meat skewers

"Nothing wrong with being a woman," I told him. "But then I'm biased, I suppose."

"Yes. Next time I will wear skirts and use the powder for my face. Go away, you."

"Good night, Atan."

He waved me off. I ate abstractedly, walking down Mourndock Street, not really noticing the food. Slowly the headache faded.

I didn't really notice the old lady, either, until it became obvious she'd planted herself in my path. She was wearing a threadbare but clean dress, an embroidered bonnet perched on her iron-grey hair. She was even shorter than me. I tried to move around her, and she shifted to check my forward progress once again.

"My pardon," said the crone. "You seem troubled."

"Whatever you're selling," I replied, "I'm very much not in the market."

"You seem troubled," she said once more, and I noticed her piercing green eyes. Everything else about her shouted 'granny,' but those eyes said something different. Something closer to predator. I pulled back. "I'm fine, thanks."

"Oh no, I don't think so. I see a darkness in those pretty hazel eyes of yours. And I see shadows gathering behind you." Her hand shot out and grabbed my wrist.

"You'd best let go of me, Gran. I don't want to make a scene on the street. But I will."

She wasn't hearing me, wasn't really paying attention to me anymore. Those green eyes had suddenly turned a stormy grey. Bloodwitch. I was having a conversation on Mourndock Street with a bloodwitch. Bloody fantastic.

"I See blood, and gold," she said, her voice gone all hollow. "I Hear a mournful howl. Fire and Death are on your trail, girl, and behind them the Eightfold Bitch makes her way to your door. One of Her Blades has noticed you. But will it find your hand, or your heart? Unclear, uncertain...."

Twisting away from her, I broke contact. My hand itched to have a blade in it, but that would have been foolish. Bloodwitches are nasty enemies. "Kerf's balls, woman, what the hells are you talking about?"

She smiled, a little wanly. Her eyes were slowly losing their grey sheen.

"Oh you have a world of trouble coming down on you, girl. Come see Mother Crimson when it gets bad. You'll find me in Loathewater." She moved to pat my hand, but I retreated. One more cryptic look and she was gone in the pedestrian traffic.

"Kerf's crooked staff," I muttered. "Aren't fortune tellers supposed to tell you how lucky you are?" But I knew my own words for what they were – bravado. I needed a drink. Bloody bloodwitches. I'd rather deal with mages any day, if I had to deal with magic at all. At least mages generally didn't bother with cryptic nonsense.

Of all those with powers—mages, bloodwitches, even daemonists—it was bloodwitches that bothered me the most. Mages could alter reality to suit their will, and daemonists gained power from the inhabitants of the eleven hells. But mages were few and far between, and I'd heard more than once that whatever power they drew on to work their magic was weakening. Daemonists, for their part, were hunted down wherever they were found, and for good reason. They all eventually tried to open a hell gate, it seemed, and the world had enough problems without hordes of demons, daemons and daemonettes wandering around it at will. Fortunately opening hell gates took considerable time and effort, and the process was, apparently, not something you were likely to miss if you were anywhere near it.

Bloodwitches, though... They were strange, and their powers were disturbing.

Let's just say I disliked the idea of someone being able to turn all the blood in my veins to rust. Add to the fact that some of them could see the future, or make the dead speak, and you'll understand why they weren't often invited to parties.

I spent some time at Tambor's wine shop, at one of the outside tables, sipping vinegar from an earthenware cup and listening to gossip.

When Tambor's closed I was in a sour mood. I've never been good at waiting. I can do it, but I don't like it. I was worried about Corbin and more disturbed by what the bloodwitch had said than I cared to admit or think about. I had no idea who this Eightfold Bitch was or could possibly be, but I knew bloodwitches were the genuine article. I'd had the misfortune of seeing one at work in Kirabor, once. I'm really not squeamish, but seeing what she'd done to half a dozen men had left me tasting my dinner a second time.

With an effort, I filed it all away for later rumination. If there was trouble on the way, it would come whether I worried about it or not.

About an hour before midnight I made my way back home to wait for Corbin, feeling aimless and surly. And worried.

Midnight came and went. I read; my mother had taught me letters before she died, and Lucernis had some of the finest and most poorly guarded private libraries of any city I knew of. But then, who steals books? Besides me, I mean. If you can read, you're probably wealthy enough to buy your own.

It was one of those slightly racy romantic histories from the past century. Normally I'd have enjoyed it, but my mind wasn't on it. I kept reading the same passage over and over, and it kept slipping away from me. Finally I tossed the book aside in disgust and settled for pacing.

Three hours after midnight my creeping suspicion had filled out into an atavistic certainty that Corbin had come to a bad end. But all I could do was wait out the night.

CHAPTER 3

Cock crowed while the sky was still black. I was out the door. Whatever had happened was probably long over and nothing I could do about it, but I couldn't just sit there. A heavy dread was slowly churning my guts. There were only two places to go. I decided to start with Corbin's house, and check at his mistress's if he wasn't there.

It was a long walk to his hovel off Silk Street, through streets mostly deserted. Few hacks worked at that hour, and fewer were likely to take me where I wanted to go. There was a baker's boy stumbling late to work, white apron trailing unnoticed on the filthy cobbles; I didn't have to be a seer to know he had a beating in his near future. There was a lamplighter on low stilts, snuffing white-yellow flame with his telescoping pole. There was the odd wagon creaking and rumbling its way towards Traitor's Gate Market, down cobbled streets. But mostly it was just blank dark windows and shuttered doorways, until I turned onto Silk Street proper.

Silk Street is where the boys and girls, and men and women in Lucernis practice the oldest profession. At that hour, there were far fewer wares on display, and those that were tended to be coarse stuff, made increasingly coarser as grey dawn seeped into the sky. Those left working were ones who had a quota to meet, a figure that had to be reached to avoid a beating or an eviction or the symptoms of one withdrawal or another. The ones who were willing to accept rough trade. One trollop in a soiled satin ball gown, his blue chin bristling out from under streaked face powder, cast aspersions on my manhood when I ignored his proposition. I would have found that amusing on several levels in other circumstances.

I had avoided their fate when I was younger. Bellarius, where I had grown up and almost died countless times, was not kind to its poor. I'd made theft my profession, and discovered quickly I was good at it. But it made me uncomfortable to see how I might easily have ended up. It always did. I deepened my scowl and ignored the various opening ploys, trudging past with my hands in my pockets.

As always, when the tired come-ons had no effect, they turned to jeers and catcalls. Anything to elicit a response. They faded behind me as I turned off Silk Street on to the nameless, barely-more-than-an-alley where Corbin's hovel was. The entire street was lined with narrow wooden houses, two and three stories high. Some needed paint; most needed to be torn down. Almost all of them were built far too close together. A few of the houses were so close to each other you couldn't have walked between them sideways. It needed only a small fire and a stiff breeze to all go up.

As I got closer to Corbin's pit, I could hear howls, and a rough old voice screeching in anger.

"Shut it! Shut up, you mongrel! Shut it, Gorm take you!" The sound of something breakable being hurled against something less breakable. The howls went on and on, heart-breaking. I've heard wolves calling to each other across snow covered hills, mournful and lonely. This was nothing like that. This was grief made audible. Other dogs in the area had begun picking it up, and other voices, rough and querulous with interrupted sleep, yelled protest in several languages. A door slammed. I broke into a trot. For people like me, there are damned few coincidences. Expecting the worst helps to keep you from getting sucker-punched—and in my world, there are always fists waiting to hammer on the unwary.

I saw the old man first. The one who'd used Gorm's name in vain. Not that there's any other way to use it, Gorm being dead and all. The old man was a greasy grey smear of nightshirt and skinny, hairy legs with knobby knees. He was swinging something that would have been a truncheon if it was shorter, would have been a club if it was thicker. His back was to me; I couldn't see what he was beating. Then I came up on him and saw that it was Bone. The geezer was bringing his stick down on Bone's spade-shaped head, again and again. The dog kept howling, and refused to flinch. Behind Bone was something wet and lumpy.

The mind takes in images in little snatches, and sometimes they make no sense at first. It looked like the dog was guarding a pile of garbage. I saw the red, and knew it for blood, and knew from the quantity of it on the cobbles that someone had died badly. But these little pieces of knowledge didn't fit together right away. There was just the gut anger at an old man beating a dog.

I plucked the stick from his hand on a back swing and rolled it around across his windpipe. He squawked and gagged and clawed at the stick. I pulled him back a few steps, turned him around and planted a boot in his scrawny backside, letting the stick go with one hand. He sprawled to the cobbles, hacking. I guessed he'd stay down for a bit, so I went to check out the dog.

With his skull-thumping at least suspended, Bone had turned his attention to the bloody lump. He was nuzzling what I recognized as a hand. When it flopped back down to the street, I saw that the last three fingers were missing. Cut off cleanly, at the last joint. Of their own accord, my eyes travelled to the corpse's face.

It was Corbin. He lay huddled at an unnatural angle, maybe a half-dozen steps from his own doorstep. Bone started up that soul-splitting howl again. Shutters were opened here and there. Cautious heads popped out, saw blood, disappeared again as if by magic. I felt a numbness take hold. I turned back to the old man.

"You see a body in the street, and all you can think to do is beat the dog that disturbed your sleep?" I squeezed the stick so hard the tendons in my hand began to creak in protest. He gabbled something unintelligible and began to scramble away from me on his backside, looking like something between a lizard and a crab. His yellowed eyes were wide. Like all bullies, he was a coward at heart. I was surprised he'd worked up the nerve to beat Bone. The mutt was eighty pounds of brindle-covered muscle, with a face that was fashioned for malign animal intent.

I let him scuttle away into his ramshackle house across the street, and I let Bone keep howling. There was nothing to be done about either. As for Corbin, I didn't cry for him. Bone was doing enough of that for the both of us. I squatted down next to him, realized I was still holding the old man's courage stick. I threw it at his front door.

I figured I had at least a few minutes, and probably much longer, before what passed for the law in Lucernis made an appearance.

CHAPTER 4

Somebody gets cut up at night in Lucernis, maybe the corpse disappears before dawn, before awkward questions start getting asked. Nobody sees anything. Nobody wants to get involved. Not in a neighborhood like Corbin's. Not usually, anyway.

I took a good look at what they'd done to him. Maybe I had an idea I would like to reproduce it in reasonably accurate detail. Maybe I just wanted to know what I was up against. I don't know. But when I moved to look over the damage, Bone stood between me and Corbin.

"Too late now. Where were you when it happened?" I realized that was actually a good question. I put my hand out to him, murmured soothing nonsense. He sniffed. I suppose he recognized me, because a little of that murderous look went out of his eyes. But he wasn't letting me manhandle what was left of his master. I settled for gently rolling Corbin over on his back. Which earned me a rumbling growl.

The damage was extensive. Somebody had worked him over with a knife. It looked as if maybe some of it was controlled, precise. Like his missing fingers. The rest just looked like Corbin had tangled with somebody in a vicious barroom brawl. Slashes on his arms, his face. Rents in his shirt suggested he'd been stabbed maybe half a dozen times, two or three of which, depending on how deep they went, could have been immediate life-enders. I'd know more if I could undress him, but I didn't really need to know any more, and it wasn't worth struggling with the damn dog over. Maybe he was the wiser. It was done, and maybe all that was left was to mourn.

I stepped back from the body and looked around. The sky was perceptibly lightening. No crowd yet. They'd show up after the law did. I walked over to Corbin's house.

The flimsy door gaped. It had been busted open from the inside; that much I could tell. The lock was engaged; the frame had given way first. I supposed an eighty pound dog could eventually have battered his way through, given sufficient motive. I glanced inside. Heavy furniture, a little dust. I hesitated. Whatever had happened, it hadn't happened in there. With the neighbors peering out behind curtains, I decided to leave it for the constables.

I ended up wishing I hadn't. The constables came around the corner as I was walking back to Bone. They knew where they were going, and they knew what to expect. Somebody had probably sent their kid down to the local watch station.

It was a pair. A fat, balding one and a young one so tall he looked stretched. Neither wore the entire uniform; Baldy had forgot or forgone his tabard, and Too-tall had substituted his deep blue woolen trousers for a paler, cooler, more wrinkled pair of linens.

Too-tall glanced at me, at the dog, at Corbin. He sighed. Baldy said, with a voice like gravel, "Can you shut that mutt up?"

"No."

He whipped out his cosh and laid it across Bone's head with a speed that belied all his fat. Bone went down in mid-howl. I took a step forward, fists tightening. I caught myself. Baldy pretended not to notice. He slipped the billy back through the leather thong at his belt and said "So what happened here?"

"I don't know. I was passing by. I heard the howling. I saw a man beating on something, so I came up behind him and took his stick away. Then I saw the body. I stayed around until you showed up."

"Just a concerned citizen, eh?"

"That's right."

"You know the deceased?"

"No." While Baldy questioned me, Too-tall was going over Corbin's corpse. Checking pockets, checking wounds. I watched him from the corner of my eye.

"Let me see your hands."

I held them out, palms down. He took a good look at my nails. No blood. He swirled a fat finger; turn them over. I obliged. No blood in the creases. Baldy looked at me, clearly not believing a word I said. He probably would have worn the same face if I'd mentioned that water was wet.

"Any weapons?"

"Yes."

He put his hand out, and I gave him two of my more obvious knives. He gave me the eye that he probably used on husbands that beat their wives, kids that cut purses, day-laborers that thumped their bosses and made off with the strongbox. The one that said he knew I was holding out on him. I kept his gaze. Finally he shrugged. "Why don't you go stand over there by the wall." It wasn't a suggestion. I went. He put my knives in his belt and turned to his partner.

"Arwin? Anything?"

"Well, he's dead, sure as shit. Somebody carved him up like a midwinter roast."

"Better let's move him out of the street."

They hauled Corbin over to the edge of the street, then Too-tall—Arwin—went back and dragged Bone over next to him. They had a muttered conversation, then Arwin went inside Corbin's house, and Baldy started knocking on doors, questioning neighbors. The geezer came out and started pointing his finger at me. He got in Baldy's face. Baldy took it for a while, then jabbed one fat finger right into the old man's sternum so hard he stumbled back, face ashen. Baldy said something, and the geezer retreated back inside his hovel, but I could see him twitch aside dusty curtains every so often.

I could have slipped off, easily enough. I think Baldy half-expected me to. I don't think he would have cared, especially. It was just another dirty little murder in a bad part of town. He didn't pin me for it. He was just suspicious on general principles. If it hadn't been for the damned dog, I would have taken off. But I could see his barrel chest rising and falling. And Corbin had paid me to keep it that way.

Then Arwin came out of Corbin's hovel, and by the look on his face I could tell things had changed somehow. He called his partner—Jarvis, apparently—and when Jarvis lumbered over, showed him something small enough to fit in one closed hand.

I heard Jarvis mutter "Isin's creamy tits," and then "better get the inspector." And I knew things were about to get much more complicated.

Jarvis made it plain that he now cared very much whether I disappeared, so I settled up against a garden wall that had been whitewashed sometime back in the reign of Orvo VII. Bone started to stir, and when Jarvis looked like he was going to beat him down again, I volunteered to take care of the dog. He shrugged. I hauled Bone up in both arms and carried him over to my spot, and kept a careful hand on his thick leather collar. Old boy was dazed. He kept licking his chops, and he'd developed a tremble. It wasn't that hard to keep him down.

We waited maybe half an hour. The sun rose higher, and the heat climbed. There was no shade. Arwin had gone off at a trot. Jarvis continued the door-to-door. A couple of night watch I could handle. An inspector would be much trickier. I was reasonably certain there weren't any little posters tacked to a wall in some constable's office featuring my face, but I didn't relish someone with brains and authority knowing what I looked like. Sometime down the road, one and one might be added to make two. But it was too late to do anything about it now. And I wanted to know what they'd found in Corbin's house.

The hansom pulled up about eight o'clock. There were no official seals on the doors. Arwin jumped out, folded down the two steps, and then a slight, middle-aged man stepped down. His hair was iron grey, cropped short and brushed forward over his long skull. He had a vaguely horsy face; prominent front teeth that his lips didn't quite cover. His eyes were mild and blue in a face that was very dark for a Lucernan. He was dressed soberly, in deep maroon velvets that were too heavy for the season. They were immaculate, but a bit threadbare. I could see where his white hose had been carefully darned. His shoes were black and polished, well-made but worn. The buckles were plain silver. He wore no jewellery.

His only concession to the climbing heat was a stiff collar undone. He glanced at me, and I knew he'd just filed away my face in the library of his mind, for future reference. He spent a minute or so with the body, then went inside Corbin's house. Jarvis followed him in, leaving Arwin outside.

They spent quite a while in there. By that time a crowd had begun to gather. Jarvis came out and spread a blanket over the body, then went back inside. Three more constables showed up, and Jarvis poked his head out to tell Arwin to go home and get some sleep. Arwin shrugged. He didn't leave.

Finally one of the new constables stepped out, looked at me, crooked a finger. I dragged Bone along with me, heavy and uncooperative and dazed.

They'd done a thorough go-through. Not that there was much there to begin with. I am familiar with the careful search, having done it myself many times. It's nothing terribly destructive. Furniture shifted to spots no one would consciously place it. Rugs rolled up and put out of the way. Wall hangings taken down. Much like someone was preparing to move house. But of course the purpose is to thump the walls, listening for hidden cavities, and check out all the undersides of tables and chairs and desks, the backs of mirrors and paintings, the mortar between stones, the joins between boards. I didn't give them good odds on finding Corbin's hidey-hole, wherever it was. He'd been too much of a professional.

The inspector was sitting at Corbin's kitchen table, going over some papers. He glanced up, took in me and Bone.

"Constable, see if you can find some water for that dog, would you?" He went back to reading.

Jarvis made a face. And did what he was told.

The inspector pointed to a chair, and I sat, still keeping hold of Bone's collar. Jarvis found a bowl and, after a second, an earthenware jug that sploshed. He put both down on the table in front of me, a little harder than was necessary. I sniffed. It was water.

"Thank you, constable." And after a second, "I'll call you if I need you." I poured while Jarvis trudged out of the kitchen. Bone wasn't interested. He sort of folded up at my feet, panting, eyes glazed.

The inspector finished the page he was reading and placed it face-down on the table. I doubt he believed I could read, but he'd noticed me glancing at the paper. Careful bastard. All I could tell from my momentary, upside-down vantage was that it was at least similar to Corbin's handwriting, and that it looked like a letter.

"My name is Kluge. Why don't we start with a few simple questions. What is your name?" He wasn't taking notes. I got the impression he didn't need to.

"Marfa Valence." There were probably ten thousand Valences in Lucernis, and a goodly portion were likely named Marfa.

"Occupation?"

"None."

"Place of residence?"

I gave him an address to one of the bolt-holes I kept the rent current on. Which of course was about to change.

"What was your relationship with the deceased?"

"No relationship."

He just kept looking at me with those mild blue eyes. I could see that his pupils were ringed with a thin band of azure. Pretty. He spoke first.

"I'm going to tell you a few things, Marfa, and then we're going to start again." He stuck out his thumb. "Judging by the wounds on the body, we are looking at two separate attacks. Three fingers were removed some hours before the fatal wounds were inflicted. That suggests torture, and I can think of too many scenarios that might fit to make this some random street slaying. If I had to guess, they tortured him, and then they let him run for a while. All the way to his house, within sight of safety. Then they finished him off, messily."

"Why would anybody do that?"

"Who knows why? Maybe for the sport of it." He sighed. I started to say something and he said in a quiet tone, "I'm not finished yet."

He held up an index finger. "The man out in the street is Corbin Hardin, known to some by the rather unfortunate moniker 'Night-Wind'; a thief with a penchant for stealing rare art of all types."

Middle finger. "Corbin Hardin was also known as Corbin Hardin det Thracen-Courune, second son of Count Orlin det Thracen-Courune. Father and son have been estranged for some half-dozen years."

He reached into a pocket and set a heavy gold signet ring down on the scarred table, one with a noble coat of arms on its flat, bevelled-edge top. I didn't try to hide the flicker of surprise that crossed my face.

Ring finger. "Corbin Hardin was a source of deep shame and embarrassment to his family while alive. But now that he's dead, that is most definitely about to change. I guarantee you, Marfa, the father will want blood. Gallons of it. And he'll get it."

Little finger. "I'm the poor sod who caught all of this in his lap, which is what I deserve, I suppose, for coming into work early. Your cooperation in this matter will ensure that any involvement you may have had will remain confidential. And you are involved, somehow. I don't think you did it. Tell me what you know, and I'll do my best to convince Count Orlin's people that you were just an innocent passer-by."

He smiled wearily. "Now, let's start again. Your name is Marfa, you've no occupation, you live at Borlick's rooming house on East Southcross. Now tell me again what your relationship was with the deceased?"

~ ~ ~

He was good at what he did. I didn't try to get too tricky. I gave him an abbreviated version of the truth. Corbin had stopped by, told me he had business that might get ugly. Told me he'd been away in Gol-Shen on a commission. That the customer had tried to stiff him. Asked me to look after his dog if he hadn't turned up by dawn. No, I didn't know what the commission was. No, I didn't know who the customer was, where they were meeting, why anyone might want to kill him.

I tried very hard to make him think I was telling him the whole truth, by telling him part of it in great detail. I described the shape Corbin was in when he came to see me. I told him what we drank, tried to remember word for word some of the things he'd said. I did my best to seem both reluctant to be telling the law anything, and eager that once I'd said my piece, I'd be forgotten. And of course I didn't say anything that might implicate me in anything. I gave the slight impression that Corbin and I had a now and again relationship of an intimate nature.

I kept the statuette out of it, and any mention of the Elamner Heirus and his flunky Bosch. I wanted them for myself. If the constabulary went barging in, the bastard would disappear if he hadn't already. And so would the other statuettes. I didn't think he was going anywhere, though. Not without the toad. Not if he was willing to kill for it.

Maybe Kluge thought I was holding out, maybe not. His face was unreadable. He presented an air of weary competence, an honest man doing his best in a job that didn't pay enough. He was going to do a kindness to someone caught on the periphery of something ugly.

Right.

I had no doubt he'd toss me straight into Havelock prison if he thought it would get him farther along. A dirty little street knifing had turned into the death of a noble, albeit a disgraced one, and people with enough clout to bury Kluge in an unmarked grave—literally—were going to be second guessing his every move soon enough. He was going to cast me back, just to see where I might lead him. I was going to have to look over my shoulder every damn where I went.

When he finally waved me away with the admonishment to make sure I was available for further questioning, he'd managed to give me sweaty palms. He got up and walked me to the door, hand politely at my back. When he stuck out a hand to shake, I took it.

As soon as his hand touched mine, the little hairs on the back of my neck stood up and a chill ran down my spine. I walked outside, pretending I hadn't noticed a thing. I swore silently.

The son of a bitch had just used magic on me. Odds were he didn't need to detail men to tail me. He'd know exactly where I was, wherever I went. I hoped that was all he'd done. I tried not to think about all the nasty little things it was possible to do with just a handshake.

Corbin's body had been removed while I was inside, and the blood mostly washed away. The smell still lingered, though, and Bone set up a half-hearted howl. I collected my knives from Jarvis, who no doubt was hoping I'd forget them. Fat chance of that. They were perfectly weighted for me, and had cost me dear.

The damned dog didn't stop his howling until we were blocks away. I dragged him along by his collar. I was going to have to get some rope. He was giving me another headache. "Kerf's withered testicles," I spat, shocking a sweet faced granny passing by.

Heirus the Elamner was going to have to wait. Hells, I couldn't even risk going back home until I'd done something about Kluge's leave-taking present. It had become necessary to get some magic of my own.

I set off for the charnel grounds. It was time to see Holgren.

CHAPTER 5

Holgren Angrado lived way the hells and gone on the other side of the River Ose, on the edge of the charnel grounds. And of course I had to walk it. No hack was going to pick me up while I was dragging eighty pounds of scarred, slobbering dog along. It was a two hour walk from Silk Street up to Daughter's Bridge, on what had to be the hottest day of the year. By the time we got there the rest of the morning had fled, and my temper was vile. At least Bone had stopped howling.

Lucernans are much like anyone else, except when it comes to death. I was born in Bellarius, myself, so I don't really understand their odd fixation with forms and observances and their peculiar ideas about the afterlife, but it seems to work for them.

There is only one true graveyard in Lucernis: the City of the Dead. It's a huge necropolis that butts up against the south bank of the Ose. Its gargantuan hexagonal wall is ten man-heights of alabaster stretching on and on. People visit, send letters to the dearly departed, have midsummer feasts there. Like any city, it has its rich districts and its poor. And like any city, if you don't pay your rent, you get the boot. Thus, the charnel grounds.

Those whose families would not or could not pay the annual mortuary tax were disinterred, and their bodies dumped with a distinct lack of ceremony in the city's charnel grounds. Which, I understand, is a bit like being taken from a civilized limbo and being cast into one of the less pleasant pits in the eleven hells. I could almost believe it, given the smell. Myself, I think dead is dead, and whatever happens to your body makes no nevermind, but like I said, I'm not from here.

Holgren was the only mage I knew well enough not to run screaming from. Why he chose to live next door to a field full of bodies in various states of rot I'll never understand. But I never asked him. I was afraid he might tell me.

I dragged Bone along dusty roads and past the occasional shack that was all there was of Lucernis northwest of the Ose. Holgren's house was low and long and dark, roofed in grey slate. It looked like it was poised to tumble in on itself. I made my way to the front door of his hovel, past the broken statuary and dead grass that made up his front garden, and banged the ancient brass knocker. And waited. And waited.

I was about to knock again when the door creaked open, revealing only gloom. There was no one on the other side.

"Holgren?" I called. "It's Amra." No answer. I shrugged, and Bone and I crossed the threshold.

My eyes adjusted. It was like any other sitting room, I suppose. More or less. A couch, dusty and torn. Delicate little tables covered with yellowing lace doilies. A porcelain teapot decorated with buttercups and morning glories. Dried flowers in a chipped vase. Threadbare rug. Less usual were the skulls and anatomical charts, the framed map of the eleven hells, the withered, claw-like Glory Hand casting feeble blue light from under a bell jar, the jars of preserved things that had no business twitching and sloshing in the corner of my eye. And the room was far cooler than it had any right to be.

I liked Holgren. I even trusted him, to a degree. But he was still a mage, and being around a mage was like being around a 'tame' lion. You could never fully let down your guard. They were just too powerful, and too unpredictable. Their motivations were too obscure. Ultimately, I think, the kind of power a mage dealt with on a daily basis pushed him, eventually, beyond mundane considerations such as right and wrong. He tended to think more along the lines of 'possible' and 'impossible', and the 'impossible' list was a lot shorter for a mage than it was for you or me.

Holgren had never been anything but polite and accommodating towards me. But there was always a first time. And considering how powerful he was, that first time would also almost certainly be the last time.

"Holgren?"

"Be with you in a moment," came a muffled reply from behind a door marked with sigils that writhed and twisted when I looked at them. I shuddered and took a seat on the couch. Bone put his rock-like skull in my lap. Almost instantly my pants were soaked in slobber. I sighed, and scratched behind his scored ears. There was a lump where Jarvis had bashed him, but other than that, he seemed fine.

A short time later the creepy door opened and Holgren sauntered into the parlor. He must have startled Bone, because the bruiser whipped around with a rolling, rumbling growl in his throat. Holgren stopped where he was, and his hawk-like eyes locked with Bone's. They stood like that for maybe half a dozen heartbeats, and then Bone shut up and dipped his head and his tail.

"You've acquired a loyal friend since we last met, Amra. Would you like some tea?"

"No thanks." I patted Bone. "Inherited, more like."

Holgren cocked an eyebrow. He was a tall, almost gangly man, with predatory eyes, a sharp nose, a generous mouth. His black hair was shoulder length and bound up in a ponytail. He was wearing black. He always wore black. Not much for fashion, this one.

"Listen," I said, "I might have brought some trouble to your door. I ran into a mage. He tagged me with some sort of spell."

Holgren pulled up a chair that had seen better centuries. Touched the teapot. The smell of chamomile suddenly wafted. He poured himself a cup.

"So tell me about it," he said.

~ ~ ~

I told him about Corbin, his commission, the favor he'd asked of me. I told him about Corbin's death and Inspector Kluge. He asked a few questions, but not many. He knew how to be circumspect, and didn't ask the questions that he knew I would be reluctant to answer.

Holgren lived on the same shadowy side of the law as me. He took commissions. That's how I'd met him. He'd subcontracted one of them to me, on the advice of Daruvner, our mutual fixer. He was a good mage, but I was a much better thief. Our skills actually complemented each other quite well, and we'd done three jobs together in quick succession. Then he'd stopped taking contracts. I found out later from Daruvner that Holgren Angrado worked only when he had to. He'd make a pile of coin, then go into semi-retirement until it ran out.

Holgren sat, legs crossed and hand to lips, digesting what I'd told him. He shook his head. "Corbin told you he'd set up the meet in a safe place. Any idea where?"

"Not really. Obviously someplace not as safe as he thought."

"He could have been betrayed."

I shrugged. Probably. There was just no telling.

"This Kluge, what did he look like?"

I described him. Holgren shook his head.

"I don't know him. I don't know what sort of power he wields. I might assume that, since he takes a civil servant's pay, he is not terribly talented, but I don't like to assume." He tapped his full lower lip with one long forefinger. He was staring at me, through me. Long enough that I started getting the creeps. "Well," he finally said, shaking himself. "Nothing for it but to see what we can see. Come sit here." He vacated the chair.

I took a deep breath, then shifted from the couch to the chair. He stood behind me, which made me more than a little nervous. He put his fine-boned hands on my shoulders. He smelled of lavender, and under that, something acrid. As though he'd been working with chemicals. He didn't smell bad, just strange. Bone looked on from where he was stretched out next to the couch, a thin rope of drool slowly stretching to the floor from his black lips. I felt a little laugh bubble up at that, but choked it down.

The hairs on the back of my neck stirred faintly. Holgren shifted his hands to the sides of my neck, then cool fingers touched corners of my jaw, then my temples. My skin tingled and I repressed a shudder. It's not that it was unpleasant. It wasn't. It's just that it was… intimate. More intimate than I was comfortable with. And the feel of his magic had a different quality to it than Kluge's. More confident, somehow. More knowledgeable. Self-assured. The difference between a grope and a caress. I found myself blushing, and was glad Holgren couldn't see my face.

"You can sense me," he remarked, a faint note of surprise in his voice. I nodded slightly, and the feel of whatever he was doing changed, somehow. Became more business-like. More formal. Almost remote. I found myself at once relieved and vaguely disappointed.

Finally he took his hands away. He sprawled out on the couch, and one hand dropped down. He rubbed between Bone's eyes with a casual knuckle, and the dog stretched out and presented his chest. Holgren scratched dutifully.

"Well?"

"Well, you were right. This Kluge marked you with a location spell. A basic working, really, but sometimes the basic ones are the most reliable. At some point during your conversation he must have collected something particular to you. Most likely a hair. Then he made physical contact with you, a simple handshake being quite sufficient."

I remembered his hand on my back, in all probability plucking a fallen hair. "That sneaky—and then?"

"And then he most probably winds that hair around something, perhaps a pin, and places the pin on a specially prepared map."

I frowned. "And then he watches the pin shift along the map as I go hither and yon."

"That's about the size of it."

"So what do I do?"

"Nothing. Right now that pin is rolling around like a sailor four hours into shore leave. He'll know you've gone to see a mage, of course, but he would have known that if I'd simply severed the connection. Better he wonder who you might know who could tie his spell in knots."

"What? Why? You're putting yourself in line for unnecessary scrutiny, aren't you?"

He smiled. "When you came here you assured a knock on my door from the inspector, I think. I'd rather he come wary and respectful. When mages meet, there is a tendency towards discovering who has the greater talent. Occupational hazard, I suppose. Sometimes making the discovery can be hard on the furniture. Now he knows that, whoever I am, I am most likely his master in the Art. It will help head off any possible unpleasantness."

"If you say so. Still, I'm sorry to have gotten you involved. I owe you."

He waved it away. "I am sorry about your friend. And interested in these statuettes, to tell you the truth. If you care to, you can come by again and I'll take a look at the one you have. If it is pre-Diaspora, I might be interested in purchasing it from you. I'd give you more than a hundred marks for it, and it will never see the open market."

"I'll think about it. I have a feeling it might be useful to me in the near future." As a lure, or a threat. "I'll stop by tomorrow if I can."

"What will you do next?"

"Get some sleep. Find out what there is to know about this Elamner that Corbin contracted with. Decide how best to approach him." How to get in, knife him, and get out with a whole hide.

"What about this one?"

"Bone? I don't know. I've got a lot to do, and looking after that slob will be a pain." I looked at the dog. He'd fallen asleep on his back under Holgren's scratching, scarred ears splayed out like little wings, tongue lolling.

"You could leave him here, for now. Until you make other arrangements. I could use the company. And he will make a nice pretence for your visit here when the inspector comes calling."

I glanced around at the various bits of bodies under glass. "You aren't in need of dog parts, are you?"

His expression was one of pained indignation.

"Hey, I was going to make you an offer. Cheap."

~ ~ ~

I managed to catch a hack just south of Daughter's Bridge. On the ride back I mulled over my options, tried to figure out what my next move was. Corbin's death had stirred up a hornet's nest.

Kluge and company would be scrambling to find someone to pin his death on, before Corbin's family came to town with blood on their mind. Heirus, I could safely assume, would still be looking for what he'd been willing to kill for. And of course some cold-eyed killers would be arriving in the next few days, come to collect their pound of flesh for Corbin's old man. From every perspective, all roads could at some point lead to me. It was too late for me to back out, even if I wanted to. I didn't want to.

There would be interesting days ahead.

CHAPTER 6

By the time I got home it was late afternoon. I was dead tired. Sleep beckoned. I checked my hidey-hole just to make sure the golden toad was still there. It hadn't hopped off. The heat was oppressive. I stripped down to my undershirt, grabbed a bottle of sweet white Gosland wine, and crawled into bed. I lay there sweating and thinking and sipping until sleep came.

Sometimes theft can be as simple and direct as a fist in an unsuspecting face, and sometimes it can be as complex as a military operation. And just like a bar-room brawl or a pitched battle, whatever plan you went in with, simple or complex, was bound to be stretched and twisted as events played out. But you'd better have some kind of plan, or you were going to get trounced. Or worse. I was planning a death, not a burglary, but in many ways that just made it easier. Taking a life was, in my experience, a damned sight less complicated than taking jewels from a hidden strongbox.

What I was facing was getting messier by the moment, however. I needed more information. I needed to act, rather than react. There was too much I just didn't know. Information had to be my first priority. Without it, I'd end up stumbling into a knife. Or a noose.

So I needed to case Heirus' villa. And I needed to brace Locquewood, Corbin's fixer. I needed to find out more about that damned toad, and I needed to throw the various dogs off their various scents and give myself some breathing room.

One last swig and I re-corked the bottle and blew out the candle.

~ ~ ~

I slept far later than I usually do, deep into the night. But it was a restless, broken sleep, between the heat and the bad dreams. In my dreams I saw Corbin hacked up there in the street, except he kept grinning at me, white teeth pinked with blood. And there was the whispering. Like he was trying to tell me things. Awful things. Terrible truths it was better not to know. Things that made my head pound and my chest constrict.

And so when an unfamiliar sound intruded, it woke me. Head throbbing, I cocked an ear to the dark. It came again; the stealthy creak of a shutter being slowly eased open. It came from the parlor.

Amateur. Should have brought some grease along, I thought, and slipped out of bed, knives in both hands. Every room in my house has easily accessible knives. I'd had a lover for a short time that found it off-putting. He went. The knives stayed.

It was near pitch black. The dark didn't bother me; I knew the layout of my own house very well and so the dark was more asset than liability. Sliding down the narrow hallway that connected my bedroom to the parlor, I kept low, presenting as small a silhouette as possible.

I caught him—it—as it was climbing through the window; a black outline against the faint glow from the moonlit street. A humanoid form; head, arms legs all in the expected places. But the head sported knobs and spikes in silhouette, and wicked looking barbs sprouted from the fingers, a dirty parody of brass knuckles.

Just seeing the outline of the thing made me want to kill it. Hate boiled out of my soul, an unreasoning, vicious hate tinged with disgust. I wanted to kill it. I had to kill it. I felt my lips pull back over my teeth, felt a snarl start way down in my lungs. I threw a knife. I aimed for the throat, but it shifted at the last instant, and the blade struck the meat of the thing's shoulder with a wet *thwock*. It hissed in pain and surprise, and toppled backward into the street. I rushed to the window, ready to cast again. It was too quick. I caught the barest glimpse of a mottled grey form loping down the alley. It was swallowed up by the dark an instant later, along with the unreasoning hate that had consumed me.

"Kerf's crooked staff," I breathed. And that was it. The whole thing, from waking to stabbing, had lasted less than a minute.

Now that it was over I began to tremble. I locked the shutter, went to the pantry and tossed down a large portion of the Fel Radoth that I'd banned Corbin from for gulping.

What in the eleven hells *was* the thing? I had no idea. What did it want? How had it found me? No idea. But I was certain it hadn't been some sort of mistake, no random break-in. I don't believe in chance. I believe in cause and effect.

As for the tide of hate that had washed over me, I had no explanation. But all of it was bound up together. Somehow. The fact that something could *compel* me to feel hate, or any emotion for that matter, made me feel a hot kind of hate toward whatever the cause was. Yes, I am aware of the irony.

The only cause I could think of was that damned golden toad.

~ ~ ~

I spent the rest of the night in a state of controlled panic, starting at every creak, every sound from the street. That thing had not been human, and it disturbed me more than I liked to admit that something could take control of my emotions.

I thought about how it could have tracked me. No way that thing had shadowed me all across the city, from Corbin's to Holgren's to my house. Not in that form, at least. But for all I knew it could be a shape changer. Still, I doubted I'd been tailed. Which brought to mind how Corbin had said he'd gotten careless himself, when he'd lost the other twelve statuettes. Something was going on, something I didn't understand. Maybe magical. Probably magical. I supposed it was possible that someone or something was looking for the statues with a different kind of sight. Hells, the creature could have sniffed the statue out for all I knew. In any case, I had to assume that the creature, presumably acting in Heirus' interests, had a way to find the statue wherever it was. Which made things more complicated than I liked.

When grey dawn crept through the shutters, I went down and looked over the alley the creature had disappeared down.

I found my knife halfway between streets. The blade was covered in a grey-green slime, and pitted with corrosion. I tapped it against a wall, and the tempered steel blade broke like chalk.

Shit. Good blades didn't come cheap.

~ ~ ~

My first stop of the day was Corbin's fixer. Locquewood had a small curio shop near the Dragon Gate. Most of his custom was from the manses along the Promenade, wealthy merchants and minor nobility who could afford the expensive baubles he sold. I would have preferred to brace him after I'd checked out the Elamner's villa, but with last night's visitor, I was feeling pressed for time. Things were starting to heat up.

I came in the back way, through the service entrance. Bollund, Locquewood's muscle, sat whittling in the back room among packing crates and scattered straw. He glanced up when I came in, then fixed his attention back on his carving. I think it was supposed to be a pheckla, but mostly it looked like a turd.

"Bollund! Still twice the woman I am, I see. I need to talk to your boss."

Bollund glanced up at me, fingered the smashed gristle of what presumably had once been his nose. He'd been a bare-knuckle fighter before becoming ensconced in Locquewood's back room.

"You don't see 'im. 'E sees you."

"Well he needs to see me. Now."

Bollund smirked. He was two heads taller and his bulk could make three of me. He wasn't impressed and he wasn't intimidated.

I pulled out the toad from my leather satchel, unwrapped its silk covering. The buttery glow of the gold drew his beady eye.

"He's got five minutes, then I'm taking this to Daruvner."

Bollund's jaw clenched. He shifted his bulk up from the slat-back chair that somehow supported him. Locquewood was a fixer, not a fence, but Bollund knew enough not to make decisions for his employer where money was involved. The toad would fit in tolerably with the kinds of things Locquewood stocked his shop with. A little older, a little uglier, a little less precious, by appearances.

"Stay 'ere. Don't touch nothing."

"Yes ma'am."

He glared at me, then disappeared though an inner doorway.

I had no interest in selling the thing, of course. Not yet, and not to Locquewood in any case. I just wanted to pump him for information. Whether I would get anything was doubtful; Locquewood's lips were tighter than a frog's arse, which was why he was trusted enough by untrustworthy sorts to be a fixer. But he might let something slip.

Locquewood appeared a few minutes later, a cadaverous dandy in pale yellow silk and bleached lace. He ran manicured fingers through thinning hair and licked his lips.

"Amra, you know the arrangement. You can't just show up—"

"I can do whatever I like when a man trusted to fix commissions gets one of my friends killed."

"What are you talking about?"

"Corbin. I'm talking about Corbin, Locquewood. The client you fixed him up with cut off a few of his more important fingers and then knifed him to death."

His pale face turned a delicate shade of green. "Why I never—that's—I don't know what you're talking about."

So Locquewood had been the fixer Corbin had used for this commission. I was fairly sure before, now I was certain of it.

"Save it. Corbin was a friend. He was killed because of this." I let him have a glimpse of the toad. If Heirus already knew I had it, I risked nothing. And Locquewood needed to know I wasn't just spouting off. "He died because of some damned statue, and because his fixer didn't check the client out well enough. That is, if you weren't in on it to begin with."

"Amra, I can assure you I, ah, am as circumspect as possible in all my business dealings. And I would never poison my own well, so to speak. I am sorry about Corbin's death. But I had nothing to do with it."

"Says you."

He got a little impatient. "What do you suspect me of? Having Corbin killed? Taking out a contract on him? Next you'll be accusing me of hiring Red Hand himself to do the deed."

"Who was the job for, Locquewood?"

"I'm sorry, I can't help you."

"Can't, or won't?"

"Both."

I could tell he wasn't going to give me anything more. That was fine. I'd planted the idea that I didn't yet know who Corbin's customer was and, hopefully, had set Locquewood on a collision course with Heirus the Elamner. Locquewood had more than two marks to rub together; I was willing to bet he would spend what it took to send a message, and keep his reputation as an honest fixer secure. How much good it would do, I didn't know. But I figured stirring up trouble would help keep eyes off me. It's easier to swim unnoticed in muddy water, so to speak. Not that I know how to swim.

I glared at him, mouth tight. He returned my gaze with a bland one of his own.

"If I find out you had anything to do with this," I hissed, "you'll regret it." And I stormed out of his back room, slamming the door.

When I walked away from his shop, it was with a spring in my step. It had been a good performance. Maybe not good enough for the Clarion Theatre, but good enough. I was certain Locquewood had bought it.

My next stop was one I enjoyed less.

CHAPTER 7

The May Queen's Dream was a red brick, three-story building on Third Wall Road, with red painted shutters and riotous flowers in every window box. It was as far from the whore's cribs on Silk Street as silk is from a sow's ear, but it was a whorehouse none the less.

A frock-coated butler offered to take my satchel. I declined, and stepped from the staid entry hall with its dark wood panelling into the lush, cool parlor.

It had been a long time since I'd been here. I'd forgotten Estra's uncanny decorating tastes. It was a huge room, but managed to convey a sense of intimacy. A creamy marble floor glowed under crystal chandeliers lit at all hours, and the walls were covered in red satin. Plush couches and chairs were arranged around the room in such a way as to create little pockets that invited conversation and intimacy. There were fine sculptures and fine paintings everywhere you looked. A bar ran the length of one wall, dark stained oak topped with pink granite. In one corner stood one of the new harpsichords, though no-one was playing it at the moment. And at the end, a grand, carpeted stairway led to the rooms above. The entire effect was somehow one of understated ostentation.

This was where Corbin had spent a fair amount of time. He came for the woman I was here to see, but also, I think, for the atmosphere. Perhaps it reminded him of the beauty he must have grown up with. Perhaps Estra had, too. They fought like rats in a bag, to hear him tell it, but he always went back to her. Their relationship wasn't placid, but it was… constant.

Only three girls lounged in the parlor. It wasn't even noon yet. A black haired, green eyed-beauty stood and glided her way towards me. Her pale skin was flawless. Her crimson lips were flawless. The cleavage that pushed out over the top of her whalebone corset was ample, and flawless. I struggled not to hate her.

"Good morning," she said. "Welcome to the Dream. Can I offer you some refreshment?"

"I'm here to see Estra. I have some news for her."

"Madame usually breaks her fast now. Shall I say who is calling?"

"Amra Thetys."

"And this is in relation to?"

"Corbin. Tell her it's about Corbin."

Something flickered in those emerald eyes. Those perfect lips gave the slightest twitch, as if they wanted to say or ask something, but knew better. Curious. She did a perfect little curtsey and glided off. I walked over to the bar and asked the elderly, white-coated barman for an ale. It was the cheapest thing they served. At the Dream, everything they served was quality, and none of it at bargain prices. But I wasn't looking forward to telling Corbin's lover he was dead. I needed something.

A few minutes later, Raven-hair, face remotely serene, ushered me into the ground floor apartments of the owner of the Dream, Estra Haig. The same taste that had furnished the Dream's parlor had turned a more intimate, cozy eye on the private rooms. Everything was sunlight and creams and pale pastels, crystal and blonde wood and greenery. Pleasing textures.

She was sitting at a small table in a beige silk dressing gown, the remains of her breakfast laid before her. She was a well-preserved, striking woman in her late forties. The morning sunlight that streamed in from the glass window showed high cheekbones and delicate crow's feet, long nose, strong jaw, and the loosening skin of her neck in equal measure. I wouldn't look that good at her age. Hells, I didn't look that good at my age. Even without all the scars, I wouldn't look that good.

She turned her grey eyes to me and smiled. We knew each other, slightly. Not enough to be chummy. If I was here with news about Corbin, I could read in her face, it wasn't anything she'd be pleased to hear. She had the look of someone bracing for bad news.

"Amra. Sit. Have you eaten?"

"I'm fine, thanks." I sat. "How are you, Estra?"

"Well, thank you."

"Listen. I'm sorry to be the one to tell you this. Corbin's dead."

She went rigid for a moment, and that haughty, aging, beautiful face went taught and still as a mask. She closed her eyes briefly.

"How. Tell me how."

I told her. About the commission, and about the Elamner. About the toad. She asked to see it, and I showed her.

"So this is what he died for," she said, and looked at it a long time before handing it back.

She asked the kinds of questions that nobody really wants to hear the true answers to. How did he die. Was it quick.

I didn't varnish it. I told her what Kluge had told me and what I saw. She asked if Corbin's fixer had anything to do with it, and I told her I doubted it. Then the questions dried up, and she just sat there, hands in her lap, staring off into nothing. She didn't cry. This one wouldn't cry.

"There's something else. Corbin was some sort of nobility. The black sheep, I guess."

"I know."

"Then you can guess that there will be heat coming down from the family. Heads are going to roll, Estra. Watch yourself, all right?"

"I have friends who will see it as their duty to shield me from any unpleasantness. But thank you for your concern."

We sat there for a little while longer, in a silence that was uncomfortable for me. I don't think she even noticed I was still there until I rose to go.

"What are you going to do now?" she asked.

"Me? I'm going make the Elamner pay."

Her eyes grew hard. "See that you do. If you need anything, come to me. Just… see that you do."

I nodded. "Give me a little time before you start looking for other, uh, alternatives, all right?"

She smiled, without a trace of mirth. "You take as long as you need, Amra. Corbin was fond of you. He trusted you. I see that the feeling was mutual. Take the time you need to do it right. But if you cannot do it for one reason or another, tell me. So that I can make arrangements. Are we agreed?"

"Yeah. That's fair."

"What will you do with that horrid statue?"

"I'm not sure yet. Melt it down, maybe. Maybe sell it. Maybe drop it in the Ose."

She nodded, face expressionless. "If you need to… dispose of it, Amra, I would be willing to take care of it for you. It's the least I can do."

"Thanks. I'll let you know if I do."

I made my way out. There were worse people to have in your corner than Estra Haig. She wielded a sort of influence in Lucernis. Her contacts spanned all classes, from brute killers to Privy Court judges to noblemen to the heads of some of the merchant families. Hells, for all I knew, she might be on a first name basis with Lord Morno himself.

I took one last glance back at her. Still the aging beauty, but something had gone out of her over the course of a few minutes' conversation. She sat as rigid as ever, but one manicured hand was white-knuckled, throttling a silk napkin.

CHAPTER 8

It remained for me to find a safe place to stow the idol. I wasn't going to be taking it along on my reconnaissance of Heirus's villa, and I damn sure wasn't leaving it at home. I could think of no better place than at Holgren's.

I stopped by a butcher's, and bought scrap and bones for Bone. He was still my responsibility, and I didn't want to press Holgren's generous impulses too far. Then I found a hack willing to take me as far as Daughter's Bridge, and walked the rest of the way.

When I knocked, Bone's deep, thumping bark started up. This time Holgren answered the door himself, with Bone trying to butt past his legs. Holgren wore a sheepish grin. I suspected they had been rough-housing. Bone grinned and drooled and thumped his tail against the doorsill. I patted his head. It was like patting fur-covered rock.

"Hello, Amra. What have you got there?"

"Treats for the beast." I passed him the packet from the butcher. "And I brought that thing we talked about yesterday."

"Excellent. Come in, come in. It's a hot day. Would you like wine?"

"That would be nice." I entered and sat down on the dusty sofa.

"Inspector Kluge came around this morning."

"How did that go?"

"Oh, fine. He was asking after someone named Marfa. I told him she was my sister, come to give me a dog. Some chitchat followed, a few questions about Corbin. I couldn't help him, and he left it at that." He passed me a glass. It was a crisp Kirabor. Not cheap.

"Sorry to bring the law to your door, Holgren."

He waved it away. "I'm glad you brought him. The dog, that is."

"So you and Bone are getting along all right?"

"I'd forgotten how enjoyable it can be to have a companion. I haven't had a dog since… for a long time."

"Well I'm glad you two have hit it off. Though I could have used him around last night."

"Oh?"

I told him about my visitor, and the effect it had had on my emotions. He shook his head.

"I've no idea what it was, I'm afraid. I've never heard of anything that fits the description. Grohl are humanoid, and a rather ghastly grey color, but they bleed red like you and I, and don't have any protrusions around the head or hands. And they wouldn't come within fifty miles of a human habitation for any reason other than to burn it to the ground."

"Whatever it was, I'm pretty sure it was after this." I unwrapped the toad and passed it to him. "I think my burglar can track that statue, somehow. I don't have any proof. I just can't think of any other reason it would be trying to sneak through my window."

"There's no telling, really. You could very well be right." He held it, and a strange look passed over his face. He set it down on the table and wiped his hand on his vest in an unconscious gesture.

"There's something more to this than meets the eye, Amra. Something distasteful. Something dangerous, I think." He looked up at me. "Have you noticed anything? Anything unusual?"

"Other than monsters crawling through my window? No. It's unusually ugly, but other than that, no. Not really."

"No strange urges? No odd thoughts crossing your mind? No sudden sickness?"

"No, nothing like that. Except—"

"Except?"

"Nothing, really. Just bad dreams and headaches the past couple of days. When I sleep. I keep hearing whispers, and breathing. I think it's just the heat."

"Maybe so, maybe no." He frowned and stared at the idol for a time. "There is something about it. Something old. Ancient. And unclean. It looks post-Diaspora, but feels far older...." He trailed off. His mind was somewhere else. He began mumbling to himself, in no language I recognized. I sat quietly, sipping my wine. One of the privileges of being a mage, I suppose, is that you can be as strange as you like, and nobody dares comment. Finally he shook himself and took a deep breath. He smiled a small smile at me.

"Would you mind terribly leaving it with me? I'd like to probe this mystery a bit further. It's very odd, almost as if—well, anyway, would you mind?"

"Not at all. You'd be doing me a favor. Another favor, actually. Just watch yourself. Apparently it's worth killing for."

He smiled an unpleasant smile. "I've ample protection, believe me. Anyone able to defeat my wards will have earned whatever they can take from me. Give me a few days, Amra, and I'll see what I can see."

I spent a few minutes being licked to death by Bone, then took my leave. Holgren waved, already distracted by the lump of gold on the table and, presumably, the old evil it represented.

~ ~ ~

Finding the villa Heirus had rented wasn't terribly difficult. I hired a hack and told him I wanted to take a leisurely afternoon ride. I put a gold mark in his horny hand and pointed him down the Jacos Road. He was happy to oblige, with a week's wages in his fist.

Walking would have been better, but there was a much higher chance of me being noticed. There isn't much traffic that far down the Jacos, and anyone walking down and then back would have been noticed by a relatively alert guard.

There were dozens of villas along the Jacos Road, ranging from weekend cottages and love nests to full-fledged farm concerns. But only three backed onto the cliffs. They were all relatively small, and crowded in on each other. It's not a huge cliff. The villas were built for the view.

The first, I happened to know, belonged to Gran Ophir, a shipping magnate. The second turned out to be deserted, and had been for years, by the look of it. Which left only the southernmost.

It looked innocuous enough at first glance. Ivy-covered brick walls about twice my height. A wrought iron gate, all curlicues and blunt spikes. Glimpses of a two-story structure screened behind lush vegetation. But the ivy was actually adder-tongue, a thorny, semi-poisonous climbing vine, and if you looked close enough you could see the occasional tell-tale glint of broken glass mortared into the top of the wall. And beyond the whimsy gate, two visible guards, armed with sword and crossbow.

I let the hack go on about a mile further, until we came to a quaint little country tavern. I had a drink in their beer garden and watched golden bees do their thing in the late afternoon sunshine. I let my mind wander.

I had seen what there was to see, and knew better by now than to try and force any sort of plan. It would all fall into place soon enough. Theft is as much art as it is craft. Reconnaissance work was a big part of that art, that craft. The villa's security, from what I had seen, was professional. I'd circumvented worse. But I hadn't seen anything but the surface.

I realized I was about to break one of my own rules. I was going to rush a job.

Usually I took at least a week to plan a break-in. I liked to observe the comings and goings, scheduled and otherwise, familiarize myself with faces and body language and study the peculiarities of the layout. To see what doors were used, and when, and by who. Which windows were opened, and which were never opened. To see if a guard had a tendency to nod, or drink, or even scratch his arse. I like to get to a place where I can grasp the rhythm of a household intuitively. The smallest thing can give you an insight which can lead to a plan. But there was no place to loiter and observe along the Jacos Road, and I had monsters trying to crawl through my window in the middle of the night, and I was willing to bet that the only way to make sure that kind of thing stopped was to kill the mysterious Elamner behind those villa walls.

When I reckoned an hour or so had passed, I woke my coachman up from where he snoozed in the shade of an old oak, and we headed back to the city. I didn't so much as glance at the villa as we passed the second time. You take what care you can.

Once back in the city, I rented a horse from Alain the carriage maker. I wasn't about to walk back to the villa.

Alain wasn't really in the practice of renting mounts, which was one of the reasons I preferred to rent from him. Another was that I'd done him a good turn once, and he felt some obligation over it. I could almost trust him. He would do right by me and wouldn't get curious as to what I might be doing.

He had a very large work yard out in the Spindles, on the city end of the Jacos Road, and half a dozen carpenters in his employ. He was an honest, stubborn, self-made man who was doing very well thanks to his skill and his wife Myra's business acumen.

I walked through the gate into his yard, and was immediately confronted with a gigantic wheeled... *thing*. Like a carriage big enough for a giant to lie down in.

"Amra! What do you think of it?" Alain called from across the yard.

"I think I pity the horse," I replied. "What the hells is it?"

"They're calling it an omnibus. Fits forty passengers."

"I have no idea what you're talking about."

He punched me in the arm. "I'm talking about making money, woman. This here omnibus will troll the length of Orange Road all day every day. People will jump on, pay their two coppers, ride as far as they want. Transport for the working man!"

"As long as the working man works along Orange Road." Which, admittedly, thousands did. It was a very long, wide road. "Does Myra approve?"

He smiled. "She approves of the fee for building it, which I'll be collecting now that it's nearly finished. She's more cautious about the investment side of things. But you're not here to talk about omnibuses. Or is it omnibi?"

"You're asking the wrong person. And I do need something. A horse for the night."

Alain picked out a grey gelding for me. From the looks of him, the horse had an appointment with the knackers in the not-too-distant future. My trust began to diminish.

"He looks ready to collapse," I told Alain.

Alain scratched his ample stomach. "He's a gentle one, is Kram. And you sit a horse like you've a stick shoved up an uncomfortable place, Amra."

I glared at him, but he was right. I can keep a saddle. Just. Growing up very poor in a city built on the side of a mountain, I didn't get much opportunity to learn. Bellarius wasn't known for its horesmanship.

Alain promised to have the horse saddled and ready an hour after sunset, and I flipped him a silver mark. Then I went home to start laying out my gear.

A funny thing happened along the way. There was a boy—well, I say boy, but he was in his late teens. He was staring at me.

He stood in the shade of the column that supports the aqueduct above Tar Street, just on the edge of the Spindles, and he had the biggest, kindest eyes I'd ever seen. He also has a shaved head, and was dressed in the simple rust-colored wrap of an ascetic. He was staring at me, and smiling a little. I scowled and his smile grew.

He didn't try to approach me. I couldn't puzzle it out, so I stopped trying. Lucernis is full of all sorts. I went on my way, but could feel his gaze on me until I turned the corner.

CHAPTER 9

I hid Kram in a copse of pin oak and hackberry about a mile from the villa, tying the lead to a low branch. I don't know why I bothered. Kram was one horse utterly uninterested in wandering. He had the look of a convict who'd given up all hope of escape, and was just waiting for death.

I didn't expect to actually enter Heirus's villa that night; all I planned to do was take a good long look at the layout of the grounds, and see what sort of security measures he had in place. And I was going to do it from the relative safety of the deserted villa next door to his. That was the plan, anyway.

The night was dark, but not as dark as I might have wished. Here on the outskirts of the city, manmade light was scarce. No street lamps, no lanterns or candles from windows close on either side of the street. There were just the stars and the moon. But the moon was almost full, and cast a bright silver light down through a cloudless sky. I have excellent night vision; that advantage would be whittled down.

I spent the next half-hour scuttling through the weed-choked ditch that ran alongside the Jacos Road, moving as quickly and quietly as I could toward the villa. It was dry as a bone, which was a blessing, but I startled the occasional creature. An opossum, a snake. A couple other things I didn't get a good look at. I am a city dweller, and had been almost all my life. I distrusted nature. It was an uncomfortable, nerve-rasping journey.

I wore a dark grey cotton tunic and trousers, and a pair of black, thin-soled boots. In one pocket I had a black silk vizard, for when it came time to cover my face. Otherwise it was a distraction. Any article of clothing you don't wear on a daily basis can be distracting, and in my line of business, distraction can be fatal.

On my back was a pack chock full of various implements and instruments of the trade, all carefully stowed so as not to shift or make noise. It was far more than I usually took to a job, but I planned to make the deserted villa next to Heirus's my base, so I wouldn't have to lug everything around the entire time. My blades were lamp-blacked, so as not to cast a stray glint at an inopportune moment. I was as prepared as I could be.

The deserted villa was nowhere near as well-put-together as Heirus's. It had a wall, but it was low and made of wood and dilapidated, sagging badly in some spots. It had been hardly more than decorative when it was new. Now, honeysuckle and morning glory and creeping laver were slowly tearing it down. When I finally reached it, I crept along the side opposite Heirus's until I found a gap wide enough to squirm through. I did, dragging my pack after me. Once inside the grounds, I crouched, and listened for a hundred heartbeats.

Nothing but the occasional call of a night gull, and the whisper of a breeze in the riotous growth that had once been a smallish formal garden. I watched the darkened, paint-peeling house for any sign of movement. Nothing. In the strong moonlight, the villa looked diseased.

And just as I had decided it truly was deserted, I heard feet crunching on a gravel path somewhere off to my left. I froze, knife in hand. I couldn't see anything; the foliage was too thick. I listened to whoever it was cross from my extreme left to almost level with my position, then heard the footsteps recede.

If I had to guess, it was a sentry, making a circuit of the yard. But I didn't have to guess. I had all night. I pushed forward, slowly and silently through the dense shrubbery until I had a clear view of the villa. It was a two story affair. I could tell by the layout there was an interior courtyard. There were very few windows on the outside, all of them too small to fit through. All the focus would be in, toward the courtyard, which would likely be tiled, with a fountain in the center. Hallways on both floors would run along the outer walls. The question was, did the builder break from the traditional villa layout to take in the sea view from the cliffs? I couldn't tell from where I was, but thought it probable.

If the grounds were being patrolled here, they were undoubtedly being patrolled by Heirus's men. Whoever was in charge of his security was no idiot. Anyone interested in gaining access to the Elamner's villa would almost certainly make use of the abandoned dwelling next door. Gran Ophir, the deserted villa's northern neighbor, wouldn't bother with such security measures. His villa was for the use of a mistress who happened to be travelling. The interesting tidbits you pick up, sitting around Tambor's.

I had a decision to make. I had planned to set up shop in the unused building and observe the Elamner's grounds from the roof. See how many guards, and what sort of rotation. Whether there were dogs. See what I could see of the interior of the villa, from a safe distance. The patrol here had complicated matters. I thought about it, and decided the risks did not outweigh the possible benefits.

I sat there in the darkness, utterly still. Two tiger moths fluttered around my head, landed on my arm. Began to copulate. I resolved to ignore them, though they were as big as my palm. Distractions can be fatal. About a half-hour later the guard made another circuit. He was armed with short sword and crossbow. The sword was sheathed, the crossbow's stock tucked into the crook of his arm. He was professional enough. He scanned his surroundings and didn't talk to himself or hum or whistle. He wore a doublet and loose, almost baggy trousers tucked into low boots. He wasn't wearing chain armor, that much I could tell. I couldn't tell from this distance if his doublet was just padded, or if iron plates had been sewn into it. Either was common.

As he moved off, away from me and in the direction of Heirus's villa, I moved quickly and quietly to my left, toward the cliffs. There was my best chance of entering the dilapidated building.

Once I got to the back of the villa it was a case of good news, bad news. The good news was that practically the entire back wall was open to the air, a series of huge windows with dilapidated shutters, to afford a view of the sea. Most of those shutters were stacked haphazardly on the ground about twenty feet away. Now it was a series of open, gaping entrances. The bad news was that there was absolutely no cover from the house to the cliff other than that low, wide stack of shutters. And there were two more guards stationed just inside the building.

I eased back into the deeper shadow of a huge hackberry, and waited some more. Listened to the dull roar of waves crashing against rocks forty feet below. Eventually the roaming guard came around the far corner and exchanged a few words with his two companions. I couldn't hear what they said over the surf. One appeared to grunt and took over the walking duties, crossbow slung over his shoulder.

I decided gaining entry to the abandoned villa wasn't worth the risk. Once you get in, you have to get out. Again I was at a crossroads. Go home, think of some other approach. Or go ahead, into Heirus's villa, practically blind. I wasn't kidding myself. If I went into that villa tonight, it would be to kill the man. I could let this go, if I wanted to. Corbin hadn't asked me to avenge his death. All he'd asked me to do was look after his dog.

Kluge's words came back to me. First they'd hacked off his fingers, then they'd let him run. Then they'd killed him, just for the sport of it.

Tonight was as good a night as any, and better for being sooner rather than later.

I trailed the roving guard at a safe distance back toward my entry point, then made my way carefully toward the Elamner's villa through the dense undergrowth that had been the front garden. I reached the sagging wall and took a look.

Between the two walls lay about ten yards of open ground that ran all the way to the cliffs. Someone kept the vegetation trimmed there; nothing grew more than ankle high. I couldn't see anyone on the wall across the open space, but I would have bet gold someone was set to watch that open space. I could see a small wooden door set into the side wall of the Elamner's villa, and about ten feet from my position, a gap in the wooden wall of the abandoned one. Where the guards passed back and forth, no doubt. Where the watcher would be stationed. No doubt the roaming guard would give the 'all's well' every time he passed.

All right, time to take a little risk.

I made my way carefully, quietly along the sagging vine-covered wall that ran parallel to the Elamner's villa, back towards the cliffs. When I reached the corner of the old house, I vaulted the low wall, to keep it between me and the watchmen stationed in the abandoned villa. Then I crawled through the shadow at the foot of the wall the rest of the way to the cliffs.

I stopped and pulled the bag of resin out of my pack, anointed both hands, and stowed it away. Took a few deep breaths. Then, offering up a brief prayer to Vosto, the god of fools and drunks, I lowered myself feet-first down the cliff face.

I descended far enough that I would be invisible to anyone not standing directly at the cliff's edge. The cliff was granite, and offered good hand and footholds. But my pack put my center of balance too far out over the water, and the rock was slick. I did not look down. If I fell, I was dead. The fall itself probably wouldn't kill me, unless I hit one of the jagged rocks down there. But there were things in the water that would finish the job. Phecklas. Grey urdu. They don't call it the Dragonsea for nothing. And anyway, I can't swim.

Slowly, carefully, blinking away the sudden sweat in my eyes, I crabbed sidewise across the cliff. I keep myself fit; I have to. But in five minutes my inner thighs were trembling and the muscles of my upper arms burned with the effort. The surf pounded and growled, an empty stomach waiting for a morsel to fall on the teeth of the rocks below.

When I judged I had gone far enough, I slowly, carefully rose up and took a look. I'd gone about three feet past the corner. Here, thankfully, there was no thorny, poisonous adder tongue to contend with. There was about two feet of rocky ground between the cliff's edge and the wall, and it was in deep shadow. It wouldn't get any better. I dragged myself up and lay on my stomach, panting. I thought I had kept myself in shape, but obviously I'd been drinking too much wine and not exercising enough. When I'd got my breath back I carefully wriggled out of the pack straps and dug out all I thought I'd need. It wasn't much, really. The small grapnel with the silk cord. Lock picks. Small flask of oil. Resin bag. A pair of heavy gloves to deal with the glass atop the wall. Weapons were already secreted on my person, more than I should ever have to use in one night.

Some thieves prefer to carry tools varied and complex. I've always preferred to travel light, unless I know I'm not going to be disturbed, or there is a need to bring something along for a specific task. This was reconnaissance work, and maybe blood work, not theft. I'd kill the Elamner if I could, but I didn't count on getting that lucky. There was just no telling what my chances were until I was inside. I slipped the vizard over my face and took up the grapnel.

The trickiest part about grapnel work is the noise. Steel on stone is a distinctive sound, in the dead of night. Which is why I wrap mine in cotton cloth. The tines will bite through the cloth if you've got a good catch, and if you don't, then you won't have to worry about steel dragging along stone when you pull it back for another cast. Not that I had to worry about any of that with the surf pounding. A bat would have been hard-pressed to hear anything.

I put my back against the wall and, silk cord coiled in one hand, lobbed the three-pronged grapnel up and over. It cleared the top of the wall, and I started reeling in line. It caught, and I tugged harder, finally putting all my weight into it. It held. First cast lucky. I worried about the glass sawing into the line. Nothing I could do about it.

The gloves were so thick they were a hindrance, but I went up the rope quickly enough, and after scanning the gloom inside for any movement, carefully and quietly cleared a wide space of the inset glass shards. Then I lay on the top of the wall on my stomach, and turned the grapnel around and dropped the line into the villa grounds.

There was a chance that the line would be noticed, but there was a greater chance that I would need a quick exit when it was time to leave, and having to recast the grapnel while people were trying to kill me wasn't something I wanted to do. You figure the odds and you take your chances. I straddled the wall, slid myself down, hung by my fingertips for a moment, and dropped down quietly into the shadows at the base of the wall.

I made my way as quietly as I could over to a darkened, shuttered window. I used a knife to slip the latch on the shutter, and then I probed gently beyond with its tip. No glass, no parchment window. Just a shuttered casement, starting at waist height.

I listened, took a peek in the crack between the shutters. Darkness and silence on the other side; a stillness that betokened an empty, lifeless room. I threw the dice and decided to slip into the room.

Opening the shutters a bare necessary amount still flooded the room with moonlight. I froze.

I was almost right about the room. It was lifeless, but it wasn't quite empty.

Sprawled on the floor with a dagger in his heart was the corpse of a man. Judging by his raw silk robes, his dark skin and his oiled, ringleted hair, he was an Elamner. Someone had chalked a protective circle around him on the parquetry. There was no blood. There was, however, a crazy grin on the corpse's face. A palpable sense of unwelcome poured out of that room, a... malevolence. As if the very air inside it wished me ill. Bad, bad magic that I'd probably be stupid to test.

Another tiger moth fluttered past my shoulder into the room, and instantly fell to the floor, lifeless.

Shit.

Something struck me then, once, twice, with blinding speed. I felt a flare of agony in my shoulder and cruel blow to the side of my head, and as I dove down into the black pit of unconsciousness, I felt once more the bile of unreasoning hate boiling up in the back of my throat.

CHAPTER 10

I don't know how long I was out. Not very long. The moon hadn't moved across the sky perceptibly. I sat up, trembling and dazed. My shoulder was on fire. I was amazed to be alive. What had hit me?

The creature that had tried to break into my place. That insane, all-consuming instant hatred was not something I was likely to forget, or mistake.

I've no idea why it didn't kill me. I would certainly have killed *it*, given the chance. With the feeling that welled up in me when it was near, I would have crawled through fire to slit its throat.

I shrugged. Now was not the time to be gathering wool. I did a once-over on myself and discovered a knot on the side of my head and a bloody shoulder.

And a missing dagger. I searched all around me in the dark beneath the window, thinking I had dropped it. It was gone. I shrugged, and sighed. Another knife lost to the creature, I assumed.

"All right," I breathed, "that's enough for one night, Amra." I closed the shutter and made my way back to the wall.

Climbing the wall was agony. I tossed the pack into the sea. There was nothing in it I couldn't replace, and I wasn't going to try and negotiate the cliff face with it. After a moment, I threw the sweat-soaked vizard after the pack. At this point, if somebody saw my face I was dead anyway.

Even without the extra burden, that twenty feet of cliff would have been torture. I doubted very much that I'd be able to go back the way I came. If I tried, I'd end up in the Dragonsea, and the scent of fresh blood would make sure I wouldn't last long. So I flattened myself down on the ground and crawled along the edge of the cliff, waiting for a crossbow bolt to find my back. I knew where it would hit. Just between the shoulder blades. A spot there the size of a gold mark burned and itched, waiting for the bolt to punch through.

When I finally made it into the slice of shadow cast by the wooden fence of the other villa, I retched, as quietly as I could. Nerves. The sour taste of bile filled my mouth again, and I quietly spat it out. At least I was breathing.

Making my way across the overgrown garden was payment for all my sins. I hadn't realized I'd committed so many. I took it slowly, everything in me just wanting to get somewhere safe, to stop moving, to still the waves of pain from my shoulder and head. At one point I started trembling uncontrollably and I was forced to lay there until it subsided, praying the roving guard wouldn't be attracted by the sound of the rattling brush.

Eventually I made it to the ditch. About halfway to the copse where I'd hidden Kram, I passed out again. I must have lain there for a long time, because when I came to, my clothes were damp with dew. I looked up at the sky. A couple of hours before dawn. I had to hurry. I pushed myself hard, and made it into the copse and to the waiting horse. He looked at me with liquid eyes that seemed to say that all life was suffering.

"Shove it," I whispered, and untied him and climbed into the saddle.

The ride back was its own brand of suffering. Every plodding footfall sent a jolt of pain through shoulder and head.

By the time I got back to Alain's, grey-fingered dawn was creeping up on the horizon. I half-fell off the horse and banged on the gate to the work yard attached to his house. After a few moments I could hear the bar being lifted, and then Alain's son Owin poked his head out. He looked at me and his mouth gaped.

"What, you've never seen blood before?"

"No. I mean yes, but not that much. Not on anybody alive."

"Are you gonna let me in?"

He opened the gate and I led Kram into the yard. Owin was exaggerating, but my shirt was ruined. If I went back out into the increasing morning traffic I would be noticed. I hate to be noticed.

"I'm going to need a change of clothes, Owin. Is there anything around that will fit?" Alain's entire family was large. I am not.

"Uh. I'll ask Mum. Just let me get Kram into the stable. Maybe you should sit down?"

"I might not get back up."

He took the horse into the narrow stable on one side of the yard, and then led me to the kitchen door of the house. I could smell bacon frying. I realized I was ravenous.

Myra, Alain's wife, was a huge woman. She had one of those handsome faces that seemed almost incongruous compared with her bulk. Huge wide eyes and perfect brows and full lips. Lustrous brown hair. She took one look at me and pulled the pan off the fire.

"What in Isin's name happened to you?"

I shrugged, which wasn't a great idea.

"Sit down. Looks like your shoulder's been torn to ribbons. And that smell! We'll have to burn those clothes. Strip out of that shirt."

Normally I would have bristled at anyone ordering me about. Not with Myra. As soon tell the rain to stop falling. Myra was Myra, an unstoppable force.

Five knives went onto the table. Myra made no comment. I had a hard time getting the tunic and undershirt off by myself. Caked blood glued them to the wound, and my abused muscles shrieked pain in protest when I raised my arms over my head. Tried to raise them. Myra helped, clucking her tongue and muttering all the while. She glanced at her son, still standing at the kitchen door.

"Owin, don't you have something to do? Whatever it is, it's not in here."

He blinked and blushed. "Ah. Yes." And he disappeared, ruddy cheeks and all. For all that he was only a few years younger than me, there was much that was still boyish about Owin.

A minute or so later I heard Alain's heavy tread come down the stairs, and put an arm across my breasts. I was in no mood or condition to be ogled by both father and son.

"Forget your modesty, Amra. There's not enough of you for me. I like my women with a little meat on their bones. And I like 'em tender, not tenderized."

I glared at him, but he didn't seem to notice.

"Great Gorm, but something got hold of you. You've got bruises on your bruises. Is that a claw mark?"

"No, it's a pimple."

Myra glanced up at her husband. "Make yourself useful and put water on to boil. Then bring me the tincture your cousin gave us, the one for unclean cuts, and that horse liniment you're always going on about. Then get me one of Owin's old shirts, in the cupboard at the top of the stairs. And then go take care of the custom."

"All right. But what about breakfast?" He cast an eye at the half-cooked bacon.

"Chew your beard, old man."

Alain did as he was told while Myra cleaned the wound, and then lumbered off to the morning's work. He paused at the door and cast one last glance in my direction.

"Will trouble be following you, do you think?"

"I don't think so, but it's possible."

He nodded and pulled down a gnarled cudgel from the wall, where it hung by a leather thong on a hook. He tucked it into his wide belt and went outside.

Once all the blood was off and the wound cleaned, Myra poured a liberal amount of some cloudy, innocuous looking tincture into each of the furrows in my shoulder. Gods, it burned. When I complained, she said "Talk to me about pain after you've birthed a child. Honestly, Amra Thetys, you sound like a man, whining about a little discomfort."

There is mercy and then there is mercy, I suppose. But her hands were deft and gentle as she rubbed the liniment on. That burned too, but in a strangely cold way that wasn't entirely painful.

She helped me into Owin's old, oft-mended shirt. I swam in it. Then she demanded my trousers.

"There's no need, Myra. Nobody will notice stained trousers. The shirt is enough. I'll be on my way and out of your hair. Thank you." I made to rise, and a meaty hand pushed me back down.

"You're on your way up to Owin's room, and nowhere else. Now out of those bloody pants, Amra."

"The longer I stay here, the more likely it is I put you and your men in danger."

"And you were in no danger at all when you pulled Alain out of that rookery where they'd drugged his ale and robbed him, and were about to cut his throat. I've waited near four years to pay that bill. Now off with your pants, or I warn you, I'll have them off myself."

"Myra, my mother died twenty years ago!"

"Isin love her soul. But at least she can't see you acting the fool now."

One more knife joined the five on the table. She clucked her tongue, but otherwise made no comment. It turned out that I needed her help to get my boots off. I couldn't bend down that far.

~ ~ ~

I slept like the dead. Through the day, and into the night. I think the only reason I woke was because I was so hungry. I was disoriented for a moment, surrounded by Owin's things, in Owin's bed. I reached for a knife that wasn't where it was supposed to be. It was a spare looking room, lit only by moonlight. A cloak hung on a peg. There was a pitcher and a bowl on a rickety stand, and a razor with a leather strop. There was a solid-looking wardrobe. There was a low table by the window, with little carvings resting on it. Creakily, I picked one up and studied it in the moonlight. It was a horse. It was beautiful. It wasn't something Owin would have bought, I didn't think. I suspected he had carved it himself. He had a master's eye, if I was right. He'd carved it in such a way that the grain of the wood flowed and accented the mane, the powerful haunches. I picked up another, a kestrel perched on a branch. It was just as lovely. He'd caught the air of regal, predatory menace in its eyes perfectly. I wondered if he even knew he was wasting a rare talent on building and repairing wagons. Or if he cared. I'd have traded the damned golden toad for one of his carvings in a trice.

The stairs were a challenge. I kept one hand on the wall and the other on my ribs. The sounds of laughter and good-natured bickering floated up from the kitchen, but they trailed off as I descended.

Owin was studiously not looking at my bare legs. Alain leaned back in his chair, mirth still lingering in his eyes. Myra glanced at me and said "Good, you're up. I was going to wake you soon, just to get some food down your throat." And she busied herself readying me a plate. I wasn't going to argue. Myra could cook. Of course, I would have eaten boot leather had it been presented to me just then.

I sat down and a plate was put in front of me. If anyone was expecting conversation out of me just then, they were sorely disappointed. Beans, capon, black bread, boiled cloudroot with a rich mushroom gravy. I made it all disappear. I looked up. Myra was smiling, Owin stared, mouth agape, and Alain just shook his head.

"What? You've never seen anyone eat?"

"Is that what you call it?" asked Alain. "No one was going to take it away from you, you know. Did you have time to taste anything?"

"Leave her alone," said Myra. "She's complimented the cook in her way."

Alain snorted, but laid off me. He changed the subject.

"Someone's been asking after you around town."

I froze, spoon halfway to my mouth. "Violent type?"

"No."

"Half-grown kid? Bald? Penitent's robes?"

He laughed. "Not hardly. But you do know all types, eh?"

I growled. "Just tell me."

"Young woman. Very pretty. Very, very pretty."

"A strumpet," injected Myra.

"A pretty strumpet. There's a thought."

"Black hair, green eyes, quality clothes."

"I don't know any—" Wait. That girl from the Dream. Estra's girl. "What's she want?" Estra knew how to get hold of me if she needed to. Why was this girl wandering around asking after me?

Alain shrugged. "She's put it about that there's a package for you at Locquewood's shop."

"I've no idea what it's about, and I don't have time for, ah, strumpets at the moment," I said, glancing at Myra, who rolled her eyes.

Owin cleared the dishes and then Myra shooed both men out of the kitchen to check my wounds. She changed the bandages on my shoulder, applying that damned tincture once more, and rubbed in more liniment. Then she brought down a parcel from a shelf, frowning. Inside were my knives, a pair of trousers she'd obviously taken in for me, my old belt, cloth for bandages, another bottle of the tincture of torture and a jar of the horse liniment. My boots were cleaned and by the door. She helped me dress, and watched with disapproving eyes while I put various knives in various places. She was the first person who'd ever seen that particular ritual.

Myra stood in front of me, hands on heavy hips, and glared. "I've done what I can. I forced some rest and food on you—well, maybe the food wasn't forced—and I've tended your wounds. I know I can't keep you longer. You're like a damned cat, Amra. If I drag you in from the rain, you'll just yowl to be let back out."

"Myra—"

"You just be quiet until I'm done. I like you, Amra, and I owe you for my man's life. You're decent and kind, however hard you may be. But I don't approve of what you do or how you live your life. Alain is the stubbornest man I ever met save my own father, yet even he doesn't usually go looking for trouble. You're going to end up dead in an alley, Amra Thetys, or swinging by your neck in Harad's Square. But it doesn't have to be that way. There's a place for you under this roof, whenever you want it. But you have to want it. Now go."

I gave the big woman a brief hug, then left. Maybe ten, twelve years ago I could have taken her up on her offer. When I was cutting purses and stealing bread to survive. Now? It was far too late for me to think of taking up any other trade, living any other life. What would I do? Marry Owin, maybe, have children, tend to the kitchen and the washing and the finances?

No, Myra. Thank you, but no. It was a good, safe, honest life you offered. But it wasn't the life for me. Not anymore. Not for a long, long time. But as I slipped out of Alain's work yard and into the night, I remembered the laughter and the amused squabbling that floated up from the kitchen table as I'd come down the stairs. And I realized there was a hole in my life, a place where a family was supposed to fit. Like a missing tooth. Or a severed limb.

CHAPTER 11

The next couple of days were spent recuperating. I didn't go home, or anywhere near my usual haunts. Instead I stayed in one of my bolt holes, a third floor garret way the hells and gone across the river in Markgie's Rest, not even in Lucernis proper. It was a sleepy little community of fishermen and caraveners perched on the north shore of the Bay. People minded their own business, and were used to comings and goings at odd hours. And it got a breeze off the ocean most of the day.

The first day was pleasant enough. I was just too sore to want to move. By the end of the second, I was bored out of my skull. So I went down to the neighborhood pub to have a drink and be alone, in company. It was pleasant in the late afternoon, sunlight pouring in through real glass windows, surrounded by dark polished wood and red and green painted tables. I'd been there once or twice before. The few customers were mostly old men, telling amusing lies about fish and women.

I'd been there maybe half an hour when the door opened and three men walked in, bringing a Kerf-damned lot of trouble with them.

Two were your typical toughs; hard men, armed with short swords and dirks. Their clothes were clean and of good quality, and they were both clean shaven. Hard eyes scanned the crowd, and their hands never strayed too far from weapon hilts. Maybe a cut above the typical tough. Armsmen. Hired blades.

The third man was something else altogether. Slightly hunchbacked, with long, greasy black hair and a sparse beard, he wore cloth of expensive cut, but there were old stains and new on his velvet tunic. One foot was twisted in, and every step looked like it pained and exhausted him. And it looked as though he'd been walking all day. In one hand he carried a fine knife; black handled and silver pommeled, the bright blade about a hand span long and three fingers wide. A knife I knew very well. I'd commissioned it, after all. It was the knife I'd lost at the Elamner's villa.

I'd sat at a bench in the corner, back against the wall. Now I was trapped.

Hunchback, who was almost certainly Bosch, slapped the knife flat onto an empty table and stared at it. The two toughs gripped the hilts of their swords. I slipped knives into both hands and quietly pushed myself back from the table.

Nothing happened for a moment. Then the knife began to tremble. Slowly it began to turn, to spin, until the tip pointed directly at me like a Kerf-damned compass pointing north. Hunchback looked me in the eye and smiled a nasty, yellow-toothed smile that spoke volumes, all of it to do with eminent harm coming my way.

I threw both blades simultaneously, one at each bully-boy, vaulted onto the table, and threw myself through the glass of the window, arm across my face. Before I hit, I heard one of the men yelp in pain. Then I was rolling on the cobbles outside. I heard a horse's shrill neighing, looked up as a shod hoof came down towards my face. I rolled aside just in time. I'd come crashing out just as a hack was passing.

There were two more sell-swords waiting outside, but it took them a second to react. I wasted no time. I was on my feet and down the street. I didn't bother to look back. I could hear the heavy slap of boot leather on cobbles behind me.

Maybe I could have outrun them. Probably I could have. But to what point? They'd follow me wherever I went. My knife would point them the way. My three knives, now. Damned magic. For once the phrase 'you can run but you can't hide' actually had some meaning. So I turned three right corners in quick succession, making a square, and came back at a sprint to the tavern. My abused muscles complained bitterly, but Hunchback was right where I'd figured he would be, lagging far behind. And far away from his toughs. Sometimes I'm so smart I amaze myself.

I came up behind him in a quiet rush and put my blade across his windpipe. He stiffened. I plucked my other knife out of his hand and said, "Where are the other two?"

"Right here. In my belt." So they were. I relieved him of those as well. I heard running footsteps rounding the corner. I spun him around to face the toughs. "Quick now, tell them to put down their swords. He hesitated, and I slid the sharp end of my blade across his stubbled neck, just enough to sting.

"Stay back! Put down your swords!" He had a cultured voice. It sounded odd coming from his twisted, dissolute body. When they hesitated, he shouted "Do as I say!" They did, breathing hard, murder in the eyes of the one I'd stuck."Good boy," I murmured in his ear. "Now tell 'em to go inside the tavern and count to a hundred. Not too fast. I'll be counting too, and I'm not so good at it. Sometimes I lose my place and have to start again. If they come out before I'm done counting I'll cut your throat." He did as he was told, and they did what he told them, and I said "good boy" again as I dragged him down the street, and into the mouth of the nearest alley. Four pairs of eyes followed our progress from tavern door and window.

"You must be Bosch." I said as we went.

He hesitated, then nodded. Carefully.

"Out of curiosity, where'd you find my knife?"

"In a planter in the garden."

"The one place I didn't think to look. Tell the Elamner he'd better back off if he doesn't want the toad melted down." I thought it best not to mention the corpse I'd seen. I still hadn't figured out what the hells it signified.

"You have the statue?"

"No, I just assumed your boss would want a golden toad. Doesn't everybody?"

"We can do business, then."

"Yes," I said. "We can deal."

"How shall we contact you?"

I yanked out a handful of his hair and pushed him into the gutter. I tucked the hair into the top of a boot.

"Don't worry. I'll find you." And then I turned and tried to make myself scarce. I was sure Holgren would know just what to do with Bosch's greasy locks.

It wasn't Bosch's men that got me. It was the Watch. Markgie's Rest wasn't the Rookery, or Silk Street. When taverns got busted up and blood got spilled, and people started running around in the street with bared blades, they came. In large numbers. Quickly.

There was nowhere for me to go. Three appeared ahead of me, and two more behind, blocking off the alley. Black, varnished billys thunked into meaty palms. One old codger with a mean eye had a crossbow and looked like he knew how to use it. Blank walls rose on either side.

"Kerf's shrivelled balls," I spat, and dropped my knife, and put out my hands.

They beat me unconscious anyway.

CHAPTER 12

When I came back to the world, I wished I hadn't.

The smell was awful. Piss and vomit and shit and fear. The stench of bodies that had forgotten what clean water was, much less soap. To draw breath was to gag. I couldn't see anything. The darkness was absolute. I felt rough straw and filth-slick stone under my cheek, heard distant screams echoing along stone corridors. Somewhere not far away a hoarse, gravelly voice kept moaning 'Mother? Mother?' in such a monotonous way that I could hear the madness behind it.

I groaned and began the slow, torturous process of levering myself up off the floor. Everything hurt. When I put my hand out to work myself into a sitting position, I planted it squarely into a pile of cold, runny feces.

"Welcome to Havelock Prison," I whispered to myself. "Mind the turds."

~ ~ ~

In the darkness it was impossible to gauge the passing of time. My cell was three paces by four, and the ceiling higher than I could reach with outstretched arms. The door was oak banded in iron, and had been gouged futilely by unknown numbers of former occupants. All the stonework was tight; there were no chinks that I could find by fingertip, though someone at some time had made a concerted if futile effort to loosen a stone in the back right corner. The stones around it were gouged and rough. A thin layer of fouled, louse-ridden straw lined the floor. I kicked it all into a corner. After a time, I stopped noticing the stench, and started noticing the lice.

All my knives were gone, of course. In the darkness I felt carefully in my boot, and came up with a single strand of Bosch's hair. I didn't see how it would do me any good now, but I wound it carefully around the back of a button on my shirt, just in case.

The wound on my shoulder ached abominably. Nothing I could do about that, or the fact that it would probably become infected in such a foul environment. Not that it mattered, really; if they had me this far down in the bowels of Havelock, I probably wasn't coming back up for anything other than a dance with the noose.

~ ~ ~

After an unknowable time, I noticed a creeping light coming from under the door. I heard muffled orders repeated at regular intervals, and sometimes blows and shouts of pain. By the time they arrived at my door, I knew the drill.

"Face against the back wall, hands on your head, eyes shut. You have until five. One. Two. Three. Four. Five." Then a bar was lifted and the door swung open. Even turned away with my eyes closed, the flickering torchlight was dazzling.

From the sounds, there were at least two, possibly three. Probably three. One to hold the torch, one to serve the food, and one to stand ready with the billy. I didn't make any trouble. I'd had enough beatings for a while. The light retreated, the door closed, the bar slammed home.

My first meal in Havelock was gruel; stale, poorly ground rye bread; and water that, from the taste and smell of it, had most likely been drawn straight from the Ose.

To this day, just a whiff of rye bread is enough to make my stomach turn.

~ ~ ~

Mother-man, as I came to think of him, was never truly quiet. Even in his sleep he would moan for her. I assume he was sleeping. And when he woke, he'd scream "Mother! I'm blind! Moooother!" On and on until they came to beat him quiet. Then, at most a few hours later, he'd start again with that monotonous call for maternal comfort.

Eventually I couldn't stand it anymore. I screamed at him, "Your whore of a mother is dead, shit brain. Shut it!" It only made him go on louder. Which made me invent ever more gruesome ends for her. Run over by a carriage. Gored by bulls, made into meat pies. Drowned in a cesspit. Gnawed to death by rats, face first. Dead of syphilis. It only made him carry on the louder, which made the guards come. They beat us both.

I found myself hoping they'd come to hang either him or me soon. I started not to care which.

~ ~ ~

My second meal was the same as the first, and my third. That was how I measured time, though I honestly couldn't have said at the time if we were fed every day or every other or at random intervals. Hunger warred with nausea, and time had no meaning.

I thought a lot. Not much else to do. I went over the entire situation, and realized they might just be holding me until the killers arrived from Courune. They'd probably want to question me before they took me to Harad's Square for my short drop into oblivion. I didn't think they would be gentle about the questions, either.

I also thought about the situation as a whole. I went over everything I knew, and everything I thought I knew. I didn't reach any new conclusions. I still thought the Elamner must have had Corbin killed, for the statue. There were thirteen, Corbin had said. Heirus or Bosch had gotten twelve, and still wanted the last, the toad, so the others must not have been terribly important to him. Not what he was looking for, perhaps. Which suggested he knew when he commissioned Corbin that the one he was looking for was in that temple, but he didn't know which one it was. Or maybe he just needed all of them.

As for the dead man in the villa, well, that reeked of magic. By its nature, magic makes no sense. It was possible Bosch had killed his boss and was running the whole show. It was equally possible that the dead man wasn't the Elamner at all. I just didn't have enough to go on to make any kind of conclusion. Didn't matter. If I ever got out, I just needed to hunt down Bosch and make him talk. Then I'd see who needed to be killed.

The thing that had tried to break into my apartment and left me alive at the Elamner's was also a cipher. Was it working for Heirus, or Bosch? Or was it something completely Other? No idea. I'd ask Bosch about that, too, next time I saw him.

After a time it all became a muddle in my mind, and I tried not to think at all. And then they finally came for me, and all I could think of was how I didn't want to die.

They put the manacles on, and the shackles, and I shuffled out of my hole with a billy in my back down a stone corridor, eyes watering at the light from the torch behind me and the smoky corridor. We went up a set of stairs, and down another corridor. This one was lit, and the cell doors had barred windows. Pale, emaciated faces stared out at us, but they were just blurs in the increased light. There was nothing wrong with my ears, though. And these prisoners hadn't seen a woman in a long time.

"Bring 'er in 'ere for five minutes before she swings! All right, three! Three minutes!"

"Just keep walking," said one of the guards behind me. I gritted my teeth and kept shuffling along.

"She shouldn't go to the gallows unsatisfied!"

"Let me impale her before you hang her!"

I kept walking, until somebody threw a handful of runny shit that hit me in the face. Then I lunged at the bastard. The guard slammed me in the kidney with his billy and I crumpled to the floor.

"Told you to keep walking." He looked down at me and sighed. His partner put his torch in an empty bracket.

"Yeah," I gasped. "I forgot."

"You won't forget again?"

"Not a chance."

"Well, everybody forgets every now and then, I suppose. You stay right there for a while."

"Not going anywhere."

He looked at his partner, who nodded.

"Gerard, I told you last time. You start throwing shit, and I'm going to make you eat it."

"No boss. I forgot, boss."

"That's what you said the last time, Gerard." And he lifted the bar to Gerard's door.

"No boss! She forgot! Everybody forgets, you said so!"

"I'm just going to help your memory along, Gerard."

They opened the shit-flinger's door and beat him senseless. And yes, by the end of it he had shit in his mouth. I won't say I liked them for it. But I certainly didn't feel bad for Gerard. In prison, I discovered, the only pity to be had was self-pity.

CHAPTER 13

They brought me to a lantern-lit room. There was a scarred wooden table. There were two chairs, both facing me on the opposite side of the table. There was a door behind the table, opposite the one they'd brought me through. They ran a chain through my manacles and locked it to a massive iron staple in the stone floor, and then they stood back, within billy-swinging distance. And then we waited. Slowly my watering eyes adjusted to the light.

After maybe five minutes the door opened and two men walked in. The first I recognized. Inspector Kluge. The second I'd never seen before.

He was a heavy, unlovely man. Deeply inset dark eyes that glittered in the lamplight. Close-cropped, receding, greying hair. Heavy, pockmarked face and thin lips. A small scar bisected one of his thick eyebrows. But he was immaculate. His wide, square nails were clean and manicured. He wore an embroidered black waistcoat over a pure white linen shirt, and his starched collar was buttoned right up to his jaw line, biting slightly into the loose skin of his neck. This man had money, was used to money. He said nothing, only took a seat and looked at me. His face was impassive.

Kluge sat on the edge of the table nearest me. He scanned a sheaf of papers that he'd brought into the room.

"You put a knife into a man's arm, and you put another knife to another man's neck. You destroyed a rather expensive tavern window. The tavern keeper will want recompense. The injured and threatened parties did not care to prefer charges, but the crown does not require them to, in order to try you for a violent crime, Amra Thetys. Or do you still prefer Marfa?"

"Amra is fine."

He put the papers aside and looked at me for a long while.

"We know who you are. We know what you are. The only reason you don't yet have a date with the hangman is because we believe you can assist us."

"You'd hang me for a tavern brawl?"

"No. For that you could spend three years in Havelock. By the time you got out, you would be toothless from the poor diet, and your body would be wasted from malnutrition. Your eyesight would probably never recover from the dark hole you'd be consigned to. You might perhaps become a charwoman. Or you could sell scraps of salvaged cloth down in Temple Market. That is the best you could hope for, Amra.

"If you swing, it will be either for theft, or for aiding in the murder of a noble. It doesn't really matter. If we want you to hang, you'll hang."

I nodded. I didn't doubt what he said. Any of it.

"Well, then, I can't think of anything I'd rather do than help you, Inspector Kluge."

He smiled. "I knew you were a sensible creature." He stood and motioned to the other, silent man. "May I present to you Lord Osskil det Thracen-Courune. Corbin's elder brother."

"I'd bow, or curtsey. If I knew how, and if I could." I rattled the chains. He ignored it.

"I am going to ask you questions," Lord Osskil said, "and you are going to answer immediately, and without prevarication. Do you understand?"

"Certainly. I have an expansive vocabulary."

"Did you have anything to do with the death of my brother?"

"No."

"Do you know who did?"

"Yes."

"Tell me who."

"I don't think so."

The guard was quick with his billy. He slammed it into the back of my thigh and I went sprawling. Chained, I couldn't raise my hands, and so I broke my fall with my face.

"Get up," said Kluge. I worked my way to my feet, nose bleeding and probably broken.

Osskil asked again. "Who is responsible for my brother's death?"

"Before I answer, do you mind if I share a few thoughts?"

A short silence, pregnant with violence. Then, "Why not," he said, face expressionless.

"If I tell you now, what's to stop you from sending me right back into that hole?"

"If you don't tell us," said Kluge, "you will certainly go back into that hole. Until they take you to Harad's Square."

I nodded. "Maybe so, maybe no. But the man who killed Corbin might never be caught then."

Silence reigned. Then Osskil spoke up. "Tell me what I want to know, and I guarantee you will go free once the murderer has been punished."

"Release me and I'll take you to bastard."

The guard reared back to smack me down again, but Osskil raised his hand.

"I'm curious about you, Amra Thetys. Who was my brother to you?"

"A friend. A colleague, so to speak."

"Were you lovers?"

I laughed. "No, Lord Osskil. Your brother and I weren't lovers."

"What were you doing there, at that house? Where they found the body."

"I went to look for him. He was supposed to stop by my house about midnight. When he didn't show up, I started to worry, so I went looking for him."

"Why were you worried?"

I suppose I could have lied. But I didn't see the point.

"Look, you know your brother was a thief. He was a good one, if that means anything to you. He stole some things for someone, and they tried to stiff him his commission. He was going to meet them that night to settle the account. They weren't nice people. He asked me to look after his damned dog if he didn't show up by morning."

Kluge sniffed. "What you aren't saying is louder than what you are, Amra."

I shook my head. "Fine. He'd acquired a lot of statues for his client, and they'd taken all but one from him and neglected to pay him. But that one they missed? They wanted it badly, or so he said. He was supposed to meet and discuss his payment. It was going to be substantially higher than originally agreed to. He called it a bad faith penalty or some such.

Obviously he went to the meet, and ran into more bad faith."

"Why did he go to you at all? Did he want help?"

"No. He wanted me to hold onto the last statue for him. I turned him down. I didn't want the risk. But I did agree to look after his dog should anything go wrong." I hoped the one lie would go unnoticed amidst all the truth.

Kluge changed the topic. "Tell me about the fight in the tavern, Amra."

"What about it?"

"Witnesses say you drew steel and attacked without any provocation. Three men walk in, you throw a knife into one man's arm and then throw yourself out the window."

"Is there a question in there?"

"Why did you attack three men, two of which were obviously swordsmen, without provocation?"

"I owed them money. They'd come to collect, and I didn't have it."

"If that was all there was to it, I might believe you. But then you lead them on a chase and return to the tavern, and hold up the man who seems to be the employer of the group. You threatened him."

"I wanted him to cancel my debt."

"Mages aren't generally in the business of loaning money to thieves. Or anyone."

"He was a mage? I doubt he was a powerful one. Well, you'd know better than I, Inspector Kluge. But I don't see why mages can't take up any line of work they want. Loan sharking. Even detective work."

He smiled a tight smile. "I think the two incidents are connected. I think those men had something to do with Corbin Hardin's death. I think you tried to brace the killer, perhaps to blackmail money for your silence, and it went awry."

"And I think I should be half a foot taller, and rich as Borkin Breaves. Thinking something doesn't make it so."

"But if I think it, Amra, if I think it strongly enough, you hang. So if I'm wrong, it falls on you to convince me of the truth."

I sighed. I ached, I was tired, I was hungry. A wave of dizziness came over me. "Do you mind if I sit?" I asked, and started to squat. One of the guards put a billy under my chin and lifted.

"Let her," said Osskil. And the club went away.

"You are too kind, lord." I got as comfortable as I could. Osskil stood up and dragged his chair around the table.

"You might not want to get too close," said Kluge.

"I don't believe she's much of a threat. She can barely stand."

I chuckled. "It's not me you have to worry about, Lord Osskil. It's the lice."

He stiffened a little. "Oh," was all he said. He set his chair down a couple of feet from me and settled in it, leaning forward to look in my eyes.

"If I give you my word you will be freed, will you tell me who killed my brother?"

I considered. He could probably be trusted. Nobles were generally particular about keeping their word. I shook my head, though.

"You don't believe I can be trusted?"

"It's not that. There's another problem."

"What other problem?"

"I swore I'd kill the bastard myself. If you go and do it, then what's my word worth?"

He just stared at me for a moment, and then he laughed. I suppose the idea of a thief worried about keeping her word was funny at that. I just waited it out.

Eventually his laughter trailed off into silence.

"You're serious, aren't you?"

"You think only nobles do what they say the will?"

"No. Most of my peers wouldn't think twice about breaking an oath. But why would you care about honor?"

"If you have to ask, you wouldn't understand. Let me ask you a question, if I may."

"Why not," he said again in that curiously flat manner of his.

"When was the last time you saw your brother? Alive, I mean."

His face went impassive. I began to suspect that's what he looked like when he was deciding whether to be angry.

"Why?"

"Because in all the time I knew Corbin, he never mentioned you. He spoke of his daughter, a little. Once he mentioned his wife, when he was drunk. But he never mentioned his old man, and he never talked about a brother."

"What are you getting at?"

"Just this. For the past three years I've drunk with Corbin, eaten with him, laughed with him and once or twice I even cried with him. If I'd wanted it, I could have slept with him, though gods only know why he wanted to, considering the mess I've made of my face over the years. But I thought at the time it would just complicate our friendship.

"We watched each other's back, and bragged to each other about scores. We lent each other money and we bet on the horses, and the cards, and the dice. The day before he died, he asked me to look after his dog. And the morning he died, I had to pull that howling mutt away from the smell of his blood. I'm the one that got to tell his lover that he'd died, and how. But somehow I'm the one who's chained to a floor, and you're the one laughing when I say I'm going to kill the man who did it."

I shook my head. I was a little bitter. "Life's a funny thing, when you think about it, lord."

"You think I didn't love my brother?" I heard a hint of roughness in his voice.

"I have no idea."

"You're right. You don't. The Corbin you knew was a different man."

"That's my point exactly. The man whose death you came to avenge was already dead. I don't know who killed Corbin Hardin det Thracen-Courune. I *do* know who killed Corbin Hardin, the thief. That's who I have a score to settle with. Who do you have a score with, Lord Osskil?"

His face paled. I thought he was going to hit me, but he stood up and turned away. The silence stretched on and on. Osskil broke it first.

"Let her go, Kluge."

"My lord, I hardly think—"

"I said let her go free. Do it now."

"But Lord Osskil—"

"Do not make me say it a third time, Inspector."

"As you wish, my lord."

Osskil stuck out his hand. I didn't know what he wanted at first. Then I got it. I put my hand in his and he hauled me up. He didn't even wipe it, afterward.

"Amra, I am lodging at the Thracen manse, on the Promenade. I hope you will call on me, that I may be of assistance to you in your... endeavor. Corbin's funeral is tomorrow at noon, at the Necropolis. You are welcome to attend." And he walked out, just like that. Kluge trailed after him, snapping out a 'release her' over his shoulder.

The guards undid the chain, the shackles, the manacles. The one who had made Gerard eat shit said, "You must have struck a nerve."

"I guess so."

"You want some advice? You walk out the gates, you keep walking 'till you get to the docks. Then you board a boat. The first one away. Because as soon as this lord leaves town, Kluge will round you up. And next time, you won't never see the light of day again."

CHAPTER 14

They kept my knives. Said they were misplaced, along with all my coin. I wasn't particularly surprised. I walked down an arched corridor to a huge set of double doors. The guard opened a pedestrian door cut into the huge left-hand gate, and the sunlight streaming in made my eyes water. The world was a blur. Street traffic was a howling din. How had I never noticed how loud Lucernis was before?

Slowly my eyes adjusted, and I set off. Three blocks from Havelock I saw a signboard featuring a straight razor and a spray of whitehearts. As soon as I walked in to the barber, a booming voice assaulted my sensitive ears.

"Oy! Out with you. No beggars in 'ere!" He was absurdly tall, and thin as a stick, and his waxed, bald head reflected the morning light. He was making shooing gestures. Probably because he could smell me from across the room. I was his only customer besides an old man dozing on a bench.

I leaned against the doorframe and lifted my left foot. I pulled and twisted the heel of my boot until it swung out, revealing the little cavity I'd paid extra for. I pulled out three gold marks and flipped one to the barber.

"My name is Dorn," he said. "Welcome to my shop, mister...?"

"Since I barely look human, I won't take offense to that."

He colored. "Don't do women."

I flipped him the other marks. I'd just given him what he'd make in a month. More than a month. "For that much you will."

"Always thought I'd been missing out on half my custom, sticking to men. What would you like today, miss?"

"If I don't get clean very, very soon, I'm going to kill someone. I'm going to need a bath. No, two baths. With hot water. Not cold, not tepid. Boiling hot. I'll need new clothes and food. No gruel, no water, and no Kerf-damned rye bread. Wine, lots of it. And I have *got* to get rid of these lice. Do you have anything for that?"

"That really works, you mean?"

"Yes."

He smiled, and brought out his straight razor. "It's not just the lice. It's the nits. And they make their home down at the roots of yer hair."

"Shit."

~ ~ ~

I stepped out of Dorn's shop four hours later, in new clothes, fed, bald, and vaguely human. The only things that hadn't gone into the fire were my boots and Bosch's single strand of hair. I still itched, but was fairly certain I had been thoroughly deloused and de-nitted. My new look drew stares. One passing matron looked at me with something akin to horror in her eyes. I was going to have to get a hat.

"Should have seen me before," I told her. She hurried off. And I did the same.

~ ~ ~

When I reached out to unlock my door, a wispy face materialized in the wood grain, opened its eyes and said "Amra." I shrieked and reached for where a knife should have been.

"Holgren is coming. Stay here." Then it disappeared. Damned magic.

I unlocked the normal-once-more door and slipped inside.

My place was thoroughly, unutterably destroyed. Someone with a lot of time and patience had taken everything apart. Every pillow was ripped open, every stick of furniture was in splinters. My clothing was charred rags in the grate. Floorboards were pried up and paintings slashed. Delicate glasswork was halfway back to the sand it had been made from. If someone had given me two pennies for the whole lot, they would have overpaid.

I checked my hidey-hole. They had found that, too. Empty. That was a good chunk of my money gone.

They'd missed two good knives and one bottle of terrible wine. That was it. That was all I had left, besides a little money on deposit with a moneylender who didn't care about the provenance of his customers' coin. That, and my very, very well protected retirement money, which I had promised myself I'd never touch until I got too old to do what I do.

Oh, well. After Havelock, I was much less upset than I might otherwise have been. Prison, I found, was wonderful for clarifying your priorities. I cleared some of the debris from a corner and sat down with my bottle to wait for Holgren.

He walked through the door less than an hour later. Holgren didn't bother with knocking. Or locks, for that matter. He took a look around, one eyebrow raised.

"Did you upset the housekeeper?"

"Ha ha. Somebody turned the place while I was in prison."

"You were in prison?"

"Don't remind me. Wine?" I held out the bottle.

"Is it any good?"

"The very best I have."

He took a sip. Swallowed, reluctantly. "That's ghastly."

"True." I took another swig. "Tell me, how is it that everybody in Lucernis seems to know where I live, when I haven't told anybody?"

He shrugged, paused. "Ah, Amra?"

"Yes?"

"What in Gorm's name have you done to your hair?"

"It's the latest fashion. You don't like it?'

"I'd always assumed *hair* was an integral part of any hairstyle."

"Sure, insult my home, my wine and my looks, why don't you."

"What are friends for?"

That took me aback a little. Holgren was likeable enough for a mage, and I trusted him to a certain degree, but friends? I don't make friends easily.

"What did you want, anyway?"

"It's about that toad you left with me. Actually, it's about what's inside the toad."

"I'll bite. What's inside the toad?"

"I'm not exactly sure."

The thing about Holgren, he doesn't realize when he's being frustratingly cryptic. Probably doesn't.

"There's a vein that throbs in your forehead. I've never noticed that before. Your hair must have hidden it."

"Will you tell me what's so important about the unspecified thing in the toad?"

"Oh. Well, that's just it. I want to melt it down. To find out."

"I might need the toad. As a bargaining chip." Actually I was surprised he'd thought to wait for my permission.

"Whatever is inside, it's ancient. Definitely pre-Diaspora. And it's powerful, Amra. The most powerful artefact I've ever personally run across."

Pre-Diaspora meant that whatever it was, it was more than a thousand years old. Possibly much, much more. From the Age of Gods. From humanity's first cultures, before the Cataclysm that killed millions and saw the survivors fleeing for their lives. The time of the Diaspora, when the gods went mad and the race of man ran screaming in every direction, abandoning an entire continent. An age of myth and legend. And powerful and deadly artefacts.

"How powerful are we talking, Holgren?"

"I believe the thing inside the statuette is, in some way, self-aware. Probably intelligent, possibly even alive."

"Magical, then."

"Yes. But not human magic. I suspect that whatever it is, it was god-forged."

"And you want to let it out of the toad? Doesn't that strike you as a tad dangerous? I seem to recall you saying something like it being 'dangerous and distasteful.'"

He shrugged. "What can I say? I've always been the curious sort."

"You mages are all mad."

"Don't oversimplify, Amra. So?"

"So what?"

"Do I have your permission?"

I sighed. "Why not?"

"Good. I'd tell you to pack your things, but I suspect there's nothing to pack."

The first faint stirrings of suspicion started to claw their way through my guts. "Why should I want to pack?"

"Well you can't stay here, can you? Not with the contract and all."

My blood went cold. Suspicion blossomed into dread. "What contract?" I said in as calm a voice as I could muster.

"I didn't tell you? Someone's put a thousand mark bounty out on you. Or your corpse, rather, but only if it's intact."

"What? When?"

"Two days ago, I think. Yes, two. Must have slipped my mind."

"How does something like that slip your Kerf-damned mind?"

He seemed slightly affronted. "Well they aren't after me, now are they? Don't worry. You'll come stay with me. It's the safest place for you. That I guarantee."

"Do you have any idea what people will do for that kind of money, Holgren?"

"Oh yes. Almost anything. But attacking a mage in his own sanctum is unlikely to be one of them."

"Why my whole corpse?" I wondered. But I already had an idea.

"I can only assume they're able to use necromantic measures to extract information. Such measures require the body to be intact to a great degree."

"They want the toad."

"They want the toad," he agreed.

I put my head in my hands. I was tired. I had sworn to kill Corbin's murderer, but I didn't see how I was going do that, since I was going to be busy dodging every back alley tough with a blade, club, rock or heavy fist. I would be looking over my shoulder every second, and waiting for assassins in my sleep.

"I should leave Lucernis."

"For that much money, there will be assassins following you to any city on the Dragonsea. Anyone who vaguely matches your description is likely to get a knife in the heart. Your best course of action is to find and deal with whoever offered the contract. Or you could match the offer, I suppose."

"Oh, sure. Can you turn around for a minute while I pull a thousand marks out of my arse?" I meant it as sarcasm, but it gave me an idea. A costly idea, but an idea.

"It was just a thought. No need to get ugly."

"Well having a price on my head hasn't improved my mood." I took a deep breath.

"We will get it all sorted, Amra. You'll see. Come, let's go." He stuck a hand out and helped me up.

"Holgren."

"What?"

"Why are you helping me?"

His brow furrowed. "Why shouldn't I?"

"Because I've landed in the shit wagon, and there's no way you're going to come away clean from this if you help me out."

He cracked one of his rare smiles. Well, rare in that it wasn't condescending. Not terribly condescending, anyway. "I like you, Amra. You're capable and you have two wits to rub together. You're good at what you do. And it won't hurt to have you in my debt. Reason enough?"

"Not really, no."

He laughed. "Gods above, but you're suspicious. Come on, the day is wasting, and the longer that dog is left alone, the greater the destruction is likely to be." He dug out a frayed piece of string from a pocket and handed it to me. "Tie this around your wrist."

"What is it?"

"Just a fetish. It will suggest to inquisitive eyes that they see nothing interesting. I don't want to fight a running battle through the streets of the city."

"Magic?"

"What do you think?"

"How long is this thing good for?"

"It should be effective for two or three days."

"How effective is it? How does it work, exactly?"

"That depends. Anyone who knows you well won't be discomfited. They'll see you just as you are. To anyone who doesn't know you, you'll be just another face in the crowd. An unremarkable one. But any physical contact will negate the effects."

"What about if I just talk to someone?"

"Well, the longer you converse, the less effective it will be. Passing pleasantries won't violate the spell. A heated discussion will."

"How much do you charge for something like this?"

"If I sold such things, I imagine I could make fifty marks or so. But I don't sell my ability, Amra. At least not directly."

"Why the hells not?"

"I just don't."

I shut up, being able to take a hint when it suited me. I tied the string on to my wrist one-handed, tightening the knot with my teeth. And then we were off.

I knew Holgren's fetish was the real thing by the time we'd got to Daughter's Bridge and not a single person had taken a second look at me despite my bald head. Holgren was a damned good mage. Made me wonder yet again why he chose to steal for a living.

~ ~ ~

Despite his professed curiosity, Holgren seemed in no rush to melt down the toad. I had expected him to toss it in a crucible and stoke the fire. Instead he rambled on about some series of preparations involving the laying of wards and whatnot. I had no idea what he was talking about, and frankly didn't much care about the details.

"How long?" I asked him.

"A day, perhaps two. Likely two. I want to take care."

"Good. I want to be around to see what's inside, Kerf knows why. But I have some errands to run. You sure this bracelet is good for another day or so?"

"If any knives sprout from your back I'll give you a full refund."

"Comforting."

"When you come back, don't bother knocking. The door knows you now, and I won't want to be disturbed."

"All right. But you should really get some rest. You look like three miles of bad road. When was the last time you slept?"

He waved that away. I wanted to ask him about Bosch's hair, but he was so wrapped up in what he was doing that I didn't. It would wait. I wasn't in any rush to confront Bosch again. As I was slipping out the door, Holgren looked up from the tome he was studying.

"Amra?"

"Yeah?"

"Be careful."

"Always."

CHAPTER 15

Fengal Daruvner had been my fixer and fence almost as long as I'd been in Lucernis. I'd met him within weeks of stepping off the boat. He had given me my first contract. He'd always been fair and trustworthy, within the limits of his own self-interest. I'd brought him a lot of swag over the years. We put meat on each other's tables.

He was a large round man with the red cheeks and nose of someone who likes his drink. He never picked up a glass before noon, and never put one down after. Behind his jolly, fatherly banter was a sharp mind. He'd survived a long time on the wrong side of the law, and he'd made so few enemies as to barely count. And those he did make ended up at the bottom of the Ose, like as not. He knew everyone, and everyone knew him. He was part of the fabric of the city. Or at least the undercity.

He ran a rank eatery on Third Wall Road. The best thing that could be said about the food was that it was cheap, and the portions were huge. I found him there, ensconced at his table in the back. His runner, a kid named Kettle because of his girth, sat behind him, dozing. Daruvner had one of his nieces on his knee, telling her some outrageous story. I couldn't remember which one she was. There were five and they all looked alike except for a bit of height difference.

He saw me as I came through the door and waved me back. I guess that meant he knew me intimately enough for Holgren's fetish to have no effect. That, or Daruvner had his own magic. Or both. I weaved my way through the crowd of late night diners to his table.

The little girl ignored me, but then his nieces always ignored everyone but Uncle Fengal.

"Amra! I see you've got the Havelock curls! I must say it hasn't improved your looks."

"I just wanted to look more like you, Daruvner. You're always saying bald is beautiful."

"For a man, yes. For you?" He leaned back and considered. "It makes you look like a penitent. Or an ascetic. It makes you look haunted, girl. Haunted and holy."

Kettle opened one eye, winked at me, closed it again. Cheeky kid.

I sat down at Daruvner's table. "That's me," I said. "Saint Amra of the second story. Got anything to drink?"

Daruvner whispered in his niece's ear. She giggled, slid down off his knee, and ran off to the kitchen. Daruvner poured winter wine into two of the thimble-sized glasses it was meant to be drunk from.

"To your friend Corbin."

"You heard?"

"Of course."

"To Corbin," I said, and sipped appreciatively. It was a little sweet for my taste, but fine. Silence stretched a bit.

"Speaking of Corbin, I got a note from Locquewood that there's a package waiting for you at his shop."

I waved that away. "I've been indisposed. I'll sort that out when I have time."

He chuckled. "Indisposed. That's one way of putting it."

"So did you know, or just suspect?" I asked.

"About you being taken to Havelock? I found out the day after. I made some inquiries, talked to a friend who owes me a favor. There was nothing I could do for you."

"Why?"

"Because you were being held on a nobleman's order."

"No, I mean why did you try to help?"

He stared at me. Then he shook his head. Then he started laughing.

"What? Did I say something funny?"

"No. That's just it, Amra. It's not funny at all. But what can you do but laugh?"

"I have no idea what you're talking about."

"I know you don't. Otherwise I might be insulted." He downed his thimble, scratched his ample belly. Gave me a mild stare. "How long have we known each other?"

"Six, seven years?"

"Eight years, almost to the day. How many commissions have I got for you?"

"I don't know. Dozens."

"Thirty-eight commissions. All of which you have fulfilled, to the very letter. You've never held out on me and you've never double-crossed me. And when you work solo, you invariably come to me to fence anything that needs to be fenced."

"I'm sure I'm not the only one."

"Don't be so sure. The ones who are as clever as you, eventually they either get too clever and try to keep a commission for themselves, or they find out they aren't as clever as they thought, and get caught. And get dead."

"Like Corbin?"

"Like Corbin? I don't know. I don't know the details, but dead is dead. The point is you're something special. To lose you would be a blow to my business. And to me personally. So I tried to see if I could pry you out of Havelock. I couldn't, but it seems you managed to spring yourself. Though I hear that you might just have been safer inside."

"That's why I'm here."

He sighed. "I suspected as much. I have a cousin in Isinglas who can set you up. I know it isn't Lucernis, but what is?"

"No, Daruvner. It's not that. I'm not going anywhere."

He lifted his eyebrows. "Are you sure?"

"Very. I have some business that won't wait."

"So what do you need from me?"

"A name."

He shook his head. "I don't know a name, Amra. You would know better than I who'd want you dead."

"Not that name. I have a good idea who's paying. I want to know who inked the contract."

Murder for hire is a nasty business, even in law-challenged Lucernis, and treated appropriately. Every contract went through layers of intermediaries, to keep any of the nastiness from sticking. But somewhere under all those layers was someone who held the money, and wrote out the contract. I'd never had cause to wonder who that was. Until now.

"That... that could be very dangerous information, Amra. I'm not sure I should tell you. I can't see how knowing will help you at all. Quite the contrary."

I shrugged. "Let me worry about that. It will never come back to you, that I promise."

"It isn't that. It's just—these are not nice people, even for such as you and me. You are an artist in your way, and I am a businessman. But these people, they are killers. In their core, you understand?"

I smiled. "Whatever you might think I look like, I'm no saint, Fengal Daruvner. I've seen death, and caused it."

"But it isn't your trade. You don't strangle old ladies in their beds to secure inheritances. You don't knife cheating husbands, you don't hurl barren wives down flights of stairs. That sort of ruthlessness is not in you, Amra Thetys, no more than it is in me. The man attached to the name you want, he is as bad as they come."

"So you know him."

"I once saw him cut a man's throat. The poor bastard was eating his dinner, and they were laughing and chatting, and then in the blink of an eye he slit the poor sod's neck from ear to ear. And then he pushed the dying man out of the chair, sat down in it, and finished the bloody food." Daruvner shook his head. "Do you know what he said to me? He said, 'Needs more salt.'"

"What's his name, Daruvner? It's not like there's no-one else to ask."

"You won't listen, will you? His name is Gavon, then. Guache Gavon. He owns the Cock's Spur, down in the Rookery."

The Rookery was a part of Lucernis that had turned cancerous over the centuries, home only to the destitute and the desperate. Morno's reforms weren't even a rumor in its narrow, labyrinthine, garbage-choked streets, and the Watch didn't dare set foot in it. People called it the Twelfth Hell. And the Cock's Spur was one of the public houses that was considered to have a 'bad' reputation there. It didn't surprise me that the owner also had a side-line in murder for hire.

"Thank you, Fengal."

"Don't thank me for telling you something likely to get you killed."

"Fine then. But I owe you."

"Do you mean that?"

"Yes."

"Then make me a promise."

"If I can."

"Don't go alone."

"Fengal—"

"I mean it, Amra. Don't go down there without someone to watch your back. Literally. I can scare up someone capable and trustworthy if you give me a couple of hours."

"Who did you have in mind?"

"The mage. Holgren Angrado."

"He's busy right now."

One eyebrow rose.

"He's already helping me, in exchange for something you don't want to know anything about. Trust me."

"Well he's sensible enough to know I'm right about this. Don't go to the Rookery without him."

"Fengal, I'm a grown woman."

"You owe me, and you promised."

"Not yet I haven't."

"But you will."

And a quarter hour later, I did. I was tired of arguing. Daruvner usually gets what he wants, if for no other reason than he has the patience of a stone.

CHAPTER 16

I hadn't told Daruvner why I wanted Gavon's name, and he hadn't asked directly. He was too polite for that. Or he knew better than to ask questions he didn't want answers to. He suspected I planned to kill the man, to make a statement. Which had its appeal, admittedly, but it wasn't what I had planned. Would-be assassins would certainly be put off if I killed the man who inked the contract on me, but I just don't have the stomach for cold-blooded murder. Daruvner was right about that. Oh, I could argue the morality of it with myself all day, and make a perfect case for putting a knife in the heart of a man who made a living being the middleman for murderers and their clients, but I couldn't fool myself. If I had to I could do it, but I hoped I wouldn't have to.

Instead I was going to try something a little more tricky. I was counting on the fact that a fixer, even a fixer for assassins, would have to honor any contract if he wanted to stay in business.

I just hoped to Kerf that it worked. If it did, no one would dream of trying to cash in on the bounty that had been put on my head. If it didn't, I'd almost certainly be dead. Either way, my problems would be over.

But before all that, I had a funeral to attend.

~ ~ ~

The City of the Dead. From the outside it looked like some mad prince's idea of a fortress, massive white walls stretching up and up, though there were no sentry towers. I certainly wouldn't have wanted to try and scale them; they were damned-near glassy and thoroughly seamless. Besides, against all that white I would have been a tad conspicuous, whatever I wore. Also, there was no need. The gate to the Necropolis was open, unlocked, and unguarded all day long. If I ever decided it behooved me to rob the dead, I could just stroll in and hide myself in a corner somewhere until everyone left. Gods knew the place was full of nooks and crannies.

There was only one gate, a thing of impressive impracticality made of oak timbers a foot thick banded with iron and inscribed with arcane symbols that throbbed with power. Next to the gate in a half-dozen languages was a notice:

The Gate Closes Half a Glass Before Sunset.
Be Ye on the Outside Before Then.
No Littering
No Blood-Spilling
No Hurdy-Gurdy Music
No Fornication

It made me wonder. Was all of this to keep the dead safe, or the living?

Once in the gate I was surrounded by mausoleums. Some were little bigger than doll houses, others dwarfed my rented rooms. Headstones and statuary squeezed higgledy-piggledy in between.

There was one gravel path. I took it, but the task of finding Corbin's funeral was daunting. The place was a giant maze.

"It's over there, on the hill with the large, not terribly well done Weeping Mother statue."

I spun around. It was the boy in the penitent's robes.

"What is?"

"Your friend's funeral."

"Who the hells are you?"

"Arhat," he said, as if that cleared everything up.

"What do you want, Arhat?"

"To pay my respects. I... failed your friend, in a manner of speaking. I'm sorry."

"Failed him how?" I asked, but he just shook his shaved head and said "Now is not the time." And then he disappeared. Literally, before my eyes.

I just stood there for a second. I mean, what would you do? Myself, I blew out a big breath of air and cursed.

"Lucernis," I muttered to myself as I made my way up to the hill he'd indicated, "gets weirder every damned day."

I was a little late. They'd already had the ceremonial meal and were cleaning up from that. Which was fine; as much as I cared for Corbin, he wasn't smelling like a flower, and despite the careful makeup he looked like what he was- a corpse propped up in a comfy chair at the head of the funerary table. It reminded me of nothing so much as some sort of gruesome child's tea party, but like I said, I'm not from Lucernis. Where I come from, somebody dies, you bury them if you have some land or burn them if you don't. You say a few words, and then get back to the business of living and grieving. Or celebrating, as the case may be.

Osskil sat on his brother's right, and three other men I didn't know took up the other seats, except for the one at the foot of the table. The one reserved for spouses or significant others. That one was empty. I wondered if Estra knew of the funeral, or if she'd simply chosen not to come.

The men were all of advanced age, with impressive facial hair. They looked so alike they had to be brothers. They were dressed in finery that looked just a tad threadbare. Professional mourners, I supposed. The other noble houses weren't going to be sending representatives; Corbin was an embarrassment. They'd all just politely ignore the whole thing.

Osskil rose and bowed when he saw me, but addressed himself to Corbin.

"Your friend Amra has come, Corbin. I told you she would. She's a bit late for the meal, but perhaps we can persuade her to have a drink with us?" The other men nodded and smiled encouragement.

"A drink would be very welcome," I managed, and Osskil made a bottle appear and filled glasses for everyone, including Corbin of course.

"Perhaps we could persuade Amra to give us a toast, Corbin?"

"Oh, I don't think—"

"A toast! A toast!" The other men quickly started up, and Osskil gave me a look that more or less said, 'Give the dead man a toast, you mannerless savage.' And so I did.

I raised my glass, cleared my throat, and said "Corbin knew—" A glare from Osskil. "—that is to say, Corbin, you *know* that I am not one for public speaking. You, ah, are a good man. I am lucky to count you as my friend."

A chorus of 'Hear her! Hear her!' from the others. I had no idea what else to say. I cast a desperate glance at Osskil and he nodded and put back his drink, so I did as well, expecting wine.

It looked like wine, and tasted like wine for the most part, but there was something else to it and my head almost immediately began to spin and my heart started thumping up in my ears. I looked at Osskil again and he tilted his head toward his brother.

Corbin sat, grinning, at the head of the table. He was looking straight at me, and I knew that grin. It was one he reserved for the petty, hilarious misfortunes of others. No malice in it, just good humor. Then he looked over at his brother, and his face sobered. He raised his glass to Osskil and nodded, and Osskil did the same.

And then the world rushed back in, and Corbin was just a corpse once more. But his cup had tumbled to the grass. Empty.

"Well. That was... unexpected." I managed. Seeing Corbin apparently returned to life, even if only briefly, had touched a nerve. It was an unlooked-for gift, but it also brought back the rawness of his loss. I wasn't sure if the trade-off was worth it.

"A special wine, in a special place, for a special man," said one of the mourners. Osskil said nothing. The redness of his eyes spoke for him.

Then it was time to bundle him up and stick him in his tomb. They just lifted him, chair and all, and walked him into the mausoleum. Put him in a patch of light from a stained glass window. Put a delicate little wrought-iron table next to him, and loaded it up with food and drink. And that was that. Or so I thought.

Osskil was the last one out. I heard him whisper 'Farewell, little brother' and saw him kiss the top of Corbin's head. Then he came out and closed the door.

The thief in me wondered where the lock was, and said so out loud.

"What need for locks in the City of the Dead? The dead know their own, Amra, as you have seen. You are welcome here, for Corbin has acknowledged you. And if an interloper were to dare disturb his rest, well, that's what the Guardian is for."

"The Guardian? I thought that was just some kind of granny tale to keep the kids out of the graveyard."

"Most assuredly not. The Guardian of the Dead is as real as you are, and ancient, and hideously powerful. The strictures posted at the gate are there to keep us living safe from it."

"Even the one about hurdy-gurdy music?"

He smiled. "Perhaps not that one. I suspect it's there just to preserve a sense of class."

"So blood, fornicating and littering all make the Guardian upset, eh?"

"Absolutely. Especially blood. Never, ever spill blood here, Amra. The Guardian *will* notice, and investigate. You don't want to meet it."

"No offense, Lord Osskil, but I'm just the slightest bit sceptical."

"Look over there. You see that mausoleum, the one with the gargoyles doing unspeakable things to each other? That's the final resting place of Borkin Breaves."

"The richest man in Lucernis?"

"Indeed he was. Still is. Inside his crypt I know for a fact are sacks and sacks of gold and jewels. I was at the funeral when they carted it all in. I was just a boy, then."

"You do realize who you're talking to, right?"

He gave me a sober look. "Please don't think about trying to rob Breaves' crypt, Amra."

"Why the hells not?"

"Besides the fact that it is incredibly gauche to rob the dead, you mean? Because when Breaves was put into his tomb, there were no gargoyles adorning the edifice. No adornment of any sort, in fact. It was just a big, ugly, plain marble cube. People were scandalized."

"Oh, please," I said. "You're saying the Guardian transformed those who tried to rob the tomb into that?"

"The Guardian has a vile sense of humor. Go and take a look. I know you won't take my word for it."

"Absolutely."

The other men had packed up all the funeral oddments and were waiting for Osskil.

"Farewell, Amra. Thank you for coming. It meant much to Corbin."

"It meant a lot to me as well." I stuck out my hand and he shook it, then held onto it for an extra beat.

"Call upon me when you are ready to move on Corbin's murderer. Please."

"All right."

He moved off down the hill with his group of rented mourners, and I ambled over to Borkin Breaves's tomb. The gargoyles were indeed doing things to each other, and by the looks on their disturbingly human faces, nobody was having much fun with it. Didn't prove anything, of course. I didn't believe a word of it. But then I doubted there was even a single gold mark in the mausoleum, either.

There was one gargoyle down low, half-obscured by weeds. Something about it made me take a second look. I pushed back the milky stalks and stared right into the scream-frozen face of Tolum Handy.

Tolum Handy was a thief who worked with Daruvner, same as me.

He'd disappeared the year before.

CHAPTER 17

It was well past midnight when Holgren and I arrived at the Cock's Spur. I'd pulled Holgren away from his 'meditation'–which to me looked suspiciously like a nap. Unless his whistling snore was actually a magely chant of sorts. If so, Bone's rumbling, snuffling snore was the perfect counterpoint.

I told him what I intended to do, and what Daruvner had made me promise. Holgren had agreed with Daruvner, in a bleary-eyed, grumpy sort of way.

I'd made one stop on our way to the Rookery, at Temple Street, north of Temple Market. At the modest temple of Bath the Silent, to be more precise. God of secrets.

Unlike its grand neighbors, there was no scrollwork, no fluted columns, no larger-than-life statuary to grace the front of Bath's temple, no maxims carved into stone and picked out in gold-leaf. His temple was built from porphyry, speckled gray and white, where others were faced with white marble or alabaster. And it was a small place, as these things go.

It was where people went to unburden their souls, secure in the knowledge someone would listen, and never tell. Holgren waited outside, insisting his secrets were his own and that he intended to keep it that way. I shrugged and climbed the well-worn steps to the small, unassuming nave.

A lesser-known aspect of Bath was that he didn't just receive confessions. He, or rather his priests, also held on to valuables. Anything that could be considered a secret was safe with the Silent One.

This was where I kept my retirement money. It earned no interest as it would with a money lender, but it also incurred no fees, and it was as safe in Bath's Temple as it would be anywhere in the world. I certainly wouldn't try to steal from him. What happened to the bodies of those who *had* tried was a secret, too.

An acolyte met me at the narrow door, quite nondescript except for the fact that his lips had been sewn shut. I'd always wondered how they ate. Another of Bath's secrets, I suppose. He led me through silent halls bathed in soft candlelight and faintly scented with some unfamiliar, musky incense. I had come to think of that scent as the smell of secrets, and for all I know that's exactly what it was.

The place was bigger inside, somehow, than it appeared to be from the street. How much bigger I didn't know, but big enough to make me believe Bath had potent magics at his disposal.

A short time later we stopped at a plain oak door, and the acolyte ushered me through.

Inside was a small, bare white room. The only furniture was a small table, on which rested eleven chains: Long, narrow bars of buttery gold cast to break precisely into ten even pieces, or staves. Ten marks to a stave. Ten staves to a chain. Eleven hundred gold marks. Which left me with about a half-dozen marks to my name once I hauled them to the Rookery.

No secrets from Bath.

I loaded the chains into a satchel I'd brought along for the purpose, and turned to go. I was surprised to find the acolyte still standing in the doorway.

"My master has a message for you."

The little hairs on the back of my neck shot up, half because of the magic that had flooded the room, half because him talking to me was very, very creepy. It had certainly never happened before.

"How do you do that with your lips sewn shut?"

He smiled, which was rather ghastly to look at. "I can't tell you. I could show you...?"

"Um. No, thanks. What message does the high priest have for me?"

He shook his head. "Not Dalthas."

"Oh. You mean—" The goose bumps were crawling, now. I shivered despite myself.

"Yes."

Bath himself had a message for me? What the hells?

"My Master bids me tell you to beware She Who Casts Eight Shadows."

"Who might that be?" But I remembered the bloodwitch's warning about the Eightfold Bitch, and her Blade.

"My master does not say."

"I'm surprised he said anything. Being the Silent and all."

The acolyte smiled that horrid little smile again. "Secrets are my master's coin. And while he is frugal, he is not a miser. He spends carefully, but that is not the same as hoarding."

"So, not Bath the Silent. What then? Bath the Very Quiet? Bath the Extremely Reticent?"

"As you like. But now you too have a secret, of sorts. You would be wise to keep it."

"Is that a warning from your master?"

"Advice from my lowly self. Those who come here to admit faults, failings, sins... well, would they come if they knew the Silent One sometimes spoke?"

I shrugged. "Bath chose to share a secret with me. I think I can stand to keep a secret about him."

He bowed his head and drifted out the door. I followed, and met Holgren on the steps. As we walked towards the Rookery, I asked him "Have you ever heard of somebody called She Who Casts Eight Shadows?"

"A goddess. Killed during the Wars of the Gods. Why?"

"I don't know. I'm supposed to beware her, apparently. But if she's dead—Did you say *wars*, as in more than one?"

"Oh yes. There were several leading up to the last. Everyone tends to focus on the last one. But what's this about bewaring a goddess?"

I smiled. "It's a secret. If you'd come in with me...."

He arched one eyebrow and frowned. And let the matter drop.

~ ~ ~

The Rookery after midnight was unpleasant. Human wreckage littered the gutters, sometimes indistinguishable from all the garbage until a head moved or a hand was held out in mute appeal. I'd forgotten how depressing the Rookery was, along with how awful the stench could be in summer.

The darkened streets fairly seethed with bad intent, along with misery and abject poverty. Bravos loitered in front of taverns and shuttered shops, passing bottles of piss ale and laughing too loudly for genuine humor. Eyes tracked us as we walked to the front of the Cock's Spur, weighed us, judged whether we were predators or prey. Or maybe that was too easy a conceit. Everyone was meat here. It was just a question of how tough the meat might be, whether it was worth the bother of bringing it down and chewing it up.

"The big fish eat the little fish," Holgren murmured, echoing my thoughts in a way, "Except, I suppose, when the little fish band together to eat the big fish."

I grunted. If these surroundings made Holgren philosophical it shouldn't have surprised me. He chose to live next to the charnel grounds, after all. For myself, it just reminded me of the bad old days. Bellarius. Another city, another time, even another life, it sometimes seemed to me. But not long enough ago and not far enough away, and if I happened to forget, I needed only to look at my own scarred face reflected in a mirror, or a stranger's eyes.

I took in the leaning, ramshackle two story building in front of us. It was all of wood, and rotting. It hadn't seen paint in a generation. The termites probably had to hold hands to keep it standing.

"Do termites have hands?" I asked Holgren.

"I doubt it. I've never checked. Why?"

"Come on," I said, "let's get this done. The sooner we're out of here, the better." And I walked in through the slightly skewed door of the Cock's Spur, Holgren at my heels.

In a place like the Cock's Spur, they don't even bother putting out chairs or benches that don't face the door. Nobody wants their back to any trouble that enters. As I came through the door, a couple dozen pairs of eyes skewered me. Well, except for the one hairy brute that had lost a beady, pig-like peeper somewhere, and in the not-too distant past, judging from the puss weeping out of the socket. He really should have considered an eye patch; if not for himself, then at least for anyone forced to look at him.

After a heartbeat, all the eyes slid right off me onto Holgren, which gave me faith in the fetish he'd given me. Or maybe it was the quality of his clothes. I heard Holgren sniff behind me.

"What's that smell?" he murmured.

"I think they're brewing ale."

"Oh. I thought it was cat urine. Is it supposed to smell that way?"

"Maybe the house recipe calls for cat piss." I'd heard of stranger ingredients, if not less disgusting. Bludgeoned roosters and the like. There was a reason I generally stuck to wine.

"I find myself appallingly unthirsty," said Holgren.

"Come on, let's brace the bartender."

"About the ingredients?"

"About the owner."

"Good idea. Take your complaint to the top, I always say." Holgren was nervous. He joked when he was nervous, I'd finally figured out. That Holgren was nervous made me nervous. Which made me pissy. I strode over to the bar along the left-hand wall where the tap man was pushing a filthy rag along the filthy bar top.

"When you're done rearranging the dirt, I want to speak to Gavon."

"Ee innt ear," the spindly man said, or something like it.

"Sorry, could you speak a human language?"

He hawked and spat. "Gavon's not 'ere."

I lifted the heavy satchel to the bar top and lifted the flap so he could see. "Get him here, and soon, or I'll let everybody in the place have a look at this. If I do that, they'll try to take it away from me, and then me and my friend will have to kill them all. That won't be good for business."

He stared at me for a second. "You couldn't take um all."

"If they take Gavon's gold, it won't matter if we could or couldn't. Not to you, anyway, because he'll kill you for pissing around instead of minding his business."

He thought about that. "That's a point. Stay 'ere."

He drifted up a set of decrepit stairs into the gloom above. Three of the bigger patrons seemed to take that as a signal of opportunity. They got up and walked toward Holgren and me, bad intent written all over their faces. I slipped a knife into the palm of my hand, but Holgren stepped between me and them.

"Gentlemen," he said, purple light suddenly arcing from hand to hand, "the tap man will be back shortly. I'm sure he'll see to refills then. Until such time, I suggest you remain seated."

Two of them saw the sense in that. One, a lean man with enormous hands, fingered something under his shirt. Some sort of talisman. I could see him deciding to place his faith in it.

"Why, I just wanted to have a word, all private-like," he said. "You being newcomers to this fine establishment and all, I thought—" and the knife came from his waist and towards Holgren's throat in a blur of reflected lantern light.

Holgren was quick, quicker than I would have given him credit for. He twisted away, and the knife blade kissed his earlobe on its way to being buried in the wall behind the bar.

The man wasn't waiting to see if his blade would do the job; he was already rushing in with those big hands clenched into fists. Holgren put his own hand out, palm forward, and that purple arcing light leaped from his hand to the would-be killer's face. Where it began to gnaw at the flesh like a hungry animal. In an instant I could see the man's teeth through a hole in his cheek. He screamed and stumbled, and clawed at his own face. He fell to the hard-packed dirt floor and screamed some more. Holgren fingered his cut earlobe. His hand came away red. He pulled a handkerchief out of his sleeve.

"That's enough, mage." A voice from the stairs, mild, a little high pitched. I glanced up and saw a supremely nondescript man drumming his fingers against the railing, the tap man behind him.

"He started it, Gavon."

"So finish it, Angrado."

"Fine." Holgren did nothing that I could see, but the weird light playing on what was left of the man's face winked out. The man stopped screaming after a few seconds. I glanced at him, then took a double take. The only wounds on his face were the claw marks he'd made himself.

Holgren leaned down, elbows on knees, and said conversationally, "That trinket around your neck has never been within a mile of a mage. Until tonight." Then he stood and walked toward the stairs. After a moment, I followed.

CHAPTER 18

"Why didn't you kill him, Angrado?" Gavon asked as he motioned us to sit at a candlelit table in the center of the upstairs gloom.

"Why should I bother?" Holgren replied.

Gavon chuckled. "You always were too squeamish for your own good. That one won't thank you for sparing him. He'll kill you if he can."

"But he can't. Not on his best day. And if I'm squeamish, what does that make you?"

"A man unconcerned with niceties."

"You mean morals. Or is it scruples?"

Gavon smiled, mirthlessly. "No one can hold a grudge like a Low Countryman, it seems."

"You would know, wouldn't you? But I'm only half Low Country, as you seemed to take every opportunity to point out."

"I believe I also said you were half a man."

Holgren grinned, and I knew things were about to turn ugly. "Mariette seemed to think I was man enough," he said. "How *is* you sister?"

And that's when the knives came out. Gavon suddenly held two huge pig stickers, and Holgren a spitting, hissing blade of white light. They were both standing, chairs knocked back.

"I'll see your half-breed guts on the floor for that," said Gavon. Holgren just smiled.

I cleared my throat. "So I guess you two know each other?"

"Oh, yes," said Gavon. "Holgren Angrado and I have a history."

I turned to look at Holgren. "You might have mentioned that," I said.

"You never asked."

"I have an idea," I said. "Let's put away the blades and do some business. Gavon, you can still kill somebody, and make a profit to boot." I heaved the satchel up onto the table in front of him. His eyes flickered to all that gold. His knives disappeared and suddenly he was smiling. He deliberately turned away from Holgren to face me directly.

"Knowing that one won't get you a discount, you know. In fact I should charge extra."

"Believe me, I am regretting his acquaintance at the moment." Holgren took the hint and extinguished his blade.

"So talk to me."

I heaved an inner sigh of relief. Outwardly, I put on my dubious face. "To be honest, I don't think you'll touch this contract."

"I have never yet come across one that couldn't be fulfilled."

"I'd want you to execute it personally."

"Now that is a problem. I don't really do that anymore. Only on special occasions, you might say."

"Well then, I'm sorry to have wasted your time." I flipped the satchel closed and began to heave it back on my shoulder.

"Let's hear it, at least," said Gavon, taking his seat again.

I took off Holgren's fetish. "You inked a contract on one Amra Thetys. I want to take out a contract on anyone who turns up to get paid for it."

He laughed outright. "Oh, you've got balls, I'll give you that. It's almost clever. I suppose you'd want it to be public knowledge, as well."

"Naturally. The dead don't care about revenge."

"What made you think I would agree to something like this?"

I put on a puzzled expression. "Money, of course. One chain just for saying yes, and ten more on the off chance you have to kill someone."

"I could kill you right now, earn the original contract, and take what you brought."

"That's what he's here for." I jabbed a thumb in Holgren's direction. "Besides, you wouldn't. Bad for your reputation, killing prospective clients."

Gavon sat back, drumming his fingers on the arm of his chair. "If I agree, I'll open myself up to all kinds of headaches. People trying to outbid contracts. It will be a mess."

"Yes. I can see it escalating, people trying to outbid each other. And every one of them paying a ten per cent, non-refundable commission to you. All that gold piling up will be very messy indeed."

Slowly, he smiled. "I do like the way you think. But unfortunately, I can't personally take this commission. I have to maintain my impartiality." He leaned forward. "I'll ink the contract, and I'll spread the word, and you will just have to take your chances that it's enough. And if the original client wishes to up their offer, well..." He shrugged.

"I suppose that will have to do." It wasn't everything I had hoped for, but I thought it would be enough. For a while, at least. I stood, and he followed suit.

"I'll be wanting my ten chains back soon, Gavon. Once I kill your other client."

"We'll see."

"I know who it is, but confirmation would be nice. You wouldn't want to help me with that, would you?"

"I'm afraid I have to keep that confidential, being part of the service and all. It's been a pleasure, Amra Thetys. May I suggest you leave through the back? I imagine there are a half-dozen cutthroats waiting for you in front by now. News travels fast in the Rookery when the news is gold-colored. Holgren, of course, is welcome to leave the way he came."

~ ~ ~

News indeed travelled fast, but Holgren blew through the motley collection of murderers waiting for us outside like an autumn storm off the Dragonsea. Quite literally. It's hard to stick a knife in someone when you're rolling down the street, being pushed along by gale-force winds. Holgren was proving to be a lot more powerful—and versatile—than I'd ever imagined. And I have an active imagination.

We made it back to civilization in time for last call at Tambor's. Holgren bought a jug, owing to the fact that I was now virtually destitute, and we sat outside at one of the scarred tables and sipped vinegar. After a silent while Holgren finally spoke up.

"You know what you've done, don't you?"

"Um, saved my own neck?"

"Yes, that. Probably. But you've also changed the face of low justice in Lucernis forever." He shook his head. "Gavon has been running the murder-for-hire racket in Lucernis for nearly a decade. Given twice as long, he never would have thought of your ploy. You've made that bastard richer than he ever dreamed, in one night."

"So you did know we were going to see him! Why didn't you tell me you knew him?"

He smiled. "As I said, you never asked. To be honest, I was hoping things would get out of hand so I could kill him."

"What is it between you two?"

"We grew up together, in Fel-Radoth. He is my cousin, once removed. We were never what you would call friendly."

"He's got to be twenty years older than you."

"One of the advantages of being a mage, Amra, is that you don't have to look your age."

"Did you really sleep with his sister?"

He shuddered. "Mariette? I'd sooner sleep with a pheckla. Certainly less dangerous, and probably more pleasurable. Guache was considered the nice one of the brood." He shifted his gaze from the bowl of wine in front of him to the street running beside Tambor's arbor, where we sat.

I don't remember what I was going to say next, because suddenly Holgren was lunging over the table at me, knocking me down to the ground. I do remember getting a hand around a knife hilt, and then the world erupting in flame.

"Stay low!" Holgren hissed, then rolled off me and sat up. He made an intricate gesture with one hand, face grim as death, and suddenly the flames vanished, leaving charred, smoking ruins around us that, seconds before, had been Tambor's arbor. And some of Tambor's other customers.

In the street, people were screaming and running. A dray horse bolted in its traces, and in its fear reduced the cart and its driver to pulp. The immediate surroundings were complete chaos, but the chaos was fleeing the vicinity as fast as it could, leaving a stillness in its wake.

I heard clapping. I looked out into the street and saw Bosch walking toward us, half a dozen swordsmen at his back. He was clapping in time with his own dragging footsteps.

"Excellent negation," he said, "especially *extemporé*. I applaud you, sir."

Holgren stood up and brushed himself off. "I am going to kill you for that," he said mildly, and sauntered out into the street towards Bosch.

"Please, let's avoid unnecessary confrontation. For my part, I apologize," said Bosch. "I had no idea a fellow magus would be in the thief's company. I will happily make amends. As soon as I secure her corpse." He pointed his stubbled chin towards me. "What do you say?"

"I say you talk too much."

"So be it," said Bosch, and another inferno burst forth from his open hands, engulfing Holgren in a maelstrom of flame. I could barely make out his form, a dark, wavering blur at the heart of a torrent of fire. I saw his smudged silhouette crumple. I saw Bosch grin, beads of sweat rolling down his face, dripping from his nose and unshaven chin. The men with him stood watching, most with mouths agape. A mage's duel isn't something you see every day.

Finally the river of fire sputtered, slowed to a trickle, failed. It was eerily silent.

Holgren was down on one knee. His clothes smoked, but his lean face was cold.

"My turn," he said, and flicked the fingers of one hand.

Bosch's body literally exploded, splattering his swordsmen and twenty yards of the cobbled street with blood and bloody gobbets of flesh. All that was left of him was his head, which fell to the ground and, I swear to Kerf, blinked for a few seconds. My stomach did a backflip at that.

"You'd best be on your way," said Holgren to the sell-swords, and they saw the sense in that. Holgren picked up Bosch's head by its lank, greasy hair. Stared into the shocked, blinking eyes.

Bosch mouthed a word and his eyes went cold and dead. Nobody home.

"Bloody hells," Holgren spat. He looked at me, and there was something feral in his eyes. "He's jumped."

"What? What does that mean?"

"It means we haven't seen the last of him. He'll be back, in some form or fashion. That's a trick you can only get by treating with infernal powers. Bosch" Holgren said with plain distaste, "is a daemonist. Let's go."

I nodded. The watch couldn't be far away. We needed to leave. "Go where?"

"Back to Gavon's. Where else?"

"But if Bosch isn't really dead–"

"He is. It's just that he's bought himself a short encore. Do you want the contract on you cancelled or not?"

"By all means, let's go see your cousin."

We set off down the nearest alley. We stopped only once, while I stole somebody's freshly laundered shirt from a second story drying pole. Holgren took it from me without a word and wrapped Bosch's noggin in it, using the tag-ends of the sleeves as a handle.

You can't just go walking around with a severed head in Lucernis. But you can, I discovered, walk around with a lumpy head-shaped item, wrapped in linen and dripping blood. I think it's just that nobody really wants to know you're walking around with a severed head, and are appreciative of the courtesy of leaving room for doubt.

In any case, nobody gave us more than a second glance, and the second-glancers made sure to move along quickly, giving us a wide berth.

Whatever Holgren was feeling, he kept it bottled up. I stole the occasional glance at him as we walked, and the best I can say was his face had gone from cold to stony. As for me, I was coming to terms with what I'd seen him do.

I have seen and caused death. It's never pretty. There is no 'right' way to kill – if you need to kill somebody, you do it any way that works. It wasn't the fact that Holgren had been so cold about turning Bosch into a red smear, and it wasn't that Bosch had met such a spectacularly disgusting demise. What bothered me was just how easily Holgren had done it. He'd decided Bosch was going to die, and just like that, Bosch was dead. Messily, spectacularly, violently dead.

That kind of raw power was terrifying.

It seemed impossible that I'd been joking with someone who could, just by wiggling his fingers, turn me into a fine red mist.

So. There was a certain reserve that sprang up between us on that walk.

When we arrived at the Cock's Spur for the second time that night, Holgren didn't make any jokes, and nobody else felt like trying their luck.

CHAPTER 19

Holgren just sort of blasted the door off its hinges and strolled in, swinging Bosch's head back and forth in a bored, idle way. The scum and villainy that was the Cock's Spur's patrons wisely remained seated and avoided eye contact. Holgren climbed the splintered wooden stairs to Guache's office. I followed.

Holgren blasted the office door, too.

Guache was sitting at his table, eating a very late dinner. Pork pie, from the smell. My satchel full of gold was still in front of him. He didn't look up, didn't say anything, didn't acknowledge Holgren in any way. He just went about shovelling pork pie into his mouth like he hadn't a care in the world. When Holgren tossed Bosch's wrapped head onto the table, Guache finally glanced at him, and that glance was pure contempt.

These two men truly hated each other, and one of them would kill the other, and probably sooner rather than later. That much I felt in my gut.

"You sent word to Bosch as soon as we left," I said.

"Before that, actually," replied Guache.

"Well there's his head."

Guache leaned back in his chair, wiped his mouth with one sleeve. "I had a cat that used to bring me dead things too. Are you applying to be my pet, Amra Thetys?"

Holgren cursed and slammed Guache out of his chair with one fist. Guache was up again in an instant, knives out, and Holgren murmured some harsh syllable and suddenly Guache Gavon was spread-eagled against the wall. His feet did not touch the ground. Strain as he might, Guache Gavon was pinned to the wall, utterly helpless and in thrall to Holgren's magic. He looked bored.

"I've brought you Bosch's head, Gavon. Now my partner is taking her ten chains back."

Gavon opened his mouth to say something, but whatever it was, was lost as a little black nightmare exploded through the window shutters.

All teeth and claws, and reeking of rotting blood and charred flesh, it was a little smaller than Bone. It smashed through the wooden slats as though they were made of paper and landed on the table, hissing and lashing a barbed tail. It had the head of a boyne beetle. If boyne beetles grew to dog size.

Holgren dropped his cousin and started another spell.

Too late. The thing snatched up Bosch's head and was out the window again before he had got two liquid syllables past his lips. I'm embarrassed to say I didn't even get a knife out until it was gone.

"By all the dead gods, what was that?" I said.

"Daemonette." Holgren spat. "We definitely haven't seen the last of that foul daemonist."

Gavon started laughing. Genuine, humor-filled laughter. I swear, tears started in the corners of his eyes. After a few seconds it seemed he was having trouble catching his breath.

"Looks like I'll be holding onto your gold for a while longer," he finally managed, then started up laughing again.

Gavon was still chuckling as we left. His mirth followed us down the stairs and out the door.

~ ~ ~

False dawn was scratching at the sky by the time Holgren and I made it back to his sanctum. He wasn't in much of a talking mood. He flopped down on his dusty couch and Bone sauntered over to him and put his heavy head in Holgren's lap. Holgren rubbed it idly and stared off into nothing.

"We know Bosch was–is–working for this Elamner, besides being friendly with creatures from hells," I said. "It only stands to reason that his boss is the one behind everything. Corbin's death. The contract on my life. The only problem is, I think the Elamner might actually be dead."

"What do you mean?"

"That's right. I never told you about breaking into his villa." I told Holgren about the corpse I'd seen, the knife sticking out of his chest, the magic that had infused the room.

Holgren gave me a flat stare. "Just to make sure, you are aware that I'm a mage, correct?"

"I know sarcasm fits you like a tailored suit, but I'm a little tired. Can you get to the point?"

"What you saw wasn't a murder scene, ritual or otherwise. It was a containment ritual. A brutal one, from the Ardesh steppes. The man you saw wasn't dead. He was just... paused."

"Paused? What the hells does that mean?"

"Paused. Suspended. Taken out of time. Put on ice. Take the knife out of his heart, and his life resumes. It's a rather tricky bit of magic, actually. You've got to slip the knife in precisely between heartbeats."

"Shit. So Bosch really is just a flunky for the Elamner?"

He shrugged. "I don't know how you come to that conclusion. Just because he didn't murder his employer doesn't mean he hasn't gone rogue. Or don't you think a daemonist would be capable of lying to, cheating on or stealing from his employer?"

I waved that away. "No, listen. This Elamner, Heirus, hires a mage, gets him to perform this ritual. It sure as hells didn't look like something you could surprise somebody with."

"No. It would require willing participation."

"What sort of person would want to be taken out of life like that? Suspended?"

"I haven't the faintest idea."

"I do. Somebody who doesn't have much time left. Someone who needs to ration it. Somebody who is sick, maybe. Dying. Maybe in constant pain. Somebody waiting for a Kerf-damned cure."

Holgren smiled. "Oh, you are clever, Amra. Perhaps a cure from the Age of the

Gods?"

I stood up and walked to the door. "Don't melt that toad down yet, Holgren. I think we need to know a little more before we do anything that can't be undone."

"Probably wise. Where are you going?"

"There's a nobleman I need to visit on the Promenade."

"I should probably say something amusing, but all that comes to mind is 'huh?'"

"It's Corbin's long-lost brother. If we're going to make a social call on the Elamner, we're going to need some hired blades. I haven't got any more money, but Baron Thracen does. And he's got a good reason to spend it."

"If you have time, perhaps you could visit Lagna's temple as well and see if that old man knows anything about the toad."

I groaned.

"What?"

"I don't like him. He's smelly and makes me feel like an idiot."

"He makes everyone feel like an idiot. He's the high priest of the god of knowledge."

"Fine. But you're going to have to lend me some money for his fee."

"It's not a fee. It's an offering."

I snorted.

"Anything you'd like me to do?" he asked, passing me a few marks.

I stopped. "Actually, yes." I fished Bosch's hair from the button I'd wound it around, handed it to him. "Do you think you can find Bosch with this, even though he hasn't got a body anymore?"

He took it and smiled. It wasn't a friendly smile. "Oh, certainly."

"If Baron Thracen agrees to help us, I'll have him send a runner to you. I want to move tonight. Or even earlier."

"That sounds suspiciously like a plan."

"No, it sounds like a steaming hot mess. We'll see if it improves."

CHAPTER 20

Osskil wasn't home.

The gate guard at the Thracen manse didn't want to tell me even that much until I gave my name, then after a muttered conference with his partner who then disappeared inside, someone higher up the servant's ladder came out and informed me that the baron was breakfasting with Lord Morno, and would be pleased to see me in the early afternoon. I guess Osskil had left instructions.

I was a little surprised that Osskil was important enough to be having meals with Morno. Lord Morno, the governor of Lucernis, generally has his hands full, what with all the political manoeuvring that comes with ruling the largest city in the West. Morno's a law and order man to his black, shrivelled soul. Governing Lucernis must be enough to make him dyspeptic. I doubt he gets much sleep.

For decades, the hereditary rulers of Lucernis were so inept and bumbling or corrupt and cruel that the king finally had to eradicate their line and appoint a governor. Morno was unlucky enough to be competent and loyal and, rumor has it, one of the queen's favorites. King Vos III is no idiot. With a queen twenty years his junior, Morno was handed the high honor of restoring the rule of law to Lucernis, which just happens to be some four hundred miles from court. Was Morno her lover? Who knows? But he's been taking it out on the city ever since.

Pirates no longer linger just off shore, and riots are a rare thing nowadays; fewer starve and many even pay at least token taxes. Morno keeps the largest city on the Dragonsea from coming apart at the seams.

Doesn't mean I like the bastard.

With a few hours to kill, I set off for Temple Street to talk to the grumpiest, most knowledgeable person in Lucernis.

~ ~ ~

"I'm old and I'm tired and it's time for my nap. Go away."

He was the high priest of Lagna, god of knowledge. Which meant he was a jumped up librarian, since Lagna happened to be dead.

Lagna's temple was big, with big glassed windows and a huge main room, or chapel, or whatever it was called, but it had seen better days. It hadn't seen a good cleaning in decades, most probably. Offerings, it seemed, were scarce. Maybe that was because people didn't value knowledge as much as they should. Or maybe it was because Lhiewyn, the high priest, was an extremely grumpy bastard with a tongue sharper than any of my knives.

I couldn't argue that he was old; his wrinkles had wrinkles and his hair was little more than a silver net across his spotted pate. He leaned on a crooked cane, and one leg looked like it was just so much dead weight. The young acolyte who had directed me to his cell in back of the book-crammed temple was probably as much a servant to the old man as he was to Lagna.

"I need your help, priest."

"That you need help is bleeding obvious," he said, taking in my appearance. "I doubt there's any help for you, though."

"How much for a little information on pre-Diaspora artefacts, specifically golden toad statuettes stashed away in ancient temples in the swamps of Gol-Shen?"

"Oh, that won't cost you anything, because I know piss-all about them. I serve the god of knowledge, not trivia. You nitwit. Jessep, show this bald, brainless twit out."

Gods, but I hated talking to this old codger. Sometimes I had to, though, when I took a more esoteric contract. It was never much fun.

"What about a goddess who casts eight shadows? Also likes knives or blades or some such?"

His eyebrows rose. "You want to know about the Eightfold Goddess?"

"No. I thought I'd ask just so you could feel superior some more."

"Now there is an interesting deity. Very few know about her, actually. Or rather, that her eight aspects are just that, and not—"

"So I've found one of your favorite topics. That's great. I've actually got somewhere to be today, though." All right, that wasn't particularly fair. I'd brought it up. But he looked like he was settling in for a long, long monologue.

"Well, then, we should start with those weapons you mentioned. I bet you like to stab things, so this should hold your miniscule attention." He sat down carefully on a three-legged stool that stood next to his pallet. They were the only furnishings in the room, so I stood. He heaved a pained sigh and straightened his dead leg out before him. Jessep stood in the corner and tried to hide a smirk.

"Some say She fashioned Her Blades from bits of the other gods," he said, "from gobbets of immortal flesh and bone that lay scattered about the battlefields of the Divine during the Age of Chaos. Thus is truth distorted over millennia.

"The truth is She was taken by Shem, Low Duke of the Eleven Hells. Her father sold Her to Shem, to be his handmaid. That one tried to rape Her eight times, but each time She left a piece of Herself behind for him to sate his lust on. Seven times he was not sated, but on the eighth his strength was spent along with his seed. And then the One Who Is Eight tore Shem to pieces with eight pairs of hands. They say that She made the Blades from his horns, his bones, his scales and claws and fangs.

"She is terrible, and beautiful, and no god or demon fucks with Her, for She is as mad as they come and eight times as nasty."

"Are priests supposed to curse?"

His bushy eyebrows went up. "What, did I offend your delicate sensibilities? I'm too old to worry about what other people think."

"Why have I never heard of this goddess?"

"You mean besides being generally ignorant? Probably because there aren't many daft enough to worship Her. She might take notice. At best, some might say a prayer to one of Her Aspects. I hear the Fraternity of Blood, that band of assassins up in Pinghul, hold Kalara as their patron deity. They aver that Red Hand is actually her consort, which if you ask me is utter tripe. Anyway, She's supposed to be dead. Not that that ever means much where gods are concerned."

"Who is Kalara?"

"The Eight-fold Goddess has, try to imagine it, eight aspects. Kalara, Goddess of Assassins, is one. Let me see if I can remember all the others. Abanon, Goddess of hate. Moranos, deity of desire, Ninkashi, worker of retribution, Heletia, font of true sight and clarity. How many is that?"

"Five."

"Then there's Husth, goddess of deception and shadows. Very popular with thieves in Bellarius."

"I've actually heard of that one. But go on."

"Xith rules death and rebirth. And that leaves Visini, goddess of decay, inertia, chaos and despair. That's eight, right?"

"Yes."

"Mind you, together they make one. The Eight-fold Goddess."

"Which is all very interesting, but what about these blades?"

"I knew you'd like the stabby bit. I'll tell you what I know, but it isn't much. I'm a priest, not a weaponsmith. Each one has some function pertaining to its particular aspect-Goddess. So Abanon's blade will use or feed on hate in some fashion, and Moranos's dagger will in some way be connected to desire. And so on."

I waited for him to continue, but apparently he was done. "That's it?" I asked.

"Well, in the presence of one, I'd rather be on the end that you hold. And given the choice I'd rather not be in the same country as any of them."

"Thanks so much for that useful bit of advice."

"They're the tools of an insane goddess, forged from the body of a demon lord. What did you expect? 'Weapon A can cut through armor as though it were butter, and weapon B lets you walk on water?'"

"Well, yes. Sort of. But I guess I see your point."

He shifted on his stool and his watery brown eyes got sort of glinty. "You came seeking information, but let me give you some advice. The world is still littered with artifacts left over from before the Cataclysm. *None* of them are safe to play with. I don't know why you want to know about the Eightfold's Blades, nor do I much care. But if by some mad chance you find one of Her Blades, or one finds you, remember one thing: Such tools *want* to be used, and to them, any mortal hand that wields them is a tool in turn. Be very, very careful. And leave your offering in the box in the foyer. Silver is good, gold is better. If you want more information you can go dig in the stacks. Jessep will help you since I very much doubt you can read. I've got to take my nap."

I turned to go. Turned back.

"One more question," I said. "A quick one."

He sighed, and gave me a long-suffering look.

"Is the Guardian of the Dead in the Necropolis real?"

"Of course it's real, you ignoramus. It's real, extremely nasty, and very unhappy with its job. I shudder to think what would happen if it ever escaped the Necropolis. Gods willing, it would stumble across you first. Now piss off."

I followed Jessep out to the stacks, which were just that—stacks and stacks of books, parchment, papyrus, scrolls and scraps. There was some sort of mad order to it, I could feel it in my bones, but it eluded me.

"So, Jessep, is there anything *not* unpleasant about that old codger?"

Jessep stopped to consider. He was a long time about it.

"Well, he makes a beef stew you'd slap your mother for," was all he eventually came up with.

Jessep did indeed help searching through the mad mess, and I did need him to read for me. What we eventually found was in a language that I'd never seen before. He'd found what I was looking for in a box of scrolls mouldy with age. Much good it did me.

On a scrap of papyrus that Jessep said was part of a chronicle of the War of the Gods was a prayer. Or a poem. Or maybe a prophecy. I'm not sure which, since the last bit was missing. Anyway, it listed the Goddesses' Blades by name. I had the youngster copy out a translation for me. Jessep was a damned good translator. He even made it rhyme:

Abanon wields the Blade that Whispers Hate,
Moranos holds the Dagger of Desire,
Ninkashi grips the trembling Blade of Rage,
With which she pierced the heart of her mad sire.

Heletia grips the Knife called Winter's Tooth,
Visini wields the Blade that Binds and Blinds,
Husth fights with the Kris that Strikes Elsewhere,
And woe betide the soul it finally finds.

Kalara hones the Knife that Parts the Night,
Grim Xith commands the Dirk that Harrows Souls;
Eight blades the Goddess has, and one
From eight will ren—

And then the rest was so badly rat-gnawed that it was useless.

My gut told me I'd just picked up a piece of a puzzle. What puzzle, and where it fit, I had no idea.

CHAPTER 21

After a quick meal of bread and cheese and small beer in Temple Market, I walked back to the Promenade and the Thracen manse. I was tired. I couldn't remember the last time I slept. Was it in prison? Surely not.

This time I was let in like–well, not an honored guest, but at least not like I'd just stepped in something rotting. A servant in Thracen livery showed me to a small study, outfitted me with some wine, tried not to look like he wanted to warn me not to steal anything, and told me Osskil would see me soon. And he did.

Such a heavy man should have lumbered, but Corbin's brother entered the room like a coiled spring waiting to be released.

"Amra Thetys, you do me honor."

"I don't know about that, but I hope to do right by you today. I appreciate your help in Havelock."

He waved that away and sat down in a chair opposite mine. "Lord Morno wasn't pleased with me about that, but then Lord Morno is rarely pleased with anything. Tell me why you are here today," he said. And I did. About Bosch, the Elamner, and the villa. About the suppositions Holgren and I had come up with regarding the 'corpse' in the villa, and the golden toad.

"We should move soon," he said when I was done. "They might flee."

I liked him even better for automatically using *we* instead of *I*.

"Holgren and I hoped you'd feel that way. Do you think you could send someone to fetch him? He should be done working on the location spell for Bosch, and I guarantee you'll want him along when you call on the Elamner. Holgren's magic is very, uh, thorough," I said, thinking of the red ruin he'd made of Bosch's body.

"Certainly. I'll send a carriage round for him at once." He rang a bell and a servant appeared. I gave him directions for Holgren's hovel.

I was less pleased when Osskil also gave instructions to have Inspector Kluge invited over.

"You've got to be kidding," I said. "Kluge? He'll screw this up just so he can pin it on me and give me a hempen necklace."

"A necessary formality. Lord Morno can't be seen to countenance private justice among the nobles, as he made plain to me this morning. Kluge's inclusion gives our action the stamp of his authority. Don't worry, Amra. I'll impress upon the inspector just how dim a view the Thracens will take of it, should you be made to pay for assisting us."

"That's all well and good, but Courune is a long way from Lucernis, and you spanking Kluge will be cold comfort to me if I'm executed."

He smiled. "Have a little faith. Both Corbin and I learned early how to be persuasive. Now explain to me again the locations of the guards."

We went over the layout again in detail, making maps. Servants came and went. Things were whispered in Osskil's ear, and Osskil wrote notes and stamped them with the Thracen seal. The notes got carried off throughout the city by liveried servants.

By late afternoon, a small army had been assembled in Osskil's courtyard. Swordsmen, halberdiers and crossbowmen milled around, talking shop. There was even a pair of Westmarch arquebusiers off in a corner, polishing their big, bell-mouthed boom sticks. They must have been for show, because their weapons, while loud as Kerf's farts, weren't all that deadly unless you stuck your head in one.

"Seems a bit much," I told Osskil.

"You saw five armsmen total when you reconnoitred the surroundings the first and second times, but there might well be more. An unknown number may be guarding derelict villa and the interior of the manse proper. And no guardsman can be on duty all day and night, so it is best to prepare for double, if not treble the number we know of."

Holgren and Kluge arrived not long after that. Holgren exited the carriage, followed by Kluge. Holgren looked amused. Kluge looked like someone had pissed down his back and told him it was raining.

"How was your ride?" I asked Holgren, ignoring Kluge. He just smiled.

"Were you able to work up a locator spell for Bosch?"

"Yes, though I'm sorry to say it's not terribly accurate." He showed me an old brass compass, currently pointing west-southwest. Towards the villa. "I might have done better with more time, but not enough to make a real difference."

"I think it will be fine. It's more insurance than necessity anyway. Let me introduce you to Baron Thracen."

"Osskil, please," said the baron, shaking Holgren's hand. "It's a pleasure to meet you, Magister."

"Holgren, please," said Holgren, smiling. Looking around the courtyard, he said "I take it this will not be a stealthy operation? A platoon of warriors marching up the Jacos Road is a noticeable thing. I can attempt a glamour—"

"Oh, that won't be necessary. Amra has come up with a means for us to arrive at the villa's gates without drawing undue attention."

"Oh really?" said Holgren, raising an eyebrow at me.

"I'm not as much of an imbecile as Lagna's priest likes to make out," I replied. "You'll see."

"Holgren, Inspector Kluge, would you care to join me, Amra and Captain Ecini, my guard captain, in the study? Time flies, and we still have one stop to make in the Spindles before we call on this Elamner. I'd like to brief you on our plan of action and receive your comments."

They did, and the baron did. Holgren made a few remarks and assured us that he could and would neutralize the death curse on the Elamner's room before we entered the building. Kluge stood there like a post.

Twenty minutes later, just as night was falling, we were on our way to Alain's.

~ ~ ~

The look on Alain's face when I showed up at his yard at the head of a small army was priceless.

"We've had some complaints about the quality of your work," I said.

"Huh?"

I punched him in the arm. "Actually we're here to borrow your optibus."

"Omnibus," he corrected automatically, taking in all the people with deadly things in their hands standing in the street outside his yard.

"Whatever. Can we borrow it?"

"Huh?"

Osskil stepped forward. "It's a pleasure to meet you, master Alain. I'd like to hire your omnibus for the evening, if that would be all right."

"It's not really mine, ser–"

"Baron Osskil det Thracen-Courune, at your service."

"My lord," said Alain, giving his forehead a knuckle. "But the omnibus isn't mine to lend."

"I assure you we will take care, and I will indemnify you and your client should anything happen to it. In addition to the rental fee, of course," Osskil reached into a belt pouch and brought out a fistful of gold.

"Of course," said Alain, taking the money in a sort of daze. He just sort of held it, as though he wasn't sure what to do with it. Myra came out from the shadows where she'd been observing the circus and took charge of the money, her husband and the situation. She gave me a questioning look and I shrugged and smiled.

She rounded up Alain's laborers, got the omnibus hitched and pointed towards the gate. Osskil had his personal coachman mount the box. The man looked half thrilled, half terrified. Our little private army climbed inside.

"Are we going to regret this?" Myra whispered to me.

"I really don't see how," I told her honestly, "but the night is still young." She *tssked* and got out of the way.

A crowd had gathered outside Alain's gate. Kluge walked out and said "Go home." The small hairs on the back of my neck stirred when he said it. It wasn't a suggestion, or even a command; it was a Compulsion. The crowd broke up.

We were on our way.

CHAPTER 22

Half the men exited the omnibus at the same clearing where I'd stashed Kram on my first visit to the villa. They would work their way through the woods as quietly as they could and assault the house next to Heirus's, where at least three guards were stationed, when they heard the signal. Which was one of the arquebuses going off, preferably in somebody's face. They moved quickly and quietly out of sight, faster than the omnibus traveled.

By the time we arrived at Heirus's gate, they were to already be in position. If anything went wrong, they had a signaller as well—the other arquebusier.

The giant wagon rolled up to the gate, and kept going. I could see the curious looks of the gate guard through the small warped windows that punctuated the omnibus's side. It was only when the back end of the omnibus was roughly even with the gate that men with pointy things started boiling out, and the guard's expression changed from mild curiosity to fear. Once everybody else was out, I jumped off and followed. I didn't see what they did to turn the gate into twisted wreckage, but it wasn't the arquebus, because I saw—and heard—that one go off in clouds of foul smelling smoke. I didn't see if it injured anyone, but I rather doubted it.

The gate guard was sprawled on the ground in a spreading puddle of blood. Two other guards were running—not towards the villa, but to the abandoned estate next door, Osskil's troops in hot pursuit.

The two guards met several of their comrades, who were running *towards* the manse from the abandoned villa, with the other half of Osskil's private army on their heels. There had, apparently been considerably more than three armsmen stationed in the abandoned villa. That's when weapons started getting thrown to the ground and hands started grabbing sky, when it became apparent that they were being assaulted from two sides by superior numbers. All told, it was over in little more than a minute.

"Now the dangerous part begins," I told Osskil, while Heirus's sell-swords were bound and stuffed into the omnibus.

We left four men to guard the prisoners. Holgren and Kluge approached the front door the way you'd approach a tiger. The rest of us, Osskil, me and a dozen armsmen, waited behind them. There was a lot of muttering between the two, and some waving of hands, and then Holgren put his hand on the door. He stood there for a time, muttering something to himself in a language I didn't recognize. His hand began to glow. Finally he turned to us.

"The wards are down, and the death curse negated. But this place is far from safe.

When we go in, follow closely."

He pushed on the door, hand glowing, and it fell to the floor with a massive boom. A stench like rotting corpses billowed out of the unnaturally dark interior. He and Kluge walked over the fallen door and into the gloom, and the rest of us followed behind.

The walls were sort of melting; sagging and peeling away from the structure underneath, like decaying flesh sloughing off bones. I felt myself very much wanting to be somewhere else.

"Daemon taint," muttered Kluge, and Holgren nodded grimly. "I've never seen it as bad as this."

"Stupid," replied Holgren. "Mad and dangerous and stupid."

"Can we just make our way to the room the Elamner is in and get out of here?" I asked. "Then we can torch the place. From the outside." I heard a muttered agreement from some of the men behind me.

"We can try, Holgren replied, "but don't be surprised if our map is useless. This place is well on the way to becoming a hell gate. Time and space only loosely apply here now."

"Let's go," said Osskil. "Enough talk." The place was getting on even his iron nerves.

Holgren nodded assent, called up a ball of light that floated ahead of us, and set off down the corridor, Kluge and the rest of us in his wake.

The corridor was too long.

We kept walking, and walking, and by my calculations should have been off the edge of the cliff and into the Dragonsea before we came to a branching passageway on the left.

Which wasn't on the map. But was filled with blood and body parts.

There were limbs and guts and feet and fingers that had been arranged in starburst patterns on the tiled floor. There was a pile of heads. Some were still blinking. One of them was wearing my face.

"Right then," I said. "Let's go back out and try to enter the Elamner's room through the window. Dealing with Bosch can wait."

More strenuous agreement from behind me. I was becoming popular with the mercenaries.

Holgren smiled, which, considering what we were surrounded with, made me like him more, oddly. "We can try," he said. "Lord Osskil?"

Osskil was staring at a rotting arm that dragged itself toward his boot, a look of sick fascination on his heavy face. Very deliberately he raised his foot and stomped down on the black, split-nailed fingers that inched it forward. He kept stomping until the bones were shattered and the thing just lay there, quivering.

"Yes," he finally said. "Let's."

~ ~ ~

The corridor didn't lead back to the entryway anymore, we discovered after at least fifteen minutes of walking. There were no branches or turnings, but we ended up in what I suppose could be called a kitchen. Assuming hells have kitchens. There was a massive hearth, and hooks dangling from the ceiling, piercing lumps of dripping flesh, swaying in an unfelt breeze. The hearth was cold, but a vaguely human form turned on the spear-like spit, charred and blackened. It didn't have a head.

The vast floor was covered in shit and offal and bile. It was utterly silent in that space, except for the faint squeaking of the rusty chains the hooks dangled from. The ceiling was lost in gloom.

A door stood at the far side of the room. Holgren marched toward it, magelight above his head. We were forced to follow or be left in the dark, though nobody, I'm sure, was keen to kick through the awful muck that covered the floor.

We were about halfway across the room when flames exploded in the hearth, roaring and glowing a hellish green-blue.

Then things began bursting out of the floor, flinging flagstones out of their way as they rose.

They were all different as far as I could tell, but each was vaguely insectile in appearance; chitinous bodies and soulless, jet-black faceted eyes, and lots and lots of stingers and pincers and barbed, multi-jointed legs. The biggest was about the size of a lapdog. But there were a lot of them.

"Back!" shouted Holgren, reversing his course toward the corridor. One of the creatures sprang for his face and he slapped it down, earning a bloody gash on his palm.

It was chaotic. Our group fell back in fairly good order, considering, but the floor was slick with filth and the creatures just kept coming. A little one, scorpion-like, stabbed its stinger down into my boot, but didn't manage to pierce down into flesh and got itself stuck. I stomped on it awkwardly with my other foot, nearly lost my balance. One of the armsmen gave me a steadying hand. The halberdiers, competent at their trade, had moved to deal with the creatures as they came at us in waves. They looked like hells' grass cutters, their halberds mowing down the vile things, scythe-like.

"Move, now, let's go," I heard Osskil say. And then I heard rattling in the chains above.

It looked like a giant crab, more or less, but moved with the speed and grace of a spider. It was bigger than me. And it was not alone.

"Keep moving!" Holgren yelled, just before a strand of what looked like vile yellow mucus shot down from above and hit him in the chest. He made a disgusted face and cut it with a terse gesture and a harsh magical syllable. Then another came down, and another, and suddenly it was raining the stuff. Men were being hit left and right—and it was sticking, and they were being pulled upward.

Demon crabs spin mucus webs, I thought. *This is knowledge I could live my whole life without.*

The first of our group to die that day was one of the arquebusiers. A strand shot down into his face and yanked him upwards into darkness. I could hear his muffled screaming. Then I could hear the crunch of a demon taking a bite out of him, followed immediately by the thunderous roar of his weapon. They both fell to the floor, unmoving, with considerable portions of their anatomy missing.

Our group had split into two during the initial attack, I realized. Holgren, Kluge, Osskil and two swordsmen were in the group closest to the hearth, while I and the rest of the mercenaries were more than a half-dozen strides away, closer to the corridor we'd entered the room from. I didn't like not being with the mages.

But Holgren and Kluge seemed to have it in hand. Holgren was blasting everything with fire, causing charred crab-bits to rain down, and Kluge had manifested some sort of whip made of light and was slicing through the strands and keeping our people from being yanked up into the darkness above. We were all still moving toward the exit.

As we got closer to the edge of the room, the less we were affected by the disgusting onslaught from above, which was intensifying around Holgren's group. The gap between us widened, and by the time we made it to the corridor, Holgren and the others were more than a dozen strides away.

Holgren caught my eye. "Go! We'll follow!" he said.

The second of our little army to die was a halberdier.

We were all so busy watching what was going on with Holgren and the others that no one had thought to keep an eye on the corridor. So Bosch, or what Bosch had become, just walked up and speared the man in the back. I only knew we were still in danger when I heard the man scream. I whipped around, ready to throw a knife.

Bosch was both less and more than he had been before Holgren had turned his body into a large red dampness. His head was the only thing organic about him. The rest of him was some mad melding of metal and magic.

He stood perhaps seven feet tall, now. His head, smiling and eyes fever-bright, was encased in what looked like a large block of amber. It rested on a large, spider-like body made of brass and iron and steel. Small lightnings played about its frame, and actinic bursts of light coruscated across it randomly, shedding sparks.

He had run the halberdier through with one of his forelegs. The man was dangling from it, feet not quite touching the floor. He was in agony.

The mercenaries were brave, I'll give them that. They rushed towards Bosch, but he interposed the halberdier between himself and their weapons, using the dying man as a shield.

"Let him go, Bosch," I said. But he ignored me.

"How do you like my sanctum, Amra?" His voice was a series of piping notes originating from somewhere in his thorax.

"I've seen nicer slaughterhouses. Let the man go, and we might let you go."

"Is that the dead thief's fat brother I see back there? Do tell him for me how his brother screamed when I chopped his fingers off, would you? If he somehow survives. If you somehow survive."

I had nothing to say to that. I just wanted to smash the abomination that Bosch had become. I wanted to throw my knife, but doubted it could pierce the amber shell his head was encased in.

The mercenary was fading fast. He was clawing at the spike in his chest, but his movement was growing feebler by the moment.

"What to do, what to do? Will you deal with me, thief? Or will you deal with *that*?" He pointed with another blood-spattered brass leg back toward the room where Holgren and the others were trapped.

"Oh come on. Do you think I was born last night?" As if I was going to turn my back on him. Then I heard it.

A rumbling, grinding sound.

Then a voice that was not a voice, but a presence in my head.

The Gate opens. But it is a tight fit, as yet.

I risked a quick glance back.

The demon webs were falling furiously, now. Kluge was keeping the area around their group relatively clear, his light-whip in constant, lashing motion, but it seemed almost impossible that those of us in the corridor could re-join them without becoming trapped. Still, I could see them, and the hellfire of the hearth. And the thing that was slowly tearing its way through it. Like some giant, bloated caterpillar with corpse-colored flesh. Holgren stood before it.

I felt it coming and darted to the side. Bosch's needle-sharp leg speared the air where my chest had just been.

"Worth a try," said Bosch in his calliope voice, and then he flung the now-dead halberdier at us and started loping down the corridor away from us, a horrid, drunken spider.

Holgren Angrado. You meet us half-way. This is… pleasant. Like a deep, cracked bell ringing in my head, I heard the voice of the demon Holgren faced. I turned around again, torn.

Holgren glanced back at us.

"Go, get Bosch!" he shouted, and then he turned to face the thing that was making its way out of the hearth. He rolled his head, stretched his shoulders, like a brawler about to enter the ring. Then he spoke a harsh syllable, and there was a sound like thunder, and the demon roared in pain and rage.

Reluctantly, I went, feeling relieved I did not have to face that thing, and feeling as though I were a coward, and determined to take it out on Bosch.

"Let's go," I said to the men with me. And we went, pounding down the hall after him. He may not have been steady on his many legs, but he was swift. We didn't lose sight of him in that long, straight corridor, but we couldn't seem to gain on him, either.

Then suddenly there was a door ahead, plain blonde wood and horribly out of place. He lost time opening it, and even more time trying to fit through it. He just had time to slam it shut before we got there.

I tore the door open. Or tried to. It was locked.

"You're a thief, right?" asked one of the swordsmen, barely out of his teens. "You gonna pick the lock?'

"The hells with that. Take too long. You're hefty, give it a good kick."

"Aye." His massive booted foot lashed out and something cracked.

"Again!"

It took three more kicks, then the door sprang open with a juddering sound.

Beyond was a room I recognized, despite the gloom. The one with the corpse sporting a knife in his heart.

Bosch was crouched over the ensorcelled corpse, his own spidery brass body humming and shivering with eldritch energies. With his head mounted atop that grotesque thing, he should have looked blackly ridiculous. He didn't. He looked vile, mad, and dangerous.

"I want you to meet my employer," he said in that pipe organ voice. "You won't like him." And two delicate, shimmering spider legs plucked the dagger from the Elamner's heart.

He came up screaming, knocking Bosch into a corner. The look in his eyes was feral. Mad. Both the angry kind and the crazy kind. He saw the armed guards surrounding him, and disappeared.

Blood and chaos ensued.

I have never seen anyone move as fast as him. I suppose technically I didn't actually see him move at all. Maybe the faintest of blurrings in the air. My eyes couldn't track him.

Osskil's little army, the ones with me and not stuck in that chamber of horrors with Holgren, started to die.

There were eight armsmen in the room with me. In three heartbeats they were all falling to the floor, throats slit, bloody handprints covering their surprised faces.

And then it was my turn.

He just appeared before me, a knife in his hand. The tip of the knife pressed ever so delicately against the skin over my carotid artery.

"Abanon-touched," he said.

"Whatever you say. You're the one with the blade."

"No. *You* have Her Blade. Or you did. I can smell it on you. You must give me the Blade. Or I will kill you."

"I have no idea what you're talking about. I truly wish I did."

He sniffed again, shuddered. His lip curled. "I also smell an arhat."

"If you say so." It's not like the bald kid rubbed himself up against me.

"Do you believe I will kill you?"

"Very much so. But I still don't have Abanon's Blade."

His eyes bored into mine. "You're not lying. So you must be mistaken." Suddenly he shuddered again, violently. His face went pale. "I will find you again. When I do, you will have found the Blade. Or you will be very unhappy in the brief span before you die." And then he vanished. The window shutters rocked slightly in the breeze caused by his passage.

"Kerf's crusty old balls," I swore, and looked around the room.

Bosch had disappeared as well. All of the men who had come with me were dead, and the bloody handprint on their faces was the signature of the most feared, deadly assassin in the world. Red Hand.

Heirus the Elamner was Red Hand, and he wanted me to give him something I didn't have, or he was going to kill me.

CHAPTER 23

"The Elamner is awake, and he's Red Hand the assassin," I told Holgren as he came through the door a few seconds later. I may have been gibbering, just a little.

"Yes, we managed to deal with the demon, thanks very much for ask—" He saw the bodies littering the floor. "What happened here?"

"I told you, Heirus is *Red Hand.* Bosch pulled the knife out of his chest and woke him up. He killed everybody. He wants me to give him Abanon's Blade or he's going to kill me too."

I watched him chew on it for a moment, then decide what question to ask first.

"Where's Heirus now?"

"Gone. But he said he'd find me again."

"We'll deal with it. We *will*, Amra. Where is Bosch?"

"I don't know. He disappeared when Red Hand started slaughtering everybody. Bosch is, uh, different now."

"I know, I caught a glimpse. It should limit his options for hiding at least. I don't see him renting a room, or doing much of anything where people can see him."

While I spoke to Holgren, Osskil posted one of the remaining armsmen at the window and the other at the door. Kluge was inspecting the bodies and the circle that Heirus—Red Hand—had been resting in. Professional curiosity, I suppose.

"First things first," said Osskil. "We need to do something about this house of horrors."

"Agreed," said Holgren.

"Good idea," I chimed in. "How do you close a hell mouth, by the way?"

"With fire, of course," said Kluge. "Fire with fire. But then you have to seal it, lest some other mad idiot reopens it."

"And how do you do that?" I asked him.

He shrugged. "With magic, and lots and lots of very big, very heavy rocks."

"That's for another day," said Osskil. "First let's get our dead out of this foul place, then burn it to the ground."

~ ~ ~

Kluge and one of the armsmen made sure nobody sneaked up on us while we hauled the bodies of the rest through the window. It was the shortest route, and besides, no one wanted to chance those hallways again. I agreed in principle; I didn't like to think of those dead men resting in the ashes of that house. I may not have known them, but I didn't have to, to want them out of there. But I was less enthusiastic about having to haul the bodies.

I'm not particularly squeamish. It wasn't handling their corpses that bothered me. It was seeing that bloody handprint on those dead faces, and knowing it might very well be me next. If Red Hand wanted me dead, then I was dead. If even a fraction of the tales told about him were true, he'd been around for generations, dealing death to kings and queens, priests and generals, merchants and even godlings all around the Dragonsea. He would disappear for years, then the all-but-impossible assassinations would start again, all with that signature bloody handprint. Red Hand was literally the stuff that legends—and nightmares—were made of.

When we'd shifted all the corpses that Red Hand had made, I turned to Osskil.

"I hate to say it, but there are two more in there." The arquebusier the demon crab had killed, and the halberdier Bosch had done for.

"I know," he said, "but we dare not risk more deaths to recover them." He shook his head. "We were not prepared. I was not prepared, not for this. We should not have continued once we knew what this place had turned into."

"I don't think it would have mattered if we'd brought a hundred men," I told him, "or a dozen mages. You didn't see how Red Hand moved. Eight men dead in the space of three heartbeats. There is no preparing for a foe like that."

He just shook his head.

"We should have burned the place to the ground right off," he said. "Never even entered at all."

"But then you'd never have known for certain Corbin's killer was done for. He might've been out having a shave when you came calling."

"I could live with that. In retrospect. I went looking to avenge one death. Now there are ten more, and my brother's murderer no closer to being dealt with."

"Such talk does not become you, Lord Osskil."

He raised an eyebrow. "That sounded rather haughty."

I shrugged and pointed towards Holgren. "Been spending too much time around that one."

It got a smile out of him at least.

~ ~ ~

Holgren and Kluge reduced the villa with magefire, which for the most part looked like normal fire. Except, you know, it was being blasted out of their hands. It *was* especially bright, even in the dim predawn light. I noted with some satisfaction that Kluge had to quit halfway through. He looked as though he'd run from the Dragon Gate to the Governor's Palace without stopping. Admittedly, Holgren didn't look much better when he'd finished. I'd have made a joke, but neither mage looked like they were in the mood.

The stench from the burning villa was more than awful, and the breeze coming off the Dragonsea was light but variable; more than once it shifted direction unexpectedly, and the vile smoke reduced Holgren or Kluge to gasping retches. It was not a pleasant chore, and to the credit of both they never complained once.

While they were about it, the rest of us loaded the dead into the omnibus along with the prisoners. Alain wasn't going to be happy about the blood. Alain would get over it.

I took a water skin from one of the men and gave it to Holgren, who was surveying the ruins of the villa. He took it with a grateful look and drank deep.

"So. You think Bosch is in there?" I asked him.

"I'm afraid not." He pulled out the compass he'd prepared with Bosch's hair. The needle pointed due East.

"I don't understand. It's pointing at the house. Or what's left of it."

"If only it were. If he were as close as that, the needle would be spinning aimlessly. He's much farther away."

"But that's the Dragonsea."

"Precisely. He doesn't need to breathe, and there isn't much to him anymore to attract a hungry pheckla."

"Kerf's balls. He's well and truly beyond reach then, isn't he?"

"Yes. For now. That one won't be content to scuttle along the sea bed for long, however. We will see him again, and sooner rather than later."

~ ~ ~

I was deeply, deeply tired. I parted company with the others as soon as we got into the Spindles, and headed toward another one of my bolt-holes to sleep, after promising to check in with Osskil and Holgren the next day. I don't know what Kluge and Osskil did with the Elamner's guards, or with the bodies. I also don't know what Myra and Alain thought about the condition they received their omnibus in. It was all in one piece, though, so they couldn't have been too upset.

I probably should have gone with Holgren to his sanctum, but it was just too far. Instead I trudged over to the herbalist's whose back room I rented and sneaked in the window.

As I crawled under the single dusty sheet that graced the cot in the dark, funny-smelling back room of the herbalist's, though, one thought kept nagging at me.

It was a little thing, and it probably meant nothing, but it kept me awake for a considerable time considering how exhausted and sleep-deprived I was. You'd think it was Red Hand, and his demand that I give him something I had no idea how to get, but it was something else.

Bosch. Gloating about chopping off Corbin's fingers.

Sure it was a nasty thing, calculated to enrage, horrible enough in its own way. But why gloat about that and not the actual murder? Why not talk about letting him run, as Kluge had mentioned, and hunting him down like an animal? That was just as cruel, if not more so.

It was a small thing, but it didn't fit.

Something was missing. Something was off.

CHAPTER 24

I slept until noon, then left the herbalist's the way I came. What the old woman thought about her mysterious boarder I couldn't say. The room was paid up months in advance and the door triple-locked from the inside, which must have seemed odd, but not odd enough to turn down easy money. That's one thing I like about Lucernans; once money changes hands, they become deeply uncurious.

At Osskil's manse I was informed that I was invited to another funeral. Or funerals, rather. Three of the armsmen he'd hired had no one to claim their bodies, and so he'd decided to inter them in the Thracen crypt reserved for retainers. It was, apparently, a rather gracious gesture on his part. They'd have a posher afterlife than they would've had otherwise, at least. It was scheduled for the late afternoon. I wasn't all that keen on going, but Osskil wouldn't be available until then. I was led to believe by his servant that he was off getting scolded by Lord Morno again.

I decided to have a very late, or rather for me a very early breakfast. At which point I realized I was thoroughly broke. I didn't trust Holgren to have any food, and didn't want to walk all the way to his house in any case, so I decided to kill two birds with one stone and get a meal and an advance from Daruvner. I'd promised to check in with him anyway.

It was quiet at his dive. No nieces, no Kettle, and very few patrons. Daruvner fed me, loaned me a few marks and then insisted I tell him everything that had been going on.

"You don't want to know," I said.

"I think I do."

I shrugged. "On your head, then, old man," I said, then filled him in about Corbin, how I'd decided to go after his killer, and how things had gone straight to hells. He supplied me with wine as I wound through the whole sordid mess, and when I was done he sat back, stared up at the water-stained, sagging plaster on the ceiling and idly rubbed his massive belly.

"There's something I don't understand," he finally said.

"You're ahead of me, then. I'm starting to feel like I don't understand anything."

"'Thus wisdom grows; in stony, unaccustomed soil,'" he replied.

"I don't know what you're talking about, but I'm sure it wasn't flattering."

"Just a quote. Look, You don't even know who killed Corbin."

"The hells I don't."

"Hear me out, woman. You've pinned this on Bosch, and his boss Heirus—"

"Call him what he really is. Red Hand."

"I'm not sure I believe that, but say that he is. Bosch admitted to cutting off Corbin's fingers, but never said anything about killing him, correct?"

"Yeah," I admitted. "That's been bothering me. But his boss is Red Hand, Daruvner. You know, king of assassins? Maybe Bosch didn't do it. Doesn't mean his boss didn't."

"You say you saw this Elamner kill a half-dozen men right in front of you. You say you know it was Red Hand because he put his bloody mark on their faces. Correct?"

"It was eight men, actually, but yes."

Daruvner leaned forward, locked eyes with me. "Did Corbin have Red Hand's mark?"

I wanted it to be the Elamner. After all the blood and trouble, I wanted it to be the obvious bad guy. But the truth is the truth, and facts are facts.

"No. Damn it."

He leaned back again, chair creaking under his weight. "I'm not saying he didn't do it. I'm not saying Bosch didn't do it. I'm not even saying it wasn't hired out by one or the other of them. What I am saying is, you've been mistaking what you think for what you know. You wouldn't do that on a job. You've let your anger cloud your judgment like you never would if this was business."

"It's not business, Fengal. Somebody killed my friend. How can I treat it as though it was just another theft?"

'But it *is* just another theft," he replied, his voice mild. "You're going to take something. Something valuable. You're going to take someone's life. You're going to take revenge. Here's where I'm very much starting to worry for you though, Amra: The consequences of a mistake on your part are the same as if you were caught lifting a cask of jewels: Death. And in this case, I'm sorry to say, you're not even sure you've got the right mark."

"A daemonist who was just about to open a hell gate on the Jacos Road and his boss, the king of assassins. I may have got the wrong villains. *May* have. But they're still villains, Fengal."

"Since when is it your job to deal with evil, Amra? You're a thief, not a hells-damned knight of the Order of the Oak. And consider this, please; while you're keeping the world safe from these very bad men, it's more than possible that your friend's real killer is out there, safe, satisfied."

"Well it's a little late now. Bosch came after me first, and I doubt Red Hand is going to leave me alone just because I say sorry and pretty please."

He rubbed his shiny head and sighed. "What can I say? You should have come and talked to me sooner. I'm deeply wise of course, but sadly I cannot undo what's already done. You've already pulled on trouble's braids."

"If you're so wise, old man, why don't you tell me who you think it was that killed Corbin?"

"True wisdom lies not in knowing the correct answer, but in knowing the correct question."

"Fine. Be that way. I've got to go. I've got three funerals to attend." I stood up.

"Don't you want to know the correct question?" he asked.

I sighed. No, I didn't. All right, yes I did, but I didn't have to be happy about it. "Sure, why not."

"Who had reason to want Corbin killed, besides the two new enemies you've made?"

"That's just it, Fengal. I have no idea."

"Well then maybe you should start trying to find out. When you have time."

"Yeah, when I have time."

"And for Isin's love, get over to Locquewood's and pick up your package. He's been bothering me about it for days, now."

"When I have time, old man!" I said as I went through the door.

CHAPTER 25

It wasn't quite as nice as Corbin's crypt, but the mausoleum for the Thracen retainers was still much more classy than any final resting place I was likely to end up in.

I met Osskil, the same three professional mourners, and two of the surviving armsmen in the necropolis in the late afternoon, about an hour before sunset. Holgren had sent his regrets and funerary tokens, claiming 'unavoidable occupation.' I think he just didn't like funerals, for all that he lived next to dead bodies.

The funeral table was bigger, but the whole ceremony was pretty much the same as for Corbin. Someone had washed the Red Hand's mark off their faces, thank the gods, and sewed them up with care. They were wearing good cloth under good armor, and their weapons were with them, shiny and sharp.

I arrived in time for the meal, which was all right. Simple fare, no meat. The three professional mourners, I found out, were brothers, though they each had different surnames; Wallum, Stumpole and Brock. I didn't try to puzzle that one out. I had enough on my mind.

Osskil made the ceremonial speech, we drank the funerary wine, and suddenly there they were, for a few moments, no longer corpses. The youngest one, the one that had kicked in the door to his own doom, looked at me with a sheepish grin on his face. Another, the one in the middle, just looked befuddled. The one on the end, a swordsman, was obviously angry, though somehow I knew it was not at us.

We toasted them, and they raised their glasses at us, the one in the middle having to be nudged by the younger one. And then they were just bodies again, and we put them in the mausoleum in the golden afternoon light.

Once the doors were closed, I turned to Osskil.

"On the day Corbin was killed, Kluge and the constables went through his house."

He nodded. "I know. I was told."

"Then you know what they found?" The letter, which according to Kluge, meant that Corbin might have been invited back into the family. That, and a Thracen signet ring. Daruvner's words had been bothering me the whole trip to the Necropolis. Who had reason to want Corbin killed?

"I know they found evidence he was a thief, and the letter I'd sent him, along with his family ring. Why?"

"The letter *you* sent him?"

"Certainly. Again, why?"

"What did the letter say?"

"I'm not sure that's your business, Amra. It's a family matter, and as much as I like you, you aren't family."

"But I was his friend, and so I'm asking you to tell me what was in the letter."

He gave me a long, hard look. "This cannot be shared with anyone else."

"You've got my word."

"My father is head of the family, but he is no longer in control of his faculties in any meaningful way. I control our interests, now, and make the family decisions. And now that my father is in no condition to object, I want— wanted my brother back. I wanted him to return to the family, to his home, to his daughter if not his wife. I wanted him to be able to be a part of her childhood, while there was still something of her childhood left. It was just too late."

I felt ashamed for doubting him. It wasn't as if Corbin, being the younger brother, could have inherited while Osskil was alive anyway.

"Now will you tell me why you wanted to know?" he asked, sounding more weary and heartsick than angry.

I really didn't want to answer him. For several reasons. But I owed him.

"There's a chance Bosch and Heirus didn't kill Corbin," I said.

"But what does that—" His eyes grew hard. "You suspected *me*?"

"No. Not really. But I wanted to make sure. You would have done the same."

That hard, cold look of his softened. "I suppose I would have, at that. But why do you think the killer might be someone else?"

"I'll tell you about it later," I said, my mouth suddenly dry and my palms sweaty.

About twenty yards away, Heirus had suddenly appeared and was staring straight at me.

Osskil hadn't noticed him there. I wanted to keep it that way. I turned away, walking slowly towards the crypt, and Osskil kept pace.

"Can I come by tomorrow?" I asked. "I'll lay it all out for you then."

"Certainly. I'll be in all day. But why not now?"

"Because I need to do some thinking first."

He gave me a long, penetrating stare. I tried to show him nothing. Finally he nodded, and started walking towards the exit. Everybody else had been waiting for him, and followed.

As the mourners streamed off towards the gate, I picked my way around headstones and past mausoleums towards Heirus. Night wasn't far off. The sun was already behind the high walls, casting everything into half-gloom

He was standing at the base of the very large, not very lovely statue of the Weeping Mother. His oiled, ringleted hair glistened dully in the half-light. His gaunt, dusky face betrayed no emotion.

"I don't have the Blade," I said to him. "I don't know where it is. I'm not holding out on you."

He seemed not to hear me. He was staring right at me, but he made no acknowledgement. I kept moving toward him, slow and careful, the way you approach any wild, dangerous animal. If you have no choice.

"Have you ever hated? *Really* hated, with every fiber of your being?" he finally asked me as I came within spitting distance of him. "True hate is a powerful thing. It can give you the strength of will to do things you never would have considered. Things you never would have believed yourself capable of. Unthinkable things. Awful and magnificent things." He took a deep breath, let it out slow. "Hate is a powerful force because it lends an impossible strength. With enough hate, you could rule the world. Or end it."

"Is that what you want to do?" I asked him. "Destroy the world?"

He laughed. "I don't give a runny shit about the world, or anyone or anything in it."

"Then by all the dead gods, what *do* you want?"

He sat down, heavily, on a cracked headstone across from me; leaned down and put his forearms on his knees. He looked tired and ill.

"I think," I said, "That you're sick. Maybe dying. I think you want the Blade because it will somehow cure you."

He laughed.

"What's so funny?"

"You think I'm dying. You don't know the half of it. *I die a dozen times a day.*"

"That sounds unpleasant."

"Well, curses aren't meant to be enjoyable. It's what I got for slaying a god."

"Um, out of curiosity, which god did you kill?'

He gave me an annoyed look. "One who needed it. One whose siblings took offense." He shuddered, looked as though he might vomit. It passed.

"How long have you been cursed?" I asked.

"How old do you think I am?" he asked.

"Forty? Maybe forty-five?"

"I'm seventeen hundred years old. Older than the Cataclysm. I saw the fall of Thagoth, and of Hluria. I was ancient when Havak Silversword was imprisoned behind the Wall. You people are mayflies to me."

"You're tired of life."

"You haven't the least idea. It's much worse than it sounds. Because of the curse laid on me, every moment that passes feels like a hundred. Listening to you talk bores me to tears. Listening to *me* talk bores me to tears. I've experienced this conversation as though it's lasted all damned day."

"I'll try and talk faster," I said, but he waved it away.

"Don't bother. You can't speak quickly enough to make the slightest difference."

"So what do you want, Heirus?"

Suddenly he was in my face. I never saw him move.

"I want the Goddess's gods-damned Blade, you stupid cow!"

"Call me a cow again and I'll stick the Blade so far up your—"

I never saw the fist, either.

I sprawled on the ground and in that bright flare of pain realization came to me.

"The toad," I said. "It's in the toad." Though if there was a weapon inside the thing, it wasn't a very big one. Maybe suitable for paring nails. But when it came to magical artifacts, who knew what was possible?

I wanted to spit out the blood that was spilling into my mouth from the torn lining of my cheek, but I remembered what Osskil had told me. You don't shed blood in the Necropolis. Ever. The Guardian *will* notice. I swallowed it instead.

"Yes, it's in the toad. Nice to see you're finally catching up."

"Kerf's crooked staff. You're worse than that priest of Lagna."

"I don't know or care what you're talking about. Just get me the toad and we can be shut of each other."

"The thing you had Corbin murdered for? I'd sooner see it dumped in the Dragonsea than in your hands."

"Your mouth moves but no sense escapes."

"You had Corbin killed so you wouldn't have to pay his fee for securing the toad. Then you put a contract out on me so you could have a necromancer get the toad's location out of my corpse. Am I making sense now?" I wasn't certain of anything I was saying, of course, but he didn't have to know that.

"Oh. I see. You're laboring under a misapprehension. I didn't have your friend killed, or hire killers to end you either. Perhaps Bosch got greedy and decided to keep the fee for himself. I don't know. I don't care."

"Why should I belie—" I didn't get to finish my sentence. A knife had appeared at my throat, pressing hard enough to draw a drop of blood. Then it was at my heart. Then almost, almost touching my eye. It didn't waver in the slightest in his hand.

"If I'd wanted your friend dead, or you dead, I wouldn't have bothered paying for it. Understand?"

"Yes."

"Finally." He stood up from where he was crouched over me. "If for some idiotic reason I'd wanted to kill your compatriot, who I hired to *retrieve* the damned toad, I'd have done it *after* I'd secured the Blade. If somehow I'd become doltish enough make a botch of *that*, I'd have brought the cooling meat of him to a necromancer straight away. And while Bosch may not be the brightest spark in the firmament, he's cunning enough to work out the same. Now. Bring me the Blade here at dawn tomorrow. Or I *will* find and kill you, and drag your corpse to a necromancer and make you tell me where you've hidden it. I will also kill both the mages and that fat lord that invaded my home."

"Alright. One condition, though." What did I have to lose?

He gave me a flat, put-upon stare.

"Go to Guache Gavon and tell him to cancel the contract on me."

"Who?"

"The Low Country trash that arranges contracts for assassination here. Or are you going to tell me that Red Hand doesn't know what I'm talking about?"

"Oh. I know him. His name escaped me."

"Tell him the contract lapsed with Bosch. Or tell him you cancel it. Whatever. I just don't want to be dodging assassins while I get the toad and bring it to you."

"Fair," he said. "I *will* see you tomorrow. One day," he said again.

"Where do we meet?"

"Just come here. I'll find you. So don't bother to run. And keep that Arhat away from me or I'll eviscerate him."

"The bald kid?" I didn't have to feign confusion. I knew who he meant, but had no idea why he wanted to avoid a teenaged ascetic. It was a strange tic of character for the King of Assassins to have. "It's not like I have him on a leash," I said, but I said it to the air. Heirus was gone.

CHAPTER 26

"**D**o you want to give it to him?" Holgren asked me when I returned to his sanctum and related my conversation.

"Do I have a choice? He's *Red Hand*, for Kerf's sweet sake. I don't give it to him, I'm a dead woman."

"That isn't what I asked, though. Do you *want* to give it to him?" The toad was sitting in the middle of some sort of arcane circle he'd sketched out on the floor with charcoal and blood. Bone wanted nothing to do with it, and kept to the corner farthest away.

"I want to have never seen that ugly thing. Sometimes we don't get what we want."

"If there is a weapon inside it, a blade forged by a goddess..."

"What?"

"When you next meet the most feared assassin in history, wouldn't you like to be holding it, rather than an ugly lump of gold?"

I sighed. "Hells, I don't know, Holgren. He'd probably just take it away from me and shove it in my ear. You didn't see the way he moves. Neither did I, for that matter, if I'm speaking precisely."

"Logically speaking, your choice is between meeting him essentially unarmed, or holding a powerful weapon. I know which I'd chose, but it's up to you. As for his speed, I think I can help you there as well. At least for a short time."

"Magic?"

"Of course." He dipped two fingers into the pocket of his waistcoat and brought out a pendant on a silver chain. The pendant was in the shape of a leaf, made of silver as well, about the size of my thumb.

"You just happened to have it in your pocket, eh?"

He smiled. "After what happened at the villa, I decided to un-crate some of my more useful, if dangerous, items."

"Speaking of the villa, that thing that crawled out of the hearth? It knew your name."

His face went hard. "Yes, it did."

"Did you want to talk about that, maybe?"

"Not particularly, no. Suffice it to say that, while I have had dealings with such creatures, I am no daemonist. If that is what you wanted to know."

I raised a hand. "Not my business."

"No, I understand that you might be concerned. Be at ease on that score." He sighed. "Back to the matter at hand," he went on, holding up the necklace.

"What is it?"

"I've made a study of longevity. Call it an interest of mine. In my studies I came across a way to, shall we say, live more expeditiously for a short time. At the cost of shortening your own lifespan commensurately.

"Can you say that without all the expensive words?"

He smiled. "It lets you cram an entire day or so of living into roughly an hour. At the end of the hour, you're a day older."

"Oh. That's not bad. I could even see giving up a week, or even a month."

"It would kill you. The aftereffects are brutal. Imagine not sleeping, eating or drinking for an entire day and night. Bad enough. A week? You might well die of thirst. A month? You'd be dead before the spell wore off. But if you need to, you can. The spell *will* let you. Best if you don't need to."

"Magic comes with a price, eh?"

"Always. Though some don't count the cost until it is too late." His expression became remote, but he quickly shrugged off whatever he was thinking about and put the chain around my neck. "No need to decide this instant. If you want to use it, just break the chain."

I thought about it while scratching Bone behind the ear. With the weapon inside the toad and Holgren's magic, I might stand a chance against Heirus. Without either I stood none, and would have to trust him not to kill me out of hand. And I still had no idea what he wanted to do with it. I honestly could not imagine it would be anything remotely good.

I was starting to believe—reluctantly—that he had not had Corbin killed. All right, he almost certainly hadn't. If I was honest with myself, I didn't want to let go of the notion of him as the culprit because he so obviously fit the mould. And because if he hadn't been the cause of Corbin's death, then there was someone else out there who was. Someone I was no closer to finding than I had been at the beginning.

That did not make him a nice person. The Red Hand had killed more people than famine had, if you believed only half the stories about him. Hells.

"Alright," I said. "Let's open up that ugly thing and get Abanon's Blade out."

"That would be a very bad idea," said the bald boy as he walked through Holgren's door, and wards, as though they didn't exist.

~ ~ ~

"Who are you and how did you gain entry to my sanctum?" Holgren's voice was calm, but I could tell he was ready and willing to unleash violence.

I recognized the boy, of course. The ascetic who had been staring at me as I left Alain's place. The one from the funeral. Arhat.

"Gaining entry to your sanctum was not difficult, magus. Magic is a rusty hammer with which to beat reality into different shapes. Philosophy, the true Philosophy, is a pen with which to alter, and hopefully correct reality."

"Arhat," said Holgren. The boy nodded.

"What do you want?"

"Please give me the statue. It is not meant for you. It is not meant for the world."

"You know this kid?" I asked Holgren.

"I've never laid eyes on him."

"But you know his name."

"Arhat? That's not a name. It's a title." He had a pissy expression on his lean face.

"Alright, I'll bite. What's an Arhat?"

"Do you remember the Cataclysm?" he asked.

"Not really, no. It *was* a thousand years ago." But he wasn't in any mood for banter.

"If you want to know why the Cataclysm happened, ask the Arhat."

I looked over at the kid. He shook his head sadly. "The Cataclysm was not the fault of the Philosophers, mage."

"Oh really? Then who was it that decided to poke and prod at the underpinnings of reality? Milk maids?"

"No. But not the Philosophers, either. A group that perverted Philosophy—"

"The point remains, Arhat, if those wise fools hadn't gone mucking about with knowledge man was literally not meant to know, *millions* wouldn't have perished—"

"Enough," I said, rather loudly. "If you two want to debate, go to the Speaker's Corner. Kerf's crooked staff, we're under a deadline here, or had you forgotten, Holgren? Arhat, you can't have the toad. Sorry about that, now please run along."

Holgren just stood there, looking mulish. The kid refused to run along.

"Seriously, go. We don't have time for you.""Please give me the statue. What is inside should stay there, in my safekeeping. I've been entrusted with it since I was ten years old. When it was stolen, I failed in my duty. I must take that duty up again."

"Look," I said, losing patience, "We don't have time for this. If Heirus doesn't get the Blade, lots of people are going to die, including and especially us. 'Please' is nice, but not nearly enough."

"The Blade was never meant to leave me. I am its guardian. I must have it back, or the consequences could be unimaginable."

I looked at him. "Corbin took it from you?"

"It was stolen from the temple."

"Some tumbledown place in the Gol-Shen swamps?"

"Yes."

I remembered the cryptic remark he'd made in the City of the Dead. "Then you're a shitty guardian. I wouldn't give it back to you in any case. Now get out."

"You have no idea what you're doing. Do not render down the statue, for the love of all."

"Tell me why. Give me one good reason, good enough to balance being slaughtered by the bloody Red Hand if I don't."

"It could end the very world."

"Well that's pretty good, I admit, but I have only your word on it, and besides, if we don't melt the damned thing down, Heirus will just kill us, take it, and melt it down himself. Nice try though. Holgren, let's do it. Or are you going to try and stop us, Arhat?"

"I will not attempt to force you to stop. But know this: What is inside the statue is like a psychic poison. If you release it, what little shielding there is between it and the world will be gone. Everyone and everything around it will be twisted beyond all recognition. Quick or slow, it *will* happen."

"Again, only your word."

"For seven years I have watched over Abanon's Blade. I have paid the price. I will show you."

And he did.

Suddenly he wasn't a fresh-faced boy anymore. Suddenly he was a nightmare, scaled and diseased, elongated slavering jaw, piss-colored eyes, taloned fingers—

And that now-familiar hate washed over me and I wanted him dead, dead, in pieces on the floor to stomp on until he was just a stain. I had a knife out and winging toward him in an eye blink, and was already following it with another in hand to gut him, but he was gone.

"You see?" he said from behind me, just a boy again. I spun around and saw that Holgren had a spitting, coruscating knife made of light under the boy's chin, and a slowly disappearing snarl on his face. Bone, silent as death, had sunk his ivory fangs into the boy's calf, and blood trickled down.

"The Blade that Whispers Hate," murmured the boy as Holgren, pale-faced, turned him loose and led Bone outside, shaking and querulous. "Do you think you can ignore its blandishments? I could not. If you release it, you'll find you have only two choices. To act on them, much to the world's woe, or to... internalize them." He bent down and ran a hand over his bleeding leg. The puncture wounds from Bone's fangs turned to puckered scars in front of my eyes, and the blood dried and flaked away onto Holgren's threadbare carpet. "I chose to take in the hate that leaked out of the Blade's prison, lest it poison the very air of the temple and the waters of the swamp. It forced upon me this duality, this alternate self that draws the hatred of others like a lodestone."

"Surely there was some other alternative," I said.

"None that I could think of. Do you mind if I sit?" he asked.

"Not my house, but feel free." I was trembling from the aftereffects of that blind hate. I sat, too. Holgren came back in and leaned against the door sill, regarding the Arhat with sharp, brooding eyes.

"You've attacked me twice," I said to the Arhat. "First you tried to break into my house, then you ambushed me when I was breaking into Heirus's villa. Why?"

"The first time I only meant to take the toad while you slept. But you woke. I did not attack you."

"You sure as hells did the second time."

"To keep you from entering the villa. If you had, you would have died. And my intent was not to harm you. But my control over the form Abanon cursed me with is imperfect."

"Why use it at all then?"

"It is strong. And it is impervious to pain."

"Why not just appear in my rooms and take the toad?"

He smiled. "I could not, otherwise I would have. The physical places where such parlor tricks are possible are limited, and random. To understand more I would need to teach you at least the fundamentals of Philosophy—"

"Mmm, no thanks. I'm a little pressed for time." And interest.

Holgren cleared his throat. "I agree that releasing the Blade would be imprudent," he said. "It still must be handed over to Heirus. There's no way around it."

"I implore you not to do so."

"Sorry. As Amra said, we have no choice."

"Well then, I will have to take it from him, then."

"Oh," I said. "He told me if he sees you he's going to do unpleasant things to your body."

"Be that as it may."

"You want to tell me why he hates you?"

"He hates all Arhat."

"Again, why?"

"He founded the Order of Philosophers. After the Cataclysm, he walked away from the Order, vowing eternal enmity."

"Sounds like there's a story in there."

"Oh yes. But one you do not have time to hear."

He stood up, and walked out the door. Holgren and I exchanged glances. He gave me a small shrug.

Somebody else knocked at Holgren's door.

"I'm becoming entirely too popular," he said with a frown. He put his hand to the door, shrugged, and opened it.

Standing at the door was Kettle, Daruvner's runner. Usually he had a mischievous look plastered on his round face, but tonight he was serious.

"Miss Amra, Daruvner wants to see you. Says it's urgent. You're s'posed to take the hack back with me." He pointed a pudgy thumb over his shoulder to the waiting carriage. "Magister Holgren should come too, an' it please him."

"What's it about, Kettle?"

He shook his head. "Not sure. Something to do with Locquewood. His man Bollund showed up at Fengal's door, bleeding like a fountain, asking after you."

CHAPTER 27

There wasn't much chit-chat in the hack on the way to Daruvner's. Holgren had taken the toad, no longer trusting the security of his sanctum, but left Bone.

I prodded Kettle to tell me what he knew.

"Bollund staggered in the eatery at supper time, blood gushing out'n him. Looked like he'd been speared in the guts. Looked like he was holding 'em in with his hands, truth be told." Kettle shuddered. "We got 'im into the back room, an' he was goin' on about a giant metal spider and askin' after you. Fengal sent me off to fetch a physicker from down the lane, and when I'd got back with 'im, Bollund was passed out and Fengal told me to go an' fetch you two."

"So Bosch is back," I said to Holgren, and he nodded.

"Who's Bosch?" asked Kettle.

"A giant metal spider," I replied, and his eyes got big.

"I thought he was just delirious."

"Sadly, no," said Holgren.

Kettle didn't seem to want to talk much after that, and I didn't want to talk too much about what might be going on in front of him, so the rest of the ride was silent. When we got to Fengal's, Kettle paid the hack off and unlocked the door to the eatery. If I'd doubted it was serious before, I didn't now. Fengal never closed, except for private parties, which he almost never hosted.

Kettle led the way back past empty tables to a storeroom off the kitchen.

Bollund lay on a makeshift cot, covered with an old horse blanket. He wasn't conscious. He was very pale, lips ashen. Daruvner was sitting in a chair near him. When he saw us, he got up and ushered us back out into the dining room.

"So Bosch attacked Bollund?" I asked him.

"No doubt. Speared him through the back and out the belly."

"What the hells for?"

He shrugged. "Because he's a nasty little git?"

"No, why did he attack *Bollund*?"

"He knew Locquewood was Corbin's fixer, and assumed Locquewood, and by extension Bollund, would know how to contact you."

"Me?"

"Of course. He wants the toad. Bollund said he's got Locquewood hostage in his shop. He sent Bollund out to tell you to bring him the toad. Alone. If you don't, he swears he'll start killing everyone you know, starting with Locquewood."

"But I don't even like Locquewood."

"That's not funny, Amra," chided Fengal.

"I just meant it's not like he's got my lover or a family member held hostage."

"Do you happen to have a lover, or any family to take?" Holgren said.

"Well no, but—"

"Locquewood was the easiest to get to, of all the people Bosch can connect to you. I was more than his match before he entered his present state, Baron Thracen is amply protected, and Inspector Kluge is quite adept at staying alive. In any case, he knew exactly where to find Locquewood, having dealt with him for the original commission. Locquewood was low-hanging fruit."

"You need to go rescue him, Amra," said Daruvner.

"Weren't you the one who told me not to be a hero?"

"I didn't tell you to be heartless, either. Bosch is your mess to clean up now."

"I'm not saying I don't want to deal with Bosch. I have scores to settle with him. I'm just saying I'm not doing it for Locquewood. Kerf's balls."

"Well, now that we're clear on that," said Holgren, "let's be on our way, shall we? Like him or not, the longer Locquewood is subjected to the attentions of Bosch, the less likely he is to survive them."

"You're coming with me?"

"Of course. I too have unfinished business with Bosch."

~ ~ ~

Kettle whistled up a hack for us. I was amazed he found one as quickly as he did, that late at night. The ride to the Dragon gate was a short one, but by the time we got there Holgren had already sketched out a plan.

"Don't enter the shop," he said as he passed me the toad. "Just call out to him, and show him the statue if you must. As soon as I can see him, I promise you he won't be in any condition to cause further trouble."

"Well that sounds simple enough," I replied. But I privately doubted it would be so easy. Bosch was mad, but he was cunning. I couldn't see him presenting such an easy target for Holgren to destroy. I would have said so, but Holgren had displayed some seriously disturbing abilities in the way of making things dead. So I kept my mouth shut, and hoped he was right.

We alighted at the end of the deserted, lamp-lit street. Locquewood's shop was in the middle of a commercial area, high-end, and nobody bought expensive trinkets like his in the middle of the night. Holgren put a hand on my shoulder, then crossed the street. We walked the rest of the way up the slight incline to Locquewood's shop.

There were no lights on in the expensive glass display windows. The door was closed. I glanced back across the street. Holgren was nowhere to be seen, but I didn't worry that he'd taken off. Much.

I put a hand on the knob and tried it. Unlocked. I pushed it open.

"Hey, Bosch," I called. "I hear you wanted to talk to me."

Silence, then a low groan, somewhere far back in the shop.

"Anybody home?" I called.

"Come in, Amra." That pipe organ voice. "I hope you've brought me my trinket."

"I think I'll stay right here, thanks. Why don't you come and get what you wanted?" I held up the toad.

"Bring it to me," said Bosch. "Now."

"No."

Locqueowood screamed. Quite a lot.

"My new limbs lack digits, but they are the very thing for poking out eyes, I've found."

"What the hells is wrong with you, Bosch?"

"Having my body disintegrated has made me churlish. Now bring me the toad, or this dandy will lose his other eye. And I should warn you, my limbs are not really suited for fine work. It's entirely possible I'll poke too deep."

"Kerf's crooked staff," I swore. I shoved the toad inside my jacket and pulled out my knives. And entered the spider's web.

CHAPTER 28

"You might as well let the dandy go," I said as I stepped into the dark interior of the shop. "It's you and I that have this dance." I walked slowly past rows of precious gewgaws and delicate frippery, giving my eyes time to adjust to the gloom. The shop wasn't all that big; I was certain Bosch and Locquewood were in the back room. The muted witchlight that pulsed erratically from the dark interior was another clue.

"All right," he said. "Mister Locquewood, if you would care to depart, be my guest."

A dull whimper was the only reply.

"It seems Mister Locquewood prefers sitting in a puddle of his own blood, Amra."

"Come out here, Bosch, and get your toad." Here at least there was some light from the street. The storeroom was windowless.

"Come back and hand it to me."

"Let's stop the games. You plan on killing me and Locquewood both, and taking the idol. I'm willing to try and save him, but not at the cost of my own life. I'm more than willing to meet you half-way, though, if you come out here now and face me. Then whoever's left standing does whatever they want."

"So you aren't going to come back here to save this wretch's life?"

I didn't like where that question was headed. "Are you afraid to face me?"

There was a jarring series of notes that I decided was Bosch's new laugh.

"I'll take that as a no. Come out. We'll settle our difference. Since you're certain of the outcome, you can always go back and finish Locquewood off after you've sorted me out."

"That would just be extra work," he replied, and then I heard a wet tearing sound, and a agonized scream that abruptly cut off.

"Oh, dear," said Bosch. "Clumsy me."

One of the things I was taught, long ago in the back alleys of Bellarius when Theiner, my friend and protector was teaching me to fight with knives, was to never, ever lose your temper in a fight. Of all the knife fighting techniques he drilled me on, that one was the most crucial. It was a hard lesson for me to learn—for any child to learn—but learn it I did.

I surprised myself a little with the hot splash of rage that sprang up at Locquewood's death. I hadn't liked him but he certainly hadn't deserved to be tortured to death. I'd like to think anyone would have felt the same, but sadly I knew better. That detached, emotionless part of my mind began to churn out bare facts in rapid succession despite my emotion.

Locquewood was almost certainly dead or on the way. My reason for being in this trap had expired. Time to leave. Holgren could burn the place down once I was out of it.

I turned and ran. Not a moment too soon, as it turned out.

Bosch had kept control of one of his hellish pets. It had been above me the entire time I was talking, waiting to drop down on me.

As I turned, I caught the barest flicker of movement from above, and then its talons raked my back, ripping my jacket and the shirt and skin beneath to ribbons. The daemonette that had retrieved Bosch's head from Gavon's. The shock of it forced a cry of pain out of me, but I kept moving. Holgren, and light enough to see my enemy, were just outside the door.

I heard a hiss and a scrabbling of talons on the hardwood floor. I knew the thing was disgustingly fast. Probably fast enough to get hold of me before I made it outside. No time to turn and cast a knife. So I turned my lunge into a sort of pirouette as I reached the door, knife arm extending out to where I imagined it would be.

I got it in the throat.

It ripped my forearm all to hells, and when we landed in the street, it was on top of me. My knife in its neck kept it from biting my face off, though it still strained fiercely to get its slavering, beetly jaws on me. Its claws were starting to do to my front what they'd done to my back, though, scoring lines of blood and fire down my chest and belly.

I got another knife into its side with my left hand. Using the two knife hilts as handles, I rolled over and arched my body away from its talons. However fierce it was, I had the weight advantage. I got it mostly on its back. Carefully, I put a boot to its neck and put my weight down on it as it twisted and writhed.

Then I pulled out both my blades and with speed and precision borne of long, long practice, I planted one in each of its faceted eyes, until the tips grated against the back of its skull.

"That's for Locquewood, I suppose," I panted, then sprang back, knives in hand. It thrashed a moment more, and was suddenly still.

Bosch faced me from the doorway.

"Impressive," he piped. "I would clap, but, you know." He raised his two blood-stained forelimbs, waggled them back and forth. Then he attacked. *Where the hells is Holgren?* I thought as I parried one of his limbs. The other tore a bloody gash along my thigh. Then I was under him, and eight metal stakes were rising and falling all around me, striking the cobbles with enough force to shatter them as Bosch did his best to impale me without actually being able to see me. It couldn't have lasted more than a half dozen heartbeats, but for that brief eternity I was certain I was going to die as I twisted desperately to avoid being punctured.

And then there was an enormous *KRUMP* sound. Above me, Bosch's body crumpled inward as if a hundred war hammers had struck it all at once.

Bosch staggered drunkenly away, the weird lights that played upon his now twisted body dimming. When they died out, he fell, motionless, to the cobbles.

"Sorry I was late," said Holgren as he staggered up to me, clutching his side. "Bosch evidently expected me as well, and prepared a reception." I looked past him, down the street, and saw a wet lump about as big as a horse but covered in scales, ichor still spurting out of it in time to a slowly fading heartbeat.

"Better late than never."

CHAPTER 29

Both of us were tired and bleeding, and I had only a bare hour or so before I was supposed to give the toad to Heirus. But we couldn't just leave the hell-spawned mess that had been Bosch and his daemonette lying there on the street. I ripped my ruined jacket into strips to bind up the worst injuries while Holgren did some magely thing to get hold of Kluge involving a prism–apparently they'd exchanged some sort of magical calling card that let them contact each other.

Once I'd stopped my blood from watering the cobbles, I offered to do the same for Holgren, but he waved it away.

"I'm going to check on Locquewood," I said, and he nodded.

"I'll wait here, and keep an eye on these things."

I found and lit a lamp in the front of the shop, then carried back to the storeroom.

He was dead. And mutilated. It was about as bad as I had expected. I hadn't known him well, but I don't think he would have wanted to survive what Bosch had done to him.

Most of him was sitting in a delicate chair behind a delicate desk. I made a mental note to ask Bollund if he'd had any family. If Bollund lived.

I was about to turn and go back out to Holgren when the package caught my eye.

About the size of my fist, it lay on the floor, half-smashed, obviously knocked there in the scuffle. Its beautiful wrapping was spattered with Locquewood's blood. I looked closer and saw my name written on the sky-blue paper it had been wrapped in. It looked like a feminine hand, one not terribly accustomed to writing.

I picked it up, heard the tinkling of broken glass from inside it. Carried it and the lantern back out to the street.

Holgren was bent over Bosch's remains, trying to wrench off the amber block that held Bosch's head.

"Souvenir?" I asked him.

"Ha. I want to retrieve it before Kluge arrives, which should be quite soon. Gavon will demand proof if you want the contract cancelled and your money back. Or had you forgotten?"

"Actually, I had." Hopefully Heirus had cancelled the contract, but a little insurance was welcome.

With an audible crack the head came free. "There, that's got it." He turned to hand it to me, saw my hands were full.

"What have you got there?"

"The answer to a mystery, maybe." I told him about Estra Haig's girl looking for me, leaving a package for me with Locquewood.

"Why Locquewood?"

"I don't know. Maybe the answer's inside."

"So why aren't you opening it?"

"I don't know. I've just suddenly got a strange feeling I won't like whatever it is."

He just looked at me.

"Alright, alright." I put the lamp down and tore open the wrapping, exposing a square little rosewood jewellery box, sadly splintered in one corner. I lifted the latch.

Inside was a scented piece of paper, folded small to fit, and bits of colored, broken glass. Broken glass I recognized from part of one green wing and from the delicate head and long, thin beak.

The hummingbird that Corbin had swiped from me the day before he died.

I fished out the note and set the box down. Unfolded the stiff, scented paper:

Madam Amra,

Corbin told me the bird had come from you, so I return it, and to show what I next write is the truth.

Corbin was my man. Madam Estra holds my indenture, and he was going to pay it, to buy it out so he and I could be together. But Madam Estra didn't like it, hated it in fact, that Corbin had chosen me to love.

I know Corbin is dead and gone. I knew it as soon as you came into the Dream to tell Madam Estra. His name on your lips and the look on your face told me all. But you didn't know about him and me. And I couldn't tell you, not there under her roof. So I want to tell you that if Corbin came to a bad end as my heart tells me he did, it was Estra Haig that did the deed, or had it done rather, because that last night before Corbin never came back to me, she told me he never would. She told me I was hers, her property, and I could no more take her man than her hairbrush could, or her dog. And when I told her that was for Corbin to say, she laughed and told me Corbin wouldn't be saying anything anymore.

Corbin told me you were a fierce one, and that if I was to find myself in trouble, you was the one to find if I couldn't find him. I'm not asking for anything, except for Corbin. If you're looking for the one who laid him low, then now you know.

I leave this with Corbin's 'connection' as he never told me where to find you.

Sincerely,

Lyra Juvis Blackdaughter

"That bitch." I hissed.

"Which bitch would that be?" Holgren asked, but I only half-heard him.

"She sat there, twisting her napkin in despair, offering me assistance in hunting down Corbin's killer, the fucking *picture* of sorrow!" I kicked the jewellery box down the street, scattering bits of colored glass along the cobbles.

Holgren carefully took the note from me. Read it. Handed it back. I crumpled it in my fist, then forced myself to calm. I smoothed out the letter, folded it back up carefully and stuck it in my pocket.

"So you're going to kill her?" he asked.

"Me? I'm a law-abiding citizen, Holgren. Especially when there's an inspector in the vicinity." I pointed my chin down the street, where a carriage had just turned the corner, with a dozen city watch trotting behind, armed with pikes.

"There's late, and then there's too late," I muttered.

Kluge didn't have anything to say to me, which suited me fine. He listened to Holgren's statement, then made a brief inspection of the shop and the corpses.

"Where's this one's head?" he asked when he got to Bosch.

Holgren looked like he wanted to feign ignorance, but he pulled his cloak back and showed the grisly trophy.

"Is there a particular reason you want that?" Kluge asked him.

"Yes."

"Do I want to know what that reason is?"

"Not really, Inspector."

Kluge let out a sort of disgusted sigh and said "Get out of my sight, both of you." Then he gave his men some instruction regarding Bosch's corpse. They got busy wrapping the thing in a canvas tarp while Kluge set about burning the demon corpses with magefire.

"You heard the Inspector," I said to Holgren.

The sky was beginning to pink with dawn as we hobbled away towards my meeting with Red Hand.

CHAPTER 30

"**I** suppose you're coming with me, then?" I asked Holgren as we made our way towards the Necropolis.

"Well, it *is* on the way home," he replied. He was smiling, but his hand was pressed against the wound in his side.

"Got any magic for healing?" I asked. My back was still on fire, and the gash in my thigh wasn't much better. Both were going to severely restrict my mobility in a fight.

"Not my specialty, I'm afraid."

"Any idea what to do about Heirus?"

"Well, you have two options, it seems. Give him the toad. Or make him take it."

"I just wish I knew what he wanted it for," I muttered.

Holgren gave a short chuckle. "What would the king of assassins want with a god-forged weapon, I wonder?'

"That's just it," I replied. "I hate to say this again, but you didn't *see* him. I did. He doesn't need any magic blade to be the deadliest thing on two legs. It's not going to make him a better killer, Holgren. You can't improve on perfection."

"He obviously made an impression on you."

I shrugged, and darted out to hail a hack that had just turned the corner. At least I wouldn't have to walk the entire way to my doom.

~ ~ ~

The gates were open when we got there.

"Why don't you go on home?" I asked Holgren as we walked in.

"I think I'll stay with you."

"There's no point sticking your neck out. This isn't your fight, never was."

"So you've decided to fight?" he replied, avoiding my point.

"It's just an expression." We got to the hill, started climbing towards the Weeping Mother statue. It really was quite homely.

"I think I know you well enough now to say that you're wrong. It's become fairly plain that you, Amra Thetys, given the choice between fighting and capitulating, will pick a fight every damned time."

"So you're saying I'm stubborn."

"Oh, yes, very much so. Contrary as well."

"No I'm not."

"Don't look now, but you're being stubborn. And contrary."

"I know you are, but what am I?"

That got a laugh out of him. But it died away quickly and his eyes got hard. I followed his gaze.

Heirus was standing directly beneath the Weeping Mother. He looked bored, and impatient.

As we closed to the last few yards, he spoke.

"You have it. Give it to me." He held out a hand.

"I have it," I replied. "But I need to know what you're going to do with it."

He cocked his head, and a confused look flitted across his face. "You know I can and will kill you, yet you continue to behave as though your needs, your *questions* matter."

"The question itself matters, not who it belongs to."

"Why?"

"Because I know you don't need this Blade to become more powerful. You are the most deadly man alive. So, Heirus, Red Hand, what do you intend to *do* with it?"

"An excellent question," said the Arhat, who had suddenly appeared a few yards away.

"I told you to keep that one away from me," hissed Heirus.

"And I told you he's not my dog," I replied.

The Arhat approached. "So, Kingmaker, Godslayer, why not answer the question? You well know what will happen if the Blade is loosed. What do you want with it?"

"What I want with the Blade is none of your concern."

"You know that is untrue. I am tasked with guarding it."

"And you have failed."

"Not yet."

Heirus moved, and suddenly the Arhat had a knife in his gut.

"Now you have failed," sneered Heirus into his face. That's when Holgren broke the magical chain around my neck.

"Remember," he whispered as it fell to the ground, "don't kill yourself." Then it hit the grass and everything changed.

With a thought, the world stood still. I looked around me, and it was like looking at a painting. Holgren stood, lips still shaped around the last sound he'd uttered. The Arhat stared into Heirus's eyes, his face only just beginning to show the agony of steel in his intestines.

I made two knives appear and began to walk towards them. "Come on then, Red Hand," I said and his head whipped around to me. "Let's see how good you really are."

He smiled and pulled his knife out of the Arhat. He actually saluted me with it. And then he flew at me, *still* a blur.

With a thought, I forced Holgren's magic to match him, and met his thrust from a half-decent guard position, knocking his knife hand away to my left with my wrist and following it with a thrust of my own with the knife in my right hand. But he had already spun away.

"You cannot sustain such magic. Either the toll it takes will kill you or I will. You cannot win."

I returned to the *Aquila* guard position, sideways to him, left arm and leg extended and right arm above my head, circling slowly, ready to strike from on high. It had been a long, long time since I'd been in anything like a formal knife duel. But you never forget. He was right, though; I could already feel the thirst building, as if I'd had nothing to drink for a long, hot day. He could just toy with me until I collapsed.

So I attacked.

I pushed the magic even harder, and came in with a showy feint to his eyes with my right while I drove my left down toward his groin. He jumped back, and back again, and gave me a shallow slice across the back of my left hand for my trouble.

"I could have had your thumb," he said, and I knew he was right.

I was good with a blade. He was much, much better.

When the cramps started I couldn't think what they were for a moment. Then I realized they were hunger pangs; hours, days perhaps of hunger compressed into an instant. I gritted my teeth against them, and the aching flesh of my back, and the ragged gash across my thigh, and pushed the magic once more, and flung my right hand blade. I was hoping—praying, really—that once it left my hand it would not suddenly slow.

It didn't.

It took him in the throat. He hadn't even tried to block it.

His eyes got wide. His mouth sagged. He made choking sounds.

And then he pulled my knife out of his neck and laughed at me.

There was no hole in his neck. There wasn't even any blood.

I sat down on the grass and put my head in my hands.

"Can I have my toad *now*?" he asked.

CHAPTER 31

"**K**erf's balls." I looked up and he was just standing there, smiling at me. Behind him, to my right, the Arhat was still dying by inches, a crimson stain spreading ever so slowly across the saffron robes over his stomach. *Why didn't you change forms? It might have given you a chance.* But he wasn't ever going to answer that question now.

I glanced behind me to my left, and there was Holgren, hand still raised from breaking the chain, infinitesimally moving back to his side.

I let go of the magic. The Arhat fell to his knees, then rolled onto his side. He was dead, or so close as made no difference. No help could get to him in time. Foolish boy. What had he hoped to accomplish?

Holgren came to stand behind me, and I could feel his power. He'd summoned up some sort of magic, and it was making the little hairs on the back of my neck fairly twist and jump.

I dropped my forearms on my knees, considered the cut Heirus had made across the back of my hand, instead of taking my thumb. Beads of blood had formed along its length.

Blood.

"You want the toad?" I asked him. "There's still one more I think you'll have to go through."

"Who? The mage?"

I shook my head, and wiped the back of my bloodied hand across the emerald cemetery grass. "They say you should never, ever spill blood in the Necropolis," I told him.

"Oh, really?" he replied. "And why is that?"

"Because the Guardian will notice. And investigate. And it's got a nasty disposition."

"Oh, I do," said a voice like a thousand tombs yawning open. "That I surely do."

It sounded as if the voice had come from above. I glanced up, and the Weeping Mother statue stared back down at me. She had changed.

There was no pity or compassion in that badly carved face now. It had been replaced with cruelty, and madness. A cold, cold wind started up, and the light bled out of the sky.

"Who shed blood here in this sanctified place?" she asked, "and whose blood was shed?"

"My blood," I replied. "His knife," I said, pointing at Heirus who, I have to say, wasn't looking all that bothered.

"I do not ask the *living*," she told me with contempt.

The tombs opened, and the dead poured forth.

I looked down the hill and saw Corbin walking towards me. Behind him were the three armsmen, and a whole host of the dead I neither knew nor cared to.

"Who shed blood?" asked the Guardian again, and half a hundred fingers, in various states of decomposition, pointed at Heirus.

"Whose blood was shed?" And the fingers moved to point at me.

"Don't forget him," I said, pointing to the Arhat.

"His blood has not yet fallen." The Guardian replied.

"Well that's splitting hairs."

"Rules are rules." She turned to face Heirus. "By what cause or right do you spill blood here?"

He sniffed. "An oath forsworn."

"What oath?"

"This one promised to bring me the statue she holds in her shirt, but refuses to give it up. Thus is she forsworn."

That massive head swivelled back to me. "Is this true?"

"I said I'd bring it, not give it to him!"

"Now who is the splitter of hairs? Tut-tut." She shook her massive finger at me, then looked at the gathered dead. "Who here witnessed this oath?"

A dozen mouldering hands raised. Including, I noticed, Corbin's. He had come to stand beside me.

"Thanks a lot," I told him, and he shrugged.

"Here is my judgment," said the Guardian. "The woman, being known to the honest dead, and having her blood spilled where it should not be, may go free." Pause. "*After* she gives up what she agreed to, here on this sanctified ground."

Bloodied, near-mad with thirst, aching with hunger and my wounds, I swore in disgust and pulled the hated toad from inside my shirt. I threw it at Heirus's feet.

"Choke on it," I said.

He bent down to pick it up, and Corbin whispered in my ear, voice slurred a little by decomposition: "When the time comes, do not let her have the Blade. We are her jailers as much as she is our Guardian. *Keep the Blade from her grasp.*"

Heirus held the toad up before his face. "Finally," he said. Then he began to whisper words that stirred the hairs on the back of my neck.

"Kerf's crooked staff," I swore. "He's a *mage* too?"

As Heirus spoke, the golden toad began to melt. The gold ran down his arm like mud and pattered on the grass, not in the least hot.

"Oh, that's a nice trick," murmured Holgren, and then all at once it was free, and that sickening feeling I'd felt when I'd tried to sleep with it in my hiding place in the wall suddenly beat down on me, on everyone there, living and dead.

Heirus held it in his hand, a shimmering, writhing thing that seemed to take on a hundred forms with each heartbeat, shedding cold blue sparks and jags of light that died out a hand's breadth away from it.

He turned and smiled at me, gave me another mocking duellist's salute.

"You asked me what I planned to do with Abanon's Blade, thief. I will tell you. I will finally, finally exit this sorry world, and be free of it and all you mayflies. Farewell."

Then he plunged the knife into his own heart.

As he crumpled to the ground, Corbin pushed me forward, shouting "Now!" in that creaky, slurred dead man's voice. The Guardian was already reaching down to pluck the Blade from Heirus's corpse. I turned the push into a lunge.

My shaking, bloodied hand got there just before her giant stone one.

And Abanon began to whisper to me, driving for a time all sense from my mind.

CHAPTER 32

The next thing I can recall: I am stumbling, shambling. I do not trust my feet or my hands or my eyes. I do not trust my breath or the taste of my own sour spit. The Blade is talking, whispering, and it has terrible, terrible things to tell me. I try to drown it out "No. No no no no no," I say, but it doesn't listen to me.

I am not in the Necropolis. I do not remember leaving. But I remember the Guardian, furious, and Corbin telling me to go to the temple. I remember Holgren pounding the Guardian with his magics, distracting her so that I could escape. I do not remember what happened to either of them.

Just get to the temple. Bath's temple. Just get to the temple, that's what the small part of my mind is saying. The part that's not being drowned by the hate, an ocean of bile pouring into my soul.

This is what the Arhat dealt with since he was ten years old? I will light candles for him in the temple of the departed. I swear it. I swear it. If I survive.

The Blade was shifting, shifting, now no bigger than a needle, now as long as a spear. I had to hold tight, very tight as it writhed in my hand.

And the Goddess's Blade whispered to me all the way.

—all these people on the street. Kill them. They deserve it and it would be so easy. Humanity, cockroaches all, deserving nothing more than being trod underfoot. What vile, foul sacks of meat, their breathing and grasping and fornicating and defecating. Shoving food into their faces, shoving their genitals at each other, shoving out more wailing, hairless monkeys at every turn who grow and grow and do more of the same. A blight. This city is a blight, a running sore on the face of the world. Scour it. These maggots deserve extinction—

An unending monologue of hate. It was all in my own voice. And the worst of it was that most of me did not disagree. I knew I was nodding my head, even as my mouth moaned out its 'no no no.'

—fucking wagon, see how it's just been left there to block the street? Thoughtless, careless self-absorbed, self centered apes all of them, just left to block the street and it's in the fucking way *but it doesn't have to be—*

The hand that holds the Blade twitches and the wagon just disintegrates into dust, along with the horse that was hitched to it. "NO no no no," I wail, and start to run.

What if a child darts out in front of me, or an old man blocks my way?

My natural impatience, magnified a thousand-fold, will be the death of—anyone. Everyone.

What if the sun shines too brightly in my eyes? What if I breathe a breath of less-than-fresh air? No. No no no. I can't carry this burden. I'm no Arhat. I cannot hold this Blade.

I run faster.

I hug the Blade tight, lest I lose hold of it accidentally again.

Soon Bath's temple appeared before me, and my 'no no no' gave way to relieved sobs.

~ ~ ~

Bath's acolyte was waiting for me on the steps of the temple. His look was serene.

"My Master cannot accept this burden," he said somehow through sewn lips.

"Oh, gods, please. I can't. I can't. I hate you. I hate him. I fucking hate him and I hate your fucking secrets you pile of stinking—" I slap my hand over my mouth.

—miserable shit never meant to help anyone or anything his only secret is the terrible things he does to worshippers in a dark back room while his god watches—

He leaned forward and put a hand on my shoulder. I hated him for it. But then I hated him for everything.

"What do you imagine would happen if a god who knew all the secrets of the world, of creation itself, felt the hate that you feel right now? No, Amra; this burden cannot come to rest with Bath."

"Then where?" I choked out. "I can't. I can't—"

"No," he said gently. "You can't either. But Bath knows a secret that he wants me to share with you." And he leaned down and whispered in my ear.

He whispered for a long time, for all that it was a single word. The word was very long, and it was forged in the fires of creation. I say it was a word, because that's how Bath chose to express it to me, but really it was a single, pure, undiluted concept.

No, it was not love. Love is not the opposite of hate. In fact, they're closer than you might think.

What *is* the opposite of love, you ask? Or hate, for that matter? I have no clue. Bath didn't share that secret with me.

What Bath shared with me was the undiluted truth of Apathy, the rat-fucking bastard, and it worked.

And what is Apathy? Best I can describe it is fatalism mixed with utter indifference. Things are as they are. Things will be as they will be. No point thinking about them, much less worrying. No point doing much of anything at all, as a matter of fact.

The acolyte whispered that terrible Word into my ear, and I collapsed on the steps like a puppet with cut strings.

The Blade poured its poison into my ear, and I no longer cared. Not about that, and not about anything else, either. Left to my own devices, I would have lain there on the steps of the temple until I starved to death or died of thirst. I was a motiveless shell. My body breathed, my heart beat, but beyond that I did nothing, because I was indifferent to everything. A mote of dust drifted into my eye and it was meant to be so. Blinking was futile.

Bath had pulled the Blade's fangs. He'd also turned me into, essentially, a breathing corpse.

"My Master did bid you be careful of the Eightfold Goddess, Amra," he said as he grabbed me under the armpits and began to drag me up the steps. "Well. Bath is the lord of secrets. He keeps them well. He will keep you well as well. What is another secret to Bath?"

He was dragging me up to the inside of the temple where, presumably, I'd disappear for good. Just another secret kept. Every blade needs a sheath.

Hate and apathy. The unstoppable against the immovable, and me being ground down in between. We were almost at the top of the stairs.

"Secrets are power," the Acolyte whispered in my ear. "How does it feel to be powerless? Useless and used? A tool for powers far greater than you?"

I felt hate for him, then. No, I felt… not hate. Rage.

I felt rage. And beneath that, terror.

Against the lifeless nullity of apathy and the corrosive torrent of poison that was the Blade's hate, rage blossomed in me. It burned and it cut and slowly made its way to my mouth as a scream.

I am no one's tool.

The echoes of that awful Word he had poured into my ear burned away to nothing, to silence. The Blade's vile whispering stuttered, stopped. The acolyte stopped dragging me and whispered a final time in my ear.

"Some secrets cannot be shared. Some secrets must be discovered."

I lay there on the steps and gasped, trembling with rage. I felt I had to stay still, or I would burn the world down.

The Blade had stopped its ceaseless, restless shifting. It was a throwing knife now. Perfectly weighted for my hand. For the first time it addressed me directly.

I will be your tool. I was meant *to be your tool. Use me, Amra.*

"Shut up," I told it. And it did.

The rage inside me screamed, inchoate, on and on. If I gave into it I knew the world would burn. I knew it. I could not let it slip its leash. Slowly, with great care, I sat up on the steps and looked at the acolyte.

"I know a secret or two as well," I told him through clenched teeth. "Secrets have no power. Not by themselves. It's the *control* of secrets that's power. Control is power, isn't it—Bath?"

He nodded. "Some secrets cannot be imparted. They must be discovered."

"And if I had not discovered this secret? Would You have salted me away in some secret place, to absorb the Blade's hate forever?"

"Yes," he said, without the least hesitation.

"At least You're honest." I climbed to my feet and carefully started down the steps. I couldn't look at the god of secrets. The rage inside me wanted to reduce him to ashes. A rage that was wholly human, wholly mine.

"What will you do with the Blade?" he called after me.

I kept walking, but said over my shoulder, "I could tell You it's a secret, but really it's just none of Your fucking business."

His laughter followed me down the strangely deserted street.

CHAPTER 33

Another secret Bath surely knew, and kept to himself, was that control is an illusion.

I'd built myself a bridge of rage, but as I walked across it, it disintegrated behind me. I had broken free of the Apathy the god of secrets had laid on me. But with the removal of the threat of being secreted away in some corner of his temple for eternity, a breathing corpse, a receptacle for the Blade's hate — with that threat avoided, it was hard to keep hold of my wrath.

The Blade was quiescent, but I didn't trust it. The old priest of Lagna was right; it *wanted* to be used. And if I did use it? What then? How could I possibly trust it? How could I trust myself? I was riding a dragon. Whatever control I believed I had, there would be a reckoning as soon as I turned loose.

And if I never turned loose? If I used Abanon's Blade as it wanted me to? Heirus was right. I could use the Blade to do awful, magnificent things with just a shred of hate and the will to see it through.

Yes, Amra. Show me what you hate, and that we will obliterate.

"I told you to shut up."

Traitor's Gate had seen better days. Better centuries, maybe. The gate itself was long gone. The pale yellow stone was fissured, and the narrow steps leading up to the abandoned guard room above were choked with refuse. But the oak door to the guard room was still relatively sound, and the lock sturdy. I should know, since I installed it myself. Another one of my bolt-holes. One with a nice view of the market, and a stupendous reek of rotting produce.

I sat in the window, on the wide ledge, looking down on the afternoon bustle. By this time of day most of the greens were limp. People haggled. Children darted amongst the makeshift tables, playing and shrieking.

I held the Blade in my hand. I couldn't put it down.

What did I hate?

I thought on it for a while. Could I actually use the Blade for some sort of good?

"Blade, could I use you to, say, kill every rapist in Lucernis?"

It throbbed in my hand. *Yes. Yes. We will hunt them down and make them pay-"*

"No. I mean right now. Can you make every rapist just drop dead."

Its silence was all the answer I needed.

What did I hate?

"Blade, can you end hunger? Poverty? Deformity in children? Can you heal the sick?

Can you do one useful fucking thing other than destroy?"

Silence.

"You're bloody useless, aren't you?"

I am the hate of a goddess made manifest. I am a Power.

"You know what I think? I think she discarded you because you were *useless*. No, more than useless. A hindrance. A liability."

I could extinguish the sun. I could rip the world in twain. I could drown nations in rivers of blood. The stones of the gate tower trembled.

"But you can't fill one child's empty belly, or cure a cough, or even get a stain out of linen."

Tools are made for a purpose. They have a function, sometimes many functions. Their existence is *predicated* on their usefulness.

A tool that cannot be reliably taken in hand, fit for no useful purpose: Was it even a tool, in any rational sense of the word?

This Blade I held wasn't broken; it was flawed from its very creation.

It must have sensed the direction my thoughts were leading, because it began to vibrate in my hand, its form flickering from one type of cutlery to another. A dull keening started up from it, and a hellish red glow.

"A workman relies on his tool to do the job at hand. His skill, his hand, guides the tool. A tool that turns in his hand should be discarded."

Yes. Discard me. Leave me here—

"But no responsible craftsman would leave a dangerous tool lying around for any fool to pick up. Even swords, meant only for killing, come with scabbards."

Then find a sheath for me. I will lie quiet.

"Ah, but every tool, flawed or not, put away or left out, holds the potential to be used again." I held it up before me, looked long and hard at its coruscating form. Felt the hate bubble up like hot bile. Let it.

"You asked me what I hate. I'll tell you. I hate *you*, you useless—"

There was a soft *pop*, and a soft sigh. In my hand was only grit and ash, and tiny bits of charred bone.

I wiped the residue on my thigh, but it left a gray stain on the skin of my palm. I didn't think that stain would go away any time soon.

After a time, I got up and walked down the steps. I still had one more job to do.

I still had to tell Osskil who'd killed his brother.

With Abanon's Blade dust, I found I'd lost my thirst for revenge. After everything that had happened, dealing with Estra would just have been an unpleasant chore. But it might still mean something to Osskil.

CHAPTER 34

It was a beautiful robe. No, beautiful did not do it justice. The robe was exquisite. Made of the finest silk, it lay in an almost liquid pool of itself, every ripple casting a lustrous crimson sheen. It probably cost what I made in an average year. It was probably the costliest bathing robe ever made. I reached to touch it, and he closed the lid of the carved, lacquered box.

"Better not," said Osskil. "Only the interior has been… treated. But why take a chance."

It was odd, having him here in my rooms. All I had for him to sit on was a decrepit sea chest. He didn't seem to mind.

I looked into his eyes, saw the flicker of some deep passion. Something hotter than rage. Something colder than revenge. Then he blinked, and shrugged, and the raw emotion subsided beneath the lordly demeanor.

"All the time we thought it was about some Goddess's artefact," he murmured, "when in fact my brother was murdered over the basest of human emotions. Jealousy."

I shook my head. "It's not so simple, I think. Estra Haig has been a great beauty all her life, and it's slipping away from her now as she grows older. When Corbin threw her over for a younger, prettier girl, it must have struck her at her core, her very sense of self." I rubbed absently at my hand, permanently marked by the Blade, or its residue. A barely visible discoloring of the skin; virtually unnoticeable compared to all the other scars I carry, and an itch that wouldn't go away. I'd learn to live with it. I've learned to live with much worse.

"Anyway, in a real sense it wasn't jealousy. It was desperate denial," I said.

After a short silence he said "Well, I suppose it doesn't matter, really. Betrayal is betrayal, and traitors always find compelling reasons to excuse their actions." His heavy-lidded gaze rested, unblinking and again hot, on the box.

"How long will it take?" I asked.

He shrugged. "Who can say? If she towels herself thoroughly first, perhaps fifty heartbeats before she notices anything. Much faster if she wears it wet. Either way, she will be a long while about the business of dying. The spasms will be ferocious. People poisoned thus have been known to break their own backs, the muscles convulse so furiously." His eyes may have shown emotion, but his voice displayed none.

I shuddered. "A terrible way to die."

"Poison is the proscribed death for traitors."

"Why?"

"Because traitors poison faith and trust."

"I mean why tell me about this at all?"

He was silent for a long time. I began to believe he would not answer. Then, "I loved my brother. My father sent me to see justice done because it was expected. But he despised Corbin. I'll never be sure why, but I think it was because Corbin favored Mother so much, in his looks. If only he'd looked a little less like her...."

He looked at me. "Because, of all those searching for my brother's murderer, only you did so not because you were ordered or paid to. Because you shamed me in that prison.

"Only you and I know the world grew a little darker at his death. Only you and I and this damned dog."

There was one other who probably knew, but I didn't bring up Corbin's lover. Best leave well enough alone, I thought.

Osskil reached down and scratched behind Bone's ears. Holgren had brought him round the day before, saying he was going somewhere for a couple of days, and that I needed a guard dog more than he did. When Osskil had first seen Bone, and been told it was Corbin's dog, he'd immediately asked if he could keep him. I couldn't say no.

"You were in on the beginning of it all," he said, pulling me back from my thoughts. "It is only fitting you know how it ends."

"Speaking of the dog," I said, changing the subject, "are you sure you want to burden yourself with such an ugly mongrel?" I hated to admit it, but I was going to miss Bone, slobber and all.

"Mongrel? This dog is a pureblood royal boarhound. He has the best lines I've ever seen of the breed. It would not be uncommon for one such as Bone to fetch more than a warhorse would. How he ended up on the streets of Lucernis, I'll never fathom."

"You're joking."

"My family breeds the finest dogs in Lucernia. I never joke about dogs."

I could think of nothing to say. We sat there for a while in silence, a thief, a baron and a royal cur. Then he rose, a beautiful, horrible death tucked under one arm.

"Thank you for the wine. If you are in Courune, and not then spectacularly at odds with the law, I would consider it an honor if you would call upon me." A ghost of a smile touched his heavy lips.

"You'll make a practice of taking in strays if you aren't careful. But all right. If I am in Courune, and not employed, I'll do just that." A thought occurred to me. "When will you send it?" I pointed at the box under his arm.

"I will call on Madame Haig personally this afternoon. We will pass pleasantries. I'll make discreet noises to the effect that she should not consider trying, in any fashion, to leverage her relationship with Corbin to gain anything from the Thracens. I will give her this gift as a token of my admiration. I wager she will think it no more than her due. And she will be right."

"What about whatever thugs she hired to kill Corbin? Will you hunt them down as well?"

He shook his head. "I don't see much point in that," he said. Silently, I agreed.

He left then and, shooing Bone before him, stepped into the gilded carriage waiting outside my door, oblivious to the threadbare crowd that had gathered to gawp at such a sight, in such a neighbourhood.

~ ~ ~

A couple of days later I found myself in Loathewater, one of the many slums of

Lucernis. The day had dawned grey and heavy with rain that refused to fall. I hadn't been able to sleep much or well, what with all the punishment my body had taken over the past few days, and so I found myself doing what I always seem to do when at loose ends; walking aimlessly, trying to keep ahead of my thoughts. Or trying at least to tread water, so to speak.

I'd set out to kill Corbin's killer. I might not have done it with my own knife, but it was done. Estra Haig was a dead woman, whether she knew it yet or not. Along the way a lot of others had gotten dead. Some had deserved it. One, at least, had desired it. But I couldn't help but wonder if things wouldn't have been better off, in the grand scheme of things, if I'd just let well enough alone.

After all, none of it had brought Corbin back.

I'd walked most of the night away and on into the dawn when I looked around and found myself surrounded by the scrap shanties and towering trees of Loathewater. The sudden feeling of being watched had pulled me out of my ruminations.

She was standing in her doorway. She, like her house, was crisp and clean and straight, though the neighborhood was dilapidated, quietly desperate, and muck-strewn.

The bloodwitch.

"Seems you've found your way to my door," she said.

"Just passing through."

"Oh, come now. I knew you'd be around. I Saw it. Come inside then, and have some tea."

"No offense, but I'd rather not."

She smiled. "We each of us do things we'd rather not. It's part of life. There are things we should discuss that are best not spoken of on the street."

I really didn't want to offend a bloodwitch. Still, I hesitated.

"Come, I'll feed you as well. You look like the type who enjoys a scone."

My stomach rumbled. I went inside.

The interior was sparse and almost harshly clean. I don't know what I expected. Jars of newt eyes and bats in the rafters, maybe. Instead it reminded me of how my mother had kept her house, all those years ago. I could almost hear her muttering "poor's no excuse for filthy" the way she had when she was scrubbing something.

There was tea, with honey, and freshly toasted scones, with raisins, all on a little table set for two. I'm not all that fond of raisins, but the scones did smell good.

"You Saw me coming? Or do you lay out breakfast like this every day?"

"I know why you don't like me, Amra Thetys," she replied. Or didn't reply.

"How can I dislike you? I don't even know you."

"But you know what I am, and what I can do. You hate the very idea of fate, and so how could you be comfortable in the presence of someone who can See it?"

I took a sip of tea while I considered what she'd said. It was true, as far as it went.

"I don't doubt you have the Sight. But I'd make a distinction between seeing the future, however cloudily, and knowing what fate has in store for someone. If fate even exists."

"Oh, it does, though I won't bother trying to convince you of the fact. But you are right in believing seeing the future isn't the same as knowing what fate has in store."

"I wouldn't have expected you to agree."

She shrugged her thin shoulders. "To see the future is to see the likeliest route of a journey. To know fate, my dear, is to know the destination. I Saw your future, dear, and I'm sorry to say that it is a dark and bloody one, for the most part."

"Was. That's over. Abanon's Blade is no more, and Red Hand is dead. I'm done with your Eightfold Bitch."

She smiled, and while there was a little pity in it, it seemed to me there was far more of something I'd call contempt. But then I generally assume the worst of people unless given a reason not to.

"I've Seen your future, and something of your fate. While you think you are done with the Eightfold Goddess, She is far from done with you. You will have truck with gods and goddesses, demigods and demons, and Powers of the Earth and Aether before you breathe your last—"

I stood up, knocking back my chair. "Why the hells would you tell me such things?"

"Because they are true."

"So *what*? What good does it do me?"

"Because you need to prepare."

"And just how the hells do you suggest I go about doing that?"

She looked down at her scone. "I don't know. That's for you to discover."

A hot flash of anger surged through me. "And there, *right there*, is why I want nothing to do with Seers. Because for all your signs and portents, however true they might be, you never offer a scrap of useful advice, and you never, *ever* offer the simplest shred of hope. Fate is a slaver, bloodwitch, and I refuse its chains."

As I walked out her door, she spoke in a quiet voice.

"That is why fate has singled you out, Amra Thetys."

~ ~ ~

Holgren found me at sunset. I was sitting on the breaker wall just north of the harbour, staring out at the darkening sea, not think much of anything, if I'm being honest.

"The sunset is in the other direction," he said, sidling up beside me and leaning on the rough stone.

I grunted. "I've seen enough sunsets in my life. How did you find me?"

"The ways of the magi are mysterious," he said with a small smile. He held out two pinched fingers. It took me a moment to see the hair trapped between them.

"You left this on your first visit to my sanctum."

I gave him a flat stare. "That's a bit creepy."

He shrugged and let the hair float down to the restless sea below us. "Speaking of hair, yours is coming in quite nicely."

I had nothing to say to that, so I didn't. The silence stretched, but it wasn't uncomfortable.

"I've got some bad news," he finally said. "Gavon is gone."

"What do you mean, gone?"

"Gone, disappeared, vanished."

"With my money. Of course."

"I'm afraid so. But Daruvner said he'd like to see us once we've recuperated. There's a commission he thinks would be perfect for us."

"Are you broke, too?"

"Not really. But I may have mentioned that I was open to commissions if you were involved."

"What? Why?"

He smiled and raised an eyebrow. "I told you before. You're capable, and you have two wits to rub together. And you do get up to the most interesting goings-on." He put out a hand. "Partners?"

I looked at him. I realized for the first time that I trusted him without question, for all that he was a mage. Realized, however much I didn't want to, that in the past few days I had come to rely on him. Realized with something close to shock that I was fine with that reliance.

And so I took his hand, and shook.

EPILOGUE

An age was ending. In the grand scheme of things, this was not such an uncommon occurrence. The Age of the Gods had been on the downhill slope for more than a millennium in any case. Soon magic would run dry, barring some unlooked-for intervention. Soon the gods and demons, those who still survived after the Wars and the Cataclysm, would take their longstanding squabbles on to some new plane of existence.

As for what would come next, well. Perhaps the Age of Humanity, of Invention, of Ingenuity. Or perhaps something entirely other.

In the Lower Realms and in the Upper, change was coming, and sentinels who had stood watch for thousands upon thousands of years were abandoning their posts, drawn to the siren call of re-creation, of rebirth, of a resetting of the cosmic board.

Soon there would be no one left to watch for the return of the Eightfold Goddess. Soon there would be no one left who knew what to watch for, or why. The signs and portents would come about, and none would be the wiser.

The first already had.

Abanon's Blade was dust, destroyed by a mortal's will.

The first of the eight seals had finally, finally been broken.

In Her hiding place, in Her self-made prison between the planes, She laughed, and stretched Her fearsome frame.

The Thief Who Spat in Luck's Good Eye

KERF & ISIN, PART THE FIRST

Another age was almost upon the world. Ancient Kerf and ever-youthful Isin had been appointed to see the present one to its close, to blow out the lamps, dust the corners, and hand over the keys to the new tenants, as it were. They toured the vast, empty plane of deities, both feeling in their eternal bones the unnatural silence, the melancholy of things ending, the excitement of things about to begin.

"Almost done," wheezed Kerf.

"Indeed it would seem so," replied Isin, patting a few stray wisps of hair back into place. "You've pulled the plug on magic?"

"Centuries ago. It drains away as we speak. What of the Twins?"

Isin snapped her fingers. "I knew I'd forgotten something! I always do."

"I had high hopes for them, alas."

"Well, it wasn't your fault, Kerf. The path to godhood may be narrow, but it is plainly marked. Though I'm afraid it was an excess of the qualities I cherish that led to their troubles."

Kerf grunted, stopped, leaned on his crooked staff. "Or a paucity of the ones I espouse," he replied. "Can't leave them in the way of the next lot, in any case."

"You rest," said Isin. "I'll deal with the Twins, and then we'll clear out."

Kerf had a sudden thought. Beneath bushy, snow-white brows, his eyes gleamed.

"No," he said. "I've got a better idea."

Isin arched a perfect brow.

"There's a thief down in Lucernis, likes to swear by my testicles, of all things. Annoyed me for years, that one." Kerf rubbed his gnarled hands together in anticipation.

"Now Kerf, what are you planning?"

"It's been ages since we've meddled with mortals. Frankly, I miss it. Might not get another chance, my dear. Who knows where we're off to?"

Isin's smile was radiant, the only kind she owned. "Oh, all right," she said. "But are you sure this thief can handle the Twins?"

"She's got what it takes to settle the matter, she and her partner, though I daresay she won't have much fun doing it."

He chuckled. "'Kerf's shriveled balls' indeed. Cheeky wench…"

CHAPTER 1

It was to have been a relaxing afternoon in the Artists' Quarter—a cup of wine, a walk along the Promenade, a show later in the evening—the final performance of The Yellow King. I'd wanted to see it for weeks, and I'd finally been able to filch a ticket. All in all, I was looking forward to an enjoyable few hours.

It didn't turn out that way. Instead, Holgren wanted to talk about money. Ten thousand gold marks to be exact.

I was sitting at one of the scarred wooden tables outside Tambor's wine shop, enjoying the first fine day of spring. Winter had held on with a tenacity almost unheard of in Lucernis, southernmost of the great cities on the western shore of the Dragonsea. It seemed everyone else in the city had the same idea as me. All Tambor's outside tables were full while the interior of his grubby little shop was deserted. Hoof, foot, and carriage traffic along the street was heavy and more boisterous than usual. There was even a warm, easterly breeze that kept the steaming miasma rising from the gutters at an endurable level. For a wonder, I was actually enjoying the rare feeling of contentment.

Holgren found me and slapped down a creased, dirty notice under my nose. It was the Duke's offer.

"This just came in with a coastal trader, Amra. The Duke of Viborg is posting it in every port on the Dragonsea apparently." He stood there with a strange grin on his face. I gave him my best annoyed look, which failed to have any effect on him.

"Well, go on. Read it."

I sighed, picked up the notice, and read. The Duke was offering ten thousand marks for proof of the existence of the legendary city of Thagoth. I pushed the sheet of parchment back at him.

"Kerf's balls, Holgren. The old buzzard is insane," I said. "That's why they call him the *Mad* Duke, you know. Besides, Thagoth is a myth. If it ever existed, it's dust and rubble now."

"But—" Holgren started.

"No buts. Look, even if we found it, you'd never get a bent halfpenny out of the old goat, much less ten thousand marks. Now sit down, shut up, and drink. Or leave. I'm busy enjoying my ill-gotten gains."

My partner leaned back on his heels and opened his slim-fingered hands in a gesture that he thought conciliatory and I found annoying. "Granted, the Duke will probably never pay, but that doesn't mean it isn't worth looking into." He signaled the barmaid and sat down at my table.

"I won't talk business today, Holgren. I won't. I have plans that run contrary to the topic."

He snorted, accepted the shallow earthenware cup the barmaid handed to him, and paid her. Tambor only served one vintage: cheap.

"You never stop thinking about business, woman. You've no idea how to relax. You've trained yourself out of it." He took a drink, made a face, and exiled his cup to the edge of the table.

"If that isn't the pot calling the kettle black, Holgren, I don't know what is."

"Perhaps. Finding Thagoth won't be business for me, however. It will be personal." He stared at me with those hawk-like brown eyes of his. It was a look I knew. He was about to get me to do something I didn't want to do.

"We need to find that city," he said, "and we need to find it before anyone else."

"What's this really about? It's not the money; that's obvious."

Holgren shook his head. "Let's speak elsewhere."

I put down a few coppers and followed him out to the street. So much for my relaxing afternoon.

~ ~ ~

He took a long, rambling route to the river Ose, dodging hacks, carriages, and the reeking contents of chamber pots slung out of windows despite a rather strict ordinance to the contrary. I walked beside him, hurrying my pace just a bit to match his long strides. I wondered what could get him interested in such a fool's errand. I had to admit to more than a little curiosity. While I'd known Holgren for a handful of years, I knew almost nothing about his personal life. He was a solitary, even secretive man. Mages are like that.

He turned off narrow, twisting Gravedigger's Row into an even narrower alley between a pair of whitewashed houses that leaned toward each other like drunken sailors on leave. At the end of the alley, we took a set of mossy, cracked steps down to the river.

The Ose ran through the city in great loops. Some sections were beautiful, ornamented with stone walkways and ancient trees whose branches fanned down to the water. Other parts abutted the back walls of tanneries, charnel houses, and squalid tenements. The stretch behind Gravedigger's Row was hardly park-like, and I pretended not to see the vague, sodden lumps that floated by, which might have been garbage, but were likely something worse.

"You take me to the nicest places, Holgren." I picked up a stone and pitched it into the water. "Want to tell me what this is about now?"

"This is difficult for me to speak of, Amra. I've never told anyone else."

"I'm honored."

"You never make things easy, do you?"

I bit down an easy retort. He was right. "Sorry. Go ahead."

"When I was a boy, I was apprenticed to a master of the Art named Yvoust. Ten years I slaved under him as an apprentice. By rights, I should have been a journeyman after seven. I had the skill and control. But I failed an impossible task he set me to, and was sent away in disgrace. He was a cruel master, prone to beat and starve his apprentices, but that does not excuse what I did in revenge.

"In my youthful pride and rage, I made a compact with dark powers and killed Yvoust using the Art. It was long ago, and I am not the boy that committed that act. Still, the lad is father to the man, and for that sin and for the bargain I made, my soul is forfeit upon my death."

I just stood there for a moment. I wasn't sure what to do or say. I put a hand on his shoulder, and he shrugged it off.

I suppose I should have been shocked. I'd never imagined him capable of such an immoral act, or such a stupid one. Except there were times growing up when I would have sold my soul to be rid of my father permanently. Times spent hiding in the muck under the house to avoid a drunken beating, or worse, times spent listening to it happen to my mother instead.

The only difference between Holgren and me was the fact that he'd had the magical power to make good on such wishes. I'd settled for a scaling knife. There were things Holgren didn't know about me, either.

"Say something," he said.

"What does this have to do with Thagoth?"

"What do you know about the legend surrounding it?"

"What everybody knows, I suppose. It was an ancient city, ruled by twin gods, a brother and sister with the power of eternal life and the power to devour souls. It and they were destroyed by a rival power, a wizard-king whose name has been lost to history."

"Close enough." He stooped, picked up a stone, and flung it into the water. "The power to grant eternal life…"

"Come on. Holgren the Immortal? I'm not sure I like the sound of that."

"I do. Better than Holgren the Eternally Suffering."

"That's what you think the Duke is after? Immortality?"

He nodded. "You've heard the stories. Bathing in the blood of the unborn. Putting a bounty on the two harbingers of death in Viborg, crows and owls. Banning funeral processions within a mile of his palace. Removing portraits and statues of dead ancestors from the palace. A dozen others, all pointing to a very particular condition when you consider them as a whole: The Duke of Viborg is scared to death of dying."

"I see your point, but what makes you think this search for Thagoth is any different from those other mad, vain attempts to fend off the inevitable?"

"This offer of his is too noteworthy, too public to simply be a whim."

"Holgren, there must be another way to settle your debt—some surer way." Some way that might actually work, I meant.

"Don't you think I would have tried by now if there were another way? Something has set him on the trail to Thagoth. While I might wish I knew what it was, it is enough for me to know that he wants to find it." Holgren clasped my hands in his. "I want and need your help, Amra. I've seen you slip into and out of places so heavily guarded a mouse wouldn't pass unnoticed. I've watched you find valuables so cleverly hidden I couldn't have located them using the Art. Dead gods, woman, I've seen you face down demons, mad sorcerers, and the living weapon of a goddess of hate. I would be a fool not to ask you for your help. Should you choose not to assist me, however, I will go on my own."

"Flattery, Holgren? You must be desperate." I pulled my hands from his and walked.

"It isn't flattery if it's true. Remember when you broke into Lord Morno's wine cellar and stole an entire crate of Gol-Shen thirty-seven? He certainly does."

"That was a lark. It's not like there were armed guards at the door. Now, be quiet, and let me think." I had to smile. I sent Morno an empty bottle every Midsummer's Eve. The bounty for the person or persons responsible had risen to five hundred marks over the years.

I contemplated the murky, filthy Ose as it slid its way to the sea. It was idiocy, but how could I refuse Holgren? He was my friend and partner; how could I not at least try to help?

"I never said I wouldn't go," I finally said. "I just said it was pointless. Where do we start?"

~ ~ ~

Holgren started at the beginning. He identified certain texts we would need, and I acquired them; the Bosk texts, notes from Mumtaz El Rathi's expedition to the west, a copy of General Velkaar's campaign memoirs, many more. Maps, histories, legends, travelers' accounts of the west, tomes of magic theory, ancient military texts—there was no rhyme or reason in what he wanted. It was all rare, hideously expensive, and generally difficult to lay hands on. I spent nearly a month tracking down, buying, or stealing what he said he needed. One particular scroll, done up in a sort of picture language I'd never encountered before, explored the lives of the Twin Gods in graphic detail. Apparently, they'd been quite a bit more than siblings if the scroll was to be believed. And the sister at least had some unwholesome appetites. I suppose gods see most things differently. Who's going to tell them they're wrong?

Holgren spent the time holed up in his sanctum, a moldering hovel hard by the charnel grounds. What he did there, he did not discuss, nor did I pry. He would prepare the odd amulet or fetish to aid me in whatever task I undertook. While I had little understanding of how they worked, I took it on faith that they did.

Holgren, on the other hand, always seemed fascinated by the most mundane aspects of my craft. Once I'd left a set of lock picks out, and some hours later, I found him squatting in front of an old sea chest I used for a table, methodically trying each pick in various positions while making notes in the margins of a book he'd been reading. When I'd told him the tumblers of the lock were rusted solid, he'd looked crushed.

It was a wet, miserable day when I returned from my latest foray for research materials. Spring had not fully sprung after all. Almost no one was stirring in the Foreigners' Quarter as I returned the spavined excuse for a horse I'd rented from Alain the wainwright. I trudged my weary way home, keeping dry the fragile map I'd acquired. As I climbed the narrow stairs to my den, I wanted nothing more than hot food, a hot bath, and a warm bed.

Holgren was pacing the rooms I rented above Burrisses' Tailors. The Burrisses were a family of immigrants from the Nine Cities who didn't care if I was a woman living on my own so long as I paid my rent. It wasn't as nice as the place I'd rented above the Korani Social Club, but too many not-nice people had somehow gotten hold of that address. I'd decided to move. I don't really get attached to places in any case. Having feelings for rented rooms was like having feelings for someone else's spouse—inadvisable at best.

"Amra!" He grabbed me by the waist. "Pfaugh! You're ripe."

"That's what three days in the saddle will do."

"Never mind. I've found it!"

"You found the city?" I pushed him away from me and sat down on the hall bench. Every bone ached from the ride. Wearily, I started unlacing my boots. "So you don't need this map I just stole from a nice widow in Coroune?"

"No. Oh, it will help prove I'm right, no doubt. I'm dead certain I have the location of the city itself."

"That's nice," I said with mock brightness. "Now get out so I can boil water for a bath, bolt some food, and go to sleep."

He looked at me quizzically for a second, then had the grace to blush a little. "I'm sorry. I know you've been killing yourself gathering all these odds and ends. I truly appreciate it. It's just that I've finally located it—"

"I know, I know. Tomorrow, I'll be suitably excited. Right now, I'm just too tired."

"Why don't you relax? I'll find you something to eat."

"Thanks." I made my way into the main room and stretched out on the floor, on the silk Elamner pillows I used for furniture. I just closed my eyes for a second, honest.

~ ~ ~

I woke the next morning. Holgren had left a tray of nuts and a bowl of blood oranges next to me along with a note in spidery silver letters in the air above my head:

See you here, midday

The letters faded as I read them. I dug up fresh clothing and headed for the baths.

The morning was hot and bright, and the streets steamed as they dried under the indecisive spring sun. Time was passing too quickly. I knew of at least three expeditions that had already set out for the lost city. There was no telling if they were headed in the right direction, but our delays had begun to worry me. If it did exist, I didn't want to get there only to find it plundered.

At the baths, I paid my penny and soaked for an hour, ignoring the comments muttered behind milk-white hands about my scarred hide. It was a little knitting circle of five women. Whenever I looked at them directly, their eyes would slide away, and the whispering would die down for a time. Then it would slowly pick back up again.

"—figure like a boy."

"Such short hair, and all those scars. Perhaps she's just come from prison?"

I kept my calm. What did they know of the world beyond their familial villas or their fathers' shops, beyond spinning, weaving, and making babies? I knew as little of their life as they knew of mine—I understood that. It's just that I didn't think their difference gave me a right to talk about them, whereas they obviously did. But of course it's always that way when you have the numbers. Men don't hold exclusive rights to bullying.

The idea of being physically ejected from the public baths for brawling wasn't appealing, so I decided to settle for flattening their purses when I left.

I put a washcloth over my eyes and turned my thoughts to Thagoth, and whether Holgren had actually located it.

~ ~ ~

Holgren arrived a few minutes late, a bundle of parchments and scrolls under one arm and a look of grim determination on his face. He cleared off the delicate Helstrum-made table I used for dining and spread out a map he had sketched and inked himself.

"Here we are," he said, stabbing the east coast of Lucernia with a forefinger. "Thagoth is almost certainly here." He moved his finger a huge distance west—about two feet on the map, which worked out to roughly two thousand miles.

"Well, that's it," I said. "We can't go after it, not if it truly is that far. If you're wrong about the location or if there's nothing left of it, we'll have wasted almost a year, maybe more, getting there and back. Be reasonable, Holgren."

"I am. I agree, the distance is daunting. Which is why I am going to attempt to gate us there."

"What?"

"According to the Bosk texts you acquired for me, Thagoth was built at the nexus of several powerful ley lines. I will transport us to that nexus. The process should be instantaneous."

"Whenever you say things like 'attempt' and 'should be,' my blood runs cold."

"Your worries are baseless. If I fail, the magics will dissipate, and the gate will not open. I'll make certain there is no possibility of you suffering any ill effects."

"And what about you?"

"I'll be fine."

"Spoken like a true liar. Tell me."

"Honestly? I don't know. There's a chance nothing will happen. There's also a chance for a whole range of effects, from the merely uncomfortable to the wholly unpleasant."

"The worst of which would be?"

"The worst of which would be my being blasted to cinders. It's a very outside chance."

"Wouldn't that sort of be missing the point of trying to find immortality?"

"Amra, if I spent my entire life avoiding danger, I would have no life at all. If I risk nothing, death and retribution will still come. Given the choice, I would rather die trying to alter my situation. I assure you, I have taken and will take every precaution I can think of to ensure my safety and your own."

I sighed and shook my head. "When do we go?"

"We could leave tomorrow, but I think I might better do a bit more research. There are indications from what I've read so far that the city is…contained, I suppose, is the best word."

"Eh?"

He leaned back, spread his hands. "When Thagoth fell, it was to a powerful sorcerer-king, perhaps the most powerful mortal the world has ever seen. He laid death magic on the environs around the city. According to the accounts of Mumtaz El Rathi, that magic was still potent a century ago when he lead an expedition there."

I began to pace. "Describe these death lands. Place-names with the word 'death' in them tend to make me very wary."

"In practical application, everything of the death lands will attempt to destroy anything not of the death lands that enter them. Grasses will reach out to bind you while more mobile creatures finish you off. Everything has some ability to kill, be it quick or slow. Or so wrote El Rathi."

"Lovely." I'd had brushes with death magic in the past, though nothing on so large a scale. I'd almost broken into a room infused with a death spell that would have killed me instantly upon entering. Now we were talking about acres of the stuff. "You're sure we won't have to deal with this? Why hasn't the city been swallowed up?"

"I can only assume the residual power of the Twin Gods keep it at bay. The city had not been overtaken at the time of El Rathi's expedition a century ago. He records seeing the golden domes of what he calls 'the Tabernacle' and other structures from the ridge above the valley itself. The death lands seem to border the remains of the city in a precise circle with the Tabernacle at the center of that circle. Could you stop pacing? It makes me nervous."

"No. This nexus you're going to magic us to, tell me about it."

"It should be well within the city and completely safe if I manage to raise the gate."

"I hope you're right, Holgren."

He cocked an eyebrow and shrugged his shoulder slightly. "I've made my calculations with the best data available. We should be fine."

"Let's leave that for the moment. What do we do once we're in the city?"

"Well, that's really more your end of things, isn't it?"

I stopped pacing, tilted my head. "I spent a month getting you research material. There was nothing in all of that to indicate what you're looking for?"

He sighed. "Amra, how often are you handed maps that say 'valuable object located here?'"

"I know a sailor down on the docks that could sell you one for every day of the month."

"My point precisely. I imagine the best place to search would be in the Tabernacle that El Rathi mentions since there appears to be some power there holding the death lands at bay. But I will know it when I find it, not before. I am quite certain it will be a difficult, possibly deadly task to locate and retrieve it. I need your skills. I know no one better at what you do."

"Not who's willing to help you with this, at any rate. No. I'm sorry. That was mean-spirited and uncalled for. I apologize."

He shook his head. "No apology necessary. You're right. No one else would be willing to attempt this. I need to keep that in mind and show my appreciation more."

"You can start by feeding me."

~ ~ ~

After an elaborate midday meal at Fraud's, we took a walk down the Promenade: the wide, straight avenue of brick that ran from the Ministry buildings to Harad's Square. It was lined on both sides by the marble-fronted, slim-columned manses owned by minor nobility and powerful merchants. I had promised myself the first day I'd arrived in Lucernis that I'd own one of them someday. I'd stumbled down the Promenade—penniless, starving and sick, and bitterly envying those who lived in such luxury. I must have stared at those great houses with real glass in their windows for an hour before the watch had moved me along. Then, I went and stole a half a loaf of bread. That had been a long time ago. I didn't have to steal bread anymore. I didn't own one of those manses, either.

The Promenade was wide enough to accommodate four carriages abreast, although no hoof traffic was allowed on it. Wealthy merchants and their wives, government functionaries, and minor nobility took to it to socialize and be seen. Much subtle business was also conducted on the Promenade—important decisions were made here, between principals, and finalized elsewhere. I'd done a fair amount of business in this fashion myself. Daruvner, my fixer, had done much more.

The Promenade was also well-policed. Lord Morno, governor of Lucernis, liked to drill his troops here. A small contingent of arquebusiers in fine new crimson uniforms was being marched around by a grizzled sergeant as Holgren and I strolled. The old campaigner kept trying to rest his hand on a nonexistent sword pommel as he barked commands.

"You see those weapons?" asked Holgren. "They are the future of warfare."

I laughed. "Those are toys. The only way to kill someone with an arquebus is to beat them with it. A good bowman could kill five times over in the time it takes just to load one." The only time I'd seen an arquebus be even remotely useful was during the assault on the Elamner's villa months before, and that was mostly as a noise maker. A trumpet would have been just as handy, and a lot more reliable.

"Ah, but how long does it take to become that good with a bow?" Holgren replied. "Five years? Ten? One can become proficient with firearms in a matter of weeks. Someday, they will be perfected; their rate of fire, range, and accuracy will be improved. People will die by the thousands without ever seeing their foe." He put a friendly arm around my shoulder. "Inventions such as these will be what drives the world, Amra, not magic." He stopped and looked at me with those piercing eyes of his.

"I want to tell you a secret," he said.

"All right."

"Magic is fading. The most powerful mages today cannot do half of what mages even a century ago could. Two thousand years ago, wars such as the one that destroyed Thagoth were commonplace. Entire empires were laid waste in a matter of days. Now, the Laws of Thaumaturgy are being superseded by the laws of the physical world. Who knows how long it will be before magic disappears completely?"

"You sound almost cheerful about it."

"Do I? Perhaps I am. Since I am in the secret-telling mood, I'll tell you another. I've never particularly liked being a mage."

"You're kidding me."

"Truly. Once Yvoust was dead, I lost the interest I'd had in the Art. What else was I to do though? I spent a decade trying to find some way out of the doom I'd created for myself. There were none—none I'd consider satisfactory, at any rate. By that time, it was the only profession I knew."

"Wait. You're saying there are other solutions to your problem besides haring off to Thagoth?"

"No, I'm not. Believe me, the cures I found were all worse than the disease." He stopped and turned to face me directly. "I have a bit more research and preparation to do. You won't see me for a few days. Will you prepare what we will need for two weeks in the field?"

"How long do I have?"

"Four days."

"All right. Will we need pack animals?"

"No. I wouldn't want to try to gate them as well as us."

"I'll have it all ready."

"Thank you. Sincerely, Amra."

"You're welcome."

He walked away then, a tall, almost gangly man in funereal black, black hair swept into a ponytail secured with a black velvet ribbon. Holgren had never much been one for fashion.

I walked a while on the Promenade, staring at the houses, trying to imagine what sort of "cures" he might have found in the past and how they could be worse than some demon keeping your soul as a plaything for eternity.

My imagination wasn't up to the task.

CHAPTER 2

Holgren appeared at dawn on the fourth day. We lugged the packs down my narrow, wooden stairs to the carriage waiting below. It was a gray, foggy morning. The driver looked like a wraith perched on the front of the carriage; the horse, with tendrils of breath writhing from his nostrils, looked like a nightmare.

"Where are we going?" I asked.

"Just outside the city proper. There's a sparse grove of alders a short distance off the Jacos Road. It's a suitable place to open a gate—not too distant, and no dwellings within a mile."

"Afraid you might cause some destruction?"

"No. I've already told you there is no possible danger to anyone but myself. I simply don't want to attract attention."

I grunted and tried to find a comfortable position. I intended to sleep the carriage ride away if possible. I've never been much of a morning person.

Sleep was a vain hope. The best of Lucernis' streets were far from smooth, and the carriage bounced and jostled us brutally. I don't know if it was him or me or the fool's errand we were about to embark on, but I was in a foul mood that morning. Later, I thought about every little detail of the ride—the smell of Holgren's soap, the low mutters the driver occasionally made, the clop-clop of horse hooves on cobblestones, and then the muted thud of them on the dirt of the Jacos Road. I thought about all the insignificant details and wondered if I would have done anything differently had I known what was going to happen.

The hack dropped us off in the middle of farmland. The morning fog had burned off during the ride. It promised to be a warm, sunny day.

The grove Holgren had decided upon was more than a mile distant. The only way to reach it was through fields of waist-high plants. I have no idea what they were, but they smelled horrible and attracted insects in droves. I made Holgren carry two of the packs. By the time we got there, most of the morning had fled. I was sweating profusely and had half a dozen uncomfortable insect bites. Holgren seemed unaffected. I dropped my pack and took a long swig of water, cursing all mages silently.

"Why don't you rest for a few minutes?" he said.

I glared at him. "Why don't we get on with it?"

"All right." He reached into his pocket, drew out a short length of red yarn, and lay it as straight as he could in the grass before him. "A concentration aid," he explained. He shouldered one of the packs and turned to face the yarn. "Stand next to me," he said.

I put the second pack on my back and held the bulky third under one arm uncomfortably. I wanted to have one hand free, just in case. I moved over to his right side. Our shoulders brushed.

"Not too close. Perhaps a few inches' distance."

He bowed his head then. He took deep, slow breaths. There was nothing gangly about him now—he was in his element, working with powers I had no ability to understand. His face took on something of the look of a bird of prey: fierce, wild, beautiful. The familiar chill that accompanied his use of power crept up the back of my neck. A breeze sprang up, and the grass swayed, then flattened as the breeze turned into a gale. I looked down at the length of yarn, and it was pulled taut as if by invisible hands. It thrummed as the wind ran across it—and then it was gone.

In its place stood a pearlescent, faintly glowing rectangle perhaps three feet wide by eight high.

"You must go first, quickly. I will follow." His voice was strained.

I took a deep breath and plunged through.

It was not a pleasant sensation. I have no words to describe it—suffice to say a body was not meant to exist in whatever nether world or space between worlds that doorway was made up of. The feeling was mercifully brief.

The first thing I saw was jungle. I smelled death, the putrid stench of corpses. I took a few gagging, stumbling steps forward, and heard Holgren follow me close behind. The wind from the gate abruptly died as Holgren let it collapse back into wherever it came from. I caught a glimpse of rust-red, stone columns just ahead of me. Then, something small, brown, and hideously fast whipped past my head.

Behind me, Holgren screamed.

If I hadn't been burdened with two packs, I could have gotten a knife out in time, could have skewered the thing before it reached him. I told myself this, and sometimes, I believed it. It might even have been true. As it happened, I did pin it to a tree with one forceful, desperate throw. It squirmed and hissed and made a high shrieking noise that drilled through my eardrums and reverberated painfully in my head.

It was just too late.

The creature had struck Holgren on the cheek—just a shallow little gash, but he screamed and screamed as if he'd been run through. I dropped the pack I'd been holding, grabbed him by the shirt front, and dragged him stumbling toward the stone columns I'd glimpsed. Around us, the bloated, waxy foliage writhed as if in agony, or expectation. I pulled Holgren after me as fast as I could go through the dense vegetation. He was still screaming. The rumbling cough of some predator sounded not far behind us. I tried not to imagine what it looked like. Holgren fell to his knees. Walking backward, I dragged him by his pack straps the last few feet. His face had begun to swell. He looked at me with agony in his eyes. His lips were drawn back across his teeth, and the only time he stopped screaming was to draw a lungful of air. I put all my concentration into pulling him forward to safety.

Abruptly, my heel touched cobbles. With a desperate grunt, I yanked Holgren fully out of the jungle and lay him on his side. I tried to get the pack off him, but his entire body had begun to bloat. I cut the pack free of his shoulders, loosened his collar, his belt, his boots. I could think of nothing further to do.

He screamed until the swelling closed his throat.

I held his hand until it was over. When he was gone, I sat there next to him for a time and thought nothing at all, felt nothing at all.

I looked down at the swollen, blackened hand in mine and thought about how ugly it was. His hands had always been so thin and delicate, almost womanly, perfectly manicured, and no calluses. They had been gentle hands. Now his fingers looked like fat, black sausages.

I closed my eyes, turned my head, and vomited. When I was done, I sat, still and cold in my soul. Then I heard it.

There was movement in the jungle. I looked up and saw dozens of eyes looking back at me. Much rustling and shifting, but nothing ventured forth to finish the job. I could feel the hate pounding at me, silent, palpable. Perhaps those eyes could feel me returning it.

I dragged Holgren a little distance away and took a brief look around. Crumbling buildings, some grand, some humble. I searched until I came upon an overgrown garden, walled in on three sides. I buried him there under a towering yew tree.

There was no spade; it was in the pack that had been left in the death lands. Knife and bowl did the job. I don't know how long it took—hours, certainly. The ground was relatively soft and the grave only about four feet deep. If I'd had the energy, I would have dug a second grave for myself since I was convinced I was going to die there in Thagoth. It just didn't seem worth the effort.

He was hideously heavy. I had to roll him into the grave. He landed face down, and I couldn't stand that, so I went in after him and eventually got him facing the sky. Using the bowl, I started filling in the grave but couldn't make myself throw dirt on his face. I dithered about that for a good while and finally decided to cut a section of canvas for covering. It went better after that.

I started to lose myself after the grave was filled in. I found myself smoothing the dirt with my hands, trying to make it perfectly level. I heard strange whimpering, realized it was coming from me. I made myself stop. I curled up there next to him with my fists pressed hard to my stomach.

Without Holgren to reopen the gate I was trapped, the last sorry resident of Thagoth.

~ ~ ~

It rained that night, a slow, gentle rain that pattered on the leaves overhead and softened the bare earth of Holgren's grave. The rain woke me, and I threw on a good wool cloak and sat under the tree, waiting for dawn.

Something nagged at me as I huddled there. There was no birdsong, no rustling of animals large or small. I wondered if, over the centuries, the death lands had somehow claimed all the city's fauna.

By mid-morning, the rain had passed. I'd begun to poke around the ruins a bit, mapping out the city in my mind, when I saw a hawk gliding and wheeling above the city. It was the first normal animal I'd seen anywhere near Thagoth. I stood there, watching it soar, envying it its freedom.

It turned slow circles, gliding slowly lower toward the walled compound of the Tabernacle in the center of the city. I assumed it must have seen some small movement and begun the hunt. I watched with interest, thinking there might be game behind those high stone walls.

The hawk descended, slowly, slower, to within a hundred feet or so of the tall, golden domes of the Tabernacle.

I heard a piercing shriek unlike anything I had ever heard before. Waves of pain shot through me, yet I could tell somehow that I had caught only the merest ripple of—of whatever it was.

The hawk caught the full force of it. It was instantly dead. Its graceful flight turned to a boneless tumble, and it plummeted into the Tabernacle grounds. Then, there was nothing but silence.

I decided to avoid exploring anywhere near the Tabernacle.

~ ~ ~

I was six months in Thagoth. I survived mainly on bark and grubs. Apparently the ancient Thagothians weren't much for gardening because almost nothing edible grew in the city. There was a small date grove. I soon learned eating too many dates was rougher on my body than not eating any at all. I found and exhausted a stand of wild chok and grazed on clover like any cow. Hunger dogged me like a debt collector.

Holgren was in my thoughts often, try as I might to push his memory away. We had met years before when he hired me to help him with a job he had been hired for. However good a mage Holgren had been, stealth wasn't his strong suit. Our abilities complemented each other. In time, we'd made our professional relationship a permanent one. We'd even become friends. I'd lost other friends, other partners in my life, and while I suspect most of them were bound for one of the nine hells, I didn't know it for certain. Not like Holgren. I thought about all the little things he'd do to aggravate me: the arch looks, the condescending remarks, or even more condescending silences. It only made me miss him more.

I wandered over damn near every inch of Thagoth in the time I was there except those buildings closest to the Tabernacle. I've holed up in vacant houses before when I was too poor to afford a place to live or was avoiding one city watch or another. The feeling of emptiness was eerie, being surrounded by signs of life and habitation, being utterly alone. Thagoth wasn't like that at all. It was much worse.

House after house, building after building, stone piled on stone, all of it empty, devoid of the smallest sign of human occupancy. The only thing I found in Thagoth to show people had ever inhabited it, besides the buildings themselves, were a few shards of crockery. No frescoes enlivened any wall, no glass in any window, no furniture, no doors, no workman's tools, nothing. Not even a child's toy. Just building after empty building, and leaf-littered floors. Thagoth wasn't a city at all; it was a vast stone skeleton placed there by the gods for the wind to play with.

I slept. Sleep was freedom, sleep passed the time, and sleep conserved energy. That was the pattern of my months—sleep, forage, explore. In that order. Until sleep began to present its own difficulties in the form of dreams.

At first, they were innocent enough. I would dream of silly things: a birthday with honeyed oatcakes, an inn I once stayed at in Elam that served barley-stuffed mushrooms in wine sauce. I dreamed of food: leg of lamb, roast hare, boiled cloudroot smothered in butter and garlic, fried bankfish… I feasted in my dreams and starved all day.

Slowly, my dreams turned to something different.

Murmuring, muttering, whispering, sharp cries, and long silences intruded on my dreams. I knew even in the midst of them that these things did not originate in any part of my mind or spirit. I woke sweating and cold despite the sweltering summer heat. Something was moving through my mind as I slept. I could feel its enormous power and its agony.

Was it Holgren, somehow reaching out to me? Did it have something to do with this place, the Tabernacle, or the death lands? I didn't know. I just wanted it to stop. After these dreams started, I began to stave off sleep for as long as I could.

I suppose that contributed to my going a little mad. I'd been rambling round the edges of the city, never too close to the Tabernacle of course, exploring. Poking around out of boredom, finding mostly stone. People of any age think alike; they tend to hide their valuables in much the same spots—under loose hearth stones and tiles, behind thin plaster, buried in gardens. Eventually, I gathered enough to buy a fine manse just off the Promenade in Lucernis three or four times over. Unfortunately, you can't eat gold or jewels. You can't bribe magic-mad monsters. No amount of wealth was going to buy me out of this trap.

One day I started flinging all that wealth out into the jungle, handful after handful of coins, gems, jewelry. I know I was screaming something, but I have no idea what. It might not even have been words.

When the last coin was gone, I just dropped down on the cobbles and cried, letting loose great, honking sobs of despair. There was nobody to see or hear me except those malevolent, ever-present eyes in the jungle.

~ ~ ~

The seasons changed and changed again before I saw another human being. A certain type of bitter nut had come into season, and I was high up in a tree, shaking one of the nut-laden branches fiercely when a glint caught my eye from the jungle across the square. The habit of years took over, and I went still. I felt exposed up there though I was above the normal line of sight. I stayed in the tree. Most of my body was concealed by leaves and branches. I lay still along the branch and watched the wall of jungle, straining my hearing.

Faintly, I heard cursing in the Gosland dialect. That vile death land foliage trembled, twisted. Through it broke the head and neck of a mule, ears laid flat. It lunged and stumbled onto the loose cobbles of the square, a huge pack on its back, trailing a sweating man in chain mail.

"Stupid beast!" he shouted at the mule. Then, he stopped abruptly, looked around, and called back over his shoulder, "Here! We are here! Tell the Duke, Iorn!" I heard a muffled reply, and the man in chain mail cursed the mule further into the square. Behind him came shouts and laughter and a troop of soldiers.

CHAPTER 3

In all, some twenty men and twice as many mules emerged from the death lands. They looked tired and travel-worn. They were also remarkably alive. That fact was far less interesting to me then than the rations I knew some of those mules were carrying. Just thinking about salt pork and trail bread made my mouth water. I was afraid they'd hear my stomach rumble from across the square. I swallowed my saliva, pressed my free hand against the hollow of my stomach, and held still.

One man stood out from the rest. Where the others led mules, he rode a beautiful bay gelding. Where the others wore chain mail, he had on gold-washed half-plate. Everything about him screamed nobility. The Duke of Viborg, I presumed. He sat there astride his horse and took a long, lingering look at his surroundings. The back of my neck went cold, and I held absolutely still: not breathing, not blinking. His eyes slid past me. For the first time in months, I forgot my hunger.

He dismounted, and I saw he wasn't a tall man. He wore his thinning blond hair shoulder-length and loose, and where the others of his party were dirty and deeply tanned, he was pale, his clothing and armor spotless. I disliked him immediately.

The party began to spread out around the square, pulling packs from mules, drinking water from skins, pulling off boots, taking a cursory look at their surroundings. Almost immediately, the Duke spoke quietly to one of the men, presumably the officer in charge, and the man began shouting orders.

"No time to gawk and lollygag, you bastards! Keep 'em moving. We'll camp in front of the temple, and that not a moment before the city has been reconnoitered. Move!"

The soldiers complied hastily, if not happily. As they made their way further into the city, they passed me by without a single glance up. When they'd gone a safe distance on, I slipped out of my tree, gathered up a few nuts in the tattered tails of my shirt, and slunk off to a secure, out-of-the-way spot on the opposite side of the city.

Six months I'd gone without seeing another soul. Here was my first and probably my only chance to escape Thagoth. I should have been thinking about these things, about how they could have made their way through the death lands—about securing some of their food at the very least. Instead, I thought about the Duke. What I'd sensed from him across the square.

I'd felt power rolling off him in waves, power I'd only felt from Holgren when he was actively working magic. I felt another sensation gnawing at my gut as I slunk away that afternoon: fear.

Several pairs of hate-filled eyes followed me as I paced a few yards away from the border of the death lands. They were intent, and malignant, and patient. I had no doubt that if I were to stick a hand or a foot past that invisible boundary, it would be bitten off or worse. The Duke and his men had to have some sort of protection that allowed them to pass safely through to the city. What was it? I beat my palm against my forehead, willing myself to think. What could it be? Magical, almost certainly. A spell laid on them? Where would they find anyone powerful or skilled enough to cast it? The Duke himself? Unlikely. Something to counter the death lands would be beyond even him.

I continued to pace, ignoring the now-familiar monsters who tracked my every move. Not a spell, then. Some sort of artifact? If so, it could be almost anything, take virtually any form. Whatever it was, it was small enough to carry on a person or in baggage—I'd noticed nothing unusual. Something as important as that would almost certainly not be left on the back of a mule. They'd want it safe, defensible.

The Duke would want it near to hand, a reassurance.

The Duke who feared death would never let it out of his possession, traveling through the death lands.

I stopped pacing, sat down, and finished my dinner of nuts and grubs. I usually feel better when I know who I have to rob. Not this time. I was out of my depth and knew it.

~ ~ ~

I crept through the camp toward where the Duke slept. He was ensconced in a silk tent while his men, those not on watch, lay wrapped in blankets on the ground. After the death lands, Thagoth must have seemed like an oasis of peace and sanity to them. They weren't particularly watchful, which suited me.

The approaching storm also suited me. Great, gray-walled clouds with lightning in their hearts already blotted out the eastern sky and were advancing rapidly on the city. With any luck, I would be able to use the breaking storm to cover my retreat if things got dicey. I just needed to get in and get the talisman before the storm woke his grace.

On my belly, I inched my way across the cobbled square in front of the Tabernacle gates to the back wall of the tent. I pulled the knife from my forearm sheath, covering the motion to prevent any stray glint of light.

Slowly, carefully, and most of all quietly, I parted the silk of the tent just enough to allow access. In the distance, thunder rumbled, and I heard an answering groan inside the tent. I cursed silently. Of course the Duke had to be a light sleeper.

I slipped into the tent. I didn't know where the talisman was or what it looked like. I did know human nature, and I knew where people tended to secure their valuables.

Working quickly and by touch in the darkness, I went through the contents of the tent. A cursory inspection of the Duke's packs yielded nothing. There was little else that suggested itself as a hiding place. As stealthily as possible, I crept over to the man himself, where he slept on a low, fur-draped cot.

I didn't bother trying to search him—I'd have needed both hands, leaving one hand uncomfortably empty of a weapon. So I just pressed my knife into the skin above his carotid artery and said, "Don't move or speak."

He woke immediately—no fog of sleep in those mad eyes.

"You'll be gutted for this," he said mildly.

"What, no 'who are you, what's the meaning of this?' Not even a 'do you know who I am?'"

He stared at me, perfectly still. His eyes were a pale blue or gray. In the darkness, they looked the color of spit. They spoke volumes, those eyes. None of it good.

"Tell you what. Give me the talisman that allowed you through the death lands, and I won't punch this knife through your neck."

He looked at me, and even in the darkness, I found it hard to meet those strange, pale eyes.

"I can die now with one thrust," he said, "or I can die slowly of starvation as you apparently are doing. I know which I choose, girl."

"I really don't want to kill you, Duke, but I will. Where's the talisman?"

"Put down the knife, and we'll discuss the matter." His tone was suddenly soothing, reasonable. I was immediately suspicious.

"Shut up."

"Really, there's no need for this. I shall feed you, and when my business is done here, you can accompany us out of Thagoth. Put the knife down. It's getting terribly heavy, you know. Why, you hardly have the strength to keep a grip on it much less threaten me with it."

"Shut up." But he was right somehow. My forearm trembled with the effort of holding the knife. I brought my other hand up to steady it, and pain exploded in my head. Suddenly, I was on my hands and knees on the ground, and the pain was so awful I wanted to vomit. The Duke was standing over me, shaking his hand.

"I believe I broke a knuckle on that thick skull of yours, my dear."

"I should have just killed you and taken it," I rasped.

He pulled a simple necklace out from under his shirt and looked at it, as if considering. "Yes, you should have. That's what I would have done." And he smiled. The next blow came from his foot. It knocked me mercifully out of consciousness.

~ ~ ~

Voices. Murmuring, threatening, screaming. Shrieks and sobs. The groan of someone in awful, terrible pain. The kind of pain no one could endure. A man's death rattle accompanied me up out of the well of oblivion. Or passed me on its way down.

I was wet, cold, and shivering uncontrollably. I couldn't feel my hands. They were off somewhere behind my back, far away. My feet were tethered to my hands, more loosely. I didn't want to open my eyes. I opened them anyway and stared into the face of a dead man. His skull had been cleaved open, and rain and blood ran down his face to pool in his open mouth.

I knew I shouldn't have opened my eyes.

I looked around, anywhere but at the corpse next to me. I was lying on the cobbles of the square, midway between the gates to the Tabernacle and the Duke's tent. One of the soldiers noticed my movement and called out. The officer came over and squatted down next to me. His face was hard, all angles and planes, and it gave nothing away.

"You got one of my men killed, you stupid, thieving bitch."

"You've got the wrong stupid, thieving bitch. I haven't had anybody killed in months."

"Shut up. Vik was a good man, a good soldier. You sneaked into camp during his watch, and for that, the Duke killed him."

"What do you want me to say? I'm sorry old Vik worked for a murderous madman?"

The man stood up and kicked me in the side.

After I got my breath back, I said, "Who needs logic when you've got a hobnailed boot, eh?"

He spat at me. "Logic? You want logic? You were going to steal the talisman and leave us all here to die. That's logic for you, you filthy thief."

"Not true. After I was out, I would have hired someone to get you all." And I might have, too.

"Right," he said.

"Believe it or not, I would have. More than your Duke would have done for me." I struggled to a kneeling position. "Look, I could have killed the Duke and taken the necklace. I'm good enough. If I'd meant for you all to die, why didn't I do that? Why did I take the chance?"

He was silent for a while. "Mayhap you're squeamish," he finally grated out.

"Believing that would be a serious mistake on your part, Captain."

"Lieutenant."

"Whatever. Look, do you even know why you're here?"

"The Duke is looking for something."

"Well, he's not on an afternoon stroll. He's looking for an artifact that will grant him immortality. If he's willing to kill—Vik, was it?—out of hand, do you think he'll have any qualms about killing the rest of you once he's got what he wants?"

"He'd never do that. There's no way he could take all of us."

"Couldn't he? He seems like the type that likes his secrets kept, and there are far too many of you to tell tales." I tried to test the ropes that bound my hands. Useless. I couldn't even feel my hands anymore.

"He wouldn't even have to kill you," I added. "All he'd need to do is leave you here."

"Having a pleasant conversation, Lieutenant?"

Even over the rain and the rumbling thunder, I should have heard the Duke's approach. The man was truly irritating.

"Just listening to this filth try to squirm her way out of death, Your Grace."

"I suggest you don't, Lieutenant. Who knows what sort of venom she might poison your ears with?"

"As you wish, your grace." The Lieutenant disappeared. The Duke looked down at me. I looked up at him.

"You've got some hellishly disturbing eyes, you know that?" I finally said.

"Hold your tongue, dear, or you'll die now instead of in the morning. I like to see what I'm doing. Make me hasty, and I'll be sure you suffer proportionally."

I thought about that a moment. "You won't kill me," I said.

The Duke arched a brow.

"You won't kill me because you need me."

"What on earth for?"

"You don't know what's in the Tabernacle, or what you're looking for exactly—not where it is, not what form it might take. You need someone like me to get it for you."

"My dear, I'm a master of the Art. What could I possibly need a thief for?"

"If you thought getting this thing yourself was your best option, you'd never have offered ten thousand marks as a reward."

"That was for proof of the existence of this city. Not for the artifact."

"You wanted someone to find the artifact and carry it out of here so you could take it away from them. It would be easier that way."

"You've strayed from educated guesses into wild suppositions now. You're boring me to boot. Good night, little thief. I look forward to seeing you in the morning." He walked away, back toward his tent.

Damn.

~ ~ ~

Three o'clock in the morning? Four? The rain kept pounding down. The Duke's men had long ago broken out their oilskin tarps. Despite the stomach-churning distaste for the dead man next to me and my fear of becoming a corpse myself, I'd managed a few minutes of miserable half-sleep when I heard someone approach. I looked up. The lieutenant. He squatted down in front of me and stared at me for a long time.

"What?" I finally mumbled.

"You're going to die in a few hours. You understand that?"

"Looks that way, yeah. If you've come to gloat, make it quick. I'm trying to get some beauty sleep here."

"I need to ask you a question, and I need you to answer it honestly if you're capable."

"Anything for you, friend."

"Do you really think the Duke will abandon us here if we find the artifact?"

"Yes. I really do. You must know what kind of man you work for."

"This is our first assignment with the Duke. He called us from the border forts to protect him during this expedition. He said he needed seasoned fighters."

"Lieutenant, did you just fall off the turnip wagon?"

"What do you mean?"

"Never mind. No, don't never mind. Don't you see? He did want seasoned fighters, ones that didn't know his reputation for treachery, deceit, and murderous madness. He needed warriors he could trust. Expendable ones."

He was quiet for a long time. I watched the idea sink in, watched his jaw harden and his eyes go cold. He got up and stalked away.

"Goodnight, Lieutenant, pleasant dreams. See you in the morning when I get tortured to death." I closed my eyes and focused on my breathing.

I heard the lieutenant's footsteps again. I looked up, and he dropped a sack next to me. He pulled out his belt knife and cut my bonds. I dropped the dead things that were my hands into my lap, stretched out my legs.

"When the blood comes back to them, they're going to hurt so bad you'll want to scream. Don't. There's food in the bag."

"Thank you, Lieutenant."

"My name is Gnarri. Now listen. This is how I see it. The only way we're getting out of here alive is if you get to the thing before the Duke does."

"That's not possible."

"Then I guess we'll all die here."

"We could take the talisman away from the Duke."

"I won't do that, not until he gives me cause. I have an oath to uphold."

"Then you're an idiot, Gnarri."

"I'm an officer in the Duke's service."

"Same thing."

"Find the artifact, or stay here and starve. Your choice."

Just then, my hands came back to life. I had to stifle the screams.

Gnarri stood up and said, "If you were really smart, you'd have noticed Vik kept a knife in his boot. You could have escaped hours ago if you were nearly as good as you think you are."

I would have told him six months of starvation had taken the edge off my normally razor-keen senses, but I was too busy paying attention to the agony in my hands. Besides, he probably wouldn't have heard me. The storm had picked up again and was screaming across the city.

~ ~ ~

I dragged myself away from the Duke's camp and hid in a dry nook where I kept my gear, devoured hard tack and jerked rabbit, and looked over my options. Nothing good. Stay here and starve, go back to the Duke's camp again and try to steal the talisman, or raid the Tabernacle and try to steal the artifact. Damn, damn, damn.

I pulled out my gear, dug out my tools and the grappling hook from my pack, and made my way through gale-force winds to the side of the Tabernacle opposite the Duke's camp. I scaled the wall and surveyed the grounds below. It was a black riot of foliage, visible only in the brief flashes of lightning.

Two choices. Either drop down into that and make my way to one of the domed buildings on foot, or try to set my hook on one of the domes and hopefully make my way in from above. I didn't relish traipsing through that jungle. Anything could be down there. However, it was going to be difficult to get a good cast in that wind. And I remembered the hawk, and its limp fall from the sky.

I finally decided to take the high road. I could always climb down if I couldn't get a good cast. And hopefully, the storm would cover my actions.

It took eight casts to get the hook set. Once it was, I hammered a small piton into the wall and secured the rope, then began to shimmy my way upward at about a twenty-degree angle toward the dome. The lashing rain mingled with my cold sweat, and I expected to die at any moment.

The storm whipped at me, buffeted me, stung my face and hands, and tried to pry me from the rope. Lightning struck the city around me, sometimes so close I could smell it. And the further I climbed, the steeper the angle grew. The rope began to sag as it soaked up the rainwater like a sponge. My abused hands ached fiercely. It was the hardest seventy feet I've ever traveled. Every second of it, I expected that unearthly shriek to turn my bones to pudding and stop my heart.

I made it to the southern dome, set my feet on the ledge, and collapsed, willing my breathing back to normal.

I was here. Now what?

The first thing I noticed was the dome was not merely golden. It was gold. One seamless sheath of gold, who knew how thick. It looked as if it had been cast all of a piece, which was impossible. There was enough gold on just the one dome to buy half of Lucernis outright. I couldn't help but laugh a little. I was the richest woman in the world if I could figure out how to haul it all away.

The next thing I noticed was what looked like vent holes at the very top, wedge-shaped, spaced evenly around the central spire. I inched up a little and saw they were in fact windows—or had been. The glass had long ago broken out of them. A few jagged shards still clung to the edges. There was something odd about the shards. I pulled one loose and took a closer look. It was a deep blue. It must have been pretty inside during the day, before the windows had broken. More importantly, I had a way in if I could figure out how to get down.

The windows were wide enough for me to slip inside, but the drop was a bone breaker. I cast a glance back at my rope. No help there; it was tied securely to the outside wall. No way I was getting it loose from where I was, and I hadn't brought a spare. The interior angle of the dome was too steep for me to try to climb unassisted. I sighed, cursed myself, and put a hand on the thin rod of the spire.

Lightning struck the spire just then, and the raw power of it convulsed my body. At the same time, a scream rose from the depths of the dome, a rising bubble of agony that was more than sound. It enveloped me and turned my own pain into a tiny corner of an agony that enveloped the world and knocked me out.

~ ~ ~

Far, far away, the buzz of a dragonfly's wings magnified a thousand times. The hum and whine of metal being tortured out of shape endlessly. I thought I could hear Holgren telling me to wake up.

Slowly, I opened my eyes but could not make them focus. Holgren's voice went away. It was replaced by another voice I could hear clearly above the hum and whine.

Wake. You must wake.

"Wha? Done my chores, Da." Something wrong with my voice. Muffled. More than muffled. Gone? No, that wasn't quite it either.

Wake, now, and do not move until you can move with purpose.

I tried to open my eyes again. I saw only blackness. "Great, I'm blind," I mumbled. Something wrong with my voice, and something was cutting into my waist, and my hands were throbbing, especially the right one.

No, not blind, only looking into darkness. You have been deafened, however.

I finally snapped back into reality. My entire torso was hanging through one of the windows of the dome. It was a wonder I hadn't fallen through. Slowly, I inched my way back from the precipice.

Come down to me now.

"I don't think so." No way in hells was more like it. Whatever it was down there was talking in my head. I'd take my chances with the Duke.

You will never overcome the Duke alone by stealth or any other means. I can aid you though.

"I'll just have to take your word on that, I guess. Now, get the hells out of my head." I slid down the curve of the dome to the ledge and took stock of myself. Deaf except for the hum and whine that threatened to split my head open. My own words were muffled things felt in my chest and throat rather than heard by my ears. The palm of my right hand was charred. My vision swam, and muscles all over my body spasmed randomly.

I'd never be able to climb back down that rope without falling. Maybe the canopy of vegetation in the Tabernacle grounds would break my fall somewhat.

Doubtful.

I ignored the voice—the presence in my mind—as best I could. Down into the Tabernacle grounds and then what? Not over the wall, not like this. Out the gate then—into the Duke's camp, then death by torture. I put my head in my good hand and held back the tears.

Come down to me. Amra. I swear no harm will come to you from me.

"How do I get down?"

Climb down the spire. It runs straight to the floor. And more.

I climbed back up the dome, grabbed hold of the spire, tightly with my good hand and then gently with the burned one, swung my legs out into the void, questing with my feet. I found the rod and locked my knees around it and oh-so-carefully contorted my shoulders through the window to grasp the rod beneath the dome with my hands. The metal was still warm from the lightning strike.

I thought the ascent up the rope was frightening. It didn't compare to the descent down that pole into utter darkness. Fifty feet? Sixty? I have no idea how far down I slid, nursing my burned palm, the rushing of my blood and that awful whine the only thing I could hear.

Almost there.

I started at the words in my mind, lost my hold, and fell the last few feet onto something fleshy, warm, wet, and alive. I felt rather than heard a low groan of pain and screamed again. I scrabbled backward on all fours away from it, heedless of the agony in my hand. Suddenly, the stone beneath me dropped off, and I tumbled backward, bashing my head against unseen stone.

Be still, Amra. You hurt yourself needlessly.

I couldn't take any more of this. No more. If only there were light—no, then I would see whatever it was that was speared on the end of that rod—

Be still. Breathe. No harm will come to you in this chamber. Be still, be calm, or I must cloud your mind. If I do so, you will never trust me afterward. I need you to trust me, little thief.

I tried to take hold of my unraveling sanity. I don't know how long I sat there in the darkness, the coppery smell of blood surrounding me until I wanted to vomit.

I am sorry, Amra, but I fear it must be done.

And then, I felt his mind enveloping mine, gently, inexorably. It was like drowning. I ceased to exist.

The next thing I knew, I'd awoken inside something like a dream. I was starting to hate dreams. First came a faint golden glow, so faint I didn't notice it until I realized I could tell the difference when I blinked.

Then, the subtle scent of incense wafted through the air, gently masking the blood smell. Some incense I'd never smelled before, gentle, not cloying. I didn't trust any of it, but it helped. I felt sanity settle more firmly in my grasp. A question floated to the surface of my mind.

"Who are you?" I whispered.

Tha-Agoth, god-king, emperor, sacrifice. Tha-Agoth the Undying, the Betrayed. Tha-Agoth the Eternal Sufferer. Tha-Agoth the Fool.

"Where are you?" came the next question though I knew the answer to that one.

Pinned to my own altar, pierced by sky-metal, punished by the fates for besting death and building to withstand eternity.

"Who put you there?"

My sister, my bride. Athagos the Destroyer, Athagos Death-Bringer, the serpent's fang, the spider's kiss, song weaver of the sirens.

"What do you want from me?"

Freedom. And in return, I will give you eternal life.

The light failed. The incense faded, as did my consciousness.

I woke knowing my mind had been tampered with. The dark and the stench were there still, but I had something to hold on to. Anger.

The past months, Holgren's death, the Duke, my battered body, eating bark and grubs, the constant struggle for survival, and now some god playing with my mind—it was enough. I was getting out of this hell-hole no matter what it took, and damn anyone who got in my way.

First, I needed light.

Mercifully, my tinder box was still in my belt pouch. Holding flint in my injured hand, I struck steel across it until I got a spark in the tinder then a twist of smoke and a small flame. Quickly, I tore a strip of cloth from my ragged shirt tails, praying it wasn't too soaked.

I will supply light if you are prepared to see.

"Shut up."

Slowly, smokily, the rag caught. I held the strip up above my head and looked around the room. Nothing but bare stone, the hint of doors to the left and right, and in the center a stone altar.

You are prepared to see. And with that, light blossomed from everywhere at once. Bathed in that golden glow lay a man on top of the altar, pinned there by the rod that ran straight up through the top of the dome.

He was the color of bronze. His hair fell in braids down the end of the altar to pool on the stone floor below. The blood from his wound trickled down the sides of the altar to do the same. There was a lot of it. The floor was awash in blood.

The pupils of his eyes were cold, bright stars, pinpricks on the blanket of his night-dark irises.

Help me.

I dropped the burning rag and approached him.

Help me, Amra. I have lain here for a thousand years, pierced through the heart, unable to die. Free me.

"I'm sorry. I have no idea how to help you." I looked away from him, down at my hands. They were covered in his blood. *I* was covered in his blood. I'd crawled through it.

I cannot affect the sky-metal that pins me. You can. You can break it somehow. It will not be easy, but I believe it is possible for a mortal. Do me this service, and I will grant you eternal life. You may leave if you choose or stay here with me and help me rebuild my empire. Please, Amra, do not leave me so.

I couldn't look at him. His situation was horrifying. I pitied him, but I didn't trust him any more than I did the Duke.

"What killed off all the animal life here?" I asked.

I do not understand the question.

"I think you do. You know my name. Root around in my brain some more, and tell me what killed the hawk above the Tabernacle."

Silence for a long time. Finally, he assented. *Athagos. She wakes sometimes. I do not allow her to feed from me, so she gains what sustenance she can elsewhere.*

"Athagos, your sister-wife? Death incarnate? She's still hanging around, huh?" I walked a few steps closer. "Tell me why she pinned you here in the first place."

Please, Amra—

"We do this my way if we do it at all. If you don't like it, take over my mind again, you bastard, and get me to do your dirty work that way." I was suddenly shaking with rage. It wasn't just toward him, but he was a convenient target.

I knew you would resent that. Very well.

We were born, my sister and I, with powers: she to cause death and I to defeat and defy it. As we grew, we also grew in power and together conquered half the world. Eventually, she grew jealous of my powers. She was forced to kill to sustain her youth and beauty. She had always abhorred death. There was a rival wizard-king, a man whose name I have since seen crushed to dust on the slow wheel of time. He poisoned Athagos' mind against me, made her believe she could absorb my powers into herself. She believed him. She believed my death would be the last she would ever need cause. I suppose it was worth it to her, for on this very altar, she lay me, drugged, and performed a fearful ceremony.

The outcome you see before you. I did not die. I cannot. The ceremony drove her mad, and the wizard-king attacked, decimating the empire and destroying my capital. To this day, his foul magics cling to the edges of my power, seeking to destroy that which cannot be destroyed. Are you satisfied? He closed his eyes and turned his head away from me.

"I wonder what her side of the story is?"

You could ask her, but I doubt she would give you a satisfactory answer. She would be far too busy consuming your essence.

"And if I free you, you'll build up your empire again."

You never knew the empire. No famine. No plague. Little warfare that affected the populace. It was paradise.

"While it lasted." I wiped the blood from my palms onto my pants. And stopped. My hand was healed, the skin neither raw nor blistered. Even the scar from a deep cut when I was a child was gone.

My blood is life. It will heal your wounds and in time grant you immortality. More quickly if you drink it.

Panic washed over me. Had I gotten any in my mouth? I stripped quickly, scrubbing myself with the blood-free portions of my clothing. I wanted nothing to do with this god or his blood, however tempting its healing properties might be. Everything comes with a price, and the bigger the thing, the bigger the price. Godly healing, I was guessing, was a pretty gods-damned big thing. I scrubbed harder.

That is not what I would call a normal reaction. Was that amusement in his voice?

"Look, I was never the one who wanted immortality. I just want to get out of this cemetery of a city, past that mad bastard outside your gate, and through hell's nine acres beyond, and back to civilization. Getting my hearing back would be nice too. You can take immortality, though, and stuff it. Look what it got you." I threw down my bloody clothes and made my way to the door. Then an idea hit me, and I went back and grabbed up the bundle of rags I'd been wearing.

You are going to leave me here. His voice was shot through with incredulity.

"I feel sorry for you, I really do. But the last thing the world needs is another power-mad ruler. It definitely doesn't need an immortal one."

Remember that I did not compel you, Amra. Remember that, and return to me when age begins to creep up on you. I will wait here though you've spat in luck's good eye.

"Where else are you going to be?" And with that, I pushed open the brass-bound door and made my way out of the chamber.

I will not stop you, Amra. Athagos will have other ideas, however. My presence is your only safety.

Stairs up, a hallway, a false start down another hallway, and I was at the massive double doors that led to the Tabernacle grounds. It wasn't as difficult as it might have been; dawn had broken, and there were ample windows in the granite walls. I pushed open one of the doors and walked out into the gray morning. The rain had slowed to a drizzle.

Quickly, I began to make my way through the dense underbrush to the nearest wall. I was planning my next move when I got knocked flat.

~ ~ ~

I lay there, stunned, unable to breathe. Even if I'd been able to hear, I doubt I would have noticed her approach.

I scrambled to my hands and knees, and my chest began to ease, the barest hint of air making its way to my frantic lungs. Eyes closed, I forced myself to take a breath. Once more. Again.

I opened my eyes and saw a pair of withered, bony feet. Slowly, I raised my head, seeing desiccated flesh hanging from shins, then knobby knees and skeletal thighs wrapped in rotting cloth. Heart hammering, I looked up into the face of the thing that stood before me. She was ancient, and not wholly human. She looked down at me, head cocked to one side. The only thing alive about her were her eyes. A stunning, unworldly blue, they bored into mine with what appeared to be curiosity. That, and hunger.

Slowly, I stood up and backed away. She followed me with her eyes. When I began to turn my body to run, she threw her head back, her arms forward, and shaped her mouth into a perfect O. The back of my neck went cold, and the hum and whine in my ears intensified to a painful level. I kept backing away, looking for anything around me I could use as a weapon. All that presented itself was a heavy stick about three feet long and crooked as hell. Transferring the bundle of clothes to my left hand, I picked it up.

Athagos—it had to be her—stopped gargling or whatever she was doing and dropped her arms. I saw surprise in those eyes when she looked at me. She cocked her head again and regarded me some more.

"I don't know what you're up to, lady, but I've got a feeling I don't want any part of it. So I'll just be going." And I began to turn again.

She was quicker than I would ever have imagined. Suddenly, she had me in a bear hug and was gnawing at my left shoulder. My left arm was pinned between our bodies. I brought the stick up against her head with all the force I could muster and felt both the stick and her skull crack. She dropped me and stumbled away.

Like an idiot, I stood there, shaking, holding the splintered stick in a death grip and staring in sick fascination at the thing that was most likely going to kill me. Already I could see her skull knitting back together. I turned and ran.

Crashing blindly through the underbrush, I stumbled away from the Tabernacle. Not being able to hear how close she was behind me put my heart in my throat and made the hair on the back of my neck stand on end.

I ran headlong into the gates. Not exactly where I wanted to be, but I didn't have time to find a spot further away from the Duke. Besides, I figured he'd be too busy dealing with old death incarnate to worry about me if it came to that.

The gates were barred from the inside by a huge timber. I knew I would never be able to lift it up off the supports, but what was there to do but try? I got a shoulder under one end of the massive beam and heaved. It didn't budge, but the end of the ancient, rotted timber crumbled. Time and weather had rotted the thing. I couldn't lift it, but hopefully I wouldn't have to.

Frantically, I searched the ground for another stick, found one about two feet long, and started hacking and punching the middle of the timber with it. Wet exterior chunks broke off, and dust from the middle sifted to the ground.

On the fourth or fifth back swing, the stick was plucked from my hand.

I turned slowly to face her, the thing that was about to end my life. I forced myself to stay calm, to keep loose, ready to take any advantage that presented itself. Every second I was alive was a second I wasn't dead.

She stood with the stick in her hand, staring at me with unblinking eyes. It was hard to tell through all the folds, wrinkles, and crags in her face, but I think she was smiling. She tossed the stick far into the underbrush, shook one bony finger at me, and launched herself.

The impact knocked me back into the gates. They burst open. I hit the cobbles of the square hard on my backside, sliding a few feet on the wet cobbles. For the second time in five minutes, I'd had the wind knocked out of me. I lay there, eyes closed, waiting to die. It took me a few moments to realize the creature wasn't on top of me, gnawing me into bloody chunks. I opened my eyes and saw her standing at the gates, straining against an invisible barrier. She must be bound to the Tabernacle grounds, I realized, or else I would have been dead months ago. I took a tortured breath.

It was about then I noticed the crossbow pointed at my head.

The Duke had it aimed right at my temple and was screaming something.

"Sorry, you mad bastard, I can't hear a word you're saying," I said in what I thought was a normal speaking voice. I looked around and saw that the Duke's men were all staring at Tha-Agoth's sister-wife. Gnarri was there, nearest the gate. I felt the chills run up my spine, and my ears began to ache again. An expression of pure agony crossed Gnarri's face, and he clapped his hands to his ears.

They were all in the same agony, all of the Duke's men, and the Duke himself had dropped his crossbow and fallen to the ground next to me. I sat up, dumbfounded, until I looked over at Athagos. Her mouth was shaped into that perfect O, her arms spread wide. The Duke and the others started to convulse, then went still. After a few moments, they all stood up in unison and started walking toward the creature like marionettes.

Gnarri was first, and even if I'd known a way to save him, I'd never have made it in time. I watched with pain and disgust as she "consumed his essence," as Tha-Agoth had put it. She clasped him around the waist with one arm, like a lover, and put her other claw-like hand to the back of his head. With her face a few inches away from his, she began somehow to *suck*. A ghostly tendril of bluish light curled from Gnarri's gaping mouth into hers, and then Gnarri's head and body slowly shriveled and collapsed, like a wine skin being drained.

In the end, all she left of him was his skin and clothing draped over her arm. Gnarri's chain mail glinted in the morning light as she dropped it and what was left of him and called the next man to her. I couldn't tear my eyes away as she consumed one after another of them. For the first time in months I wasn't hungry at all.

Then it was the Duke's turn, and I was almost too late. I caught up with the Duke in three lunging steps and snatched the talisman from the doomed bastard's neck just as he walked into Athagos' embrace. I stood there, panting, watching his slender form shrivel up to a dried husk as she sucked him dry. And all the while her features took on the glow of life, and her body filled out into that of a ripe beauty.

She tossed the Duke's skin away and looked at me, smiling. She ran a slender finger across her wide, pink lips and giggled in my mind.

I shook myself and walked away. I walked out into the ruins, stopping only to rifle the Duke's packs for a change of clothes. I've seen a lot of death in my life and caused some, but no one deserved a death like that. Except perhaps the Duke.

At least the rain had stopped.

~ ~ ~

I returned to the deserted camp an hour later. I purposely avoided even looking toward the gates. I lay down in the Duke's tent and slept like the dead all through the rest of the day and straight through the night.

Next day, I ate breakfast, rummaged through packs until I found a shovel and an oilskin, and took them as well as a mule and my god-bloodied clothes to Holgren's grave. After I got him out of the ground, I peeled off his grave clothes and dressed him in my bloody rags. It wasn't easy. Half a year in the ground had done some unkind things to him. He was starting to come apart.

I had no idea whether it would work, but what's a little vomit between friends? I wrapped his corpse up in the oilskin and tied it securely, managed to load him on the skittish mule, and went back to camp to pack.

I found a small fortune's worth of gems sewn into the Duke's fur-lined cape. Not enough to buy me a manse off the Promenade, but a tidy sum nonetheless. Enough to share with Gnarri's widow if he had one. I pay my debts.

As I rode out of Thagoth leading my string of newly acquired mules, I realized my hearing still hadn't recovered. I worried about that briefly, then decided only time would tell. If it never came back, well, an honest Lucernan trader wouldn't need acute hearing the way a thief did. Nor would a reputable fence, for that matter. But it did return, slowly. Enough that, when a few days had passed and Holgren started screaming to be let out of his canvas bag, I heard him loud and clear.

KERF & ISIN, PART THE SECOND

Kerf and Isin lounged on divans in the otherwise empty plane of deities. Resting on Isin's upturned palm lay a golden, glowing speck: Holgren's soul.

"I had a time finding him down there, I don't mind telling you, Kerf. I can't believe that lot just packed up and left. Gross irresponsibility."

"Well," said Kerf, "the Age is almost over, and let's face it; they didn't have the choicest of realms. I'd be eager to move on as well. Besides, responsibility isn't one of Evil's strengths, now is it?"

"But what of all the souls still pouring in between now and the end of the Age? They weren't being punished or even let go. They were just milling around, aimless and trapped. It's no way to run an afterlife, Kerf."

"Yes, well, you've fixed it now. The next lot can decide on a more permanent solution." He shifted, settled his hump more comfortably on the divan. "But back to the matter at hand—and might I say it is a lovely hand indeed—our friend there is almost ready to be resurrected, and the Shadow King awaits both him, and Amra."

Isin frowned. "That one!" she said with distaste. "Kerf, mightn't they have had enough? We can take care of the Twins and let them get on with their lives. The Shadow King is a tangle even *I* would prefer to avoid."

"Now Isin, the task is fairly begun. Events are unfolding apace, and I for one would like to leave this Age knowing I've helped a last pair of Heroes emerge. It *is* one of my principle aspects, hero-making."

"Yes, Kerf, I'm aware." Isin looked down at the miniscule dot that was Holgren's soul. It shone more brightly in response. Isin made a decision.

"If you get to exercise one of your aspects, dear Kerf, then I do as well," she said.

"Oh, that'll be interesting! Yes, do."

Isin smiled radiantly down at Holgren's essence. It had begun to vibrate and glow ever more brightly.

"They're a prickly pair," she said, "but we'll see if I can't get them together." And with that, she gently blew the miniscule sun off her palm.

Holgren's soul floated gently away, then began to fall rapidly down to the mortal plane.

"Off you go, then," called Kerf, "and hang on to your courage. Forget what you've learned of us, now. Oh, and see if you can't get your partner to swear by something other than my testicles? There's a good lad."

CHAPTER 4

My hearing had recovered enough in the course of a month's travel that, when Holgren rose from the dead, I heard him loud and clear.

It was on a dull, gray mid-afternoon. Winter was well under way, a chill-wet season in this portion of the world. No snow had fallen yet, and half the trees still kept their leaves.

I was riding the Mad Duke of Viborg's bay gelding and leading a score of his mules across a lush sea of grass. Originally, I'd started out with twice the number, but I'm a thief, not a muleskinner. I'd let half of them go once I'd gotten them safely away from the death lands.

The grassland ran unbroken for about five miles down to a broad, lazy river I could just make out in the distance. Beyond the river lay a dense tree line made up of a deep, green belt of firs that girded the eastern horizon. The western expanse of the continent, which some say was the cradle of humanity, lay devoid of human settlement. I am a city woman, but I have to admit I had come to enjoy the open expanses and the beauty of nature unmarred by civilization. Mostly, though, I was just glad to be free of the ruins of Thagoth and on my way home.

My hearing had returned somewhat; the din of noise from my damaged ears had faded almost completely into the background. I was enjoying the melancholy sigh of wind across the knee-high, emerald blades of grass around me when I heard another sound.

First the faintest of rustlings, shifting, cloth on cloth. Then a piercing scream and the answering bray of a startled mule.

"Get me out! Get me out of here! I can't breathe!" Raw-throated and full of panic, I still knew Holgren's voice after more than half a year without it. Alarm turned to joy in my heart, and I rushed to cut him free of his mule-borne, oilskin womb.

I had secured his corpse in a tarp, tied with hempen ropes at ankles, knees, hips, and head then secured that around the girth of the mule. I cut all the ropes quickly, and he tumbled out of his wrappings to the grass below.

He was wet, covered in what looked like nothing so much as birth waters. Steam rose off his pale, slick body. He looked like some newly hatched, gangly bird of prey. He looked wonderful. My god-bloodied rags clung to his lanky, shivering frame, shirt cuffs barely clearing his elbows, pants hardly reaching past his knees. I pulled his head and shoulders up gently, cleaned milky-clear slime from his eyes and nose and mouth, and hugged him tight for a moment. He looked up at me.

"Amra," he croaked.

"Welcome back, you lucky bastard," I whispered.

~ ~ ~

That night over a roaring campfire, I told Holgren of all that had happened since his death—of the Duke, of Tha-Agoth, of Gnarri and Athagos. Of my deafening and the god's blood that had brought him back to the land of the living. I was so glad to see him I kept even the slightest hint of reproach out of my voice. I could yell at him later for getting me stranded in Thagoth and for all that had happened after.

I'd deposited him in a nest of blankets after toweling him off, and he sat there, silent, drinking strong tea. I couldn't keep my eyes off him. I expected him to disappear at any moment or to keel over once again. I studied that angular face of his, his high cheek bones, his thin upper lip, his full lower one. I couldn't shake the image of the ruin his face had been a month ago when I'd pulled him out of his grave. Now, it was whole and perfect again save for a livid scar on his left cheek where the creature from the death lands had bitten him, ending his life through the deadliest poison I'd ever seen.

"Well," I said when I'd finished my tale, "that's about it. Now, we only have to trek across sixteen hundred miles or so of uncharted terrain, and then we're home. Simple, really, after all that."

He nodded absently, mug clutched in his hands, eyes on some middle distance I could not see.

"Holgren. Are you all right?"

He shook himself and stared at me. His eyes had always been his most expressive feature. At that moment, they were windows to a bleak landscape, and I felt sorrow for what he'd gone through. Then, he smiled thinly, and some warmth and humanity crept back into his face.

"I am all right now. And I have you to thank for it."

I shrugged.

"No, Amra. I was in Gholdoryth, the Cold Hell. Now I'm not. You saved me."

I've never been comfortable with gratitude directed toward me, not having much experience with it. Plus, it tended to diffuse all the railing at him I'd planned to do for getting me stuck and starving in Thagoth for half a year. I changed the subject.

"What was it like, hell?"

"Cold," he said. "Empty. Vast. I…I don't remember much. Let's talk about something else."

"Of course, Holgren. I understand."

"No, you don't."

I had nothing to say to that. We passed another hour in companionable quiet. By the time the fire had died down to embers, Holgren was fast asleep. I settled his blankets more snugly about him, checked the mules, and went to my own hard bed.

I lay there, running my thumb across the necklace I'd taken from the Duke, the talisman that had allowed him, and later me, to cross the death lands unimpeded. It was a simple rope chain about eighteen inches long with a cunning lobster claw clasp. It was made of some bluish metal I didn't recognize, and while it was magical, as far as I could tell, the magic was of such a specific nature that it was basically worthless. I kept it as a memento, a souvenir—and as a reminder to listen to my gut.

Right then, my gut was telling me I had missed Holgren just a bit more than a business partner should. I told my gut to shut up and go to sleep, and I followed suit.

~ ~ ~

Holgren was up before me and had built the fire back up a bit. He'd found his pack among the mules and dressed in his own clothes. What he'd done with the rags I'd put on him I didn't know or think to ask. Not then.

He was standing on a little knoll a few yards away from camp. It was hardly more than a swell of ground on that wide plain of grass. His eyes were closed, his hands stretched up toward the sky. He was taking slow, deep breaths of crisp morning air. A lazy smile played across his face.

"The world is a fine and beautiful place, Amra. It's good to be alive. Tea there near the fire and jerked meat."

I grunted at him and walked a ways off to relieve myself. When I returned, he'd unrolled the map he'd sketched and inked months before.

"You haven't charted out the return trip?" he asked.

"I'm no cartographer. I've just been following the rising sun."

"Well then, we'll just have to estimate." And I spent the next hour describing the terrain I'd traversed over the last month between bites and sips, giving him my best guesses as to distances traveled.

"I wish I'd thought to bring a compass. Still, you've been traveling latitudinally for the most part, so no harm done there." He fiddled with the map a while then set it aside.

"We don't have to spend months traversing uncharted terrain, you know. I can open another gate—"

"No."

"It's only a month's journey back to Thagoth, and you've got the talisman this time."

"No. Absolutely not. I'm not going to let Tha-Agoth have another crack at my mind or yours."

"He didn't force you to free him before."

"A mistake he will most likely remedy if we return. I won't do it."

He sighed.

"Let's get moving," I said. "I'd like to get to that river. The mules need watering, and I'd like to take a bath. I'd think you would too."

"Yes. Yes, of course. Sorry."

We got our mules going again and reached the river in less than two hours. It was broad and shallow, and the mules drank greedily. The gelding, who I'd taken to calling Dandy, drank almost daintily, as if to distance himself from the disgraceful manners of the mules.

Holgren had pulled out his map again and was sketching in the last bit we'd traveled.

"Can you start filling the water skins?" I asked him. "I'm going to clean up."

He raised a hand in distracted assent.

I pulled a lump of the late Duke's soap out of a pack and walked a little distance downstream. The Duke had been a fastidious man and his taste in soap expensive if a bit perfumed for me. I stripped and jumped in.

The water was frigid. I gasped and proceeded to scrub myself up vigorously and quickly.

It was on the third or fourth dunk, as I was trying to get all the soap out of my hair, that I noticed something across the river on the thin ribbon of bank between river and tree line.

It was one of my mules. What was left of it. It had been hacked to pieces, its guts strung up in the trees. The mule's severed head was staring sightlessly at me. It had been stuck on a branch that jutted out of a log half submerged at the river's edge. The neck had been hacked at raggedly, and red gobbets of flesh hung down from it almost to the river, blood pinking the water near it before being carried off by the flow. Flies crawled all over its open eyes, its froth-flecked nostrils—

I sprinted up the bank to my clothes, yelling for Holgren all the way.

As I made it to my pile of clothes, I felt the familiar chill along the nape of my neck and knew Holgren was performing magic. He ran up to me, holding a glowing sphere in one hand. I pointed to the mule's head as I quickly dressed.

~ ~ ~

We decided to take a detour.

"No animal would do that," Holgren said. "Kill, yes, but play with the remains? I don't think so."

"I'm just wondering how the mule got across the river in the first place."

"No telling. Mules are intelligent beasts. Perhaps it broke its hobble in the night and just wandered off for a drink."

We were backtracking a mile or so then planned to parallel the river for a few more miles before we started looking for another ford. Holgren looked a little ridiculous riding a mule. His long legs didn't quite hang naturally. But Dandy wanted nothing to do with him.

"Bloody as it was, what was done to the mule shows at least some level of intelligence," he continued. "I'm curious as to who or what makes those woods home."

I was going to tell him I'd used up all my curiosity in Thagoth, but then I was being strangled.

It was the necklace I'd yanked off the duke's doomed neck. It had tightened suddenly. I couldn't breathe. I gagged and hacked and clawed at it and fell to the ground.

Holgren was right there beside me, alarm in his eyes.

"Move your hands, woman! *Move them*!"

I stuffed down the panic enough to drop my hands from my neck. He put his own on the necklace and muttered a few liquid syllables, eyes closed. There was a thunderclap and a brilliant flash of light, and Holgren flew back half a dozen feet. Mercifully, I could breathe again.

Holgren got up and came back over to me. I panted raggedly.

"Thank you," I rasped.

"Don't thank me. My spell failed—rather spectacularly at that. The necklace…decided to let you go."

"What do you mean?"

"Just that. Let me see it again. This thing has to come off."

"Kerf, yes. Get it off me."

He tried for nearly an hour to no avail. Finally, he sat back on his haunches and huffed.

"It's powerful, and it's complex. I don't know if I could remove it in the best of conditions." He looked around, plainly missing his sanctum. "These are not the best conditions."

"You've got to get this thing off me. I mean it."

"I can't. I'm sorry. I have been able to decipher something of its nature, however. As far as I can tell, its purpose is to make the wearer go…*some*where."

"What are you talking about?"

"Put simply, the necklace didn't like you traveling back the way we came."

"But the Duke must have come this way. He definitely traveled west to get to Thagoth in the first place."

"As I said, its nature is complex. I'm seeing only part of the weave of commands embedded in it. Very fine work, actually."

I swore again.

Holgren went on and checked the campsite. I stayed with the mules. I whiled away the time trying to get the necklace off, and succeeded in making my neck even more raw. The clasp had frozen shut, and it refused to break.

Funny how it had slipped right off the Duke's neck just before Athagos had sucked him dry. The clasp had just opened when I snatched it from him.

My neck was hot and stinging when Holgren returned.

I sighed and scratched my head. It required an act of will to keep my hands from straying up to the necklace and trying to rip it off.

"Well, do we go forward or try to go around?" he asked. "It's your neck, so to speak, so perhaps you should decide."

I gave the chain another tug and stood up. "Let's try to avoid the mule butcher's territory if we can. Let's see how far this thing will let me get."

~ ~ ~

It let me get about six miles downriver before it started choking the life out of me again. I whipped Dandy back the way we'd just come and set him to a canter. The necklace eased almost immediately.

"You handled that adroitly," said Holgren from mule-back.

"This is not something I want to get used to," I rasped. "You're the mage. Figure something out, for Kerf's sake."

"For what good it will do, I'll try again when we make camp. Speaking of which, I would only loosely term this daylight." He gestured at the sky. There was still a decent amount of light in the west, but night was falling rapidly.

"Fine. You make camp while I hobble the mules."

He nodded, dismounted, and started pulling open packs.

Once camp was set up and we'd eaten, he sat down in front of me and peered at the necklace again.

"They used similar items in Elam before slavery was outlawed. Kept the slaves from running off. What you're wearing is much more complex, however."

"I'm not interested in a history lesson, oddly enough. I want it off."

"I'll try. Of course I'll try. I just don't hold much hope." And he bent back to the task at hand.

I ignored his breath on my cheek and the inadvertent touch of his fingers on my bare skin as best I could. This was neither the time nor the place, I told myself forcefully.

An hour passed. He dropped his hands and leaned back.

"It's no use. I'm sorry. The spells laid on it are seamless, and I still can't see what all went into the making of it. There's nothing for me to get hold of to try and unravel. I'm afraid if I try anything truly invasive, you'll get hurt."

"So be it," I said with more conviction than I actually felt. I was tired of thinking about the damned thing.

The next morning, we forded the river and went into the woods. I was jumping out of my skin at the slightest sound, and Holgren held his power ready for an instant casting. I could feel it, that crawling sensation in the back of my neck. It gave me some comfort.

The woods were sparse enough that we had a decent view of our surroundings and no real trouble leading the mules. There were birds and squirrels and rabbits, but we saw no sign of larger game.

Holgren called a halt at midday, and we ate a sparse meal. Then, we continued on much as before.

It wasn't until late afternoon that we saw anything out of the ordinary. A wall.

The wall was ancient, vine-choked, and tumbledown. In its day it must have been massive, but we had no trouble leading the horses through one of the many great rents in it. Beyond, a small city in even worse shape than Thagoth had been. Tumbled granite blocks and raw winter grass was all that remained. If the stones had not been obviously carved, I might have been tempted to believe it was some natural, if odd, meadow.

No stone stood atop another in all that great space save for an odd, low, stepped pyramid in the center.

"Night is coming," Holgren said. "Might as well camp here."

"Alright. I'll look around and gather firewood."

"Be careful. I sense the residue of old magics. Very faint, but best be cautious."

"Any idea what this place was?"

He shook his head. "No telling. So much was lost in the Diaspora. It might be Trevell, Hluria, or one of a dozen other shattered cities."

As I wandered closer to the pyramid, I realized there was a large, stone bowl at the top and, almost invisible in the daylight, a fire was lit in that bowl. I climbed the steps of the pyramid to get a closer look, already thinking that this place was inhabited, probably by the mule killers, and that we needed to get moving before they came back. But something was compelling me, more than my natural curiosity, and even as I was thinking how stupid it was, I was moving closer to that fire.

A pale blue flame burnt in the bowl, feeding on nothing. Stone and flame was all. With a sense of disbelief that quickly transmuted to panic, I saw myself sticking my hand into the flame.

The meadow and everything in it melted away.

CHAPTER 5

I stood in the center of a great, gray, stone hall whose walls rose up into darkness. Dozens of staircases and hundreds of hallways stretched away in every direction and at impossible angles. I could not imagine what it would have taken to build such an edifice, beyond sheer insanity. Torches flickered wanly, imparting a dull, will-sapping gloom rather than honest illumination.

The whole fantastic place reeked of age and abandonment—no, not abandonment exactly. Buildings get abandoned by the living. This place wasn't for flesh-and-blood mortals. I couldn't imagine people actually inhabiting that space.

There was nothing about the place that I even remotely liked.

"A thief," said a voice high above. "Nothing to steal here, I'm afraid. Any treasure you take from my halls must be earned, oh yes."

"Who's there?"

"I ask the questions here, and you answer them as you can. I am the judge, and you are the judged."

"I'm here to be judged?"

"You placed your hand in the flame. Therefore, some part of you wishes to be judged. Some shame compelled you to do so."

"You'll forgive me if I don't take your word for it."

"Well, if you have had a change of heart, just walk out through those doors behind you. You might survive."

I glanced back. Massive, black double doors beckoned, easily twenty feet tall. I turned back around.

"What happens if I just leave without being judged?"

"That depends on your undischarged guilt. In Hluria, the law has always been an eye for an eye."

I didn't like the sound of that at all. "So you're saying—"

"No more questions. It is time for judgment."

A light appeared on a staircase high above me, one that could only have been used by spiders and flies since most of it was upside down. Swiftly, it began to descend, and all the while, the voice spoke on, sibilant, insinuating.

"So many crimes," it said, "so many to choose from. But you don't consider theft a crime, do you? Not a moral one. 'Take what you can from those who don't need it, and take punishment, if it comes, as punishment for stupidity, not wrongdoing.' Isn't that what your crippled teacher told you? Ah, but you'd rather forget old Arno, wouldn't you? All he did for you, all he taught you, and you left him to die in that shack in Bellarius."

"What? It wasn't like that—" I hadn't thought of Arno in years. He'd been my mentor, more of a father than my father had ever been. He'd taken me in, showed me how to steal bread without getting caught. How to pick a lock. How to pick pockets. How to scam unwary merchants out of pocket change. He'd been a fine thief before he got caught, and the magistrate broke all the bones in his hands. Then, he'd been a fine teacher before the lung fever took him the winter after he took me in. When he started coughing up blood, we both knew what it meant, and he drove me out of his shanty lest I catch it as well.

He'd died within a week.

"All that he did for you, and you let him die alone. If it weren't for him, you'd never have seen your eleventh birthday."

"Arno chose to die alone. If I had stayed with him, we wouldn't be having this conversation. I'd be dead along with him. I know the debt I owe him, you bastard."

"Do you? Perhaps you do. That was hardly the worst thing you've ever done, though."

I didn't like where this was going, not at all. I'd let a lot of things stay buried in the past for good reason. The light had gotten much closer, but it was still high above. It seemed to be carried by a robed figure, though I couldn't make out much detail.

"What's the point of this?"

"For the third time, I ask the questions here. Do not make me tell you again."

"Or else what?" I regretted the words as soon as they left my mouth.

It was silent for what seemed a long time but was likely only seconds. The figure was almost at the bottom of the stairs, hidden by a corkscrew turn.

"Else I will show you what you least desire to see." With those words, I felt a sick dread begin to worm its way through my guts.

The figure descended to the floor, suddenly somehow right side up. It held a lamp high, illuminating its face, and laughed. I screamed.

Its face was the face of my dead father. Guilt and terror crashed down on me.

I couldn't face it wearing my father's face. I couldn't. I fled into the labyrinth of passageways, past staircases and intersections and dust-choked, empty rooms in that hellish, twilight world. I scurried away like a rat, a cockroach. Like the nothing that I was. I fled. The voice followed wherever I went, just a step behind.

"What was it like, plunging the knife into your own father's back? Could you feel the blade strike bone, the shock of it run up your arms? Could you hear the steel grate along his rib? A clumsy kill, but you got better at it, didn't you? You learned to keep your blade parallel to the ground. You learned where to thrust and why. You learned to kill quickly and quietly."

I ran, panting, down another torch-lit corridor. I remembered everything. I remembered my father. I remembered the time after his death, before Arno took me in. Death struggles over scraps of food or begging territory, pitched battles on rooftops and in alleyways, filthy, starving boys and girls dying alone and terrified. Not me. Never me. I remembered the mantra I would mouth silently as I rocked myself to sleep every night: I *will* survive. I *will* survive. I *will* survive…

I rounded a corner and plunged down darkened stairs, the voice hard on my heels.

"How he must have screamed though. Even in his drunken stupor, it must have been agony, feeling his own daughter's blade in his back, in his lung. Feeling his life seep away. Unable to breathe once you pulled that filthy scaling knife out of him and his lung collapsed.

"Do you remember how he writhed, bloody bubbles at the corner of his mouth, mewling like a dying kitten? Do you remember his feeble kicking? How he clawed at the floor? Do you remember? Do you? Of course you do, Amra. You remember very well."

And I did. I remembered the night I killed my father in perfect detail. I remembered coming home to a darkened house, hearing my father's fists thudding into my mother's body, her dazed pleas for forgiveness and mercy. My mother, who didn't even know what she was begging forgiveness for, whose only failing had been choosing a viper-mean drunkard for a husband.

I had picked up the scaling knife from the muddy ground next to the loose, splintered front steps where it lay next to a pile of fish guts. The worn, wooden handle was tacky with fish blood and viscera. Flies buzzed clumsily around the pile of guts and fish heads in the chill autumn air, and inside, my mother was being beaten. Yes, I remembered.

I walked into our one-room hovel on the dying edge of Hardside, found my father hunched over the prone figure of my mother, beating her face in with a cold, wordless fury. I remember his fists hammering down again and again, methodical, almost workmanlike.

And yes, I remembered holding that filthy, slender, single-edged knife over my head in a two-handed grip and driving it down into my father's back with all the force my eleven-year-old body could muster.

I'd held my mother's unconscious body, cradling her bloody head in my lap as my father bled his life away on the floor next to us.

She never woke up.

The terror and sick guilt of what I'd done were suddenly replaced by anger. I knew then that my emotions had been manipulated. Gods-damned magic.

"So many have died around you, at your hand. How very many deaths you are tangled up in, little thief. How great your guilt must be."

"No," I said.

"No? Are you unrepentant then? Will you not plead for mercy, for forgiveness as your mother did before she died?" I could feel his breath on the back of my neck. I balled my fists at my side, took hold of my remaining fear, and strangled it to death.

"No. I won't. What deaths I've caused, I regret for the most part, but I've rarely had any choice, and I've never killed for profit or pleasure. Only survival, mine or others'. If you know so much, then you have to know that, too." I took a deep, ragged breath. "Was I supposed to lie down and die? Everyone has the right to try and survive if they can. I won't beg forgiveness for it. Not from you. Not from anybody." I steeled myself and turned around.

A tiny, blue-white flame bobbed at eye level, somehow casting a warm, golden glow. No robed figure. No father's face.

"Spoken truly, Amra. I've waited centuries for one like you to come to me. You were almost too late. The umbrals attack even now."

"What are you talking about?"

"You are the one. Receive my mark." The flame flew at me, *into* me. It didn't burn. That hellish maze disintegrated around me. I fell to the cold, coarse winter grass and into another kind of hell entirely.

~ ~ ~

I was on my back at the base of the pyramid. Night had fallen, and massive, shadowed creatures roamed the ruins. The stood half-again as tall as a man, and were as wide as three. Their wicked blades, long as me and curved, flashed in the moonlight, but every movement the creatures made was warped, blurred, like ink in water. It was as if they were shadows and smoke made flesh.

Holgren stood near me, flinging bolt after bolt of pure white fire at the attackers with little effect.

"Oh, Kerf," I swore.

One, the largest of them, was bearing down on us. It swung a blade as long as I. Each swing was measured, precise, the space of a slow heartbeat. The thing was a juggernaut. Nothing Holgren threw at it did more than rock it in its course. It was going to be on us in three or four more strides.

I estimated the distance between us and it, watched the rise and fall of its sword. I timed it as best I could, hoping the thing had poor reflexes.

Just as another of Holgren's bolts splashed harmlessly off the thing and its sword began a downward sweep to the left, I darted out toward it, knife in hand. I heard Holgren call my name and felt the whispering passage of its blade on the air near my head. I swung the knife up toward the cleft between its massive thighs.

My blade shattered like a cheap wine bottle dropped on paving stones.

Not the servants, but their Master, hissed the Flame's voice in my mind. I cursed and rolled through the thing's legs, pulling my last knife.

It turned quickly to try and face me. I kept behind it, and it kept turning.

"This is not a long-term plan," I muttered.

It swung its blade behind its back and nearly took my head off. I'd found only a momentary respite.

It had to see, I reasoned. Which meant it had to have eyes. I hoped. I sprang from the muddy grass onto its massive back, clawing for purchase. Its skin felt like nothing so much as a bankfish's underbelly: cold and soft and smooth in a distasteful way. I slipped an arm around what I had to assume was its neck and began to poke at where a face generally went. I jabbed less fiercely than I might have otherwise. I couldn't afford to lose my last knife.

I have no idea whether I had much of an effect. Holgren screamed at me to drop—but he was too late. I heard the low, terrible hum of a blade slicing air in the split second before it connected. I knew I was dead. I didn't have time to see my life flash before me. I didn't even have time to curse. It struck me in the neck.

It should have decapitated me. I felt the links of that cursed necklace bite into the flesh of my neck under the weight of that terrible blow—and then the monster's sword bounced away and buried itself in the shoulder of the creature I was clinging to. Thick, black blood sprayed up from the wound and drenched my face. It stung and smoked and smelled much like the death lands had. I dropped instantly, retching and clawing the stuff away from my eyes and mouth with my free hand. I landed hard on my back and instinctively rolled away. Good thing I did. The one that had been cleaved fell on the space I'd just quit. It made no sound, and it didn't get back up.

The creature that should have decapitated me was still very much alive, though, and was right on top of me. It had left its sword in its brethren. It crouched above me and with thick fingers began to probe its own stomach. I scrabbled back on my elbows in the slick grass. A fissure appeared there on the thing's torso that stretched from groin to neck. The thing pulled it open wider, revealing a blackness that beggared the darkest cave. A sigh escaped that black opening, and I swear it formed whispered, groaning words.

"Come to me, my love. Come inside…"

"Not on your best day," I muttered, and hurled my last knife into that perverted talking womb.

The fissure closed with an elastic snap, and the creature rose up with fists raised, ready to pummel me into the earth. I heard Holgren uttering more strained, liquid syllables. I didn't want to be anywhere near when he was done. I was positive whatever Holgren was about to unleash would be quite unhealthy for me if not the beast.

I started running, sure I'd never get out of the creature's reach in time. The top of my head tingled where its fists would come down and turn my brains to jelly. All my hair began to stand on end. I didn't dare look back.

Holgren uttered a final word, and lightning pounded down out of a cloudless sky. Once. Twice. Again.

I looked back over my shoulder, and the thing stood, fists raised above its head, smoking and sizzling. It wasn't blurry anymore.

I saw then that it did have a head of sorts, a massive bulge atop its torso with three holes spaced in a triangle, point down, in the center of it. It had no neck to speak of. Slowly, almost imperceptibly at first, it began to topple. When it fell, the ground shook, and the meadow echoed with the impact, leaving a momentary silence in its wake.

The rest of the creatures hardly seemed to notice. They were too busy bearing down on me and Holgren. They formed a terrifying skirmish line, weaving a wall of steel before them as they came. Holgren was face-down in the grass, unmoving. He'd told me once that when a mage exhausts his magic, the least they could expect was to lose consciousness. I hoped like hells that was all that was wrong with him.

Not the servants, but their Master, the Flame hissed again. *Flee, Amra.*

I fled. Scooping him up under the armpits, I pulled Holgren back from the creatures. I was delaying the inevitable. They'd mow us down. I couldn't move fast enough carrying him.

"Holgren! Wake up, you heavy bastard!" Nothing.

Inside the pyramid is an escape, of sorts, hissed the Flame. *The doorway is hidden.*

"How do we get in?"

How did you enter before?

The monsters were coming, relentless. There was about a forty-foot gap between them and us, and it was narrowing by the second.

We could escape. Through that pale fire at the pyramid's point. Now, it was a race.

I got a better grip on Holgren and, digging for every scrap of strength and speed I had, dragged him up the stepped slope of the pyramid as quickly as I could. I held Holgren by his shirt to keep him from sliding back down the pyramid, hoping he would be transferred along with me to the Flame's halls beyond. I reached up over the stone bowl's lip to touch that pale blue fire. That's when one of the creature's swords came whistling down from out of the dark to cleave the bowl of fire in two.

What happened next was over in a matter of moments. I looked back over my shoulder, and the creature was raising its sword again to bisect me this time. But its blade was now coated with a living, dancing flame that was crawling rapidly toward the sword's hilt. As the sword descended, pale blue flame found the inky flesh of the creature's hand.

The effect was explosive.

The creature disintegrated instantly, along with pretty much that entire side of the pyramid. The roar of the explosion was like nothing else I'd ever heard. The blast threw me back onto what was left of the stepped side of the pyramid and ripped Holgren from my grasp. I landed hard, my right arm twisted behind me. I felt the bone of my upper arm snap. The stone beneath me groaned, shifted, and suddenly gave way. I tumbled into darkness. I struck something, bounced, and then lots of rocks beat my body to a pulp. I don't know how big the one was that nearly took my head off, but it was big enough. The pain was excruciating, nauseating.

Luckily, I passed out before I vomited. I hate vomiting.

~ ~ ~

I don't really remember much of what passed after that. Hours flew by, and I drifted in and out of consciousness. I was pinned in the rubble, legs immobile, facing down into the great hall where I'd first faced the flame when it was wearing my father's face. In the dim moonlight, I could see that rubble and earth made a perilous slope from the meadow above down to the hall's floor, perhaps forty yards from top to bottom. I was somewhere in the middle.

At one point I started to cough, which brought on agony from my shattered arm. I suppressed it before I passed out and just lay there for a time, concentrating on each breath.

You have survived much, said the flame suddenly in my head. *You will live to survive more.*

When I could talk again, I asked a question. It helped take my mind from the wreckage of my body.

"Hey, Flame. What the hells are you?"

I am what the Sorcerer-King discarded when he attempted to become immortal.

"That's about as clear as mud."

All your questions will be answered, in time. For now, save your strength. Dawn comes, and with it your hope of rescue.

"Flame? Hey. Flame?" But there was no answer.

It *was* getting lighter though nearly imperceptibly at first. After a time, the pale morning light filtered down enough for me to make out more of my surroundings.

From my nearly upside-down position on the rubble hill, everything took on a crazed perspective. I knew exactly where I was, and it would have been just as crazed if I were right side up. The mammoth hall was still mostly intact. Staircases still beggared gravity; hallways still stood at impossible angles and at random spots in those cliff-like walls. At the far end of the hall, I could just make out those two huge, black double doors. I looked to my right. A few yards away rose the spiral staircase that the Flame had descended.

High above, one of the shadowy monsters was speared through the back on the jagged tip of the stair's central support. Its limbs hung limp, boneless. It might have been a huge, ugly doll. Eventually, when the sun rose high enough to shine straight on the corpse, it sort of dissolved, leaving behind a tiny, shriveled husk.

The rising sun also illuminated more of the hall below me. The pyramid had just been the tip of a vast madhouse. I couldn't imagine what it had taken to build such a thing, or why anyone would have bothered.

"I suppose it will make a good tomb," I muttered. As the light grew, my consciousness dimmed.

~ ~ ~

It must have been close to noon when I woke again, this time to a massive shift in the rubble. I was far gone. I didn't know where I was anymore and was none too certain of who I was. I only knew I was in pain and that I was thirsty. I opened my eyes but couldn't focus properly. I saw a wavering silhouette above me, coming closer. Slowly, it came into focus. It was Holgren. He picked his way down to me carefully, taking forever. Relief flooded through me. He was alive. He was here.

"Where the hell have you been?" I croaked. He just smiled, thinly, and said "Hush now."

My mind wandered far and away, into the deep recesses of memory. It's one way to escape pain. And Holgren couldn't help but cause me pain as he freed me.

~ ~ ~

I awoke to distant birdsong. I smelled winter rye, felt the weak sun on my face. I tried to move and found I was wrapped up like an infant in swaddling clothes.

I was lying in a makeshift bath made from an oilskin tarp supported by cut saplings. Pinkish water covered me to the chin. Something was different besides that. It took me a while to think of what it was. Then, I remembered. I was supposed to be half deaf and in agony. I was neither. I looked around. Still in the clearing. The yawning pit that had been the Flame's pyramid was some distance off to my left. The sun was brushing the treetops behind it on its way to bed.

"I didn't know if it would work," Holgren said from behind me. "The blood was old and dried, and I had no idea how much potency was left after my own resurrection. I thought it best to return it to a liquid state."

Tha-Agoth's blood. Ugh.

"Can you hear me, Amra?"

"I'm not particularly fond of blood baths, Holgren. Can you get me out of here please?"

He pulled me out of the bath, undoing the strips of rag that bound me. I found I was shaky and weak' and had to lean against him during the whole procedure. He felt my right arm, tenderly at first.

"Any pain?"

I shook my head.

"Excellent." He held me at arm's length. "Look at you," he said. "Not a scratch, not a scrape."

I shivered. "Not a stitch of clothing either. I'm cold, Holgren."

He looked at me again, then, with different eyes. He blushed and turned his head. "Yes, of course. Sorry. Let me set you down, and I'll, ah, get your things. Here's a blanket."

"What happened to you after the pyramid collapsed?" I asked him as he collected my clothing, which was in a tidy pile near the bath.

"I woke as I was being thrown through the air. You'll have to tell me just what happened to cause that. The remaining creatures set on me drove me back into the woods. I didn't have a thimbleful of power left." He handed me my clothes and took my hand.

"I'm sorry I left you for so long."

"Don't be an ass. What good would you have done me dead?"

"I should have done something."

"What? Jumped in after me, broken your legs? We'd both be down there dying right now. You did the right thing, Holgren. The only thing."

I tried to pull my hand away, to start dressing, but he held it firm. Those eyes of his searched my face. "When I saw you fall, Amra, I…" He let go of my hand, raised both of his in a helpless gesture. "I don't want to lose you."

It was my turn to blush.

"Turn the hells around so I can get dressed." I explained to Holgren how the pyramid had exploded as I dressed. It was a slow process. I was healed, but I didn't have much strength or coordination. My fingers fumbled on buttons and ties. I strapped on the knife sheaths, though I no longer had any knives to go in them. But without the familiarity of the knife-rig on my body, I'd still have felt naked.

"How did you escape the creatures?" I asked him.

"I didn't really. They would have gotten me eventually. When the sun rose, they just melted into the ground. Their power is limited in that way, at least. Gods know they're powerful enough."

"What are they, Holgren, and why did they attack? You can turn around now, by the way."

"And will they attack again? I don't have any answers."

I also remembered what the Flame had said when I'd been dying down below about being what the Shadow King had discarded. And there was that shriveled corpse of the monster, still speared on the jagged tip of the staircase down there. Not enough answers, too many questions.

"We need to get going ourselves before those bastards show up again."

"Let me just collect some of your bathwater before we go." He poured out the contents of the water skin and then submerged it in the pink water I'd been soaking in.

"Do you think it will be any good anymore?"

"Only one way to find out. I can't imagine it will hurt at any rate."

"Did you find Dandy or any of the mules?"

"Yes. Dead. I'm sorry. I'm also sorry to say that we'll be eating mule for the foreseeable future. It's all there is."

"Damn." I was going to miss our beasts of burden and not just for sentimental reasons. I'd have been hard put to outpace the monsters fully rested. I had no chance now, weak as I was.

"What do we do now?"

"For now, we go to ground."

~ ~ ~

It was a long way down to the mound of rubble I'd been pinned on. Holgren and I made it down with the aid of a rope. He lowered me then climbed down after. From there, we carefully picked our way across the floor of the Flame's dismal foyer.

The—umbrals, hadn't the flame called them?—hadn't liked the pyramid's blue fire one bit, but it was out now. Would they hesitate to chase us down here? I just didn't know enough about what was happening to guess. One thing was for certain—if they came again that night, I didn't have the strength to fight or to run.

Holgren and I made camp in one of the empty rooms. He brought down firewood and started a fire, then he pulled out canvas-wrapped chunks of meat and began to roast them over the fire.

"You need to eat something, Amra. You can't do much more tonight, I think."

Mule steak. Great. But it was true. My stomach was a gurgling void, and if the umbrals showed up just then, I'd barely be able to crawl away. As the pieces cooked, he doled them out, and I ate mechanically, bite by tough bite.

When we were done, I lay back on one of the blankets Holgren had salvaged from our packs. We were in a high, nearly inaccessible chamber deep inside the Flame's labyrinth. I didn't feel terribly safe. The shadow raiders weren't exactly smart, but just then, I could only think of one thing that frightened me more: Athagos. I remembered how she had sucked all those men dry and shuddered.

"Are you cold?" Holgren asked, and I shook my head. "No. Just thinking unpleasant thoughts. I'm fine."

"Do you want to plan now or in the morning?"

"What are our options? We have limited supplies, we can only go where the necklace lets me, and these shadow creatures could set on us any time from sunset to sunrise."

"It will work out. You survived Thagoth. You can survive this." A thought crossed his face. "I just realized I never got a chance to ask you what happened with the flame."

"Nothing I care to talk about right now." I didn't want to go into the details. Killing your father is a very personal thing, no matter how you look at it.

"As you wish," he sighed. "I'm going to scout about. Get some rest." And he was off into the labyrinth.

I stifled a yawn, bunching up a blanket to use as a pillow. I made myself as comfortable as possible on the cold, stone floor and settled down for desperately needed sleep.

~ ~ ~

It was deep in the night when I woke with a start. I looked around the dim chamber, trying to figure out what had woken me. I stared at the dying fire in the center of the room for a while and Holgren's snoring form on the other side of it. I closed my eyes again.

Wake. Little thief, I have something to show you.

The Flame. I sighed. "What do you want?" I whispered.

As I said. I have something to show you. Come. A tiny, golden flame popped into being in the air above my head and floated toward the corridor.

"This better be good," I muttered, and rose from my makeshift bed.

I followed the bobbing flame out into the corridor, around a corner, and down another corridor that I didn't remember seeing on the way in. From there, it led me down a set of dusty stairs.

Those stairs went on and on. They finally ended in a long, high chamber lined with twisted pillars. The Flame stopped at the base of the stairs. At the other end of that chamber was a simple wooden door, about six feet high by three wide.

I may go no further. The answers to many of your questions are behind that door.

Something about this felt wrong. Part of being a successful thief is relying on your instincts. That innocuous door was making mine very nervous.

There is nothing inherently dangerous to you beyond. But there is much that is…unpleasant. What you feel is much like a stain, left over from the past. The Flame actually seemed uncomfortable.

"Why don't you just tell me what's in there? That way, we can both avoid any unpleasantness."

I cannot. This, you must see for yourself. No harm will befall you in these halls.

I took the last few steps down into the chamber and started walking toward the door. I was sick of mysteries and riddles. I wanted some answers. As I approached the door, the small hairs on the back of my neck tried to rip themselves out of my skin. The entire underground labyrinth practically radiated magic, but whatever was behind that door was something else again.

I began to have third and fourth thoughts about what I was doing. I kept walking. A sort of pressure began to build, gently at first, like a friendly hand trying to turn me aside. A few steps later and I was walking against a strong wind. A few steps more and I was trying to push myself through a stone wall. I gritted my teeth and closed my eyes and put one foot in front of the other, straining with all my inconsiderable might. Just as I was about to give up, the resistance vanished.

I opened my eyes. The door stood in front of me: plain, unadorned, innocuous. There wasn't even a lock. I had no tools to probe with, but I inspected the frame and flagstones around it as best I could, searching for any tell-tale signs of alarms or traps.

Nothing else guards the door. You are free to enter.

"I guess I'll just have to take your word on it." I put one hand on the knob, turned, and pushed. The Flame was right. Inside was much that was unpleasant.

CHAPTER 6

I suppose it could have been called a throne room. It could also have been called an abattoir or a mausoleum.

The room was about forty feet long by thirty wide, low-ceilinged, dressed in pale marble. It was lit by four blue-burning braziers, one at each corner. Walls, ceiling, and floor were all spattered with old, dried blood. Desiccated corpses strewed the floor.

The bodies were contorted, their withered faces eerily similar in their expressions of agony—or was it ecstasy? The ancient finery they wore was stained black with massive quantities of dried blood. In the center of the room was a low dais on which stood a high-backed chair that faced away from me. On the far side of the room, a pair of bronze-sheathed double doors took up most of the wall. That was it except for the chilling residue of massive magics.

What answers was I supposed to learn here?

I nudged the nearest corpse—one with a jewel-hilted dagger sticking out of its chest—with the toe of my boot. The corpse collapsed into a pile of dust: clothing, skeleton, and all. The dagger clattered on the floor. I turned to go.

A chill wind started up from nowhere, and the braziers flickered and dimmed. Shadows began to play on the walls, creating moving shapes I know I didn't imagine. My imagination isn't that fertile. Or perverted. I turned back around quickly. I didn't want my back to that room.

The wind picked up and blew the corpse dust into a vaguely human shape that searched the room with hollow eyes. It darted from corner to corner as if it was searching for something, pushed by or riding on that corpse-wind. It paused every so often as if to sniff the air. And then the voices started.

Not human voices. No human throat could have produced those sounds. If time, madness, and desolation could talk, they would have given tongue to voices like these.

Who disturbs our rest? Who…who…can smell their blood…can hear their heart… But where? Can taste their fear… No one comes here… …Flesh and bone…Is it pretty? Is it food… …Where… Wherewherewherewhereoh WHERE?

"Right here," I said, praying the Flame had been right about nothing being able to harm me. My words seemed to take them aback. The voices quieted to a murmur, and the dust ghost stopped its frantic search. It hung nearly motionless, half obscured by the chair in the center of the room.

Master, it moaned. *Someone has come.*

"I know," said a mild, elderly voice that emanated from behind the chair's back. "Go back to your rest," it said, and whatever power held the ghost's tenuous form together abated. The dust-ghost broke apart and drifted to the floor.

I snatched up the jeweled dagger from the floor. It was good to have a blade in my hand again though I doubted it would do much good if things came to violence.

"Come here where I can see you, my dear."

I shook my head. "I don't think so."

"That you stand in this room means you know no harm may befall you, necklace bearer, Flame's champion. Indulge me. I cannot come to you and would not harm you if I could."

The voice was cultured and kindly. I distrusted it completely. I stayed put.

"You've come for answers, no? These I can supply."

"Fine. If you try anything, I'll skewer you."

A chuckle was the response. I picked my way carefully along the edges of the room, careful not to disturb any more of the corpses and careful not to come too close to the dais. I wanted a clear shot at whatever was sitting in that chair if I had to take it.

As I came around, the chair's occupant became more and more visible. He was old—ancient. His wrinkles had wrinkles, and there were a lot of them to see since he was completely naked. Not a pleasant sight. I stopped in front of him, several arm-lengths away.

He sat, utterly still. One hand lay on the chair's arm rest; the other was a twisted claw drawn up across his chest. His head was cocked to the left, almost as if he'd fallen asleep. All his limbs were shriveled and with more than age. His joints were great, knobby bulges, but the rest of his limbs were hardly more than sticks. He was completely bald, and an intricate pattern of tattoos spiraled from the top of his head down to an inch or so above his white eyebrows. The design was of a repeating pattern of arcane-looking symbols. Age had not distorted them. They were crisp, sharp-edged, and pitch-black. The tattoos seemed to hover just slightly above the old man's skin.

The only thing that seemed alive about him were his eyes. They glittered with a keen intelligence and tracked my every move.

"Not a pretty sight, am I?"

"I've seen worse," I said truthfully.

"I was born this way, you know. Cursed by the gods, my parents said. As if an unborn babe could have done anything to offend the gods."

"Everybody has it hard growing up. You said you have answers for me? Good. I've got a lot of questions."

He stared at me, and a small smile played across his lips. "The Flame made an interesting choice in you," he said. "Very well; ask your questions, and I will answer them as I can."

"Let's start with you. Who the hell are you?"

He chuckled again. "I'm no one."

I have never been a particularly patient person. I have learned to be cautious, but it's been a hard-won skill. Just then, I'd used up all my patience, and caution seemed to have deserted me. I stalked over to the wrinkled riddler and stuck the knife under his chin. In my best back-alley voice, I said, "Don't toy with me. I'm not in the mood. Answer my questions straight, or you'll be wearing a second smile."

He looked down at the knife as best he could from his cockeyed position then looked up at me.

"As you wish." But there was no fear in his voice. I lowered the dagger.

"I spoke truth," he said, "though not plain truth. I am no one now. What I once was—it has been erased from history. How I came to be what you see before you is a long tale."

"Just give me the juicy bits."

Another chuckle. "A millennium ago, I was a king and a mage of the highest order. My power stretched over nearly half the continent. Armies marched at my command, and magic bent the world to my will. It was not enough. I could prolong my life, but not indefinitely. I could assume other, healthier forms, yet eventually, I always needed to return to the seat of my power, this twisted shell you see before you. I wanted more."

It didn't take a genius to make the connection. "You're the Sorcerer King that destroyed the Thagothian Empire."

"I was. I am that person no more."

"A thousand years to think about it made you a new man?"

"No, dear. I am literally only the animated husk of the Sorcerer King. When I said I was no one, that is exactly what I meant. There is no soul, no spirit in this flesh."

I chewed on that for a bit. "You seem pretty lively to me. What animates you?"

"Ah, now you strike at the core of the conundrum. Can a mirror see itself? Can a coin be minted so thin that it has no edge? Which is more important: words or the space between them? But to answer your question in a way satisfactory to you: Magic. In ways too arcane for even me to fully fathom, I must exist that the others may."

"What others? I don't know what you're talking about, and I'm starting to think you don't either."

"Forgive me. It has been a thousand years since I last held a conversation. I will endeavor to speak more plainly—though the finer points of the Art may be lost on you."

"I'll try to muddle along," I said as I stuck the knife in my belt and eased back from him. He smelled…unpleasant.

"You see these corpses all around you?" he asked. "Powerful mages in their time. My *khordun*, my coven. When mages link, their powers grow exponentially."

"I've never heard of such a thing. I didn't even know it was possible."

"Such a joining was rare even in my time. There are…dangers involved. And difficult trade-offs."

"Such as?"

"One will rises to gain dominance in the *khordun*. The strongest will. The others are subsumed eventually, leaving little more than vessels of power—animate shells with only a rudimentary intelligence and no free will. And once a *khordun* is formed, it is a perilous thing to attempt to disband it."

"So all these mages became your slaves? Did they know it would happen?"

"Of course not."

"Did you?"

He just smiled wanly.

I shook my head. "You were a very bad man, my friend. I'm glad you're not still roaming around loose. Now, what does this have to do with what I need to know?"

"You know of the fall of Thagoth. You know of the Flame and the Shadow King. And now, you know of me. What conclusions can you draw, I wonder, from these disparate facts?"

"You're the one that's supposed to be answering questions."

"Indulge me. I beg you. I had an interest in riddles once."

Impatience struggled with natural curiosity. What *did* all these things have to do with one another, if anything? I tried to make the facts hang together.

"The Flame is connected to this place, somehow. That much I know. It told me these halls were his. Perhaps the Flame was some sort of punishment on you."

"That's a pretty picture, but you've left out most of the pieces."

"Look, you withered-up old husk—" And it began to come to me. I remembered what the Flame had said as I lay pinned in the rubble. *I am what the Sorcerer King discarded when he attempted to become immortal.* I looked around the chamber, at all the bodies. The corpse I'd kicked with the knife in its chest. Hadn't its own withered hand been on the hilt?

"You tried something, some ceremony to get you power, to get you immortality, didn't you? You tried it, and something went wrong. Now, there's three of you. The Flame, the Shadow King, and you. Two sides to a coin and its edge."

Again that dry chuckle. "Very good, my dear. You have a facile mind. But what of Thagoth? How does it come in to our little passion play? How does it figure in to our sordid equation?"

What had Tha-Agoth told me? Something about the wizard-king poisoning Athagos' mind. The ceremony that was supposed to kill Tha-Agoth. But he couldn't be killed. Was that what went wrong? I didn't have enough information to be certain.

"You tricked Athagos into trying to kill her brother," I guessed, "but it didn't work. Somehow, that fouled your own ceremony, didn't it?"

"Some coins can indeed be minted without an edge, it seems. Athagos and her brother were and are inseparable. Or at least the method I employed to pry them apart failed when everything said it should have succeeded. The very moment that my domination over reality itself seemed assured, the core of my being was sundered. Flame and Shadow, light and dark."

"And you."

"I am no one and can affect nothing. I suffer an eternity of impotence, trapped in this form I hate so much." A single tear escaped the corner of his eye and disappeared into the folds and crags of his leathery face.

I felt no sympathy for him. Tha-Agoth, yes, but not him. He'd brought it on himself.

"Look," I said, "we've been rehashing the past, and it's been interesting, but I need to know about what's happening right now. I've got problems of my own. You said you had answers for me, so start answering."

"I will answer if you ask."

Where did I start? "Who is the Shadow King? Is there any way to escape his creatures? The Flame said it had been waiting for me—for what? Why is it so secretive? You called me necklace bearer. What is the necklace, and how the hells do I get the Kerf-damned thing off?"

The Flame could go to hells if I could get the necklace off. Free of it, Holgren and I could steer clear of all this and make our way home.

That damned chuckle again. "Which question would you like answered first?"

"Tell me about the necklace." If I could remove it, the rest of my questions were mildly interesting at best.

"Come closer, then, and let me see it."

"Why did you call me necklace bearer if you don't know what it is?"

"I know its form, but not its intent. You wear a slave-chain. I made many such in my time."

"And that really makes me want to trust you." But I stepped forward. I wasn't afraid of him, but he definitely made me uncomfortable. Perhaps if he'd had some clothes on.

"Bend down. I cannot see it very well." I did so. I didn't like it. A delicate scent of putrefaction rose from him, more noticeable the closer I got. I suppressed a shudder.

After a time, he said, "That will do."

I backed away. He was silent for a while. As the silence stretched on, it also stretched my patience.

"Well?"

"The Shadow King has learned to work with the material world more intricately than I would have given him credit for, and has lost no skill or subtlety in the Art. That, or he has enlisted other minds and hands to do his will."

"I don't care about all that, old man. I just want to get it off my neck."

"Then you must place it on the neck of the one it was intended for."

"What?"

"This slave chain was fashioned to bring Athagos to the Shadow King. Does he seek to complete the ceremony interrupted so long ago? But no, she alone would not suffice—would she? I wonder…" He was obviously talking to himself more than me. His eyes stared at some middle distance. Then, they snapped back to my face.

"Where did you come by this?" he asked.

"I took it off a doomed man's neck in Thagoth."

"Were you near Athagos at the time? You had to have been, but how could you have been? She would have consumed you."

"She tried. She failed."

The old man looked at me with new respect. "The Flame chose well indeed, then, when it chose you. But back to the necklace. It was meant to draw Athagos to the Shadow King. Somehow, it found you instead. It must have sensed her power when you took it."

I remembered how it practically leapt into my hand when I took it from the Duke's neck. Where had the Duke gotten hold of such a thing? I'd probably never know. It didn't really matter. I had much bigger things to worry about. A dark realization came to me, and fear flowed like icy water through my body.

"So the only way to get it off is to get Athagos to put it on? But it won't let me go back to Thagoth. It's herding me. To the Shadow King. Kerf's balls!"

"What will he make of you, I wonder? He's cast his net for a goddess and caught a sneak thief. What are the chances of such a mishap?"

"Too good for my taste. What will he do if I can't avoid him?"

"He will use you. In some form or fashion, he will turn events to his advantage. It is what I excelled at. Even more than magic, it was my true Art—using others to do my will. Such is learned early when one is crippled. In order to survive, others must be coerced or convinced to do one's bidding."

"What does he want? Why does he want Athagos?"

"He wants power, my dear. He is consumed with the desire for it. Any action he takes may be attributed to that motive."

"So Athagos will give him power. How? And for what?"

"As to the how—it might be as simple as using her as an instrument of his will. Can you imagine the death goddess loose in the world, free of the restraint of Tha-Agoth? Doing the Shadow's bidding? But I think he wants her for another purpose."

"What other purpose? And why do you think so?"

"As to the what, I cannot speak with certainty. He may have worked out an alternate ritual to steal Athagos' innate abilities. Or it may be for some purpose I have not thought of. A thousand years presents opportunities and new insights. I know his will, not his thoughts."

"Why do you think he wants Athagos for something other than turning her into a weapon?" I could imagine her destroying armies, subjugating nations single-handedly. What were Holgren's arquebuses compared to that?

"He is as trapped as I ever was, dear. He cannot affect the larger world. He is chained to the spot where I was to have been resurrected as a god. It is not enough for him to send minions out into the world; he yearns to be free with a passion only the crippled can ever understand."

"Oh, I think I understand something of it." I wanted only one thing: to go home. To be free of this thousand-year-old knot of intrigue, madness, and obsession. It had nothing to do with me. The gods only knew how I'd stumbled into it.

"The will of the gods cannot be fathomed," the old man said, as if reading my thoughts, "but it is clear to me that you are here for a purpose, one of serious import. I cannot help but believe it has something to do with the Shadow King. The Flame has chosen you."

"What exactly does that mean? I've had enough mystery to last me a lifetime. Tell me."

"If I am the edge of the coin, then Flame and Shadow are the opposing faces. What good there was in me passed to the Flame, and all that was evil to the Shadow. The Flame seeks to burn away the dark. The Shadow yearns to engulf the light. The Flame chose you as its instrument."

I laughed. "Maybe I don't want to be anybody's instrument. Did anybody think of that?"

"A tool has no say in what hand wields it or how it is used."

"I'm no one's tool, old man. Not if I can help it."

He said nothing, only kept his glittering eyes on me.

"Is there anything else I need to know? How does the Flame intend to destroy the Shadow King?"

"I do not know the thoughts of either, only their general intents."

"Then I guess I'd better go to the source." I started picking my way through the corpses to the exit.

"What do you intend to do, my dear?" he called as I opened the door.

"What I do best. Survive. And I'm not your dear."

He chuckled. "One more thing, thief. You played my game, and so I will reward you with a little extra knowledge: I did not trick Athagos into betraying her brother. *She* approached *me*. What riddles might you be able to solve with that tidbit, I wonder?"

His chuckles followed me out of the room.

~ ~ ~

The Flame waited for me at the foot of the stairs. I marched toward it, building up a thunderhead of harsh words to unleash on it as I went. Before I could begin, it stopped me cold with its own words.

The Shadow King begins his assault. We must hurry. It flitted up the steps, and I followed at a run.

"You said this place was safe!" I panted.

I said it afforded an escape, of sorts. It does.

"Why did you let us get comfortable, then? Holgren and I could have been well on our way."

Your only safety lies in the destruction of the Shadow King. Only you can accomplish that. And you needed to see what you just saw and speak to the one you just spoke to.

We reached the top of the stairs, and the Flame bobbed down the corridor that led, eventually, to the great hall with its sundered roof.

"The Shadow King? You're his enemy," I said. "You destroy him. I never asked to be a hero."

Which is why you are suited for it. Hurry.

I felt the slightest trembling under my feet. A little dust began to sift down from the walls and ceiling. We rounded another corner, and ahead lay an opening to the great hall, some forty feet above its stone floor.

"What is that? Umbrals?"

No. Much worse. It is a Sending, a creature from another age the Shadow King found and allied with. It will tear these halls apart, if it must, until it finds what it seeks.

I ran up to the entry and looked out. At first, I saw nothing but stone walls, twisted stairways, and rubble. Two sets of stairs led down to the floor from my vantage point, each hugging the wall on either side of the entrance. Far to the left were the massive, black double doors. Nearer at hand to the right was the rubble mound. *Nothing unusual,* I thought, until I looked up.

Dozens of great, inky tendrils were snaking their way through the opening, feeling along the walls and the mound of rubble. The shortest was four or five times as long as me. If shadow could be made flesh, that was what these things were made of. My own flesh crawled at the sight. In a way I cannot express, I knew I looked on something wholly evil.

The thing that those tentacles were attached to began pulling its way into the opening.

A servant of the Shadow King, said the Flame as the fiend slithered its slow way down into the great hall, *but not his slave as the umbrals are. He will unleash worse things on the world in time. You will help me destroy him.*

I barely heard the words. All my attention was glued to the monstrous shape easing its way inside. Its body must have been a hundred feet long and its thin, many-jointed legs twice that. The shadowy tentacles I'd first seen sprouted from the thing's head, which was long and sleek and gleamed dully in the starlight. Its jaws were as long as I and lined with double rows of silvered teeth. A long, black, whip-like tongue unfurled and snaked this way and that, touching, tasting. I had taken it for a smaller tentacle at first. Its eyes were smoky, black orbs that ate the light.

But its body was the worst. What I took at first to be mere bumps pebbling its shadowy hide were not bumps at all. Spaced unevenly along the thing's torso were hundreds of distorted faces. As I looked on them, I realized they were all moving, screaming, in silent agony. As I watched, one of the faces bloated, swelled, and popped—and out plopped a miniature version of the fiend. It fell to the floor, shook itself, and scurried off into the deeper shadows.

"Oh, this is bad," I said. Then, I had the presence of mind to withdraw further into the corridor.

You have only the merest inkling, the Flame replied.

"What the hells are we going to do?"

There are two exits from my halls besides the opening above. One begins at the Gate below.

"Those black doors at the end of the hall?"

Yes. The other does not concern you. It is too small for you to traverse. The Sending hunts you, Amra. Or rather, it hunts the person that wears the necklace.

"It thinks I'm Athagos."

And it will not be gentle with you if it catches you. Athagos is nearly indestructible.

"Where do those double doors lead to?"

They will lead you to your fate. Hurry. You are almost out of time.

The Sending hung spider-like from the gap in the ceiling now, secured there by its long, twisted legs. Its body swayed slowly in some unfelt breeze. It seemed to be in no hurry. Another face had popped; another small nightmare had been released. I tore my eyes away from it and looked at the Flame.

"Can't you do anything?"

I am the small decent fraction of a soul twisted beyond recognition. I have survived this long only by hiding. It is you who must do what must be done. I can do little more than guide.

"But—" The Flame blinked out of existence, and Holgren pelted into the corridor, calling my name. I wondered why the Flame appeared only to me—was it only that it had been hiding for so long that it had become habit, or was there some stricture I didn't understand at play?

"Amra!" Holgren cried. "Where have you been?" He took me by the arm. "We need to go. Trouble is coming."

"It's already here." I pointed out to the monstrosity. It had settled in to birthing more nightmares. They fell from its torso by the dozen. The floor below was alive with them. Holgren looked down. Even in the gloom, I saw his face blanch.

"We've got to get out of here," he said. "There's no way we can deal with that."

That was one of the things I liked about Holgren—he wasn't one for false bravado. That sort of thing generally gets people killed.

"Our only way out is through those doors at the end of the hall," I said. "We're going to have to get around those things. Somehow."

"What? That's suicide. We'll never get past that—that nightmare."

"We have to. There's no other exit."

"How do you know that?" His eyes searched mine, brow furrowed.

"It's a long story, and we don't have time. Trust me."

"I do, but—"

"No buts. Help me figure out how we get by that thing. And all the little nightmares it's spawning."

He looked at me a little longer, his hawk-like eyes searching my face; then, he turned to the task at hand. He looked down again at what lay below. "You're the expert at stealth. What do you think our chances are of sneaking by?"

I shook my head. "I'm comfortable skulking around in shadows. Those things *are* shadows. Our chances are rotten." The miniature nightmares were everywhere now, slinking into dark hallways, slithering up and down those twisted stairwells. Gravity meant nothing to them. Half a dozen clung to the very walls and ceiling of the hall.

"Well then. If stealth won't serve, let's try diversion," he said. "Do you have a knife?"

I handed him the dagger I'd picked up in the corpse room. He took it—and then almost dropped it. He looked as if I'd handed him a pile of offal.

"Where did you get this thing?" he asked. Then, he shook his head before I could answer. "Never mind. There's no time." He squatted down and pricked his finger with the tip. Slow, fat drops welled out, more black than red in the gloom. Several fell to the floor. He smeared them into the crude outline of a man then wiped the tip of the blade and smiled up at me.

"A little trick I picked up in the Low Countries. I think you'll like it. If it works. Your turn."

"How can you perform Low Country magic?"

"My mother was a Gol-Shen witch. My father was a Gosland mage. Stick your hand out."

I was tired of blood: tired of losing it, tired of bathing in it, and tired of looking at it. But I didn't have time to grouse. I stuck out my hand and he pricked my thumb. I squeezed on it with my other hand until blood welled up.

"Careful," he said. "Don't mix it with mine."

"I thought only women were supposed to be able to perform this sort of stuff," I said as I let my blood dribble to the floor, careful to keep it away from Holgren's.

"They are, but it's more tradition than anything else. My mother wasn't terribly traditional." He used his clean hand to sketch out a female form with my blood.

"How much longer? One of those things could come in here at any time."

"If you'd stop asking questions, it would move along a bit faster."

I took the hint and shut up. He hunkered down over the blood drawings and began to rock back and forth. A strange, low keening came from his throat that I'd never heard before.

I took a step back. Low Country magic tended to be vicious, as befitted a region with a centuries-old tradition of vendetta. Whatever he was doing, he damned sure needed to hurry.

Holgren began carving the air with the dagger. At first, I didn't know what he was doing. Then, something began to form before him at the direction of the blade. Slowly, too slowly for my taste, two figures began to take shape. After a moment, I recognized Holgren's features in one and mine in the other. They were sketches at best, but they didn't have to be much more. I knew what they were now: blood dolls. Sacrifices built of blood and magic, given shape by a mage's mind, made to do one thing convincingly. Die.

As I said, Low Country magic tended to be vicious. Even purely defensive magic. Centuries of occupation by one conqueror after another had really had an effect there.

Holgren's blood doll was barely more than a scarecrow. He'd given it the merest suggestion of a face, a long hank of hair, and a dark robe. The one he made for me was a bit more. Its short, brown hair was artfully if simply arranged, and its face was free of any scar or blemish. The nose was long and straight, the almond-shaped, green eyes perfectly balanced. My own thin lips were fuller on that face, and I would have needed cosmetics to get them as red as he made them. I fingered my oft-broken nose and wondered if he were mocking me or if this was how he really saw me.

I looked away from the blood doll, uncomfortable on several levels.

"Hurry the hells up, Holgren."

Finally, he was done. He stood up and stretched and looked at his creations.

"They won't last long," he said, handing me back the knife.

"Then let's get to it."

"Step two is to divert attention from ourselves while they draw it. I've got something that would serve, a fool-the-eye, but I would need an hour or more to prepare it."

"No time for that. I've got a better idea."

"What?"

"Let's run like hell."

He smiled shakily, and I returned it.

"Ready?"

He nodded. Then said, "Not in the least."

"Send them down the right set of stairs. With a light, if you can?"

He nodded again, and the blood dolls came to life. A glowing sphere of light popped into being above the false Holgren's hand, and they both turned in unison and pelted into the hall and down the stairs. I counted to three, grabbed Holgren's arm, and took off.

Fear is a funny thing. It can kill you, but it can also keep you alive if you learn to ride it instead of fighting it. Arno taught me that. It heightens all your senses. It lends your feet wings. In its grip, time slows, and you have time to read to events that you would not have normally. Or so it seems. I should know. Fear has been a near-constant companion for much of my life.

I heard it before I saw it, just the faintest scrape on stone. We had just cleared the entryway and were taking the left-hand set of stairs in great bounds. Holgren had already pulled slightly ahead of me with those long legs of his. I spared a glance back to see how the blood dolls fared and caught a quick impression of a hundred shadows racing toward their tiny light. That's when I heard that faint scrape on stone from just above, about three feet away from my ear. I knew without thinking that not all of the monsters had taken the bait.

Before I'd even decided to, my arm shot out and plunged the dagger into the thing's head.

Would a normal blade have worked? Probably not. That one did. It still held a residue of powerful magic. Awful magic. It pierced the thing's skull as if it were an eggshell, and the creature fell from the wall to land behind me, dead. That was the good news. The bad news was that one of its tentacles brushed my hand. It was the briefest of contacts, but my whole arm went numb for a moment, and I lost the dagger. At least I was alive.

We reached the bottom of the stairs and high-tailed it toward the double doors, which stood some twenty yards away. The blood doll's light had gone out by then. It didn't matter. We were almost free. Besides the one I'd slain, there were no shadow creatures on our side of the hall that I could see.

I had forgotten the mother of all bad dreams above us.

A tentacle as wide around as a Borian pony slammed down in front of us, cutting off our route to the double doors. It could just as easily have crushed us. I guess it liked to play with its food. Holgren, just ahead of me, skidded to a halt and backed up, muttering and gesturing. I doubted whatever he was preparing would be any more effective against this thing than his previous attempts to kill the raiders.

I looked up at it. It looked down at us. With a voice like wind whistling among tombstones, it giggled.

"What's so damn funny?" I shouted. "Whatever you're going to do, do it."

"Amra—" Holgren muttered. I ignored him. Holgren wasn't much for bravado, but sometimes, it had its uses.

The tentacle coiled around the two of us, drawing tighter, threatening but not yet touching. That awful giggling continued all the while.

"Be prepared to make light," I murmured to Holgren. "Some bright light."

You ask me what I find amusing, little one? I was Sent to snare a goddess and instead find an alley rat and a hedge mage. Is that not amusing?

"Not particularly, no."

I am amused, though the master will not be. Your skulls will make fine wombs for my beautiful children.

"Out of curiosity, how does that work, that skull-womb process?"

It's quite simple, actually. I bite your heads off and eat them. You won't die though. Not immediately. My babies need a host still able to experience torment, you see.

"I do see. Thank you for clearing that up. I've got one more question if you don't mind. What blind excuse of a cross between a giant squid and a spider would have the poor taste to impregnate you? Judging by the stupidity and sheer ugliness of your children—"

With a snap, its tongue retreated into its mouth, and it lunged.

"Now, Holgren!" I screamed. I closed my eyes and waited for those silvery teeth to descend and rip my head off. I had gambled our lives on the fact that these were creatures of shadow. The spell that Holgren cast wasn't deadly. It was in fact one of the simplest spells I'd ever seen him perform. The power he invested it with, however, was awesome.

Light blossomed from his fingertips and engulfed the fiend's head, but to call it simply light is to say a sea contains a little water. It was as if a heatless sun had sprung from his outstretched hand. Closing my eyes just wasn't enough. I threw my arm over my face, and still, my eyes pained me.

The mother of monsters wasn't giggling anymore. She was shrieking. The light began to fade, and I risked a squinting glance up. She was pulling herself back out of the hall, her long, vicious head no longer visible, hidden behind the brilliance of Holgren's spell. I couldn't look at her directly.

I looked down at the floor around us and saw with satisfaction several black, shriveled husks, tentacles now only wavering piles of ash. The little ones had been more susceptible to the light.

"How long will the spell last?" I asked, surveying the damage.

"Not much longer. Hurry." His voice was strained.

We bolted toward the doors. His spell was already fading. The hall had begun to groan and tremble. The mother of shadows was going to tear the place apart.

I spared a glance back. I immediately wished I hadn't. She was thrashing through the opening above, ripping stonework away in her haste and fury. She made no sound now except for the violence of her passage. Ichor dripped from the great, black orbs that were her eyes.

We reached the doors and pushed for all we were worth. Each door was massive and made of black basalt. We groaned, sweated, cursed. Nothing, nothing—and finally, mercifully, movement. The door had moved enough for us to slip out. I grabbed Holgren's arm and yanked him through. Beyond was a cavernous darkness.

"Let's go." I started off.

"Wait," he said. "Help me close the door."

"No time. Let's move."

"I'm going to set a Binding. It's worth the delay."

"I hope you're right."

We shoved the door closed, and he worked a quiet magic. Time stretched. Impatience is hardly the word for what I felt, but railing at him would only break his concentration.

"It's done," he finally whispered. "It will buy us more time."

I didn't waste time on words. I started running. My eyes were not adjusted to the dark after Holgren's light show, but it was a huge hallway. Our footsteps and our panting echoed back from the matte black walls. It was mercifully free of obstacles, but still, one or the other of us would stumble. Holgren created another light, but it was a puny thing. I suppose it was all he could muster.

If the Sending caught us this time, we were worse than dead. And she was coming. She pounded out her fury on those doors, booming, shuddering blows that made the very air tremble. I found an extra bit of speed.

Time is impossible to measure when you're running in abject terror. The booming grew fainter after a time, until it was barely audible over our gasps. For a fractured moment, I began to think it possible the doors might hold indefinitely. Then, Holgren abused me of the notion.

"The binding weakens," he panted. "Faster, Amra." I went faster.

We didn't get much further before the doors gave. When they collapsed, her shriek echoed down the passageway before her, a chilling howl that voiced her triumph and our doom. I felt it as much as heard it, and my imagination tormented me with images of the monster and her progeny coming for us, swarming over the rubble of those giant slabs to hunt us down.

The most maddening thing was the silence. She said nothing more after that one shriek, and shadows make no sound when they move. I spared a glance back and saw a boiling darkness rushing down the tunnel toward us. It overtook Holgren and me before we'd gone three more paces, and when it did, it became near pitch black. Holgren's magelight cast no more illumination than a glowing ember.

"Just keep running," he gasped. Holgren had pulled ahead of me with those lanky legs of his, so it was him that smacked into the wall at the end of the passage. I heard the meaty thud of his body connecting with solid stone in time to pull up before I repeated his performance.

"Are you alright?" I asked.

He grunted. And I took that as a yes. I began to run my hands along the wall, praying there was a door. If not, we were finished, and the Flame had a very odd and distinctly unfunny sense of humor.

At first, I felt only stone, and panic washed over me anew. Had we missed a door or a passageway in our headlong flight? Then, my fingers brushed past stone into an opening. I explored it with blind hands and found it big enough for two abreast.

"Thank you," I whispered.

I helped Holgren to his feet and pulled him after me through the opening. The Sending at least would not be able to fit through though her children would. She would have to tear open a hole big enough for her monstrous bulk. That would take time.

I was barely a pace in when my foot encountered a step. Up, thankfully. If the stairs had led down, we would have taken a tumble and broken our necks in the dark.

I hauled Holgren up the steps, holding him by the waist and guiding him. He seemed dazed by the run-in with the wall. His light had disappeared completely.

"Faster," I urged him. "We have to go faster."

I smelled it first—that algae-ridden, vaguely fishy smell that large bodies of water tint the nearby air with. We were close to an exit and fresh water.

We were near an exit. Hope flared briefly, then died down. If it was still night, we were probably still doomed whether we made it outside or not. Daylight was our only hope.

The stairs went up and up. I could hear them, now, behind us, the faint skittering of claws on stone. I spared a glance back but of course could see nothing. I looked up—merciful gods. High above us, made small by distance, stood the faint outline of a doorway.

Fear is a powerful motivation. Fear mixed with hope becomes a grand sort of magic. I thought I had given my all before. Now, even hindered by a groggy Holgren, I fairly flew up the stairs. There was light beyond that door.

Two hundred yards or more separated us from escape. I couldn't be sure how much distance separated us from the Shadow King's creatures, but that gap was shrinking by the second. I kept my eyes on the approaching exit and did not look back again. Gray dawn filtered through the doorway, and as we approached, it illuminated our steps. I was already going as fast as I could, but the simple fact that I could see where I placed my feet was a relief. We narrowed the distance, second by second, step by step.

I could hear them swarming up the stairs now, and it was only with an act of will that I kept from looking back the way we'd come. Either we'd make it or we wouldn't. I refused to waste any time looking back.

"Come on, partner. Not far now. Hurry. Please hurry, Holgren." He did his staggering best. I could hear the wind on the water above now. I could also hear our pursuers scrambling up the steps, near enough to hit with a cast dagger if I still had one.

My head was just level with the top of the stairs when the first tentacle wrapped itself around my boot heel and sent me sprawling. Instinctively, I kicked out and connected with nothing. Another wrapped itself around my leg and a third. I tried to pull myself up the stairs but was yanked back.

"Go!" I screamed at Holgren. He stood there a few steps above me, dazed confusion showing on his face. He didn't move. I felt a burning indignation for him at that—that he was going to die because he'd addled his brains running blindly into a wall. What an idiotic way to go.

And then the sun rose over the horizon, and the first glorious shafts of golden light found their way into the stairwell. The tentacles that trapped me fell away. A putrid, burning stench flooded the stairwell. I was free.

I gained my feet, grabbed Holgren's hand, and stumbled out to gaze on the most beautiful sunrise I'd ever laid eyes on.

CHAPTER 7

The first thing I saw on exiting was the sun rising over a distant line of low, brown mountains. Even without the added spice of a sudden reprieve from death, it would have been a beautiful sight. As it was, tears welled up at the sheer grandeur of it. I wiped them away with the back of a hand.

We stood on a stone ledge about five feet wide and twenty long. Both the landing and the stair's exit were hewn from the face of a cliff whose rough, gray bulk rose thirty feet or more above us and twenty down. The landing ended in sets of stairs down on either end.

In front of and below us, the rays of the rising sun gilded the rippling waters of a vast lake. It stretched on for several miles to the east and was perhaps a mile wide from north to south at its narrowest point.

I helped Holgren to a sitting position against the cliff face. The blow he'd taken to the head worried me. They could be dangerous. I should know, having practically made a career of them.

"Holgren. Stay awake now. You need to stay awake."

"All right," he said, eyes squinted shut. I pried open one lid and then the other and checked the size of his pupils. Sometimes, with a bad head injury, differently sized pupils meant serious damage. Or so I had been told. Holgren's seemed to be fine. He pushed my hand away from his face and put his own hands over his eyes.

"Don't go to sleep, partner."

"I won't. I can't. I'm in too much pain."

"Good. I'm going to take a look around. Don't wander off."

"Ha," he said in a pained voice. If he was feeling up to even weak sarcasm, I assumed he would be all right. I gave his shoulder a brief squeeze and got up to see what I could.

I found an ancient stone quay at the base of the stairs, crumbling and algae-slick. There were no boats of course. I looked to the right and left, hoping for some sort of path to shore. All I found was cliff wall for a hundred yards in either direction, slime-coated near the waterline. To the left, where the cliff curled away and diminished, jumbled rocks met the shoreline. To the right, the cliff fell away even more. A marshy area filled with waxy reeds stretched off for an uncertain distance beyond it. No telling where the marsh ended and solid ground began.

I supposed it would be possible to swim to either side, but there was a fundamental problem with the idea. I'd never learned how to swim. Even if I'd wanted to, there had been no one to teach me.

I had spent much of my childhood in Hardside, a seaside slum just outside Bellarius proper. Most working men there were fishermen. To my knowledge, there isn't a fisherman or sailor alive on the Dragonsea who knows how to swim. Better a quick death by drowning, it is reasoned, than a slow one which will almost certainly end in having your legs ripped off by one or more of the gray urdus or the pheckla that infest those waters. They don't call it the Dragonsea for nothing. So. Swimming. Not one of my many skills.

I sighed, scratched my head, and climbed the stairs again to consult with my partner. I tried not to think about what fate held in store for us after night fell, but it was impossible not to. Be it the shadow raiders or the mother of nightmares and her children, we would be overtaken in short order and then—I remembered that hideous talking chest cavity of the shadow raider and the agonized faces on the torso of the spidery shadow fiend. I felt despair begin to creep over me.

"One thing at a time," I whispered and took long, deep breaths. The first order of business would be getting off this cliff and onto solid ground. After that, whatever happened, happened. Maybe Holgren would be able to think of something.

I climbed back up the stairs and sat down next to him. He had moved back to lean against the cliff face. One hand shaded his eyes; the other picked at a ragged edge of his cloak. Cloak—I had lost mine somewhere, some when. Which meant I'd lost the gems that had been sewn into the hem as well. An inane thought bubbled up to the surface of my mind, and I laughed out loud.

"I could use a little humor too," Holgren grated.

"It's nothing. Just a stupid thought, not really funny at all."

"Share it with me anyway."

"I've lost the Duke's gems. We'll have to call the whole adventure off. You know I don't work without pay."

He smiled. "You call what you do working?"

I grabbed his hand and squeezed. Strained and stilted as it was, it was good to banter with him. When I tried to pull my hand away, he held on to it more tightly.

"Amra," he began, but I cut him off.

"I know, Holgren. But I make it a practice never to become involved with business associates."

"Don't joke, woman. This is difficult for me. And I may not get the chance to say it again."

"Holgren—"

"No. Let me say what I have to say." He shifted, sighed, and proceeded not to say anything. I knew him well enough to know he was organizing his words just so. There was no point trying to rush him.

I studied his face and realized for the first time—allowed myself to realize for the first time—how truly beautiful he was. Not handsome. Handsome is a matter of looks and dress. Lanky, scarecrow Holgren might be considered good-looking by some, but handsome was a stretch. But he was beautiful in ways I could hardly find words for. I was vaguely aware that it had something to do with the way he moved his hands, the way he smelled, the emphasis he would invariably put on certain words, and a thousand other things. It scared me to death, that realization. I waited for him to speak with a strange mixture of terror and anticipation.

"I don't know if you remember," he said, voice low and serious, "but last year, I lent you twenty marks—"

I punched him dead in the ribs.

"Ow! All right, all right! Mercy, Amra," he cried, managing both to smile and grimace as he hugged his ribs.

"You bastard," I growled.

"Do I have to say it?" he asked.

I just glared at him.

"Very well. I'll say it. I love you."

A dozen things to say occurred to me ranging from sarcastic to syrupy. I settled on kissing him.

I wouldn't say I was comfortable with my body. I have an endless list of complaints. No one had ever mistaken me for a raving beauty, nor would they ever. A boy, yes—and I've exploited that fact on numerous occasions when it served me.

I suppose that would have been the perfect time, there on that ledge with the sun rising and the water lapping and a gentle breeze and all. The odds of our ever getting a second chance to make love were worse than slim. But I wasn't ready. I just wasn't, and the truth was I didn't know if I'd ever be.

When I pulled away from him, more abruptly than I meant to, he seemed to sense something of that. He reached out gentle fingers, and I guided them to my lips, kissed them.

"It's all right, Amra. Whatever comes, it's all right."

And despite it all, I actually believed him a little. He drew me into an embrace, and we sat that way for a time, me with my head on his chest, him resting his chin on my head.

"Tell me we're going to make it through this."

"We will, somehow. There has to be a way. We'll find it. I promise." He sighed. "It's my fault we're in this mess to begin with, so I'll get us out."

"I chose to help you find Thagoth. I knew there were risks involved. Neither of us could have imagined the things that have happened since. Not the Flame, not the Shadow King—say, I haven't told you all that's happened."

I sat up and proceeded to tell him all that had transpired, leaving out the nature of the trial the Flame had put me through. I had no desire to relive that. He stopped me only a few times during my retelling to clarify a point or describe something in greater detail.

When I was done, the sun stood another finger-width above the horizon, and my throat ached a little from talking so much.

"So that's what happened to Hluria. The histories say little more than that it descended into chaos shortly after the Sorcerer King's victory over Thagoth."

"But is there anything in all I've said that will help us?"

"Well, it's encouraging that the Shadow King is tethered to one location. I do wish you'd thought to ask where."

"I can't think of everything. Besides, I've got a feeling we'll find out soon enough. But back to my question. Can you think of anything in what I've told you to give us some sort of advantage?"

"I don't know, Amra. Nothing that I can see right off. But something may come. Let me think on it a while."

I suppose it was too much to hope for that he could find some way out of our doom just for my wishing it. Still, it was disappointing. I got up and stretched and looked out at the glinting, rippling waters of the lake. It reminded me a bit of the bay of Lucernis…on the infrequent occasion I'd seen it in the morning light. It didn't really look like it much at all, but it was the largest body of water I'd seen in the better part of a year.

I missed Lucernis. I missed decent food and the public baths and wine and my bed and—was that a boat out there in the distance?

At the same time I thought I saw something, Holgren called out.

"I sense a mage coming this way. He isn't bothering to damp his powers, and they are considerable.”

“I think I see who you’re talking about. There’s a boat out there on the lake, coming toward us. I can’t make out much more. Is he actively casting?”

“No, not that I can tell.”

“Well, what do you want to do, partner?”

He struggled to his feet. “I say we go down and greet our visitor. Perhaps he holds a key to our escape somehow.”

“I’m not counting on that.”

“Let’s just count on each other, then, and see what this new turn of events might mean to us.”

“Fine, but I don’t have the energy to battle another minion of evil right now. If he’s come to do unspeakable things to us, you’re going to have to deal with it on your own.”

“As you wish. Help me down the stairs, would you? I’m still a bit dizzy.”

I led him down the stairs and out onto the quay. “Mind your step,” I told him. “It’s damned slippery out here."

“I’m fine, Amra.”

I squeezed his hand. We stood that way, shoulder to shoulder, waiting for the mage to arrive. I tracked the slow approach of the boat with my eyes, Holgren with the inner sight of the mage-born.

Slowly, it drew closer. After a time, I could tell it was a long, narrow punt. A robed figure poled it across the lake with practiced ease and deceptive speed. That lake was big and, if a boat could be poled across the length of it, fairly shallow. I realized then that I probably could have made the shore after all. Too late now.

As the boat glided closer, I felt the hairs on the back of my neck begin to stand up. “Are you sure he isn’t casting?” I asked in a low tone. Sound can travel a surprising distance over water.

“Quite sure. This mage holds more power than any I’ve ever seen. Much more than me, I’m afraid.”

“Well. I’ve never met a mage yet who was immune to a knife in the throat.” Of course, I didn’t happen to *have* a knife just at that moment.

“Let’s try to stay positive until circumstances force us to become otherwise, shall we?”

“All right. I’ll play nice.”

As the boat drew even closer, I noticed the pole used to propel it was three times my length, which made me feel better about not trying for the shore. I also noticed that the mage was a woman, which surprised me.

It’s not that I’d never heard of female mages, but I had never actually seen one. They were rare unless you counted bloodwitches. Women excelled in blood magic. Low Country women were accorded an extra measure of civility based on that fact alone—you just never knew who you might be insulting. The one I'd met in Lucernis the previous year hadn't done me any harm, though she'd told me some things about my future that I hadn't liked. Things that seemed to be coming true, more or less.

This was no Low Country mage, though, blood or otherwise. She was as brown as a nut, and her hair was straight and dark. As she drew closer, I could tell her eyes were a brown that could almost be called black. Such a combination of physical features was as rare in the Low Countries as ice in summer.

Just where she was from, I couldn’t say. Somewhere far to the east of the Dragonsea, most likely.

When she had approached to within fifty feet or so, she pushed off with the pole one last time and lay it down in the punt at an incline, wet end on the boat’s bottom, dry end sticking out the back, rising at a slight angle above the water. She took a wide stance in the center of the punt. The boat slowed as it approached the quay. When it came abreast of us, it was moving at the pace of a leisurely stroll. She hopped out onto the slick, stone quay a few feet away from us, lithe as a dancer, then stuck one foot back out over the water and stopped the punt.

"Good morning," she said. "I've come to collect you."

"Who the hells are you?" I asked. Holgren tutted me.

"Forgive me," she said with false heartiness. "Goodness only knows what you must be thinking. First thing's first. I am Ruiqi. I'm afraid I only know you by inference. I suppose there could be others about that match your descriptions, but it's highly unlikely, no? They don't call these the Empty Lands for nothing."

Her name pretty much confirmed my ideas as to her origins. It had a distinctly Chagan flavor.

"What exactly do you want?" I asked.

"As I said, I'm here to collect you. If you prefer not to accompany me, you're certainly welcome to wander about on your own, but I'm sure you're well aware of the dangers once night falls."

"Where is it you intend to convey us, Ruiqi?" asked Holgren. Mages tend to talk like that in each other's company, I've noticed. Won't bother with one word if three will do and won't use a little one if they can think of a big one to take its place.

"Why, to my master of course. I'd think that was obvious."

"I'll bite," I said. "Who's your master?"

She looked at me as an adult would a particularly slow child.

"The Shadow King, my dear. The Shadow King."

It's probably a good thing I didn't have a knife. I settled for glaring at her. It wasn't very satisfying.

"He's sent me to convey his sincerest apologies for the treatment you've received thus far. It has been a case of mistaken identity."

"You mean he collared me instead of Athagos."

"Oh. You've worked that out, have you?" Her tone rode the edge of condescension.

"Indeed," Holgren replied.

"Then you know how dangerous my master's intended quarry is and why he felt it necessary to employ the methods he has to secure her. Empires have risen and fallen in the vast span of time he has waited for her."

"History concerns us less than future events, Ruiqi," said Holgren. "You've acknowledged the fact that we are not your master's quarry. What does he want with us then?"

"The Shadow King wishes to discuss a matter with you. It involves the necklace your companion wears."

"If he wants this Kerf-damned necklace back, I'd be more than happy to give it to him. In fact, why don't you take it to him? Just show me how to get it off, and I'll hand it right over."

"I'm afraid it isn't that simple."

It never is.

"I cannot free you of the necklace," she continued. "Certain conditions must be met. Come with me, and all will be made plain. The Shadow King wishes you no harm."

"No? You could have fooled me. What were those raiders doing two nights ago, giving in to high spirits? And the Sending? I suppose she was just trying to throw a scare into us. Do me a favor, and don't bother to lie. You're no good at it."

"As I said, my master expected another to be wearing the necklace. The umbrals were on…other business when they came across you and recognized you as the necklace bearer."

"What about the other one? She knew I wasn't Athagos. She didn't care."

"Shemrang is often willful. She will be castigated." She raised her hands in a conciliatory gesture. "Truly, my master wishes neither of you harm, but he requires the necklace you wear. If you do not accompany me, you will leave him little choice but to compel you to come to him. He has sent me as proof of his desire to avoid such measures."

"He's already tried to 'compel' us. It didn't work out quite the way he planned, did it?"

She gave us both appraising looks. "Somehow, I doubt you'll be able to resist his invitation again come nightfall. Be sensible. Why take a hard road when there is a much easier route? In the end, the necklace will draw you to him no matter what. That is its function."

I didn't trust her, and I damn sure didn't trust her master, but she was right. The necklace wasn't going to let me go free. If the beasties of the night didn't get me, I'd end up going to him on my own. He had me whether he wanted me or not. It was only a matter of time. Kerf's crooked staff.

"Fine," I said. "Go. Wait here for me, Holgren. I'll be back as soon as I can." No reason for him to stick his head in the noose. I was the one wearing the necklace.

"Don't even think it. Where you go, I go."

"I don't want to argue about this, Holgren—"

"Then don't. Just accept the fact that I'm coming with you because I am."

I pulled him aside. Ruiqi turned her back to our whispered conference with a smirk.

"That's stupid," I hissed. "How are you going to rescue me from the clutches of evil if evil is clutching you as well?"

"Don't be so melodramatic. If anything happens, our best chance of dealing with it is together. I wasn't able to be there for you in Thagoth. I will be for this. Nothing you say will sway me."

"You had a good excuse, being dead and all. All right, fine. I could use the company. She gets on my nerves."

He smiled. "I don't think you're her favorite either. Try not to antagonize her. She's too powerful."

"I promise nothing."

"You've decided then," she said. "Good. Time flies, and my master waits."

"Keeps you on a short leash, does he? Keep your robe on. We're coming."

I helped Holgren to the punt, and he settled in the center while she held it steady. I would have liked to have sat in the back to keep an eye on her, but that was where she poled from.

When we were settled, she pushed off, turned the punt around with practiced ease, and set out for the far side of the lake and the Shadow King. The lake was larger than it looked from the cliff. Ruiqi poled us along for nearly an hour before we caught sight of the far shore.

During the ride, I decided to do a little digging.

"Ruiqi. Can I ask you a question?"

"If you must."

"From everything I've heard, this Shadow King isn't a particularly nice individual. Why do you serve him?"

"For power of course."

"I see." Though I didn't. Not really. "Care to elaborate?"

"No."

"Suit yourself." I looked out into the green-brown water and at the wooded shoreline sliding by at a deceptively lazy pace.

"So how'd you get so good at boating?"

"Practice."

"Where?"

She cast a suspicious look my way. "Why would you want to know?"

"I'm working on my conversational skills. Holgren seems to think I can be a little abrasive when I first meet someone." He grunted behind me.

"Imagine that," she said.

"So?"

"So what?"

"So where did you learn to pole a punt?"

I didn't think she would answer, but she did after a fashion.

"On a lake much like this one. Like this one, that lake was slowly being strangled by plants and accumulated silt. In a century or so, this will all be marsh most likely."

"What a pleasant thought."

"Change is nature's way. What cannot or will not adapt disappears, to be replaced by something more able to survive. Or something more willing. You would do well to remember that when you meet the Shadow King."

"I'll keep it in mind."

"*Listen to me*," she hissed in an entirely different tone, one filled with pain, anger, and not a little fear.

I whipped around to see her face twisted in some inner agony. Her body, too, was twisted to one side, abnormally so. She looked like a completely different woman.

"*Listen to me. Don't anger him. Don't balk him. You* will *live to regret it.*" And just like that, she stood up straight again and snapped back to the snide, overconfident woman we'd first encountered. I just stared at her, open-mouthed.

"What are you looking at?" she asked, brow furrowed.

"Nothing. Sorry." I turned back around and looked out at the water, shaken. Something was very wrong with our gondolier. Whatever power she'd gained from the Shadow King I was willing to bet came with some serious tradeoffs. I didn't feel sorry for her, but I found it hard to keep my animosity sharp. I didn't feel like baiting her anymore.

I kept quiet the rest of the trip. So did everybody else. Including her second voice, thankfully.

I don't know what I expected to find on the far side of the lake—something akin to the death lands, perhaps, all twisted foliage and vile monsters. The reality was far different and far more dangerous in its innocuousness.

We came to a simple wooden dock with a dirt path that led off through knee-high grass into a stand of evergreens. Sparrows flitted and chirped in the grass and the trees. It would have been the perfect spot to put up a cabin. There was nothing to hint at the power that resided beyond.

"Nice place. Yours?"

"No."

She let the boat ground itself on the muddy shore next to the dock.

"Follow the path. A meal has been prepared for you. I have been instructed to assure you it isn't poisoned or drugged. My master will speak with you after nightfall."

"Are you coming with us?" Holgren asked.

"No. I have other business to attend to. Just follow the path."

When I got Holgren and myself on to the muddy shore, she pushed off again. I didn't wave good-bye. I don't think her feelings were hurt.

"Well, partner, let's go climb inside the dragon's mouth," I said as I led him off toward the path.

"We're well inside the mouth. Let's go see what the belly of the beast looks like."

"How's your head?"

"A little better, not much. Hurts like all hells. Hard to concentrate. I'm barely up to counting fingers or casting most spells."

"Which is different front your normal state in what way?"

"I should turn you into a toad for that."

"You couldn't turn a profit on Silk Street wearing nothing but a bow."

~ ~ ~

The path led us, eventually, to a pretty little sun-dappled glade. A low block of some glassy, black stone stood in the center of it, and food had been piled high atop it. Fish, fowl, red meat, fruits, vegetables, bleached bread, fresh butter, flagons of wine—there was enough food for a dozen people. I figured I could handle my half, but Holgren had always been a picky eater.

"Well, he's laid out a hearty last meal."

"Indeed."

"What do you think?"

"My head thinks we'd be fools to touch it. My stomach has a conflicting opinion."

"I know what you mean." I looked at all that food, and my stomach rumbled as if on cue. "Oh well," I muttered and tore off a drumstick.

"So much for caution," he said and joined me.

I ate until I was in danger of becoming sick. Six months starving in Thagoth followed by a month of soldier's rations had left me virtually incapable of moderation. That meal was good.

Holgren showed more restraint. To him, food was little more than fuel, which is an attitude I can't really understand. Good cooking is as much of an art as sculpture or painting.

When I was done, I lay back on the grass in the early afternoon light and waited for the first pangs of poison to shoot through my gut. Holgren and I made small talk. I looked around the glade and felt a measure of contentment. I suppose that was the intended effect, and I suppose, too, that I should have mistrusted it. But a person can only go through so much horror and suffering and face so much death before she begins to become inured to it. At that moment, I'd had my fill.

A nonchalant sort of fatalism had overtaken me. I had a full belly. I had Holgren. I had a short space where nothing was trying to kill me or worse. And there was nowhere to run. The necklace held me as surely as the bars of any prison. All I could do was wait for events to unfold and keep my eyes open for any opportunity that presented itself. Most luck is made.

Afternoon passed to evening. Holgren lay napping on the grass beside me, and fireflies began to appear in the gloom beneath the trees. It was a pleasant sight, reminding me of early childhood summers spent with my grandmother before she'd died, when my father had still been able to get caravan work—

Fireflies? In winter?

"Holgren, wake up. Something's happening." I nudged him in the ribs, and he came up quick and clear-headed.

"Powerful magic is at work."

I looked around, and the trees were melting away like phantoms. The lights I had taken at first for fireflies were expanding, brightening, and aligning themselves along intricate geometric lines. They bled into one another until solid planes of glowing, green light came into being. Walls formed hundreds of feet high. Even the meadow grass retreated back into the ground and was replaced by some hard, flat surface. As these new surroundings took shape, that eerie, green light faded to be replaced by weak starshine. The walls took on the appearance of tangible shadows. Precise as every angle was, there still seemed to be something organic about the structure in a way I couldn't pin down.

When everything stopped shifting, we stood in the courtyard of a huge fortress. Walls surrounded us on three sides. The fourth side of the courtyard, behind the obsidian block, was taken up by a massive archway, beyond which lay only a shadowy void. It was the entrance to a massive structure that stretched up and blotted out the stars. I craned my head back and saw a confusing welter of walls and windows and eaves and high above them a thin spire that seemed to pierce the sky itself. No human hands could have built such an edifice.

Welcome to Shadowfall, said a rich, disembodied voice. It was familiar. It was a younger version of the voice the Sorcerer King's crippled husk had owned.

Ruiqi will be joining us momentarily, the voice continued. *Please enter, and make yourselves comfortable.*

I glanced at Holgren. His face was unreadable. I took hold of his shoulder, and we went through the arch.

I thought I had experienced discomfort when I entered the gate to Thagoth that Holgren had conjured up months before. This was something else again. It wasn't pain, but was as if every particle of my body was taken apart, studied, sniffed over, tasted, and put back together in a fraction of a second. It was over almost before it began. As I stepped through the archway to the room beyond, I felt an impulse to scream that dissipated before I had a chance to act on it.

The room was much like any drawing room with a hearth in one corner containing a small, flickering fire. Two upholstered chairs were drawn up beside it. I glanced back at the archway, and it was now the size of a normal door. Beyond, I could see nothing but shadows.

I apologize for the brief discomfort, but I find such measures save time. Now, I know just who—and what—partakes of my hospitality. Welcome, Amra, Flame-chosen. Welcome, Holgren, resurrected mage. Please take a seat. We have much to discuss.

Holgren and I seated ourselves.

"Why don't you join us?" I asked. "I like to see who I'm talking to."

Your partner spoke closer to the truth than you guessed when he jested about being in the belly of the beast. Rather than being in the room with you, it would be closer to the truth to say I am *the room. I can, however, create a manifestation if it will make you more comfortable.*

"It doesn't really matter to me, I suppose. And I doubt it makes much difference to Holgren. Though I thought you wicked types liked to make people uncomfortable as a general rule."

Have you ever considered the notion that every so-called hero is actually a villain from someone's perspective? The reverse also applies, as in any equation.

"I don't tend to think of such things. I'm a more practical person. I try not to let the larger issues distract me."

The flames in the hearth sort of rippled and twisted, and out of them stepped a man of medium height. He was naked and bald. Those same tattoos adorned his skull. Shadows sloughed off him like dead skin and drifted like ash to the floor at his feet.

He was handsome in a boyish sort of way though his eyes were two dead things that reflected no light. I sort of had to squint to see the resemblance, but he could have been a younger, able-bodied version of the Sorcerer King.

"I understand just what you mean, Amra." He raised a finger absently, and another chair appeared. He sat down and thankfully crossed his legs.

"I too am what you might call goal-oriented," he said. "Which gives me hope that we can come to an understanding this evening. But here is Ruiqi now with refreshments."

She came in the room through the arch, still wearing her ochre robe, carrying a tray on which rested a flagon of wine and two small, crystal glasses. She knelt between Holgren and me, eyes downcast. Nothing showed now of the haughty, powerful mage from this morning. The tray she held trembled slightly, and sweat beaded on her upper lip though the room was cool despite the fire.

"Not right now, thank you," I said. Holgren shook his head. She rose and, walking backward, retreated to a far corner where she stood and held the tray with white-knuckled hands. She kept her eyes firmly on the floor.

Was this some sort of subtle statement on the Shadow King's part? If he was trying to intimidate me, it was pointless. I already feared him as much as I feared anything. I did feel an odd stab of pity for Ruiqi, though, to see her so cowed. I suppressed it. I had my own problems.

"We needn't waste much time, I shouldn't think," said the Shadow King. "You know my interest in you has to do with the necklace. You know its intended recipient was Athagos. Let's discuss what I require from you."

"I told her, and I'll tell you, nothing would make me happier than for you to take this necklace back. You'll be happy, I'll be happy, and we can all go about our business. I don't see what there is to discuss. Just take it."

"In a perfect world, that would be precisely what I would do. Alas, we do not live in a perfect world—not yet, at least. There are two ways to remove the necklace, Amra. The first requires your death."

"I can't say I like that one much at all."

"I'd assumed as much. That fact alone should make the alternative more palatable."

"What is the alternative?" Holgren asked.

"Amra must return to Thagoth and place the slave chain on the neck of the one it was intended for."

"Let me just work this out aloud," I said. "You made the necklace, but you can't take it off me?"

"No. I only guided the making of the slave chain. I did not fashion it myself. If I had, we would not be having this conversation as the chain would fully acquiesce to my will."

"May I ask who did make it?" Holgren asked.

"The Duke of Viborg. A talented man, given his limitations."

"Ah. I see. Thank you."

I wanted to get up and pace. I didn't. "So you can either kill me and get somebody else to cart it back to Thagoth—which I have to assume isn't your first choice or you wouldn't bother to get all chatty—or I go back to that hell-hole myself and get Athagos to try it on for size."

"Essentially. I have enough control over the Duke's creation to redirect its focus and allow you to return to Thagoth."

"It all sounds very plausible, doesn't it? Except that I'm actually a dead woman either way. I only survived Athagos last time by sheer chance."

"You are a resourceful woman, Amra. You'll think of something. Or not. Honestly, it is of no concern to me so long as Athagos dons the chain."

"It's not your problem, in other words. What if—hypothetically, you understand—I refuse to go?"

He smiled, but it didn't reach his eyes. They were lumps of coal.

"There would be nothing hypothetical about your death, I assure you. You would still bear the necklace to its destination. Believe me when I tell you death is no bar to my will."

"You'll forgive me for saying so, but where I come from, dead is dead."

"Ruiqi. Be so kind as to show our guests what I mean."

I didn't like the sound of that at all. "That won't be necessary, really. I have a vivid imagination."

"I find object lessons powerful motivators."

Ruiqi set down the tray and stepped closer, to within arm's reach. She kept her eyes cast to the floor. Slowly, she began to pull her robe over her head. Delicate ankles were exposed, then graceful, muscular calves, dark skin glowing like burnished copper in the fire's light. The hem of her robe rose higher to expose knees and thighs, as graceful and toned as a dancer's or an acrobat's.

It was just above her groin that her body changed from most men's dream to anyone's nightmare. As she slipped the robe over her head and let it fall to the floor, I couldn't help but stare in sick fascination at all the damage. The woman had no right to be walking around or poling a punt or even breathing, mage or no.

Something had torn great chunks from her torso. She had been partially gutted. Blood-slick lengths of intestines—what remained of her intestines, I should say—lay coiled in the depression just above her hips, held in place by Kerf-only-knows what force. All flesh on the left side of her abdomen was gone from ribs to navel. I could just see the tips of the vertebrae of her lower spine peeking out, orange in the fire's light. Her ribcage wasn't much better. It had been cracked open and a fist-sized section removed, exposing splintered ribs and her purplish, beating heart.

"Ruiqi has, in the past, sought to cross me in certain matters," the Shadow King said. "She has learned the wisdom of obedience. Haven't you?"

"I have, master," she replied.

"You may dress now, and leave us."

"Thank you, master." There was no hiding the tone of relief in her voice. She put the robe on quickly but left the room with a measured gait. I suppose her master disapproved of haste.

"You will return to Thagoth, Amra, and collar the death goddess. If you manage to survive, I wish you a long life. Our business will have been concluded. Have you any further questions?"

"Why do you want Athagos?" I asked.

"I'm afraid you wouldn't understand."

"I would," said Holgren.

"Indeed, you might. My motivations should be the least of your concerns, however."

Holgren nodded. "As you say."

I stood up and grabbed Holgren's arm, fairly yanking him out of his chair. "Well, I suppose we should be on our way. It's a long trip back to Thagoth, and I'm sure you'd like to have Athagos here as soon as possible, whatever you want her for. Will you be provisioning us? We lost everything in your creatures' attack."

I wanted to get the hell away from him—it, whatever—as soon as humanly possible before my smart mouth earned me missing chunks of my anatomy. Just thinking about it made me shudder.

"Provisions won't be necessary. I shall open a gate for you."

"That's great, but what about after? If we manage to survive securing Athagos for you, we'll be hard-pressed to make it home."

"In your own words, that's not my problem."

I had nothing to say to that. Ruiqi came back in then and stood just inside the archway with her eyes downcast. "All is prepared," she said in a subdued voice. "Follow."

I hooked an arm through Holgren's and followed her out. My mind was already turning to the question of surviving Athagos. I had to find some way to deafen myself again, preferably in a temporary sort of way. I weighed the chances of simply stuffing my ears with cotton or wax. It was a hell of a chance to take, and I'd only get one shot. Perhaps Holgren had some magical way to achieve my deafening. Once we were well away from the Shadow King, we were going to need a planning session.

Ruiqi led us back through the arch, this time without the disconcerting side effects, into the courtyard beyond. The Shadow King was already there, standing off to one side. A circle of ghostly blue fire about eight feet in diameter ringed the glassy, black block now.

"Holgren, please enter the circle." The Shadow's voice was cool, a trifle too nonchalant. It rang alarms in me.

"This isn't anything like what Holgren did to summon up the last gate."

"The observations of a magic-poor thief do not interest me."

"Then let me rephrase—what the hell is going on?"

Ruiqi blanched. Her eyes grew wide and she shook her head. *Don't,* she mouthed.

Again, the Shadow smiled. His eyes weren't made of coal anymore though. More like lightless pits of doom.

"Enter the circle, Holgren. I will not tell you again."

Holgren leaned into me. "We're nearly free," he murmured. "Whatever will happen, will happen. I love you." And with that, he walked forward until he crossed over into the circle. He brushed against the obsidian block. And began to scream.

"You motherless—" I screamed and rushed to Holgren and found myself suddenly on the ground. The circle of flame had repelled me. I tried again. I couldn't cross the boundary of the circle. My body refused to. I could reach my hand up to the circle but could not force it past the edge of the ghostly fire, couldn't break the plane no matter how hard I tried.

Holgren fell to the ground as I watched and curled up there in pain next to the block.

"I have other endeavors on which to spend my power," the Shadow said. "The circle makes his abilities available to me to open the gate. The side effect is painful and unpleasant."

"Then hurry up and open it."

"Perhaps you haven't noticed, but it is I who commands here."

"Fine. Please open the gate!"

"You can do better than that, Amra."

"Tell me what you want me to say, and I'll say it!"

Holgren was going into convulsions on the floor. Foamy spittle was collecting at the corner of his mouth. His head smacked the block with every spastic jerk.

"Draw your example from Ruiqi," he said.

"Please open the gate…master." I forced the word out. What was a word in comparison to the agony Holgren was going through? Words are cheap.

"Much better, Amra. Much better though I might question your sincerity. Don't feel as though you've compromised any vestiges of honor or dignity in acknowledging my station. Once Athagos comes to me, the entire world will bend to my will. You have only done what everyone will in time."

"Whatever you say. Master. Please stop. You're killing him. How can he help me in getting Athagos for you if he's dead?"

"Holgren will not be joining you in Thagoth." The circle of flame sputtered out, and Holgren's convulsions subsided. I ran to his slack body and cradled his head in my lap. He was still breathing.

A pearlescent gate opened in the center of the courtyard a few feet away from us.

"I would never kill a member of my *khordun*," the Shadow King said. "Not in any permanent sense. If you doubt me, ask Ruiqi. Holgren will go a long way in replacing the Duke. His death was a vexing inconvenience and one I've learned from. Holgren will remain here."

The bastard had taken Holgren against his will. He would be a slave just as much as Ruiqi, and if the husk had been telling the truth, they would eventually become mindless, will-less vessels for the Shadow King to draw power from. Ruiqi seemed well on her way already.

I remembered the ghost formed from corpse-dust in the husk's throne room and his sighing, *"Master, someone has come."* Not even death would free Holgren from the *khordun*.

It was then I knew I would have to destroy the Shadow King, whatever the cost. Not for the Flame, not for any god, but for Holgren. With that certainty came a cold inner peace and a clarity of purpose that allowed me to see what I needed to do.

It might not work. It probably wouldn't work, but it was our only chance for survival. I looked up at the Shadow King with tears in my eyes. Those I didn't have to fake.

"Master, I would like to say good-bye to him before I leave. Please. I'm begging you." This one wanted slaves, wanted power. Wanted to show his power, I hoped.

He smiled again, waved an indulgent hand. "As you wish."

I felt Holgren stir. His eyes fluttered open, and a groan escaped his lips. "Oh, gods," he whispered and began to shudder. I tried to haul Holgren to his feet, but he was practically dead weight. I had to get him standing if what I planned had any chance of success.

"Ruiqi, will you help?"

She hesitated then, when her master didn't object, bobbed her head and helped pull him upright. I worked it to where we staggered a pace or two closer to the gate. I didn't know if it would be enough.

"Hurry up. I waste power keeping the gate open while you dally."

"Yes, master. Just one last embrace." I put my hands to his face and kissed him, thoroughly. Ruiqi looked away. I wrapped my arms tightly around his waist and looked into his eyes and saw a pain there that had nothing to do with his body.

"Say good-bye, Holgren," I whispered. Then with every scrap of speed and strength I had, I flung us both toward the pearlescent, glowing gate.

The Shadow King's scream of rage rang across the courtyard. Holgren shrieked in time. The gate shrank even as we hurtled toward it.

CHAPTER 8

When Holgren opened the first gate to Thagoth, we went through one at a time. When we plummeted through this one together, I found out why.

Stepping through that first gate had been unpleasant. To disappear from one place and reappear in another the next instant wasn't a natural act, and my body had known it. This time, both Holgren and I occupied the same non-space, the same space between here and there, the same fissure in reality. We shared an intimacy that living things were not meant to know. There are no reference points, nothing to proceed from. It was as if our very souls mixed and intermingled. I saw—I felt—just who he was, his own essence, whatever made him *him*. And he saw and felt me. For that brief eternity, we became each other. It was terrifying and elating. Then it was over.

We hit the ground hard with Holgren on top of me. The familiar, putrid stench of the death lands forced its way into my nostrils. I suppressed my gag reflex, breathed through my mouth. I pushed Holgren off me and looked back to see if anything was coming after us.

Something was.

Through the rapidly dwindling gate hurtled Ruiqi, a look of abject terror on her face. Was she trying to escape the Shadow King, or had she been sent to do his bidding? I wished that I had a knife.

Most of her made it. The gate contracted down to nothing just after her knees cleared. The double amputation was instantaneous. Her scream was a twin of the one Holgren had uttered months before in this very spot.

She fell to the ground next to us and writhed and shrieked in the dark. Blood spurted from the stumps of her legs, dark gouts spraying the hideous foliage around us as she twisted in agony. I saw the pale, fleshy flowers of a thorny shrub bend down to catch her blood.

I couldn't leave her like that. She had tried to warn me of what the Shadow King was capable of, had tried to help in her own way. However she had fallen under his sway, she had obviously tried to balk his will more than once with horrifying results. I didn't trust her or even like her, but walking away from her was beyond me.

"Help me out if you can, Holgren. We've got to get tourniquets on her legs. Rip some strips from your cloak. I'll find sticks or something to twist 'em with."

"Alright." His voice was weak but certain. He began to rip at his threadbare cloak. I searched around the area with blind hands, trying to find a stick or even a rock, something to tighten the strips of cloth around her stumps and stop the bleeding. I came across a moldering piece of canvas.

It was the remains of the pack I'd thrown down months ago in my haste to drag Holgren to safety. I searched some more with greater hope.

The contents were scattered far and wide. I found the shovel I'd missed while burying Holgren and, after a few seconds, a pickax. I rushed back over to them.

"Is she still breathing?" I asked while I fit the shovel's handle in the loop that Holgren had left in the bandage on her right leg.

"Yes. She's passed out, thankfully. Give me the pickax." I did, and he pulled the remains of her legs further apart so that our unwieldy tools wouldn't collide as we cranked down on the bleeding stumps.

The gushing slowed to a trickle as the strips of cloth bit cruelly into the flesh just above her knees.

"We'll have to secure them now. I didn't tear enough strips off."

"Give me your cloak." He handed it over. He held on to the handle of the pickax, and I sat on the shovel's handle and tore more strips from the remains of his cloak, starting them with my teeth when they were too stubborn to be torn by hand. Then one leg at a time, we secured the handles to her thighs.

I stood up and looked at our makeshift physicking. The effect was unsettling. Where her lower legs should have been, the shovel's blade and the head of the pickax stood out. But I thought it had saved her life for the moment. If she could die at all.

"Let's get someplace more comfortable," I said. "Necklace or no, I don't like being out here."

"It isn't my favorite spot either," said Holgren.

Together, we managed to hoist her up and carry her past that abrupt demarcation between the death lands and the ruins without jostling her too badly. I directed Holgren to the nearby garden where I'd buried him and spent my first night in Thagoth.

We laid her flat on the grass and proceeded with the grim task of bandaging her stumps. The remains of Holgren's cloak served. As we padded each stump with cloth and secured them tightly to the remains of her legs, I wondered if we had truly done her a favor in saving her life. When it was finished, I sat down with my back against the garden's yew tree and rested for a moment. I looked around at my surroundings, at Holgren's crumbling, open grave. A thought came to me, and I smiled. History wasn't repeating itself exactly, but it had begun to rhyme after a fashion.

Would Ruiqi die as Holgren had? Could she die? I wondered if we'd eventually have to put her in the grave I'd dug for Holgren. At least I'd have a shovel this time instead of making do with a bowl and a knife.

A knife.

"I'll be right back," I said to Holgren and walked back toward the death lands.

"Where are you going?"

"To get something I left here months ago. And to gather firewood. We're going to have to cauterize her wounds."

"What a pleasant thought."

It was still sunk deep in the trunk of the tree out in the death lands where I'd pinned the thing that had killed Holgren. I pried my best blade loose, using both hands and eventually a foot for leverage. I'd paid dearly for that knife, had it made and weighted specifically for my hand.

The tree had begun to grow around the blade. The corpse of the little beastie was long gone, or else I would have taken its skull to Holgren as a souvenir. He was always one for picking up odd, sometimes disturbing items.

The knife was in remarkably good shape save for a bit of rust and discoloration.

Maybe it was foolish, even pointless considering the types of horrors I'd seen and was likely to encounter, but just holding that blade in my hand made me feel better. It was more than a weapon. It was a link to life before Thagoth. I stuck it back into its long-empty sheath and walked unmolested back out of the death lands, into Thagoth. The necklace had its uses.

While I was out, I gathered deadwood for a fire and swung by the remains of the Duke's camp to gather up some of the supplies I'd abandoned there when I left the first time. The Duke's silk tent still stood in the center of the square though it had begun to sag. Various supplies were scattered all around, tossed about by more than a month's worth of weather. It was a forlorn scene.

It was also dangerously near the Tabernacle gates and Athagos, but Ruiqi needed blankets. I tried not to think about those stumps too much. We had probably saved her life for the moment, but I had no idea whether she would survive the night. We could only cauterize the stumps to prevent further bleeding and infection. And if we got the chance, we could try to secure some of Tha-Agoth's blood and treat her with it.

I knew a sufficient dose would probably regenerate a limb—when I'd pulled Holgren's corpse out of the ground, not much flesh had remained. Hell, it might even heal her other wounds. The ones inflicted by the Shadow King.

Getting it would be the problem. And I still didn't know what her intentions were toward us. We might have to kill her if it came down to it. I didn't like the thought of saving someone's life only to turn around and take it, but I would if she gave me cause. If she was killable.

If not, I supposed we could hack her into lots of little pieces, as revolting as that would be.

No, I didn't want to kill her, and I didn't want her to die for a number of reasons, not the least of which was I had a feeling in my gut that she was a key to our survival. Her knowledge alone made it worth saving her. Who else could we question as to the Shadow King's capabilities, his plans, his weaknesses? Forewarned is forearmed and all that.

I loaded up the supplies in an oilskin as quickly and silently as I could in the dark and lugged them back to the garden with such thoughts for company. When I returned, Holgren was asleep, curled up on his side like a child. It had been a long time since either of us had had any real rest. I felt my own exhaustion, looking at him. The business of survival had kept it at bay.

I decided to let him sleep until I'd built up the wood for a fire. Then, I'd need him to start it and hold her down while I did the deed.

I eased my bundle to the ground and pulled out a blanket, covered him with it, and turned to get another for Ruiqi.

"Why did you save me?" Her voice was a strengthless whisper. I pulled out another blanket for her and a stack of tarps to elevate her legs with.

"Why?" she asked again.

"Because I couldn't just watch you die." I moved over to her and put the blanket around her. I avoided looking at her legs and didn't want to look her in the eyes. It didn't leave much to look at.

"I've done nothing to you. Why don't you let me die?"

"Is that what you want? To die?"

"Look at me," she hissed. "Wouldn't you?"

"There's an outside chance we can get your legs healed and even the other damage. I don't promise anything."

"Don't you understand? This is the only place in the world I can slip his yoke. I don't want to be healed. I want to die here, outside his power and beyond his call. I want it to end here while something still remains of me. Before I become a mindless reserve of power for him. Before he breaks the world to his will."

I lifted her bloody stumps up as gently as I could and positioned the bundle of tarps under them. It must have been painful, but she gave no sign. I suppose she was used to enduring pain. When I had accomplished that, I turned to face her.

"Now you listen to me," I said. "You aren't taking the easy way out. I don't know how you came to be with that monster, but you've helped him in his plans, willingly or no. You've incurred a responsibility, a debt. You know what the Shadow King is, what he plans, what he is capable of. Whether you like it or not, it's your responsibility to help stop him. You can die when you've helped me accomplish that, not before."

"You've no idea what you're talking about. He cannot be stopped. To even think of opposing him is madness."

"You see? It's thinking like that that got you where you are." I pointed to Holgren, rage building inside me. "Look at him. He did nothing to deserve being roped in by the Shadow King, but the same fate waits for him as waits for you. I won't have it. He doesn't even want to be a mage for Kerf's sake. You *will* help me figure out a way out of this doom, you selfish, self-centered bitch, or I'll show you what it really means to want to die. Do we understand each other?"

She blinked at me, and I saw realization come to her through her agony and misery.

"You're serious, aren't you? You are actually going to set your will against the Shadow King."

"I'm not going to give Holgren up to that bastard."

"You love him enough for that. Remarkable. Stupid, but remarkable."

"Just get some rest if you can. After I get a fire going, we're going to have to cauterize your wounds. Prepare yourself as best you can. I haven't got anything to dull the pain."

"Pain and I are intimates."

I looked at her and could think of nothing to say. I turned away and lay down next to Holgren, wanting just to be close to him for a few moments before I woke him and had him start the fire. My tinderbox was long gone.

What we had experienced going through the Gate—until now, I hadn't had time to really think about it. But looking at him, I remembered and felt closer to him than I'd ever felt to anyone, any time. It was a pale shadow of the actual experience, remembering, but it was more real to me even still than the chill winter wind or the susurrus of the wind in the yew tree or even the breath in my body. I bent down to fit my body against his, stealthily so as not to wake him.

I needn't have bothered. He woke as soon as I touched him.

"Amra?" He sat up and looked at me, and I saw reflected in his eyes some of what I felt tempered by an internal pain. I knew that pain. It had been mine as well for the short, unending moment we'd been connected by the gate.

"Go to sleep for a while more. I'll wake you in a few minutes."

"No. I meant to wait for you. I just nodded off. We need to talk."

"It'll keep. You need rest."

"Amra. The Shadow King. He—"

"He forced you to become part of his *khordun*. I know."

"A *khordun*," he said, voice flat. "Such a simple word for what he did. Such a bland one for that particular kind of rape and enslavement. Such a thing has not been accomplished, or even attempted, for hundreds of years."

"That's not exactly true though, is it?" I said, looking over at Ruiqi. "He's revived the practice."

"Unfortunately. I was taken wholly unaware. It was an…invasive procedure. He has complete control of my powers outside the bounds of Thagoth, I'm afraid. And every time I use them, be it at his will or my own. I will fall further and further under his sway. It will erode my willpower, sap my sense of self, and leave me a gibbering creature fit only to do his bidding." He shook his head and gave me a half-wry, half-bitter smile. "My powers have grown considerably though."

"I know. Just being next to you has the hairs on the back of my neck at attention." I rubbed at them with one hand, absently.

"I think I understand why he has no power here," I continued. "It's the same reason the death lands only encroach so far. Tha-Agoth's power keeps them and the Shadow King at arm's length. It's why he needed the Duke and now me to get Athagos for him." I pointed a thumb at Ruiqi, who was now sleeping fitfully nearby. "But why, if that's so, doesn't she die of her original wounds? She certainly wants to end it."

"It is not the Shadow King's power that sustains her but her own. He has etched his will into her deeply enough that she cannot help but follow his order to live." He shook his head. "She is trapped in the prison of her flesh, and her will is not wholly her own. It grieves me. And it frightens me as well. I do not want to share her fate."

"Then we have to figure out a way to destroy the Shadow King. It's as simple as that."

"I hate to say this, Amra, but perhaps it would be best if we never left Thagoth. If we deny the Shadow King what he wants, namely Athagos, we deny him the means to do whatever it is he so desperately wants to do."

"We can't stay here forever. The food won't hold out."

"I know."

Did he mean what I thought he meant? I looked into his face and saw that he did. "Kerf's grizzled beard, Holgren, you're as bad as her. Why do you people think death is any solution? It's not. It's the end to any possibility of winning through!"

"I don't want to die. If we free Athagos, however, the Shadow King will gain powers never before unleashed on the world. I don't know exactly how he will accomplish it, but I know without a doubt he's found some way to harness Athagos' powers and direct them at his whim. He will turn the world into a charnel house, and whatever remains standing will survive only to serve him. I sensed some of that when he took me. His vision of the future is as bad as any version of hell you can imagine. You heard him—death is no bar to his will. He will destroy and enslave, and there will be no power in the world great enough to stop him."

"You don't know that. The old Sorcerer King failed once."

"The Shadow King is not the Sorcerer King. And he's had a thousand years to think about what went wrong and correct the original mistake."

"Even if you're right, dying here will only delay him. He'll lure another mage to him as he did the Duke and Ruiqi, I suppose, then fashion another necklace, and the whole damned thing will only start over again with no one to oppose him."

"Magic may fade completely before he is able to accomplish such a feat."

"Are you willing to bet our lives on that? Are you willing to bet the fate of the world? You told me months ago that it was better to die trying to alter your fate than just to die giving in to it. Are you telling me now, after having died, that you'd rather do that again than try to get free of the Shadow King?"

He thought on it for a while, brow furrowed. "No," he finally said. "I suppose not."

"Good. The next person I hear talking about dying gets a kick in the head. I'm sick of it."

He gave me a wry grin. Obviously, he thought I was joking.

"So be it. Now that we've decided we want to live, the first order of business is figuring out how to accomplish it."

"We won't do it by hiding in Thagoth; that's for damn sure. We have to get out of here and destroy the Shadow King."

"Excellent goal. How do we accomplish it?"

"I'm hoping our maimed friend over there will give us a clue." I turned to look at our now-sleeping patient. I prayed she had some kind of an answer because the sole one I was able to think of could only be called desperate.

"Like I said, it'll keep. But her legs won't much longer. I need you to start me a fire, partner."

He did, and when the knife blade was as hot as it was going to get, he woke her and secured her legs.

Intimate with pain or no, her screams filled the night until she passed out. It was not pleasant. I had to heat the blade a dozen times. When it was over, I was more tired than I can ever remember being. I curled up next to Holgren and went to sleep to the rhythm of his deep, regular breathing. Thankfully, the smell of his particular, wonderful scent replaced the sickly-sweet stench of her charred flesh.

~ ~ ~

If I had hoped to get any immediate answers out of Ruiqi, I was disappointed. Soundlessly and without either of us noticing, she had somehow disappeared while we slept. My cursing at her absence woke Holgren.

"She can't have gotten far," I said. "Come on; let's go find her." I started off toward the death lands, figuring she'd crawled that way like a wounded animal to have those hideous creatures destroy her.

Holgren laid a hand on my arm. "Not that way," he said. "Over there. I sense her presence in that direction." And he pointed west, toward the Tabernacle.

"Kerf's crooked crutch! Hurry, before she manages to crawl inside." I set out at a dead run, Holgren trailing behind. How big a lead did she have? How fast could she be dragging herself? We might come on her just as Athagos began to consume her. If that happened, we'd be dead as well. Damn Ruiqi for putting us in greater danger.

What remained of Thagoth's streets radiated out from two squares on either end of the Tabernacle, something like a double spider web. There were only two main thoroughfares that ran straight from those squares to the edges of the death lands: one north and one south. We were at the extreme eastern edge of what remained of the city.

I didn't bother to keep to the streets. I led Holgren through broken buildings and over mounds of rubble, through smashed courtyards and roofless towers on a direct route to the Tabernacle. I'd learned those old stone bones better than the city of my birth during the half-year I'd spent there.

As we approached the Tabernacle's high wall, I slowed and motioned Holgren to do the same. "Where is she?" I whispered, and he pointed dead at the Tabernacle.

"Damn her." I moved to the edge of the wall and took a peek. The gates stood slightly ajar. There Ruiqi lay, half in the Tabernacle grounds. She was not moving. I pulled back and tried to think of what to do.

She might already be dead, but Athagos hadn't gotten to her if she was. She wasn't a deflated skin sack. I thought long and hard about leaving her there. If she was already dead, I would risk myself needlessly trying to save her. If she was alive, then saving was the last thing she wanted.

But I didn't really care what she wanted. There was a chance she knew something that would help us destroy the Shadow King. Was it important enough to risk my life trying to save her, that chance? I looked over at Holgren and decided it was.

"Is there any way to make someone temporarily deaf?" I asked him.

His brow furrowed. "I've never tried. I suppose I might be able to, given time…"

"Time we don't have. Listen to me. If something happens, don't come after me. There'll be nothing you can do. I mean it. You'll be the only one left to oppose the Shadow King. Promise me. Promise, Holgren."

I didn't think he would. He was silent for so long. Finally, he nodded.

"Good." I leaned over and kissed him. Then, before I could change my mind, I jumped up and sprinted for the Tabernacle gates.

As I ran toward her, I took in the situation as best I could. The gates were open outward into the square though they were only made to open inward. There was about a three-foot gap between the gates. The right-hand one hung at a slightly drunken angle. The massive bronze hinges had pulled away from the rotting wood of the gates when Athagos had hurled me through them. Ruiqi was on her side in the gap between them, one hand curled up near her face and the other stretched forward, into the Tabernacle grounds. Blood had begun to pool around the stumps of her legs. She had lost her bandages along the way, dragging them across loose cobbles. Twin trails of blood stretched back out of sight toward camp.

But she still seemed to be breathing. I had to give her credit; she was as stubborn in her way as I was in mine.

I didn't want Athagos to even suspect we were there. She couldn't leave the temple grounds, but she damn sure could draw us to her. I didn't know what her range was and didn't want to find out. I brushed aside the memory of Gnarri deflating like a speared puffer fish and Athagos' mad smile. It wouldn't be my fate. Not if I could help it.

I altered my route, angling away from the narrow opening in the gates just a bit so as not to present a target to anything inside. I was waiting for that bone-chilling shriek of Athagos' to catch me in mid-stride, Waiting for it to strike me down and take control of my body and deliver me to her so that I could be sucked dry. Some people say fear of the unknown is the worst. They haven't seen anything truly worth fearing.

It wasn't an eternity exactly, but that run across the square seemed to take a very long time indeed. When I reached the opened door, I was panting and sweating. I was a foot or so away from Ruiqi's prone body. I took a second to steady my breath and listen for any sign of movement on the other side. I heard nothing.

The partially opened gate, while affording some extra cover, would also make it more difficult to pull her back from the grounds. The angle was wrong. I'd have to twist around the gate to get a solid grip on her. Moving to the other side would make it easier, but it would also, however briefly, present a silhouette, a moving target. I decided to risk it.

Heart in my throat, I moved as quickly and quietly as I could to the other side of Ruiqi. No unearthly wail turned my bones to porridge. I bent down, grabbed a double handful of her robe, and yanked her back away from the entrance. She was surprisingly heavy for someone missing as much of their body as she was. I didn't get her clear of the entrance on the first pull. I mouthed a silent curse and yanked again, more forcefully. This time, all but her hand cleared the threshold. A final tug and she was completely in the square. I gave a quiet sigh of relief. Too soon as it turned out.

You have returned, Amra, sooner than I had hoped. And with a companion or two.

Tha-Agoth. My heart skipped a beat then started thumping madly. I hadn't thought he could make contact with me so far away from his prison.

"Just a little visit," I whispered as I hoisted Ruiqi on my back. "I'm not staying long."

You have reconsidered my offer?

I shifted the unconscious mage around until I got her arms flopped over my shoulders. Then, I got a good grip on her lower arms and teetered to my feet.

"I'm entertaining the possibility of helping you." I said. "Don't pressure me, and stay out of my mind, and maybe we can work a deal." I staggered across the square toward Holgren.

As you wish.

"Swear you'll stay out of my mind, Tha-Agoth. You know I hate it."

I will not tamper with your mind, Amra, nor go digging through your memories. That I swear. But I cannot communicate with you without making contact with your mind.

"I suppose that will just have to be good enough."

Return to the square when you are prepared to talk. I will be waiting.

"I know you will be. Now go away."

Silence. I prayed Tha-Agoth wouldn't go hunting around in my mind. His sister may have betrayed him, but I was willing to bet he wouldn't look kindly on us sending her off to the Shadow King. If he saw in my thoughts what I intended to do—I didn't know what he was capable of, and I didn't want to find out. Not under those circumstances.

Holgren met me a few yards away from the edge of the square. Together, we hauled Ruiqi out of sight of the Tabernacle, and I let her drop to the street more roughly than I intended. I didn't feel much guilt. She had put us in stupid, unnecessary danger. I sat down, put my hands on my knees, and took deep breaths, resting and trying to regain some calm.

"I sensed something," said Holgren, "some power there when you were bringing her back."

"Tha-Agoth. I'll tell you about it. Not here."

He nodded, gestured toward Ruiqi. "Ready?"

"I suppose." I hauled myself to my feet.

"Remarkable, the kind of willpower it must have taken to crawl so far." He grabbed her under her arms. I got a backward grip on her legs, and we heaved her up and started back toward camp.

"Sure," I panted, "give me the messy end."

"We can switch if you'd like."

"No. This end is lighter. I'll take the tradeoff."

We toted her back to camp and treated her wounds again as well as we could. They would probably become infected. It would be a terrible way to die. After we'd done what we could, I secured her to the tree with a length of rope salvaged from the Duke's camp. I didn't want her wandering off again. If she decided to use magic—well, Holgren was more than a match for her now though that kind of pissing contest would only benefit the Shadow King in the end.

I decided to worry only about the things I could do something about. Magic wasn't one of them. Breakfast was. I looked up at the sky; the sun had barely risen two fingers from the time we'd woken. Had it only been an hour or so? It seemed much longer.

"Well, partner," I said. "I guess it's time you sampled the fine cuisine Thagoth has to offer."

"Lovely," he said. "Do you need help?"

"No, you keep an eye on her. This won't take long. Not much of a menu."

"Tell me about Tha-Agoth when you come back."

"I will, but I want to talk to Ruiqi first."

~ ~ ~

"I owe you six months' worth of meals," he said over a breakfast of dates that were well past their prime. I'd decided not to bother digging up any grubs. He wasn't hungry enough yet, and I was in no hurry to reacquaint myself with their taste or texture. I'd passed on breakfast entirely, in fact. My last encounter with dates had left a vivid, lasting impression on memory and body. When I got hungry enough, I knew where the grubs congregated. I was willing to put that off pretty much indefinitely. The bitter nuts I'd been harvesting when the Duke showed up, I was holding in reserve. What was left of them might have to last a while.

"Six months of *good* meals."

He looked up at me and smiled. Then, he turned his attention back to the rotten dates. His smile faltered as he looked down at his less than appetizing breakfast. I think one had a worm in it.

"It helps if you close your eyes and try not to breathe through your nose," I suggested.

"Does it?"

"Not much but some. It could be worse. At least dates don't squirm."

"This one here does."

"Think of it as a two-course meal then."

I caught motion out of the corner of my eye. Ruiqi was stirring.

"I'll just go have a chat with her. Enjoy your breakfast." I rose and gave his shoulder a brief touch. He grunted noncommittally and poked at one of the dates with a forefinger. I don't believe I'd ever actually seen him look glum before that. I couldn't help but smile. Many's the time I'd wished he was alive and suffering what I was suffering during my first stay in Thagoth. Sometimes, wishes come true.

Would Ruiqi's? I sat down next to her on the cold grass, just looking at her for a time. Her hair was in her face but did not obscure the distant, pained expression there. She was lost in some internal hell. I don't think she even noticed me until I brushed the hair away from her face. Then, she jerked away and cringed.

"How did you end up with the Shadow King?" I asked.

"I have a right to die," she spat.

"I agree. No one should have to live forever if they don't want to. Especially not as a slave."

"Then why don't you let me die?"

"Because I need you. I need your knowledge. You had a hand in setting all this in motion, and now, you have a responsibility to help us stop it."

"I didn't do anything to you. Or him."

"You didn't try to stop it from happening either."

"I would have been punished."

"That doesn't free you of the responsibility."

She began to tremble. Tears welled up in her eyes. "I will never be free of responsibility. Never. Until I die. Duty. Oh, gods." She dissolved into tears then and a sort of keening. I was fairly certain she was losing her mind. It wasn't pleasant to witness.

"Amra," said Holgren, "leave her be for now."

"I will if she answers just a few more questions." If I waited, I was afraid she might be too far gone to answer.

"Ruiqi. Tell me something that will help me defeat the Shadow King."

"It is impossible."

"I refuse to believe that. He has to have some sort of weakness. We know he has trouble operating during the day. We know he is confined somehow to the area he called Shadowfall. How can we use that to our advantage? Give me something, Ruiqi. Tell me where he and his creatures go during the day."

"The umbrals bury themselves. Shemrang has many hiding places—anywhere the sun cannot touch. The mountains to the east of Shadowfall are riddled with caves."

"What about the Shadow King? Where does he go when the sun comes up?"

"He doesn't go anywhere. He cannot. Not until he subdues Athagos. He can only command his creatures and send his will out into the world to affect events indirectly."

"What do you mean?"

"He manipulates events, actions. Subtly, so subtly that you think it is your own idea, to go one way and not another. To take a ship to the Wild Shore instead of trekking across wilderness. To take a mountain trail instead of a forest path. All the while, you believe you're on a trail of your choosing. And then you're standing in front of his altar, and he is offering you refreshment and rest from your journey. He's offering you power to destroy your enemies. Immortality. A chance to remake the world. You see your hand reaching out to touch his black prison. You think it is your own will moving your hand, but is it? Is it really? Ask your lover if it was his choice to be snared."

"It was not my choice." Holgren had come up behind me. I'd been concentrating on her tale. I hadn't noticed. He sat down beside me.

"No one would choose to become part of a *khordun*, especially not with such a beast," he continued. "Not the renegade apprentice of a murdered master and certainly not an adept of the Order of the Dawn. That's what you are, aren't you?"

Even I had heard of the Order. Powerful mages bound to serve the throne of Chagul. Aridhall Flamehand had decimated them centuries before in open battle, but that was Aridhall Flamehand. The stuff that legends were made of.

Ruiqi shook her head. "What I was makes no difference. Now, I am a slave. You say no one would choose such a fate, but you are wrong. The Duke of Viborg did. The fool actually believed he could pit his will against the Shadow King. Use him to gain power. He was allowed to think they were equals, as he had great skill in fashioning artifacts."

"The Duke is dead, and no one is mourning his loss. You two are still alive. I intend to keep it that way. Tell me something I can *use*. He has to have some sort of weakness. What about that stone block? Is that what he is tied to?"

"I don't know."

"I think you do. Is that why you were punished—because you tried to destroy him? Did you try to destroy that block?"

"Leave me alone!" She curled up into a ball, face buried in her hands. I had pushed her too far. I looked at Holgren, and he shook his head. I sighed.

"I wish I knew more about how the original ceremony was supposed to work," he said quietly. "What is the stone's significance? Why is the Shadow King tied to that particular area?"

"It was where the Sorcerer King was supposed to be resurrected. Or so he said."

"That's odd. Not in the Flame's halls?"

"Not from what I was told."

"Let's try to reconstruct the events. The Sorcerer King convinces Athagos to slay her brother somehow—"

"By piercing him through his heart with a sixty-foot rod made of sky-metal, to be exact. But he says it was her idea, not his."

"Be that as it may, it was somehow supposed to supply the Sorcerer King with the element necessary to transform him into an immortal, all-powerful being. The ceremony takes place in his sanctum and involves the members of his *khordun* committing ritual suicide. He is expecting to be reborn on the other side of the lake, miles away from his sanctum. In that spot is an obsidian block or altar."

"Well, the husk didn't have a mark on him. He wasn't killing himself. Maybe he intended to go to the block later to complete the ceremony."

"Perhaps." He picked at the grass as he spoke, brow furrowed. "Athagos fails to kill her brother, pinning him to his own altar for an age instead. He is unable to break free of the rod that pierces him. Athagos is driven insane—though not necessarily by the act. The Sorcerer King's ceremony is botched, and instead of being transformed into some sort of god, he is split into three separate entities: the Flame, the Shadow King, and the physical husk."

"Well, you've summed it up nicely, but how does it help us?"

"You said the Flame told you he was the part that was discarded in the attempt, correct?" I nodded.

"Somehow, the old sorcerer was trying to mirror effects. A sort of grand scale sympathetic magic. Tha-Agoth was to die; what was to become the Flame was to be discarded. The deaths of his khordun would supply an enormous surge in raw power to work with for a brief few moments. But was it more than that? Was it somehow meant to attract or mesh with Athagos' need to kill?"

"Death stead," said Ruiqi, voice raw, much to our astonishment. She turned to look at Holgren.

"What?"

"The death stead. An ancient ritual. No one of the Order has performed it in centuries. No one has had the power. It is a way for a mage to send his spirit out, to draw back the spirit of one who has just died. It kills the mage."

"You think the old sorcerer killed his *khordun* to work a version of this 'death stead' ritual?" I asked. "What for?"

"To guide Tha-Agoth's soul to the block!" said Holgren. "He was going to trap it there and use it somehow to further his ends. You're right, Ruiqi. I believe we're on to something."

"Tha-Agoth didn't die though." I'm good at pointing out the obvious.

"Exactly. The ceremony must have required a soul to inhabit the block. The Sorcerer King had already laid the groundwork of the transformation—he was going to forfeit one part of his soul anyway, the part that became the Flame. What was left was what became the Shadow King, and it was sucked into the prison prepared for Tha-Agoth."

"So we need to destroy that black block."

Ruiqi made a rasping, choking sound that I recognized after a second as laughter.

"What's so funny?" I asked her.

"Ask him." I turned to look at Holgren.

"That block isn't just stone. Layer upon layer of protective spells have been placed on it. I know of no force in the world that could even mar its surface."

"How do you know this?"

"I tried when the Shadow King took me. I hurled every scrap of power I had at it. It was like throwing a twig at Havak's Wall. If destroying that block is the answer, then there is no answer."

"Just because you couldn't do it using the Art doesn't mean it can't be done. Or if we can't destroy it, we could try hauling it off during the day, dump it in the lake—"

"You asked how I received my wounds," said Ruiqi. "I will tell you. I tried destroying it both with magic and without. It amused him. I failed. And was punished."

I thought about it. I tried to think of some other option, but it seemed there was none. No matter what, the Shadow King had to be destroyed, and desperate situations call for drastic measures. I resigned myself to the only course of action available, much as I didn't want to. I could see no other way.

"That black block is the key," I said. "I know it is. If we can't destroy it, then we're just going to have to enlist someone who can. I don't think he's going to like our methods though."

"There's no mage alive today powerful enough to contend with the Shadow King," said Holgren. "Besides, we're trapped here."

"Not a mage," I said. "A god. Tha-Agoth. Start working on a way to deafen me, Holgren. We're going to send Athagos to the Shadow King. Then, we're going to send her brother after her."

CHAPTER 9

"You want to free Athagos *and* Tha-Agoth. Do you really think it wise?" Holgren was looking at me as if I were talking nonsense.

"No. I don't. Truth be told, I think Tha-Agoth is as bad in his way as the Shadow King. But we don't really have a choice. Once we release Athagos, we lose our only way out of Thagoth, namely the necklace. She isn't going to let us stroll along with her through the death lands. She'll most likely try to hunt us down. The only safe place will be in Tha-Agoth's chamber. Only he has the power to keep her at bay." I raked my fingers through my filthy hair and continued.

"He is also the only being I know who's powerful enough to take on the Shadow King. And honestly, given the choice between a world ruled by Tha-Agoth or one ruined by the Shadow King, I choose Tha-Agoth. At least his vision for the future doesn't include death and destruction—that I'm aware of. It may not come to that. They might destroy each other and leave the world to itself."

"That's wishful thinking at best." Holgren drummed his fingers on his thigh. "We're meddling with forces far more powerful than any that walk the face of the world today, hoping to manipulate them into doing what we want. There's no guarantee we won't make matters far, far worse in doing so. Is this really the right thing to do, Amra? I just don't know."

"I don't know either. I really don't see how things can be worse than the Shadow King ruling the world, but I suppose it's possible. Let's look at it this way though: Have you got a better idea?"

He pursed his lips, shook his head. Those fingers kept drumming though.

"All right, then. Maybe Ruiqi will help you figure out a way to keep Athagos from sucking me dry while I collar her. Remember, it's her voice that is her weapon. I'd rather not be permanently deafened, but I'll take it if there's no other choice." I was hoping that perhaps, if Ruiqi had some task to occupy her, she would stop trying to kill herself for a few minutes. If this worked, I could get her the blood that would save her life and heal her wounds. Then, she could do what she pleased. If that was suicide, I couldn't stop her. I hoped that with a whole body, she'd see there were benefits to living.

"Ruiqi?" Holgren said. "Will you help?"

She had her eyes closed. She took a deep breath and exhaled slowly. "This is madness," she said. It was something like her original voice now. Confident, even a little arrogant. I took it as a good sign.

"So it's madness. So what?"

"You've no idea of the true nature of Tha-Agoth, do you? His sister did not try to destroy him on a lark, you know."

"I'm sure he has character flaws. I can't imagine they're any worse than the Shadow King's."

She had nothing to say to that.

"So answer the question. Can you help Holgren?"

"Perhaps. Either we can deafen you or silence Athagos. Actually, a combination of effects is the better route. It affords a greater chance for success."

"How do you propose to silence her? Get anywhere near her, and she has you. She took a score of men at once, marched them to her one at a time like marionettes, and sucked them dry. She's death on two legs."

"And I am the legless, undying thing. We are a fitting match."

"Are you trying to get at something, Ruiqi?"

She looked at me. "I will help you, but in return, you must let me die." I started shaking my head, and she raised her hand. "Death is my only escape. I choose to die at her hands. In doing so, I promise I will aid your plans."

"No. Absolutely not," I said, but she wasn't listening.

"Holgren will help me prepare. When Athagos takes me, my death will trigger a spell that we will have prepared, one that will incapacitate her for a short span if all goes well. It will give you time to place the necklace on her and escape to Tha-Agoth's temple. It is the safest way."

"It's murder."

"You asked for my help. You insist I have a duty to discharge, a debt to pay. I have helped you as I can, and I am willing to help you further in this. But I have a right to die as I see fit. I can do nothing more for you. This last act will serve both our purposes."

"Holgren, tell her it's not going to happen." I looked at him and saw from his expression he wasn't going to tell her any such thing.

"I think she's right, Amra. She's done all she can. To force her to continue living strays from good intentions into enmity."

"You can't mean that!"

"I'm afraid I do. Even fully healed, her will would not be her own outside the confines of Thagoth. She's been under the Shadow King's rule for too long; she would be a tool forced to commit acts she abhors. If Ruiqi chooses to defy the Shadow King by dying, I believe it is her right." Holgren put a hand on my knee, and I brushed it aside.

"It's gutless cowardice," I said.

"Call it what you want; it is my choice." She pulled herself to a sitting position. "I will find a way to free myself one way or another."

"Fine. You two work on the plans for the execution. I'm taking a walk. I'm not interested." I got up and walked away toward the ruins.

"Amra. Please." Holgren caught up to me and put a hand on my arm. I shook it off.

"This goes against my very nature, Holgren. You know that more than anyone."

How could he not know? I had lived through things that would—had—killed others more capable than me only because I refused to give up, to give in. Survival was ingrained in me. The experience we'd shared in the gate had shown him that.

"What is right for you isn't right for everyone. There are some things more important than survival to some people."

"This goes a long way from surviving or not surviving. It's murder."

"You're wrong. I love you for wanting to save her, but you're wrong. At worst, it's sacrifice; at best, it's a release for her. And it isn't your choice. It is Ruiqi's."

"Call it whatever you want, Holgren. The fact remains that if we follow this plan, she's going to die. Instead of trying to stop her or talk her out of it, we're going to help her do it. You might not think of it as murder, and she might want nothing else. Think about this, Holgren; we're going to let Athagos suck her very soul from her body. You don't know what that means. I do, damn it. I'd rather help her slit her wrists than watch a repeat performance."

He had no idea what it was like. Neither of them did. "If you'd seen what Athagos is capable of, what's going to happen when Athagos takes her, you'd both be a damn sight less glib about it."

"Glib is far from accurate, Amra, and you know it. Don't you see? This is the only sure way for her to be released. She hasn't died from the wounds inflicted by the Shadow King, and she's not going to die from the loss of her legs either even if they putrefy. Lopping her head off probably wouldn't kill her. The Shadow King commanded her to live, and that's exactly what she'll do to the limits of her power. Only Athagos' embrace will set her free."

"Some freedom, to be consumed. Sure, she'll be free of the Shadow King, but her soul will be eaten. Think about that for a minute." I crossed my arms and fought for calm. It was elusive.

"Maybe you're right," I continued. "It doesn't really matter though, does it? Right or wrong, it's going to happen whatever I say. So go on back and prepare. Just leave me alone right now. I'll be back."

"As you wish." The look on his face was sorrowful. Even as angry as I was, it pained me to see him so. I stalked off into the ruins, feeling an ache in my heart that I couldn't fully explain.

~ ~ ~

The highest vantage point in Thagoth was atop a crumbling, rust-colored, roofless tower on the far north side of the city a block away from the surrounding death lands. I climbed to the top floor and sat in the wide oval of the west-facing window. With feet dangling, I looked out at the nightmare landscape the Sorcerer King had wrought. It wasn't any prettier from five stories up. How much damage hate and envy could do, given sufficient power.

Maybe Holgren was right. Maybe the world would be better off without magic, but I suspected that power would just take some other form. The effects of its abuse would remain about the same: death for the powerless in some form or fashion. Humanity was all too predictable.

Be it spells or swords or some improved arquebus, the mighty would take by force what they wanted and leave bodies in their wake. It sort of made my profession look noble by comparison. I've never taken anything from someone who had less than I did.

I cast my sight out beyond the death lands, to the edge of the valley, to the horizon and the wispy tendrils of clouds moving away to the north. It was one of those bright winter days that are deceptively sunny. Step into shadow, and you could feel the cold sucking at your body heat. It was going to be a frigid night. It might even snow. I hadn't seen snow in years—it rarely got cold enough in Lucernis, which, while not one of the reasons I'd moved there in the first place, was one of the reasons I'd stayed.

I was angry at Holgren for agreeing to help Ruiqi kill herself and that we were going to profit from her death. Sacrifice was idiocy. There was nothing noble or glorious about it. But what was I to do? Follow her through life making sure she never got the chance to kill herself? Keep all sharp things away from her? Tie her down, force-feed her? If she was going to do it, no measure I took would be enough in the long run. The chances of any of us making it through the next day or so were awful anyway.

It didn't make the situation any more palatable.

I pulled myself out of the window and lay on my back, staring up at the sky. From this position, with the walls blocking out the surrounding terrain, I could be anywhere. Sky is sky. I tried to pretend I was in Lucernis or Coroune or even Bellarius—anywhere but Thagoth. It was no good. The silence, the lack of street noise and human voices was too different from any of the places I tried to imagine myself away to. Would I ever get back to Lucernis or anything approaching civilization? When would the nightmare end?

I looked up at the sky and slowly accepted my situation. I was in Thagoth, and tomorrow or the day after, we were going to confront Athagos and probably die. If we survived, we would face Tha-Agoth and possibly die. If we survived that, we would eventually face the Shadow King again and almost certainly die. There seemed to be a large probability of Holgren and me dying in the near future. I really didn't like it. Not only because I very much wanted to live but because I wanted to live alongside him. My heart ached when I thought of all the things we wouldn't get to experience if we failed to survive our multiple dooms. Then, it hit me. I smacked my forehead with a palm and got to my feet. Eventually, even I can realize when I'm being an idiot.

There was one thing we still had time to share.

I made my way down the uneven steps of the tower and back to camp. Holgren looked up at me, and I put a finger to my lips. Ruiqi was sleeping again. I grabbed a couple of blankets, turned back toward the city, and gestured for him to follow me. He did so with a look of puzzlement on his face. I led him to another walled garden, one with springy turf and a shattered fountain that still trickled pure, sweet water. There, I spread the blankets out and began to undress. He looked at me with a sort of amazed bemusement on his face. I took my filthy shirt off and, taking his head gently in both my hands, bent it down so I could kiss him. My heart was pounding in excitement for once instead of fear.

After a deliciously long time, I broke away and started pulling my boots off. He just stood there.

"The sooner you strip," I said, "the sooner we can help each other clean some of the grime off. I'll be much less distracted if I'm not worrying about how badly I stink."

I may have had a head start, but he managed to get undressed before me. The water of our bath was breathtakingly cold. We warmed up rather quickly, though, afterwards.

Somewhere along the way, I managed to tell him I loved him. It wasn't nearly as hard as I thought it would be. In the rush of it all, I wondered distractedly why I had made such a fuss about saying it or showing it.

~ ~ ~

It was with more than a little regret that I disentangled myself from Holgren's sleeping form and started dressing. The sun was setting, and the cold could no longer be ignored. But I didn't want to leave our little pocket of peace and happiness.

The wind had picked up. A frigid gust blew through the garden and plucked the blanket off Holgren. He grunted and shivered and felt around for me with one hand, eyes closed.

"Wake up, lover. Time to face the future, such as it is."

"Mmm. In a bit. Come back. I'm cold."

I finished buttoning my shirt and knelt down beside him. I ran my fingers through his long, tousled hair. How could I have known him so long and not seen just what he was, what he meant to me?

"Get up, and get dressed, Holgren, or you might get frostbite on some very uncomfortable spots."

He cracked one eye open and regarded me. "I love you," he said.

"I love you too. Now, get up, you lazy bastard, and help me gather firewood. Tonight's going to be a cold one. We'll need to move Ruiqi indoors as well. Don't want her to die before it's time."

"Amra, please—"

"Sorry. I'll leave it alone from now on. I promise. It won't be an issue after tonight anyway."

He nodded, stretched, and started getting dressed. "Tomorrow morning, then?"

"If you and she are prepared."

"We will be. The preparations are minimal and not terribly complex. All I will be doing is supplying her with an extra measure of power as most of hers is absorbed in keeping her body functioning."

"I didn't know mages could lend out power."

"Normally, they can't. We are now members of the same *khordun*, though, so it's a simple matter in this case. One of the few advantages of the situation and poetic in that it might ultimately lead to the Shadow King's downfall."

"Here's hoping. Come on. It'll be dark by the time we get back to camp, and we still have to move to a better shelter."

Holgren and I moved Ruiqi and our few belongings to a windowless building nearer the Tabernacle, one that still had most of its roof intact. The wind had really started to blow with the coming of night, and the temperature was falling fast.

We built a fire up in one corner, huddling in blankets around it, Ruiqi propped up against a wall and Holgren and I nestled next to each other. Damp wood hissed and crackled in the fire, and the wind moaned and shrieked. All three of us were cold and hungry. Ruiqi was talking to Holgren.

"Adepts of the Order are taught to make even their deaths serve the will of the Emperor. It is what we call the *argilleh*, the last blow. In the days when battle mages were an integral part of warfare, sometimes even in defeat, those of the Order would secure victory for the armies of the Empire by preparing themselves in just such a way as you will help me prepare."

"Aridhall Flamehand killed dozens of the Order at the battle of Isinglass," I said. "Or so the story goes. Why didn't their 'last blows' kill him?"

"Flamehand was unique. No one before or since could match the kind of control or mastery of the Art that he achieved. And no one had the raw power that he possessed, not since before the Diaspora. The Order at that time was rotted through with evil and ineptitude. Flamehand was a blessing in disguise. After Isinglass, the Emperor reshaped the Order and cut out what deadwood was left. Some trees need drastic pruning in order to survive and thrive. So it was with the Order."

"Which is all interesting but strays from the point. Can you say with certainty that your *argilleh* will knock Athagos out?"

"I cannot promise it, no. I believe there is a very good chance it will succeed. Between Holgren and me, we should be able to muster sufficient power to produce the intended effect. I offer no guarantees."

"Then I want you two to work on a way to temporarily deafen Holgren and me as well."

Ruiqi nodded. "Prudent and already discussed."

"I think I've got a way to produce such an effect," said Holgren. "I do wish I had access to my sanctum."

"I wish I had a bottle of wine and a leg of lamb." I shivered and drew my blanket tighter around me. "If it gets much colder, we might not have to worry about tomorrow. We'll freeze to death in our sleep." I wrapped my blanket tighter still and lay down on my side on the leaf-littered floor, scooting as close to the fire as I could. The front of me sweltered while my backside froze. Such is life.

I watched the flames and listened with half an ear as Holgren and Ruiqi talked about theorems and paradigms and occasionally uttered sounds I recognized as magical triggers.

Magic was at heart a simple matter of impressing your will on reality, or so Holgren had explained to me long before. In practice, it was rarely that simple. It seemed that mages could spend weeks on the simplest of tasks though usually when somebody was paying them for their time rather than results.

Without even realizing I was tired, I soon fell into an uncomfortable sleep.

~ ~ ~

Holgren woke me sometime before dawn. He had replenished the fire, and it burned higher and hotter than before. Good thing. It had begun to snow while I slept. The part of the room open to the sky had grown a snow-drift overnight. I watched as more flakes swirled in, driven by the howling wind.

"At first light, we're going to carry Ruiqi to the gates," Holgren whispered. "I wanted to talk out our plans."

I looked over at her. She was still sitting up, propped against the wall. She was in some sort of trance state, motionless, arms raised to the sky, palms up. Her breathing was so slow as to be nearly imperceptible.

"She's preparing herself. And so should we."

"Did you figure out a way to deafen us?"

"Yes, but only briefly. And if you speak at all, make any sound with your voice, the spell will unravel. Remember that. Don't cry out, no matter what, until you're sure it is safe to do so."

"I'll do whatever it takes where Athagos is concerned."

"This is what we came up with while you slept. We will carry Ruiqi to the gate at dawn as quietly as possible. I'll perform the deafening, and we'll stay out of sight in the square, much as you did when you dragged her back yesterday. Ruiqi will open the gates and call Athagos."

"The gates are already open."

"No, they're slightly ajar. She plans to get the goddess' attention quickly. You'll see. When Athagos takes her, the *argilleh* should render her unconscious for at least a few seconds, hopefully longer, allowing you to transfer the necklace and us to slip past her into the Tabernacle."

He leaned back and stretched. "After that point," he said through a yawn, "planning becomes futile. Can you suggest any changes or improvements?"

"It may take a long while for Athagos to respond to Ruiqi, whatever she's planning to do. Our deafness might wear off before that happens. I'd prefer to approach the Tabernacle from the opposite side and use Ruiqi's suicide as a diversion. Unfortunately, I've got to hang around and drop off the necklace." I looked at him. "That doesn't mean you have to."

"Where you go, I go. No arguments."

"Alright. What's involved in renewing the spell, then, if it wears off before Athagos is incapacitated?"

"Let's just say we don't want that to happen."

"Then what have we got to plug our ears?"

"I'd love to have some wax, but there's nothing except cloth. Or dirt, I suppose. I really doubt we can fashion anything that would do the trick."

"We'll just have to hope for the best then."

He squeezed my hand and smiled. "We *will* make it through."

"Of course. Don't we always?" But I wasn't sure about this time. Not at all.

We spent what remained of the night in each other's arms, sharing warmth. Ruiqi sat as still as a statue, the only sign of life the slow rise and fall of her chest. Prepare as she might, though, I doubted anyone could truly be prepared for death at the hands and mouth of Athagos.

As daylight crept up on us, she stirred at last. She lowered her arms and placed her palms against her forehead then put her fingertips to her lips and finally let her hands settle in what remained of her lap. "Please take me to see the dawn," she said, voice serene. Of all her voices, that one disturbed me the most. I think. No one should be that calm facing imminent, certain death.

We lugged her outside and found a low, stone wall to perch her on so she had an unobstructed view to the east. It was still snowing and bitterly cold. There was no way she could actually see the sun rise, but it didn't seem to matter to her. Or perhaps she found it fitting.

She let a couple of tears escape though she smiled that serene smile all the while. After a few minutes, she said, "I am ready," and we helped her off the wall and carried her to her doom.

~ ~ ~

It was slow going through the snow-filled streets. One of us was constantly slipping. Finally, Holgren called for a halt and put Ruiqi on his back, getting a grip on her legs above the stumps and having her cling to his neck. I walked ahead, plowing some of the snow out of the way. I don't know that it went any more quickly after that, but there were fewer spills.

The moment I stepped into the square, Tha-Agoth's voice filled my head.

What are you planning, little thief?

I stopped abruptly, and Holgren bumped into me. "What's the matter?" he asked, and I held up a hand.

"You said you'd stay out of my mind," I said to Tha-Agoth. "Is your word good or not?"

I said I would not enter your memories, and I have not. I made no such assertion in respect to your companions.

"We do what we have to. I hope you can understand that. We have no choice. When we're done, we'll free you. That I promise."

Behind me, Holgren stiffened. "What are you doing?" he whispered. Not to me.

"Tha-Agoth! Get out of his mind!"

How dare you? How dare you deliver my sister to that monster? The ground beneath our feet trembled, and I caught an image of him twisting on his altar, beating his fists against the stone, the rod tearing at his flesh and fresh blood welling up.

He would not break free. If he hadn't yet, he wasn't going to.

"What choice do we have?" I asked him. "What do you owe her? Have the past thousand years taught you nothing? She betrayed you! If things had gone as planned, she would have killed you! Why would you want to protect her?"

Silence for a time. Then, less furious, *She is my twin, my sister, my wife. Whatever she has done, I will always love her in ways you cannot imagine. I cannot allow that dark mishap you name the Shadow King to have her.*

"And I have to send her to him. But I will free you as well, Tha-Agoth, and hopefully, you can bring her back. Only you can stop the Shadow King once and for all. Surely, a thousand years pinned like an insect have given you a taste for revenge."

Revenge is foreign to my nature. I will do what must be done, thief, but there will be a reckoning and not only with the Shadow King. Justice is not revenge.

"I'll accept that. Now, leave us alone to do what we must."

If she is harmed—

"I know. I know. Quiet, please." I waited a few seconds, and when he didn't respond, I motioned Holgren forward. I didn't have to tell him to go as quietly as he could.

We trudged and stumbled past the wreckage of the Duke's tent to the Tabernacle's massive gates. There, I helped Holgren lower Ruiqi to the ground. When we had her safely deposited, I bent down and whispered in her ear.

"It's not too late to change your mind."

She looked at me and just shook her head, that small smile still playing on her lips.

I got up and crept over to Holgren, who had taken his station two steps away behind the left-hand gate. I looked at her and wondered what she might have become had the Shadow King not netted her. I didn't really like her, maybe because she was too much like me in a way. But I had begun to respect her. What a waste.

She took one deep breath then gestured with the first two fingers of her right hand. The right-hand gate responded by flying open, slamming against the wall and shivering to pieces. The booming crash that accompanied it would have woken the dead. I was certain it had gotten Athagos' attention.

In an abnormally loud, commanding voice, Ruiqi cried out, "Athagos! Come to me!"

Holgren touched my forehead with one suddenly glowing fingertip. The world went silent. I kept one hand on the necklace and my eyes on Ruiqi, waiting for some sign of Athagos' approach. I measured time by my speeding heartbeats.

It was somewhere around thirty beats that I noticed Ruiqi's eyes grow wide. At thirty-five, she had begun to writhe and shriek—in silent agony. I couldn't hear her screams, but I could imagine them all too well. I hated it. I felt the necklace twitch under my fingers. At forty heartbeats, she had collapsed. At fifty, she was crawling across the threshold of the Tabernacle, pulling herself along through the snow, hand over hand. The necklace was squirming on my neck like a snake. I was glad I couldn't see what would happen next. I'd seen that grisly trick far too many times already. I began to believe we might survive.

Too soon. At about fifty-five heartbeats, I was preparing to take a peek around the remaining gate when my hearing returned. I was in sudden agony. Beside me, Holgren fell twitching to the snow-covered ground with a scream forcing its way past lips thinned in pain. I pitted my will against the force that was suddenly rushing through my body, ripping from me all control to my limbs, but it was impossible. I fell to the ground beside Holgren and felt my consciousness pushed back to some far, dusty corner. I was reduced to a spectator in my own body.

Athagos' magic had taken control. I no longer even had the power to scream. My body rose with the jerking, puppet-like movements I'd seen in the Duke and his men. I walked into the Tabernacle behind Holgren.

I couldn't direct my eyes, but I could make out Ruiqi's truncated form deflating in

Athagos' embrace just fine with my peripheral vision. I waited and prayed for her last blow, her *argilleh* to kick in as the storm intensified.

When Athagos tossed Ruiqi's hide away and licked her lips, I knew despair.

Athagos looked at me. She was beautiful. Her eyes were the same as her brothers now: stars ripped from the night sky rather than that unearthly blue I remembered. Her skin was the same flawless bronze. Her long, black hair floated loose around her shoulders, drifting on unseen currents of power. And her generous, pink mouth was curled into a smile.

So good to see you again, she said to me without speaking. *I enjoyed our last meeting. You bring such lovely gifts.*

"Go to hells, you crazy bitch." I tried to say it, but of course, I couldn't speak. Apparently, the thought was enough.

My madness passes. I suppose I have you to thank for that. The mind heals more slowly than the body, however, and the process is more taxing. I require further sustenance. These magelings are much more…satisfying.

Holgren was next. I couldn't even close my eyes. After everything that had happened, we were both going to die in Thagoth after all.

Athagos stretched her arms out, and Holgren jerked and twitched his way into her embrace. The rage and despair I felt defied words. She snaked her shapely arm around his waist, cradled his head—

Then it happened. Athagos' eyes grew wide, and she flung Holgren away and started clawing at her chest. I felt her grasp on me slip the tiniest fraction.

I poured all my will into driving her out. Slowly, painstakingly, I began to re-exert control over my body, one digit at a time. Athagos fell to the snow-covered ground, still clawing at her chest. She had dug great, red furrows in her flesh now though they healed as I watched. Her limbs began to twitch, and she screamed—not with any magical element but a scream of rage and agony.

And then in mid-thrash, she fell utterly still.

I rushed all the way back into my body the way the tide races in to shore. I stumbled my way over to Athagos' beautiful, frightening form, ripping at the necklace on my way. It came off immediately. I threw it at her head.

It caught her on the jaw and fell down to the hollow of her throat. From there, each end snaked its way around the back of her neck; after a moment, I heard the faint snick of the clasp closing.

"It was made for you, you bitch. Hope you like it." I would have kicked her, but I didn't have the coordination yet.

"No time for that," gasped Holgren. "She'll wake any moment. Hurry."

We staggered off toward Tha-Agoth's dome, stumbling like drunks through the storm and deepening snow. Holgren was right. I didn't want to be around when she woke up. She'd rip us to shreds.

It was easier to find my way this time despite the storm. I knew where I was going, and the dense foliage had thinned out with the onset of winter. I had just spied the doors to the Tabernacle itself when Tha-Agoth's voice sounded in my ears.

She wakes, Amra, and she is displeased. Eagerness mixed with a strange reluctance filled Tha-Agoth's mental voice.

"Holgren—"

"I heard. Run!"

We ran, neither of us daring to look back. Ours was a headlong rush to the dubious safety of Tha-Agoth's prison. Bare branches whipped at our faces; snow-hidden roots sought to trip us up. The storm was intensifying. An already bitter wind had become a howling monster intent on driving us to the ground and burying us, one white flake at a time. And behind us, death was shaking off a dead mage's final spell. It was a sad state of affairs that I had become at least somewhat accustomed to such situations. It didn't lessen my fear in any way, mind you, but I no longer found it incredible.

The granite bulk of the Tabernacle proper came into view, and I led Holgren toward the entrance of Tha-Agoth's gold-topped dome through the wind-whipped, driving snow.

I located the doors quickly enough. It was the massive snowdrift blocking them that slowed us.

The entrance was situated in the cleft between the two domes, partly sheltered from the wind. Snow blew in but didn't get blown back out. If the doors had opened inward, it wouldn't have been a problem.

Such is life. We clawed at the drift with numbed hands until we'd cleared enough away to try and open one of the doors. Together, we pulled on one of the massive, carved handles. Slowly, too slowly, the door began to inch outward.

It opened a couple of hand spans, and then she was on us.

What have we here? Two mice seeking shelter from the storm?

I looked back out at the grounds. I didn't see her anywhere. I looked back and saw that Holgren had got the door open just enough for one to slip in.

"GO!" I screamed and shoved him through the opening over his protests. Then, a cold hand had me by the nape of the neck, and I was suddenly cartwheeling through the air.

I tried to tuck into some sort of roll, but instead of the ground, my body connected with the trunk of a massive oak. I fell to a heap at its base. I didn't move for a long while. I couldn't even think about moving. The only reason I knew I was still alive was because of all the pain.

I heard Holgren scream my name and then the thunderous boom of the door slamming shut, only slightly muffled by the storm. I wanted to look up and see what was going on, but I couldn't seem to move my head.

I am saving him for later, little one. He will keep. You and I have matters to discuss first. First matters. Matters of discussion, you see. You do, don't you?

"I don't know what you're talking about." It hurt to speak. It hurt to breathe. Slowly, I willed my hands under me. Tremblingly, they responded. I wasn't paralyzed. I would be dead soon, but I wasn't paralyzed. It's the little things that keep you going.

I pushed myself up to a kneeling position, steadying myself with one hand on the oak's ice-crusted trunk.

You know. Do you know you know? Yes. I think so. In an eye blink, she appeared before me. Her backhand sent me skidding through the snow, face first. When I came to a stop, I spat blood and rolled over again, trying to gain my feet.

"How can we have a discussion if you keep pummeling me?" I groaned.

Discussion. Yes. We were having a discussion. Sometimes, I find it difficult to concentrate. Please forgive me. She yanked me off the ground by my collar and held me at arm's length. My feet dangled inches from the ground. She studied me, turning me this way and that.

This is it, I thought. She's going to do it. I fumbled for my knife. Hopeless, but I wasn't going to just give in. I'd try to get her in the throat, maybe cut her vocal cords—

She gave me a tooth-loosening, lip-splitting slap and shook me till all thoughts of going for my knife were jarred loose. It reminded me of growing up. The bad old days.

How can we have a discussion if you insist on trying to harm me?

"You always play with your food, or do you have a point you're getting to?" A slow, stupid, doomed sort of anger was starting to well up in me.

Ah, the mouse bares its teeth. The harvest comes home; the owl is in the orchard. The Shadow leashed the earth, you know, but couldn't teach it to sing.

"You're raving mad, you know that?"

She threw me down to the ground and sat down before me. She smiled again, a sunny, carefree smile that revealed perfect teeth and sent shivers down my spine.

Oh. Yes. I know. It comes and goes. I don't want to kill you, actually, but I probably will. I would like to apologize to you in advance for that.

"Apology not accepted, you crazy bitch."

She brought her hand up to her neck and toyed with the necklace I'd put on her. Well, at least if I died, she wasn't going to fare much better.

Tell me about the chain.

"Just a pretty trinket. Don't you like it?"

I never saw her move. She just had me by the throat all of a sudden. I felt my windpipe begin to collapse under the pressure of her grip.

No lies, now. It makes my thoughts whirl, skirl, float away. And then all that's left is the hunger. Understand?

I tried to gag out a yes, settled for a nod.

Good.

She released me, and I drew in a tortured breath of frigid air.

"Slave chain," I choked out, "made for you. Shadow King. Go—to him."

I don't know what kind of reaction I would have expected from her. The insane are, almost by definition, hard to predict. I can say without reservation that I did not expect the reaction my gasped words caused.

Her face lit up like a child presented with a new toy or an unexpected treat. She actually clapped her hands together and laughed exultantly. She dragged me to her. One hand cradled the back of my head, her other arm snaked around my waist. It was going to happen—she was going to suck me dry.

And then she was hugging me tightly, so tightly my spine creaked. She buried my face in the hollow of her neck. I drew a breath and caught a whiff of lilacs. Death smelled like lilacs.

You are joy's messenger, little mouse. I will not harm you, oh no. How could I?

She kissed the top of my head then pushed me away into the snow and ran fleet-footed toward the gates. I watched her go, the realization that I was still somehow alive and apparently would remain so for the time being slowly sinking in.

Just before the falling snow obscured her completely, she stopped and turned to look back at me.

Gnaw through the bar of my brother's cage, mouse. Set him free to follow me. But take your time.

And then she was gone. "Kerf's lice-ridden beard," I muttered and staggered to my feet. I had to find Holgren.

I found him just inside the Tabernacle. He was slumped against the wall, head lolling at an unnatural angle. He was breathing in short gasps, like a dying fish. The wall behind him was daubed with one long streak of blood where his head had been bashed against it and he'd slid to the floor. Athagos must have hurled him against the wall and then come after me.

I pulled his head to a more natural angle, hoping to help his breathing, and began to realize just how massive his injury was. The back of his head was a sticky, bloody mess. I examined it more carefully by touch, as gently as I could. I resisted the panic welling up in me. It wouldn't help. The back of his skull was crushed. It was more than crushed, actually. It was pulverized.

I'd watched him die once. I wasn't about to go through that again. Not after what we'd shared. He needed Tha-Agoth's blood immediately. I put my shoulder against his abdomen and levered him up using the wall until I got to a standing position. I wouldn't be able to carry him far, but I didn't have to. I just had to make it to Tha-Agoth's chamber.

I staggered off down the hall toward it. "No problem, partner. We'll just get some of that good old blood that brought you back before. Don't you worry now, Holgren. Don't you worry; do you hear me?"

He couldn't hear me. But the words weren't for him anyway.

When I reached the stairs down to Tha-Agoth's chamber, it was with relief. Then, I ran into an invisible wall. The stairs were blocked. It could only be Tha-Agoth.

"Let me come down," I panted. Only silence answered.

"Tha-Agoth, let me down. He needs healing. He's dying."

You took her from me. You sent her to my enemy.

"I had no choice. You know all this."

Silence.

"If you don't let me down to get healing for him, I swear I'll let you rot down there. You'll never see her again, and you'll still be pinned to that stone when the Shadow King puts the entire world to torture. He will have won because you were pouting like a selfish child. Is that what you want?"

Silence.

"Answer me, damn you! Is that what you want?"

It is not.

"Then let me come down. Now."

Come.

I made my precarious way down the stairs as quickly as I could then rammed the door open with the heel of my hand. I lay Holgren down gently on the blood-washed floor in the gray light that filtered in from the broken windows high above.

I didn't look at Tha-Agoth. He wasn't my favorite person at that moment.

Holgren had stopped breathing. I turned his head to the side and scooped up handfuls of blood from the floor. I dribbled it onto the back of Holgren's skull then pried his jaw open and filled his mouth with it. Seconds stretched to minutes. Nothing happened.

"Why isn't it working?" Panic began to well up in me in earnest. I fought it, but it felt as if my heart was being sliced to ribbons. I looked at Tha-Agoth. His head was turned away.

"Why isn't it working?" I asked again.

I don't know. But I knew he was lying.

"Tell me, Tha-Agoth."

I don't know. Perhaps his bond to the Shadow King prevents the healing.

"You're lying. I can sense it." I stood up and walked over to him. He refused to look at me. I put my hand on his chin and turned his head toward me. Those star-filled eyes blazed up at me.

"Listen to me. If he dies, I'll leave you here and the world be damned. I swear it. I'll walk out into the death lands and let the beasties have me for a snack to make sure I don't go soft and change my mind."

I could turn your mind now, thief, and make you help me.

"No you can't. You'd already have done it. I've had a while to think about our first encounter. If you had been able to make me free you, you would have. After a thousand years, *anybody* would have done whatever was necessary to get free. You didn't because you couldn't. And you can't now. If I'm wrong, prove it. If I'm right, you'd better stop playing games because I'm your only hope."

No response.

"I'll take that as an admission. Now why isn't the blood bringing Holgren back?"

Because I do not wish it to.

"Why?"

You took her from me. Why should I give him back to you?

"You pathetic piece of—" I choked the words down. They wouldn't do any good and would probably only make matters worse. I began to see why Athagos might want to get rid of her brother. I leaned in closer.

"If the fact that we're going to free you isn't enough, consider this: He's just as much a victim of the Shadow King as you are of the Sorcerer King. You might say he's a fellow victim; we both are. To allow him to die when you have the means to save him makes you both a murderer and party to the evil that put you in your own personal hell."

I leaned in closer and whispered in his ear. "It makes you at least as guilty as your own worst enemy."

He closed his eyes and rolled his head away from me. *Perhaps I'm beyond caring.*

"For your sister's sake, I hope not. You're the only chance she has. If you want to spare Athagos from the Shadow King's attentions, you'd better bring Holgren back to life. If I can't have him, I'll make sure you can't have her. That I promise you."

He looked back at me with those star-torn eyes, and I stared into them, unblinkingly. He looked away. Eventually.

Very well. But expect no more healing from my blood for either of you.

Behind me, Holgren choked his way back to life and along with him, my heart.

CHAPTER 10

I rushed to Holgren as he scrabbled onto his side to retch out a mouthful of god blood. It afforded me a view of his knitting skull. Seeing the shards of bone jostle themselves back into place and the scalp crawl back over the skull beneath wasn't pretty, but I could have asked to see nothing that caused me more joy.

I knelt down and put an arm around his middle, pressed my cheek to his, and whispered in his ear. "Don't you ever die on me again, you whore-spawned excuse for a mage. I couldn't stand it."

"My mother…wasn't a whore. She—ah, gods my head hurts!—she was a witch. Not the same thing at all." He boosted himself up to a kneeling position with my help.

"Besides, I don't die on purpose, you know."

Enough. Free me. Now.

I kissed Holgren quickly then helped him to his feet. There was work to be done.

~ ~ ~

"Oh, this isn't good at all." Holgren had both hands wrapped around the rod that speared Tha-Agoth. He had been muttering arcanities for the better part of an hour.

"What is it?" I asked him as he let go of the rod and stepped away from Tha-Agoth.

I've given you back your life twice now, mageling. You are indebted to me. Do not fail.

"The hells you say," I told Tha-Agoth. "I pulled his rotting corpse out of the ground the first time and had to coerce you to bring him back the second. He doesn't owe you a damned thing."

Without my blood, he would still be decaying in the garden where he was buried.

"I would prefer not to be talked about as if I weren't present. I'd like it even more if you'd both be quiet. This is difficult enough without listening to you two bicker. I've still got a headache."

Holgren cracked his knuckles, stepped further back from the altar and stretched. "The magics employed to fashion this—thing—were powerful in the extreme."

It has thwarted all my attempts to destroy it for a millennium, mage. It was specifically designed to kill me though in that, it failed. Its nature should not be proof to your mundane Art, however.

Holgren looked down at Tha-Agoth, eyebrow raised. "How much do you really know about the laws of thaumaturgy, may I ask?"

It is a subject that holds little interest for me. The power I possess is drawn from a different source.

One far more powerful.

"Not in this case, it would appear. Let me state the situation as concisely as I can. A mage is able to produce effects in direct correlation to two conditions: the raw power he possesses the ability to tap and the strength of will he is able to exert on that power to shape reality. It gets a bit more complicated than that, but to illustrate the point, consider this rod. It is the product of magic. It was created by a mage powerful enough, a mage possessing the requisite strength of will, to fashion something that could trap a god for an age."

I fail to see your point.

"That's because I haven't *made* it yet." Holgren rubbed at his eyes, took a deep breath. I guess dying made him irritable.

Then make your point, mage. You waste time.

"This rod isn't subject to the same laws that govern other physical things. A mage forces his will on reality when he uses the Art to the extent that his power and will enable him. Part of the reality of this rod, as envisioned by its creator, is that it is indestructible."

There is no indestructible object. It must have a weakness.

"You're absolutely right. There is one set of conditions that will allow us to break the rod. But you aren't going to like it."

What conditions must be met, mage?

"The Sorcerer King was good at what he did. He knew that it would take a greater power than even he possessed to best a god. He took that into account when he set about creating your doom.

"Tha-Agoth, It is your *own* power that sustains and strengthens your enemy's weapon. You must have noticed your weakened condition?"

Yes.

"The rod leaches your power away and turns it against you. The more you struggle against it, the more power you lend it. Artfully clever, actually."

The chamber was silent. If I understood what Holgren was saying, there was no way to free Tha-Agoth that I could see. I had faith, though, that Holgren would find a way. If he didn't, we were doomed.

"What can be done?" I asked. Holgren glanced at me then looked down at the god.

"I have only one solution, and it isn't certain or easy."

Tell me.

"We're going to have to kill you in order to save you," he said.

What foolishness is this? I cannot be killed. Do you understand nothing?

"I understand more than you do in this case. The rod feeds off your energy. I need for the flow of energy from you to the rod to cease or at least falter before I can attempt to impose my will on it. A massive trauma, such as beheading, should do the trick."

You expect me to allow you to behead *me? Your humor escapes me.*

"I'm pretty sure he's serious," I told Tha-Agoth. "Holgren doesn't have much of a sense of humor."

"Not at the moment, at least."

This is insanity.

"Nevertheless. I do wish there was another way. There isn't, not that I can think of." Holgren spread his hands and shrugged.

"Once he's beheaded, how will you break the rod?" I didn't think a shovel and pickax would do it. That's all we had in the way of tools.

"I'll use the Art. Destroying it is as much a matter of ripping through the mesh of commands that infuse the rod as breaking its physical reality. Once I've accomplished that, a sharp blow should suffice."

"Will you be able to manage it?"

He gave me a flat stare. "There's only one way to find out. With the additional power made available to me through the *khordun*, it is at least possible. I will do my best."

Do more than your best, mageling. You will not be allowed to take my head more than once.

"I don't expect to fail, Tha-Agoth. Failure dooms us as much as anyone. But I cannot guarantee success. That is the reality of the situation. Accustom yourself to it."

I started toward the stairs. "I'll go fetch a sword from the Duke's camp. You two try to get along while I'm gone. We all need each other, like it or not."

~ ~ ~

It took me forever to find a sword in the snow.

Just inside the gate, a score of armed men had met their fate at the hands and mouth of Athagos. Most of them hadn't even been able to draw their blades. They'd hung at their sides, utterly useless, inches away from hands that did not their owners' bidding but Athagos'. What a way to die.

It should have been a simple thing to find one sword in a relatively small area, but the snow made it a frustrating, agonizing task.

I finally came upon the hilt of a sword, my hands frozen nearly lifeless after almost half an hour of questing blindly through the snow. I pulled up my prize and disentangled the sword belt from the chain mail shirt it was attached to with difficulty.

When I finally managed it, I pinned the sword in its scabbard awkwardly to my chest with a forearm and buried my numb hands in my armpits.

I slogged my way back to the Tabernacle through the storm as quickly as possible. I couldn't imagine Athagos would stick around, especially after the way she had acted when I told her about the necklace, but why take a chance? She was seriously, deeply insane.

But cracked as she was, I was fairly certain her main goal in life was getting as far away from her brother as possible. There was something between them that I didn't really understand, more than Tha-Agoth's seeming obsession with his sister-wife, more than Athagos wanting to cause him harm. I felt as though I were staring at a puzzle with an unknown number of pieces missing. Everything pointed to Athagos wanting to get rid of her brother, yet she'd told me to free him just before she left.

Except she was raving mad, and nothing was beyond her. Including hanging around the Tabernacle, waiting to make a snack of me.

I shook my head in disgust. Enough of logic chasing its tail, I told myself. Just get on with the business at hand.

I didn't relax until I'd made it back inside and then only by a few degrees. Tha-Agoth didn't exactly put me at ease.

Back in the temple, a tense silence reigned. Tha-Agoth was motionless, eyes closed. What he was thinking, I couldn't even begin to guess. Having his head chopped off might not kill him, but it was still going to be hideously painful.

As for Holgren, he was squatting in one blood-washed corner, elbows on knees, thumbs pressed against the bridge of his nose. Whatever he was doing had the hairs on the back of my neck trying to loose themselves from my skin.

"So," I said more loudly than I intended, "are we ready?"

Make the stroke clean, thief. One blow only if you can manage it. I'll not have you carving on me.

"I'll do my best. Holgren, are you ready?"

"As ready as I can be." He stood up and walked over to Tha-Agoth. "I wish—"

"—you had access to your sanctum. I know. You don't. So let's move on."

He smiled half-heartedly and looked down at Tha-Agoth.

"Forget the rod," he told the godling, "and concentrate solely on healing the damage we are about to cause. I want as much of your power diverted from the rod as possible."

You do not forget a spear through your chest, mage.

"Do the best you can." Holgren turned from Tha-Agoth and looked at me. "Once you've finished the beheading, I want you to swing on the rod at my signal. However much I may weaken it, physical blows will still be necessary. And do try not to hit me, Amra."

"You take the fun out of everything."

Holgren moved to the other side of the altar, across from the doors. I lined myself up with Tha-Agoth's neck, planted my feet, and took a few practice swings. The sword's balance felt all wrong; it was far too long for me, and the grip was slick. I didn't have to fight with it, though. I just had to hit a stationary target or two. I hoped I could cut through with one swing—beheadings were a grisly business. There was a reason the condemned paid their executioners to do their best.

Satisfied as I was going to be with the weapon, I stepped forward until the last few inches of the blade hovered just above Tha-Agoth's neck. He looked at me with those star-filled eyes of his but said nothing. He turned his head and looked up at the snowflakes swirling in from the broken windows far above.

"Are we ready?" I whispered and looked at Holgren. He was kneeling down, and his hands clasped the rod just above Tha-Agoth's chest. His head was bowed. He looked to be praying, almost.

"Strike when you will," he said, voice muffled, "but wait for my signal before you swing at the rod."

"Alright." My palms were suddenly sweaty, making the sword hilt even more slippery. I thought about wiping them dry but decided against the delay. The sooner this was over, the better.

Holding the sword in two hands, I lined up the blade along Tha-Agoth's throat. I took a deep breath and pulled it overhead. With a wordless cry, I whipped it down on the god's neck with all the force I could muster. The edge of the sword stayed perpendicular to the ground, thankfully, and bit into Tha-Agoth's neck with a meaty smack.

The shock of impact rode up my arms, and I nearly lost hold of the hilt. Blood sprayed up, hot rivulets of it splashing my face and torso, but I'd done it.

"Again, Amra!" Holgren's voice was strident. I looked more closely at the cut I'd made. I'd failed to cut all the way through. Tha-Agoth's head was still connected to his body by a thin strip of flesh at the back of his neck. His body spasmed. His torso tried to curl into a backbreaking arch, but it was held in place by the rod. His head was already reattaching itself to his body.

"Cut again, Amra! Quickly!" Holgren's voice was rough with strain. I cursed, dropped the sword, and severed the remaining scrap of flesh with my knife. Then, I pulled Tha-Agoth's head a little away from the rest of him and scrambled for the dropped sword. It might have been my imagination, but I thought I saw Tha-Agoth's eyes tracking my every move. I know he blinked.

A greenish, pulsing glow began to suffuse the room, emanating from the point where Holgren clutched the rod. It lit his face, gave him a diabolic look. His lips were pulled back from his teeth, and his forearms trembled with the effort of his magics. A low groan began to force past his teeth, growing slowly louder.

"Holgren?"

The green glow suddenly turned to a burst of brilliant red, and Holgren flew back from the rod as if he'd been hurled away from it by an invisible giant. He slammed into the far wall and slid down to the floor. Then the unnatural light died and was replaced by the weak winter light from far above.

I dropped the sword and ran over to Holgren. He was already climbing to his feet. The palms of his hands were burned.

"What happened?"

He let me help him to his feet. "I failed," he said, voice tight. "I don't have the power to destroy the rod. It's been feeding off him for an age. Its reserves are vast."

"So we can't break the rod. We'll just have to try something else."

"What else is there?"

I looked back at the rod, the altar, the beheaded god. Good question. What else was there to try? The rod was indestructible. We could try to break the altar using the pick, but that would take weeks at best. I watched Tha-Agoth's head slowly reattach itself to his body, and an idea came to me.

"So the rod won't break. We don't need it to."

"What have you thought of?"

"We need to get him free of the rod, not the other way around."

Holgren looked at me, and I saw understanding spark in his eyes. "Why didn't I think of that? Brilliant!"

"I know. Come on, let's do it before he has a chance to object."

Object to what?

Too late. "We're going to free you," I said. "It's going to be painful."

You will not sever my head from my body again. His voice was full of pain and a little fear.

"You're absolutely right." I walked back over to him and picked up the bloody sword.

Tell me what you intend to do.

"We can't break the rod, so were going to cut you free."

I have been struggling against it for centuries with no effect.

"You're also weak as a kitten. You don't have the physical ability to pull yourself free of the rod. If you did, you'd have escaped long ago. Now, do you want to be free or not?"

Yes, he hissed.

"Then prepare yourself. As I said, this is going to hurt. A lot."

The rod was about two inches in diameter and had speared him roughly through the heart or near enough. I would have to cut more than a hand span's worth of flesh and bone from the rod to his side. And I'd probably have to do it more than once considering the rate at which he healed.

"Holgren."

"Yes?"

"I want you to stay on the other side. Start pulling once I get enough of his chest cut away to free him. I don't want to have to keep hacking at him. Pull him by his right arm."

"Alright."

It was easier to think of him as a pig or a cow about to be butchered. I wasn't sure I could go through with it otherwise, immortal or no. I wasn't particularly squeamish, but this was going to be gruesome. Not that beheading him hadn't been, but…

"Put your left arm above your head and stretch out your right for Holgren to pull on." I didn't want to hack his arm by accident. He did as I asked, and then there was nothing left to do but start cutting.

The main difference between beheading someone and butchering them is the screaming. It's hard to scream when your vocal cords have been severed along with the rest of your neck. When chunks are being taken out of your chest, you can scream just fine though the blood from your punctured lung works its way into your throat and mouth and gives the screaming a wet, bubbling quality. And when you're a god, you can stream right into someone's mind so they get the full effect.

I couldn't very well tell him to be quiet. I gritted my teeth and hacked through flesh and ribs, clearing a bloody path for Holgren to pull him free of the rod. I kept hoping he would pass out. He didn't. Tha-Agoth healed with amazing rapidity.

We resorted to a constant tugging on Holgren's part and methodical hacking on mine. It might have gone a little more smoothly if I'd thought to cut out a wedge-shaped portion out of the god's flesh, but I didn't until later. So I had to sever reconnecting flesh continually.

At last, Holgren gave a yank. Tha-Agoth fell to the blood-washed floor of his temple in a limp, shrieking heap. I let the gore-drenched sword slip from my fingers. It fell to the stone floor with a metallic ring. I was exhausted. I felt as if I'd been hauling nets all day, something I had never been fond of as a child. I was drenched in blood. On the positive side, none of it was mine.

Tha-Agoth's shrieks began to subside. I looked over at Holgren, and he looked back at me, smiling. "You did it," he said.

Free. Tha-Agoth rose from the floor, one hand on the altar for support. A golden glow began to gather around him. I could see the wound I'd caused healing over completely.

Free, he said again, and the golden aura grew in intensity. He stretched out his arms, threw his head back, and howled. It made the very stones tremble. There was an undeniable—glory, I suppose—about him. I knew I was in the presence of a power, something greater than me. Greater than I ever would be. I shrugged the feeling off as much as I could. I began to have second thoughts about what we'd just done.

Tha-Agoth beat furiously on the rod that had pinned him for so many years with both fists. At first, nothing happened. Then, the rod started to bend under the assault. Tha-Agoth unleashed a flurry of blows, hands bloody. Finally, the rod snapped about two feet above the altar. Tha-Agoth wrenched the short length of rod from the stone that supported it and hurled it away toward the stairs.

So much for your indestructible object, mage.

Holgren took a step back from him a bit too late. I'd have backed off when fists started flying.

Tha-Agoth grabbed him by his shirtfront and lifted him off his feet. Holgren made no move, but I felt magic gathering around him. It wouldn't be enough, whatever he was preparing.

"Think very carefully about what you do next, Tha-Agoth," I said.

You sent my sister to my enemy. For that, I should kill you. But you freed me from an age of torment. What should I do with you two?

"Why don't we just call it even and start fresh? We aren't your main concern, Tha-Agoth. We want the Shadow King destroyed as much as you do if not more. We're your allies."

The enemy of my enemy is not necessarily my friend.

"We share a common goal, damn it. What happens after the Shadow King is destroyed doesn't really concern us right now. We've got to get to Athagos before she gets to him. Frankly, we don't have time for this."

Tha-Agoth dropped Holgren, who stumbled but did not fall, still holding on to energies he'd summoned.

I know truth when I hear it.

"Good. What do you suggest we do next?"

Now, I go and look at the whole of the sky for the first time in a thousand years instead of mere slivers of it. With that, he walked across the chamber, through the doors, and up the stairs.

I looked at Holgren. He shrugged. We followed Tha-Agoth up into the wreckage of his city, Holgren ahead of me. I stopped and surreptitiously picked up the short piece of rod that Tha-Agoth had flung toward the stairs, securing it under my ragged shirt in my belt. It was mostly instinct that made me do it. I had a vague, itchy feeling that it might come in handy at some point.

~ ~ ~

How much has time undone, Tha-Agoth said upon entering the Tabernacle grounds. *The gardens have run riot.* Something close to shock suffused his features. What did he expect after a thousand years?

"I'm afraid you haven't seen the half of it yet," I told him. "Wait until you get out into the city. Though a lot of the destruction is covered by the snow."

Yes. The weather is inclement. He glanced up at the sky. The wind suddenly died, and the snow stopped falling. Just like that. Then, the cloud cover began to thin away. The sun broke through. I could feel the temperature begin to climb.

I began to understand just how powerful he actually was. A hope for surviving the Shadow King began to grow within me, tempered by a certain feeling of dread for what might happen after. We had unleashed a power on the world that would probably, for good or ill, change it forever.

Tha-Agoth started off toward the gates. We followed him through the melting snow. When he saw what had happened to his city, I thought he was going to cry.

He turned in slow circles, taking in the destruction. The feeling of loss and sorrow rolled off him in waves.

How fate must hate me to allow this to happen.

"I don't know anything about fate. I do know a little about time. Nothing lasts forever."

He stared at me, a grim expression on his bronze face.

Not so, Amra. I will show you otherwise. He set off to the north. Holgren and I followed. What else could we do?

Tha-Agoth climbed the tower I'd gone to the day before—was it only a day? We followed. "What are you planning?" I asked him as we went up the cracked stairs.

You shall see.

"If it doesn't have something to do with catching up to your sister, we're wasting time."

There is time enough for this.

"I guess I'll just have to take your word on it since I have no idea what you're going to do."

He didn't respond but just kept climbing the steps. When we reached the top floor, he went from one window to the next, looking out at the corpse of Thagoth.

It was now completely free of the last remnants of snow, dreary desolation ringed on all sides by the death lands. Then, impatient with his limited ability to see, I suppose, he gestured with one hand, and the roofless walls of the tower fell away, leaving an unobstructed view on all sides. The stones didn't fall really; they just disappeared.

Now, you will see. What has been done can be undone. What time has destroyed, I can mend here in this place. First, I will cure the disease that eats away at the edges of my domain.

A wind started up, blowing outward in all directions from Tha-Agoth. That golden glow suffused him again, only this time, it was swept up by the wind and formed a pulsing, shimmering whirlwind with him at the base. Powerful gusts battered us. I fell to my knees and held onto the edge of the tower's precipice. Holgren followed my lead.

The storm grew to an intensity that threatened to pluck us from the tower top. Tha-Agoth gestured, throwing his arms wide. The whirlwind of light surged outward in all directions. It hit the death lands with a mighty rumble.

The scale of the change was massive and instantaneous. Demented vegetation turned to ash, swept away by that light-suffused, cleansing wind. Horribly mutated predators were caught in it, died, and decomposed in the blink of an eye.

It was finished in the space of a dozen slow breaths. The wind just ceased to be, and the golden light winked out. Tha-Agoth had swept the remnants of the Sorcerer King's death magic away from the limits of the valley, scoured the earth around the city clean of any taint of it. I looked out on that newly discovered terrain and saw tumbled stones and bare, red earth. Dreary as it was, it was a beautiful thing to behold.

I am far from finished. Observe.

I looked up into his starlight eyes then back out on the red, stony wasteland that had been covered by the death lands. First, I saw nothing. Then, I glimpsed movement out of the corner of my eye and felt the first tremors. The ground was spewing up stones.

What the Sorcerer King's magic tore down, what time's patient fingers pried apart, I will rebuild.

Hewn stones flew through the air in a complicated dance, re-knitting buildings, streets, fountains, garden walls, statues. The very dust of crumbled stones was drawn together like iron filings to a lodestone, obscuring much of the magic playing out before us in a howling, rust-colored storm.

When the storm was done, we saw Thagoth standing in its true splendor for the first time in over a thousand years. It was breathtaking. The shattered ruins I'd wandered through for six months hadn't given me a true sense of the beauty of the city.

It put Lucernis or any of the great cities of the Dragonsea to shame. Where most of them had grown up in haphazard fashion over the course of centuries, the city that now lay before me was planned with care and thought given to the placement of streets and fountains and garden spaces. Perhaps one of the great builders or architects could have appreciated and understood it more, a Lohen or a Kanikesh, but I understood well enough that Thagoth was of a piece. The last detail had been planned before the first stone was ever laid. It saddened me that it was, despite its resurrection, still a dead city.

Patience, Amra. Patience and faith. My work is not yet complete. You see only bones.

Fountains sputtered to life first as their workings knitted back together below ground. Water splashed on stone and caught the light. Then green things began to reappear across the city—trees shot up, vines climbed walls and sprouted flowers, hedges burst forth in spots that had lacked something I couldn't name before, and lush grass rushed across bare expanses of earth like a frantic, green tide, changing the primary color of the city from rust red to emerald green.

"How can you do this? I know you're powerful, but—"

This is my city. The earth and the stones of the earth here take their color from the blood I shed to create it and to keep it safe. It is mine. Time itself cannot destroy it if I will otherwise.

"But it's still lifeless. Cities are meant to be inhabited. Your people are long since dust."

He smiled. *The ones that fled the cataclysm, I can do nothing for. Those whose lives Athagos took I can do nothing for. All others I cradle in my palm. My blood is life eternal. What the earth has taken to its bosom, I can call back into the light. Your knife, please.*

I handed it over to him, and he plunged it into his palm unflinchingly. Then, he flung the resulting blood droplets out and away from the tower.

Awake, you sleepers, he muttered as he walked around the tower top, slinging blood in every direction. *Death is only a dream.*

And they came. A vast humming filled the air, and thousand-year-old corpses reassembled themselves out of the tiniest bits of matter, suddenly appearing one after the other on lawns, in streets, in doorways. They stood and stretched for all the world like sleepers awakening from a thousand-year nap. It was powerful magic.

They had lost their lives here. Even after an age, some infinitesimal portion of their physical selves still remained in this place. It seemed to be enough for Tha-Agoth to work with.

"Nothing is ever truly destroyed, I suppose," said Holgren.

Come, awake. I call to you, my people, my children. Time is no bar, and matter no barrier. Come. One by one they woke from death, hundreds of men, women, children—an entire bronze-skinned race that had not walked the world in a thousand years. Straight-limbed and handsome, each and every one, they looked up at their emperor and god with an expression of wonder and rapture. They uttered no sound. And Tha-Agoth looked down on them with what I can only call a look of paternal affection.

My children, he said. *My people. I am eternal, they are eternal, denizens of this eternal city.*

That was all great and wonderful but had little to do with the doom pressing down on the rest of the world. I had had enough of wonders. I wanted to foil the Shadow King, save Holgren from a fate worse than death, and go home.

"Can I have my knife back now?" I asked.

~ ~ ~

He decided to start out as the setting sun touched the rim of the valley. Tha-Agoth had called up the warriors of his people to accompany us, and the rest went back to their daily lives as if nothing had happened. That in itself was bizarre, but the truly unnerving thing about the Thagothians was that none of them spoke. Not a word, not a sigh or a chuckle or a hum. Not even the children. They walked around their resurrected city with content smiles plastered on their faces, like half-wits, or sleepwalkers.

Thagoth was not a city I wanted to spend any more time in, whether the death lands were gone or not.

What Holgren thought of the situation, he kept to himself. He was hardly more talkative than the Thagothians. When I asked him what the matter was, he shrugged and squeezed my hand lightly with his own burned one. We were sitting out of the way of things, against the outer wall of the Tabernacle.

"Everything depends on what happens now," he said. "I'm nervous is all."

"Don't be. We've made it through everything else. We'll make it through this as well."

He smiled and nodded then pointed out to the square where warriors were assembling around Tha-Agoth. They wore ancient bronze breastplates and helms and nothing by way of armor below their waists except for pale, linen breechcloths and sandals. They carried huge, bronze shields and long, bronze-tipped spears. They looked like something out of legend. I had no idea what good they could possibly do in the coming struggle, but they'd look good doing it.

Tha-Agoth himself had donned a suit of armor that reminded me of a shimmering body of a dragonfly. His long braids hung free and heavy down his back. He held no shield or weapon. I suppose he didn't need them. I suspected the armor he wore wasn't much more than ceremonial since he was immortal. I felt that sense of awe catch at my heart again as he stood amidst his troops, and I squashed it. Then, Tha-Agoth turned and started walking down the main thoroughfare through the city. The soldiers fell in step behind him in two columns.

"I think it's time to get going," Holgren said.

"All right, partner. Let's go face the future." We hitched ourselves upright and fell in behind the last of the ancient warriors, two ragged afterthoughts among the shining host.

~ ~ ~

Tha-Agoth ripped holes in reality for his troops to march through. Holgren tried to explain what he was doing, something about folding space. All I know is the god would rip at the air with his hands, and before us would suddenly be a ragged, pulsing hole that opened on an area a mile or more distant. Everybody would troop through, and the process would be repeated.

In this fashion, we moved through the night, skipping over miles and miles of terrain. At that pace, I estimated it would take us no more than two days to reach Shadowfall, perhaps much less. Not as swift as a gate, but definitely faster than walking or riding.

Once out of the valley, though, we encountered the tag end of the snowstorm that Tha-Agoth had banished from his city. It sputtered out quickly enough, leaving the land under a silent, white blanket. After the third or fourth leap forward, I made my way up the lines of silent soldiers to talk to Tha-Agoth.

We would make better time in daylight, he said, *but to delay until dawn might mean arriving too late.*

"Athagos can do this as well?"

Yes though not as well as I.

"Can you sense her?"

Always. She is somewhere ahead. I follow her trail.

"What will you do when you catch up to her?"

I will rip the cursed chain from her neck and send her home.

"And then?"

I will destroy the Shadow King.

"How?"

Slowly and painfully.

"That's not exactly what I meant."

It is all you need to know.

"This coming encounter affects all of us. You may need Holgren and me. You are perhaps the most powerful being I've ever met, but the Shadow King scares me silly, and I don't scare easily."

He is a worm that I will crush underfoot. Be sure you are not standing too near when I do so, little thief. I have not forgotten your betrayal.

I shook my head. If he didn't realize by now that we had done only what we had to, he never would.

"I'm not your enemy, Tha-Agoth. Nor is Holgren."

Of course you aren't. You are nothing in the grand design. You spurned the gift of immortality. You delivered Athagos to my enemy. I do not consider you an enemy. I do not consider you at all. He turned away from me and ripped another hole in reality.

"Well, it's nice to know where I stand," I muttered as the Thagothians shouldered past me into the pulsing rift.

It was some time around midnight when the first attack came. I'd stopped counting the rifts we'd walked through. I was tired, hungry, and concentrating on keeping up with the seemingly indefatigable Thagothians. I didn't doubt Tha-Agoth would leave us behind should we start to lag. If that happened, Holgren would almost certainly fall under the Shadow King's sway. We had to keep huddling under his protective aura.

We'd just stepped through a rift into a dark copse mostly free of snow when the umbrals hurled themselves out of the ground, huge swords whirring. Blood and body parts few in all directions.

It was a perfect ambush.

It was doomed.

In the first few seconds, Tha-Agoth's foot soldiers were being decimated. I saw one man split in two from skull to crotch, the umbral's sword cutting through his breastplate like it was cheese. The monster reversed its blade with blinding speed and beheaded another man. All this in the space of two seconds.

The remaining soldiers formed a hollow square around their god, leaving Holgren and I to fend for ourselves. Holgren was already uttering the harsh syllables that would call down lightning. I stood there, useless, knife out.

Then, the soldiers opened their mouths and screamed.

It wasn't exactly like Athagos' power. There was a thinner quality to the shriek, a less powerful feel. Still, it turned my bones to jelly and had Holgren and I twitching on the ground. The thought came to me that Tha-Agoth had been speaking literally when he'd called the Thagothians his children. His and Athagos' with powers to match. No wonder they didn't talk.

Around us, the umbrals stopped in their tracks and crumbled to dust. When it was over, their terrible shrieking stopped. The darning needles in my ears withdrew, and control of my body returned to me. I turned over and dry heaved the nothing that was in my stomach.

Tha-Agoth moved among the fallen warriors, spending drops of blood to resurrect them. I sat up and helped Holgren regain his feet.

What foulness is this? said Tha-Agoth. He was standing over one of his slain warriors, dribbling blood from his freshly cut palm into the gaping mouth of the corpse. Nothing was happening.

"Looks like the Shadow King has found a way to kill permanently," I croaked.

Impossible. My blood is life eternal. He tore at his wrist with the head of a snapped spear and let the resulting gush of blood coat the man's gaping chest wound. There was no change.

Holgren wobbled over to a pile of dust that had been one of the Shadow King's beasts. He touched two fingers to the giant blade that lay nearby then drew his hand back as if it had been scalded.

"There are foul magics woven into this blade. The Shadow King has found a way to destroy souls." He looked up at Tha-Agoth. "You won't bring any of them back. There's nothing to *bring* back, I'm afraid."

Tha-Agoth rose from where he knelt next to the slain soldier, starlight eyes afire.

He is a scourge, a blight on the world. He must be destroyed.

"He also seems to know your line of march," I said. "Perhaps we should deviate from it a bit, just to keep him guessing." I didn't want to catch a stray blade. I might not have much of a soul, but what I did have I wanted to keep. And since it seemed that Holgren and I would be twitching on the ground every time there was a skirmish, I'd just as soon avoid any more violence along the way.

Tha-Agoth had other ideas.

Let them come in their hundreds. I will destroy them all.

"Holgren and I along with them, most likely."

Perhaps. That is not my concern.

"Well, it is mine. But forget about us. How many more of your men are you willing to see die? Did you bring them back after a thousand years to blithely see them perish?"

I will not let the Shadow King sway me from my path.

"Then you're a fool," I said. He didn't bother to respond.

~ ~ ~

We went through three more ambushes by the umbrals that night. Each time, we spent most of the melee twitching on the ground, waiting for death. It was one of the darkest nights I've ever lived through. I can think of little worse than the feeling of utter powerlessness that possessed me that night.

By the third attack, Tha-Agoth had lost more than half his troops. Perhaps thirty remained. Those left still wore those beatific, untroubled looks on their faces. They were serving their god, sure of their destiny despite his inability to bring them back to life. They were idiots led by a dangerous deity.

After the last umbral attack, Holgren took me in his shaky arms and buried his face in my neck. "Leave, Amra," he whispered. "Walk away now. Go back to Lucernis, and leave all this behind. Go home."

I raised his head and put two fingers to his lips. Then, I put my hand over his heart. "This is my home now," I said. "No more talk of me leaving, Holgren. I'll see this through to the end."

"You're a damned fool," he said, and a thin smile touched his lips.

One thing I couldn't figure out was why Tha-Agoth didn't just destroy the umbrals himself. After what he'd done to the death lands, I thought it should have been child's play for him.

"I believe he only wields that sort of power in Thagoth," said Holgren when I mentioned it. "If you remember, he said something about that place being special to him because of the blood he shed to protect it."

"So he isn't the all-powerful being he seemed this afternoon."

"I really don't think he is, else he would have had the entire world under his sway a thousand years ago."

"Let's just hope he's powerful enough to finish the Shadow King," I said.

We suffered no more attacks from the shadowy umbrals that night. As dawn approached, I began to believe we might be safe for another day. I should have remembered the mother of monsters. Shemrang.

Athagos. You are close now, said Tha-Agoth to himself. *I feel you.*

He stood staring through the dark to the east. *I feel you, moving through the night, a shadow among the shadows. I can almost smell you. I can almost hear your breath…* He shuddered, the longing plain on his face.

I didn't pretend to understand what strange emotions they held between them. Forgetting the fact that she was his sister, how could he want her when she had betrayed him and doomed him to agony for a thousand years?

Neither was human, I finally decided, and human morals, human emotions, and motivations simply did not apply.

After a time, he shook himself and ripped another hole in reality.

Inky tendrils of distilled night shot through the opening and tore him in half.

Tha-Agoth screamed. The rift began to collapse. The tentacles pulled Tha-Agoth's upper half through the collapsing rift as the smaller nightmares poured through to finish the soldiers. They were hideously fast, faster than they'd been when we'd encountered them in the Flame's halls.

Holgren had to stay with Tha-Agoth. If he didn't, he was finished. I shoved him through the closing rift and prayed as Tha-Agoth's shrieking soldiers lay me flat and twitching. I hit the ground hard, facing east. The rift closed completely.

I waited for death to come in the form of one of Shemrang's offspring. Out in the distance, perhaps two miles away, I saw a great blossoming of light, pure white mixed with warm gold, and prayed that Holgren had been able to drive Shemrang and her children away again.

The Thagothians dispatched all of the creatures that had swarmed through the gate but at a high cost. Only twelve of Tha-Agoth's men remained. I survived, I think, mainly because I wasn't a moving target. They likely mistook me for dead.

Once the shrieks died away and control returned to my body, I stood on shaky legs and tottered off to the east.

"Let him be alive," I muttered to myself. Behind me, the Thagothians heaved up the lower half of their god on broad, bronze shoulders and followed me. Or at least they moved in the same direction as I did.

The sky was lightening in the east. Soon, the Shadow King's creatures would have no power above ground. If Holgren still lived, we might be able to make it to Shadowfall before night and destroy the massive, black block that I suspected housed all the Shadow King's power. If Holgren was dead… He wasn't. He couldn't be. Completely unacceptable.

I stumbled into a shaky run.

~ ~ ~

False dawn had taken the sky before I arrived at where I thought I'd seen the magelight flare, allowing me to take in my surroundings more fully. Snow had not fallen this far east. I realized we were fairly near the river where Holgren and I had first met the umbrals. We'd traveled much further than I had realized.

We were on the edge of the great expanse of grassland that led down to the river in an area of thorny shrubs and scattered, wind-twisted trees. The ground was uneven. I stumbled more than once. All the while, I scanned the horizon for some sign of Holgren or Tha-Agoth. I saw nothing, had seen nothing since that burst of light.

I found them in a shallow depression nearly hidden by the surrounding brush. The upper half of Tha-Agoth lay bleeding in sparse, graying grass. His eyes were closed. Holgren lay not far away. At first, I thought he was dead, and a stabbing pain ripped through my heart. Then, I saw the slow rise and fall of his chest.

He drove the creatures away. It cost him dearly. Tha-Agoth regarded me with his starlight eyes. I ignored him. His followers would arrive soon with his lower half, and he'd be as good as new.

I went to Holgren and turned him over. His face was bloody, his clothes shredded. Shemrang or her children had gotten hold of him at least briefly.

"He saved your life," I said. "Heal him."

No.

"How can a god be so petty?" I asked. "How can you refuse aid to someone who freed you from a thousand years of torment?"

If he lives, I will forgive him his betrayal. More, I will not do.

The others arrived. Tha-Agoth busied himself with putting his body back together. I cradled Holgren's head in my lap and wiped the worst of the blood from his face. He breathed shallowly but did not wake.

Tha-Agoth and his men were ready to go in less than half an hour. Holgren still hadn't woken.

"Tha-Agoth," I said. "I need your help. If you won't heal him, at least have your men carry him. If he gets too far from you, he will become the Shadow King's creature. It will be another victory for your enemy."

At first, I thought he would refuse even this, but he simply nodded, tight-jawed, and one of the soldiers discarded his shield and threw Holgren over his shoulder.

Tha-Agoth stared off to the east, into the rising sun. *She fords a river,* he said. *She is very close now.*

"Then she's also very close to Shadowfall." I said. "We should be able to get there long before dark and take the Shadow King at his weakest."

First my sister, he said, *then my enemy.*

"What if she doesn't want to go back to Thagoth?" I asked him.

She will do as I say. But he sounded less than certain.

"If you say so."

She will. She must. It is only the necklace that forces her away, the filthy necklace that you put on her.

I said nothing but began to wonder. A thought occurred to me: Just who had bound her to the Tabernacle grounds, and why? I had suspected things were not as they had seemed and never had been. The feeling grew in me.

The next rift opened on the bank of the river where I'd had a mule's head staring back at me as I'd bathed. It was the last Tha-Agoth would open.

From here, we follow solely on foot. She is very close now. He forded the river, and we all followed. Once across the water and into the trees, he stopped and sniffed like some predator tracking its prey. Tha-Agoth moved forward, a little to the south, and we followed.

I kept an eye on Holgren, checking periodically to make sure he was still breathing. It ate at me that there was nothing more I could do for him. That Tha-Agoth would do nothing for him I tried not to think about as the rage it engendered made me want to plunge my knife into his godly back.

We moved through the woods. After a time, I thought I began to recognize where we were heading. It wasn't anywhere I wanted to go. My suspicions were confirmed when we emerged into the clearing that had once contained the Flame's pyramid.

She has gone to ground there, said Tha-Agoth, pointing toward the gaping hole I'd helped create.

"That's what I was afraid of," I muttered. More than likely, it was also where Shemrang and her vicious children had gone to ground as well. Tha-Agoth might be able to survive being ripped in half, but Holgren and I wouldn't.

I tried again to reason with him. "Tha-Agoth, please listen to me. Let me lead you to Shadowfall now. If you destroy the Shadow King, Athagos will be free, not to mention Holgren. You don't have to waste time getting rid of the necklace if you destroy him. Going down into that pit is only asking for trouble."

No. Athagos first. I will deal with the Shadow King only after I've found my sister.

I sighed. Exactly what I'd expected, but I had to try. "Be ready to deal with Shemrang and her offspring again, then. Only this time, Holgren won't be able to drive her off since you won't heal him."

He said nothing, only climbed down into the darkness. The rest of us followed. I had no doubt it was going to be bad down there in the dark. I just didn't know how bad.

KERF & ISIN, PART THE THIRD

On the plane of deities, Isin was berating Kerf.

"How do you know it isn't the Shadow King's reign that is about to begin?" she asked. "If we had taken care of the Twins ourselves as I suggested, none of this would be happening. His influence would have been limited to those he could trick to coming to him. In time, he would have faded away as magic did. Now, he's poised to usher in an age of death and darkness!"

Kerf leaned heavily on his crooked staff, the weight of worlds seemingly settled on his uneven shoulders.

"Isin, calm yourself. Death and darkness are *always* waiting to sweep down on an unsuspecting world. Sometimes, they even prevail. But it is our function to aid mortality, not protect it from all possible harm. Free will entails responsibility, oh goddess of the kind heart and lovely smile."

"Don't try to flatter me, Kerf. The fact remains that the Twins are our responsibility. They aren't mortal. They were destined to join us. I should never have let you persuade me to let those poor mortal dears try to settle the matter."

"You've grown attached to them, is all. You have a sentimental investment in them. So do I. I've taken a real liking to that foul-mouthed, foul-tempered woman and her partner. But the very nature of heroism entails just such life-or-death endeavors as they're undertaking. When this is over, they'll be stronger, wiser, and more fully human than they ever would have been had I not set them on the trail of Thagoth."

"That is cold comfort if they die, Kerf, and you know it. It isn't even your real motive. You're an inveterate meddler."

"And the world is a better place for it. Do I have ulterior motives? None that I haven't already revealed. I don't want to leave this age hero-less. Is that so terrible? Who knows what this next crew will be like? Just because our time here is at an end doesn't mean our responsibility is as well."

"Don't start prattling about responsibility to me, you old scoundrel. I'll say it again: The Twins were our responsibility. They're our children after all."

"I hadn't thought it possible, but you are even more lovely when you grow wroth, fair Isin. Why did I ever let you go?"

"Kerf—"

"Isin, I've felt every pain of every mortal I singled out for greatness, be it physical, mental, emotional or spiritual. I have suffered every ill of Aridhall Flamehand, of Halfa the

Wanderer King, of Havak Silversword and a dozen-dozen more both famous and obscure. And now, I add Amra Thetys and Holgren Angrado to the list. I know what I ask of them, and I pay as surely as they do. Look at me. I was not always a hunchbacked, crippled old god. You know that."

Isin relented a little, touched Kerf's lined face with one cool, soft hand. "I know, Kerf. I know. And to me, you're still that brash youth that won my heart when the world was young."

Kerf grabbed her hand in his own and pressed it to his lips. "Ah my love, perhaps in the next age, we will discover what we might have been together. It is my one regret, you know. Choosing duty over love."

"You are what you are, Hero Maker. I knew that when I took you to my bed. Now hush. I want to pay attention to what's happening. And if those lovers lose their lives or worse, you'll regret it for a dozen ages. Do I make myself clear?"

CHAPTER 11

I tried to keep my eyes everywhere at once as we made our way down the mound of rubble to the hall's floor. I scanned every shadowed recess, searching for signs of tentacled nightmares. I had half-expected Shemrang herself to be waiting in the great hall. She was too massive to fit anywhere else. She wasn't there, but that didn't mean her offspring weren't. Attack could come from anywhere at any time.

I was not afraid—that emotion seemed to have been burned out of me. My only concern was for survival—mine and Holgren's. Instead of fear, a cold, muted anger suffused me. It had much to do with the pigheaded god and his twelve silent soldiers descending ahead of me, the murderous, mad goddess they tracked, and the thing made out of nightmare and shadows that we would have to face very soon now. And the shadow's creatures. Mustn't forget Shemrang and her get.

It was a bleak feeling that made me colder and harder than I had ever been before I discovered what I felt for Holgren. Seeing him slung over one of the soldier's shoulders like a lump of meat, refused healing by the one he'd saved from being torn to shreds—I discovered what it truly meant to have a hard heart. Tha-Agoth might be our only hope of defeating the Shadow King, but if I ever had the chance to do him ill, I would seize it. I promised myself I would leave him twisting in the wind.

When we had all descended to the stone floor of the hall, Tha-Agoth sniffed the air like an animal.

She was here just moments ago. Which way though? Which way has she fled?

"She could be anywhere," I told him. "This place is a labyrinth. It could take days to find her. While you're searching, she could slip by you and be taken by the Shadow King. Destroy him now, Tha-Agoth. It's the only sure way."

He didn't even glance in my direction. *This way, I think. Yes.* He strode off toward the stairs where Holgren had made the blood dolls, and his men followed.

So did I, cursing them all silently and keeping an eye out for spider-limbed, tentacled monsters.

Tha-Agoth may not have needed light to make his way through pitch-black stone corridors, but I certainly did. Since his men did as well, he called into being a golden glow that suffused his body and drove the darkness back. The light also made him a target. I wished fervently that when we were attacked, it was him the beasts would go after and not the soldiers. Holgren would most likely suffer should they be attacked.

Tha-Agoth would pause periodically to sniff the air or bend down and touch the stones of the floor with thick fingers. Then, he would resume his hunt.

In this fashion, we made our way through dusty corridors for what felt like hours. I began to suspect Athagos was leading us around in circles on purpose. The thought came to me that she planned to keep us from reaching Shadowfall for as long as possible—probably until nightfall, when the Shadow King would be most powerful.

I turned it around in my head. It felt right even if I couldn't understand why she'd do it.

Eventually we were headed toward what I realized was the old Sorcerer King's sanctum. Was Athagos leading us there on purpose? Did she have some reason to go there, or was it chance or her madness? I had no answers, nor could I see what difference it really made.

We descended the stairs that led to the sanctum. Tha-Agoth paused there at the base of the stairs in front of the door to the lair.

I sense something, he said, head cocked to one side. *Some power.*

I didn't enlighten him. I owed him nothing. Perhaps the husk that had been the Sorcerer King had a surprise left for his age-old enemy. Or Athagos had something in store for her brother. In any case, I wanted no part of it. I had a feeling that unpleasant things were about to happen in that unpleasant place.

When the Flame started whispering in my mind, I nearly jumped out of my skin. I'd forgotten all about him.

Do not enter the sanctum, the Flame's voice hissed in my head. *Neither let the mage enter if you value his soul.*

"We'll just wait out here if you don't mind," I said to Tha-Agoth.

Do as you will. It matters little to me. I tapped the soldier who was carrying Holgren on the shoulder and said, "Let him down."

He helped me lower Holgren to the floor. I checked Holgren's heartbeat. It was thready. Huge welts on his neck and face oozed pus where the monster's tentacles must have touched his flesh. He looked as close to death as he could be without actually being dead. If I'd had any impulse to warn Tha-Agoth of the danger that lay ahead, Holgren's condition squashed it.

The god pushed open the door to the sanctum. Nothing happened. He stepped inside. His men followed him in. Still, nothing happened. I could see a slice of the room through the open door—a bit of wall, the torso of one contorted corpse, the pale, blue light of a brazier and obscene shadows dancing on the wall. Then, those ghostly, gibbering voices started shrieking, and the door slammed shut with a thunderous clap.

Even with that thick door closed, I could hear the sounds of carnage and millennium-old hate being vented.

The ghost-khordun feeds, whispered the Flame. *Their hunger is a thousand years old and insatiable.*

"Why didn't they eat me before? And where the hells have you been?" I asked.

You are my chosen. They can sense you but cannot harm you. And I have been here, as always.

The hallway shuddered, and I felt magic's chill hand on the back of my neck. Blood began to seep through the crack underneath the door. Battle raged on for perhaps three or four minutes, then a perfect silence descended.

As I was about to get up and put an ear to the door, it exploded outward, torn to splinters. Tha-Agoth strode out of the hall and into the corridor, his face a bloody mask, his dragonfly armor ripped to shreds. He held the stunted husk of the Sorcerer King up above him by the neck.

YOU DARE? YOU ARE NOTHING! Tha-Agoth slammed the king's body against a wall. Bones splintered. The husk's tongue lolled out of his mouth, and his withered face was purple.

Where is she, worm? said Tha-Agoth, punctuating each word by beating his opponent's head into the wall. *Where is Athagos? Where? Where?*

"He can't answer you if he can't speak," I pointed out.

Tha-Agoth threw the wreckage that had been the Sorcerer King to the floor. There it gagged and coughed but did not otherwise move.

Answer me, or I'll rend your desiccated flesh from your bones.

It took me a moment to realize the husk was laughing.

"You can no more destroy me now than I can destroy you, godling. I am beyond death. As I can affect nothing, so too can nothing affect me."

That's when Tha-Agoth started ripping his limbs from his body. Tha-Agoth was definitely affecting him, in my opinion. It wasn't a pretty sight.

When the husk was nothing but head and torso, Tha-Agoth leaned down and spat into his face.

I will ask you once more. Where is my sister?

"Somewhere in the labyrinth," he rasped, "and soon under the sway of the Shadow King. More I cannot say."

Then your usefulness is at an end. And Tha-Agoth put his fist through the husk's wizened face and tore his head from his body. I shuddered. If what he'd told me was true, even in that state, the old bastard wasn't dead. I wondered briefly what it might be like to live through such a thing. My mind couldn't encompass it.

Tha-Agoth stood and shook bloody gobbets of flesh and brain from his hand. I got up as well and stood in front of him. Perhaps not the best time to confront him, but time was in short supply. Night was coming.

"Listen to me now. Abandon this search. You know where she's going, where she has to go. If we waste time searching for her here, it may well be too late. Please listen to reason."

He shook his head. *She is here. I sense her.*

"She could be anywhere! Do you really think you were following her trail when you entered that room? It was a trap!"

No. She was here. That was no illusion.

"Then she led you here on purpose, hoping to destroy you or at least slow your pursuit. Have you forgotten how she tricked you a thousand years ago?"

Some of his certainty seemed to crumble.

She was swayed by that one, he said, indicating the remains of the Sorcerer King.

"Why she did it doesn't matter, only what she did and will do. For whatever reason, she doesn't want you to catch her. If you waste time down here, you will lose her to the Shadow King forever, and the entire world will be enslaved. Think beyond the moment, for Kerf's sweet sake! We know where she has to go. Why not wait for her there?"

He relented. I didn't think he would. He was as mad in his own way as his sister: obsessed with her to the point of unreason.

Take me to this Shadow King.

~ ~ ~

Tha-Agoth would not help me carry Holgren, the bastard, so it was slow going.

Hurry, mortal. Time flies.

I had Holgren slung across my back. Every tottering step threatened to be my last.

"You won't heal him, and you won't help me carry him, you godly sack of dung, so you can take your 'flying time' and choke on it." We were making our slow way down the passage that led to the stairs and the lake. I had no idea of the time. I hoped it was still daylight.

He is a burden. Leave him.

"He's only a burden because you refuse to help. He's also the only reason I'm helping you at all. You'd better remember that."

I do not need your help.

I stopped and lowered Holgren to the ground. "Fine," I said, pulling out my knife. "I'll just end his life here so he doesn't become a mindless slave to the Shadow King. Then, I'll get along home and leave you to find Shadowfall on your own. Maybe you'll find it before your sister does. Maybe you'll be able to keep the Shadow King from snaring her. I don't really care anymore, you selfish, obsessed, immortal puddle of vomit. Godhood was wasted on you, you miserable tick."

I thought he was going to kill me. The rage on his face was plain. Maybe no one had ever spoken to him in such fashion. I stood my ground, waiting for his divine fist to punch a hole in my very mortal face. He trembled with anger, and his hands balled at his sides.

"Do it if you're going to," I said quietly. "But make sure you kill Holgren as well. He would not want to survive as a pawn of evil."

I cannot kill him nor heal him, just as I cannot rifle through your mind. I swore I would not. My word is final. I cannot go against it.

"You've got a twisted sense of honor then. Are you going to kill me or not?"

No.

He said it as though it caused him physical pain to do so. I should be so lucky.

"Then help me carry him if you want to get to Shadowfall before Athagos." He stood there for a little while longer, eyes shining. Then, he scooped Holgren up in his arms, like a parent would a sleeping child. I sheathed my knife with trembling hand and set out once again for the stairs and the ledge and the lake. Beyond that, I didn't contemplate. One thing at a time.

We made the ledge above the lake. It had snowed but only a little. A light powder dusted the ledge. The lake wasn't frozen, not even at the edges. The sun was bleeding its life away in great, red streaks behind and above us. Darkness was creeping in ahead. We had wasted the day down below and would face the Shadow King in all his power.

Where to now, Amra? Tha-Agoth asked. *Where will Athagos go?*

I pointed out to the other end of the lake, which was lost in gloom and a pale, acrid smelling fog. "There," I said. "The far shore, or rather a short distance beyond. You should be able to see Shadowfall construct itself any moment now. Kerf knows it's big enough to be seen from here."

Tha-Agoth lay Holgren gently down and started for the stairs. *I cannot be encumbered now,* he said.

I heaved Holgren onto my back and staggered after Tha-Agoth. In my heart, I held little hope for Holgren or myself, but I would see it through to the end. There was nothing else to be done.

Tha-Agoth made his way to the stone quay where we'd first met Ruiqi and stood there, staring out at the approaching gloom. In the distance, green planes of light had sprung into being. Shadowfall was assembling itself. The Shadow King had woken. Tha-Agoth stood looking out at it. He seemed bemused by the sight.

There lairs my enemy, he said. But there was another enemy much closer.

The fog-shrouded surface of the lake exploded up and outward. Shemrang, mother of monsters, raised her black, steaming bulk out of the murky waters of the lake, snared Tha-

Agoth with tentacles made of night, and dragged him down under the water. It was over in a heartbeat.

I just stood there for a moment, stunned and soaked, staring at the roiling water. Then I laid Holgren down on the slick stones of the quay, drew my knife and the length of rod that had pinned a god for an age from my belt, and jumped in.

I don't know how to swim, so really, I don't know what I was thinking. I suppose I wasn't thinking, in fact. All I knew was Tha-Agoth was the key to defeating the Shadow King and freeing Holgren and to saving the world. And Shemrang had him. She might not be able to kill him, but he was of no use to me torn into a thousand little pieces, his severed head giving birth to monsters. So I went in that murky water to get him back.

That lake was cold, choked with weeds, and black as pitch now that night had come. I struggled toward where I thought Shemrang must be, kicking and sinking. I wasn't going to make it. My lungs began to burn with the need for air almost immediately, but I couldn't even tell which way was up after a few seconds. I could barely see my own hand in front of my face. I thought I had used up all my fear over the past months. I was wrong. It was an awful, terrifying experience.

I didn't have to find Shemrang. She found me. One giant, questing tentacle latched onto my thigh and dragged me through the water toward her. I hacked at it with my knife. It did not seem to affect her in the least. She didn't loosen her grip. Quite the contrary. The tentacle snaked around my chest and squeezed, forcing air out of my tortured lungs. Everywhere exposed flesh met tentacle, it burned.

Ahead of me, a burst of golden light shot through the gloom. I could only assume it was Tha-Agoth. It didn't rival Holgren's magelight. I don't think it actually harmed Shemrang all that much. She still had me firmly in her grip. It did allow me to see the battle that raged between the two as I approached. Tha-Agoth was being constricted in much the same way I was. He was having much better success at causing Shemrang discomfort. Much as she had torn him asunder, he was shredding tentacle after tentacle with his bare hands. A desperate hope flared in me that we might survive. That hope died as suddenly as it was born when Shemrang maneuvered Tha-Agoth within range of her gaping, serrated maw.

She snapped his head off with one bite.

The golden glow slowly faded from around his decapitated corpse, now set free to float down to the bottom of the lake with a dark cloud of blood to mark its passage. It was my turn next.

I suppose she didn't consider me much of a threat after Tha-Agoth. I had no doubts she was still harboring a wee bit of resentment over the unflattering things I'd said about her and her children. She wanted to torment me before she finished me off. She rose up from the lake, dangling me in front of her long, narrow face. I gasped a tiny bit of blessed fresh air, as much as my constricted lungs would allow. The tip of her leathery tongue lapped at my face.

Not as savory as a god, gutter thief, but you will do. And the mage as well.

I'd have snapped off a witty retort, but I could barely breathe. Besides, none sprang to mind. My arms were free of her embrace, so I let my knife speak for me.

I nearly severed the last inch or so of her tongue.

Apparently, it was a fairly sensitive organ. Her shriek was quite loud. Then, I was rushing toward her mouth head-first. Dropping the knife, I got a two-handed grip on the rod and prayed.

My timing wasn't perfect nor my aim. I'd intended to wedge the bar between her jaws, thus staving off my imminent beheading. Instead, the jagged tip of the rod caught her about a foot or so below her eyes. It parted her strange, sleek flesh and continued on into the interior of her head as if she were composed of warm butter. And I thought she'd screamed when I nicked her tongue.

She tried to fling me away, but I held on to that tentacle for dear life, wrapping my thighs and free arm around it as tightly as I could. I didn't want to end up in the lake again or smeared against the cliff wall.

I clung to her, burning, hoping something else would come to me.

She started pounding me against the lake.

I'd always thought of water as being soft. When you're hurled against it, it isn't soft at all. I suppose it isn't as bad as being smacked against stone. It wasn't a feather bed either.

After the third or fourth time, I knew I had to do something other than just hold on. She was hurt, but how hurt, I didn't know. First thing's first. I had to get Tha-Agoth's head back, and it was inside her. I was going to have to retrieve it for Holgren's sake.

The things we do for love.

On the tentacle's next upswing, I took in the situation as best I could. It was going to be tricky. I'd only get one chance.

It is amazingly difficult to judge distances and angles when you're clinging to a lashing, writhing monster of a tentacle. Try it sometime; you'll see what I mean. The tentacle flew downward and smacked me into the water again. I was getting very tired of that. On the next upswing, I launched myself, hoping I would get it right. I very much doubted I'd get a second chance.

I'd planned to land behind her head so that I could drive the rod into the base of her brain. It would make everything else so much easier if I didn't have to deal with Shemrang's writhing. It didn't turn out that way. My vault carried me up over her half-cleaved, screaming head.

I landed down around the middle of her back, among the faces that pebbled her flesh. I stuck my hand in one of the mouths unknowingly. It gnashed down, and I nearly lost a finger. I pulled my hand away and began to slide down her slippery back toward the water. That wouldn't do.

Tha-Agoth's head was somewhere inside, so I went looking for it. The rod parted her flesh with a terrifying ease. Black, viscous blood welled up immediately, and her shrieks took on a new urgency. She began to flail around her back with the tentacles that ringed her head. They buffeted but did not dislodge me.

"Hurry up and die, you bitch," I muttered. And I dug deeper, clearing great gobbets of flesh as I went. And all the while, I tried to figure out where she kept her stomach.

I don't have words to describe the foul stench of Shemrang's innards. It was worse than the death lands if that gives you any indication. It was distilled essence of corruption. The vomit I choked out as I made my way through the meat of her was a sweet smell in comparison. Somewhere along the way, she collapsed and was still, save for a twitch, a tremble that felt like an earthquake as I mined my way through her putrid body.

I have never been afraid of enclosed spaces—my profession had put me in tight spots many times over the years. As the foul meat of Shemrang pressed in all around me and I clawed my way into stench and darkness, though, I felt an unreasoning fear begin to creep up on me. She was dead, and clawing through her carcass had me more terrified than when she was about to snap my head off.

The workings of a mind are strange indeed.

I was all the way inside her corpse and running out of breathable air when I finally hit her windpipe, or gullet or whatever. It was large enough for me to crawl through in a prone position, and air and lake water trickled in from her mauled mouth. It was also coated with an acidic slime that stung my eyes and ate away at my skin. I headed south toward what I assumed would be her version of a stomach, or maybe womb.

I found Tha-Agoth's head lodged in a crevice just before the passage opened up into a place I really didn't want to go. Dead or not, I'm certain Shemrang's stomach was not a healthy place to be.

It wasn't difficult to find Tha-Agoth. His head still glowed faintly. He'd gotten hold of the slimy wall with his teeth and was hanging on with a tenacity that, while admirable, was also gut-splittingly funny in a horrible sort of way. Maybe it was just me. He certainly didn't seem amused.

I picked his head up by the hair, looked into his face, and said, "Do you have *any* idea how deep you are in my debt now?" His only response was a slow, shuddering blink.

I carved a way out for us with the rod, straight up from where I'd found the god's head. I slithered out of the monster's corpse not unlike how I'd seen her children born. Once free of the vile meat of her, I collapsed on that nasty hide and took in great gulps of relatively fresh air. None of the faces that dotted her torso moved anymore. They were all slack and gray. I hoped they'd been released with her death.

Shemrang floated on the surface of the lake like some immense bladder. Roughly a third of her bulk was above the waterline. I could tell she was sinking, slowly. I had to figure out what to do next. I glanced over toward Holgren. He was still lying on the stones of the quay, undisturbed by the battle that had just taken place. I couldn't tell if he was still breathing from this distance and in the dark, but he wasn't moving.

First thing's first. I had to get Tha-Agoth his body back. I figured it would be easier to bring his head to his body rather than the other way around. The only trouble was I didn't know exactly where his body was. That and the whole not-being-able-to-swim thing. I held the god's head up and looked him in the face. He was hurting. He'd get over it.

"Hey, Tha-Agoth. Do you have any control over your body right now? Blink once for yes, twice for no."

Blink-blink. Scowl.

"Any bright ideas as to how I can find it?"

Blink.

"Can you tell where it is from here?"

Blink.

"I'll call out directions. Blink when I get it right. West?"

Nothing.

"East?"

Nothing.

"North? South?"

Nothing. Nothing.

"I've run out of directions, my friend."

Blink-blink. Scowl. Then he mouthed a word: *down.*

"It's underneath us. It's underneath her." And she was sinking fast.

Blink.

I took a deep breath then another. It was time to jump back in before Shemrang's bulk buried Tha-Agoth's body. I got a good hold of Tha-Agoth's long braids and the length of rod. Before I could think too much about what I was doing, I jumped back in the foul lake. The water hadn't gotten any warmer or any more breathable, but at least it washed most of Shemrang off me. I was able to hold on to my breath better this second time, and the weight of my waterlogged clothes, Tha-Agoth's head, and the rod made sure I found the bottom rather easily.

I took a second to secure the rod in my belt again, wishing I'd thought to do it before

I dove in, and began to search by feel along the muddy, weed-choked lake bottom. If I occasionally dragged Tha-Agoth's face through the silt, what can I say? It was dark, and I'm no swimmer.

I felt the bulk of Shemrang's corpse pressing down on me, figuratively if not yet literally. My lungs began to burn with the desire for fresh air. With the threat of immediate, horrible death removed, I was able to control my emotions and my lungs a little better this time around. Still, time was trickling away, and my fear was mounting. I was going to have a hard time just getting back to the surface. Once there, I wasn't sure if I could make myself go under again.

When the ache in my lungs became a clawing beast, I gave up and planted my feet on the bottom to kick up—and I felt the rubbery give of flesh under my ragged boots. Quickly, I found what I'd stood on—a thigh—and followed with my hands the way bodies are usually put together, along buttock, back, and shoulder to get to the neck. Briefly, I wondered what would happen if I stuck Tha-Agoth's head on backward, but the need to breathe was overpowering. I shoved his head down on the stump and fled toward the surface, using Shemrang's body to claw my way up.

Sweet air waited for me at the surface. I imagined Tha-Agoth would follow shortly. I clung to Shemrang's slowly sinking corpse and willed my limbs to stop shaking, but once the fear subsided, the cold took over.

It was maybe twenty yards to the quay. I figured I could make it. I'd mastered up and down in the water. How hard could across be? I never got the chance to find out.

I clung to Shemrang's side, eyeing the quay and judging distances. Then, I noticed movement above. I glanced up at the ledge, and there she stood. Athagos.

The little mouse has wicked teeth, she said and began to descend the stairs. *I do like you, thief, yes I do. You are the very definition of surprising.*

"Stay away from him," I chattered. I meant Holgren, but she misunderstood me. Or maybe chose to misunderstand me. It's hard to say, what with her being stark raving mad.

Oh, he's no threat to me, that one. I led him by the nose when he still had one. Now that he doesn't even have a nose, how could he trouble me? The king of shadows. What a poor kingdom that is, always dependent on the brilliance of others for your very existence. She'd reached the bottom of the stairs now and was walking out onto the quay.

"Whatever you say. Why don't you just run along then and do whatever it is you plan on doing?" And get the hell away from Holgren.

Oh. I am. I just wanted to leave a message for my brother. You'll be so kind as to pass it on?

"Whatever you want."

Tell him I look forward to our meeting on the other side. We've put it off long enough.

"I'll make sure he gets the message."

See that you do. With that, she ripped a hole in reality much as Tha-Agoth had done repeatedly to get us here. I'd never seen it from the other side. I don't know what I expected. Darkness, perhaps, or the pearlescence of a gate. It was neither. It was—nothing. Not blackness, just…nothing. When it disappeared, if that's the right word, so had Athagos.

So had Holgren.

"Tha-Agoth!" I screamed. "Hurry up and re-capitate, you sorry excuse for divinity!" I knew he couldn't hear me. Sometimes, screaming isn't about that.

Finally, Tha-Agoth broke the surface a few feet away from me, graceful as a fish. I kicked out wildly toward him, obscenities boiling out of me all the way and water leaking in.

Be still! he finally roared and got an arm around my chest. He lifted my head out of the water and went easily, gracefully, toward the quay.

Now, tell me what has happened. I did, including the message Athagos had asked me to give him. He went very still.

"We've got to hurry," I said. "There's no time left. Work your damned magic, and get us over there."

I...can't, he said and continued on to the quay.

"What do you mean you can't? You've been obsessed with getting your sister back, and now you say you can't? What the hells are you saying?" We made it to the quay. He lifted me out of the water, and I climbed up. He followed.

I can't. I won't. It's over.

"I clawed my way through that monster's belly to get you back. I saved you from a fate literally worse than death. You owe me. Don't you dare tell me it's over."

You don't understand. If I continue after Athagos, it may mean my death. It may mean both our deaths, hers and mine.

"What are you talking about, mister 'I can't be killed?'"

He wouldn't meet my eyes.

"Answer me, damn you!"

There is a way. It will destroy us both. I hid it from her. I kept it from her because she desired it so badly and I so much wanted to live. She has puzzled out what it is. That is what her message means.

"Too bad."

Don't you understand? I could die.

I took a deep breath and forced down my frustration. Talking to him was in some ways like talking to a spoiled child. A powerful, deadly, spoiled child that I couldn't take over my knee.

"Look," I said. "I don't really care what sort of problems you two have had in the past. I don't care whether she wants to die or if you don't. It's this simple: She's gone to the Shadow King. She's taken Holgren. You owe Holgren, and you owe me, us poor mortals who deal with the very real possibility of dying every single day. If you think I'm going to be sympathetic because there's an off-chance you might kark it, you've got to be out of your mind." I shook my head, turned away. "I figured you for a lot of things, Tha-Agoth, but a coward wasn't one of them."

You dare call me a coward?

"When you run away from your fears? I certainly do. They wouldn't call it courage if it was easy."

I owe you nothing.

"If you really believed that, we wouldn't be standing here having this conversation. You'd be high-tailing it back to Thagoth."

He stood with his arms crossed, looking out at the lake. I was silent, letting him make his own way toward what had to be done though every fiber of my being wanted to scream at him to hurry the hells up.

At last, he dropped his arms, took a deep breath, and said, *Let us pay a visit to the Shadow King, then.*

I let out a deep breath, and took stock. I was sopping wet and freezing. I'd lost my best and only knife for the second time, and I'd lost Holgren for, what, the fourth time? How many times could I twist events in my favor?

As many times as it took, I told myself firmly. You keep trying until you're dead, and then, you try some more. We were going to get out of this mess. We were going to destroy the Shadow King and free Holgren.

I ignored the niggling little voice in the back of my head that said, "What if Athagos has already sucked him dry?" I had Tha-Agoth at least. And near three feet of monster-killing metal. It would have to be enough.

"The Shadow King's stone is about a hundred yards east of the lake," I told Tha-Agoth. "We're fairly certain it contains his power. It might even *be* him in a sense. After dark, it's behind those walls." I pointed toward Shadowfall where it rose up against the stars, faintly glowing, massive.

They will afford him little protection. He stared out toward Shadowfall then glanced at me. *Stay behind me, little thief, during the battle that ensues. I will protect you as I can.*

"I'll take care of myself. You take care of the Shadow King." But I was begrudgingly touched. "Let's get to it. Remember, you must destroy the stone, Tha-Agoth. Everything else will sort itself out if you do."

I will do what I must.

He gestured. A rent appeared before us, and I followed him through, heart in my throat.

~ ~ ~

We came out on the wooden dock on the far side of the lake. I expected to be attacked immediately. Everything was still and silent. Shadowfall clawed its way to the stars ahead of us, through a thin screen of trees. Pale starlight, a newly risen gibbous moon, and Shadowfall's faintly glowing bulk were our only illumination.

I clutched the oddly warm rod with both clammy, shivering hands and followed Tha-Agoth into the tree line. He moved as silently as a wraith. I wasn't exactly noisy myself. Perhaps the Shadow King had exhausted all his troops. Maybe he just didn't give a damn whether we came calling or not—or he wanted us to. In any case, no night-spawned monsters came out to greet us as we made our way through the evergreens.

I was strung tight as a wire, waiting for the ambush that had to come.

It never came.

When we followed a bend in the path and came upon an open archway into Shadowfall's courtyard, it was almost disappointing. Almost.

Through the arch, I could make out the square, black stone in the center of the courtyard. Just to the left stood Athagos, one hand on a hip, the other pressed lightly against her mouth in a contemplative, philosophical manner. She was regarding a heap on the ground that I recognized immediately as Holgren.

He was between Athagos and the stone, hunched over and face-down, knees to his chest. The palms of his hands were fitted against the sockets of his eyes. There was no way he'd been positioned like that. He was conscious, then.

Welcome, Tha-Agoth. Welcome, Amra. We've been waiting for you. The Shadow King's voice rolled out from no particular direction, pleasant, amused.

Please, don't stand out there in the cold. Enter.

Tha-Agoth strode into the courtyard as if he owned the place. I followed, looked around for the Shadow King's manifestation. It wasn't here this time. I looked back at Holgren, but he hadn't moved.

"The stone," I whispered to Tha-Agoth. "That's his power. Destroy it, and we've won."

Tha-Agoth glanced at me then made a beeline to his sister, ignoring the stone completely, damn him. I think I knew then that we had lost.

He put his hands on Athagos' shoulders. I moved to one side to keep all the players in view. This was not how it was supposed to go. At some point, I was going to have to go for the block myself, but I had a feeling if I just went up to it and started whacking on it with the rod, I wasn't going to get very far. Something told me—the Flame?—that things had to fall in line, and they hadn't yet. It wasn't time. I only hoped I would know when the right time came around.

Come with me now, Tha-Agoth told his sister. *Back to our city, to our people. All is forgiven, and the future stands before us. Come.*

She stared into his eyes for a long time then put a gentle hand to his cheek. He sort of leaned into it and closed his eyes. Which is when she spat in his face. He took a startled step back.

All is forgiven? No, brother. I have forgiven you nothing. I'll not go back to your city and imprisonment. I will not return to our children, the fruit of forced union. I am free of your yoke, free of your attentions. I will remain so. Forever.

My love—

I've never seen anyone move as fast as her except Red Hand, the King of Assassins, and technically I suppose I hadn't actually seen him move at all. He'd moved too fast for the human eye to follow, when he wished.

One moment, the two godlings were standing there, Athagos airing their soiled laundry, and the next moment, Athagos had her hand *inside* his chest and her mouth locked on his.

I suppose it was a parting kiss, of sorts. I felt a trickle of that awful power of hers in my body, scouring my soul and making me twitch. They toppled to the ground, and Tha-Agoth's robust, bronze flesh began to shrivel slowly. He got his hands round her neck and began to squeeze. I didn't think it was going to do much good.

She is crushing his heart, said the Shadow King merrily, *as she sucks away his vitality. His blood may be life eternal, but only while his heart beats. That rod you hold should have stopped his heart front beating a millennium ago, but he moved just enough at the last instant. It crippled but did not kill him. She will finish him this time. Better late than never, I suppose.*

"Won't she die, too?"

Oh, yes, normally, she would. The bond between the Twins is unlike any other. They are tied to each other, body and soul, whether they like it or not. But of course I can't allow her to die in such a fashion. Once they've died, their very essences will be trapped here. I have great plans for such power. Just as I have for you.

I didn't like the sound of that.

I underestimated you, my dear. You tricked me. You caused the death of not one but two of my khordun and stole a third away from me at least for a time. You defeated my umbrals and destroyed Shemrang, a creature so old and wicked and powerful that I was at pains to make her obey me. I would be very angry with you indeed if I weren't so impressed. You will be a valuable tool.

"I'm nobody's tool."

I believe you will discover otherwise. Think on this, Amra: If you are of no use to me, then I have no reason to spare you, do I? Too, I hold your lover's soul in the palm of my hand.

I suppose he had a point.

Now be quiet, and do not bother me, he said. *I have waited to see Tha-Agoth die for a very long time.*

I shut up and feigned interest in the gruesome show. Tha-Agoth was struggling and putting up far more of a fight than anyone else I'd seen Athagos slurp down.

He wasn't going to make it. His skin began to sag off his bones. The hands that had tried to pry his sister off him now beat feebly at her head. Blood trickled from her hand's point of entry into his chest. All in all, I'd seen more pleasant things.

I weighed all the options and with a little regret decided it wouldn't be such a bad thing if the Twins took each other out. Theirs was an old and apparently ugly story that had nothing to do with me.

The Shadow King did. I hoped the rod would do to the block what it had done to

Shemrang. It was all I had going for me.

I didn't try anything tricky or fancy. I just walked up to the block and, with every ounce of force I could muster, rammed it down onto the stone's wide, black surface.

I flew in one direction, and the rod spun end over end in another.

I told you not to bother me, Amra.

When the cobwebs cleared, it was very quiet. I clambered slowly to a standing position and took a look around. Athagos was prone on the ground, not breathing, not moving. Next to her was Tha-Agoth's skin. It was crumpled into an untidy ball. His braids were bigger than the rest of his remains. It was a little sick-making. Or maybe it was just the pain.

That was…satisfying, said the Shadow King. *Now. Pick Athagos up, and lay her on the block.*

"Do it yourself," I muttered.

How soon they forget. I think it is time for another object lesson.

I was expecting him to magically rip portions of my anatomy from me. I didn't get off that lightly.

Holgren twitched, stirred, then stood up. His eyes were wide, and the veins in his temples throbbed. I felt the presence of magic creep up my neck. I braced myself—the Shadow King was about to do something unpleasant to Holgren. And he did after a fashion.

Holgren twitched, cocked his head, and screamed, "NO!" Then, his hand shot out toward me, and I was in agony. It was as if molten lead had replaced the marrow of my bones. I fell to the ground, writhed, shrieked. There was no more me. There was only the terrible pain.

It stopped as abruptly as it began. I curled up into a ball and panted.

Place Athagos' body atop the block, Amra.

If it had just been my pain, I might have held out until I died. Very, very doubtful but at least possible. It wasn't just my pain though. It was Holgren's as well. The Shadow King's display of power would hurt Holgren far more than it hurt me.

I crawled over to Athagos' body and began to drag her to the block. I didn't look at Holgren. I couldn't. I had failed him.

"I'm sorry, Amra. Oh, gods, I'm sorry," Holgren whispered.

Be quiet, said the Shadow King.

I finally got Athagos up on top of the block, head lolling, arms trailing off the edges. I stepped back and sort of tumbled down to a sitting position, every bone aching. The Shadow King's voice let out a strange little hiss.

Finally. Freedom at last and the power of the Twins to shape the world in my image.

Holgren collapsed then, and the stone began to melt away in an odorless vapor. It was over. We'd lost. I sat there for a moment, bitter with defeat and despair. I wasn't going to get up again. Everything seemed pointless.

I glanced at Holgren. I'd failed him. He had counted on me, and I'd failed him. I didn't even have a knife to end his suffering with.

It was about then that I noticed a subtle change in the light, a flickering. I looked around for the source and found it outside the archway. A large, flickering fire was gliding rapidly through the air toward me. I closed my eyes, rubbed at them with the heels of my hands.

Now, my time comes, said the Flame.

I opened my eyes again, and it was bobbing gently in the air in front of me. I tried to understand the words.

All is not lost, Amra. On the contrary. You now have the opportunity to destroy him.

"What are you talking about? It's over. Tha-Agoth is dead. We lost."

It is doubtful whether Tha-Agoth would have been able to defeat the Shadow King in any case. Listen well. The Shadow King is in the process of transferring himself from his stone prison to the goddess' body. He can do nothing to protect himself while that process takes place. If you strike now, you can destroy him.

Hope flared then dimmed. My natural facility for suspicion I suppose. It was just too easy after all that had happened.

"What's the catch?"

I will be destroyed along with the Shadow King, but I do not think that was your meaning. The 'catch' is that you will almost certainly be destroyed as well.

"That's a damn big catch."

Choose, Amra. Little time remains. Soon, the process will be complete and the opportunity lost. He is vulnerable now and only now. End him.

"And end myself in the process?"

I ask you to do nothing I will not do myself. Your spirit will not be consumed, at least, as mine will, and the pain will be fleeting.

"That's not really a great selling point."

I am not trying to sell you anything. Hurry. Decide. The process is nearly complete.

I glanced over at the block and saw he was right. The block had melted away to a chunk of blackness about the size of a skull. Athagos' body lay suspended in the air above, arms dangling, her hair rippling in unseen currents.

Once the block disappeared, the Shadow King would have a body to walk around in and the power of the Twin Gods to wield along with his own. If that happened, the world was in for a very bad time. On the other hand, if I did something about it, my time was up. Decisions, decisions.

Death isn't lying down for a long nap or getting up from a card game or any of those feeble attempts to pull its fangs and make it an almost cozy occurrence. It's the end.

If you've seen someone die, especially someone you know—once you've seen them make the great transformation from a living, breathing person with likes and dislikes and annoying habits and pet foibles and a history and all the things that add up to make a person unlike any other there has ever been or ever will be—once you see them make that great and terrible transformation into so much cooling meat, you know you will do whatever you can to keep that from happening to you for as long as you can.

Or at least I did.

True, I passed on Tha-Agoth's offer of immortality, but there were too many strings attached. You can go too far the other way too. Look at what the Sorcerer King had done, and all that had come of it. You can stall death. You can cheat it for a time. But even gods die.

I made my decision.

I stumbled over to the rod where it had rolled next to Holgren. I knelt down and touched his ashen face. Whatever happened, I was going to make sure he got out of this. I kissed his eyelids and tried not to think about all the things we wouldn't get to do together. I grabbed the rod and made my aching way back to Athagos. The block had melted down to a sliver, maybe the size of a fat man's finger. Not much time left.

Athagos' body floated at hip level, where the top of the block had been. I put the tip of the rod against her chest, just to the left of her breastbone.

A little further over, I think, said the Flame. He floated just above Athagos' chest.

"Who's doing this?" I groused but repositioned the rod.

It is a good thing you do, Amra. I chose well in you.

"You just do whatever it is you have to do. I don't want this to be for nothing."

I took a deep breath and slammed the rod down into Athagos' perfect, dead flesh. The Flame dove into the opening I created, and Athagos sat up in mid-air and screamed with the

Shadow King's voice, eyes open, blazing.

The world disappeared in pain and darkness.

The Flame was right about one thing, at least. The pain was mercifully brief.

~ ~ ~

They fought in the space between life and death, the Shadow and the Flame. I was a spectator, trapped.

It was a vast, empty plane, and on it, an overwhelming blackness ate away at a tiny point of light just as the light struggled to burn away the dark. I have no idea how much time passed as I watched them. I'm not sure time really had any meaning there.

"They'll continue that battle until the end of time," said a voice off to my side.

I turned and saw a shriveled-up old hunchback leaning on a cane a few feet away.

"It isn't all that much different from what goes on in every soul," he continued. "Good struggles with evil eternally in each of us, doesn't it?" He peered at me beneath bushy brows.

I had the feeling I should know him. I shook my head. "Most people die, though," I said. "Then, it's settled one way or the other."

"Not necessarily. There are some very old souls roaming the world, you know. And the afterlife isn't an infallible system. Take your friend the mage, for instance. He was slated for an uncomfortable afterlife despite being a rather good sort."

"Who are you?"

"For someone as intimate with my anatomy as you seem to be, I'd think that would be obvious." He smiled as I puzzled on that one. I gave up. I had more pressing questions.

"Is this my afterlife then? If it's a heaven, I can think of better ones. If it's a hell, then I guess I got off pretty lightly."

"It's neither. You've sort of fallen through the cracks, so to speak."

"Oh. What do I do now?"

"Go back, Amra. Go back to your body, back to your life. The world isn't finished with you yet, nor you with the world. The afterlife will wait."

"What, just like that?"

He raised a bushy eyebrow. "Did you want it to be more difficult? I can arrange a harrowing trial or–"

I raised my hands in a pacifying gesture. "No, no, I'm absolutely fine with not difficult. Just point the way."

"Just turn around."

I did, and there was a door much like one of Tha-Agoth's rifts. Through it, I could see Holgren. It was daylight, and he was awake and hugging my slack body to his chest. Tears coursed down his cheeks.

"Go on then," said the old man. But as I started toward the doorway, he called me back.

"One more thing, Amra: Choose what you swear by a little more carefully from now on. You never know who might be listening." He smiled again, and then, he was gone.

I stepped through the doorway and found myself in Holgren's arms.

I couldn't think of any place I'd rather have been.

...AND EVERYTHING AFTER

We stayed there along the edge of the lake, too battered in body and spirit to start the trek home immediately and too intent on each other to care much about the world or the future. We said and did the things that lovers say and do, and never you mind about the details. We were alive, and we had each other. We'd won.

We set up camp for the winter in the Flame's dusty stone halls. Winter storms buried the land and froze the lake. It would have been hard going for us if we had tried to travel. I was far weaker than I wanted to be. My body, knowing the daily threat of annihilation was passed, simply refused to be mistreated any further. Holgren surprised me with his ability to trap game and to forage. Perhaps if I'd been trapped in Thagoth with him, I would have fared better.

One evening over a meal of rabbit and arrowroot, Holgren told me a decision he'd made.

"I never intend to work magic again."

"What? Why?"

"As I said, I haven't enjoyed it for years. And when I hurt you—"

"That wasn't you, Holgren. It was the Shadow King."

"It doesn't matter. I'm through with magic."

I gave him a hug. "Fine, if that's what you really want. But what are you going to do instead?"

"Something will come up, I'm sure. First, let's get home. One thing at a time."

I was feeling rested, and then restless, before winter was ready to turn things over to spring. I spent a lot of time wandering, poking around. Eventually, my rambling led me to the Sorcerer King's chamber.

~ ~ ~

His corpse lay rotting in the hallway outside. Whatever had animated him for so long had finally given out. I don't think he minded. I know I didn't.

The ghosts of his khordun were departed as well, for which I was grateful.

It was behind the bronze-sheathed double doors on the far side of the room that I made my big find. I had never seen so much gold in one place save for the gold-domed Tabernacle in Thagoth. It lay in heaps on the floor, coins minted with the Sorcerer King's likeness on both sides. No coin tosses in his kingdom, I suppose.

We took away with us enough, come spring, to last us several lifetimes, which I was more than happy with. I was less than happy with the direction we took—back to Thagoth. I never wanted to see that city again. Holgren pointed out the fact that it was a month over familiar terrain to a place he could open a gate, or half a year crossing unknown territory and foraging along the way. Reluctantly, I agreed.

We took our leave of the Flame's halls on a windy day in early spring and made an uneventful journey back to Thagoth. When we arrived some twenty-seven days later, the city was once again a deserted ruin. I suppose it fell when Tha-Agoth did. At least the death lands had been destroyed.

It was full dark when we arrived. We camped overnight, and the next day, Holgren opened a gate to home.

~ ~ ~

The Burrisses had auctioned off all my belongings for back rent. I can't say I blamed them; I'd been gone for nearly a year after all. Were they supposed to store all my belongings in the off-chance I'd reappear? Still, it hurt not to have anything left of my own.

There were a few items of sentimental value that I sorely missed: a tortoiseshell comb that had belonged to my mother, my first set of lock picks that Arno had given me, and the remaining bottles of Lord Morno's Gol-Shen.

Holgren was homeless as well. A fire had swept through the upper end of the city about the same time we'd first encountered the umbrals, destroying block after block of tenements, hovels, and shanties. It was whispered that Morno had had the fire set, or at least had not been in any great hurry to contain it. But the fact that the blight known as the Rookery was still left standing put paid to that notion in my mind.

There had been rioting, put down by Morno's arquebusiers in the end when the mob had tried to storm the governor's mansion. Whatever the case, many of the poorest parts of Lucernis were ash. Beggars slept on every corner, it seemed, and Holgren's sanctum by the charnel grounds was no more. "I was never terribly fond of the smell anyway," was his only comment.

As Ruiqi had said the day I met her, change is nature's way.

We took up residence in one of the better hostels on Arrhenius, a few blocks away from the banking houses. I began to make discreet inquiries as to the disposal of our newfound wealth. I preferred to pay a banker's fee as opposed to the heavy tax levied against foreigners in Lucernis. And to be honest, I didn't want to exist on any tax roll. Anywhere. It was all too possible that someone, somewhere, might make an unwanted connection. My past was spotty enough.

I have discovered it is very difficult to be both rich and anonymous, whereas poor and anonymous go hand in hand. Very difficult, but not impossible. Once I'd converted our wealth to a more spendable kind, I went looking for a place for us to live. Naturally, I looked around the Promenade.

I had enough money, but no one seemed to want to sell. Not to me, at least, or to the clerk I'd retained. It was an exclusive club, the owners of Promenade real estate, and money wasn't enough to get me invited. I brooded over it for a time and almost decided to give upon the notion.

Then, I met one Harald Artand over a game of cards. Harald was the eldest son of some Lucernan lordling. His father owned one of the smaller manses on the Promenade, down near the Dragon Gate. The father, Lord Artand, didn't even live in the place. He just kept it for when he was in town on business. Harald stayed there in a sort of disgraced exile.

It seemed young Harald had a great fondness for, and terrible luck with, the horses, and the cards, and the dice. And his family, however noble they might have been, weren't made of money.

To make a long story short, I let him crawl into my pocket until only his stockinged feet stuck out, and then I buttoned him up. It took two months. At the end of three months, I had forgiven his debt and bought the manse outright, though for half my original offer. I'm not rapacious, but I'm not a charity either.

Holgren, forswearing his powers and unfazed by it, rented a warehouse out by the docks and began to tinker. He'd spend hours there, absorbed in tearing apart arquebuses, examining the innards of locks, setting fire to things, and generally making an unholy mess. When he wasn't in what I came to call his workshop, he was out around town badgering smiths and tanners and bakers and tailors and tinkers and chandlers and stonemasons and glassblowers. He also seemed to attract others infected with his peculiar madness. At any time of the day or night, there would be two or three men, and even sometimes women, in his shop, setting things on fire, making an unholy mess, and grinning like idiots. I had no idea what they were doing, but it made him happy. That was all I needed to know.

At the end of the day, he'd come home and explain the latest theory he was exploring, and I'd pretend to understand what he was talking about. I'd tell him about the latest financial endeavor I'd sunk some of our money into be it spices from beyond Chagul or property in what people had begun to call the Charred Quarter. He'd nod and smile and pretend he was interested, and we'd eventually wander off to bed, happy just to be with each other at day's end.

Perhaps it sounds boring, but given the choice between boredom and excitement—well. I'd had all the excitement I cared to. Several lifetimes of it.

And boring was fun. While it lasted.

The Thief Who Knocked on Sorrow's Gate

THE KNIFE

It did not know impatience.

It had existed for more than a thousand years. It had been created to fulfill a single purpose. After a thousand years waiting for the proper conditions, then a century of stealthy, careful manipulation, and then twenty years of outright meddling in the affairs of mortals, its purpose was now very nearly fulfilled.

The Knife that Parts the Night had instigated two wars, along with all the plague, famine, and suffering that followed. It was responsible for tens of thousands of deaths.

It did not know impatience, and it did not know remorse.

The Knife had manipulated events to ensure that hundreds, perhaps thousands, of refugees, mainly war orphans, would flee to Bellarius, hoping the City of the Mount would be a refuge from the madness further south. Those hopes proved to be worse than false. The Knife made sure of it.

The Knife did not have a conscience. It had purpose, frightening intelligence, and vast power.

The Knife observed with keen interest the children who flooded the city, found no aid, and, crushed by the weight of destitution, desperation, and hunger, became petty thieves, then cunning criminals, then—as often as not—cold-eyed killers. But most keenly, it observed the handful that became consummate *survivors*. Those who died were not, of course, mourned though the Knife remembered them. The Knife remembered everything.

It had to be children, or so the Knife had determined centuries before. Adults simply weren't malleable enough. And the Knife needed to mold an individual with a very specific set of characteristics.

Someone quick-witted.

Someone with an almost inhuman will to survive.

Someone who could inspire loyalty, even love.

Someone with the ability to overcome desperate, brutal situations against hopeless odds.

Someone who, under the right set of circumstances, could be manipulated into doing what the Knife required of them.

And that someone had to be female.

The Knife that Parts the Night did not know impatience or most of the other basic human emotions. But it did know satisfaction and anticipation. As it set the final series of events into frightful motion, it felt both.

Its purpose was very nearly fulfilled.

CHAPTER 1

On Halfa's Night, one of the rowdiest of Lucernis' festival nights, someone sent me Borold's head in a cedar box.

I was home alone, savoring a nice Gol-Shen red and rereading Dubbuck's epic and amusing *Iron Witch*, when someone came knocking at the door. At first, I ignored it, thinking it was a group of drunken revelers come to serenade the big houses on the Promenade in hopes of festival largess. Then, whoever it was found the bell-pull and started pulling. And pulling. And pulling.

I sighed and went to answer the door, cursing all drunkards and wondering, not for the first time, whether it really wouldn't be best if Holgren and I hired some sort of live-in servant. I was the one who had wanted the big house on the Promenade. I'd never considered how much effort it would take to keep even a small manse in something approaching a decent state. It was built to be run by a staff, and there was just Holgren and me knocking about the place. Sometimes, I felt like a squatter in my own house. Usually, it was when the neighbors stared at me with disdain.

Holgren couldn't have cared less one way or the other, but I had a sort of bone-bred repulsion toward the idea of a maid or serving man. I suppose I'd seen my mother scrub too many floors she wouldn't otherwise have been allowed to walk on, wash and mend and embroider too much in the way of clothing she would never be able to afford to wear. And I'd seen my father drink away what little she made, which brought my thoughts back to the drunk fools outside. I had the sudden, strong urge to cut the bell pull and wrap it around somebody's throat.

But when I opened the door, it wasn't a group of wine-sotted minstrels. It was a sailor, a merchantman by his scruffy port jacket and ragged canvas pants. Under one arm, he held a wooden box.

"Ye'r Amra Thetys, then?" he said with a distinct Bellarian accent.

"What do you want?"

"I'm here to give you this, then, amn't I?" He held the box out to me. "If ye'r Amra Thetys."

"What is it? Who sent it?"

"As to what it is, it's a box, innit? I don't know the tall chappy's name what give me the box neither. He only said give it to Amra Thetys, who lived down by the Dragon Gate. And even with that, I had a time finding you."

"What did he look like?"

"Not really sure, mistress. He were all wrapped up in a night-black cloak, an' I might've had overmuch to drink."

"And you've come from Bellarius?"

"I come from all 'round the Dragonsea, mistress, if you take my meaning, but that's where I was given this to give to you. Are you goin' to take it, then?" He glanced over his shoulder at the lamp-lit, boisterous crowd staggering up and down the Promenade, clearly itching to spend his leave out there on the street rather than at my door. I couldn't really blame him. The wine and the ale flowed freely, and the revelers, both men and women, seemed to have abandoned anything approaching morals or common sense. Many had also abandoned important parts of their attire, though everyone I could see still had on a mask of one sort or another.

"Fine," I said, more to myself than to him. I wasn't born naturally suspicious, but I picked up the trait fairly early. I took the box gingerly, surprised at the weight of it, and set it down on a dusty table there in the entry hall. When I turned back to close the door, the sailor was still there, hand half-out. I dug a silver mark out of a pocket and put it in his grimy palm. He looked like he was going to ask for more, but I closed the door in his face. Maybe if he hadn't been so energetic with the bell.

I took my time with the box, checking for nasty surprises. There was nothing obvious. Just a well-put-together box, about two hand-spans square. The only way to be truly sure it was safe was to have somebody else open it with me in another room, but what can I say? The list of people I would use that way had grown remarkably short. Eventually, I shrugged to myself and pried open the lid with a knife, holding my breath. The breath-holding part turned out to be a good idea.

The first thing I saw was a loop of brown hair, braided and tied off just like it was meant for a handle. What it was a handle *to* was down in gray oakum fibers, the stuff that's left over when you pick apart ships' ropes once they'd outlived their usefulness. I briefly considered slapping the lid back on and just living with the curiosity, but even as I was thinking it, I put three fingers into the loop and lifted up.

The reek of Borold's decaying flesh invaded the room. There was no note, only Borold's noggin, open eyes gone squishy and his heavy, vaguely pig-like face slack and greenish-gray. I recognized him almost immediately despite the decay and the intervening years.

I gagged a little. I'm not exactly squeamish. I've seen and done some foul things, but *you* get a rotting head sent to you and see how you handle it.

After I got my stomach under control, I took a good look at my grisly package. The cut itself was amazingly clean, as if Borold's head had been severed with one blow. While this was certainly possible, it was by no means an easy thing to accomplish. Unfortunately, I'd had first-hand experience at decapitation—but that's another story. Such a cut spoke of either an experienced headsman or a wicked-sharp blade. Perhaps both.

There was a brand on his forehead. It had been done, it looked like, while he was still alive. Or at least while he was still fresh. Not that I'm an expert on such things. I'd seen the brand somewhere, something much like it at any rate. It was the Hardish rune for "traitor." Well, almost. Something like a downward-pointing dagger with three successive cross guards, or quillons, of equal length. Except the middle quillon was missing from the brand. I set the head back on top of the now-loose oakum fibers it had been packed in and backed away into the next room to get a clean breath.

Who had sent it? Who had done the deed? Probably, but not certainly, the same person. Someone who knew that I knew Borold, who had cause to believe I would care whether his head had parted ways with the rest of him. Did I? Not particularly. Not anymore.

And who was Borold? In years past, he had been a wharf-rat in Bellarius, a tough, and a bully. An altogether unpleasant boy who, I was sure, hadn't grown any more likeable with age. He'd hurt me once. Badly. I'd been one of the few gutter children he couldn't cow into giving him "tribute"—scraps of scrounged food or pilfered coin. I suppose I set a bad example, so one afternoon, he'd sneaked up behind me as I sat on the sea wall, watching the waves crash against the rocks, and damn near knocked my head in with a paving stone.

I had reason to wish Borold dead, but fifteen years or thereabouts had dulled the edge on that particular desire.

Someone else, it seemed, had decided that late was better than never. And I had a fair idea who it might be.

Damn.

I took a few deep breaths and went back to Borold. I don't know exactly what I was looking for. Something, anything else to tell me my suspicions were wrong. Or right for that matter.

There was just the head, the cut, the brand, the box. And the oakum, old rope fiber used mainly for caulking boats. Maybe there was something in that, maybe not. It was common enough stuff though not generally used for packing.

The brand drew my eye again. If there was a message in all of this, that was it. I just wasn't sure I knew the language. If it meant Borold was a traitor, well, that wouldn't have surprised me. But who goes to the trouble of making a brand and gets it wrong? It could be some noble's chop, I supposed, or some warlord's, as unlikely as that was in Bellarius. More likely it was the symbol of one of the crews, the street gangs in Bellarius that made up the bulk of the shadow guild there. I just didn't know. It didn't even occur to me that it might be some magical symbol until I traced a fingernail over where that missing middle stroke of the rune would have been if it were indeed "traitor."

Borold started screaming then, a shrill, tortured scream that didn't stop, never had to draw breath from lungs no longer attached. It was a scream that spoke wordless volumes about agony and mindless terror. I should know. I've heard the like.

The hairs on the back of my neck stood up; whether from the magic or the shock, I couldn't say. I pushed Borold's face into the oakum so that it would dampen the sound somewhat and slammed the lid back on, hastily hammering nails back in with a knife pommel. I could still hear him. Kerf's beard, the neighbors could probably still hear him, and I no longer lived in the Foreigner's Quarter, where screams of pain were most often met with shouted curses to shut the hells up.

I dumped out one of Holgren's countless chests, put the box in it, and padded it all around with blankets and pillows from around the house. Then, I went looking for a shovel.

~ ~ ~

Holgren dragged himself in from the workshop about an hour before dawn, smelling of chemicals and singed wool. He found me in the bedroom. I'd already packed and made all the preparations necessary for my trip. Money can make things happen, whatever the hour. It just takes *more* money on Halfa's Night.

He took one look at me, at my bags, opened his mouth, closed it again. A twinkle sprang up in his smoke-reddened eyes. "There's a hack waiting outside. Was it something I said?"

"I *should* give you hells about spending all your time down there at that madhouse of yours," I replied. It didn't actually bother me. He'd given up magic, the Art, after being forced to use it on me—painfully. If experimenting and inventing one silly thing after another made him happy and kept him occupied, who was I to complain? I had my own interests to keep me amused.

He came over and put his arms around me. I leaned into him briefly, but the fumes coming off him made my eyes water. I gave him a quick kiss and pushed him away.

"I have to go to Bellarius. An old friend may be in trouble. It might be nothing, but I have to make sure."

"I'll throw a few things in a bag—"

"No. Just me. My ship leaves in two hours with the tide. I was going to stop by the workshop if you hadn't arrived in time."

"But I've always wanted to see Bellarius."

"Nobody *wants* to see Bellarius, Holgren. It's a pit. And it's best if I go alone. There are people I'll have to deal with who won't say mum if you're with me. You'd wind up sitting on your hands in some inn or public room when you could be here, trying to blow up half the city."

"Unfair. We haven't had a fire in months."

I pointed to the charred hole in his shirt. He glanced down at it. "Not a large fire, in any case."

"I'll be back in a month, hopefully less. Assuming this is all just me worrying for nothing."

"When you worry, it's never for nothing." Holgren stripped off the shirt and sat down on the edge of the bed, his chest pale and lean. "What's this all about then? Who's this friend who's in trouble?"

"He may not be in trouble at all. But I received a disturbing message tonight." Which was now buried in the back garden. I could have told Holgren about it, could have used his magical expertise, I supposed. But he'd left magic behind, and had a good and sufficient distaste for his former profession. I respected that. "I'm just going to check things out is all. I owe Theiner that much."

"A childhood friend, then." Holgren knew something of my childhood. Enough to know it wasn't dolls and skip-rope.

"Yes. Now, come here and give me a kiss. I've got to go."

He got up, but instead of kissing me, he went to one of the many chests that lined the walls. An inveterate pack rat, was my Holgren. So long as nothing exploded, it didn't bother me. He'd been doing lots of experiments with gunpowder. Enough that I'd made him promise to keep the stuff out of the house.

He rummaged around for a few moments then came to me holding a black velvet bag and a smallish wooden case.

"Traveling gifts," he said and smiled. He handed the box to me and took a silver necklace with a bloodstone pendant out of the bag.

"No thanks, lover." I'd had a bad experience with a certain necklace not so long ago in the Silent Lands. I wasn't fond of jewelry in general anymore.

"Wear it for me, Amra. If it leaves your skin for more than a day, I will know. And I will come."

"Dabbling in magic again?"

"It still has its uses. Someday, it will fail utterly, but until then, I will use it if it can help keep you safe."

I was touched. Holgren hadn't wanted to be a mage even when he was a practicing one despite his formidable power. "What's in the box? More mystical artifacts?"

"Oh, no. Something I take much more pride in."

"Guns?" I knew he'd been working on some smaller version of an arquebus. And he knew my low opinion of firearms.

He shook his head. "Open it."

Inside was a brace of throwing knives, ivory-handled, single-edged, elegantly simple. I picked one up. It was perfectly weighted for my hand.

"I was saving them for a special occasion. You'll find they hold an edge quite well."

"You made these? They're beautiful."

"Helped make them. I owe you a few knives, no?"

"All right. Thank you. I'm certain I won't need them or the necklace, but thank you."

"I don't like seeing you in danger," he said, face tightening briefly.

We were a pair. Even after a year together, we both found it hard to share our emotions. But then, after the things we'd been through, most times, that wasn't necessary.

"I've got to go." I slipped the necklace on, feeling it warm to my skin almost instantly, and put the knife case into a graceful old sabretache I'd lifted from an annoying cavalry officer. The fashionable idiot had worn it low enough that it had slapped his knee. I wore it higher up, against my thigh, like the non-idiot I was. The knife case didn't leave much room for anything else.

I'd have to have sheaths made for them once I'd reached Bellarius; they wouldn't fit in my current rig. I stripped it off and hung it on a hook. Over the last year, I'd decided to limit myself to two knives on my person at any one time in an effort to better play the respectable woman of business role. It wasn't easy. I felt, if not naked, at least under-dressed.

It was time to go, or I'd have to wait another day at a minimum for the next outbound berth.

"Come back soon," he said. "You know how I fret."

I kissed him, letting my mouth say in one way what it had trouble saying in another. It occurred to me, as his hands tangled themselves in my hair, that a month was really rather a long time to be apart. I let my hands run down his bare, pale chest. Lean, but muscled, and scarless since being regenerated by Tha-Agoth's blood. My own body was nearly as unblemished save for the stain that Abanon's Blade had left on my palm and the scars on my face that were far older and apparently beyond the power of a demigod to erase.

"A month," I said, grabbing his waist. "That really is quite a long time."

Judging from his reaction, it seemed the same thought had occurred to him.

An hour later, the hack I'd hired was making unusual speed down to the docks. I wondered as the cobbled streets jounced me around inside the carriage if I'd miss my boat. Just at that moment, I didn't really care.

CHAPTER 2

I'd sent a messenger to secure the first berth available to Bellarius. It happened to be on a ship called *Horkin's Delight*, a three-masted carrack, lateen rigged. It reeked of turpentine and dried fish. I had a hunch that it was both faster and more maneuverable than it looked. I was sure it was at least sometimes a smuggling ship. Not that that bothered me, especially. I wouldn't have to deal with any nonsense about a woman traveling on her own. I *would* have to keep a sharp eye on my belongings, but I would have done that in any case.

I climbed up the rope ladder thrown over the *Delight's* side, grateful to be off the bobbing, pitching deck of the lighter I'd hired to row me out. False-dawn was creeping up on the sky. I was met by a small, paunchy man in stained finery much too big for him. Horkin, I assumed.

"You're almost late," he said, taking in my disheveled hair and mis-buttoned shirt as my traveling chest was whipped up from the lighter by two of the sailors.

"And you're almost making a point," I replied.

He laughed, a surprisingly rich, deep laugh. "Oh, we'll get along fine, you and I." He hooked a thumb toward one of the sailors roaming the deck, preparing to get underway. "Haemis will show you your berth after you show me your coin."

I produced three gold marks and put two into his palm.

"Right fine," he said, smiling. "I'm Captain Horkin. Just remember, you're cargo. Stay out of the way."

"I know my way around a boat."

"Then you'll know when you're in the way," he replied, and whistled up Haemis to lead me below decks. Haemis lifted my chest without even grunting, and I followed the silent, muscle-bound sailor down into the depths of the *Delight*. After surveying the dark, filthy closet that was my cabin, I decided that Horkin was far too easily delighted. And that I'd be sleeping above deck when the weather permitted.

~ ~ ~

Night on a ship. It always made me feel small. The wind and the waves and the creaking of wood and rope, and nothing else for miles and miles. And, as a passenger, nothing to do but think.

I was sure it was Theiner. No one else knew what Borold had done to me that day. And while Theiner might have told someone else, I doubted it—and doubted too that anyone besides Theiner would think I'd want such a grisly favor. Come to think of it, I couldn't see why Theiner would think I'd want Borold's head, not after all these years.

I shook my head, tried to clear away all the questions that couldn't yet be answered. Theiner was mixed up in all this somehow; that much was fairly certain. Just what "all this" was about, I had no idea. Nor would I until I got to Bellarius. But something was wrong. Theiner wasn't the type to bestow grisly presents, like a cat bringing home some gutted toad or thrush. Nor was he the kind to send cryptic messages. Certainly not magical ones. Theiner was shrewd, plainspoken, and practical. That's how I remembered him, at least. But it had been years.

Theiner, the Theiner I'd known so long ago, was as decent a boy as the streets of Bellarius allowed him to be. I could still recall his broad, farmer's face, the shock of blond hair that stuck up from the back of his head, and the dusting of freckles across his nose and cheeks. He looked slow, almost simple, but there had been a sharp mind inside that thick skull of his. Sharp enough to keep him alive for years on the streets of Bellarius after war and plague and famine had dumped hundreds, perhaps thousands of unwanted children onto a city already bursting at the seams.

He'd never let the constant grind of survival take away his sense of right and wrong. If it hadn't been for him, I wouldn't have made it through my first week on the streets there. He'd taught me how to survive, and taught me too, that there were some things worse than not surviving.

"Two things you never do for money, little one," he'd told me. "You never sell your body. And you never take a life. The one you give away or maybe it gets taken, and the other you do if you have to, and do it smart and quick and sure. But you don't sell such things. Some things are worse than dying, eh?"

I'd just nodded, then, taking on faith that what he said was true. And after all these years, I've still never sold my body or my blade.

I sighed, tried to get comfortable in the moldy hammock I'd got Horkin's grudging permission to string up on the quarterdeck, stared out at the stars above the Dragonsea. Whatever Theiner was up to, unless he'd changed far more than I thought possible, he was driven to it by some sense of right and wrong, some sense of justice. Or because he was forced somehow. But still, it wasn't adding up.

Despite myself, I thought back on those bleak, terror-filled days before I finally escaped Bellarius for good, before Theiner helped me stow away on an outbound ship. I remembered the Blacksleeves roaming the night streets, slaying the gutter children where we slept in doorways, ferreting us out of rooftop hideaways and abandoned buildings and deserted cemeteries. They said that a mage was working with the Blacksleeves, that it didn't matter where we hid. I believed it then. Hells, I believed it now. It was why I took the chance of being found out as a stowaway and tossed overboard, meat for pheckla or gray urdus.

The Syndic and the Council of Three had finally had enough of our petty depredations, I suppose, or maybe it was the shadow guild culling the herd, getting rid of those too stupid or unlucky to eventually recruit. In any case, someone in power had finally had enough and decided starvation and disease and abject poverty just weren't doing the job fast enough. And so came what was referred to in polite society as "the Purge" when it was referred to at all. Such a simple phrase for the mass murder of street children.

I looked out into the night, and the slow rocking of the *Delight* showed me stars and water, stars and water. I drifted off to sleep and dreamed of hundreds of head-sized boxes floating on the swells of the Dragonsea, and a shadow darker than the night that moved across the stars. It laughed, that shadow, and the laugh was like distant thunder.

~ ~ ~

It was a cloudless, golden autumn morning when we came in to Bellarius' wretched port. It took nearly two hours to warp in to the dock; enough time for me to remember just how much I loathed the place. When it had been over the horizon, I could loathe it in an abstract sort of way. Once it was in front of me, my disgust became more visceral. I wanted to just turn around and go back to Lucernis.

The Bay of Bellarius is a natural, deep-water harbor, sheltered by the bulk of Mount Tarvus to the east. The Mount's western slope is—was—covered by increasingly fine houses, and then the spire-tipped towers of the Gentry, and then the Riail, the Syndic's palace as you neared the summit and the Citadel. To the north, the bay is sheltered from the worst weather by the black face of the Rimgurn Cliffs, which are really an extension of the mount. Lining the cliff top and the narrow stretch of land beyond are more houses of the well-to-do and then the Lesser Lighthouse and the sea. Perhaps there had been a Greater Lighthouse at one time; now, the Lesser was also the Only.

To the south is Hardside proper, a low, muddy spit of land good for little except growing shanties and generation after generation of poverty. Beyond Hardside are the marshes, home to smugglers and fugitives and the odd witch or black magician. Between Hardside and the Mount is Bellarius proper, known to one and all as the Girdle.

Every few years, the sea would rise up to sweep away most of Hardside, which is, I suppose, why those of means never bothered much with it in land-short Bellarius. It was Hardside where I was born and bred. It was Hardside where my father had killed my mother, and I had killed him.

I looked out at it all as we made our slow, tedious way to port. The Girdle and the high houses of the Gentry were ugly. Bellarius was an ugly city, no way around it. Graceless and cramped. Hardside though—Hardside just looked diseased.

~ ~ ~

I paid Horkin his other gold mark and climbed down onto the bleached boards of the pier, which was already filling with beggars, hawkers, thieves, working girls, and the occasional family member waiting to greet the *Delight*. My chest would follow shortly, but I kept Holgren's box of knives on me in my sabretache.

Some people keep talismans. Some kids have a favorite doll. Knives comfort me, and I needed a bit of comfort, coming back to Bellarius. Don't judge.

As soon as my foot met the tar-stained wood, I felt an instant of sickening dizziness. For a moment, I couldn't seem to draw a breath. It passed almost instantly though, and at the time, I put it down to suddenly solid footing after eight days aboard ship.

"Aya, lass!" Horkin called, leaning over the rail. "We'll be in port for a fortnight. Make your way down to the Pint and Anchor if you want to lose some marks at dice."

I waved to him then paid a burly fellow with the body of a war god and the face of a simpleton to toss my sea chest on his shoulder and follow me. Then, I weaved through the crowd toward the Girdle to the north of the docks. I was a little unstable due to my newly acquired sea legs. Dicing wasn't on my mind. I wanted a decent meal, a bath, and a glass of wine while I mulled over what to do next.

I'd made it about halfway down the pier when I heard my name being called over the babble of the crowd. At first, I thought it was Horkin again and turned back a little impatiently. It wasn't Horkin. A scabby, black-haired youth was swaggering toward me, face set in a practiced scowl. I was familiar with the look. I'd worn it myself at his age. He was carrying a letter.

I let him get close, my hand dipping idly into the sabretache. He had the letter in his left hand; his right swung free. As he came toward me, I shifted so that I was a little to his right. Before he could say anything, I hooked my left arm through his right. Instantly, we were two friends easy in each other's company. Except my other arm, extended across my midriff, had a knife at the end of it that poked firmly but gently into his scrawny side. He stiffened.

"Keep your mouth shut, and don't make trouble," I said, my tone pleasant and calm, "and you won't get punctured." I led him down the pier, my hulking porter following along, mindful of nothing but what foot came next.

"Look, lady–"

"Shut it," I said again, and poked him a little. He shut it. Smart kid.

Someone—Theiner?—knew I was coming, and maybe on what ship. It could have been good guesswork, or the kid could have been staked out here, waiting for someone who fit my description to show up. Or it could have been magic at work, or something else that hadn't occurred to me yet. The boy, or to be fair, young man, had to know something. I glanced around, trying to see if anyone had been set to watch him but saw no one who showed interested in us. Didn't mean a thing. Have I mentioned my suspicious nature?

My first thought was to haul the kid into the first dark alley I came across and make him talk, but I couldn't be sure he didn't have someone set to watch him. I didn't want our private conversation interrupted by his mates or employers. I just wanted answers.

"Who sent you?" I asked him as we neared the end of the dock. I glanced at his face, noting the first growth of downy beard on cheeks and chin and above his upper lip, the stubborn set of his jaw. I poked him again with my knife.

"Thought you wanted me to keep my gob shut," he muttered.

"I'm a woman. I get to change my mind. Get used to it."

He snorted, and I liked him a little better for it.

"Who?" I asked again.

I felt the chill hand of unleashed magics grope the back of my neck just as he opened his mouth to speak. Whatever the kid was going to say was lost in the crumping roar of the dock behind us being blown to bits.

CHAPTER 3

Most believe the eleven hells are all savage infernos. I happen to have it on authority that at least one of them is in fact bitterly cold; but in any case, it was as if a huge hand had risen up out of some flaming hell-pit of the more traditional sort and slapped me and the boy sprawling.

I must have flown a dozen feet before touching down again and skidded a dozen more across splintered planking that bucked and swayed and peeled skin from my arms and face. Smoldering chunks of wood and flesh rained down around me. Someone close by was shrieking in short, sharp, monotonous bursts. I smelled burning cloth and hair, realized it was coming from me, from my shoulder and the back of my head. I patted out the flames with stupid, trembling hands and looked around me, trying to understand what had happened.

Nothing would hang together at first. The world was screams and smoke and fire and people running, some away from the dock, some toward. I looked back and saw that the dock that I had just walked down was flaming wreckage, most of it floating in the Bay. The *Delight* was on fire, as were two or three other ships. There were bodies and parts of bodies everywhere, lying on the remains of the dock, floating in the water, tossed into the burning rigging of the nearest ships. It was wholesale slaughter, and I felt—knew—that it had been meant for me.

The youth was a yard or so away from me, unmoving. His arm was folded under him at an unnatural angle. The letter he'd carried was nowhere to be seen. My knife, miraculously, was right next to me rather than in me. I picked it up and put it in my belt while absently still staring at the boy. As I looked at him, a woman rushed past, her face sheeted with blood. Unseeing, she kicked the boy in the face. Uncaring, she stumbled on. I dragged myself up and grabbed him by the collar. I wanted to get him off what was left of the dock or at least to one side so he wouldn't be trampled to death. He was my only source of information, after all.

He proved to be heavier than he looked. A balding merchant in gaudy, singed velvets stopped to help. His face was white, and his hands shook, but he got the boy's good arm around his thick neck and dragged him off the dock and onto gray cobbles and, after a quick nod in my direction, hurried back toward the conflagration. I felt the odd urge to follow him, to help where I could well up inside me, but common sense overruled it. If the fire had indeed been meant for me, the best thing I could do for all involved would be to go far away as fast as I could.

Bells were ringing now, clamoring, being taken up throughout the city. I could see several Blacksleeves, members of the watch, pushing their way through the frantic wharf-side crowd like fish swimming upstream. Fish with truncheons that they used freely. It was time to go. Bellarius' peacekeepers were brutal and efficient when it suited them.

The youth was twitching and moaning now at my feet. I gave him an open-handed slap to the face that had his eyes open and his good hand searching for the knife at his belt. The one I'd already made disappear.

"Blacksleeves are coming," I said. "Can you walk?"

He nodded, face gray with pain, and I helped him climb to his feet.

~ ~ ~

It was to Hardside that we made our way. The place I'd lived until I was ten. The place I'd killed my father. The place he'd killed my mother.

It felt like going home, and I dreaded it. But Hardside was the closest and easiest place in Bellarius to go to ground.

I thought that I knew Bellarius, particularly Hardside, but as we stumbled and shambled down refuse-littered, grimy "streets," I realized that more than a decade had changed details I remembered. I don't know why this should have surprised me, but it did. Perhaps because my memories were so vivid if mostly horrid. I felt a strange sense of indignation that the streets and buildings were not trapped in amber. Stupid. Nonsensical. Would you curse a knife that gave you a scar for growing dull or rusty? Gods only knew how many times Hardside had been washed away by flooding and rebuilt since I'd left.

The youngster, whose name was Keel, directed me to a dingy, once-whitewashed cottage with the bleached bone hanging above the lintel that denoted a chirurgeon. It was dilapidated as all hells and probably one of the nicest buildings in Hardside. I banged on the door, heard snores and then muttered imprecations from inside, and banged harder. Eventually, an evil-looking, foul-smelling troll of a man poked his head out. His gray hair stood up in kinks above his sallow face, and I could tell by his bloodshot eyes and drink-reddened nose that he was more than halfway down the neck of a bottle. But once he saw my bloodied face and Keel's ashen one, he got it together and hustled us into his lair, which was far cleaner and more orderly than I had expected.

"You have coin?" was the only question he asked, and once satisfied as to the answer, he went about examining and then setting the boy's arm with expert, if trembling hands. He was efficient about it, though not particularly gentle. He had me hold Keel still while he aligned the bones. For his part, Keel bit his lip bloody but did not cry out. Stupid bravado, but I knew well enough that stupid bravado could be an asset on the streets of Bellarius.

"You've got a two in three chance of this healing straight and true," he told Keel as he bound the splinted arm to the youngster's chest, "and the Lord Councilors' healers could do little better. As for you," he said, addressing me but not looking away from his work, "There's a stack of clean rags in that cabinet and a basin of fresh water on the table to your left, though no mirror. Clean off the blood as best you can, and I'll see if you need stitches presently."

I did as he instructed and realized after most of the dried blood was off my face and palms that, beyond having to pull a few splinters and wearing scabs for a time, I had escaped remarkably unharmed. When the bone-setter came to look at me, I waved him off.

"What's your name?" I asked him.

"Hurvus. You'll need unguent and plaster for that cheek unless you want to chance scarring."

"Do I look like I care about scars?" I asked. He just stared at me. "Fine. How much?"

"Two silver." It was an outrageous sum for what he'd done.

"You'll have four, but we'll need a room for the night. And a meal that you'll go and get from someplace that serves edible food."

"This isn't an inn, woman."

"No, but it isn't exactly a thriving practice either, now is it? Five silver."

"I like my privacy."

"Don't push it, or I'll take my coin elsewhere, and you'll be drinking small beer instead of spirits."

His lip lifted in a tick that was half a smile. He held out a drink-tremored hand, and I put down three silver into his palm, showing him two more before I tucked them away.

"Room there past that curtain," he said, and went out to secure us dinner.

I helped Keel into the room, which was a narrow little space with a cot, an uncomfortable willow-branch stool, and a clean chamber pot. Keel lay down on the cot, trying to look like he didn't want to throw up from the pain, and I eased myself down on the creaky stool.

"Time to talk," I said.

"Not in the mood," he managed through clenched teeth.

"I know. I've been there. But we need to talk while we have privacy. Our landlord's a wine-belly, and if there's anything worth selling in our conversation, I don't trust him not to sell it when he's down on his luck and out of alcohol.

"First question: Who gave you the letter to give to me?"

"Ansen."

"Ansen who?"

"*The* Ansen."

"Oh, come on. Do I look stupid?"

"You think I don't know how it sounds?" he got out through gritted teeth.

Ansen. The Just Man. A Bellarian myth. A hero from centuries ago who promised to return when needed, according to legend.

"Don't play with me, boy."

"Not," he managed, then leaned over and retched into the chamber pot. I was inclined to believe him. Or rather believe that he believed it. He was in too much pain to try and be funny.

I went out to get a few clean rags, both because Keel hadn't had the greatest aim and because the smell of it had me more than half on the way to vomiting myself. I hate puking. I steeled myself and went back in, breathing through my mouth.

I cleaned up the worst of it, forcing myself not to gag. Keel lay on his good side, eyes closed, panting.

"I'll have him give you something for the pain when he gets back," I told him. "Now, the man who gave you the letter. He told you he was Ansen, and you believed him just like that?"

"No. Not just like that. He *was* Ansen. Is again."

I sighed. "Keel, Ansen lived three centuries and more ago. He was just a peasant who led a revolt that made things better for some for a time. He wasn't a mage or a god, he didn't have any power over death, and he certainly isn't going to come back and save Bellarius in its darkest hour, whatever the legend says."

Keel didn't say anything to that. He just shook his head then lay there and panted, eyes closed.

"All right. That's enough for now. Get some rest."

I left the room and threw the soiled rags into the low fire in Hurvus' main room, then sat back in one of his two chairs and watched them burn. I had no idea who Keel's Ansen might really be. But I'd bet marks to coppers it wasn't some peasant legend come crawling out of the grave.

I wanted to know what had made Keel believe such a fairy tale. He was obviously a bright kid. Too bright to be suckered in by such a bombastic lie, I would have bet, had I not just learned better.

Whoever was pretending to be Ansen, for whatever reason, must've been very slick indeed. And "Ansen" had had a letter waiting for me on my arrival. Somehow, that was connected to the inferno the dock had turned into to welcome me home. I don't believe in coincidences.

"Gods, I hate Bellarius," I whispered to myself, and poked bits of the fouled rags deeper into the fire.

I don't believe in coincidences, and I don't like people knowing where I'm going to be and when I'm going to be there before even I do. I was being used in somebody's game, and the game stank of magic. Again.

Reluctantly, I pulled Holgren's necklace off and tucked it into a secure inner pocket against my heart. I didn't want to bring him into this, whatever *this* was. I didn't want to be in it myself. But with the amount of magic I'd already encountered on my first Kerf-damned day back, I saw no choice but to call out for his help.

He didn't want to be a mage. He didn't want to use his considerable power in the Art ever again. But he would, for me, without hesitation.

I didn't feel like I had the right to ask him to do so, and I didn't want to ask him. But I could *feel* something in the air, something subtly, deeply wrong. Without Holgren, I was very much afraid I wouldn't even be able to see the threat coming before it was far too late.

A day for him to know I'd taken off the necklace. Eight days from Lucernis to Bellarius, weather permitting. Another day just to make the gods happy.

As the light faded outside, I pondered where I could best go to ground for a ten-day.

~ ~ ~

It was full dark when Hurvus returned. He'd obviously filled his skin while he was out. His hands had stopped trembling. He brewed a willow bark tea for the boy and forced it down his throat, then put some foul-smelling plaster on my cheek and a liniment on my hands. Then we ate, he and I. Black bread, clam soup from a clay pot, a quarter wheel of a young, gray cheese. When it was plain that Keel wasn't going to be eating anything, Hurvus ate his share of the soup and more of the cheese as well, and wrapped the rest up in cleanish linen.

When he'd sucked the last crumbs from his graying beard, he looked up at me with those bloodshot, still-clever eyes of his and said, "People looking for you. At the public house."

I felt a knife of fear slide into my guts but didn't let it show.

"Do they know where to find me?"

"No. Not from me."

"Why not?"

"You still owe me two silver. Besides, I didn't like the look of 'em. Or the smell."

"Blacksleeves?"

He shook his head. "No. Don't know what. Don't know what you're into. Don't want to be part of it."

"We'll be gone in the morning."

He nodded his head then stoked up the fire a bit. With the falling sun, the temperature was dropping. After a time, he put the poker away, put a bottle of cheap stuff by his chair, and settled in.

"What did they look like, these people who were looking for me?"

"Two of 'em. One a bruiser, shaved head. The other a weaselly type, expensive clothes, silk and ermine and lace. Looked like he looted it off a corpse if I'm honest. The both of 'em smelled like the marshes. Were asking after a woman looked hard and an injured gutter boy, maybe together, maybe alone."

"Marshes, eh?" Smugglers? Who knew? "Did anyone else pipe up?"

"They weren't offering a reward, only threats. People 'round Hardside, they don't pay much attention to such. Unless they got a personal stake."

That much, at least, hadn't changed. I sat and stared at the fire while he filled his pipe, thinking. They'd get around to checking bone-setters soon enough, whoever they were. Hurvus would be on their list. Best I moved on with Keel before dawn. I couldn't just leave the kid. He didn't know anything about me, but that wouldn't stop them from beating him to death to find it out, most likely, if they had anything to do with the fire. And I still had questions to ask him. I had too many questions all around.

They must have set someone to watch Keel, else they wouldn't have known I might be with him or that he was injured. That they didn't know if I was still with him probably meant they'd lost track of us in the confusion following the explosion. In any case, they had the brains to search Hardside. Which was too bad, really. I prefer any possible enemy to be as stupid as mossy rocks.

Well, if they were looking for me low and I wasn't ready to face them, then I'd hide myself up on high. I had enough to take a room at one of the posh inns near the top of the Girdle. And I had enough to hire a few thugs of my own if it came to it. I just didn't want it to.

Mainly, what I needed was information. There was too much going on, and I didn't understand any of it.

I glanced over at Hurvus. He had nodded off in his chair, pipe gone out and dangling from his mouth. I gently nudged his chair with a boot tip, then harder when that had no effect. He sat up, snorting and blinking.

"I have a few questions. I'll give you gold if you can answer them."

He wiped his eyes with a thumb. "I'll answer if I can."

"You heard of anyone masquerading as Ansen lately, come back from the dead?"

He snorted. "Every year, it seems. The Syndic and his Council don't get any less popular as time goes by only because once you hit bottom, there's no further to go. If it weren't for the Telemarch sitting up there in his Citadel, I don't doubt the mob would've burned down the Riail long ago. But it's hard to start a revolution when the other side has an archmage on the payroll."

"So what's the story of the latest Ansen, then?"

"I honestly couldn't say beyond slogans scrawled on walls. 'Return the people's power' and such like."

I grunted. "If I wanted to find somebody on the quiet, who's the best person to talk to?" I knew of one professional information broker in Bellarius, but I would much rather not use him if I could avoid it. I tried to keep the professional and personal separate wherever I could.

Hurvus shrugged his shoulders. "The Hag; who else?"

"Kerf's crooked staff, she's still alive?" She'd been ancient when I was a girl and more than half legend. But I knew where to find her. Everybody in Hardside knew where to find her. It made it easier to avoid her.

"Let me ask *you* a question," Hurvus said. "Why do you want to know all this?"

I thought about it a long time before I answered him. Decided to be truthful, Kerf only knows why. "I was born and raised in Hardside, Hurvus. I know you know it; you can hear it in my speech as surely as I can hear it in yours."

He nodded. "There's no mistaking the Hardside drawl, sure. Though yours has gone soft around the edges."

"I've been away a long time, and coming back's not something I ever planned on doing."

"So why have you? I know it's your business and none of mine, but if I were less of a wreck and managed to climb out, nor hells nor the dead gods could drag me back. But it's too late for the likes of me." He took a swig from the bottle as if to prove his point.

"I have a debt to pay," I told him, "and the marker finally got called in."

He looked over at me, and even drink-fogged, his eyes were appraising. "You sit there in your raw silk trousers and bleached linen shirt and dagwool waistcoat, carrying knives the like I've never seen except on noblemen who had no least clue how to use 'em properly, wearing boots that cost what most people make in a year, offering me gold to tell you what anyone would tell you for the time of day, and you tell me you came to Hardside to pay a *debt*? Don't talk rubbish. Whatever you are, however you made your moil, you could've sent somebody else to settle it."

I shook my head. "It's not that kind of debt. And coin won't cover it."

"What will, then?"

"I don't know. Maybe nothing. Maybe blood. Probably blood. Maybe my life." Whatever Theiner needed, I owed. And would pay. And that, I finally admitted to myself, was why I hadn't wanted Holgren along.

He was quiet for a while. When he spoke, his voice was rough with drink and with some obscure emotion. "I had a debt like that once."

I cocked my head. "How'd you settle it?"

He smiled, but there was nothing of humor in it, just some old, private pain. "I never did. Or I still am. Can't decide which it is anymore." And he took a long, long drink from the bottle and stumbled off to his bed without another word.

I banked the fire and dug out a blanket from my pack, then went to sleep there on the floor, one of Holgren's gift-knives in each hand.

My last thought, before sleep overtook me, was that I really didn't want to go and see the Hag. That was the nicer of her two names.

Her not-so-nice name was the Mind Thief.

CHAPTER 4

Morning was a gray smear in the eastern sky with the last stars still twinkling in the west over the Dragonsea. Keel was groggy and pale-faced, but he'd live. I got us moving through streets populated only by us two and a surprisingly large number of sparrows, even for Bellarius. Sparrows were—well, not sacred, exactly, but favored. There was a local god who watched over them. Had a shrine in the Girdle and everything. I had no idea why there would be a god who watched over sparrows or why anyone would bother to build a shrine to him, but it was harmless enough, and I'd heard of stranger. And much more repugnant.

Anyway, sparrows were thick on the ground that morning. People were not. And so I wasn't expecting any trouble.

The thing about Hardside is that there's no law—only a thin tissue of custom. Oh, sure, Blacksleeves might occasionally come down from the Girdle to roust a few shanties by way of making a point or to search for some particular miscreant who did a bad thing to someone with some pull, but there's no Watch in Hardside, no authority to go running to when the bonds of civilization are tested. You've got your family and friends, and possibly your neighbors, who *might* lend a hand out of enlightened self-interest when things get ugly. Might. If they're not too drunk, too hung over, too shattered on hell weed, or just plain worn down too far by an existence defined by deep, relentless poverty.

Point being, when the two shit-heels Hurvus had described to me the night before appeared from around the corner of a driftwood shanty as Keel and I were on our way to see the Hag, I knew without thinking there was just me to deal with them. Keel was useless, and nobody else was going to interfere, however it turned out. No passerby was going to get involved, not that there were any at that hour of the morning. In Hardside, you deal with trouble yourself. Or it deals with you. Either way.

It was plain they weren't expecting to see us. The big one stopped dead in his tracks when he spied Keel. The smaller one took a couple of extra steps before he realized his partner had stopped, but it only took him a heartbeat after that to figure out the situation.

"Been looking for you, Keel," said the big one. "Moc Mien wants to see you."

I glanced at the kid. He'd turned even whiter. "Ah, fuck," he whispered.

"I take it you know them?" I asked.

"Yeah." He looked like he was going to bolt. I put a hand on his arm. I still had questions for him.

"Let's go, Keel," the big one said. "Say goodbye to your lady friend."

"I don't think he wants to go with you," I said.

"He doesn't have a fucking choice," said the big one. The one that looked like a dissolute merchant sniggered, exposing rotten teeth. The big one cut him an annoyed glance.

"Why's that?" I asked.

"Because Keel's part of Moc Mien's crew, though he seems to have forgotten that fact." He wasn't really talking to me. His eyes never left the kid's face. "He took Moc Mien's mark and Moc Mien's coin, and now, he takes Moc Mien's fucking orders. In short, whoever the fuck you are, young Keel doesn't have a choice because he already *made* his fucking choice when he *joined the fucking crew*. Now, come the fuck along, Keel. I'm not going to say it again."

Keel surprised me. Broken-armed and obviously scared spitless, he still stood up straighter and said, "No."

"Ah, fuck," said the big one. "It was already bad, kid. Now, it gets much worse." And he and his partner started forward through the muddy excuse for a street.

So I pulled out Holgren's gift knives, held them low and away from my body, points down.

"He said no."

They were still maybe ten feet away. Both of them pulled up at the sight of steel. The little one brought out a chopper of his own, pure marsh-blade, meant for chopping through undergrowth and stubborn roots. It would do a person's limbs or neck just as well. He smiled his black, crumble-toothed smile. The big one frowned.

"I don't know who the fuck you are, but if you want to go knocking on sorrow's gate, don't fucking cry if it opens."

I smiled. "You say 'fuck' too much. You should expand your vocabulary."

The littler one jumped forward, chopper raised high. So I threw the left knife. You don't hesitate in Hardside.

It got him in the neck, in the hollow at the base of the throat, and he went down, choking on blood and Lucernan steel. I felt nothing, and some part of me that belonged in Lucernis, not Hardside, worried about that in a distant, abstract sort of way.

The bruiser was already wading in as well, unconcerned about his partner, betting I wouldn't cast my other knife, betting I didn't have another somewhere I could get to before he got to me. He was right.

If he could get hold of me, it would be over quick. He was probably triple my weight, and he had on the velvets—gutter gauntlets, thick, leather gloves with iron plates sewn in all over, good for bashing faces in and blocking and grabbing blades. He looked like he knew how to use them.

So I rushed into him, diving at the last instant below a surprisingly quick attempt at a grapple. And once I was down in the muck between his legs, I shoved the other knife up into his crotch.

You don't hesitate in Hardside, and you don't ever fight anything but dirty.

A slab of meat like him, he probably would have shrugged off a knife in the arm or leg. One in the chest would have disabled him if I planted it right, but he wouldn't have held still long enough for me to make certain, and even if I hit something vital, it might not have taken the fight out of him quick enough. So I drove the knife into his crotch and ripped it out the back, feeling the blade scrape along something bony and pelvic along the way. And he screamed and fell to the ground and screamed some more, all the while writhing and clutching his privates.

I felt something then. My nerves were buzzing, my whole body trembling in reaction to the sudden violence, and I wanted to vomit.

He wasn't going to live through that kind of wound. So I made myself do the right thing though all I wanted to do right then was run off somewhere and puke my guts out then squat and hug my knees till the trembling stopped. But the kid was standing there, watching me with big, round eyes in a pale face. So I made myself get up and cut the man's throat with a shaking hand. His writhing didn't make it any easier. Then, I went and removed my knife from the corpse of the other one, wiped the blood off of both on his stench-laden cloak, and put them in my belt. Carefully. I really needed to have sheaths made.

Less than a minute had passed.

Welcome home, Amra, said a voice in my head that I assumed at the time was my own.

I shrugged it away and said, "Let's go," to Keel. My voice came out colorless and harsh, even to my own ears.

"Wh-where?" He was just standing there, staring at the bodies.

"We still need to see the Hag, don't we?" I walked over and grabbed his good arm. He shook me off.

"After *that*?" His face was the picture of incredulousness.

I squinted at him. "What should we do, boy? Go light candles for them at the temple of the departed?" But I knew how he felt. When I'd seen Holgren turn Bosch into a bloody mist just by snapping his fingers, I'd had a similar reaction though I hadn't voiced it at the time. Sudden, ferocious violence *should* be something that takes us aback. Seeing two men turned into corpses in less time than it takes to lace up a boot isn't something a healthy-minded person should be able to dismiss with a shrug. But honestly, there was nothing to be done about it after the fact. The doing had already happened.

"Well?" I prompted him. "What do you think we should do now, Keel? Go up to the Girdle, find a bench in Jaby cemetery and contemplate the fragility of life?"

"I don't *know*," he said. "I don't know *what* we should do."

"Well, I do. We have business to attend to. We're going to attend to it."

"No offense. Really, no offense. But your business isn't my business. And I don't want it to be."

I gave him a flat stare. "I just killed two members of your crew—"

"Former crew."

"They disagreed, but never mind. My point is, your business just became my business. And that means my business is now yours as well."

"Um, that doesn't really make logical—"

"I've got the knives, Keel, and I've got the will and ability to use them. If I say my business is your business, then that's the Kerf-damned way it damned well is. Is that logical enough for you?"

He nodded. He was not wearing a happy face.

"Here's some more logic for you: If you think the only ones who just saw this were us and the sparrows, you're dreaming. Someone in one of these shit-shacks saw what happened and will run to your 'former' crew boss and tell the tale for the reward they're sure to get. Your crew boss *will* find out about it sooner rather than later. Which means we both just went to war with—Moc Mien, was it?"

He nodded.

"Now, would you rather go to war broken-armed and friendless or with me?"

He thought about that, but not for long. "With you," he said.

"Good. Now, let's get away from this cooling meat. The Hag isn't getting any younger."

I started walking, and he followed after a few seconds as I knew he would.

As we walked, he kept shooting me furtive looks when he thought I wasn't looking. But there isn't a damned thing wrong with my peripheral vision. It finally got annoying enough that I said, "What?"

"No offense, but you don't look like much. Not like Mouse."

"Mouse?"

The big one you, uh…"

"The second man I killed."

"Yeah."

"What's your point?"

"How did you get so hard?"

"I'm exactly as hard as Hardside made me."

"I grew up in Hardside. I'm not like you."

I could have told him that Hardside, that Bellarius fifteen years before, had been hell on earth for ones like me. I could have explained about the numbness that seeps into you when your every waking moment is a struggle not to wind up dead and how I felt that chill stealing back into my soul with every breath I drew of Bellarian air.

I could have explained to him that outside of Hardside I was just a semi-retired thief, not a stone killer. I could have told him that I would probably be having nightmares about what I'd just done for weeks, that the shock of my knife against the bone in Mouse had felt almost exactly the same as when I'd stabbed my father and the knife had grated along a rib.

He wouldn't have understood any of it. And that was a good thing.

"You're right, kid," I said. "You aren't like me. Be thankful for that."

He kept staring at me with that look that said he had more questions.

"*What?*" I said exasperatedly.

"Did Hardside make you quick like that too?"

"Huh?"

"I never saw anybody move that fast. Nobody. Ever."

"What are you talking about? I'm just quick. It makes up for being small, some."

He looked at me like I was telling a joke at his expense. "Nobody is that quick."

"You never met Red Hand."

"The king of assassins. You're saying you did?"

"As a matter of fact." I didn't mention the fact that Red Hand had beaten me in a knife duel so easily it had bored him, that he'd actually made fun of me.

"Now I know you're just fucking with me."

"Language, Keel. Language."

As we walked away from the two bodies in the street, all the sparrows suddenly rose up in a storm of tiny wings and flew off in a ragged cloud toward the Girdle.

CHAPTER 5

I could have quizzed the kid while we walked about his letter and the supposed Ansen who'd had him deliver it, but I was in no mood for talking. I was still shaken by the aftereffects of the slaughter I'd just committed. I figured there was time. He was smart enough to stick with me while Moc Mien wanted his hide. And if he did get a sudden case of stupid and disappeared on me, well. Somebody had sent me one letter. They could send me another.

Hardside doesn't really have a beach. It's mostly mud flats or rocky tidal pools until you get to the water. Except for the Wreck.

On the rare occasions that a storm blows from just the wrong direction, there are, inevitably, fishing boats and even the occasional ship blown up and broken on the rocky jumble called the Wreck, where they are immediately scavenged by all and sundry. But that's not why that little spit of jagged rock is called the Wreck or at least not the only reason.

The Wreck is where madmen and lepers, and some say the Hag's enemies, end up, camping out and scratching a meager existence, catching what was to be caught in the jagged margin between land and sea. Mostly clams and crabs, I'd imagine. I'd never had cause to investigate.

At the furthest extent of the Wreck, there is something very, very different. It's a galley, a fifty-oared penteconter, unlike anything that plies the waters of the Dragonsea today. Or, possibly, since the Cataclysm. At any rate, it's ancient.

And made completely of stone.

The hull, except where a great rent lets in the sea? Stone. The oars, those that are not sheared off? Stone, as well. The rowers, or let's be honest here, the galley slaves, some dead at their benches, others forever pulling, mouths open in a silent rictus of strain or pain are also stone though they're difficult to see since they are mostly submerged.

And *that* is what the Wreck gets its name from.

I've no idea what happened. But that ship is no sculpture. Even after however many hundreds of years since whatever doom it was befell that ship, it still stinks of magic. Somehow, unimaginably long ago, that galley broke itself upon the rocks and then immediately became a part of them.

That was where the Hag lived, in the tiller's shed of a doomed stone ship with the sea sloshing in the unfenced oarsman's pit beneath her and madmen and lepers outside her door.

She didn't get many visitors.

Neither the madmen nor the lepers gave us any trouble. They seemed to want nothing to do with us and scurried away from us as soon as we appeared, some glaring, most just hiding in the jumble of rocks, waiting for us to pass. Their camp was pitiful. A single driftwood fire, a few moldering, greasy blankets, a pile of clam shells, another pile of gull bones and feathers. And a stench. We passed by quickly and were at the galley within a few minutes despite the hard going through the rocks and Keel's difficulty climbing. Then, it was just a short drop down onto a narrow margin of stone deck. A wooden plank crossed the oarsman's pit, obviously installed in recent memory, and fetched up against a raised platform and the tiller's shed. The doorway was covered by a heavy, moldering tarp that barely shifted in the breeze.

Everybody knew where the Hag lived, and nobody went there unless they were desperate.

I wasn't desperate exactly, but I wanted to find Theiner as quickly as I could and get the hells out of Bellarius as soon as possible. The Hag knew things, and what she didn't know, she could find out quickly for all that she never left her boat. The question was, what would she ask for payment? The rumors growing up had been rife and horrific. Had they been based on anything even close to the truth?

"Only one way to find out," I said.

"Find out what?" Keel asked. I'd forgotten he was there.

"Nothing. Let's go."

"I'd rather stay here." He looked like he was going to wet his pants.

I shrugged. "Suit yourself," I replied, and made my way across the plank to the canvas that served as the Hag's door.

"Enter, Amra Thetys," said a low, melodious voice before I could call out.

So I did.

~ ~ ~

The small space smelled unpleasant. Not foul, but like the room of a very old person unaware of their own smell. There was a little light from the curtained doorway and a little more from the hole through which the great stone tiller plunged into the sea below. There was nothing else in the room but the Hag and the chair she sat in.

She was sitting in a cane-backed, wooden chair. Her hair was iron-gray and straight, and it fell to the floor. She wore an old-fashioned linen dress, yellowed with age but clean. Her hands were in her lap. Every finger had a ring, and her nails were very long but well-maintained.

Her face was lined and pale, and her eyes were milky orbs that shimmered faintly in the gloom.

"I'm sorry I haven't any place for you to sit, Doma Thetys," she said, and I was struck by her voice. It wasn't old or weak in the slightest. She could have been a singer.

"That's all right. I don't imagine I'll be staying long. What's a 'doma' if you don't mind my asking?"

"Just an ancient form of address. The meaning is akin to 'mistress.'"

"I see. Just call me Amra."

"Very well. And you may call me Lyta."

"I'll do that." I cleared my throat.

"Yes," she said. "I know you aren't the most patient of women, Amra. So down to business."

"If you don't mind."

"I don't," she replied. "You want to know where your friend Theiner might be."

"You're pretty good, Lyta, I'll give you that. How do you know my name or what I want?"

"I know many, many things," she said with a small smile.

"Are you a bloodwitch?"

She laughed. "No, my word, no. I'm something much more powerful than that."

It was on the tip of my tongue to ask her just what she was, but then I realized I probably didn't actually want to know. Idle curiosity rarely payed in any coin but trouble, and I had enough of that.

"All right," I said instead. "You know what I want. What do you want from me in return?"

She sighed, and her hands twitched in her lap.

"I want your memories," she said.

I blinked.

"Oh, not to keep. Just share them with me. You won't be harmed in the slightest, and you won't forget a thing. You'll just be giving me a copy, as it were."

I blinked again. "I can think of a half-dozen different reasons why that would be a bad idea without even half-trying."

My profession, however retired I might be at the moment, required secrecy. People don't like it when you steal very valuable things from them and tend to go to great lengths to find out who took their shinies. Everyone I knew and even half-cared about would also be at risk from some very bad, very powerful people if my name ever got out in connection with some of the jobs I'd done. Daruvner, Holgren, perhaps a dozen others.

Not to mention the fact that just because she *said* I wouldn't lose any memories didn't mean I wouldn't. I mean, how would I know? How could I ever be sure?

"That's just not an option, I'm afraid."

"Oh, that is a pity."

"I could pay you in a more standard fashion. Money is very popular nowadays, you know."

"Do I look like someone who has use for coin, Amra?"

"You might appreciate a more comfortable chair."

She smiled. "You don't trust me."

"I don't even know you. And most days, I barely trust even myself. No offense, Lyta, but I'm not going to let you root around in my memories. I had a godling do that once. Never again."

She leaned forward, suddenly intent. "What godling, may I ask?"

"A question for a question?" I replied, and she smiled again. There was no emotion in her smiles, I'd realized, any more than there is in a facial tic.

"The answers to some questions are worth more than others."

"You know my question. What payment will you take other than my memories?"

"None, I'm afraid."

"There's nothing you want? Really?"

She sighed. "Nothing you could buy, beg, borrow or steal, Amra Thetys."

"Are you certain of that? You know my name. You know I'm not one for idle pleasantries. You should also know that if there's something you want, there's a very good chance I can get it for you if it's physical and portable."

She laughed, but it was tinged with bitterness. I knew she wasn't laughing at me.

"Tell me," I said.

"I do desire something. And it is indeed physical. Portable, however, would be stretching the definition."

"Just tell me," I said, leaning against the wall.

"It is a stone, brilliant white, oblong, inscribed with arcane symbols, and layered in puissant sorceries; it stands half a man tall and three wide…"

It was my turn to laugh. "You want the Founder's Stone."

"I do indeed."

"The Syndic wouldn't like that. That's where he puts *his* comfortable chair." In the Great Chamber of the Riail, the Syndic's palace. The throne room.

"Nevertheless. That is all I desire, Amra Thetys, and all I will take in payment for the information you seek besides your memories."

"You want to rule Bellarius?"

"I do not. I want only the Stone."

"Why?"

"Because it is mine, and was taken from me when this city boasted four mud huts and this harbor sheltered nothing greater than copperbark boats rowed by headhunting savages."

"I sense a story there."

"You do, I'm sure." But she said nothing more, and I didn't press.

After a short silence, I pushed myself off the wall and said, "Well then. If I happen to stumble across the Founder's Stone on one of my walks, I'll be sure to pocket it and bring it to you."

"Yes, do that if you don't mind. And Amra, you should be aware that I will require both your memories *and* the Stone to secure my assistance once the spirits of the slain speak to you."

I frowned. It was a sad state of affairs that I had come to a point in my life where cryptic statements from mysterious and powerful people were almost expected.

"I have no idea what that means," I replied.

She nodded. "You do not, yet. Good day, Doma Thetys."

"A pleasure, I suppose. Good day." I pulled the tarp aside and stepped out into the bright, morning light. I'd just have to try and find Theiner the hard way. There's a reason shortcuts are generally not well-traveled.

The kid was still where I'd left him, squatting on the rocks above the galley and flicking chips of stone into the restless wash below. He saw me and half-raised his good hand.

"Still got your mind?" he asked. Only half-joking, I think.

"As much of it as I went in with at any rate," I replied as I crossed the plank and joined him. We started back towards Hardside

"Did you get what you wanted?"

"I did not."

"What did you want, anyway?"

"I'm looking for somebody. The Hag was the quickest way to find him. Now, I have to put my ear to the ground and knock on doors."

"Hopefully not at the same time."

I laughed. I was starting to like this kid.

When we got back to the madmen's camp, there was someone waiting.

CHAPTER 6

He was squatting over the meager fire, warming his hands. The normal residents had vanished completely. Dressed in a particolored cloak and wearing a frockcoat and leggings at least a decade out of fashion, he was shaven-headed with tattoos covering the shiny dome. His face was long, his eyes dark, his skin pale. Magic poured off him in a cold, unseen river, making the hairs on the back of my neck stand.

I'd met someone else with tattoos something like that. The Sorcerer King. He hadn't been a nice person for all that he'd helped me. I was instantly wary. One hand slipped to a knife hilt. The other shot out to check Keel's forward progress.

The mage stood and executed a shallow bow. He was a tall one.

"Amra Thetys, greetings."

"That's two people this morning who've had me at a disadvantage," I said, tense but polite.

"Your reputation is such that it precedes you," he replied, ignoring my polite request for his name.

"What reputation is that?"

"Master thief. God-touched. *Blade breaker.*"

"That's a lot to unpack," I replied. "Let's start with the last one."

"As you wish."

"I've broken many blades in my life. I'm hard on cutlery."

"You broke a Blade forged by a goddess, powerful enough, perhaps, to cleave the world in twain. I would *very* much like to know how you managed such a feat."

"I expressed my dislike for it using harsh language."

"Amusing."

"And true."

He waved a long-fingered hand. "This is getting us nowhere."

"With all respect, Magus, I don't even know your name. I'm not asking for flowers and a nice dinner, but if you want something from me, you're being a bit brusque about the getting of it."

He smiled as insincere a smile as I've ever seen and bowed again. "My apologies. I am long removed from polite courtesies. My name is Fallon Greytooth. I am indeed a magus."

"And how did you know my name, Master Greytooth? Or where to find me?"

"I have been waiting for you to come. It was inevitable. I felt you step on that dock yesterday. And so did…others."

"I'm not really fond of cryptic comments, Master Greytooth, and I've already had one this morning."

"Then let me be direct: tell me how you broke the Blade that Whispers Hate."

"I did tell you. You weren't listening."

"I *am* listening. Attentively and patiently, which is something that I am not terribly good at if I am honest. Tell me, Mistress Thetys, how you destroyed the Blade. And I will give you information you require in return." He glanced at the penteconter. "A much more reasonable price than others have demanded, no?"

"Do you know where Theiner is?" I asked.

"No. I've no idea where, or who, this Theiner you seek might be. But I have other information that, I assure you, is of far greater import."

"Will you swear by your name and power that what you tell me is true?" Holgren had told me about that one. It was old-fashioned and formal and wouldn't stop any mage who wanted to lie. But this Greytooth seemed like an old-fashioned, formal kind of fellow. I figured it couldn't hurt. And I also figured if I didn't tell him what he wanted to know, things might get ugly. Mostly for me.

"I will so swear. If you will do the same."

I blinked. "I can swear by my name, sure. But I don't have any power to swear by."

He stared at me for a moment, disbelief etched on his long, thin face. Then, he uttered a quick bark of a laugh.

"Do you understand yourself so little, then? I can't decide if that makes you less dangerous, or more."

"I have no idea what you're talking about."

"I believe you," he replied then stood a little straighter. "I swear by my name and on my power that what I say to you is true and that I harbor no intention to deceive. I told you that I felt you step on the dock yesterday. So did the Knife."

"What Knife?" I asked, a feeling of dread welling up from my gut.

"The Knife that Parts the Night, sister weapon to the Blade that Whispers Hate, which you destroyed." He frowned and shook his head in a parody of distress. "I think it is unhappy with you for that."

"Kalara's Knife is here? In Bellarius?" I asked. The sick dread I felt started to choke me. I never wanted anything to do with the Eightfold Goddess again as long as I lived. Which wouldn't likely be long if one of her sentient weapons was looking for me.

"Kalara's Knife is here," he affirmed.

"Do you know where?"

In answer, he pointed back to the bulk of Mount Tarvus.

"In the Girdle?"

"Higher."

"Among the Gentry? In the Riail?"

"Higher."

The Citadel. The Kerf-damned Citadel. Where the Telemarch, probably the greatest living mage in the world, kept *his* comfy chair.

The Eightfold Goddess had eight aspects, each of which wielded a weapon, a Blade.

The Blades were eight intelligent, powerful magical weapons She'd left lying around in the world when She died. Or pretended to die. Or split into eight separate goddesses. Whatever. So I had been told by the most knowledgeable and most insulting man in Lucernis.

The Blades had been fashioned from the bones and fangs and scales and talons of Her demon lord husband, whom She'd slaughtered, and suffused with Her will and Her madness.

And Her power.

It had not, apparently, been the happiest of marriages.

The one I'd encountered, the Blade that Whispers Hate, had been crazier than a sack of rats and had essentially pounded my mind into hate-filled pudding until Bath, the God of Secrets, had intervened.

Oh, he hadn't saved me. He was all for putting me away in a small, dark room for the rest of eternity as a catatonic human sheath for the Blade to keep it—and me—from running amok. But he did give me the smallest of nudges toward wrestling with the Blade's will and winning.

It had worked. But it had been a close, close thing. If I'd tried to do what others before me had done—use it or contain it—it would have eaten me up and spat out an Amra-shaped marionette to do its bidding. Or worse.

Instead, I'd turned its power against itself. And it had crumbled to ash and bone chips in my hand. The same hand that was now itching and burning like I'd stuck it into an ant hill.

I very much doubted such a trick would work a second time against another Blade. I didn't even know what power this Blade used. The Blade that Whispers Hate had lived up to its name. It had done exactly as advertised—unceasingly, corrosively. Maddeningly.

But the Knife that Parts the Night? What did that even mean? The best I could come up with was that it could see in the dark, which was a decidedly underwhelming power for one of the Eightfold's toys. Kalara's Knife was a mystery except for being bad, bad news.

Anyway, it didn't matter. I was *not* going to get involved. I was here for one reason only: to find Theiner and help him however I could. Once I'd done that, I was on the first ship, boat, or floating log out of here.

"You seem to be disturbed by my tidings," Greytooth said.

"That's because I'm sane. What do you want from me, Magus?"

"I've already told you. Repeatedly. I wish to know how you destroyed the Blade that Whispers Hate."

"It won't help you."

"How could you possibly know what would help me?"

"You are a mage. Almost every mage I've ever met craved power like a drunkard craves a bottle. Unless every ounce of your will is determined to destroy that Knife, it will take you and twist you and make you into its tool." I took a step forward. "Listen to me, Master Greytooth. You can't reason with it, bargain with it, or threaten it if it is anything like the Blade I encountered. If you try, it will have you. All you can do is fight until you or it is destroyed."

"And how exactly did you do that with the Blade that Whispers Hate?" he replied, ignoring everything I'd said but the last bit. I sighed. Handing out sound advice is generally a thankless task even with rational people. Try it with a mage sometime.

"I destroyed the Blade that Whispers Hate by using its own power against it," I told him. "It offered to destroy whatever I hated. I hated *it* with every fiber of my soul and unleashed that hate on it, and it crumbled in my hand. I swear it."

His cold, hard eyes searched mine for a few seconds. Then, he nodded. "I thank you, Mistress Thetys. Good day." He turned and walked a few steps toward Hardside, and then, he just disappeared.

I stood there for a moment, staring at the empty space where he had been. I'd seen that trick once before. It wasn't magic, apparently. It was, according to a boy who was now dead, philosophy. Master Greytooth wasn't just a mage. He was one of the famed, and generally hated, Philosophers.

The group of gentlemen that had set off the Cataclysm a thousand years before.

"Uh, Amra?"

"Yes, Keel?"

"Is your life always like this?"

"Is my life always like what?"

He waved his good arm toward where Greytooth had disappeared. "Um. That. Powerful and mysterious people appearing and disappearing, talking to you like you were a barrel full of gunpowder sitting next to a bonfire."

"Don't be ridiculous," I said. "Nobody talks to barrels. That would be crazy."

"Ha. Ha ha."

"Come on. Let's go get some breakfast. Your sense of humor might improve once you've got some food in you."

CHAPTER 7

I was, by all the dead gods, not going to eat at a slop house in Hardside or even wharfside if I could help it. And I could. So we walked around the edges of Hardside proper and fetched up against South Gate in about half an hour. The gate guard took one look at us and stuck out a hand. Palm up. I flipped a silver mark into it, and he went back to doing what he did best, which was as little as possible. He couldn't even be bothered to keep kids from painting graffiti on the wall, it seemed. Within a dozen yards of the guard post, I saw two penises, a pair of improbably large breasts, a suggestion that the Syndic do something anatomically impossible, and the Hardic rune for "trap."

The last made me hesitate. After my experience with Borold's gourd, I was a little sensitive where Hardic runes were concerned. It was the closest thing there was to a thieves' language, and it wasn't uncommon in many cities on the Dragonsea. But out in public as graffiti? No, I'd never seen it used in that fashion. To my mind, it was a message or a warning. But to whom? And about what exactly?

The guard was giving me the eye, looking like he might want to take an interest in me loitering after I'd paid him. I wasn't in the mood to talk to any Blacksleeve, lazy or otherwise, so I moved along, a few steps behind Keel.

There was some invisible line. I crossed it as we walked through the gate. I felt it, a repeat of the sudden dizziness and the momentary inability to breathe I'd experienced when I'd disembarked from the *Delight*. It was accompanied this time by an almost indefinable mental pressure; an instantaneous sense of entrapment that settled on my mind like a spider web with a million fine, sticky strands.

What I had shrugged off on the dock as a bad reaction to returning to land after days at sea was, I was now certain, me sensing very bad magic aimed squarely at me. I grabbed the kid by the arm—the broken one as it turned out as it was closest—and started running. He cried out in pain.

"Move!" I shouted.

It wasn't fire this time.

The Girdle side of South Gate is all narrow, cobbled lanes and narrow graystone shop-houses three and four floors high. They weren't in the best shape because South Gate wasn't the best of neighborhoods, but they weren't slums either. There weren't any slums in the Girdle. That's what Hardside is for.

There were people out on the street: a knot of workmen with sawdust in their hair, a butcher's boy delivering a dripping packet, a knife sharpener trundling his grinder down the street. When the bilious, green fog started seeping up from between the cobbles in the street, nobody seemed to notice for a moment. Then, the butcher's boy tripped and fell.

The fog coalesced and rushed toward him. In an instant, it enveloped him completely. He was invisible inside but not inaudible. He screamed. And then, the scream was choked off. The fog drifted away from him seconds later, and what was left was wet bones in an untidy pile of clothes.

The fog had gotten thicker.

"We need to get off the street and up high," I told Keel and abruptly changed directions, heading for the nearest door. It was a tailor's shop. Behind me, I heard the knife sharpener curse and then his shorn-off scream. People were popping out of the buildings all around to see what was going on.

"Get back inside!" I screamed, hoping it would do some good. But knowing human nature, I doubted it. I risked a glance behind. It looked as though my shouting had attracted the fog's attention. It was forking in two directions above the remains of the knife sharpener, half of it floating toward us rapidly, the other half spreading out along the street.

It was moving fast.

We reached the tailor's shop. I shoved Keel in ahead of me and slammed the door.

I caught a quick glimpse of the interior. Dusty and disheveled. The tailor looked much like his shop and was gabbling something; I've no idea what. Bolts of cloth were stacked on a low table near the door. I grabbed one, took a handful of the ragged edge, and flung the rest down to the floor, unwinding it. I whipped out my knife and started cutting.

The fog had eaten the butcher's boy, but it hadn't touched his clothes.

The tailor and the gate guard were screeching now. I felt a hand on my shoulder, then Keel snarled at him, and the hand went away.

Good kid.

There were more screams coming from the street now. A lot more.

I started stuffing the cloth into the space between the door and the frame, starting at the floor, hoping I'd be quick enough.

I wasn't.

"Amra!" came Keel's warning cry, and I looked up to see the fog boiling in all around the sides and top of the door.

"Go!" I cried and flung myself backward, but it was too late.

A tendril of the fog struck out at me, viper quick, and latched on to my right hand.

The first touch was fire. Then, it burrowed in under my skin, and I screamed.

You, said a voice in my head. Then, *Yes*.

The fog suddenly hardened, became something slick, rubbery. Dazed, I watched the transformation. It started at my hand and rapidly traveled back up the tendril. When it reached the door, it flexed, and the door shattered into splinters. It started pulling me outside.

My hand was in agony. It felt as if the tendril had wrapped itself around the bones in there. It was solid now. It took me a dazed moment to realize that meant I could do something about it—or at least try.

I pulled out my other knife and cut the tendril. Or at least I tried to. But the blade passed through it as if it were still just so much fog. Kerf-damned magic.

Suddenly, I felt an arm around my waist, pulling me back or trying. Keel. Brave kid. But the pain in my hand became pure agony. I screamed.

Interference, said the voice in my head. Then, *Kill it.* Another tendril snaked through the door.

"No!" I screamed and felt the mountain tremble somewhere down beneath my feet.

The fog paused.

It talks, it said. *It hears.*

I talk, I said to it in my mind. *I hear.*

Do not resist. No more interference.

"Let go of me," I said both to it and Keel.

And both of them said, "No."

"Back off, Keel," I grunted. "It'll kill you or pop my hand right off if you don't. Maybe both."

"Damn it," he muttered and let go of me.

It yanked me through the remains of the door.

It dragged me out into the center of the street.

I could see dozens of other tendrils of fog retreating from doors and windows all along the street, all contracting toward a central mass, which I was rapidly being pulled toward.

"Stop," I told it.

No.

It yanked me into the heart of its central mass. The world disappeared in a green blur. The fog plunged down my throat, into my nostrils, rubbed up against my eardrums.

Now, you cease, it said matter-of-factly.

Along with the terror and the agony, rage boiled up inside me.

NO! I screamed silently at it and sensed again, somehow, Mount Tarvus tremble beneath me. And then, my flesh began to burn. My skin, my throat, my lungs.

NO! I shrieked again with all my will as I felt first my eyelids and then my eyes begin to dissolve and dissipate.

NO, I decided with all the force of my will. What was left of my hand, where Abanon's Blade had turned to dust, throbbed in sympathy. And I felt the world crack just a little.

I'm a thief, not a mage. I've seen massive magics done and been both healed and badly hurt by magic, but I know no more of the doing of it than I would know how to fly by watching birds. Holgren would probably be able to describe what happened so that it sounded clear, concise, and rational. There was nothing clear, concise, or rational about what happened next as far as I could tell.

It felt as if some metaphorical wall had cracked open, and through it streamed a blinding light. I knew, without knowing how I knew, that the light was meant for *me*, mine to shape. Mine to use. Mine to make with. To make what?

Anything. It was pure, undiluted possibility.

As my skin boiled away, and I shrieked silently in agony. I grabbed onto that light, let it fill me. Let it suffuse me. Let it harden me. Let it force the fog from my lungs, from my hand. And as the fog retreated, the light mended all the horrid damage caused.

No, said the fog monster.

I pushed the light outward so that it did not just fill my body, but surrounded me in a cocoon of radiant power.

No, the fog said again.

I opened my newly regenerated eyes and saw the world and the world in between.

I lay on the cobbles, curled up like an infant. Beneath me, deep down in the heart of Mount Tarvus, I sensed a restless ocean of power, of possibility. Here was where the light poured out from for me to use. I glanced up at the fog, wavering uncertainly above me, and saw a black, smoky thread in the center of it, the end nearest me twitching back and forth like the tail of an angry cat. I followed the thread with my eyes and saw that it plunged down into the street then ran under it, maybe a foot or more beneath it, and went…somewhere. I couldn't see the other end.

"Where do you go, I wonder? Who's at the other end?"

I grabbed that twitching cat's tail and pulled.

Cobbles and packed earth flew as the smoky thread was yanked out of the ground. The thread writhed, trying to escape, but I wouldn't let it. Hand over hand, I pulled on it, pulled more of it out of the ground, creating a new ditch there in the center of the street. Cobbles flew, but none could touch me.

"I'm coming for you," I told whoever or whatever was on the other end of that thread.

Apparently, they heard me, whoever they were, because they cut the thread. I fell backward on my rump, and the thread just dissipated in my hands.

"Bastard," I said. Then, I passed out.

CHAPTER 8

I woke again when Keel started slapping my cheek with his one good hand. I opened my eyes and saw only the same mundane world I'd ever seen before that day. I was where I had fallen in the street.

"Trying to give me rosy cheeks?" I said or tried. What came out was more like, "Trrgmpfh mrgle chuuh?"

"Gorm on a stick!" he said, a particularly vulgar epithet, seeing as how Gorm had died via impalement. "Are you all right?"

I tried to speak again, got no better results. I settled for raising one hand and waggling it back and forth from the wrist. *So-so.*

"I don't know whether to help you up or run away screaming. What the hells just happened?"

"Not. Really sure," I finally managed, and with his help, I got to my feet. I felt weak. And very, very hungry.

"Do you need anything?"

I pushed away from him, stood on rapidly steadying feet. "We need to get away from here." Blacksleeves would eventually show up now that all danger had passed. "And I need food. Lots and lots of food. And wine."

"Do you want to talk about—"

"Gods, no. Not yet. I need to think. For a while."

"Because it sure looked like you—"

"Keel."

"Yeah?"

"I don't *know* what happened. I swear to Kerf."

He thought about that for a moment then said, "You're a very scary lady."

"Call me a lady again, and you'll have reason to be scared."

~ ~ ~

It was not the most expensive eatery in the city. Not even close. It wasn't nearly high enough up Mount Tarvus. It was, however, the one place I remembered well enough after fifteen years to go to without having to ask directions.

The thing that made the Garden memorable, or at least impressed me as a street rat, was the fact that there was indeed a small water garden in the center of the place with ferns and mossy rocks and big, bright fish circling lazily in small pools.

I'd seen it from above; the garden area was open to the sky with the eating area surrounding it on all sides being roofed. It was no challenge at all to climb up there and watch the fish and the rich (rich to me at least, at the time) stuffing their faces with all manner of foods I had no names for then.

It was an Elamner eatery back then and still was, as we discovered when we went inside. It was smaller than I remembered and more dingy, though that might just have been due to the passage of time. But the smell of the cooking was just as good as my memory insisted.

The man at the front smiled and led us in. As with most Elamner establishments, it was all low tables and cushions instead of chairs. Elamner eateries also meant searingly spicy food, mostly grilled, and awful wine. I was fine with everything but the last.

Once he'd seen my silver, the man sat us in a quiet, screened corner and at my request sent a boy to fetch a bottle of table Fel-Radoth that I knew from experience would go well with the meal. Then, he assigned someone to hover unobtrusively while we ate—a fine line to walk, but the girl managed well enough.

Both of us were hungry. Not much talking got done as dish after dish appeared and disappeared. Finally, neither of us could eat anymore, and as if on cue, tiny cups of *veul dom* appeared before us, the after dinner drink Elamners claim aids digestion. I'm not partial to it myself. When it became apparent that Keel was, I pushed mine toward him.

"Time to talk," I said. He nodded.

"You're a mage. Why hide it? You could have just told me."

"I'm *not* a mage, and it's time to talk about *you*, numbskull, not me."

"I *saw* you. You went from wet meat to not a mark on you in a heartbeat. You re-grew your *eyes*. Then, you got up, floated above the ground, made that killer fog go *poof*, and destroyed most of Southgate Street. But no, you're not a mage. Not possible." He rolled his eyes.

"Look, I don't *know* what happened, Keel. It sure as hells has never happened to me before. If I am a mage, no one would be more surprised than me."

He stared at me. "You're serious," he finally said.

"Completely."

"That's…that's awesome and terrifying all at the same time."

I grunted. I was suddenly very, very tired.

"Look," I told him. "I was going to interrogate you about your pal Ansen, but I just don't have the energy. Do me a favor. Take me to an inn, somewhere nice. Then, tell Ansen to come meet me there. Say, tomorrow afternoon."

"All right. You want nice, or very nice?"

"I've got money and don't want to share my bed with any creepy crawlies."

"Follow me then."

I paid, and we left.

~ ~ ~

The innkeeper was fat, bald, dainty, and unimpressed with me and Keel. His inn, the Copperbark, was smallish but very, very well-appointed.

"I want a bed," I told him as we entered his brightly lit common room.

He raised a plucked eyebrow. "I'm not sure this is the right establishment for you. I believe you'd be more comfortable wharfside. Something with an hourly rate, perhaps."

I turned to Keel. "Did he just call me a whore?"

Keel shrugged. "Maybe he meant me. I'm younger. And prettier."

I turned back to the innkeeper. "I changed my mind," I said. "I want a suite. You *do* have a suite, right?"

"Very amusing," he replied. "Now if you don't mind, I have guests with coin that I need to see to."

I pulled out a doeskin purse from an inner pocket. There were enough gold marks in it to keep me in a place like that one for half a year. Say one thing about Bellarius; it was far cheaper than Lucernis. I tossed it to him, and he caught it, visibly surprised by its weight.

"Let me know when that runs out. Meantime, I'll want a bell to ring for service. And I'll want you to answer it personally, day or night."

Money doesn't make anybody better than anybody else. But it can make servants out of those who believe it does.

The suite had a sitting room complete with couch and stuffed chairs; a bedroom with an enormous, curtained bed; a balcony behind heavy, expensive drapes; and a bathroom with an actual copper bath. Everything was meticulously clean and neat and of a very high quality if a bit precious for my taste.

I made sure the innkeep knew Keel was free to come and go as he pleased then dragged myself to the bedroom, threatening death to anyone who disturbed me as I closed the door. Then, I fell face-down onto the feather bed. I think I was asleep before I hit the mattress.

~ ~ ~

I woke sometime in the night to the muted sound of rain on the roof and on the balcony. I lay there in that enormous bed for a long time, but I couldn't get back to sleep. One thought chased the next through my head. Finally, I gave up, lit a candle, and started pacing up and down a monstrously expensive Helstrumite carpet.

You'd think I was thinking about my using magic. You'd be wrong. I didn't want to think about that because it made absolutely no sense and scared me spitless. When I finally saw Holgren again, yes, I'd unpack that mystery and pore over it with him, try to figure out what had happened. But on my own, I wasn't even equipped to ask myself sensible questions much less come up with reasonable answers.

What I couldn't keep my thoughts away from were the attacks on me at the dock, then at South Gate. Two magical attempts on my life.

I didn't really have any doubt that someone was trying to end me using magic, and they weren't concerned about others getting dead in the process. For the life of me, though, I couldn't get a handle on *why*. No doubt there were a few people out there in the world that would like to see me dead. Most of them were people I had stolen very precious things from. But those people wouldn't know who exactly had stolen their shinies. Unless I was very, very unlucky, they would *never* know the identity of the person who'd robbed them. And anyway, you didn't hire a mage to kill a thief. You hired a guy with a knife and a bad reputation.

It was the magic that didn't make sense. It was the use of magic, and maybe my sensitivity to it, that nagged at me. I was pretty sure these two things pointed to who and to why someone wanted me dead, but if they were clues, they were written in a language I didn't read.

I'd always been sensitive to when magic was being actively used around me. I'd never met anyone else who could feel it though—but it's not like I go around asking people. When Holgren had first discovered I could sense him working magic, he'd been surprised but not exactly dumbfounded. But then I couldn't imagine Holgren being dumbfounded by anything. Ever.

Just how unusual was my talent, exactly? And was it something that improved over time? I'd never before been able to feel with such clarity the shape or form or whatever the correct word was for what a spell was and how it worked. I had at the dock and had again, even more distinctly, at South Gate. I recalled with absolute clarity the feeling of a giant spider web settling on me, shuddered, and resisted rubbing my skin free of magical webs that weren't actually there.

Was this increased sensitivity to do with me or the particular magic that had been used? I just didn't know enough about magic to even make a guess. But I was more than half-convinced that these spells had been laid down ahead of time and left to wait for me to come along and trigger them. The first at a place I was more than likely to arrive at; perhaps the other docks were similarly spelled. I wasn't curious enough to go wharfside and jump up and down on docks to find out. Unless I had to.

The second at South Gate. I was willing to bet all three of the Girdle's gates had been fitted out with a nasty surprise for me—

A series of truly frightening thoughts occurred to me then.

Were these traps set to keep me out, or keep me in, or just to do me in, whichever way I was going?

Would these magical traps *reset*?

Would I be able to leave without being attacked if I retraced my route?

Were they only placed at strategic choke-points in the city that I was likely to pass through, or were they scattered randomly around Bellarius?

Kerf's dirty beard.

~ ~ ~

I slept again for maybe four hours—surprisingly deeply, considering. Then, the most damnable itch on the palm of my hand woke me up.

It could have been my imagination. It could have been the last, wispy remnants of a fading dream that I saw as I opened my eyes. But the palm of my Blade-stained hand was glowing faintly blue for an instant after I pried my sleep-gummed eyes open.

Even sleep-stupid, I made the connection. After all, the faint discoloration was still there, where Abanon's Blade had disintegrated at my will.

It could have been a dream. Sure. Kerf's crooked staff, what did it mean? I had no idea, other than trouble.

At least the itching had faded along with the glow.

I got up.

I needed to see how deep into the trap I actually was. And I needed to decide what I was going to do about it.

I passed Keel on my way out, sleeping with his mouth open on the couch in the sitting room. Asleep, he looked even younger. Really just a kid. It seemed I was stuck with him for a while. I thought about that, decided I didn't much mind.

The night watchman bowed as I went out into the chill pre-dawn. The rain had stopped, but I knew it would be back. It was the season for cold, wet rain, and once it settled in, it would go on, off and on, for days, even weeks at a time. I was going to have to get a cloak. Hells, I was going to have to get a whole wardrobe. Nearly everything I owned had burned up on the dock.

I hate shopping. Fortunately, I had enough money to make the shops come to me.

~ ~ ~

Southgate Street hadn't been repaired yet. It looked like it hadn't been touched at all. The deep furrow in the cobbled street had collected a little rainwater and a little rubbish, but the whole area looked exactly the same as it had the afternoon before, barring the early gray light and the sparrows.

There were thousands of sparrows on the street, on window ledges and rooftops, and criss-crossing the air between me and the gate.

Hopefully, they'd be the only witnesses if things went horribly wrong and I was killed by magic and my own stupidity in unleashing it for the second time in as many days.

I walked along the crumbling edge of the furrow I'd somehow created using the magic that seemed to now reside inside me or beneath me. I tried to sense something, anything, of that magic, either an echo of the previous day's goings-on or anything still waiting for me or in me. I felt nothing at all. Not a single hair on the back of my neck stirred. No mystic sunlight appeared to my inner eye or whatever. Everything seemed to be perfectly mundane.

As I got closer to the gate, I had to slow my pace. It wasn't the unsure footing that was the problem. It was the sparrows. They kept darting under my feet, as if they wanted to block my path. The closer I got to the gate, the more suicidal they became. It finally came to the point where there was nowhere left for me to place a foot that wasn't already taken up by several fragile little bird bodies.

I tried to take a step forward, to scare them out of the way. I couldn't. They wouldn't budge. I wasn't walking any closer to the gate unless I was willing to kick or squash a few sparrows.

"This is ridiculous," I told them. They had nothing to say in reply.

"The gate's only three or four paces ahead. I can easily jump the distance even flat-footed, you know." Yes, I was actually talking to sparrows. Yes, I knew it was crazy.

Even more crazy was that they seemed to understand me, for as soon as the words were out of my mouth, hundreds more sparrows launched themselves from the surrounding rooftops and swarmed the air between me and the gate, creating a living, swirling, winged curtain that blocked my path.

Of course, the only thing stopping me from walking or jumping through the gate was my own reluctance to injure a few small, fragile birds.

It was enough, that reluctance. That and the fact that somebody or something obviously thought me passing through the gate wasn't the greatest of ideas and would rather I didn't do it. That made me very, very curious.

"All right, all right," I sighed. "I know when I'm beaten. But I think I'd better have a talk with your boss."

As I walked away from the gate, the sparrows rose up in a storm of wings and flew once again in a ragged cloud to somewhere deeper in the Girdle. I followed them at my own, non-winged pace.

CHAPTER 9

I had to stop and ask the way several times. It was at the end of a very long alley that was more vertical than horizontal and mostly made up of steep, worn sandstone steps that were almost more easily climbed on all fours.

The shrine of the God of Sparrows wasn't exactly what I'd expected. I'm not sure what I expected, actually, but what I saw before me certainly wasn't it. A huge, ancient tree in the heart of the Girdle? If anyone had told me such a thing existed, I'd have called them a liar. Land is scarce in Bellarius, and any patch of ground big enough to grow a tree is big enough for a building of one sort or another. In the Girdle, growing things were confined, literally, to pots.

It was thick-boled if not especially tall, and it grew out of the slope of Mount Tarvus at a gentle angle. Exposed, gray roots as thick as my thigh formed a recess at the base of the tree maybe big enough for three adults to sit in if they were especially friendly.

The hodgepodge nature of the city's growth had created a small, mostly level courtyard in front of the tree, maybe eight paces wide by ten long, and the rocky slope the tree grew out of climbed upwards for maybe twenty paces behind it before ending at the featureless, plastered wall of the building above. To the left and right, dry-stone walls had been erected with hundreds of nooks and crannies in each, all of which were filled with sparrows, sparrow nests, and little scraps of prayer notes. The tree itself was also chock-full of sparrows, constantly flitting hither and yon.

The courtyard was carpeted with sparrows, all in constant motion, groups of ten or twenty or more coalescing and breaking apart to reform elsewhere, flashing brown and white and black wings and bright eyes, intent on their own business. They took no notice of me now except to avoid my tread. It all seemed very natural and peaceful until I realized the sparrows made no noise at all. No chirping, not even the smallest rush of air on wing.

Once I noticed the silence, my skin began to crawl a little.

Someone was sitting inside the little root-cave. All I could make out through the sparrow-roil was that the person was small, had their back to me, and had long, black hair. I shuffled forward carefully. Sparrows darted out from under my feet. When I was about halfway to the shrine, the figure inside turned and smiled at me.

She was maybe ten years old and cuter than a basket full of kittens. Which made me distrust her instantly.

"Hello," she said. "Are you her?"

"I suppose that depends on which her you mean."

"*Her.* The one the God has been waiting for. I think you must be. He said you had some wicked scars."

"Scars I have, certainly," I replied, consciously keeping my hand away from my face. "And I think He's been trying to communicate with me, your God."

"Oh, He's not *my* god. He's the God of the Sparrows."

"But He talks to you?"

"Yes."

"So you're His priestess?"

She laughed. "He talks to me, but I'm not His priestess. He doesn't have anything like that, or at least He doesn't anymore. Not for a long, long time."

"So what are you, then, to the God of Sparrows?"

"I guess I'm His friend." She waved her hand. "As much as He loves His birds, they're not very interesting to talk to, you know."

"I'd imagine not."

"So you want to sit down?" she asked, so I squatted down next to her on the hard-packed dirt.

"You said He's been waiting for me?"

She nodded.

"Why?"

"He said He needs to tell you some things. He said there's something you need to do, or all of us are going to die."

I blinked. "Well," I finally managed. "That would be bad."

"Yes," she replied.

I waited a while, but apparently, the girl had said all she had to say about that.

"So, does the God want to talk now? Or…?"

"Oh, yes, any time you're ready."

"I suppose I'm ready now."

"Did you bring a knife?"

"A knife? Well yes, I've got a couple actually."

"All right then. Just go ahead. I'll be here; don't worry."

"Um, just go ahead and what?"

"Give him blood, silly."

"See?" I muttered. "Never trust kids who are cute as baskets full of kittens."

"Huh?"

"Nothing," I replied. "Talking to myself."

"You shouldn't talk to yourself. People will think you're crazy."

"Kid, why does the God of Sparrows need *blood* to talk to me?"

"Oh. He wasn't always the God of Sparrows. Before that, He was the Blood God. But He did something the other gods didn't like, and they made Him watch over sparrows instead. He says He likes it better now." She shrugged. "I guess sparrows are better than human scarri—sacar—"

"Sacrifice."

"Yeah, that's the word. Anyway, He still needs blood to talk to you, at least the first time."

"Did you give Him blood the first time?"

She nodded. "On accident. I was playing here. I fell down and split my lip on that root there," she said, pointing to one by my knee. "Then, He was in my head. Or really I was in His, I guess. Now, He can talk to me anytime as long as I'm here. Though He doesn't really talk."

"Wait, does he talk or not?"

"Sort of. He understands what I say, but He talks back in pictures. Sort of." She shrugged. "Talk to him and see."

I blew out a breath and pulled out a knife. "All right. Here goes."

I pricked the fleshy pad at the base of my thumb and squeezed until a bright drop of blood welled up. Then, I pressed my hand against the root.

The world kind of half went away.

I mean, I knew my body was still sitting there at the base of the tree next to dangerous kitten girl, but I knew it in a very distant, abstract sense. I had to concentrate to make the connection. And most of my concentration was taken up with where I now sort of was. Which was someplace very, very different from Bellarius.

I suppose it was a temple. The space was cavernous, brown stone walls stretching up and up out of sight, impossibly high. It was a long space lit by flickering braziers every twenty feet or so. A deep, dark, jagged fissure maybe a hand span wide ran the length of the floor. The floor was tiled in gold bars. As in actual, buttery bars of gold as long and wide as my foot. Thousands of them. I tore my eyes away from them. Reluctantly.

At the far end was a throne made of the same stone as the walls. At a glance, it was big enough for half a dozen giants to sit together comfortably. It, too, was cracked down the middle. One half leaned drunkenly against a wall. Some rubble was scattered around the throne's foot. Somebody was sitting on one of the chunks of stone.

I walked forward.

He was big. Muscular, bald, bronze-skinned as Tha-Agoth had been. Naked as Tha-Agoth had been. Generously endowed and utterly unselfconscious about it.

But where Tha-Agoth had been unarguably handsome, this guy's features were brutal, and an old, deep, furrowed scar creased his skull. He looked like a killer or, I guess, a blood god. One that had mellowed considerably though. His face showed no anger at least, and his eyes, beneath thick brows, were mild.

I got to within a few feet of him and said, "The God of Sparrows, I presume."

He nodded.

"You wanted to talk to me."

He nodded again.

"Why?"

An image filled my mind. Bellarius from above. Or more precisely Mount Tarvus. It was as if I were floating in the sky, a bodiless eye, seeing the whole mountain below me.

Time sped up. The sun set three times. When the sun rose a third time, Mount Tarvus exploded, taking all of Bellarius with it. The destruction was total, brutally swift, and too incredible to really grasp. All that was left of the city and the mount was a huge, gaping hole that the sea rushed in to fill.

Then, the vision was gone, and I was standing in front of Him again. "Kerf's bunched back!" I swore. "In three days?"

He nodded.

"Why?"

He pointed to my hand. The one that had held the Blade that Whispers Hate when I destroyed it. Then, He showed me another vision: the Citadel at the top of Mount Tarvus. Where the Telemarch lived. And, according to Fallon Greytooth, where the Knife that Parts the Night currently was.

"I don't really understand," I told Him. "I've got something to do with Bellarius becoming a smoking hole in the ground?"

He nodded.

"Then I should get the hells away from here."

He shook his head emphatically. He showed me the Citadel again.

"I should go to the Citadel?"

He nodded.

"And do what?"

He showed me a picture of the Citadel again then an old man with a long, dirty beard standing on a balcony. Then, He showed me a picture of blood.

"I've got a bad feeling the old man is the Telemarch. The world's single-greatest mage. Am I right?"

He nodded.

"And you want me to go to the Citadel. Meet him. And spill his blood."

He nodded.

"You want me to kill him."

He nodded. He was good at it.

"And If I don't? Is this some kind of threat? Why should I trust you?"

He shook his head. Then, He showed me Mount Tarvus exploding again. But this time, He showed me pictures of the kid at His tree being blasted limb from limb, and sparrows dying in their thousands, and His tree shattered into splinters.

"So. You're not threatening me. You're just telling me what will happen if I don't kill the Telemarch."

He nodded again.

"Leave that aside for a moment. *Why* will all this happen?"

He pointed to me, to my hand, then showed me a picture of a knife.

It was nothing like Abanon's Blade. That one had shifted form constantly and thrown out sparks and jags of painful, unearthly light.

This one was just a little, crystal sliver, maybe as long as my index finger, with a black hilt. It glowed faintly, blue-white, and the glow pulsed like a heartbeat. It floated in the air above the Telemarch's head, point down, slowly spinning.

"Sorry, I just don't get that part," I told him. He nodded, looked frustrated, shrugged helplessly.

"You can't make it clearer than that, can you? It's too complicated to do with pictures."

He nodded His head.

"Why me? Why not you? You're a god."

He just shook his head a final time and pointed to me and to my hand. Then, I was suddenly back at the tree, next to the kid. I shuddered.

"He's nice, isn't He?"

"Er, He's not mean anyway. Have you been inside His throne room?"

"Of course. That's where I talk to Him. He says it's His mind."

If that's His mind, it's cracked. Literally, I thought to myself, *which means everything He just told me is suspect at best.*

"If that's His mind, where is His body?" I said out loud.

She patted the nearest root. "He's the tree now. That's what the other gods did to Him. And the sparrows are His eyes, of course."

"Of course. How could it be otherwise?"

"'Zactly," she replied, serious as a justicar.

"What's your name, anyway?" I asked her.

"Cherise."

I felt a little stab of emotion at that. "That's—that's a good name," I managed. "It was my mother's name. I'm Amra."

"Sounds like a boy's name," she told me.

"It's one of those names that can go either way." I got up. "Well then. Thanks, kid. Cherise." I turned to go.

"Are you going to do it?" she asked.

"Do what?"

"Save the city. I don't want to die."

"I'll be honest with you, kid. I don't know if I can. And I still don't know why your friend the God of Sparrows thinks it has to be me." Or if I should believe anything He'd just told me. I was leaning heavily toward crazy god talk. Or crazy god pictures. Or whatever.

She scrunched one eye up and regarded me. "It has to be somebody, doesn't it? And it can't be Him; I mean, He's a *tree* now. And it can't be me. I can't even stay out after dark."

"All valid points," I acknowledged.

"So I guess it's you. He's pretty smart, you know, even if He can't talk properly. He sees everything His birds see. And He's really, really old."

I rubbed my forehead. When did I go from being a thief to some sort of hero? When exactly did that happen, and how could I possibly not have noticed? And most of all, why *me*?

"Tell you what, kid. Let me have a good think, and I'll get back to you."

"All right. But you'd better hurry. We're all going to die in three more days, you know."

"That's what I've been told, yeah."

CHAPTER 10

Funny thing. At the tree, the sky was cloudless, the sunlight gold on the leaves and the courtyard, and the sparrows, of course. But once I was in the alley on my way back to the inn, the temperature plummeted, the sky became leaden gray, and a cold wind came down off the Dragonsback range to skirl around Mount Tarvus. That miserable, chill Bellarian autumn rain was coming again.

When I got back to the inn, I was assaulted by the most delicious odor: roast beef. I realized I was ravenous and sat down in the common room rather than take my meal upstairs. The innkeep served me personally, a little white cloth on his arm and a deeply unhappy look on his pudgy face. I tore into the meat, ignorant of anything else around me until a lace-cuffed, hairy, manicured hand intruded on my field of vision. A hand that snapped its fingers. A hand attached to a man who was obviously one of the Gentry. The powdered wig was a big giveaway. He'd snapped his fingers in my face to get my attention.

"You, girl. Can you afford that meal?"

"What the hells is it to you?"

"If you're in need of coin, you can accompany me this afternoon. Once you've bathed and dressed suitably."

I raised an eyebrow. "Accompany you?"

"Indeed. I find myself at loose ends. You can amuse me." He said it like it was a rare honor.

"I think I'll pass."

He stared at me as though I had suddenly started speaking in tongues. Then, some idea occurred to him and slowly seeped into his face.

"Ah. You are a lover of women then."

"No, I'm what you might call a misanthrope."

A slick, mean grin crawled across his face. "Mis-an-thrope. That is a very large word for such a chit of a girl. Are you quite sure you understand its meaning? I'd have said you were a bit of gutter tail myself."

I rolled my eyes and did that trick where my knife is suddenly poking up somebody's nostril.

"Misanthrope. It means 'piss off right now' in Lucernan."

He did. The innkeeper wasn't happy. I didn't care. I pushed the suddenly flavorless beef away along with the dirty feeling the Gentry idiot had smeared me with and stared out the window and the low, gray sky. Rain was coming for sure.

Once it arrived, it would linger for days, maybe weeks on end, constantly inconstant.

Of course, I wouldn't have to worry about that after a few days, now would I? If I did nothing, I'd be blown to bits. If I did what the God of Sparrows wanted me to, I'd be dead in some other hideous, magical way once the Telemarch and Kalara's Knife were finished with me.

If the God of Sparrows wasn't mentally damaged to the point of derangement.

If I ran away like a sensible thief—

Could I run away? Leave Bellarius to its fate? It had left me to mine all those years ago. Part of me truly believed this stinking city deserved to be wiped from the map. All of it. Every brick and shingle. It wasn't the sanest part of me, but it was very persuasive.

I wasn't going to save Bellarius. That was impossible. Kill the world's most powerful mage, who happened to also possess one of the Eightfold Goddess' Blades, all on the say-so of an obscure, mentally damaged deity? Oh, please.

So the question I was really facing was pretty straightforward.

Was I going to bugger off before Mount Tarvus maybe, possibly erupted, or was I going to ignore the conversation I'd just had and continue on looking for Theiner?

Decisions, decisions, said the voice in my head that sounded almost like my own.

"Oh, shut it," I told the voice. "I'm feeling crazy enough without hearing voices added into the bargain. Not that talking out loud to myself is helping matters."

~ ~ ~

Since my traveling chest had been destroyed along with most of the dock when I arrived, I had exactly what I was wearing in the way of clothing, which wasn't warm enough, was rather singed, and in all truth was starting to smell. So when I got back to the Copperbark, I summoned the innkeeper and told him what I wanted. I was not going out amongst the shops of the Girdle and suffering looks down noses until I put gold under them.

Keel was nowhere to be seen. I shrugged to myself. I was sure he'd turn up. If not, he was his own man. I hoped he'd taken my message to Ansen, but if not, I wasn't terribly concerned. I had plenty of other things on my plate. Like finding Theiner.

Within half an hour, two tailors and their assistants and baggage had arrived along with a leathersmith. I bathed while waiting for them and then met them in the sitting room wrapped in an enormous and dangerously soft towel. The innkeeper might have been a self-important little class monger, but he had taste. I reluctantly changed into a bathing robe and let them start measuring.

If the tailors disapproved of my unladylike sartorial requirements, they wisely kept their opinions to themselves. After all, I was paying triple to have my order finished by day's end.

They finished up and started muttering to each other, and then the leathersmith silently took the measure of my waist and chest, showing no embarrassment whatsoever and pointedly ignoring the fact that the tailors had just done it before him. Then, he measured out Holgren's gift knives. Then, he asked me when I'd be wanting my sheaths and harness.

"As soon as possible," I replied.

He grunted. "Cheap, fast, or good. Choose only two."

"The last two. But nothing fancy required."

"I'll be back at dinner time then," he grumbled and stalked out.

The tailors left soon after with a long sheet of scribbled notes and a hefty deposit, which left me short of hard currency, as I'd known it would. The next person in was a gem merchant, a wizened old Pinghul gentleman shadowed by a very large, very hard-eyed guard. I showed him three of the smaller jewels I'd brought with me. He inspected them with his loupe and a spelled talisman then quoted me a ridiculously low price. I laughed, countered with a ridiculously high price, and we set to bargaining. Ten minutes later, we'd exchanged gems for coins, and he'd bowed his way out, a small smile on his face. He'd gotten the better of me but not by much.

I had lunch in my rooms, and then, there was nothing more to do until my new clothes arrived, since what I'd been wearing had been whisked away to be laundered and mended. Or possibly burned, considering the innkeeper's personality.

Now, with suddenly enforced idleness pressing down on me, my conversation with the God of Sparrows came unbidden to my mind. I very much wanted to ignore it, to forget it. It was ridiculous.

It is rarely wise to ignore messages from gods, said the voice in my head.

"Maybe, maybe not," I muttered. Maybe He wasn't deranged. But doing what He wanted me to certainly would be.

Assuming He wasn't crazy as a box of frogs, what *was* I going to do? Was I going to high-tail it out of Bellarius, leaving everyone to be blown to bits? Or was I going to go on a suicide mission to assassinate the Telemarch, on the say-so of a blood god who had been turned into a tree by his fellow gods for, presumably, being a not-nice fellow?

There was a knock on my door.

"Take that, ridiculous decisions," I muttered and sat on the couch, put one knife on the table in front of me and another down in the cushions at my back.

"Come in," I called.

The door opened, and Keel popped his head in. "You're not naked or anything?" he said, staring at me in my robe as only a teenage boy can do.

"Don't make me hurt you, Keel."

"I told him what you said about meeting him," the kid replied, coming into the room and putting his eyes on the curtains rather than my legs.

"Ansen?"

"Yes."

"And?"

"He's, uh, not coming," Keel replied, sitting down on one of the overstuffed chairs.

"Color me surprised."

"But he gave me this to give to you." Keel took out a crumpled letter from inside his waistcoat and handed it to me. This one I took. But I didn't open it.

"Why do you believe in this guy, Keel? What makes you believe this man is a three-hundred-year-old hero returned from the dead?"

His face sobered. He looked me in the eye. "Maybe he isn't. Maybe it really is impossible. I know you don't believe it, and you obviously know a lot of things about a lot of things. But if he isn't Ansen, the real Ansen, he might as well be. There's nobody else out there fighting for what's right."

"Are you sure that's what he's doing? What makes you think this whole Ansen persona isn't just some elaborate scam?"

"Con men and grifters don't feed the poor. They don't kill bent Blacksleeves. They don't start rebellions."

"Small time grifters don't, no. But maybe this guy is playing the big game."

"What do you mean?"

"So he's not out fleecing the poor for what little they have. That doesn't mean he's not using them all the same."

"For what?"

"For a power base. If this Ansen character is starting a rebellion, he needs, you know, *rebels*, now doesn't he?"

"You're wrong," he said flatly. "He doesn't use people."

"Maybe I am wrong. For your sake, I hope I am. But if your rebellion *is* successful, and that's a staggeringly large 'if' considering the fact that the Syndic has the Telemarch to stomp all over pitchfork-wielding rabble, we'll see who ends up sitting in the Riail, passing laws and collecting taxes. If it's your Ansen, try not to feel too used and bitter about it."

Keel gave me a look that was both hurt and disgusted at the same time. "I don't like you very much right now," he said, getting up and walking out.

"Sometimes, I don't like myself very much either," I said quietly to the closing door.

After a moment, I remembered the letter in my hand and opened it.

Amra Thetys, Greetings –

My apologies for not being able to meet with you personally. Circumstances make such a meeting inadvisable. I beg your understanding.

Keel informs me that my first message to you was lost during the incident on the dock (and I thank you for looking after my young associate). Its essence was this: the man you are seeking lodges at Number 7, Ink Street

– A.

"Well," I said to the empty room, "I guess I know what I'm doing tonight."

CHAPTER 11

"**K**erf's hairy warts," I whispered to myself when I found No. 7 Ink Street.

It wasn't all that big a building, but it was the finest one on a street full of scribes, copyists, chandlers, and accountants. People and businesses that, by and large, made decent money. Fully half the first floor was taken up with leaded, glass windows. I could see a couple of people moving around inside and dimly make out clerk's desks lit by oil lamps.

The sign hanging from the eaves read:

SWAINPOLE & SON
FACTORS—CHANDLERS

I'd never seen the building before; in fact, I'd never set foot on Ink Street in my life. But I knew who lived in that house. I'd heard my father shout it at my mother more than once.

Why don't you go back to Ink Street, Cherise fucking Swainpole? That's right; they won't fucking have *you anymore!* What followed next was usually a slap.

I was standing in front of my maternal grandfather's house. The man who'd refused to let her marry my father, not that I'd have disagreed with him if I'd been around. The man who'd disinherited my mother when she'd gotten pregnant with me.

That, I had a problem with. Ultimately, it meant she'd stayed with my father because she'd had nowhere else to go. Ultimately, it meant him beating her to death. Ultimately, it meant years on the street for me, fighting for food and being hunted like an animal.

Yes, I had a problem with that and those who lived in the house that stood in front of me. Enough of a problem that I found myself considering burning the house down to the ground. Arson seemed fitting, somehow, for a house I had never been allowed to set foot in.

What, by all the dead gods, had Theiner been doing living *there*?

Abruptly, I decided I didn't want to know. It wasn't worth it.

"Just let it go, Amra," I whispered to myself. "Just walk away." But I couldn't take my eyes off the place.

Coward, whispered a voice in my head. I'm pretty sure that one was my own.

There was a face in the window now, a man's face looking out into the street. Looking at me. I turned on my heel and started walking away. I heard the door open, the bell ring.

"Amra?"

I kept walking.

"It *is* you, isn't it?"

I kept walking.

"I'm your uncle. Ives. Your grandfather's dead."

I stopped. Turned around. Looked at him. He had the same eyes as my mother. As me.

"How do you know who I am?"

He smiled, a little sadly. "You look very, very much like your mother. Except—"

"Except for the scars," I finished.

We stood that way for a while. Then, he said, "So why don't you come inside for a while?"

"Too many reasons to count," I replied.

He nodded. "All right. I understand. But just stay there for a moment, will you? I've got something to give you."

"Whatever it is, I don't want or need it."

"I think you will want it. It was your mother's."

He had me.

I still really didn't want to. Which probably meant that I should.

"All right," I finally said. "I'll come in."

~ ~ ~

He led me past the front office, where two silent clerks sat at desks writing lots of numbers in big ledger books, down a short hallway, and into a cheery, brightly lit kitchen. There he sat down at a sturdy, scarred table and gestured me to sit as well. I slid onto the bench opposite him.

"What do you want to give me?"

He reached under his broad, linen collar and pulled from around his neck a silver locket on a chain. He put it on the table between us and leaned back.

"You could have given this to me on the street."

"I did offer," he replied. "But the light is better here."

I picked it up and pressed the catch. The locket popped open.

My mother, no older than sixteen, smiled up at me from the palm of my hand. Fresh, happy, beautiful.

Unbroken. Like I'd never seen her while I was alive.

"Gesher painted that before he got too famous to do miniatures. When your mother left, she gave it to me and asked me not to forget her."

I snapped the locket closed.

"But you did."

He shook his head. "I did not. But I was four years her junior, and our father was a hard man. When he disinherited her, I was only twelve. There was nothing I could do." he shifted on his bench. "I tried to sneak out once, to bring her money. He found me before I even got outside the Girdle and beat me bloody. I couldn't leave my bed for a week."

"Sure, I can understand a boy of twelve being cowed. But my mother died ten years later. In all that time, she—we—never heard from you once. Were you still so afraid of your father when you were fifteen? Seventeen? Twenty?"

He looked down. His hands were clasped together. White-knuckled.

"Yes," he finally said.

I stared at him. Contempt bubbled up from my gut and choked me.

"My father was a monster, a drunk, and, let's face it, a murderer," I said. "But at least he wasn't a coward."

"You're right; I should have found a way to help your mother and you. But do you know what your grandfather said to me as he kicked me in the ribs until several of them broke?"

"I have no idea."

"He said, 'If you ever try to help that whore that was your sister again, I'll have her and her whelp killed, and by all the dead gods, I'll make you watch. And you will know, boy, as she screams her life out, that it's all your fault.'"

He looked up at me. "My father was a monster too. Never doubt it."

I looked down again at the locket in my hand. I nodded. I heard the truth in his voice. "So I have monsters on both sides of my heritage."

He leaned forward and placed a finger on the locket. "But you also had her."

"Not for long enough," I forced out.

He looked away while I cried.

I don't cry. But for my mother, I did. I don't really want to talk about it. When it was over, I put the locket around my neck, safe under my shirt.

"Do you need money? A place to stay?" he asked.

"I do not."

"Is there anything that I can do for you?"

I thought about that. Thought about my mother. Thought about my time on the streets. Shook my head.

"The time for doing is long past, Uncle. Your offer comes years too late."

He seemed to slump inward. He nodded. "I understand," he replied.

"There is one thing I want," I told him.

"Anything."

"A man lives here named Theiner. I'd like to know what he's doing here and how you met him."

"Theiner did live here, yes. But he died last week. I'm sorry, Amra. I know he was your friend."

I was taken aback. I didn't know how to respond. Or even what to feel.

"How?" I finally asked. "How did it happen?"

"I don't know. He didn't go to work one day. Daymer sent a lad around to check on him since Theiner hadn't missed a day's work in years. We knocked, but there was no answer. I unlocked the door, and we found him sprawled on the floor, dead. There wasn't a mark on him, and his room was as neat as it ever was." He leaned back, blew out a breath of air. "It could have been a natural death."

"But you don't think so," I said.

He shook his head. "I don't, and I can't tell you why. He was young, younger than me at any rate, and far healthier. Sure, fit fellows drop dead sometimes. It happens. But…"

"But what?"

"Theiner worked at Daymer's ropewalk during the day. But in his free time, he did something else. Something dangerous. Very dangerous."

"Maybe you should tell me everything from the beginning. Like how you met him in the first place."

He smiled a little. "I met Theiner after your grandfather died. When I went looking for you."

"You looked for me?"

"I did, near ten years ago. By then, you were long gone across the Dragonsea and disappeared. I was relieved that you'd at least escaped the Purge even if I could find no trace of you. By then, Theiner was a young man, and when he found out who I was, he punched me in the face." He smiled and shook his head ruefully. "It took him a while to believe I wanted to help you. Over the course of a few weeks, we became friends. He told me about you, what you were like, what you had been through, and how he admired you."

"He admired me?" I laughed.

"He did. He said you were the most relentless person he'd ever met and that he wished he had half your will." He grew serious, then, and looked me in the eye.

"It was about that time he decided he was going to make an accounting for the purge. He decided he was going to do what he could to make those responsible pay for their actions."

"Madness. You talked him out of it, right?"

"Wrong. I financed him."

"You're joking."

"I am not." He spread his arms wide, looked around. "This business your grandfather left me is very profitable. I have no wife, no children, no family at all except you, and you were lost, I thought, for good. Theiner became almost a younger brother to me, and he had a good cause that lacked funding. You knew him. He was as honest and earnest as the day is long. I considered it money well spent, and in truth, it wasn't all that much money. He refused to work for me or live off the funds I gave him. Every copper I gave him went to uncovering those who had a hand in planning or executing the Purge."

"And just how far did he get in this one-man quest for justice?"

"I don't really know. I could show you where he spent the money and what for. He kept meticulous records for me though I told him time and again it wasn't necessary. But results? I don't know. We decided almost at the outset that it would be safer if I didn't know any of the names he unearthed."

"I guess it wasn't safe enough for him," I said.

"Considering what he was doing, he was making enemies of some dangerous and potentially powerful people."

"Precisely. The only thing that I can't work out is why they would bother to make it look natural. They could have had him knifed him in the street just as easily. Or even just made him disappear."

"Maybe they were afraid someone wouldn't leave it alone in that case."

"Maybe. There's just no telling."

"Where is he now?"

"I put him to rest up in Jaby."

I raised an eyebrow. "I don't know if Theiner would appreciate rubbing elbows with the Gentry, even in death." Jaby was a cemetery within spitting distance of the houses of the Gentry.

My uncle smiled. "I rather think he would have approved. He had a quirky sense of humor, did our friend Theiner."

"Did he? He must have grown it after I left."

"When you knew him, there probably wasn't much to joke about."

"True enough." The picture my uncle was painting of Theiner was a strange one. Theiner as some sort of vigilante, yes, I could see that to a degree. But I still wasn't seeing Theiner as a man who would be lopping heads off, stuffing them in boxes, and sending them across the Dragonsea. But there was no one else who knew what Borold had done to me, damn it. Which left me with the rune on Borold's forehead as the only clue, and magic as the only answer. Which was no answer at all.

I made a decision, knowing as I did so that I would almost surely regret it. "I need to have a look at anything that was Theiner's. You haven't thrown his belongings out yet, have you?"

"No, his room hasn't been touched. It's all just as he left it. There wasn't anyone to give his things to, not that he had much; nor is there anyone who needs the room." He sorted through a ring of keys at his belt and pulled one off. He handed it to me, holding just the tip. As if he were afraid our fingers might touch. I took it and nodded.

"He had his own entrance, in the back. The stairs are right outside the door there," he said, indicating a door on the far side of the kitchen that led outside.

"Thanks. I'll find my way."

He jerked his head in assent and sat down again at the table, putting his chin in his hand. His eyes traveled over the dining room but in an abstract, unfocused way. As if he wasn't sure just what to make of the day's events.

I felt exactly the same.

CHAPTER 12

Theiner's garret was at the top of a set of sturdy, wooden stairs in the house's attic. I unlocked the door and stepped inside, holding up the lamp I'd taken from my uncle's kitchen. I fit the key in the lock but stopped before I turned it.

Here I was, at the end of my search. I could just leave it here, turn around and walk back down the stairs. Keep walking, down to the docks. Take ship. I'd come to Bellarius to find out what Theiner was up to. What he was up to was lying down and not ever getting up again. He didn't need my help with that.

I stood there for a long time, hand on the key. Finally, with a muttered curse, I turned it and pushed open the door.

It was a small room with a single window next to the door, a sloped ceiling with exposed beams. It was a little musty now that no one was inhabiting it. On one side stood a narrow, wooden bed with a thin mattress and an even thinner pillow covered by an old, soft-looking quilt. On the other side was a narrow table and a rickety, wooden chair. At the far end was a tiny wardrobe with a tiny, steel mirror nailed to the door and a tiny table holding a pitcher and a basin. And that was it.

Except I knew that wasn't it. There would be more. Theiner would have a hidey-hole here somewhere.

I checked the bed, the table and wardrobe, and found nothing more than a few changes of clothes, a knife, fork and spoon and, under the bed, a pair of boots that had seen much better days. They were caked in grime and smelled like a particularly vile strain of cheese.

I checked the basin, the pitcher, the tiny little wash stand. I checked behind the mirror. I checked the floorboards and the ceiling and the beams. I checked the walls for hidden cavities.

Nothing. Nothing at all. Everything was painfully neat, tidy, clean—

Everything except the boots.

"Disgusting but clever, my friend," I said to the air and, breathing through my mouth, stuck my hand into one and then the other of the boots.

Crammed into the toe of the second was what I was looking for. I fished it out, a many-times folded sheet of paper.

I dropped the boot and unfolded the paper. I couldn't read what was written there; the room was too dark and the writing almost unbelievably small. I brought it and the lantern over to the table and sat down to try to decipher the incredibly close, cramped writing.

It was a list of names with annotations. The names meant nothing to me, but Theiner's notes meant something more:

Adok Frees, Blacksleeve, Murdered three in front of witnesses. Deceased.
Garl Lenst, Former Blacksleeve, Now Justicar Lenst. Murdered two. 12 Coln Street.

Almost three dozen names in all. Borold's wasn't among them. More than half were still alive. A long list of child killers. I suppose I should have felt more, felt something. Anything. But I didn't, really, until I got to the end of the list. The one at the end of the list stood out because of the note that Theiner had underlined.

Affonse Yarrow. Blacksleeve Commander. Retired. Murdered dozens. Address unknown.
He knows the mage's name.

I stuffed the list into a pocket of my new silk waistcoat, grabbed the lamp, and walked out. My hands were sweaty. After years of believing without proof, here at last was confirmation that there really had been a mage finding street rats for the Blacksleeve death squads, that it really hadn't mattered where we'd hid.

We'd never had a chance, any of us.

If I hadn't left, I'd almost certainly be dead.

I locked up and went back downstairs.

Uncle Ives was still sitting at the table, this time with a mug in front of him.

"Did you find anything?"

"I did. Maybe why Theiner was killed. Do you want to know?"

He thought about that for a while. "Yes. But no. What will you do?"

"Honestly, I'm not sure. I need to think. To decide."

"I understand."

"Thank you," I told him. "For…thank you."

"Are you sure you wouldn't like to stay here?" he asked.

I shook my head. "I'm also into things right now that you're safer being away from and knowing nothing about."

"All right," he said, but I don't think he believed me.

"I'll come back again once I've taken care of my business."

"I hope you do, Amra. Niece."

I forced myself to give him a brief hug, which made both of us uncomfortable. Me more than him, probably, since as soon as we touched, the small hairs on the back of my neck stood up.

Uncle Ives, if that's who he really was, was a mage.

I kept my face neutral as we parted. "Goodbye, uncle," I managed. Then, I was out the door.

CHAPTER 13

I brooded on it all night. Ansen's note. Meeting my uncle. Finding Theiner's list then discovering Uncle Ives, if that was really who he was, was a mage.

It stank like week-old fish. It stank from so many directions I didn't even know which one stank the worst. I have a very suspicious, pessimistic, and fertile imagination. The ways that the situation could be rotten were almost limitless, and I didn't have enough information to make any sort of reasonable guess as to what exactly was really going on. But someone, somewhere was trying to play me, to make me believe… What, exactly?

That I had an uncle. That said uncle knew Theiner. That Theiner had been on a one-man crusade to right the wrongs of the Purge.

A mage had helped track down gutter kids. The man who said he was my uncle was a mage. It would be very, very easy to stick those to bits of knowledge together and make an assumption. Too easy, maybe.

I spent a good hour pacing my rooms, staring at the locket my supposed uncle had given me.

It was her. Of that, there was no doubt. The miniature portrait in the locket was of my mother. And if it wasn't a Gesher, it was the best forgery I'd ever seen. I'd had the opportunity to see a full-sized Gesher up close. Yes, it was for a job. No, I'm not going to talk about it. But there was a reason Hurin Gesher was the greatest living portraitist on the Dragonsea, and when you'd seen one of his works, you wouldn't mistake it for anyone else's. At least I wouldn't.

The thought crossed my mind that the locket could be spelled, that I should get rid of it. But I couldn't make myself do it. I finally slipped it into my pocket, where it kept company with Holgren's necklace.

Sometime after midnight, Keel came back, forcing me out of my brooding. He flopped down on the couch. It was an awkward flop, him being effectively one-armed.

"I forgive you," he announced.

"That's nice. For what, exactly?"

"For being a negative, suspicious hope-killer."

"Oh, that. You haven't even seen the tip of the knife on that, I'm afraid."

He snorted.

"Do you know what your buddy Ansen's note said?" I asked him.

"No idea."

"You didn't sneak a peek before you gave it to me?"

He snorted again. "I can't read. Well, I can read my own name, but that's about it. So unless it said 'Keel Fenworth' a bunch of times, his message was safe with me."

I wasn't surprised. You could probably count the number of people in Hardside who could read on one hand.

"What kind of a name is Keel anyway?"

"An awe-inspiring one."

"As in 'keel over and die?'"

"Ha ha."

"As in 'well I'll be keel-hauled?'"

"What kind of a name is Amra? Sounds like something you take when you've got the runs."

"Better than being named after a ship's bottom."

"My ma said my da named me Keel because without its keel, a ship could never make it where it wanted to go," he said, serious now. "Without its keel, a ship will always be pushed off course by wind and tide. He wanted to make sure I always had a way to get where I was going."

"That's actually sensible. Your da knew a thing or two."

"Yes. He did." It was the first time I'd seen the kid serious and sad. Obviously, he'd lost his father, and just as obviously, it *had* been a loss. Unlike mine.

He shook himself out of it fairly quickly. "So? What kind of a name is Amra?"

"The kind of name you get when your father wants a boy and gets a girl," I replied.

"It's not a Bellarian name. Not even a boy's name."

"No. I don't know where my father got it. The only other Amra I've heard of was a pirate king from Nine Cities a long time ago." I shrugged. "My father was unpredictable." By which I meant irrational, which was a nice way of saying half-crazy. Among other things. I didn't want to talk, or think, about him, so I changed the subject.

"What does he look like, this Ansen?"

"Huh? I don't know."

"Oh, come on, Keel. Aren't we past that sort of thing by now?"

"Really, I don't know. I've only been in the same room with him a few times. His face is always covered. The Blacksleeves *are* looking for him, you know."

"How many people listen to this guy?"

"I'm not really sure. A lot of people, I think, but any time he talks, it's only to a few people at a time. He says we have to be cautious for now."

"How do you know how to contact him?"

He sat up and shook his head. "I can't talk about that. Please don't ask."

"All right." It was important, but not important enough to torture it out of him, which was likely what I would have had to do. As long as Keel could make contact, and I had a hold on Keel, it would suffice. "Listen, Keel, you know I'm looking for someone. The letter Ansen had you deliver to me told me where he lives. Lived. I'd like to know how Ansen knew I was looking for Theiner in the first place, how he knew Theiner, and why he bothered to give me the information that he did."

"I don't know anything about that."

"I know you don't, and if you did, you probably wouldn't feel comfortable talking about it. I respect that. But you can pass on the message for me."

"Sure, I can do that. You want to write a letter?"

"I'd rather not. Just mention it if you get the chance."

"I will. But I don't know when." He yawned.

"Fine. Meanwhile, I need to pay a visit to Daymer's Ropewalk. Any idea where that might be?"

"Wharfside. I'll take you."

"I doubt they're open at the moment."

He rolled his eyes then rolled over on the couch. "I didn't mean now," he mumbled into the cushion.

I sat there until I heard his muffled snores. It didn't take long. When you're young, you can stay up for days. You can also fall asleep at the drop of a hat.

I went to bed but not to sleep, not for a long time. I missed Holgren's arm around my waist, his forehead against the nape of my neck, his long legs tangling with mine.

The rain came and went all night.

~ ~ ~

When we got to South Gate, I steeled myself and went through the gate, waiting to feel some malicious magic wake and try to kill me.

Nothing.

Happily disappointed, I continued on, following Keel. We fetched up at Daymer's ropewalk a few minutes later.

A ropewalk is just a Kerf-damned long building where they turn almost-rope into rope used for ships. To be fair, the rope they make in such places is thicker than my arm and damned long, which I suppose is impressive in its own way, but it didn't really excite my interest. To me, it just looked like a lot of sweaty men pulling on rope. Holgren, on the other hand, would have been fascinated by the process. But Holgren wasn't here.

I wasn't in much of a mood to dance about trying to get information about Theiner. I just wanted to confirm that he had indeed worked there. I wasn't taking much of what "Uncle Ives" had told me on faith, and Theiner's day job seemed the easiest thing to verify.

I asked around for the foreman and was pointed to a man who was as big as a house with his shoulder muscles bulging up damned near to a level with his earlobes. I lay a gold mark in his rough hand.

"You had a man named Theiner who worked here. I need to know anything you can tell me about him."

He put the mark back in my hand.

"I don't know anything about anything. Good day to ye."

I grabbed his paw and shoved the mark back in it along with an equally shiny friend of the same denomination.

"Just tell me what you know about Theiner, and I'll be out of your hair."

He got an annoyed look on his face, took my hand, pressed the marks firmly back into it once more, and curled my fingers around them.

"No."

"Why the hells not?" I asked, exasperated. I wasn't paying three gold for a simple bit of information.

"Because I don't know you or why you want to know what you want to know and because you're a rude little chit."

Behind me, Keel stifled a laugh.

I sighed and stuck out my hand, this time without any gold in it. "I'm Amra Thetys. What's your name?"

"Kubo," he replied, "Kubo Daymer." His hand engulfed mine. He shook it. When I got it back, it wasn't too badly mangled.

"Master Daymer, I'm trying to find my friend Theiner. I think he might be in trouble.

Any assistance you could give me in finding him would be greatly appreciated."

"That's better. Money don't serve for manners 'round here. This ain't the Girdle. As to Theiner being in trouble, I couldn't say."

"What do you mean?"

"If it's the same Theiner who worked for me, he quit years ago."

~ ~ ~

I described Theiner, and Kubo allowed as to how that certainly sounded like the fellow he'd employed. If memory served him correctly, Theiner had had trouble showing up for work on time due to unspecified nightly activities. Finally, he'd told Daymer he wouldn't be working there anymore. That was all the ropewalk owner remembered after more than five years.

We left. I bought us bowls of stew from a streetside vendor, and we washed it down with small beer. I wasn't feeling particularly talkative, and Keel seemed to sense that even if he didn't know what was going on. When we'd finished, I told him to get lost for the day. Then, I set out for Ink Street.

I was passing an old, badly dilapidated warehouse when I saw another rune marked on the swollen, mold-eaten door. I knew that one too. Hardic only has about a hundred runes total. It was a good, easy written language for illiterate thieves to pick up, if rather limited when trying to get across complex concepts. The rune scrawled on the door ahead of me was simple enough to understand.

Murder.

I kept walking.

Got a dozen steps away.

Turned back.

"You're an idiot," I told myself. But I had to know.

I made short work of the lock. The whole mechanism just fell out of the rotted wood with a judicious application of force. But the door itself was swollen into its frame. After a considerable amount of grunting and shoving, I got it open enough to slip inside. I got a knife out and stepped to the side so that I wouldn't be silhouetted by the light from outside and stood perfectly still, letting my ears inform me while my eyes adjusted to the gloom.

The place was empty and had been for a long, long time. The flagstone floor was now an algae-slick pond. I could hear a steady drip drip from the leaking roof and nothing else. Until I did hear something else. The slightest whisper of sound from the far side of the building. I might have imagined it.

I pulled out the other knife and walked slowly across the empty space toward the sound.

At the far end, there was just the foreman's windowless cubby, a small room maybe eight feet deep by a dozen across. The flimsy door was torn off its leather hinges and lay on the floor quite some distance away from the frame, like it had been thrown there.

Knives out in the defensive posture that Theiner had taught me so long ago, I entered the dank cubby.

There was a desk, furry with moss, and a broken chair. I couldn't see anything else in the deep gloom. Except—

Something under the desk. Something whitish.

I took a step closer, squatted down.

The white I'd seen was a skull. There was a skeleton to go along with it, dressed in rotting clothes.

I held still. Listened very carefully. Nothing. And in this small room at least, nowhere for any potential enemy to be hiding.

I eased myself around so that I would be facing anything that decided to enter the foreman's cubby and looked over the remains a little closer.

It was a kid. I don't know how old; I'm no expert on that sort of thing. Maybe ten years old? Not a toddler, not an adult; that's all I could tell for sure.

Something had caved in the left side of the skull.

The body had been stuffed into the space under the desk. Even as small as it was, it had been a tight fit. I knew in my gut this had been a street rat, futilely trying to hide from the Blacksleeves. Another victim of the Purge.

I didn't hear anything. There was no noise, but I caught the slightest flicker of motion in the doorway. I sprang up, knives out. Maybe I saw something, a darkness moving against a dark background. Then, it was gone.

Maybe I imagined it.

I scanned the warehouse, but it was empty. There was nowhere for anyone to hide. After a couple of minutes, I gave up, telling myself it was just nerves, not really believing it. Then, I went out, bought a few yards of linen, came back and wrapped up the bones and then took them to the temple of the departed.

~ ~ ~

I stayed at the small, badly maintained temple until the votive candle I'd bought guttered out. The bones made a depressingly small bundle in my lap. The bench was uncomfortable and cutting off the circulation in my legs. I lived with it.

They could have been my bones just as easily. It could have been my body stuffed into the knee-hole of a desk for more than a decade. Murdered then crammed out of the way like rubbish. How many more were out there in the nooks and crannies of the city? How many more stuffed in crawlspaces, up disused chimneys, dumped in cesspits, and discarded in unmarked graves? I couldn't begin to guess at an exact number, but I had a good idea of the digits. Hundreds.

Hundreds. And nobody would remember them. Except for people like me, survivors of the Purge, nobody cared.

Finally, I got up, found one of the volunteers that doled out the candles and kept the temple tidy, and put the bundle in his arms.

"This one needs a home," I told him.

Once he figured out what he was holding, he tried to give it back to me. I didn't take it. "This is not a cemetery, mistress, just a place to remember the departed," he said.

"Yeah, well, nobody remembers this one. Not even his or her name."

"The temple isn't for the dead; it's for the living," he replied not unkindly.

"Make an exception," I told him and dug out one of my more precious gems. "Find this kid a place to rest here in the temple. That fire opal will keep this place in candles and brooms for a while. The roof is leaking. The benches are torture devices. You could use the donation; don't pretend otherwise."

"All that is true, mistress, but it's also true that the temple is not a place to lay anyone to rest."

"According to who?"

"Well, tradition, I suppose."

"Then start a new one. There's no god to gainsay you. Not here." The temple of the departed was a purely mortal place, owing no allegiance to any deity, living or dead. No god had lent a hand to this murdered street rat in life. They could piss off in death as well.

"But...but where? Where will we put this?"

"I don't know. That's up to you. Anywhere will be better than where it's been the last decade and more. Just give the bones a little dignity for pity's sake."

"All right. I suppose we can do something."

I turned to leave. Turned back.

"Put up a plaque."

"A plaque?"

"It should say, 'Victim of the Purge.'" I put another gem in his hand.

"All—all right."

"Good. I *will* be back to check. Take care of it. And thank you."

I left the attendant standing there, holding the bones of a murdered child in one hand and a small fortune in the other, with a look of consternation on his face.

~ ~ ~

Number 7 was still there. But it wasn't the same place I'd visited the night before.

The leaded glass windows were grimy and cracked. The signboard was faded, its paint peeling. I made my way to a service entrance on a side alley, made short work of the lock, and entered.

Nobody had lived or worked there for quite a while. Dust covered every surface, including the floor. It was undisturbed except for a couple of tracks leading back and forth from the front door to the kitchen.

Only the kitchen showed any sign of recent use. Or at least recent cleaning. The ashes in the grate were fresh at least, and the table, benches, and floor were dust-free. A couple of the lamps had clean windows, fresh wicks, and a decent amount of oil.

I did a quick search of the upstairs rooms, ones I hadn't seen on my previous visit. The entire upstairs was bare. Not a stick of furniture. There might have been a cellar, but I didn't bother to check.

I went out, climbed the stairs, and checked "Theiner's" room.

It, at least, was exactly as I had found it the night before.

"What the hells is going on?" I said out loud.

Nobody answered, not even the little voice in my head.

CHAPTER 14

I spent the rest of the day sorting truth from lies, fact from fiction, and emotion from reason. I was angry at being manipulated. Furious, actually. I was also confused as all hells as to what the point was.

Fact: Somebody had sent me Borold's head marked with a magic-infused rune. Those same sorts of runes had warned me of a trap and led me to a years-old murder.

Fact: Somebody with magic, and lots of it, had tried to kill me. Twice. I had somehow tapped into some sort of power that lay deep in the heart of Mount Tarvus, and used it to regenerate my own flesh and drive off one of the vicious magical attacks.

Fact: Someone purporting to be Ansen had sent me to the old family home, where a mage purporting to be my uncle had given me a locket with my mother's portrait (real) and a story about helping Theiner hunt down those responsible for the Purge (part of which, at least, was false).

Fact: The God of Sparrows wanted me to believe the whole city would be destroyed in two days and that me killing the Telemarch was the only way to avert that. Fallon Greytooth wanted me to believe that Kalara's Knife was in Bellarius, probably being used by, and in turn using, the Telemarch. And that it wanted me.

"Well, Amra," I said to myself as I paced my rooms, "that's an impressive number of facts you've got gathered up there. But what do they all mean?"

They didn't hang together neatly. They didn't hang together at all, really, that I could see. Oh, I could take various pieces, glue them together with a liberal dose of guesswork and supposition, and get any number of pictures. But none of them were pretty. All of them were logic-challenged to put it kindly. The only thing I could really divine from all that had happened was that someone was trying to run a game on me. That and Bellarius was bad for my health and peace of mind.

Mysterious, powerful, nameless entities toying with my life kind of scared me spitless. I don't like being scared spitless and couldn't do anything about the mysterious or powerful parts, so I decided I'd work on the nameless bit. I didn't happen to have a name, so I made one up.

"Chuckles will do," I said to myself.

The only way not to lose the kind of game I found myself in, whose rules were obscure and whose players were cyphers, was not to play. And to give said cyphers ridiculous names.

By late afternoon, I'd reached a decision. It wasn't one I was entirely happy about, but then those sorts of decisions are fairly uncommon in any case.

I'd come to help Theiner. Theiner was elusive, possibly dead. It was time for me to go.

Theiner's list, if it was real, was far heavier in my pocket than paper had any right to be. But I was not some vigilante, some instrument of justice. I certainly wasn't going to be hunting down bad people for things they'd done fifteen years before. Not because they didn't deserve it; they did. They deserved all the pain and suffering it was possible to visit upon a living thing. No, I wasn't going to start, or continue, some campaign of retribution because *I* deserved to have a life and had been lucky enough to survive and to build one.

Vengeance would suck that life away from me as surely as Athagos had sucked the life out of the Mad Duke of Viborg and his men back in Thagoth, if more slowly. It would consume me. I knew that. I'd been down the revenge road with my friend Corbin's murder, before Thagoth. Revenge hadn't been nearly as sweet as I thought it would be, and it had gotten a lot of people killed unnecessarily who'd still be walking around Lucernis instead of decomposing, if I hadn't gone looking for my own personal justice.

If I went looking for those responsible for the Purge?

In all likelihood, I'd become a monster. There was a sea of rage deep down in my soul. It had taken years for those dark waters to become still. When I'd first arrived in Lucernis and the terror had abated, I'd been angry all the time. At everything. I'd learned quickly enough to channel that rage, that energy, into productive things like making money and not getting caught. But I wasn't going to pretend that I had anything approaching a normal life.

I had more scars than those on my face. I wasn't about to start cutting them open again.

Stirring up that rage was not something I wanted to do. I couldn't.

Not if I wanted to stay *me*. And I was finally, after decades, fairly content with myself.

"So. Sorry, Theiner. I tried," I said to the lengthening shadows that were slowly coating the room in autumn gloom. "Sorry, Sparrow God, Blood God. I really hope for Your sake, and Your little friend with my mother's name, that You're just mentally damaged and delusional.

"Goodbye, Bellarius. Time for me to go." Holgren would forgive me for his unnecessary trip. If he got upset, all I had to say was, "Thagoth. Six months. Eating grubs and bark."

"Sorry, Chuckles, but your game is no fun. Time for me to go," I whispered again.

But you just got here, said the voice in my head.

~ ~ ~

There was one place in Bellarius—or Hardside, actually—that I wanted to go to. Well, *wanted* might be a stretch. Say rather that I felt obligated to go to and didn't feel reluctant about. If I was going to be leaving, I needed to go there first, and any magical traps be damned. I had a quick dinner in my rooms, threw a bottle of Gol-Shen in my sabretache, and went out into the chill evening.

They'd burned down his shack and him in it of course. I'd watched them do it after he died. You didn't take chances with something like lung fever. But I knew exactly where it was or had been.

Arno had been much more of a father to me than my own ever had. I'd had him for six months before he drove me out of his shack with a stick and coughed curses and tears lest I catch the lung fever as well. Six months. Long enough to teach me what I needed to know to survive as a thief. How to pick a pocket and a lock. How to cut a purse. How to tell good coin from bad and gems from glass. How to move as silent as a shadow, and how to avoid notice in a busy street. He trained my hands and feet, my ears and eyes. But most importantly, he trained my mind. He taught me how to *think*, even when my fear threatened to choke me.

He gave me everything I've ever really needed to survive. And all he ever asked for in return was food and the occasional bottle of wine. Blacksleeves had caught him years before I ever met him, and the magistrate had ordered every bone in both his hands broken. Then, they'd kept him in a cell long enough to ensure they would never heal properly. Then, they'd let him go, laughing. The funny thing was, he told me, they'd pinched him for a theft he hadn't actually committed.

Yeah. Funny. Ha ha.

Anyway, after that, his thieving days were over. But he could still teach, and when he found me hiding in the muck under his shack, clutching my mother's comb and the knife I'd ended my father with, he took me in and proceeded to teach me everything he knew.

I was a much better thief now than he had ever been. But I would never be a better person.

After he died, I was truly on my own, navigating an endless, perilous path between the everyday dangers of the streets, the Blacksleeves, and the street rat gangs.

I survived. Many, many more did not. The difference was what Arno had taught me about theft and what Theiner had taught me about knives, and eventually, when the purge was at its height, Theiner's help in stowing away on a ship bound for Lucernis.

I retraced my route down to South Gate. The street was still torn up. I walked through Hardside to the place where Arno's shack had been in the shadow of the Rimgurn cliffs. The whole area was deserted despite the ground being rather less waterlogged than most of Hardside. Common wisdom in Hardside had it that the stretch of ground where Arno had built his shack was cursed, poisoned with some sort of dark energy. He hadn't believed it; he called it superstitious nonsense.

Maybe he was right, maybe not. But nobody else had died of lung fever that season. At any rate, the place was shanty-free for quite some distance around.

My feet led me up the slight, almost imperceptible rise almost of their own accord. Of course, there were no charred beams, no ash drifting in the still air. That was just my memory. But half-hidden in the coarse weeds that passed for grass in parts of Hardside, I found without even trying the motley collection of scavenged bricks and cobblestones Arno had laid down in front of his shack and had called his stoop.

"A man, and even a girl, needs a place to sit outside of an evening without their arses getting muddy," he'd told me once as we sat there and watched the sun set over the Dragonsea.

I sat down in my old spot and imagined him there, to my left, grizzled chin pointing seaward as he hugged his knees. I pulled out the bottle of Gol-Shen, prised out the cork with a knife and long practice, and took a swallow. Stared out at the stars and the ceaseless sea. To the north, the stars were disappearing. Rain was coming again.

"Brought you some of the good stuff, old man," I whispered and poured the rest into the ground.

I never heard it coming. It literally didn't make a sound.

I looked up from pouring out the wine, and there was someone—some*thing,* sitting next to me, where Arno had once sat.

It looked human. Sort of. A young man with sad eyes and some sort of brand on his forehead. It was also a flayed corpse, dressed in smoke and shadows. Wet meat and white tendons and damp, pink bone, teeth exposed by a gaping hole in one cheek, and all of it hidden, exposed, hidden again in a restless cloak that seemed torn from the night sky. All this I took in, in the instant it took for me to drop the bottle, whip out both knives, and drive one toward its throat.

It blocked my thrust with enough force to make my wrist go numb. The knife in my left hand slid from suddenly nerveless fingers. Then, almost as quickly as Red Hand, it punched me in the face.

My head snapped back, and I went sprawling. My vision went black around the edges, and I saw stars, swarming like agitated fireflies. Felt the hot blood gushing from my nose and down my lips and cheek.

"We don't want to hurt you," it said in a voice like cemetery gates creaking in the wind. "Don't do that again."

Get up. Get up. I still had one knife. I started to roll over, away from him, intending to come up in a fighting crouch. As soon as I started to shift, an iron grip pinned my wrist to the ground. I froze. My vision cleared. Those sad, soulful eyes were inches from my own. I recognized the brand on his forehead now. It was the Hardic rune for justice. An image of Borold's rotting noggin flashed through my mind.

"Listen," it said.

"I'm listening."

"They are all going to die," it said.

"Who're they?"

"All the souls in this city."

I got it. Suddenly, I got it. Or at least I thought I did. "You're Chuckles," I said.

"We are Justice." The way it said it, you could hear the capital "J." It should have been funny. It wasn't, not in the least.

"So it says on your forehead," I replied. "What do you want with me?"

"You are the witness. You must see and understand."

"Why me?"

"You are the witness."

"You sent me Borold's head, didn't you? You lured me here." It was just a wild guess, but the rune was kind of a big coincidence.

"You are the witness," it repeated. It wasn't really an answer.

"Get off me."

It did. I rolled over, sheathed the knife I was holding. Took a corner of my cloak and staunched my bleeding nose. Kept it in view. It just stood there, impossible, gruesome. Once I'd got the bleeding more or less under control, I said, "So you're going to kill everyone in Bellarius, and you want me to watch."

"Yes."

"And what did an entire city do to deserve death?"

"This city killed innocence. Over and over and over."

"I won't argue that. But not everyone in this city is guilty."

"Bellarius must die."

"That's not justice. That's mass murder."

"Yes. And that is what makes it just. One mass murder for another."

"What are you? Who are you to decide the fate of thousands?"

"We are Justice. We are legion."

"I have no idea what you're talking about."

He stared at me for a time then seemed to come to some decision. "You are the witness. You must understand."

Suddenly, its hands were on either side of my head, and its eyes had locked mine. I fell into them.

I was running down an alley, scared out of my mind. The fear blocked out the agony of the cuts and weeping sores on my bare, freezing feet, the hunger that gnawed my belly hollow. My breath came in ragged gasps, pluming in the cold night air. The Blacksleeves were coming, and I was going to die. I had to run, run faster, run furth—

The crossbow bolt took me high in the back. The steel head sprouting suddenly from my thin, bony chest. It had pierced a lung. I stumbled, fell, sprawled on my side on the frigid cobbles. Nothing had ever hurt like this before. I curled up around my pain, around the bolt.

Footsteps approached.

I opened my eyes, stretched out my hand, opened my mouth to say please.

The billy came down on my head again and again until my skull cracked then shattered, and all the light in the world went out.

My eyes fluttered open. It was still holding my head, staring into my eyes, my soul.

"One," it said.

"I—"

It was dark and smelled of mold and rotting wood. I was crammed into a tiny space, tiny even for my tiny body. I was trying to breathe silently. I was terrified they could hear my heartbeat. I was terrified of the spiders and centipedes I could feel crawling over my face, down the neck of my filthy shirt. I wanted to scream. I dared not scream or even breathe.

On the other side of the wall, I could hear footsteps on the warped floorboards of the abandoned warehouse. The insects began biting, and their bites were like fire. I thought I would go mad with it, with having to stay still as they stung me over and over.

It was a good hiding place. It was a safe hiding place. Too small for Blacksleeves to fit. Too hard to find, I told myself over and over, silently.

Until the ax bit into the wall above my head, and I started screaming.

They dragged me out once the hole was big enough, the jagged, wooden teeth of the demolished wall ripping deep furrows into my flesh. They threw me onto the floor. One sat on my back and held my arms. Another ground my face into the floorboards, keeping my head immobile.

The third parted my head from my thin shoulders.

"Two," it said.

"Wait—"

I was very small, and didn't understand anything. I hadn't eaten in a long time. The fever wasn't getting any better. Somehow, I'd made it to the city with the others. They said there would be food, but no one had given us any food.

One girl sat me in a doorway and said she would come back. She told me to stay where I was. I stayed there all day, and the fever climbed higher. I watched people pass by. I called out to a few, but all of them ignored me. Every single one.

The girl never came back.

As the sun set, the fever that I'd carried all the way from Elam finally drove me down. I fell from where I was sitting in the dirty, piss-reeking doorway and sprawled out into the narrow street. The last thing I remembered, before I lost consciousness and then my life, was a man kicking my arm out of his way. His shoe was brown, the toe scuffed, the copper buckle tarnished.

"Three," it said, and I tore my head away from its grasp.

"Enough!" I shouted and scrambled back, panting.

This thing in front of me. It was a conglomeration of the souls of murdered children. Of the street rats that had been slain or allowed to die in the Purge. And it wanted justice. Another unintended consequence of the Telemarch's attempt to revive magic?

"How many?" I finally managed. "How many are you?"

It shrugged. Shook its head slightly. Not that it didn't know; rather, the question didn't really matter. "All."

"And you're going to kill everyone in the city."

It just stared at me, sorrowful eyes and glistening flesh.

A horrible sort of realization was born in me. "In a couple of days, Mount Tarvus really is going to explode, isn't it? Everything will be destroyed."

"Yes."

"Is that your doing?"

"No."

"Then what is this all about? What justice is it you're going to lay on this city if it's already doomed?"

It nodded. "Now, you will understand." It leaned forward, slowly, never taking its eyes from mine. Put a careful, bloody hand on my knee. For the first time, some emotion crept into its voice. It wasn't happiness.

"You *left*. You escaped. Once you were gone, they stopped hunting *us*.

"You're saying the Purge stopped once I left Bellarius?" I knew it had ended soon after I'd escaped to Lucernis but not when exactly. It wasn't something they put notices up about. The implication of what it—they—had just said hit me.

"You think the Purge was meant to kill *me*?"

"When you left, it stopped."

"That's what people call coincidence, for Kerf's sake." But I didn't believe in coincidence. I believed in cause and effect.

"It wanted *you*. It took *us*. Now, you will witness. And then, you will join us."

It exploded into hundreds of sickly, green corpselights. They rose into the air, higher, higher, like Chagan fireworks, until they were almost indistinguishable from the mundane stars above. Then, they began to fall.

They did not make it back to the ground. It was as if they met some invisible barrier and smeared themselves across it. Met or made it. Slowly, the shape of the barrier became plain.

Bellarius was now trapped under a dome of slowly fading corpselight from the peak of Mount Tarvus to the end of the longest wharf. Above the Citadel, unfading, another Hardic rune burned in cold corpse fire.

Guilt.

I got up, picked up my other knife, absently stuck it back in its new sheath, and started walking. I was going to check. Of course I was going to check. But I knew with complete certainty no living person would be leaving Bellarius before it exploded.

CHAPTER 15

The souls of murdered gutter children had passed judgment on an entire city and sentenced it to death. And then—

And then, they'd decided, I was going to join them in whatever sort of conglomerated afterlife or post-life had become their fate.

I had been on the verge of leaving Bellarius to its fate, and try as I might, I couldn't muster up much sympathy for the city even though I knew it was deeply, heinously wrong. There was no excuse for murdering tens of thousands, the vast majority of them having had nothing to do with the Purge.

But to my knowledge, no one had offered shelter to the street rats before and certainly not during the Purge. No one had hidden them—us—from the death squads. No one had fed or clothed us. Not one person. I didn't even remember a single kind word. Just curses, kicks, thrown stones, and backhanded slaps when I'd gotten too close to any upstanding citizen and been noticed.

I had been treated exactly like vermin. A rat, a cockroach. We all had. Every hand, and I do mean *every* hand, had been turned against us.

How was it possible that an entire city would treat children in such a fashion?

That deep, dark sea of rage stirred within me at the thought. Storm winds had started to blow in my soul.

How would it be possible for those murdered shades to feel anything approaching compassion, mercy, or forgiveness? In a frighteningly real way, Bellarius had planted the seeds of its own death with every murdered street kid. I understood that like few could. I have a marrow-deep repulsion toward the idea of fate, but even I couldn't help but feel what was happening to the City of the Mount was the next best thing to destiny, to inevitability. And if I couldn't bring myself to call it justice, I still could not convince myself it was completely unjust. Not from the dead's perspective anyway.

I would have had more sympathy for the dead, however, if I wasn't as trapped and doomed as everyone else.

I walked out to the end of Aloc Pier, the longest of the docks wharfside, ignoring the drunk, slurred questions of the single guard stationed there. I could still see, faintly, the corpselight prison wall shimmering just an arm's length away off the edge of the pier. I reached out and tried to put my hand through it. I felt nothing, but my hand would not break that almost invisible barrier no matter how hard I pushed.

"Hey! What're you doin'?" The drunk guard behind me. He stumbled up next to me, squinting first at me then at my hand.

"What'n hells is that?" he said and reach out to touch the barrier.

"Maybe you shouldn't—" I said but too late.

As soon as his hand met the corpselight, he froze. His eyes grew wide. The corpselight crawled up his arm in a heartbeat then wrapped around his head. He never screamed. It released him an instant later, dissipating, and he fell to the salt-stained boards of the pier, dead.

The guilt rune was branded on his forehead.

I was pretty sure the same would happen to anyone who tried to leave Bellarius. Except for me, apparently. I was here for the duration.

I left him there. He wouldn't be the last. The spirits of the slain had passed their judgment. Which meant that the Hag had known this was going to happen. She'd told me her price would be my memories *and* the Founder's Stone once the dead talked to me.

But her price for what? I'd assumed she'd meant for finding Theiner, but that seemed highly unlikely in light of recent events.

I started walking to the Wreck. I had a feeling she'd be expecting me.

The rain I'd seen approaching from Arno's stoop began to fall, soft and cold.

~ ~ ~

The madmen's camp was deserted. Not even a fire. The war galley was a stony as it ever was. The sea still rushed in and out of the great hole in the hull. But I could see a faint light leaking out of the tiller's shed, past the tarp.

I didn't bother knocking.

The room was very dark except for her eyes. They glowed like fire opals. Looking her in the eye would have ruined my night vision, so I settled for looking at the air over her shoulder and her hands.

She hadn't moved a muscle since the last time we'd spoken as far as I could tell.

"You knew this would happen," I said.

"What 'this' do you mean exactly, Doma Thetys?"

"This situation we're in now. Bellarius about to disintegrate, and the souls of murdered children making sure nobody escapes before it happens."

"Yes. I knew."

"What are you?" I asked.

"I am the Hag, the Mind Thief. Or so they call me, no?"

"Tell me who and what you are," I insisted.

"I am Elytara Mour, Queen of Trevell, Avatar of the Goddess Mour."

"Trevell I've heard of. It was destroyed during the Cataclysm."

"It disappeared during the Cataclysm," she corrected.

"Normally, cryptic statements like that would drive me insane, but tonight, I just don't have the energy. Who was Mour?"

"It doesn't matter. She *was* destroyed in the Cataclysm. No one worships Her anymore, and few even remember Her."

"Why do you want my memories, Lyta?"

"For several reasons. Information. I don't get out much. Entertainment. I've been alive a very long time, and experiencing the memories of others helps to stave off the inevitable madness that confinement paired with longevity brings."

"What else?"

"What makes you think there is something else?"

"There's something else. I don't know how I know it, but I know it. Why do you want *my* memories?"

"You have lived a very interesting life. Much more so than most who seek my assistance. Is that not enough?"

"No. You have some other purpose."

"All right. Mour had a sister."

"That's nice."

"Her sister became the Eightfold Goddess."

"Ah. So?" I asked, but I didn't much like where this was going. That's what I got for asking.

"Consider it a familial curiosity on my part. I am Mour's avatar. A part of her remains in me though She is no more. That part of me wishes to know the doings of Her sibling. You have experienced something of the Eightfold. I want to see those memories."

"Tell me; were Mour and her sister what you would consider close?"

She laughed softly. "They were bitter rivals from birth."

"Mour couldn't have been that bad then," I replied.

She waved a hand. "As I said, it doesn't really matter. She is gone, never to return. The Cataclysm did what the Wars of the Gods could not."

"A couple more questions. Why are you here, like this?"

"When Trevell was about to fall to the Cataclysm, I fled with my consort and the Founder's Stone."

"Just left everybody to die, did you?"

"I did not. You have no idea what the Stone truly is. No one does in this benighted, magic-poor Age."

"So tell me."

"It *is* Trevell. Every soul, every stone, every tree and tower and toss pot."

"Um. What?"

"The Cataclysm raced across the land, an unstoppable tide of unreason, first sickening and then severing every bond of nature and logic. Up became down, light became dark, the blood in your veins might turn to water or wine or molten lead. The very air might become poisonous vapor or simply disappear, leaving countless thousands to suffocate like fish on land. You could not trust your senses. Silk could suddenly cut skin like razors. Between one moment and the next, your eyes might see something a thousand leagues or a thousand years removed. Reality itself was collapsing. Most living things died. Some became monsters. A few became dark powers, not far removed from gods.

"I did the only thing I could. I called upon the goddess to save Trevell, and she did. My city is there in the Founder's Stone, the greatest transformation the world has likely ever seen. We took the Stone and fled, seeking a place to rebirth Trevell, far from the consuming chaos of the Cataclysm. Mour was destroyed holding that tide at bay, giving us the time necessary to escape."

"That's…that's incredible," I said.

"Whatever challenges you face, yours is a quiet Age, Amra Thetys. You are blessed."

"You'll forgive me if I don't feel particularly blessed," I replied. I take death very personally, especially my own. Which was rapidly approaching.

I squatted down, leaned my back against the wall. My face hurt from the punch I'd received, and my wrist ached from my blocked strike. "How did you end up as you are now?" I asked her.

"My consort, Kyphas, was a powerful mage. Eventually, he grew weary of the search for a new land in which to wake Trevell. We argued many times. I wanted to continue the search, to go as far as possible from the lands which had fallen to the contagion. He believed we had journeyed far enough. I suppose he was right," she said. "In the end, the Cataclysm never did reach the Dragonsea.

"When we were wrecked upon the rock here during a fierce storm, he unleashed magics that he had, somehow, been preparing in secret. I was battling the storm; his treachery caught me completely off-guard. He carried me, senseless, to this room and trapped me here. I cannot leave; I cannot die. I believe he intended to return, to set me free once he had woken Trevell. He did love me. But he overestimated his own powers. He could not call the city forth from the Stone; only I, the Goddess' avatar, can do that.

"Love me or no, Kyphas was proud to a fault. Instead of returning to me and admitting defeat, he built the first crude iteration of the city that stands here now. Bellarius. The City of the Mount. The Archmage of Trevell died the chieftain of a mud-walled village, his throne a split log atop the Founder's Stone."

"And you've been here ever since."

She nodded.

"Now, you want my memories and the Founder's Stone. What do I get in return?"

"If you manage to avert the disaster that rapidly approaches Bellarius, the spirits of the slain will not simply disappear. As things stand, they are content to contain the city's inhabitants. If the city fails to be destroyed, they will fall on the city like the judgment they are, killing every living thing.

"I, and only I, can keep them from doing so. But not while I am trapped here. And in order to escape, I must have the Founder's Stone."

"The God of Sparrows, the souls of those dead street kids, and now you have all confirmed that Bellarius is going to end badly. But I still have no idea why, except that it has something to do with the Telemarch."

"What do mages want more than anything else?" she asked in reply.

"Generally speaking? Power."

"Correct. True in my day, true today. But magic is fading."

"I'm aware of that. What's your point?"

"If you were the most powerful mage in the world, would you be happy about that situation?"

"Probably not. But as far as I know, there's not a damned thing anyone can do about magic going away."

"The Telemarch believes he has found a way to bring it back. Or at least create a reservoir of magic, of power for his own personal use. A very, very large reservoir."

A chill crept over me. "Let me guess. He's using the Knife to do it."

"You are clever when it suits you, Doma Thetys."

"What's that got to do with you? Or me, for that matter? Or with Bellarius being leveled?"

"The power he is gathering, it isn't truly magic. Or rather, it is magic that hasn't been refined. It's chaos. Pure possibility. The Telemarch believes he has it safely contained, but that is impossible due to the nature of that which he is attempting to contain. How can one contain the essence of possibility?"

"That's a little too philosophical, or maybe semantic, for me to tackle. I do better with more mundane questions." But that word, *possibility*, itched in my mind.

"That power has been leaking out from day one," she said, "and reacting with the mundane world in unpredictable ways. There are things out there in the city, Doma Thetys. Impossible things, that can *do* impossible things, that *know* impossible things. They are not nice, and they are not sane by any reasonable definition. But they are not what concerns us now.

"In a few days, the safeguards that hold that chaos more or less contained are going to fail. Catastrophically. They are already crumbling. Bellarius will become a waking nightmare before it's finally destroyed. It is even possible that we will see a short encore of the Cataclysm before the final curtain."

"And all of this is somehow because of me. Or so the God of Sparrows seemed to think."

"It is, I'm sorry to say."

"Nothing you've yet told me has any connection to me at all."

"You know how these Knives work, Doma Thetys. You have experience."

"I do. Though how you know that is beyond me."

"It's not important now. What is important is this: the Telemarch is using the Knife that Parts the Night. What do you think the Knife is doing in return?"

I sighed. I knew the answer to this one. "It's using the Telemarch in turn."

"Absolutely," she replied.

"How do you *know* all this, Lyta?"

"Do you know who Mour's lover was?"

"I have no idea. I'm not really up to date on the love lives of dead gods, sorry."

"Bath."

The God of Secrets. The Silent One. Except He talked sometimes. He'd said a very bad word to me once. I still hadn't forgiven Him.

"What's your point?"

"Bath shared some of His secrets with Mour. Including the getting of information by unusual means. I know things, Doma Thetys. I am Mour's avatar."

"Fine, fine. Kerf knows I'm not interested in Bath's pillow talk." An unbidden image of Bath kissing somebody entered my mind. I shuddered. The two times I'd met Bath, he'd been masquerading as one of his own priests. Those guys *sewed* their *mouths* shut.

"So," I said. "The Knife set all this up on the off chance I'd decide to visit Bellarius after fifteen years so it could destroy me along with the rest of the city? Seems like chopping down a tree to make a toothpick." But actually, I hadn't returned on some off-chance, had I?

"I could not say what the Knife wants. The Telemarch, however, is terrified of you and wants you to die as soon as possible. The moment you appeared in the city, he began pouring more power into his reservoir at a reckless rate. He will kill everyone in a few days if he does not stop. Or isn't stopped."

"The Telemarch is afraid of me?" I laughed.

"Aither is afraid of his own shadow. I believe the Knife has twisted him to be that way, but that, admittedly, is speculation. What is not speculation is the fact that you scare him spitless for whatever reason. He set traps for you throughout the city long before you ever arrived."

"I've run into a couple."

"And you are still here. Perhaps he is right to fear you."

"The first was too slow. The second wasn't, but I had…help."

"What sort of help, may I ask?"

"I sort of found some magic of my own. I don't really understand it."

"You 'found some magic,'" she repeated, amusement in her voice. "Was it lying in the street then?"

"No. Beneath it, actually. Deep down in Mount Tarvus. I was dying, and I felt it down there, and I reached out to it, or maybe it reached out to me. It gets confusing. It was like sunlight. Or…"

"Or pure, undiluted possibility," she finished for me. "I think I know why the Telemarch fears you, Amra Thetys."

"Why?" I asked. But I was afraid I already knew the answer.

"Because, somehow, you have access to the power he has been building up for more than a decade."

"The power that's going to destroy Bellarius in a matter of days?"

"The very same," she replied.

Silence settled between us. I thought about my situation. In order to save myself and the city, I needed to steal a two-ton slab of stone from the Syndic's throne room, cart it all the way down the Mount, through the Girdle, out the gates, through Hardside, and to the Wreck. And that was the easy part. After that, I had to kill the Telemarch and, probably, break another of the Eightfold Goddess' Blades. And there was still a list of names in my pocket, one of which, I realized, I very much wanted to see crossed off. Though how I was going to do any of that escaped me at that moment.

"We're all well and truly screwed," I muttered.

She laughed.

"What's so funny? This isn't the least bit amusing."

"I've been a prisoner for a thousand years. My perspective is slightly different from yours, I suspect."

"I just hope you aren't as batshit crazy as the last thousand-year prisoner I freed," I replied, standing. Though Tha-Agoth hadn't been as blatantly insane as his sister.

"I look forward to finding out," she replied. "Will you share your memories now or once you've brought me the Founder's Stone?"

"I'll wait if it's all the same to you. I prefer to do the impossible before the unpleasant."

"As you wish, Doma Thetys. As you wish."

~ ~ ~

Past the Girdle, on the increasingly steep slope of Mount Tarvus, were the houses of the Gentry.

Carved into the rock of the Mount itself, their façades built vertically for the most part, the rising towers of the Gentry vied, each against the others, to look down on who and what was below them. Elevation equaled status. The higher up the slope, the more elite the house—and the House. For those lower down, building up was some sort of partial remedy. Or maybe they just wanted to block the views of those higher up. I don't know. The Gentry might as well have been another species as far as I was concerned. I didn't spend much time trying to puzzle out their mindsets.

Anyway, the mad jumble of towers and spires had always struck me as singularly ugly. But it afforded me a large number of vantage points to climb to, from which I could get a closer look at the Citadel and the Riail. I had no idea how I was going to break into the two most secure, well-guarded buildings in Bellarius, but I figured taking a look at them from somewhere closer than the Girdle was a good start.

I chose a house whose thin tower was particularly ugly, ornamented with so many stone friezes that climbing it was child's play even in the rain. The seal on the gate was of a stylized hart wearing a crown, its neck bent back at an improbable angle, its hooves kicking up flames. Whatever. Heraldry wasn't my strong suit.

The single guard wasn't asleep, but he wasn't exactly wary, either. I slipped over the ornamental wall as quiet as a shadow and began to climb the tower on the northeast side, out of his view. I peeked in one window and realized the tower was wholly for show. Inside was just a staircase, no space for rooms of any sort. It was just a folly. Which meant all of the living portions of the house were carved into the Mount. I stifled a laugh.

The Gentry, those high and mighty nobles of Bellarius, basically lived in caves.

When I reached the top, I hung an arm over the rusted weather vane and took a long look at the Riail.

It was like a pale, stone necklace adorning the throat of the Mount. It was a graceful building, especially for Bellarius. Level upon level rose up like layers of a cake, buttresses and arches and spires graceful in the glow of hundreds of lanterns. For all that, it wasn't especially big. There just wasn't enough land to work with that high up the Mount.

Small or not, I knew nothing of the interior. I certainly didn't know where the throne room, and the Founder's Stone, was located. Visiting the Syndic wasn't something I'd had the opportunity to do when I'd lived here.

I was going to need plans of the building or, failing that, a description from someone who had been inside and seen the interior well enough to describe it with some accuracy.

I thought I knew where I might get the first as well as plans of the Citadel. Both would cost me, but you can't spend money if you're dead. The second wouldn't be terribly difficult either if likely less useful.

I looked up higher to the Citadel, where it loomed just above the Riail, brooding and heavy where the Riail was graceful.

The Citadel was just a massive, square, squat tower built of a stone so gray it was almost black. It took up the peak of the Mount. Windows of random shapes and sizes pierced its sides in random places. No getting around it, the Citadel was an ugly piece of stonework. Worse, I could intuit nothing of the layout from its exterior.

I studied it a while longer, then sighed and prepared to climb back down.

Something moving through the air caught my attention. It was far too big to be a bird.

Rising into the air from somewhere below the Riail, but above my position, was a man. He was too far away to make out facial features; he was turned away from me in any case. But I recognized the particolored cloak he wore, even in the gloom of the night and the softly pattering rain.

Fallon Greytooth. Magus. Philosopher.

What the hells was he doing?

When he had floated up until he was level with the Citadel, he whipped his hands in the air in some sort of arcane, sorcerous gesture. With a squeal of tortured metal, the grate that covered the window was ripped out of the wall along with a goodly portion of the stones the grate was attached to. Greytooth made another gesture, and the grate flung itself out over the city, far enough that it would end up in the Bay. After a moment, Greytooth himself flew at amazing speed through the dark, gaping hole he'd just ripped open.

Nothing happened for two, three, four heartbeats. Then, a blazing gout of fire shot out of the window followed immediately by a low, loud roar and a loose-limbed body in a smoking, particolored cloak. Greytooth was hurled with vicious force out and away from the Citadel. I watched him fall, his terminal arc ending down in the Girdle. I knew where he'd landed. Jaby Cemetery.

"Well, that's fitting, I suppose," I whispered to myself, shaken.

If that's what happened to Greytooth when he stormed the Citadel, I didn't want to think about what was going to happen to me.

I waited a few minutes more, but nothing else happened. The citadel was as dark and quiet as it had been before Greytooth's intrusion. Apparently, the show was over. I started back down again.

At some point during my climb down the tower, I realized that I had decided to go and check out Greytooth's body. I must have been getting morbid in my old age.

~ ~ ~

The bastard was still alive.

Oh, he didn't look good. He'd crashed down atop a little mausoleum, crushing the lead roof and cracking the marble-fronted walls. He lay there, unconscious, in a pool of his own blood. What parts of him that weren't charred were bloody. But he still had all his limbs and digits.

I assumed he was dead until he coughed.

"Kerf's bunched back," I muttered. "You're a tough one."

His only response was a groan.

I got up onto the remains of the mausoleum and, with not a little difficulty, dragged him down to the ground. He was not small. Once there, I nudged him in a relatively blood free place. Eventually, his eyelids fluttered open.

"Are you going to be dying in the next hour or so?" I asked him. "Because I'm not hauling your dead body through the streets. That sort of thing never ends well."

He didn't laugh. Some people have no sense of humor.

I got his arm around my neck and him more or less to his feet.

CHAPTER 16

"Like a stain, it soaks into the fabric of reality. Between the warp and weft of what is, is what might be. For those who want it badly enough. For those not concerned with consequences. This is what Aither, the Telemarch, has done." Fallon Greytooth knew lots of big old words.

He'd been coherent enough to direct me to his lair, which hadn't been all that far from Jaby. Greytooth was staying in one of the lowest and smallest of the houses of the Gentry. It was, apparently, deserted. He didn't offer to explain how he'd ended up there, and I didn't ask. And yes, it was almost completely carved into the rock of the Mount. It was dusty, cold, dark, and barely fit for human habitation despite its expensive furnishings.

We were sitting in a cramped, close room whose ceiling was low enough to make me uncomfortable. Greytooth couldn't have stood up straight in it even if he were capable of standing. Which he wasn't at the moment. He was slumped on a very expensive, very old couch that had not been made with comfort in mind. The bloodstains he was getting on it would never come out, I noted absently. I was sitting on a stool. I'd found a bottle of wine in a cupboard though there were no glasses. The bottle stood between us on an ugly little gilt table. Two oil lamps smoked and blackened the ceiling, making the air grimy and my eyes itch.

"He used the Knife that Parts the Night to cut open reality, to get himself some power," I replied. "I know."

"He used the Knife to attempt to bring magic back into the world. In so doing, he evoked the law of unintended consequences. And we will all be destroyed by it. Unless he is stopped."

"I know that too. So go stop him. You're the Philosopher, the mage."

"What do you think I just attempted to do?"

"Commit suicide?"

He gave me a sour smile.

"You can't have it both ways, Mistress Thetys. Either I should be trying to stop him or running away from certain death. Which would you prefer?"

"I'd *prefer* to be back in Lucernis, drinking bad wine at Tambor's and watching people pass by on the street, shaking my head at their poorly thought-out fashion choices."

"This conversation is going nowhere."

"All right, how about this: other than the Telemarch, you are almost certainly the most powerful and deadly person in this piss-pot of a city. You seem to want to stop him. You failed once, but you survived. It goes to reason you should try again with a better plan."

"Oh, you want to talk reasonably. All right. I tried, and failed, to stop the Telemarch. I failed to destroy the Knife. I failed to avert the coming disaster. Your turn."

I glared at him. "I'm just a thief. A retired one at that."

"You are more than that, and you know it. Whether you like it or not."

"Look. I already saved the world from evil once, maybe twice, depending on how you count such things. I've paid my dues. If you failed, I have absolutely no chance of succeeding."

"I am powerful. But the power that resides in the Citadel is beyond me. I tried to intercede. The Knife slapped me down as though I were a child. What else would you have me do?"

"The same thing you'd have me do, I suppose."

"If you will not, then I will try again. But I will fail. Again."

My temper snapped. "What makes you think *I* won't fail, Kerf damn you?" I shouted.

"I don't know that you won't," he replied calmly. "But the Knife *wants* you, Amra Thetys. That presents opportunities open to no one else."

"How in the cold hells do you know that? Or any of this you've been talking about? Just what, by Kerf's dirty beard, is the connection between you Philosophers and the Eightfold's blades, Greytooth?"

He reached out a bloodied hand, grabbed the wine bottle, and took a healthy slug. Then another one. Put the bottle back carefully.

"Do you really want to know?"

"I asked, didn't I?"

"'Moranos holds the Dagger of Desire,'" he said.

I stared at him for a second. It sounded familiar. Then, I remembered where I'd heard it before. "I'm aware of the poem. Or most of it, anyway. The copy at Lagna's temple in Lucernis is missing the end bit. What's your point?"

"Do you remember the Cataclysm?"

"Why do people always ask me that? How Kerf-damned old do I look?"

"What the renegade Philosophers who caused the Cataclysm a thousand years ago desired most was to understand the workings of reality itself. What they did not realize, sadly, is that which is observed is changed by the very fact of its observation."

"You're saying one of the Eightfold's Blades caused the Cataclysm?"

"Caused it? No. Men caused it. But the Dagger of Desire made it possible."

"That's just word games, Greytooth."

"Perhaps. It doesn't really matter. To answer your original question, the Order of Philosophers is tasked with tracking down and securing the weapons of the Eightfold Goddess so that nothing like the Cataclysm may ever happen again." He leaned back on the couch, pain and exhaustion plain on his long face.

"Your job is to find and secure the Blades. Not destroy them?"

"We didn't even think it was *possible* to destroy one of Her blades until you did it."

"So how many have you managed to 'secure' then?"

"At the moment, none."

"*None*? After a *thousand years*?"

"At one time, we had six contained. That was a century ago. Since then, they have, one by one, managed to breach their containments or subvert their guardians. The last we lost was the Blade that Whispers Hate. Which leads us back to the matter at hand."

I got up. Started pacing. In that small cave of a room, it was unsatisfying. It reminded me of my cell in Havelock prison only with less feces on the floor and gaudy furniture.

"Everybody who's anybody in this stinking city is pushing me to go kill the Telemarch and destroy the Knife, and you all seem to think I'm the only one who can do it, but not one of you can give me the least clue how to go about it."

"I planned my assault with great care. Much good it did me."

"You flew into a window and tried to burn the Telemarch to a crisp. You call that planning?"

"I bypassed a dozen layers of guards and wards. I attacked with what should have been an element of extreme surprise. It afforded me the best chance of success. Or so I thought. I did not give sufficient weight to the Knife's capability or independence of action."

"You thought the Telemarch controlled the Knife, not the other way around."

"I had hoped their union was of a more equal nature. He is the Telemarch, after all."

"Have you ever actually held one of Her Blades?" I asked, and he shook his head. "He's a meat puppet for the Knife, Fallon. Never doubt it. And now, the Knife knows you're out there trying to get it. You showed your hand, put its guard up. If surprise was an option before, I very much doubt it is now."

He sat up straight though it caused him obvious pain. "Do you want to know how I would go about it if I were you?"

"Oh, yes, please. Enlighten me."

"I would just walk into the Citadel."

I stopped pacing and turned to stare at him.

"Did I do something to you to make you want me dead?"

"I'm completely serious. The Knife *wants* you. I don't know why, but it does. I think you are the only person in the world who could just walk up to it and take it."

"That is the most spectacularly stupid idea I have ever heard in my life. Let's assume you're right, and the Knife wants me for whatever reason. I have it on very good authority that the *Telemarch* wants me to become a greasy red smear, the sooner the better. Do you think he will just let me take his shiny away from him?"

"Didn't you just call him a—what was that lovely expression you used? Ah yes. Didn't you just call the Telemarch a 'meat puppet' for the Knife?"

"Yeah, well, the Knife didn't keep him from laying deadly traps for me all around the city, did it? He might be some sort of gibbering tool, but he obviously has *some* free will left to him. And anyway, the point is moot. You did notice what happened to the sky earlier tonight? And the big 'guilt' rune floating over the Citadel?"

"I did. I considered it a situation to deal with after I'd dispatched the Telemarch and the Knife."

"Good job you failed then." I explained what the Hag had told me, that the city would just die a different death if the Telemarch's disaster was averted. When I was done, he steepled his fingers in front of his face and lost himself in thought for a while.

"You say she needs the Founder's Stone."

"That's what she said. Though how in hells I'm going to steal a two-ton slab of rock out from under the Syndic's ass—" Oh.

Oh, sometimes I have a thought, and it approaches being clever.

"What is it?"

"I think I know how to do it. I need some more information to make sure, but it's at least possible. But I'm going to need your help."

"You have it. Whatever it is and if it is within my power."

I left him shortly thereafter to recuperate and made my way back to my inn. Along the way, I slowly became aware that someone, or something, was watching me. I knew it with perfect certainty though I saw absolutely no evidence. Once, I heard what might have been the soft scrape of a foot on a rooftop. Or it might have been something completely different.

Suspicion? Paranoia? Considering the life I'd led, it was entirely reasonable for me to assume that everyone and everything was out to get me. Far too often, that assumption has been dismally accurate.

I made it back to my rooms no worse off and none the wiser.

CHAPTER 17

It was abysmally early in the morning, which generally meant for me that it was almost time to sleep. Instead, I was squatting at a low, rickety little scrap-wood table in front of one of the many, many kef shops in the Keddy Glam neighborhood of the Girdle. The kef was good. I'd drink it more often if it wasn't so gods-damned time-consuming to make. Or if women on their own were more welcome in Helstrumite establishments. But I wasn't there for the kef, and I hadn't picked the place.

I'd sent Keel to set up the meet when I'd returned to the inn. He'd been happy to get out but doubtful about delivering a message that late at night.

"Don't worry about it," I'd told him. "Coin never sleeps. There'll be somebody up to take the message."

He had come back with the details on where and when the meet would take place, and I'd let him sleep a couple more hours while I paced my room and turned the situation over in my mind.

As morning approached, I'd woken Keel, who'd been snoring away again on the couch in the sitting room, and sent him down to the Wreck to ask the Hag a simple, very important question: How much of a physical beating could the Founder's Stone take without being damaged?

Keel hadn't liked the second errand. Not even a little bit.

"She's dangerous," he'd complained, rubbing his eyes with a knuckle of his good hand, "and scary as all hells."

"*I'm* dangerous and a lot more likely to stick you. Especially since you snore like a rabid goat."

"Rabid goat? That doesn't even make any sense."

"Go, whiner. And try not to get noticed by your crew along the way. I'll be too busy with my own stuff to save your ass again."

"Pffft." With that and a yawn, he'd headed out the door, and I'd followed him a few minutes later to keep my very early morning appointment.

The measured, cultured voice of a Keddy priest washed through the streets from the temple a few dozen yards away, magically enhanced. It was morning prayer time. I don't speak more than a few phrases of Helstrumite, so I had no idea what he was saying. But based on the Keddy religion's dim view of women, I disagreed on principle.

I was waiting for Hoddy Marza. Marza was an information broker. Fengal Daruvner, my fixer in Lucernis, had distant family ties to the Marzas and, much more importantly, a current business relationship that was apparently mutually beneficial. So playing on Daruvner's name, I'd reached out via a note delivered by Keel and secured a meeting. I could have gone to him when I'd first arrived, to find Theiner, but I didn't like to use business contacts for personal matters. And I didn't like Keddy Helstrumites. And I didn't trust information brokers.

Those who dealt in information were untrustworthy on principle, to my mind. The fact that someone was seeking information was information in and of itself and potentially worth payment from someone else somewhere. I always assumed that whatever I might say to such a person would eventually find its way back to ears that would have an interest. Which is why I usually let Fengal deal with such matters and gave him his cut. It's also why I hadn't gone to Marza first when I was looking for Theiner, even more than the fact that I just plain dislike Keddy adherents. My fondest wish is to be utterly unknown. To everybody. But life rarely grants us our fondest wish.

I could have used an intermediary to meet with this Helstrumite. It might even have made more sense to send a man. Which is probably why I hadn't gone to the trouble. Let this Keddy talk to a woman as an equal, as a client. Let it stick in his throat.

That, and the list of people I would trust to go to a meet for me had exactly two names on it—Fengal and Holgren—and neither of them happened to be available. Besides, who knew me in Bellarius now? I wasn't staying long enough, one way or another, to worry about any long-term issues with identity.

I needed three pieces of information. I was looking for an old man who was, at least nowadays, nobody. At least, I didn't recognize his name, and neither had Keel, so either he'd changed it or he'd never risen much in the city's power structure however important he might have been in the Blacksleeves fifteen years ago.

I also needed detailed plans of the Riail and the Citadel. I didn't have time to case them myself seeing as how the city was going to become a big hole in the ground come the next morning.

A few minutes after the morning prayer had finished, worshipers began clogging the streets. I'll give them this: The fear of being trapped, unable to leave, that seemed to be slowly gripping the rest of the city seemed nonexistent here. The Helstrumites were going about their daily business as if nothing unusual was happening, unlike the confused, frightened gabbling I'd passed on my way to the meet. Too bad that business included looking down on me. I suffered a few hostile glances before Marza appeared in front of the kef shop, unwinding a red prayer cloth from around his face and head.

He was a handsome man and pale in the way most Helstrumites are with close-cropped, platinum blond hair and sky blue eyes. He looked to be in his early thirties, on a par with me. His smile was brilliant and disarming. If you didn't know better.

"Amra Thetys," he said, spreading his robes and squatting opposite me. "It is a pleasure and an honor to meet you."

"Oh? And why is that?"

"You are Bellarius' most famous daughter, at least in the circles that you and I travel. Your deeds rapidly approach legend."

"I have no idea what you're talking about," I said, straight-faced.

"Of course you do not. Just as you would have no idea that the Governor of Lucernis is missing an entire crate of an almost mythical vintage, or that a cask of Westmarch fire opals disappeared one day from the most secure vault of the most powerful banking concern on the Dragonsea, or—"

"Like I said," I cut him off. "Don't know what you're talking about." He was good. Too good. Information like that, if it got out, could get me dead. Which is why he'd said it, of course. To show he was worth the fee he was going to charge me. And to make me nervous. Nervous people let things slip and didn't haggle nearly as hard over fees.

"As you say," he replied. "How is Fengal Daruvner?"

I smiled. "Fat, happy, almost completely bald. Surrounded by nieces that he spoils shamelessly."

"It's a pleasure to hear that," he replied. "When next you see him, please tell him the Marzas send their regards."

"I will."

"To business, then. How may I be of service today?"

"A few things. First, I'm looking for someone here in Bellarius. All I have is a name and some speculation as to what he was into fifteen years ago."

"And what was this mystery man into fifteen years ago?" he asked.

"Exterminating street rats."

Marza's face froze then suddenly became blank, devoid of any emotion. I was pretty sure I knew why. Fifteen years ago, he was probably a street rat much like me; a refugee driven northward to Bellarius by war, plague, famine, or a combination of them all.

"And what would you wish of me?" he asked lightly.

"I told you. I'm looking for this man. You are a master of information. I'd like you to inform me of his whereabouts."

He leaned forward slightly. "Why would you wish to know such a thing? What is revenge to you? You left Bellarius. You escaped."

I could have asked him why he wanted to know. I could have said it wasn't his concern. I could have lied to him. Instead, I just told the truth.

I locked eyes with him and traced the scars that marred the left side of my face with one finger. "I didn't get these plucking my eyebrows, Hoddy Marza."

He nodded slightly and leaned back again.

"You remember when the killing started in earnest," I said. It wasn't a question. If he lived through it, he remembered. "No matter how well-hidden we were, they found us. And ripped us apart. The man I'm looking for, he's the only one left who knows the mage that made it possible for the Blacksleeves to find us no matter where we went to ground."

He didn't agree or disagree. He didn't confirm or deny being a street rat during the time of the death squads. But I saw the slightly flushed tone on the fair skin of his face, the slight, almost imperceptible flaring of his nostrils, the sudden jumping of the artery in his neck above the high, tight, stiff collar.

I leaned back and smiled a small, tight smile. "I thought I might pay this man a visit and do a little reminiscing. If I can find him."

Marza cleared his throat and signaled the shop boy, who brought him a steaming glass of kef. He sipped from the steaming glass before he spoke.

"This name you have. I and others have been seeking just such a name for a very long time. Despite considerable effort and gold, and not a little ingenuity spent on the search, such a name has not surfaced. Out of curiosity, may I ask how you found it?"

"I didn't. A friend did." Supposedly. Though I had my suspicions. But I wasn't getting into that with Marza. My plan was to get the man's location, have a nice chat with him, and find out if the list was real or a pack of made-up rubbish.

"I understand. Your 'friend' would no doubt prefer to remain anonymous."

"He won't care. He's dead." Maybe. "His name was Theiner."

"This man, this name. You understand he will be wanted in his own right. Not just for what he knows but also for what he did."

"Wanted? By who?" In one sense, I knew exactly who. People like Marza. People like me. Survivors. But he understood my question.

"There is an affiliation, I suppose is the best word, of like-minded individuals who have an interest in…*chastising* people such as this man whenever they are found. Members are all over the Dragonsea, including here in Bellarius, of course. I'm surprised no one ever approached you."

"Well, I make a practice of being difficult to find."

"There is that." He smiled. "My point is, this affiliation will very much want to have a representative present when you meet with this man."

I thought about it. I leaned toward "no" but didn't want to offend Marza. So I put the question off.

"I'll think about it. But Marza, I'm not doing this for some group I never heard of before just now."

"If it is a question of money—"

"You know it isn't."

He nodded.

"Your 'affiliation' can have what's left of this old bastard when I'm done talking to him. Once I get what I want. I don't plan on killing him. I want the one whose name he knows." I pulled Theiner's list out and passed it to him. "They can also have this."

He took it but did not unfold it.

"What is it?"

"A list. Lots of names there along with what they did and where they are now. Some are apparently dead. Every name on it will have to be verified, Marza. I can't vouch for it not being a pack of lies. Don't take any of it on faith."

He nodded again and made the paper disappear inside his robes. I noticed his hand trembled slightly. "Many thanks, Amra Thetys."

"So. How much for finding this man?" I asked him.

"As you said, this isn't a question of money. The list you just gave me would have more than covered the fee in any case. If it's genuine."

"If, yes."

"Just tell me the name, and I will find him."

"Affonse Yarrow. It's on the list as well."

"You said you need a few things. That's one."

"I also need a map of the Riail and the Citadel. And I need them today. Actually, I need everything today."

He laughed.

"I'm serious."

"Let's pretend that's possible. Can you tell me why? It's not a question I usually ask, but…" He spread his hands, raised one eyebrow in amusement.

"Because tomorrow morning, Bellarius is going to cease to exist unless I do something about it. And to do something about it, I need those maps and time to plan."

His face slowly sobered. "You're serious."

"Unfortunately."

"Does this have something to do with the wall of death that's gone up around the city?"

"It does."

"What you ask is not a small thing. You say the city will be destroyed if you do not get maps of the Syndic's palace and the Telemarch's sanctum, the two most powerful men in the country. On this, I have only your word. However, if I am caught getting or giving you such information, I will absolutely and unequivocally be executed even if you only hang those maps on your wall as mementos."

"If you can get me those maps, all our chances for survival improve. If you can't, I understand. I'll just have to make do without them."

He shook his head. "I don't even know if it's possible."

"You know your business best," I said, standing. "I need them by tonight or not at all."

"Wait," he said.

"Yes?"

"The city is about to be destroyed, you say. You are, it would appear, determined to save it. And yet you are still looking for a man whose crimes, and knowledge, will cease to have any meaning in a day if you fail."

"That's about the size of it, yes."

"Why?"

"I have to take care of Theiner's business before it's too late, now don't I? I came back to this cesspit to help him. I was far too late; he was dead before I ever boarded ship. But he had unfinished business. I can at least try to clean up the worst of it before everything is blown to hells." It sounded good at any rate.

"I'm not sure I understand the logic, frankly."

"That makes two of us," I replied. "But it's something I need to do. And that's enough." I didn't have time to explain the feeling in me. Somewhere, there was a mage who ferreted out street rats for the Blacksleeves, who found their every hiding place, and who ripped away any shred of safety from them. From us. And all the while, he remained hidden, anonymous, and safe—denying us what he himself had apparently guarded jealously. Still guarded, fifteen years later.

I wanted to take away from him what he had taken away from so many. I wanted to rip him out of his hiding place and leave him exposed, vulnerable to anyone who wanted to take a bite.

Maybe I wouldn't have been so determined if I hadn't discovered a child's skeleton stuffed under a desk or experienced the dismal, terrifying deaths of three pitiful street rats. Probably not. I'd spent a great amount of time and effort putting the past behind me. But I *had* found those bones and experienced those deaths just as if they were my own.

It had changed things for me.

I gave Marza a leave-taking nod and set off back toward the inn to wait for Keel and the Hag's answer. It was only a piece of what I needed to keep Bellarius standing. But…

One thing at a time.

~ ~ ~

I heard whimpering coming from an alley I was passing. That wasn't an especially remarkable thing in the grand scheme of things, not in any city I'd ever been in. I'd almost certainly have passed by without a second thought or a single glance if something hadn't told me it sounded like Keel.

There aren't any coincidences in my world, and I expect the worst pretty much all the time. If it sounded like Keel, it probably was him. If he sounded like he was in pain, he probably was. I turned into the alley, hand on a knife.

It was rubbish-choked and rat-infested. They scattered away from me as I took cautious steps, scanning the heaped garbage for the kid.

I didn't find Keel. But I found something else.

He looked like a moving pile of garbage, one among many, and he smelled much worse. It was only with some difficulty that I made out the human bits: head, with two eyes, a mouth, and a nose where it definitely shouldn't have been. The two expected arms, ending in rather unexpected and brutally malformed hands, resembled nothing that came to mind. I couldn't make out any legs. He—it—dragged itself toward me on its arms. It blocked all of the narrow alley's far end.

It was a revolting sight. Somehow, I knew that this thing had once been a normal human. It wasn't anymore. Now, it was a moving mound of trash and offal with a carrion stench to go along with it. It mewled piteously. It also blocked my way. I wasn't stupid enough to think it wasn't, in some fashion, dangerous.

"Do you like my pet?" a voice behind me asked.

I half-turned, keeping rubbish-man in sight.

Mage. I felt the power trickling from him. It was more than just a familiarity with the breed. There was a feeling down in the pit of my stomach almost any time I was around one, including Holgren, that hadn't been there before Abanon's Blade or before Thagoth. Not unless they used their magic on me anyway. I couldn't really pretend anymore that I hadn't been changed by my experiences. Just *how* I had changed, and what it meant, I had no clue.

This one was tall, taller than Holgren, with close-cropped, silvery hair, a strong-boned face, sturdy frame. He wore a simple tunic and trousers and well-made boots. A few silver rings shone on his long fingers. His eyes were mild.

I stuck a thumb at the rubbish man, who was still inching toward me and making pitiful sounds.

"Is that yours?"

"Indeed. I'm rather proud of my handiwork there. It's a tricky thing, keeping someone alive through such an extreme transformation."

"You made that out of a person?"

"He deserved it, I assure you. Killing was too good for him. Literally."

I shrugged. "Not my business."

"You are a difficult woman to approach. I apologize for waylaying you. I mean no disrespect—or harm."

I believed that about as much as I'd believe a tooth-puller who said I wouldn't feel a thing. But I kept quiet and kept an eye on him and his awful pet. My hands itched for my knives, but I kept them loose and open.

"Did you know, Mistress Thetys, that powerful creatures are being birthed in Bellarius as we speak? That old things, long sleeping, are waking in dark places?"

"Can't say that I did," I lied.

"Many are already about. Many more will swarm, like flies to rotten meat, to feed at the trough of power the Knife has cut open. I've seen it, and what I see is never wrong."

"That's kind of a mixed metaphor, but I've been guilty of the same. Go on."

He smiled. It was the least genuine smile I'd seen all day.

"The Knife *wants* you, Amra Thetys. I have seen it. Others will have as well. And they will try to use you to influence the Knife, to secure its power for themselves alone. Some will seek to partner with you, others to make you their slave. Some, of course, will simply seek to eliminate you."

"Is that what you'd like to do?"

"I've already said I wish you no harm. I just want you to go far, far away and never come back."

You and me both, I thought, but my mouth said something different.

"Now why would I do that? Bellarius is my home town."

"Bellarius is a sty, and you hate it here. I've seen that as well. I am not enamored of the place myself—but I rather think there will be great changes very soon. You wouldn't recognize the place, I assure you."

"There's a slight problem with the whole 'me leaving and never coming back' proposition. Maybe you noticed the light show last night? Nobody is going anywhere. Bellarius is locked up. Anyone who tries to leave gets dead very fast." Well, except for me, apparently. But while I seemed to be safe from being killed trying to leave, I *was* as trapped as everyone else.

"Oh, dear. That *is* a problem. One I'm sure you will resolve in time though. I understand you are frighteningly resourceful. I wouldn't take too long coming up with a solution, however. Say, by the end of the day?"

"You still haven't told me what I want to hear," I said.

"Which is?"

"What are you offering for my hasty departure?"

He smiled again and snapped his fingers.

The revolting thing in the alley shrieked and writhed, and a portion of its form distended. Rotting flesh shifted and thinned, revealing another face.

It was Keel. Maybe I *had* heard him after all.

He was imprisoned within the monstrosity, bound and gagged by ropes of intestine and crepuscular tentacles. He wasn't moving.

"Completely unharmed, I assure you."

I turned to face the mage directly. I wasn't angry. What I was feeling was too cold to be called anger.

"Oh, see now, you shouldn't have done that."

"And why, pray tell, not?"

"Because now, I have to kill you."

He smiled. Then, he laughed. He made a pass with his fingers, and the gibbering nightmare shrieked again. I glanced back. The ropes of intestine binding Keel were tightening.

"He is completely unharmed. That can change very quickly."

I didn't know if I could summon it again or control it if I did manage to call it up. It had only come to me the once, at South Gate, and then, to the best of my understanding, because it was reacting to something in the magic that had been thrown at me or maybe my rapidly approaching death.

I simply knew that I could never, ever allow anyone to control me through fear. Not fear for myself or fear for the safety of others. A mad mage named Bosch had tried that on me once, and I'd half-knuckled under. And he'd murdered his hostage anyway. I wasn't going to bow to that sort of blackmail again.

I *was* willing to bet Keel's life that if the mage that controlled it was dead, the monstrosity he'd created would die along with him.

Maybe that made me a not nice person. I don't know. I'd consider it a gray area.

I sort of reached inside me and called out, and it was there, just like that. I could feel the rent now, down deep, deep under Mount Tarvus. I knew what it was now thanks to the God of Sparrows and the Hag. Pulsing power, for all practical purposes, to do anything I wanted. Absolutely anything. To reshape reality. I felt a deep, seductive temptation to…change things.

But whatever I did, I had to give it form. If I didn't, if I didn't take care to channel it, form it, *constrain* it, it would very likely scour me out of existence as soon as I tapped it. That much I knew instinctively.

So I did what I had seen Holgren do once.

I smiled as I'd seen Holgren do that night in Lucernis, the night Tambor's arbor had burned.

Just like Holgren, I said, "My turn." And I flicked my fingers just as he had, imagining the same destruction he'd visited on Bosch happening to the man in front of me, willing the power pulsing down in the rent to flow up through me, through my hand, and into the smiling, kidnapping magus in front of me.

That night, Holgren had turned his opponent's body into a bloody mist. I'd actually been frightened of him then, of his power, of his absolute willingness to use it to end a life without a shred of hesitation. I hadn't understood him very well back then.

What happened when I tried imitating his spell—it made me terrified.

Of myself.

An invisible but palpable wave of pure force leapt from my hand. The mage just disintegrated before my eyes, every eyelash and toenail.

So did the building behind him. And the one behind that.

And the one behind *that.*

I don't know how many people I killed that day.

I stood there for a long time, horrified by the destruction I had caused. Long enough for shrieks of fear to start up in the neighborhood. Long enough for people to start running toward the strangely tidy destruction. Long enough for a haze of dust to drift into the alley, composed surely of masonry and furnishings and people—

Behind me, a ragged, gagging cough. I turned around.

Keel knelt in a vast pile of rancid meat, hacking and gagging and pulling intestine from around his neck and arms and legs. He looked up finally and saw me.

"What in hells is going on?" he said.

I just shook my head.

"Where are we?"

Finally, I shook myself out of the shock that I had fallen into and moved to help him.

"It doesn't matter," I replied. "We're leaving."

CHAPTER 18

When we got back to the inn, Keel was still shaken. So was I. The horror of what I'd done, inadvertent as it might have been, threatened to choke me. But I put it away, buried it deep, ruthless with myself. I would deal with it later. When there was time. If there was time. If all of Bellarius went up in a cloud of dust, then three buildings full of Kerf-only-knew how many people was nothing—

Stop it, Amra. Just stop, I told myself.

"This kid needs a bath," I told the innkeep as we passed him on the way to the stairs, "and I need something stronger than wine. Send both up as soon as you can."

The man bowed sarcastically, which was an impressive skill, I had to admit.

As soon as I unlocked and opened the door, I knew something was wrong. The door connecting the sitting room to the bedroom was open, and there was a cold breeze blowing through both rooms. Which meant the balcony doors were open. I'd left them closed and latched.

I blocked Keel from entering the suite and drew my knives.

"You've got a nice view here," came a Hardside voice from the balcony.

"Why don't you come over here and let me get a view of *you*?" I replied.

I heard slow footsteps approaching. I brought up a knife, ready to throw.

That broad, farmer's face was older now. A few wrinkles around the eyes and on his forehead had joined the freckles on his cheeks and across the bridge of his nose. His hair was still blond but cut close to the scalp now; no cowlick sticking up from the back anymore. His blue eyes were as intense and determined as I remembered them but not nearly as kind.

"Amra," he said. "Been a long time."

"Theiner."

He smiled a little at that. "Not for a while now. These days, everybody calls me Moc Mien."

He was average height and wore clean, loose-fitting, dark gray silks. I noticed his boots were soft-soled. I suspected he'd trod intentionally heavily to let me know he was approaching. Everything about his demeanor spoke of a cat-like grace. His hands were plainly visible and empty.

Theiner was Keel's crew leader.

"I've been looking for you," I told him.

"I know. Wish we could've met under better circumstances. Bottle of wine, good meal, reminiscing about the bad old days. All that."

"Want to tell me what the hells you're doing in my rooms?" I asked.

He sighed. "I came for that little bastard cowering in your shadow," he replied.

"So. You're Moc Mien?" I asked, not ready to delve into the issue of Keel just yet.

In reply, he gave me a shallow bow.

"Why the name change?"

"Theiner is a farm boy's name, not one to attract respect, much less fear. Might as well be called Turnip Boy. Moc Mien, on the other hand…"

"Chagan, isn't it?"

"It is. Means 'peaceful life' or some such. Not that anyone around here would know that." He shrugged.

"I'm not calling you 'Moc Mien,' Theiner."

"You can call me whatever you like, Amra, as long as you hand over the kid."

"I'm not going to be doing that."

He sighed. "We go back a long way. I don't think I have to remind you that you owe me."

"That's why I'm here, actually. I got your present."

He stared at me blankly. "What present?"

"Borold's head."

"Borold? What are you talking about?"

"Somebody sent me Borold's head in a box. You're about the only person who'd have reason to believe I'd want it."

He shook his head. "I haven't seen Borold in years. I certainly didn't chop his head off and send it to you. I've got better, and less insane, things to do with my time."

I sighed. "I was afraid you were going to say that." If Theiner hadn't sent the head, that meant I *had* been lured to Bellarius. But for what and by whom? Exhaustion, both physical and mental, settled on me like a smothering blanket.

"I'm tired, Theiner. Really tired. Can we have this discussion another time? I had no sleep last night and a very rough morning."

"I know."

"You know what?"

"That you didn't sleep last night, and your morning's been busy. I've been shadowing you since you left the Wreck last night. For a master thief, you're not particularly aware of your surroundings. Maybe you're getting ol—er, complacent."

"I *was* being followed. I knew it!" Paranoia? Kerf's shriveled balls.

"Did you mean to destroy those buildings this morning, by the way? It seemed a bit…excessive."

I was not going to talk about that.

"What do you *want*, 'Moc Mien?'"

"I told you. I want Keel."

"And I told you. You can't have him. Sorry."

He sauntered over to the couch and sat down. Leaned back, stretched his arms out behind his head. Laced his fingers, put his hands behind his head. Stared at me. "You know I can't allow him to just leave the crew consequence-free," he said.

"I know that wouldn't play well," I acknowledged. A crew leader couldn't be seen to tolerate that kind of blatant insubordination, or they wouldn't remain crew leader for long. But that wasn't my problem. I knew, however, that Theiner was going to make it my problem. He didn't really have a choice if he wanted to remain in charge of his crew.

"You can come in, by the way," he said. It's your room, after all." I was still standing in the doorway. I wanted Keel out of his line of sight.

"Are you going to try and make a move on the kid?" I countered.

"Not for the length of this conversation, at least," he replied, so I put away the knife and sat down opposite him. Keel walked in behind me and closed the door. He was obviously scared, obviously trying not to show it. He leaned against a wall, as far from Theiner as he could get without being too blatant about it.

A few seconds later, there was a knock on the door, and the innkeeper entered with a tray. On the tray was a carafe of water, three small glasses, and a bottle of root: clear, distilled spirits. He set the tray down and looked at me, pointedly ignoring Theiner and Keel.

"Shall I delay the bath?" he asked me.

"Yes, thanks. Did you know I had a visitor?"

"Not until I heard voices. I went back for an extra glass since I heard no screams of pain or bodies falling to the floor."

"You are a consummate host."

He rolled his eyes and left.

I poured myself a splash of root, threw it back, coughed and shuddered, then mixed a little more with water and settled back into my chair. I really was tired and not in the mood to deal with this. Theiner watched me with calm, cold eyes all the while. Keel was behind me; I had no idea what he was doing.

"Aren't you going to offer me any?" asked Theiner.

"You helped yourself into my rooms. You can help yourself to a drink if you want it."

As he mixed himself a drink, I asked him, "How much?"

"How much what?"

"How much to make this problem go away?"

"It's not that simple. Keel didn't just try to quit the crew. He got *political*," said Theiner, disgust plain on his face and in his voice. "He mouthed off about how we should be trying to overthrow the Syndic rather than taking from our fellow oppressed citizens."

I glanced back over my shoulder at the kid. His face was a little red, but his jaw was hard. Embarrassed but stubbornly sure of his belief.

"Ansen really has a way with words," he muttered. "Probably because he speaks the truth."

Theiner snorted. "Believe what you want, boy, but you were happy enough to join the crew when it meant a full belly and a roof over your head, you ungrateful little shit."

"I *was* happy," Keel replied. "That was before I knew better. The Syndic and the Council of Three *want* us down in the mud, preying on each other. It keeps us from looking up and seeing who's *really* keeping us from climbing out of the muck."

"Yeah, well, when you figure out how to off the Telemarch, then you can talk to me about revolution. While the archmage takes the Syndic's pay, things will remain exactly as they are, you stupid git."

"Enough," I said. "You two are giving me a headache. Keel, please shut up. Theiner, I understand your position, but I won't be giving Keel up to you. And honestly, you and everybody else in this city have bigger things to worry about. Or haven't you noticed the wall of death sealing the city off from the rest of the world?"

"That's a problem I can do nothing about," replied the crew leader who had once been my friend. "Young Keel, there, is a problem I *can* do something about. In fact, he's right at the top of my list of chores."

"If you've been shadowing me for the last dozen hours, you know there are some very bad things happening in Bellarius, Theiner."

"There are very bad things happening in Bellarius every single day, Amra. I'm one of them."

"Oh, gods, spare me the menacing patter. I'm not some pot-bellied shopkeeper you're looking to intimidate into paying protection money. Tomorrow morning, the whole city is going to become a smoking hole in the ground. It seems very likely that I'm the only one who has a chance to stop that from happening. I don't have the time or the patience to listen to your extortion speech."

He raised an eyebrow. "I see why you and Keel get along so well. An idealist and a thief with delusions of grandeur. Tell me; how are you going to stop the supposed destruction of an entire city?"

"I don't know if I *can* stop it, but I do know that I don't have time to be dodging you and your crew while I go about trying."

"Then give my wayward lamb to me, and get on with your heroics. I'll applaud when you're finished."

I slammed the glass down on the table. My patience had evaporated. "Why don't you cut me some Kerf-damned slack, *Moc Mien*, and put your vendetta on hold until lunch time tomorrow? Surely, you can keep your crew under your thumb for that long. If the city's still standing then, we can revisit this conversation."

He gave me a long, flat stare. Finally, he spoke, and his voice was deadly serious.

"I don't know if I can give you that long. There are internal pressures in the crew that you know nothing about. I can give you few hours. Then, I'm going to have to come for Keel. How you respond at that time is up to you, but think on this: I could have put a dagger in your back at any time over the last dozen hours, whatever freakish powers you seem to have now. I didn't out of respect for the friendship we once had despite the fact that you killed two of my crew.

"You owe me, Amra. Without me, you'd never have got on that ship, not on your own, and like as not, you'd have died in the Purge. I didn't help you to put you in my debt, gods witness, but you're there nonetheless."

"Are you really going to let this come to bloodshed, Theiner?" Fifteen years was a long time, but we had been close back then. Too close for the nonsense I was hearing now.

"I got no choice, Amra. Do you see many *former* crew leaders puttering around?"

I looked down, picked at my nail. He was right about that. Being the boss of a street crew was dangerous. Being the *ex*-boss of a street crew meant you were a corpse, one way or the other. Whoever took your place wouldn't just let you spend time with your knitting. You'd always be there, a whisper, a shadow falling over every unpopular decision the new fellow made.

He let the silence stretch a bit then said, "You can pay the debt on your own, or I can *make* you pay. That's something I've got good at over the last few years. That's not patter. It's the cold, hard truth. Just ask Keel. And remember who taught you knife-work in the first place."

With that, he stood and walked toward the door of the suite.

"Theiner," I called.

He paused. "What?"

"Did you ever meet my uncle?"

"You have an uncle?" he replied, obviously annoyed. I'd stepped on his parting speech.

"I have somebody who claims to be my uncle. Says you punched him in the face when he went looking for me ten years ago."

"I remember. Some fellow came around asking after you, yes. There was some family resemblance, sure, but I didn't like him. He got a little too insistent. I popped him in the nose. He made himself scarce."

"That was it?"

"That was it."

"Thanks."

"A day, Amra, at the most," he reminded me. Then, he turned to Keel.

"I'll be seeing you again soon, kid," he said in a mild voice. Keel played at being a statue. Then, Theiner was gone.

I closed my eyes and leaned back in my chair. Let out a sigh. For all the bad, very bad, and stunningly bad news that had come my way since I'd gotten back to Bellarius, the conversation I'd just had made me feel the worst. Powerful entities trying to kill me? Sadly, nothing new. The threat of horrific destruction looming? Somehow, I'd become almost inured to the concept.

Choosing between giving up the kid to be, at best, maimed for life or fighting my oldest living friend to the death? That put some serious cracks in the shell of numbness I'd grown since my return.

"If you want me to get lost, I understand," Keel said quietly.

"What I want is for you to take a bath," I replied, forcing myself out of my funk. "I thought you smelled bad *before* you got a big hug from Rubbish Man. Kerf, was I wrong. Oh, that reminds me. Did you manage to see the Hag before you got swallowed?"

"Isin's love, you're just full of compassion, aren't you?"

"I'll work on that. Just as soon as I'm someplace that isn't about to be ripped apart by fell magics. Well?"

"I saw her. She said, and I quote, 'The Stone is indestructible. It will survive the city's death, should you fail. As will I.'"

I grunted. No wonder she'd laughed when I said we were all screwed. But it was good news. It meant my plan had a chance of success.

A few minutes later, the innkeeper arrived, servants trailing him with pails of hot water. Keel complained that he couldn't get his clothes off with one arm.

"Use your teeth," I said.

CHAPTER 19

Marza came through on the first item I'd asked for not long after Keel had finally managed to get undressed. Unfortunately, he wasn't able to accommodate me on the others.

Keel was splashing around in the tub in the bathroom, complaining that he couldn't reach half his body what with one arm broken.

"If you think I'm coming in there to help, you're out of your very tiny, teenaged mind," I shouted back from the couch.

There was a knock on the door. I went over and opened it, free hand on a knife hilt.

The man was very large, very tanned, and very scarred. The sword slung from his hip was nearly as long as I was tall.

"Mistress Thetys?" he rumbled.

"Maybe. Who's asking?"

"Hoddy Marza sends his regards and the address you requested."

"That was fast."

"Hoddy Marza also regrets to inform you that he cannot secure the other information you requested within your specified time frame."

I blinked. "You talk real good for a sword-swinger," I said.

The armsman said nothing to that, just regarded me levelly with mild, competent eyes.

"So what's the address, big man?"

"The Trise. Seventh house on the left, coming from wharfside. Gray stone; weathered, yellow shutters. Your item of interest is at home now."

"Thanks. And my thanks to Marza." I dug a silver mark out and offered it to him. He ignored it.

"I'm to go with you," he said, "and I'm not on your payroll."

"I don't need a guard."

"I'm not guarding you. I'm to collect whatever is left when you're done and deliver it to some other people."

"Ah. Well then. I suppose we should go."

I shouted to Keel that I was going out, got a muffled acknowledgment, and then we were on our way to the Trise to have a chat with Affonse Yarrow: old man, suspected child murderer.

~ ~ ~

The house was just a house. A little run down, peeling paint on the shutters. A little grime around the door's handle. But it was just a house. I couldn't help the irrational thought that evil people shouldn't live in innocuous-looking places.

The armsman's name was Springsweet. That didn't fit either, not that I was going to tell him that. He didn't seem to have much of a sense of humor anyway. I *did* tell him to wait a short distance away, out of sight. I didn't want old man Yarrow spooked when he answered the door.

Once Springsweet had moved off an appreciable distance, I knocked. There was no answer. I knocked again and waited some more. So I pulled out a knife and started banging on the wood with the pommel. Finally, it was yanked open.

"Isin's thighs, what the hells do you want!"

He didn't look evil at first glance. He just looked old and grumpy. Stick-thin, yellow-white hair in disarray, wearing an oft-mended nightshirt in the early afternoon. I knew without having to think about it this old bastard lived alone. The only thing that put me off about him were his eyes. They were still sharp. And cold.

"You're Affonse Yarrow." It wasn't a question. Marza wouldn't have made a mistake about that. "I want to come in and talk to you.

"What makes you think I want to talk to *you*?"

"Because I'll pay you for the conversation," I lied. "I don't imagine a Blacksleeve's pension is so generous that you couldn't do with a little more coin. Or a lot more coin, depending on what you have to say."

"What's it about?"

I shook my head. "Not on the street."

He thought about it a moment. Looked around the street. Opened the door wider.

I went inside.

He sat down on a sagging, greasy couch there in his front room. I sat across from him in a chair whose stuffing was slowly bleeding out onto a diseased-looking carpet. The whole interior of the house that I could see looked dim, dingy, and unhealthy. More like a lair than a home. *That's more like it*, I thought.

"What do you want to know?" he asked, his voice casual. His face was mild, but his eyes were devoid of emotion if not calculation. His gaze traveled up and down my body, but there was nothing sexual about it. Something told me this man didn't have much of an interest in sex, maybe never had. He was just taking in details.

"I want to know the name of the mage who helped the Blacksleeves track down street rats during the Purge."

"And you'll give me money for that name?"

"Sure. How much do you want? I've got lots. Name your price." My mouth was saying the right words, but my heart wasn't in it. I kept seeing an untidy pile of bones stuffed under a desk.

"I think you're lying," he replied. "In fact, I know you're lying."

I raised an eyebrow. "Well, that's not a very nice thing to say to someone you just met."

"I'm not a very nice person," he replied.

"That makes two of us. Look, Yarrow, I've got a lot to do and not a lot of time to do it. I could go into a big, emotional monologue about all your wicked deeds and how you should pay for your crimes, but Kerf's balls, we both know it would be just so much wasted breath. Just give me the name, and I'll be on my way. Or don't give it to me, and let things get ugly. I'm fine with either option."

"You interest me," he replied, his expression of mild interest never changing.

"I'm thrilled," I replied, but he continued on as if he hadn't heard.

"Your accent, for example. Ostensibly Lucernan, but down at the roots, it still carries the grimy residue of Hardside. Your vocabulary—in the same sentence you use the word 'monologue,' you swear by Kerf's testicles. And your clothing as well. Beyond the fact that you dress as a man, every item you're wearing is perfectly fitted and of the highest quality, and yet you display not a single stitch of ornament or adornment."

"So?"

"So you interest me." And then he sat there and stared at me with his old man's watery blue eyes, his stone killer's eyes. I put up with it until it got old. Which was about three seconds.

"Right then," I said, getting up to stick a knife to his throat.

"Who are your parents?" he asked me suddenly before I made it to my feet.

"My parents are dead."

"Ah. Were you a war orphan or a plague orphan?"

This old turd hadn't earned the right to be nosy about my past. "I'm a dead parents orphan," I snapped.

"If you tell me what happened to your parents, I'll tell you what you want to know," he smiled. "I will tell you the name you want so badly to hear."

I didn't believe him for a moment. I knew, without knowing how, I would have to drag the mage's name from him, syllable by bloody syllable. And I was fine with that because this old child murderer was a dead man, whatever happened. Springsweet was waiting outside to make sure of it.

"Well?" he asked, and I smiled back at him.

"My mother was a clerk's daughter from Ink Street. My father was a caravan guard when he was sober. I was born in Hardside. One evening when I was almost ten, my father beat my mother unconscious, then kept beating her. I stuck a knife in him to make him stop. He stopped. My mother never woke up."

I found myself suddenly standing over him where he sat on his dusty, faded couch, my hands itching for my knives.

"So what kind of orphan am I? Not war. Not plague. I suppose you might call me an orphan of poverty. Or just plain, unadorned, shitty luck."

He sniffed, and his lip curled. It was the first honest emotion that had touched his face the whole time I'd been talking to him. "You're still a street rat." He placed a casual hand on the back of the couch.

"Oh, I'm much more than that. Now, tell me the name."

"It's—"

For an old man, he was still fast. The casual hand on the back of the couch sprouted a stiletto, and he drove it at my midsection with a speed and force that seemed impossible considering his age and frailty.

I'd been waiting for it. Once a cold-blooded killer, always a cold-blooded killer.

I arched my abdomen out of the way of the stiletto's wicked point, grabbed his bony wrist with my left hand, and brought my right elbow down on his thin forearm.

The sound of bones breaking is unmistakable.

I dragged him down to his filthy carpet, on his belly. Sat on his back. Pulled the stiletto from his loose fist. Ignored his moans.

"I believe you were about to tell me a name," I murmured in his hairy ear.

"You c—"

I slammed a fist down on the broken bone. He screamed.

"The name."

"Piss on you," he panted. "Filthy street rat."

"I'm only going to ask once more. Then, I'm going to break the other arm. Then, I'm going to tie you to a chair and go see some fellows I know down in Hardside," I lied. It wouldn't do to tell him the truth and leave him no hope. He'd clam up as like as not.

"I'm going to tell them there's an old man named Yarrow tied to a chair in his house on the Trise, who used to be a Blacksleeve back during the Purge. Maybe they'll remember you. Even if they don't, they will consider it their duty to send you on to whichever hell you've earned in as slow and painful a way as possible. They just aren't civilized like me. Never having left Hardside, their *vocabularies* are sadly lacking.

"Now, did my little *monologue* bore you? Or are you ready, by *Kerf's hairy balls*, to give me the name?"

He was silent for a little while except for some panting. Then he spoke in a broken, quavering old man's voice.

"Aither. The Telemarch. Much good it will do you," he panted.

"You're lying. The *Telemarch* got his hands dirty hunting down street rats? Come on, Affonse. You can do better than that." I put a knee his broken arm and ground down on it until he writhed and screamed.

"The Telemarch ordered it! Aither *ordered* the Purge, I swear to Gorm!"

"All right, Affonse. All right. I believe you." Kerf's dirty beard, I did believe him. I wished I didn't.

I got off his back, kicked the stiletto into a corner. Wiped my hands on my thighs. I left him moaning on his filthy carpet, walked out the door, and nodded to Springsweet, who was waiting at the foot of the steps.

"He's all yours," I said and walked away. I didn't look back. I had no interest in whatever was going to happen to Affonse Yarrow. He was a twisted little monster of a man who would soon meet a fitting end, and I didn't need or want the details.

I felt unclean. Like I'd just wallowed in a pool of filth. I very badly wanted a bath.

No time. I had a much scarier monster than Yarrow to deal with, and I still didn't know how I could possibly do it.

CHAPTER 20

I wasn't getting the layouts of the Riail or the Citadel from Marza. That was a problem, but not an insurmountable one. I was pretty sure there was one person who could give me what I needed. So I climbed higher up into the Girdle to have another chat with the God of Sparrows.

On the way, I had a good think about the Telemarch. Everything, it seemed, was pointing me to him, from Greytooth to the God of Sparrows, from Ansen and his false note to my dear, mysterious, lying, vanishing "Uncle" Ives. Everything since before I arrived in Bellarius, actually; Borold didn't chop his own head off and send it to me for a laugh.

About the only person who didn't seem to be involved in any way was Theiner. He might well do his best to knife me in a few hours, but at least he wasn't trying to run a game on me. It's good to be able to count on old friends. Did I wish Theiner and I had had a happier reunion? Of course. But the thing was, anyone who hadn't been through what we'd been through would almost certainly see him as a cold, murderous bastard. I'd escaped; he'd stayed in this hell-hole. By his own lights, by the standards that we'd both grown up with, Theiner was a fucking paragon of virtue. He wasn't lying or cheating, and he wasn't giving me cold steel in the back. No, I had no hard feelings towards Theiner, strange as it might seem. He was giving me the most important thing a street rat could give to another: respect. And it was costing him with his crew. Pushing thoughts of Theiner aside, I went back to picking at the whole sordid mess surrounding the Telemarch. Manipulated into it or not, I had a stack of reasons as high as my head to want to go and make the Telemarch dead. From the fact that, according to Yarrow, he was responsible for the Purge to the fact that, according to everybody in a position to know, he was inadvertently about to destroy the city and me with it, it seemed like a good idea for the Telemarch to stop breathing. It seemed simple. Not easy, by any stretch of the imagination, but simple.

Too simple. Someone wanted very, very badly for *me* to kill the Telemarch. Or at least attempt it. And that just didn't make much sense on its face. Sure, I'd survived my share of scrapes, but at the end of the day, I was not on the same level as Aither. Not even close. He was an archmage, for Kerf's sake, while I was a thief. Maybe I had powers. All right, three destroyed buildings said I had access to some real, deadly power. But those three destroyed buildings, and all the people inside them who'd suddenly disintegrated, also said I had no idea what I was doing with it. Being able to tap that power didn't make me a mage. It made me a disaster waiting to happen.

A disaster—

I stopped still in the street. People moved around and past me, muttering.

Maybe I didn't need plans for the Citadel after all. Maybe I didn't need to break in and confront the Telemarch.

Maybe all I needed was to call up that power again, flick my fingers, and watch the Citadel and everything in it transform to dust, drifting away on the wind.

It couldn't be that easy, could it?

Could it?

I started walking again, faster.

~ ~ ~

The sparrows were in a frenzy. They swirled this way and that in the courtyard, no longer silent, a storm of wings and piercing, distressed cries. Kitten girl—Cherise—was nowhere to be seen.

"Something's wrong, huh?" I asked them. They didn't answer. So I went to talk to their boss.

I walked up to the tree and put a hand on a root, not bothering to sit. Immediately, I was in the God's throne room, or mind, or whatever.

He was agitated. Pacing up and down, making fists. His brutal face wasn't in the least mellow now. He looked exactly what I would imagine a blood god should look like.

He didn't bother waiting until I'd walked up to him. He sent me a picture almost immediately.

The kid. Cherise. Being dragged away from the tree by Blacksleeves, screaming and crying.

"Where?" I asked, walking up to Him. "Where did they take her?"

Another picture.

The Citadel.

"Kerf's crooked staff," I cursed. I wasn't going to be disintegrating the Citadel with a child inside it. Which I suspected was the point of her being taken. Someone knew far too much about how my mind worked. "When?"

He showed me a picture of myself leaving Yarrow's house.

Somebody knew what I was likely to think of before I even thought of it? Shit.

"All right. I'll try to help. I'm going to kill Aither anyway. Or at least try. But first, I have to take the Founder's Stone from the Syndic."

He showed me a picture of Cherise again, her screaming, tear-streaked face. His message was plain enough.

"Listen. This is about more than her. You told me so Yourself. If I walk into the Citadel now and somehow succeed in killing the Telemarch, that girl will die anyway along with everyone else in the city. You must know the spirits of those murdered in the Purge have turned Bellarius into a prison. They've sentenced everyone in it to death. If the city doesn't explode, they'll just kill everyone themselves. In order to stop that from happening, I *need* the Founder's Stone. So first, I get the Stone, then the girl. I don't like it any more than You, I swear to Kerf."

He kept making fists. Big, brutal fists. His lantern jaw was clenching and unclenching, the muscles on either side working, bulging out. Finally, He nodded.

"I need to know the layout of the Riail, specifically the throne room and everything between it and the wall closest to the Bay. I also need to know the layout of the Citadel. I'm sure You've seen both."

He showed me the Citadel from the outside. A sparrow tried to fly into one of the windows. It just disappeared in a puff of feathers before it broke the plane of the opening. Its tiny body, what was left of it, drifted to the ground.

"Not the Citadel then. Damn. What about the Riail?"

This time I was, apparently, perched on the stone railing of a long balcony. To my right was the Bay of Bellarius, sparkling in the sun. To my left, graceful, stone arches and beyond them a big room. In the room was a big, white block of stone. Glowing runes chased each other across its surface. Sitting atop the stone was a gilt chair. Sitting in the chair was a heavy man, chin on his fist, surrounded by men in armor.

Finally, some good news. If the Founder's Stone was that close to the outer wall of the Riail, it made the first part of my plan much more likely to succeed.

"Is there anything else You know or can do to help me?" I asked him.

He shook His head, frustration, rage, and desperation all evident there. Then, He was suddenly still, as if a thought had occurred to Him, or perhaps He'd made some important decision. He reached up above His head and, from thin air, pulled down a green, heart-shaped leaf. Carefully, slowly, He opened up the top of my waistcoat with one massive finger. With the other hand, He tucked the leaf into the inner pocket where I kept Holgren's pendant and my mother's locket.

"Um, thanks? What am I supposed to do with it though?"

He shook His head and smiled a little sadly. Shooed me away.

"I guess I'd better go, then," I told Him. "Time is running out."

He nodded, and I was back at the tree. The sparrows, while still agitated, weren't quite so frantic.

I had very little time and a lot left to do.

CHAPTER 21

Fallon Greytooth was still recuperating in his cave. He didn't look like he was up for what I needed him to do, but he assured me he'd be ready by evening. Yes, time was running short. Yes, I was going to break into the Riail and steal the Founder's Stone. But I wasn't going to do it in broad daylight. I was desperate, not insane. That and there was still one small part of my plan that I didn't quite have worked out. A detail, really.

For all that I'd mocked Greytooth for his "careful" planning in assaulting the Citadel, my own plan to relieve the Syndic of the Founder's Stone wasn't all that different. Seeing Greytooth rip out that window grate, along with a goodly portion of the wall it was attached to, and fling it out into the Bay had given me the idea. Lyta had confirmed that the Founder's Stone wouldn't be damaged, whatever we did. The Sparrow God had shown me enough of the layout of the Riail to reassure me we wouldn't have to blunder around the Syndic's palace trying to find it, probably fighting Council guards all the while and blasting holes in walls to get the Stone outside. In a very real sense, this wasn't going to be a burglary; it was a simple smash and grab.

It was just that the *scale* of it was so much bigger than shattering some display case and bolting with the loot before a guard could nab you. Or stab you.

That and making sure the Stone landed where we needed it to.

"Can you guide the Stone's flight?" I asked Greytooth.

"To a degree."

"How fine a degree though? Could you land it on the deck of a ship, say?"

"I don't say I *couldn't* hit a moving target, but I do say that I would be very surprised if I managed it."

"How about a ship that that hadn't moved in, oh, a millennium or so?"

"Still doubtful. Such a target is very small, Mistress Thetys. Unless…"

"Unless?"

"Well. I would need a magical lodestone of sorts. Something to call to the Stone in its flight. It would take some preparation."

"How much? How long?"

"What time is it now?"

"Mid-afternoon. Which you would know if you didn't live in a cave."

"Give me until midnight then. I'll also need something from the location where you want the stone to land."

I thought about that. I didn't see how I could even scratch Lyta's penteconter much less break a piece off and bring it to Greytooth. A thousand years being assaulted by the sea hadn't put a mark on it.

"Would sea water be good enough?"

He gave me a look that said, "Don't be daft." "Does sea water stay in one place?"

"All right, how about a scrap of tarp?"

"Has the tarp been in the same place for an appreciable amount of time?"

"Years, probably."

"Then yes. That will suffice."

We talked over my sorry excuse for a plan a little more, searching for anything that would increase its chance of success. Basically, it boiled down to "get to the Founder's Stone without getting killed, launch it out across the city and make it fetch up in Lyta's lap without getting killed, and then run away before we got killed."

The scariest part was the fact that Greytooth would be very busy during almost the entire job, leaving me to keep the Council guards from sticking lots of holes in us. I said as much to Greytooth.

"They're trained warriors, and there are likely dozens of them. I'm a burglar, and last I checked, there was only one of me. They'll hack us to pieces. Isn't there any sort of edge you can give me of the magical variety?"

"Wouldn't it be easier to hire some blades of our own?" he said.

"No, actually, for two reasons. First, as soon as you told any mercenary what the plan was, they'd laugh their heads off, leave, and report us for the reward they'd be certain to get. Second, it would be almost impossible to sneak enough people in to make a difference. So. Magic?"

He blew out a weary breath. "I'll think of something. But I'm no battle mage."

"Do your best," I told him. "I'll be back. I've got to go get you your target."

Another thing about living underground is the fact that you have no idea what the weather is up to. When I opened Greytooth's door, I discovered it was now pissing down rain: a cold, pitiless rain from a slate-gray sky. I drew the hood of my cloak up over my head and waded out into the deluged streets. This far up the Mount, the streets were more vertical than horizontal, making them the next best thing to waterfalls.

"Gods, I hate this city," I muttered.

~ ~ ~

It was dark by the time I arrived at the Wreck. As furious as the rain had been when I set out, it had died down to a miserable drizzle by then. I was thoroughly soaked and in a foul mood.

Lyta was, surprise, at home.

"Once again, welcome, Doma Thetys," she called out as I reached the tarp that served as her door. I pushed it aside and entered.

"Don't suppose you've got a fire hidden somewhere," I asked, keeping my eyes from her glowing ones.

"Alas, no. I don't really feel the cold."

"Lucky for you."

"To what do I owe this visit?"

"I'll be doing my damnedest to deliver the Stone to you. Tonight. I need a piece of your front door to do so."

"You are welcome to it," she replied without any perceptible change in her tone. I might have been asking to borrow an egg or a cup of flour for all the emotion she showed.

"I'd have thought you'd be a little more excited at the prospect of getting the Stone and getting free," I told her, cutting a corner away from the tarp and pocketing it.

"I find it doesn't suit to become excited by prospects, Doma Thetys, only realities."

"In other words, you'll believe it when you see it."

"Precisely."

"I suppose I can understand that," I replied, rising. "Well, if all goes well, you'll be seeing something believable sometime after midnight." I pushed the tarp back, preparing to leave.

"Amra."

"Yes?"

"Aren't you forgetting something?"

My memories. She still wanted them.

"I was kind of hoping *you* would forget, actually."

She shook her head. "Mour is insistent."

"Mour is dead."

"Nevertheless."

I sighed. "All right. Now's as good a time as any, and later might be too late. Let's get this over with. What do I do?"

"Give me your hand," she replied, stretching out her own in the gloom. I crossed the short space between us, leaned down a little, and put my right hand in hers.

As soon as our hands touched, there was a spark, a shock, the kind you might get from a door knob after walking across a carpet on a cold, dry winter's day. I pulled back instinctively, or tried to, but her grip was suddenly vise-like and painful. She was far stronger than her old lady body had any right to be.

"I thought you said this wouldn't hurt a bit, Lyta."

She didn't reply. Her eyes grew brighter. Her long, white hair began to billow about her head. Her grip on my hand was getting painful. Bones started grinding against each other. And the stain left by the Blade that Whispers Hate began to glow.

"Abanon? What do you here? What fool let slip your chains?" The words were coming out of Lyta's mouth, but it wasn't Lyta's voice.

"Lyta? Better let go now. I'll be needing that hand later to get you the Founder's Stone." I was starting to sweat despite the chill.

"Mad shard of a mad sister, I will not *let you free. You are a stain, a poison, and one I will not countenance."* And then she started strangling me with her other hand.

I couldn't knife her. I needed her. But if I didn't do something quickly, she was going to crush my windpipe. So I punched her dead between the eyes with my free hand and with a strength born of not a little desperation. And maybe something more. Certainly I'd never hit anybody else that hard in my life.

She flew back, chair and all, breaking both her hold on my hand and my neck. Her head smacked hard against the stone deck with a very serious sounding thud. Her lights went out. Literally. The room was very dark. I backed off until I was just inside the doorway and pulled the tarp open to let in a little more light.

After a few seconds, she began to move. She opened her eyes, and they glowed faintly once more, opalescent. She made it to her knees and leaned against her overturned chair. Her long hair covered most of her face.

"Are you going to try and kill me again?" I asked her.

"No. I apologize. That was Mour, not me. I think it best we do not touch again."

"Sounds very reasonable to me. Mind telling me what just happened?"

"You did not destroy the Blade that Whispers Hate, Doma Thetys."

"The hells I didn't."

"No. Listen to me. You used your will to disintegrate it. A very unlikely achievement and the only thing you could have done to keep from becoming its pawn. But you did not destroy the Blade. You overpowered and overwhelmed it. You took from it its physical form, its ability to act on and in the world as an independent agency."

"So what's the Kerf-damned problem?"

"In doing so, you became Abanon's avatar." She stood, righted her chair, and sat down in it once more. As if nothing had happened, she pulled her hair away from her face and tucked it back over her shoulders.

"That's impossible," I told her flatly.

"Do you not think I know something of being an avatar of a goddess?"

"Do *you know* the things I've been through since I destroyed the Blade? If I'd had access to some sort of power, anything *like* the power that the Blade had, then everything to do with Thagoth would have been child's play instead of the worst half-year of my life."

"You, Amra Thetys, are the living vessel of Abanon, Goddess of Hate, and one of the eight shadows of the Eightfold Goddess. I swear it."

I shook my head. "You're either lying or crazy. Either way, you're wrong."

She had nothing to say to that. The silence stretched. I realized I was angry, so angry my hands were trembling. There was no time for this.

"Can you actually save the city from the spirits," I spat at her, "or was that just crazy talk as well?"

"I can and will if you get me the Stone."

"So we're done here?"

"We are. For now."

"For good, you mean. As long as you follow through on your end of the bargain. And you'd damned well better."

I walked out without another word.

I walked through Hardside toward the Girdle, wet, cold, and shaking with rage, unaware of my surroundings. I didn't know what sort of game the Hag was playing or what she hoped to accomplish. But by all the dead gods, she *had* to be lying. There was nothing to lend credence to her story. I'd had the Blade pouring its bile straight into my mind. I knew the sound of its voice, the *feel* of its awful, corrosive power better than anyone except the young Arhat, who had guarded it for years until Corbin had stolen it.

Better than anyone living, in other words.

If it was still inside me, somehow, I would *know* it.

Wouldn't I?

The only answer was a damnable itching on the palm of my hand, which was no comfort at all.

The rage had left me by the time I got to the Girdle, leaving in its wake a sick feeling of dread in the pit of my stomach.

That rage would flare again once I got back to Greytooth's.

CHAPTER 22

This time, Greytooth wasn't alone.

He'd finally started a fire in the grate, which helped with the light and didn't with the smoke. When I walked in, he was cross-legged on the floor, bent over a very big, very fat book. At the far end of the room was a man with his back turned to me, studying a dusty, broken, gilded clock.

"Master Greytooth," I said in greeting. "Who in hells is that you've got with you?" Entertaining visitors right before breaking into the palace of a country's ruler seemed somewhat inappropriate.

"Amra," replied Greytooth, not looking up from his book. "You suggested we would require magical aid in our endeavor. I procured it." He gestured to the man. "May I present to you the Just Man, Ansen."

The man turned around to face me.

"Hello, Uncle Ives," I said, and then I was across the small room and pounding his face with my fist. I got in three good blows before Greytooth pulled me off.

"Amra! Have you gone mad?" he said, pinning my arms. Which left my legs free. I managed a good kick to Ansen's privates, which doubled him over in a very satisfying fashion. I'd like to say that even though I was furious, I still had enough sense not to stick him with a knife. I'd like to say it, but it would be a lie. The truth is, I wanted to *hurt* this man who had pretended to be my family, who had, through his deceit, caused me to cry over my mother. I wanted to cause him pain, and a knife was just too impersonal.

I only stopped because Greytooth made me. I felt his magic run cold fingers down my spine in the instant before it took hold, locking every muscle of my body rigid. It was not a comfortable feeling.

"You assault a guest in my *home*?" Greytooth growled, staring down at me where he'd dropped me on the floor—and not gently. "How dare you? By what right?"

"She has the right," wheezed Ansen from out of my view. "I deceived and manipulated her in a very personal manner. Let her up, Magus."

Greytooth glanced at Ansen then looked back at me. "No more melees, Mistress Thetys. I warn you, this is not a tavern." And then my muscles were my own to move once again. I climbed to my feet, ignoring Ansen and Greytooth. Went over to the cabinet where the wine was kept, pulled out the first one that came to hand, and uncorked it with a knife and an expert twist. Took a long swallow, didn't taste it. Stared at the wall for a while.

"I'm not working with that piece of filth," I finally declared.

Greytooth sighed. "I've no idea what has passed between you two, nor do I find myself caring. We need assistance in order to meet our objective. Ansen can provide it. His interests are aligned with ours, time is desperately short, and the consequences of failure, need I remind you, are dire in the extreme."

"So what's your point?" I asked, turning to face him. He looked like he was about to kill me, so I put up my hand and said, "I hear you. You're making perfect sense. But I can't trust him, Fallon, and what's more, *you* shouldn't trust him either. He'll use us both to get what he wants and leave us twisting in the wind once he's got it."

"Do you even know what I want?" Ansen asked.

"I'm guessing you want me to punch you in the face some more, or else you wouldn't be talking."

"I want the Syndic and the Council of Three thrown down. I want the whole damned *Riail* pulled down. I want just rule for Bellarius and all of Bellaria, an end of the depredations of the—"

"Tell him to shut his mouth, Greytooth, or I swear by all the dead gods, I'll shut it for him."

"You'll do no such thing," replied Greytooth. "Ansen," he continued, "*please* be quiet."

"Look, Fallon. This is very simple. You can't trust him. Deceit is what he's all about apparently. What we are about to do, it's too damned important to risk bringing this liar and fake in on it."

Greytooth stared at me, his long face gloomy, the tattoos on his bald head shifting restlessly.

"There is a simple way to resolve this," he finally said. "Master Ansen, will you consent to a Compulsion?"

"What kind?" Ansen asked in return.

"Truth."

Ansen didn't look pleased at the prospect. "If I must," he replied.

"What are you talking about?" I asked Greytooth.

"Simple magic. A Compulsion of truth, imagine it, compels the subject to speak only truth for the duration of the spell. It must, however, be agreed to voluntarily. I cannot force the spell upon him."

"Are you sure it will work?"

Greytooth didn't bother to reply to that.

"Fine, fine. Can I also ask him questions?"

"You may. It would be up to him whether he chose to reply. He will be compelled to tell the truth. He will not be compelled to talk if he doesn't wish to."

"I don't like it," I said, and sat down on the couch with my bottle.

Greytooth had Ansen sit in a chair, put the first two fingers of his right hand on Ansen's lips, and muttered a few liquid syllables. I felt the chill of active magics brush the nape of my neck. Then, Greytooth sat down next to me.

"Do you intend to betray us or otherwise see our plans to take the Founder's Stone fail?" he asked Ansen.

"No," Ansen answered.

"Do you intend to aid us in that endeavor to the best of your ability?"

"Yes."

"Why are you helping us?" I asked him, and Greytooth gave me a glare.

"Because taking the Founder's Stone will help to weaken the Syndic's grip on power and hearten the masses, making them more likely to rebel. And because I am assured that if we don't steal it, we are all going to die."

"Are you satisfied now, Mistress Thetys?" Greytooth asked me.

"Nowhere near," I told him, looking him straight in the eye. Then, I turned back to Ansen.

"Why did you pretend to be my uncle?"

"I didn't."

"What do you mean?"

"I *am* your uncle. Your mother's brother, just as I told you. That was not a lie then or now. Nothing I told you about our family was a lie."

"But you certainly did lie about knowing Theiner."

He smiled. "That's not a question."

"Why did you lie to me about Theiner and his list?"

"Would you have liked it better if I'd said, 'Hello niece, I'm your long-lost uncle. By the way, I'm also a revolutionary leader, a middling mage, and I've got a sideline in hunting those responsible for the Purge. You know, on my idle days?'"

"You didn't answer my question. Why did you lie to me?"

"Because I didn't want you to think me mad. I wanted you to have the list of murderers I'd compiled over the years. I wanted it to be your choice what you would do with it. Burn it or cross each name off in their own blood, whatever would serve you best. It's a grisly sort of present, I know. But then we are grisly sorts of people, Amra, aren't we?"

They say nobody knows you like family. I shook the thought away.

"I went back to Ink Street after I found out you'd lied about Theiner. The place is deserted and has been for a long time. Why all the illusion? Why pretend you lived there, that the business was a going concern, employees and all?"

"I shut it all down once my father died. A factor's business is a dirty one, Amra. You buy over debts from businesses in distress, and then you squeeze those who owe. Your grandfather made a lot of money from it because he was ruthless. Having a conscience is a liability."

"You didn't answer my question."

He sighed. "What can I say? Illusion is my specialty. Caution and subterfuge keep me alive. It's second nature. And maybe I wanted you to get a sense of normality or constancy about some part of your family history. I'm not really clear on my own motives, Amra, and unfortunately, Master Greytooth's spell can't make me tell a truth that I don't actually know."

I frowned. It wasn't a satisfying answer, but apparently, it was all I was going to get. I moved on.

"You had a letter waiting for me before I ever reached Bellarius. How did you know I was coming?"

"I'm a mage, and you are a blood relative. It wasn't that difficult."

"Why did you kill Borold?"

"Who?"

"Borold. The man whose head you shoved in a box and sent to me in Lucernis. Did that somehow slip your mind?"

"I've never, to my knowledge, killed anyone named Borold. And I definitely never sent you anyone's head. That I would remember."

"Is your spell still working?" I asked Greytooth.

"Yes."

"Are you *sure*?"

"Don't be insulting," he replied.

"Shit." I'd pinned most of what had happened to me on Ansen, or rather Ives, once

I'd found out he'd lied to me about Theiner. It wasn't that simple. I admitted to myself that I had been ignoring evidence that had pointed in other directions. There was still an unseen player out there trying to run a game on me. Someone who had started the whole ball rolling with Borold's decapitation. The brand on Borold's forehead pointed to the spirits of the victims of the Purge, as did the runes I'd found wharfside and in the Girdle. And the big one in the sky over the Citadel.

They had pulled me to Bellarius just to witness and experience its demise. Which seemed more than a little insane. What good would it do for me to witness the death of the city if I was going to be killed along with everyone else? What good was a dead witness? Wasn't the point of a witness to tell what she had seen?

"Are there anymore questions?" my uncle asked. "This spell is beginning to make my brain itch."

"Mistress Thetys?" Greytooth asked.

"I can't think of anything else right now," I admitted. Grudgingly.

"Then let us get to work. Time is in short supply, and this has been an unwelcome distraction."

~ ~ ~

Less than an hour later, we were standing at the foot of the Riail, out of sight of the main gate. I'd suggested Greytooth fly us all up as he had done at the Citadel, but he'd disabused me of that desire. First, he couldn't carry another person while he levitated. Second, he and Ives could not cast any magic whatsoever before they set foot inside the Riail. Every external wall of the entire building was warded, and using magic would set those wards off. None of us would survive that, or so he said. I had no reason not to believe him.

So. It was up to me to climb the dozen yards to the balcony of the throne room, tie a rope around something, drop the other end of said rope down to my accomplices, and keep any guards distracted while Ives and Greytooth climbed.

What could possibly go wrong? said the voice in my head.

I couldn't risk throwing a grappling hook and didn't have one in any case, so I had the joy of free-climbing the ridiculously smooth wall, coiled rope slung over a shoulder, bandolier-style. I also didn't have any resin. I also hadn't really been keeping in shape. I was supposed to be retired, for Kerf's sake.

The wall was marble-faced, polished smooth and made slick by the miserable drizzle that had started up yet again. Each rectangular block was about a yard wide and two feet tall. The space between each block was just enough to stick a knife in; not nearly enough for a finger hold. The only thing in my favor was the fact that the wall wasn't completely vertical; there was roughly a ten-degree slope to it in my favor likely because it served as a retaining wall as well as a keep-intruders-out wall.

"Sorry, Holgren," I muttered, drew my knives, and wedged the blade of the first lengthwise into the highest join I could reach. I hated to think what I was doing to the edge of the blade. And I hoped to hells the knives were strong enough to take the punishment I was about to mete out to them. If the tang broke, I'd be holding a very nice hilt as I fell, feeling like an idiot. Until I hit the cobbles. Then, I'd be lucky to feel anything.

Slow and easy, I pulled myself up, careful not to shift my center of gravity. My boots were soft-soled enough that I got a little purchase in a lower join. It helped some. It helped much more that I was small and didn't weigh much.

Slowly, carefully, I reached up and wedged the next blade in sidewise. Set myself. Wiggled the first blade out. My arms were already starting to complain.

"Not bad," I heard my uncle murmur. I blocked him and everything else out. One slip of attention and I'd be coming right back down. I did *not* want to have to start over again. My whole world was balanced on two knife edges.

It went remarkably well until suddenly, it didn't.

I was more than halfway up the wall and had just wedged the left-hand blade when I heard a *crack*.

It wasn't Holgren's gift knife. It was a tile of the marble facing of the wall, the upper one where I'd wedged the right-hand blade. The torque I was forcing on the mortar that attached it to the brick wall behind it made that mortar fail.

The marble tile fell away, and all my weight suddenly hung from the left-hand knife. I had to force myself not to flail around. My left arm burned with muscle exhaustion and the sudden strain, and my hand was slick with sweat. I found a toehold on the area of now exposed brick and as quickly as I could got the right-hand knife wedged.

"Kerf's crusty beard," I whispered, suddenly drenched in sweat. I realized I'd never heard the marble tile hit the ground but didn't waste time or concentration investigating. Greytooth or Ives must have dealt with it. If the gods were kind, Ives had broken the tile's fall with his face.

The rest of the climb was torture, but uneventful torture. I rose to eye level with the balcony floor, did a quick scan, saw no one, placed one knife carefully and quietly on the floor, got an arm around a stone railing, sheathed the other, and slipped over onto the balcony, muscles burning.

I knelt down on the shadowed balcony for a few seconds, scanning the dim, candle-lit interior of the throne room. What I could see of it from my position. I saw no movement. It appeared empty. Of course, there would almost certainly be roving guards, and I had no idea what sort of rotation they'd be on. I hastily got the rope secured to the railing and dropped it over the side.

Ives came up first. He wasn't nearly quiet enough for my taste, and by the time he made it over the railing, he was panting like a bellows.

"Quiet," I hissed.

Too late.

They must have been stationed around the corner; I hadn't risked putting my head into the throne room proper. I heard them a scant second before they stepped onto the balcony, fully helmeted and wearing breastplate, gorget, greave, and vambrace. Their swords were drawn. It was a mystery to me how they moved so silently in all that metal; magic must have been involved.

They were Council guards, not Blacksleeves. They weren't down in it every day, extorting and blackmailing, bullying and, yes, murdering. But they were part of the vast machine that kept the Syndic and the Council of Three in power, and that made them guilty enough in my book. Besides, I didn't have a choice.

I rammed one knife into the eye-slit of one guard's visor to the hilt. It hit no bone, so it went into the eye and then the brain. The guard just sort of froze in place. The other raised his sword for an overhead strike. Stupid. I slammed my other knife into his now-exposed, unarmored armpit. The sword tumbled from his grasp, clanging down onto the stone floor, and he screamed.

So much for the quiet part of quick and quiet.

The first one started to jerk violently and toppled backward. I snatched my knife back, whirled back around to the second, pushed his visor up, and planted both my knives into both his eyes.

His second scream withered away.

I ran back to the railing, ignoring Ives, who was just now getting to his feet. Greytooth was still hanging onto the rope. He was almost at the top, but he looked worn out.

"Hurry up," I told him, reaching down to help him over. "We don't have much time now."

Once Greytooth had cleared the wall and the wards were laced into it, he stood up straighter, and much of the pain evident on his face vanished as he uncloaked his abilities. I felt the chill rush of magic pouring off of him once more. But it was Ives who had the next dance.

"Stand aside," he panted as more Council guards came pouring in from three separate entrances.

Ives stepped forward to meet them. I felt him call up his magic. He made short, low, chopping gestures with his hands and the leading Council guards went sprawling, as if something had tripped them. Those behind just leapt over them, swords out.

"That's all you've got?" I asked my uncle.

"No," he replied and made a circling gesture with his right hand followed by a thrust to the right.

The swords of those guards to the right of him ripped themselves out of their owners' hands and flew off to the far end of the room, tumbling and clanging and then just disappearing.

"Master Greytooth?" he said, voice strained, while he repeated the performance with his left hand and to the guards to the left.

"They're still coming," I noted.

"But now they don't have sharp things. And they'll be somewhat distracted momentarily.

"How?"

"They'll see what I want them to see. Just get Greytooth to the Stone."

We rushed forward toward the Stone, I on Greytooth's left, Ives on his right, and the Council guards met us halfway.

After that, it was pure melee, a dozen unarmed but armored Council guards against us three. Ives called up a blade made out of light, much like I'd seen Holgren do. He was muttering arcanities all the while. I had my own more mundane knives. Greytooth didn't seem to have anything in the way of a weapon and didn't seem concerned.

The Council guards were professional and brave enough, I'll give them that. Knowing they were facing a mage who had just disarmed them, they didn't hesitate. They waded in, determined, it seemed, to bring us down by force of numbers and gauntleted fists. But they were attacking each other as much as they were attacking us. I wondered briefly what Ives was making them see, but then I had no time for anything except not dying.

It wasn't the best time I'd ever had. Most of it was a blur of fists and feet, me slashing and dodging and planting a knife in any exposed, unarmored area I could find. A gauntleted fist clipped my ear; a steel-capped knee rammed itself into the small of my back. I snarled and slashed. There was no rationality, no cold planning. I just fought for my life like a wild animal.

I caught a glimpse of Greytooth paralyzing a guard much as he had done to me. Ives' knife was a radiant blur in the corner of my eye, cutting and burning. There were grunts and screams, some of them coming from me.

And then, suddenly, it was over.

We were surrounded by guards. We were standing, more or less. They weren't. They were sprawled across the marble floor, some dead, some paralyzed, some squirming and moaning. My left ear felt wet, and at the same time, it burned. I reached a hand up and discovered it had been *torn* somehow. Lovely.

"The target, Amra," said Greytooth, and I reached into a pocket, pulled out the scrap of tarp, and passed it to him. He stepped over an unmoving guard and slapped the scrap onto the Stone. Muttered something. The scrap of canvas attached itself as securely as if it had been glued in place. Then, almost as an afterthought, Greytooth heaved the Syndic's gilded throne off the top of the Stone. It clattered on the marble. I heard some part of it crack.

"That was a satisfying sight," Ives said.

"Stand aside," Greytooth said, and Ives and I moved out of the way in opposite directions.

Greytooth stood in front of the stone and called up his power. He gestured, uttering liquid syllables, and the Founder's stone rose, slowly, into the air. He walked backward, toward the balcony, somehow never missing his footing amidst the sprawled Council guards, and the Stone followed him as obediently as a pet.

He gestured again, and it rose slightly higher. He stepped under it, turned to face the Bay, put his hands on its lower surface. Stood that way for a moment.

"Hurry the hells up," I muttered. I wanted to shout it, but I didn't dare break his concentration. I was under no illusion that we'd dealt with every guard in the Riail.

Greytooth's incomprehensible words grew louder, and with what sounded very much like a command, he suddenly threw his arms forward. The Stone flew out into the night like an arrow.

I glanced over at my uncle, and he smiled at me.

"We did it," he said.

Then an arrow suddenly sprouted from his chest.

CHAPTER 23

I whirled around to face the room once more, cursing myself bitterly for being distracted watching Greytooth.

Dozens more Council guards poured into the room, some with bows, some with crossbows, at least three with arquebuses.

Greytooth cried out in pain. From the corner of my eye, I saw the quarrel sticking out of his shoulder. He staggered back. Hit the railing. Tumbled over it and down.

"Drop your knives," said one of the guards. One with gilded armor.

I looked at my uncle. He was on the floor now, shuddering and spitting up blood. And then he wasn't. His face went slack, his body still.

Gone.

"Drop the knives *now.*"

"Go to hells," I replied.

"Never mind, Captain," said a new, tired-sounding voice from behind all the men in armor. "I'll speak to her as she is. Have your men put their weapons away. Bows down." The guards parted for a heavy, bejeweled man. They did what he said. They didn't look happy about it, but they didn't argue.

The Syndic.

I threw a knife at him on general principle. It bounced off an invisible, magical shield maybe a foot from him, clattered to the floor.

"Got that out of your system, now, have you?"

"You killed my uncle."

"*I* didn't kill him. And he broke into my house. Besides that, he'd already been tried *in absentia* for treason and fomenting rebellion and sentenced to death. A much worse death than he, in fact, received."

"You knew he was Ansen."

"Indeed. Just as I know that you are Amra Thetys."

"And how do you know that?"

"What's the use of being a despot if you can't even get information when it is required? Informants abound in the City of the Mount."

"What do you want?"

"I want to know why Aither wants so badly for you to die, among other things."

"Ask one of your informants."

"Sadly, informants do *not* abound in the Citadel. Those I send generally come back to me in chunks. Aither can be crude."

"Why don't you ask him yourself then?"

"The Telemarch and I aren't on speaking terms. We find mutual feigned ignorance of each other's existence, on most days, to be mutually beneficial. Tell me why he so very badly wants you to die, Mistress Thetys, and I will let you go free."

I smiled. "Even if I believed that, I wouldn't tell you."

"Why, pray tell?"

"Because you're a leech, sucking this city dry. But mostly because you killed my uncle. If you want something, it's my new purpose in life to make sure you don't get it."

He sighed. Stuck a fat finger in his ear, wiggled it around a little. Wiped the finger on his gold-embroidered velvet vest. Charming.

"I'll try once more. Tell my why Aither so badly wants you dead, why he ordered me—*me*—to have the city turned inside out until you were found. Tell me why he fears you so."

"Why the hells should I tell you, assuming I know the answer? And please don't bother to lie about setting me free."

"Oh, it isn't a lie. If Aither fears you, you must be a real danger to him. I've been saddled with that mad bastard for nearly two decades. If there is a palpable chance that you can lay him low, I will set you on your way and wish you well. But I must know *why* he fears you. Should you fail to end him, I want avenues of approach to try on my own."

I made a decision. If the Syndic wanted to know why the Telemarch was afraid of me, I'd do more than tell him. I'd *show* him.

"I'll give you your answer," I told him, reaching down to the rift, questing for that vast, seductive power at the heart of the Mount.

It was there, and it rushed into me, warming every particle of my body but not touching the chill in my soul.

"Pay attention now," I told the Syndic. "I wouldn't want you to miss this."

I concentrated, felt the power straining to be let loose. I flicked my fingers just as I had done at the mad mage, willing the Syndic to just disintegrate. I was focusing on him alone, but I didn't particularly care if the guards behind him caught any excess. I felt the power release and strike him, unerringly.

Nothing happened.

He raised an eyebrow. "Did you think the Syndic of Bellaria went about unprotected from magic?" he asked me. "Come now."

"That's a fair point," I allowed and tried something new.

Pure, undiluted possibility at my fingertips, suffusing my body.

Uncle Ives had wanted to bring down the Syndic, the Council and the Riail. He'd given me a list of murderers and a locket with my mother's portrait.

I gave him a gift in return.

"You're protected from magic. You're also proof against knives."

"Indeed."

"What about hunger? Or thirst?"

He gave me a quizzical look.

"I like the idea of you buried under tons of rubble, slowly dying of thirst. Let's do that."

I pulled down the Riail on top of the Syndic.

CHAPTER 24

It was easy. Frighteningly easy. I wanted the building to come tumbling down, and it did.

Cracks ran up the pillars and the walls like lightning, and chunks of stone began raining down. Then, the entire ceiling began to collapse, bringing all the upper floors crashing down.

I ran for the balcony. A chunk of marble column clipped me in the shoulder. It hurt. A lot. I didn't let it slow me. Behind me, I heard screams. I hoped they were from the Syndic but didn't stop to check.

The floor began to open up as well. I ran faster. The noise was tremendous.

I made it to the rope and started down. Too late. The stone railing of the balcony shattered, and I fell. It occurred to me just as I was about to hit the cobbles that I hadn't really thought out my attack all that well.

Rather than the cobbled street, I hit something relatively soft. But I hit it hard, flat on my back. The wind was thoroughly knocked out of me. Dumbly, I was still holding onto the rope, the end of which was still tied to a chunk of the stone railing and falling rapidly right at my face. I ducked my head at the last instant, and the chunk shattered against the street, spraying me with sharp-edged chips of stone.

When the lacerations stopped, I opened my eyes.

The Riail was gone. Just gone. All that was left was clouds of dust billowing up in the night sky and the lower wall that I'd scaled. And that wasn't looking too good. In some places, it was just cracked; in others, the pressure of all the rubble had broken through the wall and spilled out down the Mount, little avalanches of the remains of the Syndic's palace.

As tombs went, it was a pretty good one for my uncle. I think he'd have appreciated it. I pushed my thoughts away from that. It wasn't hard. When you can't force your lungs to draw breath, it sort of consumes your attention.

After a while, I got my breath back. Everything was quiet. When I could think again, I began to wonder why I wasn't a broken pile on the road. I wheezed my way off of what I'd landed on.

What I'd landed on was Greytooth.

He really wasn't looking good. Unconscious, quarrel in his shoulder, one leg twisted at a gruesome angle. But he was still breathing.

I got up on shaking legs. Grabbed his wrists. Started pulling. There was no way I could support his weight, so dragging was the best he was going to get. His house wasn't that far away but far enough to make me groan just thinking about how far I was going to have to drag him.

At least it was all downhill.

I hadn't got him far when alarm bells started pealing throughout the Girdle.

~ ~ ~

I got him to his house. He never woke despite all the punishment he had gotten along the way. That probably wasn't a good sign. I didn't dare pull the quarrel or even do much in the way of setting his leg. He needed a professional. Luckily, the bone-setter who'd taken care of Keel was on the way to the Wreck. I had to make sure Greytooth had gotten the Stone where it needed to go before he'd dived off the balcony of the Riail. If he hadn't, then there was a lot of work to be done getting it there and not a lot of time.

I hoped he'd managed it. I hoped he'd survive and be able to finish the job if he hadn't managed to get the stone to the Wreck. Maybe that was cold, hoping he'd recover just so I could get the Stone to Lyta. At that point, I didn't much care considering what *I* had to do soon enough.

I also hoped Hurvus, the chirurgeon who'd taken care of Keel, was sober. I was just full of hope.

I'd rather have been full of expectation.

I left Greytooth on his ugly, expensive couch, unconscious and dripping blood. I wasn't feeling exactly spry myself, but I'd learned to deal with pain over the years. I couldn't ignore it, but I could push it into the background. When I left, I didn't bother locking up; Keel might have been able to pick the lock, but Hurvus surely wouldn't be able to.

The inn was along the way. I decided to stop off and change out of my torn, bloody clothes. I didn't need to attract attention, especially not from any curious Blacksleeves, who'd certainly be worked up by the Riail's collapse.

It turned out that I needn't have worried about that, but caution is rarely wasted.

Keel was pacing the parlor when I got back.

"Where the hells have you been all day? What the hells happened to you? What the hells happened to your *ear*?"

"It's not important. I need to change clothes and get down to Hardside." I walked into the bedroom, closed the door, stripped off my ruined, expensive new clothes.

"Amra, what's going on?" Keel asked through the door. "The whole city's going crazy."

"Probably because the Riail just collapsed," I shouted back.

He pulled the door open. "Are you shitting me?" he said, face flushed. Then, he noticed I was naked, and his face flushed some more.

"Keel, I'm about to cut parts off of you that you'll *really* miss."

"Sorry, sorry!" he said. He didn't sound sorry. But he closed the door again quickly enough.

I dressed hurriedly and, holding one of the inn's towels to my still bleeding ear, went back out to the parlor. The innkeeper would likely have a fit about his bloodstained towel. Which almost made up for having a ripped ear.

"The Riail is really gone?" he asked, bouncing around as only a youngster can do.

"The Riail is really gone."

"And the Syndic?"

"He's under the rubble somewhere. If he's still alive, then he's indestructible. But I'm pretty sure dehydration and starvation will do the trick."

"Yes!" Keel shouted. "This is Ansen's chance!"

I took a deep breath. "About Ansen. I've got some bad news for you, I'm afraid."

"What? Don't give me any more crap about him being a huckster, all right?"

"It's not that. He isn't. Wasn't. He really was a just man, if not *the* Just Man." He was also my uncle, but Keel didn't need to know that. Nobody did.

Keels face sort of scrunched up. "What do you mean, 'was?'"

"Ansen died in the Riail tonight."

Just like that, the kid's spirits went from high to low. All that boyish energy just left him. He sat down heavily in a chair and stared at the floor.

"Wait," he said. "How do you know all this? How can you be sure Ansen's dead?"

"I was there, Keel. So was Greytooth." I put a hand on his shoulder. "I've got to go. I need to get a physicker up to Greytooth. He's badly injured. Hurvus is competent. I'll need you to lead him if he's too soused though. And then I need to get down to the Wreck."

"All right."

Thunder rumbled up the Mount. Or I took it for thunder at first, but then it happened again. And again, regular as a heartbeat if a little slower. I quickly realized it was far too regular to be anything natural. *What now?*

"What the hells is *that*?" Keel said, echoing my thought.

I felt a weird slithering in my inner pocket, the one where I kept Holgren's necklace and my mother's locket. I felt a moment of panic, sure that the locket had indeed been spelled and that I was about to die some horrible, magical death. Had I been right to be suspicious of my uncle after all? I stuck my hand into the pocket and whipped out the contents, flinging them across the room.

The locket and its chain bounced across the carpet and fetched up against the door.

Holgren's necklace refused to leave my hand. It was writhing like a snake, and its bloodstone pendant shone with a deep, red light. The light pulsed like a heartbeat in time with the thunder.

"What the hells is that?" Keel asked again, looking at the pendant as it pulsed and gyrated in my hand.

"*That*, my young friend, is reinforcements."

CHAPTER 25

I ran to the balcony, Keel right on my heels, gabbling questions I didn't really hear.

Out there in the Bay, someone was making a furious effort to break through the wall of death put in place by the spirits of the murdered street rats. Brilliant, actinic light flared against the barrier, steady as a heartbeat, forceful as a battering ram and louder than thunder. I was much too far away to see any details, but I knew who it was.

Holgren was knocking, and one way or another, he *would* find a way in. Determined didn't even begin to describe Holgren when he set his mind to something.

I realized I was grinning from ear to ear.

"You're early," I whispered, "and just in time. Thank the gods."

"Huh?" Keel replied.

"Better stop ogling me when I'm naked, kid," I told him. "That's my lover down there. He's not really the jealous type, but he can turn you into a toad."

"Really?"

"No. But he *can* turn you into a red stain on the cobbles with a flick of his fingers, so behave when he gets here."

"*If* he gets here," Keel replied.

"Oh, he will, kid. He will. He always comes through. Come on."

"Where are we going?"

"To meet him."

As we left, I scooped up the locket and put it back safe in its pocket. I slipped Holgren's pendant back on over my head and tucked it in underneath my shirt. I figured he would get the message.

~ ~ ~

The streets were a madhouse.

We had to skirt two separate riots. The mobs were hurling cobbles torn from the streets at armored lines of Blacksleeves, whose naked blades shone orange in the torchlight and red with blood. I've no idea what exactly they were rioting about. I doubt they did either. There were too many excesses, to many brutalities endured over the course of too many years to point at one and say, "That's why this is happening." It was just a breakdown of order, a kind of pent-up madness that was finally being let loose. The inciting event, if there even was one, was immaterial. The Riail was a pile of rubble for all the city to see. It was enough.

The riots were easy enough to avoid. The looters were less so. They seemed to be everywhere the Blacksleeves weren't. Shutters were being torn off windows, and glass shattered everywhere, it seemed. Figures, both male and female, young and old, were scrambling in and out of shops with all manner of goods in hand. Some wore makeshift masks. Most hadn't bothered.

Keel looked scared out of his wits.

"Just don't pay them any attention, and they'll do you the same favor," I told him. But I kept my knife bared as a precaution and a warning.

Once, I saw something that definitely wasn't human cross the darkened street in front of us, climb a wall with what looked like four arms, and disappear onto the roofs above us. An overpowering smell of burned cloves and spoiled milk lingered in its wake.

The seals on the Telemarch's reservoir of power really were failing.

We made it wharfside without incident, which seemed almost a miracle. I led Keel to Aloc pier, where Holgren was trying to batter his way in. With every strike of his magic, the barrier put in place by the spirits of the murdered street rats shed coruscating sparks of whitish-green light that fell and faded before they reached the bleached boards of the pier and resounded like a gate being struck by a battering ram. From that distance, I could see him making passes with his hands. Each time his hands stilled, the barrier was struck by his magic. And then, he would begin again.

He saw me before I'd taken three steps onto the pier, but he didn't pause in his assault.

When I made it to the end of the pier, I said, "Hello, lover."

He was standing in a little dory that bobbed on the waves but otherwise didn't move from its position. There was no anchor other than his will. His face and hair were sweat-soaked despite the cold.

"Amra my dear," he said. "We need to talk about your ideas on gardening." He gestured again in that arcane fashion. Sparks flew. The barrier boomed.

"Why's that?"

"They are disturbing." Gesture, sparks, boom. "You do know that burying a head—" gesture, sparks, boom "—*won't* actually sprout a new person, don't you?"

"Ah. You found Borold."

"Was that his name?" Gesture, sparks, boom. "I'd just been thinking of him as 'the screaming head fellow.'" Gesture, sparks, boom.

"How long do you think this is going to take, Holgren?"

"Hours."

"We don't have hours," I said. I put my hand against the barrier.

I'm pretty sure you can hear me, I told the spirits. They didn't respond, but I thought I felt their attention.

The man who ordered the Purge, I don't know if you know, was the Telemarch. I'm going to go and kill him. Or at least try. I'll have a much better chance of success if you let this fellow who's knocking come in.

They had nothing to say to that.

Please let him in.

I felt them reach a decision. *He can come in,* they told me, *but he will not be allowed to leave. Do you understand?*

"I do," I whispered and hoped to hells I hadn't just gotten Holgren killed.

The barrier between Holgren and the pier sort of peeled back, and Holgren jumped up from his bobbing boat, graceful as a cat. I was hugging him before he'd even straightened up.

"You're early," I said, my arms around him and my face pressed against his coat. "I didn't expect you for a few more days." Which would have been far, far too late.

"You buried a screaming head in our back garden. The birds kept landing and then immediately flying away. Eventually, I went to investigate. Also, I got bored and a little lonely without you." He stroked my hair with those long, fine-boned fingers of his.

I squeezed him tighter then let him go.

"Well, Bellarius is anything but boring just at the moment," I said.

"So I noticed on my way in. Care to catch me up?"

"Oh, you know. The usual. Mad archmage about to destroy the city, one of the Eightfold Bitch's Blades at the center of things, mysterious and powerful beings meddling in the affairs of mortals. Total breakdown of order in the city, as you can tell."

He glanced past me, toward the Girdle, where the sound of rioting and the smoke and glare of several fires were obvious. "I see. Is there a particular reason for that anarchy, or is it just an excess of high spirits?"

"I might have had something to do with that," I admitted.

"I was afraid you were going to say that. What did you do, Amra?"

"I sort of killed the Syndic by pulling down his palace on top of him."

He rubbed his face with his hands.

"He deserved it."

"No doubt. And the friend you came here to help?"

"He's fine. He'll be trying to kill me any time now, but he's fine."

"Well then. What's next on the agenda?"

"Well, first, we need to release the human avatar of a dead goddess from her thousand-year prison, and then send a physicker to a Philosopher who's got a quarrel in his chest and a broken leg. After that, we're going to take a walk up the Mount to the Citadel and assassinate the Telemarch. Pretty full list of chores, actually. Could use a hand if you're free."

"Amra?"

"Yes?"

"How do I put this delicately? You are very much a grown woman, but I'm not sure you should be let out of the house on your own anymore."

I snorted. "Given all the things that have happened in the last few days, I'd be very content to become a shut-in. If I somehow manage to survive the night."

"Can I ask why we're about to kill the most powerful mage on the Dragonsea?"

"Sure. If we don't, the whole city will explode come morning.

"Given the state it's in right now, I'm not sure how you could tell the difference."

"Easy. Right now, there's a mountain. In the morning, there'll only be a smoking hole in the ground."

"Ah. And who's the young man standing behind you, looking rather twitchy?"

"That's Keel. He's sort of a stray I decided to keep."

"All right. But you're cleaning up after him. Anything else I should know?"

"Tons. But there just isn't time. Except for one thing. It seems I have access to magic. Sort of."

He raised an eyebrow.

"Very quick version is this: the Telemarch used the Knife that Parts the Night to cut open a hole in reality and bring magic back into the world. People who know better than me say it's unrefined magic, chaos, and pure possibility. That's what's set to blow the city apart. It also seems that I have access to the reservoir of it that the Telemarch created, maybe because of my connection to Abanon's Blade. Anyway, the Telemarch isn't keen on sharing power, which is why he's been trying to kill me. I've tapped it twice. The first time, it saved my life. The second time—the second time, I accidentally destroyed some buildings with it. And the people inside those buildings."

"She was saving my life at the time," Keel chimed in.

Holgren studied my face. If there was anyone in the world that I would talk to about how killing loads of innocent people made me feel, it would be Holgren. And maybe I would talk to him about it someday. But not then, not there, not even if we had the time, which we didn't. He seemed to intuit that.

"All right," Holgren said again after a few seconds.

We started walking down the pier. "Where to first?" Holgren asked.

"Better send help to Greytooth. He's tough, incredibly tough actually, but he looked bad when I left him. Then the Hag."

"The Hag?"

"She's the living avatar of the dead goddess I mentioned. Been trapped on a ship since around the Cataclysm."

"She's scary," Keel added.

"More than you know, actually. But we need her."

"I really need to visit the jakes," Keel said to nobody in particular.

CHAPTER 26

Hurvus was moderately sober but unwilling to leave his house. I shoved a handful of marks into his palm, described Greytooth's injuries, and told him if the patient died, I'd replicate the same injuries on him. He packed a bag and set out for Greytooth's lair, grumbling all the while. But hurrying. I sent Keel along with him, both to help if it was needed and to make sure Hurvus didn't make a detour into some tavern. I didn't think he would, but with Hurvus in possession of a pocket full of marks and a drunkard's thirst, *thinking* wasn't enough. Keel was insurance.

Also, Keel would be useless in the rest of what was to come. Worse. A distraction. Better he was out of the way.

For his part, Keel was happy not to have anything to do with the Hag. Can't say I blamed him really.

Holgren and I set out for the Wreck.

I really, really hoped Greytooth had managed to get the Stone onto Lyta's penteconter. If he'd missed, it could be anywhere. Knowing my luck, "anywhere" would probably mean in the Bay. In which case, we were all dead.

"Now that we have some privacy," said Holgren, "is there anything else you want to tell me?"

"Um. I love you?"

"I love you too. That's not what I meant."

"What did you mean?"

"Everything is coming apart at the seams here. In my experience, that doesn't just happen by chance. What are we really facing?"

"One of the Eightfold's Blades. Kalara's, the Knife that Parts the Night. It's toying with me, Holgren. I can't prove anything, but…"

"But?"

"There's something of a chance that when I destroyed Abanon's Blade, I became her avatar. There might well be a connection between that and this. I think we aren't going to make it out of this one if I'm being honest."

He was silent.

"Say something."

"I noticed you've only got one of the knives I gave you."

"I lost the other in the Riail, sorry. What's that got to do with what I just said?"

He smiled. "You really are hard on knives." He stopped walking, put his hands on my shoulders, looked me in the eyes. Smiled. "If I was Kalara's Knife, Amra Thetys, I'd be very, very worried."

It's good to have one person who believes in you. Especially when you're having a hard time believing in yourself.

"Knowing you, I brought you a replacement." He dug into a pocket of his black longcoat and came up with something that looked like a newborn arquebus.

"That's not a knife."

"I didn't say I brought you a replacement knife, just a replacement. I made it myself."

"It's not even a quarter the size of an arquebus, and an arquebus isn't much more than a toy."

"It's not an arquebus. It's a pistol. A flintlock pistol, to be precise, not that that means anything to you, I know."

"What am I supposed to do with it?"

"Well, first, keep it from getting wet, or it's no better than a club. You cock it by pulling this hammer back, then you point it at the person you want to perforate and pull this trigger. There'll be a loud bang, a cloud of evil-smelling smoke, and hopefully a fresh corpse. The closer you are, the better your odds."

"How many shots?"

"One."

"One?"

"Do we have time for me to go through reloading?"

"Not really."

"Then one shot. If I know you, it will be enough."

"If you say so, Holgren."

"I do."

I stuck it in an outer pocket after giving it one last dubious look-over. It's not that I doubted Holgren or his weapon, it was just that I was a creature of habit. I knew knives. I trusted knives.

"Thanks, I guess. Now, let's go save the city."

~ ~ ~

I explained the situation with the spirits of the dead and with Lyta and the Founder's Stone on the way. Holgren was intrigued, but he kept his comments to a single, "I wish there was time to speak to her about the world before the Cataclysm." Endlessly curious was my Holgren.

I didn't get into Lyta's belief that I was now somehow Abanon's avatar. If we survived the night, there would be time enough to pick it over and decide if she was lying. If we didn't, well, the problem would solve itself, now wouldn't it?

The Founder's Stone had indeed made it onto Lyta's galley if just barely. One corner was roughly a foot from the tarp that served as her doorway. The other end of it stuck out over the sea, resting on the low railing of the penteconter. It was in no danger of tipping out into the bay, thank Kerf. Could have been worse.

Other than the Stone, nothing seemed to have changed on the ship. With Holgren behind me, I pushed open the tarp.

Lyta was still inside the tiller's shed, still sitting in her chair.

"Lyta," I said.

"Amra," she replied. Then after a moment, she nodded to Holgren. "Magister."

He bowed briefly in return and murmured, "Doma."

I cut him a glance. "How do you know—forget it. No time." Holgren raise an eyebrow and smiled.

I turned back to Lyta. "There's your Stone."

"Indeed."

I waited a second. She didn't seem to have anything more to say.

"Did you need an invitation?"

"I need the Stone to break the plane between this room and the outside world. My prison is this room, not the entire ship."

"Kerf's lice-ridden beard! You might have mentioned that earlier!"

She shrugged. "I did not think you would succeed in removing the Stone from the Riail."

"Is this some sort of joke to you?"

"It is not." She sighed. "A millennium in durance may have made me…hesitant."

"Hesitant about *what*?"

"Freedom. Responsibility. Re-entering a world changed beyond recognition."

"Too gods-damned bad," I spat at her. Then I turned to Holgren. "Hold that damned tarp open, would you? Better yet, tear it down."

He got busy with that without a single question. I walked over to Lyta, stood behind her chair.

"What are you doing?" she asked.

Checking to make sure Holgren was out of the way, I said, "Giving you the swift kick back into reality that you apparently need." And then I did just that, lashing out sideways with one foot, sending her chair and her skittering across the short distance between her and the Stone. The two front legs of the chair pitched up against the low sill of the doorway, and she tipped forward, screaming as she broke the plane between the tiller's shed and the outside world.

She landed heavily on the Stone. She lay there, unmoving. For its part, the chair crumbled to dust. For a few seconds after that, nothing happened, nothing at all. A sudden, sickening thought occurred to me: What if leaving the tiller's shed had killed her?

Shit, shit. Hells and shit.

Then, I saw the change begin.

Spreading slowly out from wherever the Stone touched, the penteconter was changing. The stone deck and rail were transforming back into their original wood.

I glanced over at Lyta. She was not moving, but that ancient, brittle, dingy-white hair was shifting to lustrous black, the color creeping down from the roots to the tips.

"Amra," Holgren said.

"Yes?"

"I think it would be prudent to get off this ship before the transformation is complete."

"I want to make sure she follows through on her end of the bargain and takes down the barrier."

"If she chooses not to, I don't think you'll be able to force her. Not now that she's been reunited with the Stone."

"If you say so."

Careful not to touch the Stone, we crossed the plank and clambered onto the rocks. Watched the ship transform back into a vessel of wood and rope and canvas. Watched the oarsmen become flesh and blood once again, clamber up out of the flooded galley pit and cling to the rails, confused, gabbling to each other in a language that had not been spoken for hundreds of years.

When the ship was, once again, a ship, albeit a holed one, Lyta stirred, staggered to her feet.

She was a beauty. Black hair, pale skin, gray eyes. But thin, on the edge of emaciation.

She stared at me. Her face was cold. Her crew called out to her; she ignored them.

"Your turn," I shouted to her. "I held up my end of the bargain."

She nodded once, sharply, then put one hand down on the Stone and the other up in the air.

The dome of death that enclosed the city flared, greenish-white. The stars dimmed and disappeared, and a keening filled the air.

The dome fractured. The keening rose in pitch and volume. I clapped my hands over my ears. It didn't help. All at once, the dome disintegrated, reverted back into the hundreds of corpselights I had seen shoot into the sky just two nights before. They swirled in the sky, shining points being sucked down into a gyre whose eye was the palm of Lyta's hand.

They did not go willingly. But they went. Slowly at first, one by one, then in an ever-increasing stream, they rushed down, spinning faster than my eye could follow, a whirlwind blur of light.

And then suddenly, they were gone, and it was silent once more save for the beating of the surf and the slap of thousand-year-old canvas, the creak of millennium-old wood.

"Catch," Lyta called out to me and threw me something.

I caught it. It was a little, round, clear green stone no bigger than my thumbnail. It looked like glass. It wasn't.

"What do I do with this?" I asked her.

"That is entirely up to you. Partings, Doma Thetys. I will not say farewell." Then, she turned away from me and, with a gesture, repaired the rent in her ship's hull. She spoke to her crew. They began to bail. She did not look at me again. After a moment, I put the bead of souls down into the pocket that held the locket with my mother's portrait and the Sparrow God's leaf.

"I think we've been dismissed," Holgren said.

"Suits me," I replied.

"She called you Doma."

"So?"

"Do you know what Doma means?"

"Yeah. Similar to mistress. So what?"

"It's not similar to mistress. It doesn't translate all that well into Lucernan, but basically she just called you a Power."

"Not sure what that means, and just at the moment, I don't care. I'm glad to part ways with her. I didn't really enjoy her company." But I liked the next person we were calling on much less.

CHAPTER 27

When we entered South Gate, Holgren staggered and went to one knee. Vomited.

"Holgren," I shouted, convinced the Telemarch was attacking again. But Holgren put up a hand.

"This place," he said, getting to his feet. "It's very, very wrong."

"It must be the rift," I said. "It's breaking down its containment faster now."

"Worse," he replied. "It's poisoning my well."

"What do you mean?"

"I mean my own power is being affected by what's happening, and not in a good way. I think it's best if I don't cast any magic until I absolutely have to."

"All right. No worries," I said, but what I meant was, "Oh, hells." If Holgren couldn't count on using his own power, our chances of surviving the night had just gone from extremely unlikely to "Ha. Ha-ha-ha. Ha."

Well. I had never really expected to survive my appointment with the Telemarch anyway. But I'd been more or less resigned to that when it had just been me going down. Now, it was Holgren as well, and I couldn't stand the idea. But I knew better than to tell him to leave me. He wouldn't any more than I would leave him.

"Let's continue on, shall we?" he asked, starting to walk up Southgate Street, which had still not been repaired.

"The barrier is down now," I said as we walked. "We could just collect Keel, and Greytooth and Hurvus I suppose, and leave." And leave a little girl with my mother's name alone and imprisoned in the Citadel until it exploded.

"We could," he replied, "but I know how you hate to leave things half-finished. Makes you twitchy and grumpy. Impossible to be around, actually."

"Really?"

"Really."

"I did not know that. Is that why you spend so much time at your madhouse, I mean warehouse? To get away from me?"

"Absolutely."

"Considering your delicate health at the moment, I'm not going to punch you in the stomach the way I want to."

"You are the very soul of compassion, Amra Thetys. Has anyone ever told you that?"

"I just don't want to get any vomit on my boots. They cost me dear."

In such a fashion, we walked through the Girdle and into the territory of the gentry, skirting riots and whole blocks of burning buildings. Dawn, and the city's destruction, were about three hours away.

~ ~ ~

"Hello, Amra."

He was good. One moment we were walking up a deserted street, and the next, Theiner was just there, leaning against the granite wall of the next Gentry house up from us. I stopped. Holgren looked at me.

"Theiner," I said, both in greeting to Theiner and by way of introduction to Holgren. Two birds and all that.

"Time's up, Amra." The rest of Theiner's crew appeared out of the shadows, about twenty of them, blocking every exit. He had a surprisingly large crew. Which meant he was doing very well.

"You couldn't wait three more hours?"

"I'm afraid not. Moron Fisher over there called it to a vote as was his moron right." He pointed a thumb at an oily, fat-faced crewman, who in turn crossed his arms and gave his best stubborn look. I noticed the rest of the crew gave the guy a wide berth. The majority might have voted with him, but they weren't fond of him, looked like.

Theiner sighed. "Now, you either hand over the kid or we get to get physical."

I patted my pockets, shrugged. "I don't happen to have Keel on me just at the moment."

"Yeah. He's at the mage's house. I know."

"So why bother talking to me about it? You know where he is; why not just go and fetch him?"

"Because Keel isn't really the problem anymore, now is he? When I said, 'Hand over the kid,' I meant it more in a metaphorical sense. As in, stop fucking about in my crew's business, and let me deal with my crewman's transgressions."

"No."

He peeled himself off the wall and stretched his neck. "All right then, old friend, let's get down to business." He pulled out two slim blades and went into the *aquila* position, the guard stance he himself had taught me so many years ago, feet sidewise, one knife high and circling above his head, the other out and ready to engage.

I felt the chill of active magics on my neck.

"I'll burn you all down where you stand," Holgren declared, but his face was ghastly pale, and he was shaking. I put a hand on his shoulder.

"No, Holgren. This I have to deal with in my own way. It has to be like this. I owe him."

"You owe him your life?"

"Yes."

He looked grim as death. Finally, he let go of his magic, slumped a little. "If he kills you, I *will* kill him, Amra."

"I expect nothing less," I told him and gave him a kiss. Then, I pulled out my own knife and went to duel my oldest living friend.

With only one knife, I took a crouching, head-on stance, the blade's cutting edge facing him and parallel to the ground.

"Where's your other knife, Amra?"

"Lost it in the Riail earlier."

"Why didn't you say so?" He cast his upper knife, and it stuck in the oaken gate of the house to my right, passing dangerously close to Moron Fishhead along the way. For his part, Moron flinched then blushed. Then looked furious.

Theiner changed his stance to mirror my own. He had the reach of me, and he was stronger than me. The first counted for a lot and the second not much in a knife duel. But what counted most of all was quickness.

I didn't know if I was quicker than he was. But I thought it likely.

"Are you sure you want this dance?" I asked him.

"I'm sure I don't. But here we are." And he lashed out viper-quick at my abdomen. I felt the tip of his knife rip the fabric of my waistcoat as I sprang back. He pressed me immediately, all one continuous, sinuous motion. The knife dove toward my abdomen again, a third time, which turned out to be a feint, flying up toward my throat. I twisted my head out of the way struck his forearm with my own, knocking his knife arm off the line of attack and opening up his side. He spun away before I could make the thrust. Before I could make myself make the thrust.

I couldn't do it, I realized. Even if I was faster, even if I got the opportunity, I could not take Theiner's life. Even with all the doom rumbling down on us, I couldn't make myself climb over Theiner's body to try and save the city.

I owed him.

"Maybe you really are getting old," he said. "You used to be quicker."

"I never had to stick anybody I called a friend back then."

"You do what you have to do, Amra. You let emotions get in the way, you hesitate, you're dead. I taught you that a long time ago. Did you forget?"

"No. I just don't agree with that bit of wisdom anymore."

"Then you're going to lose this fight."

"No way I can win it, no matter who bleeds," I said, lowering my blade.

He'd been impassive the entire time; now, he looked angry. "Get your knife up, Amra."

"You'd kill me just because somebody named Moron Fishhead didn't like your leadership style? Really?"

"My name's *Maron*," seethed the bulgy-eyed, blubbery-lipped crewman, "an' it ain't Fishhead!"

"Raise your blade, Amra. I'm not going to say it again."

"How about this? Banishment for Keel. He never comes back to Bellarius. I'll see to it. And I'll make reparations to the crew for the inconvenience he and I have caused." I deliberately turned my back on Theiner and looked over the crew surrounding us.

"Well? How about it, gentlemen? Is that fair enough? If Theiner kills me, which he almost certainly will, you get nothing except dead by dawn at the latest, and probably much sooner when my partner here does ugly, unfixable things to your bodies with his magic. If you accept my proposal, on the other hand, you get rid of a troublemaker, and coin in the bargain."

They were an ugly, hard, not-very-nice lot, but they were not, on the whole, stupid. Well, except for Moron.

"We had a vote already," he said.

"You can have another. Everyone who wants to listen to Moron over there, get your hands up."

There were no takers. Except for Moron.

"Everybody who wants to make some coin, keep Moc Mien as your crew leader, and see the backside of that insufferable twit Keel for the last time, say, 'Aye.'"

There were a few responses, but most of them were waiting to see how Theiner would react.

"Take Fishhead along with you, and you've got my vote," said one fellow with a wine stain birthmark across half his face. That got more than one grunt of agreement and a murderous look from Fisher. He'd just got two unflattering nicknames in one night, and they were the kind that stuck. I worried briefly that I'd pushed him too far but then dismissed it. He had to be torn down so that the crew would be more likely to vote for Keel's banishment. Nobody wants to be associated with an idiot.

I turned back to Theiner. Pulled out my purse. Held it out to him.

"Looks a bit small," he said, still holding his knife. "You sure that will split a dozen ways?"

"There are some choice gems in there; don't worry."

He put his knife away and picked the purse up off my palm. He leaned in close.

"You always were quicker than me," he whispered in my ear.

"Was, am, always will be," I murmured and took a step back.

I heard the rush of feet behind me, saw the alarm in Theiner's eyes. Spun sideways just as Fisher came upon me, a knife already plunging down at my face.

And then Holgren made him explode. When Fisher reached me, it was as bloody mist and gobbets of flesh. His knife flashed by my ear and clattered harmlessly on the cobbles. The rest of him splattered against me and Theiner.

"Thanks, I guess," I said to Holgren while wiping blood out of my eyes.

"Don't mention it," he replied, but his face was frighteningly pale, and he was trembling. I was afraid he was going to collapse.

"He doesn't look so good," Theiner said to me, ignoring his own fresh coat of blood.

"He'll be fine. Goodbye, Moc Mien. Fare well."

"You really going to try and off the Telemarch?"

"Not much choice."

"Then I wish you all the luck."

"Care to tag along?"

I'll give him this much, he actually looked like he wanted to. Or at least was considering it. But he shook his head.

"My authority has been tested enough for one night. If I asked them to storm the Citadel, they'd laugh me down to the Bay. And if I leave them alone and go with you, they're like as not to change their minds and go and stick Keel for the sport of it."

He stuck out a hand, and I shook it. The way he looked at me was the way you might look at a friend about to be executed. False bravado masking sadness and a little relief that it wasn't you mounting the block.

CHAPTER 28

I had to support Holgren for a portion of the way, but by the time we were standing in front of the Citadel, he was doing it by himself.

"Greytooth thinks I can just walk into the Citadel unmolested because the Knife wants me," I said to him.

"I suppose we're about to find out if he's correct," Holgren replied.

"Me. Not you, lover."

"So I am supposed to just wait for you here while you run your errands inside? Come now."

"Can you do anything more, magic-wise, without fetching up your dinner?"

"Only one way to find out," he said, smiling, but his face was pale as whey, and he was covered in a cold sweat. I couldn't make him stay, though, as much as I wanted to. And I needed any edge I could possibly get. Holgren, even virtually incapacitated, counted.

"On your head then," I said, and pushed on the massive, iron-banded, oaken door. It swung open without even an ominous creak.

We went inside. Nothing struck us down. It was a good start.

The interior was gloomy with only the dim light of the overcast night stealing in through barred windows. But the layout wasn't all that complicated. The first floor was one big room, empty except for a set of stairs smack in the middle of it. We entered and began to climb.

The second floor was exactly the same except for a few dusty, empty crates and a painting on an easel covered by a dingy cloth. I elected not to uncover it.

The third floor was also the second-to-last by my estimation. It looked like a library. Dust covered everything, even with several large, shutterless windows to circulate the air. I knew Holgren was out of sorts when he didn't give the titles on the shelves even a cursory inspection.

There was one more staircase in a corner.

"Ready?" I asked him.

He raised a hand, waggled it in a so-so gesture.

"Guess that'll have to do."

I started up the stair, knife out, Holgren behind me.

I saw Cherise as soon as my head was above the level of the floor. She was sitting in a corner, knees to her chest, eyes closed. She was obviously frightened out of her wits, but I didn't see anything that was immediately doing the frightening.

"Cherise," I whispered.

She opened her eyes, saw me.

"Don't come in here," she whispered back, raggedly.

I took a look around the room again. Nothing except an ugly, tasteless, wooden door shaped like a giant skull.

"I'm going to have to if we're going to rescue you, now aren't I? What's the problem?"

She shook her head. Her eyes were huge. "It will get you," she whispered in a tiny, almost inaudible voice.

"There's nothing here right now," I said and climbed the rest of the stairs.

Come calling at last, said the voice in my head that I was sure, by this point, was Chuckles. I ignored it.

I walked over to Cherise and put out a hand. "Come on then. Your tree friend is very worried about you."

Slowly, eyes darting everywhere, she raised her hand toward mine as Holgren came up behind me.

As soon as he left the stairs, it attacked.

It coalesced out of thin air in the center of the room: huge, nasty, ugly. Its thin, long face was not human, nor were the mismatched eyes and gaping mouth, the hair like long, black wires, the skin the color of a rotting corpse. It was eight feet tall or more. Impossible to tell what sex it was. If it even had a sex.

"*Told you to NOT TO MOVE!*" it shrieked at the girl and raised a ragged-taloned hand to strike her.

I thrust my dagger through its throat. The dagger went through it, as did my arm. As if the thing wasn't really there at all. Or as if *I* didn't exist as far as it was concerned.

It slapped the girl, leaving bloody lines across her cheek.

I thrust again. Got the same results.

I felt Holgren call up his magic. Turned, saw him scream and collapse to his knees, the palms of his hands against the floor, arms shaking. He vomited up a thin, bloody bile. I felt him let go of his magic. He kept hacking, retching, and heaving.

"*Another one? Get in the corner!*" the thing shrieked at Holgren then threw him next to Cherise. He hit the wall hard. Cherise screamed.

"*Be quiet!*" it screamed in her face, and she covered her mouth with her hands. The thing slapped her again anyway. Dazed, Holgren reached out and pulled Cherise to his chest, covering the girl with his own body.

"*Both you stay there! Both you don't move! Both you be QUIET!*" The thing started raging around the room, tearing at its own hair, pulling it out in chunks. What fell to the floor disappeared like smoke.

"What the hells are you, and how do I end you?" I said out loud.

It is the greater portion of the Telemarch's insanity, Chuckles said to me. *As for ending it, you could try summoning the power of the rift.*

Chuckles was right. I could have. But I might well have ended up killing Holgren and Cherise. I just didn't have the control I needed to risk it. Standing above a sea of power that was mine to summon with a thought, I was helpless. The knowledge made me sick with impotent rage.

It boiled inside me, the rage I kept locked up, afraid of letting it loose and destroying the world. Afraid of becoming my father, destroying whatever was within reach because the true target of my anger was unreachable, unknowable, impossible to admit. It was another kind of sea, just as powerful in its own way as all that chaos down in the rift. Just as dangerous.

So I had locked it up long ago, that rage, and buried it deep. Most days nowadays, I forgot it was even there. But I never pretended it had gone away.

It would never go away.

Every second I spent in Bellarius rattled the chains I'd wound around it, chains that were very close to snapping. And with the near-limitless power buried beneath my feet, waiting for me to tap it—damn near *begging* me to tap it—

I took a shuddering breath and took a mental step back from the precipice.

"That's what you want," I told it. "And if you want it, then by Kerf's crooked staff, you won't get it from me, Chuckles."

Then this portion of the Telemarch will torture your friends until they expire or, in approximately two hours, Bellarius ceases to be, replied the Knife.

"I'll make you a deal. Let them go, and I'll do what you want."

I do not control it. Nor, at this point, does Aither. It will certainly not let them leave. If they are quiet and still, it won't molest them overmuch. Ultimately, there is only one route to salvation, and it lies in wresting from Aither the power contained in the rift. It will wither, albeit slowly, without that connection. Up to you. I *will continue, come what may.*

"You know me very well, don't you?"

Intimately. Though I confess I do not know why you insist on calling me Chuckles.

"You know what I'm likely to do before I do it, sometimes before I decide to do it. You know what I will resist doing and what sort of pressure to apply to make me do it anyway."

I am a very intelligent Knife.

But you're not a mind reader, I thought. *Not really. And that gives me a chance.*

Its silence gave me all the answer I was likely to get.

"Well then, Chuckles, I guess we'll do it your way," I lied. "Holgren, Cherise, just hang on. Don't move; don't talk. I'll be right back."

I put my last knife in Holgren's hand and pushed open the door.

~ ~ ~

The Telemarch's audience chamber, or throne room, or whatever you wanted to call it, was dismal. Almost as depressing as the cell I'd inhabited at Havelock prison. The floor wasn't strewn with feces, but it *was* a windowless stone cell, dank with mold and filled with stale air and not much else. It was a sight bigger than my cell, and the Telemarch had a big, ugly slab of a stone chair where I'd had nothing, but at the end of the day, the greatest mage on the Dragonsea lived like a prisoner. Which, I suppose, was exactly what he was. His jailer floated over his head, point down, providing the only light in the room. I walked toward him slowly.

"They named me the Telemarch. Do you know why? Do you know what it means?" He sounded old and colorless and very tired.

He was sitting on the big, ugly stone chair. It was throne-like but only because of its size. Everything else about it was distinctly un-grand; it was very big and brutally ugly. He almost looked like a child sitting in an adult's chair. His robe was ragged, his short, white hair ragged, his face very pale, very wrinkled. Cataracts blighted both eyes.

"Enlighten me, why don't you." If he wanted to gabble, I was fine with that. It would afford me the chance to get close to him before things became deadly.

"It means I am unsurpassed at measuring things from afar."

"That's distinctly underwhelming, if you don't mind me being honest."

He shrugged. "You underestimate such a power. Most do because they misapprehend what it is I can measure."

"All right, I'll bite. What can you measure?"

"Anything. Anything at all."

"Would you like me to clap?"

"For example, do you know what your soul is like, Amra Thetys? Would you like me to measure it for you?"

"Not really, no. But I'm guessing you're going to anyway."

"Please understand that some measurements are of the metaphysical sort. Let me have a look at you then."

"I don't see how you can have a look at anything, honestly, with those cataracts."

"At the top, a layer of detritus and thorns. Below that, a fertile layer of soil, surprisingly fecund and surprisingly thin.

"Below *that*, broken glass: jagged, sharp, and blood spattered. That layer goes down deep, yes it does.

"Below that, oh, below that, you have horrors chained up, the likes of which I have rarely seen. I am more than a little surprised that their howls haven't yet driven you mad."

"I learned how to make them behave a long time ago."

"Really? That is something I would like to know more of."

"Sure. If they get too loud, they don't get any dessert." I was two arms-lengths away from him now. Close enough.

"I am unsurpassed at measuring things from afar, not only in space but also in time."

"Oh Kerf, I thought you were done."

"I saw a danger to me amongst the street children sixteen years ago. But even I could not tell, at such a temporal distance, who among you would eventually present a mortal threat."

"So you ordered the Purge."

"I did."

"How'd that work out?"

"It remains to be seen."

"I'll give you a clue. If it hadn't been for you instigating the Purge, I wouldn't be here right now, ready to burn you down to grease and ashes. You provided me the motivation to do what you wanted to prevent by having hundreds of children murdered. Congratulations."

"Yes, well. Ready and able are two separate things. You will never wrest control of the Rift from me. You will try, and you will die." He shifted on his stone throne, looking small, withered, and wretched. The Knife turned slowly above his head, silent now, its slowly pulsing light the only illumination in that barren room.

Outside, I heard two muffled screams. The first must have been the creature's. The second was definitely Holgren's. Enough wasting time.

"Right then," I said. "Let's get down to it, shall we?"

"As you wish.

I felt him summoning up the power in the rift. It was an incredible amount; more than I could ever dream of calling or controlling. Where Holgren's magic was a chill on the nape of my neck and Greytooth's had sent chills down my spine, Aither's summoning of power actually sent shudders through my body. I was glad I'd gotten as close to him as I had.

I pulled out Holgren's flintlock pistol, pulled back the hammer, and shot him in one of his milky eyes.

His head whipped backward and cracked against the stone back of his throne. Powder burns stippled and blackened his face. He slid slowly downward, body limp, leaving a red smear on the chair's backrest. The power he'd summoned dissipated. The Knife fell from the air and lodged itself in his unmoving chest. Smoke from the pistol's discharge slowly spread out across the room.

Well. That was unexpected.

"I bet it was."

You do not believe in the efficacy of firearms.

"But I do believe in the efficacy of Holgren-fucking-Angrado. Implicitly. And nothing magical was even going to scratch the Telemarch, now was it?"

Pick me up, Amra.

"Why the hells would I do that?"

If you do not, then the rift will collapse, and Bellarius will die. The Telemarch could not contain the power in the rift, not indefinitely. You, who are definitely not the Telemarch, will be annihilated if you try.

"You're absolutely right, Chuckles. Good thing I'm not going to try and contain it then, now isn't it?"

What do you intend to try instead?

"Oh, wouldn't you like to know."

Whatever it is, it will fail. Anything you might have thought of, I thought of first. I know *you, Amra. In a very real sense, I* created *you.*

"Oh, really?"

Yes. Did you think Aither decided to instigate the Purge all on his own?

"Are you saying you gave him the idea?"

Yes. Not that he was aware of my influence.

"Now why would you go and do a thing like that?"

To create the conditions that would, in turn, create someone exactly like you.

"I suppose you also started the wars between Helstrum and Elam, then, to flood the streets of Bellarius with raw materials, so to speak."

Yes.

"Really? I was being sarcastic."

Really. I was being factual.

"And the spirits of the dead street rats? Did you call them up as well?"

They were already here but impotent. Leakage from the rift gave them power. I gave them…direction. I couldn't have you running off, as sensible as that might have been.

"So you caused hundreds of children to be murdered, and then you used their shades to further your own plans."

Waste not, want not.

"You are without a doubt the worst person I've ever met, and you're not even a person."

I am as I was created to be. Just as you are.

"And just what was I created to be?"

The ultimate survivor.

I smiled. I knew then that my plan was going to work. Too bad I wouldn't be around to gloat about it.

"You know, I should have died fifteen years ago," I told the Knife. "In a way, every day since I stowed away on that ship has been something of a gift. Unearned. I always wondered why Bellarius was so consistently cruel to us street rats. I've been to many places since I left and seen cruelty in a lot of different colors but nothing so consistent as what this city dished out to the street kids. It made me hate Bellarius, truly hate it. I just couldn't understand it. It didn't make any sense. Until now."

Indeed. I suppressed every natural impulse towards pity or compassion when it came to the street children. It was imperative that they, that you, *learn to rely solely on your own abilities.*

"Why?"

I am the perfect tool. I require a hand perfected to wield me.

"You're lying. By omission if nothing else."

Perhaps. It doesn't matter. Either you pick me up or you and the city are destroyed, and I start again. I do not know impatience.

"I thought you'd say something like that. Thank you. It makes it even easier to do what I need to."

Explain your meaning, Amra.

"Nah. You'll see soon enough."

If you do not pick me up, I will make sure the girl outside this room, the one who bears your mother's name, will die alongside your lover.

"Not really sure how you can manage that, but best not to take any chances," I replied, and pulled out the leaf that the God of Sparrows had given me. Let it fall to the floor.

There was a massive ripping sound, as if the very air had been torn, and the God appeared. Not as a tree, thank Kerf, but as I'd seen him when I'd talked to him, massive and muscled and fierce.

He sent me a picture of Cherise.

"She's right outside the door. So is my friend. His name is Holgren. I would very much appreciate it if you could destroy the thing that's tormenting them and take both of them out of this wretched place if you can, quickly. I've got to deal with the rift and the Knife."

He nodded, put a hand on my shoulder. Squeezed until my bones ached. He looked sad.

"You're not going to survive this, are you?"

He shrugged, showed me a picture of his tree. Leaves were shriveling and blowing away by the hundreds.

"Better hurry then."

He showed me another picture of the city. Buildings were melting like candles. People were just dropping dead in the street for no reason that I could see. A river of blood had suddenly appeared and was washing everything away on the Street of Owls. The message was plain enough. The containments on the rift were failing spectacularly.

"Guess I'd better hurry too."

He gave me another brutal squeeze. Then, he walked out of that dismal chamber to take care of the person that meant the most to him and the person that meant the most to me.

I was satisfied. It was time.

I'd always known, somewhere deep down, underneath all the broken glass that Aither had talked about, that this city would end me. But I'd never imagined I could take the architect of all my sorrow along on the way out.

I reached out for the power, the possibility in the rift, and it answered me as eagerly as it always had.

Whatever you are going to attempt, it will fail, the Knife told me. *The only way to save yourself and the city is to pick me up.*

I was full of power now. My skin itched with it. I felt like a wineskin filled to the point of bursting.

What was possible? Anything. Anything within the bounds of my own limitations in calling the power. Anything within the limitations of my own will and imagination. That's what magic was, Holgren had told me a long time ago. The intersection of the mage's will and power. You had to believe utterly in the change you forced on reality, and you had to have the raw power to make the change stick.

Summoning up every shred of will and concentration I possessed, I took myself, the Knife, and the rift out of existence.

The magic that I'd pulled from the rift left me. Nothing else, as far as I could tell, had changed. I could still feel the rift somewhere below me, immense, immeasurable. The Knife was still stuck in the Telemarch's corpse. The room I stood in had changed not a whit.

What have you done, Amra?

"Good question." I walked over to the door that led to the antechamber. Opened it.

There was no antechamber, no creature, no Holgren, no Cherise. There was nothing.

Literally nothing. A void, blacker than black, except for a cloud of roiling, golden light far below.

I assumed that was the rift.

"Kerf's hairy balls," I said.

Well. I suppose it's a good thing I do not feel impatience or boredom.

"Oh yeah? Why's that?" But I wasn't really paying much attention. I was staring out into the void.

You have torn us out of time and space. Welcome to eternity.

"I'm stuck with you for eternity? Fantastic. I was sure we'd just cease to exist, damn it."

We did as far as the rest of reality is concerned. I can of course bring us back. If you pick me up.

"I'd rather bite off my own tongue and choke to death on it."

The Knife had nothing to say to that.

I knew I meant it at that moment. I'd literally rather die than return to reality with that thing in my hand. But what about a few days from now? If time and its consequences still applied in the place I'd brought us to, I'd be mighty hungry and dying of thirst. I'd be desperate.

Best not to take a chance.

I dug out a gold mark, flicked it out the door and into the blackness beyond. Watched it spin away from me, light from the rift below reflecting off its surface until it went further than my eye could see.

Amra. Do not do something that cannot be undone. Think again.

"But that's the whole point," I said as I walked over to the Telemarch's corpse. "Doing something that can't be undone so I don't have the chance to change my mind." I grabbed Aither by a grimy ankle and pulled him off the throne, taking care that I wouldn't come into accidental contact with the Knife.

I created you to survive. You will not survive without me.

"That's ultimately where you made your mistake," I said, dragging the corpse, and the Knife lodged in its chest, to the door. "I *am* a survivor. If I pick you up, there won't be an *I* anymore. *I* wouldn't survive *you*. So you've got to go."

Let us come to an accommodation then.

"An accommodation? With you?" An image flashed through my mind. Bones stuffed under a rotting desk. "Never."

I got the corpse to the edge of the door and dropped the ankles. Stepped over it so that I could push it out.

The Knife pulsed a sudden, blinding flash of blue-white light and burned itself to ash in an instant. Aither's corpse opened its eyes, one still a bloody, gaping hole but the other now glowing with the same blue-white fire as the Knife. His skeletal hands shot up, grabbed me by the waistcoat, and pulled me down with an iron grip. I punched him as I went down, but it made no difference. He was already dead, and the Knife didn't care about any damage done to the corpse.

He shifted his grip with lightning speed, putting one hand on the back of my neck and pulling my head down to his. I fought it with everything I had, planting my palms on the floor on either side of his head and bracing my arms, but I was overmatched. I could hear the withered muscles in his arm tearing. My mouth was open, my teeth gritted with the strain. Our faces were inches away from each other. A bead of sweat dropped from my forehead and fell into the ruin I'd made of his right eye.

He exhaled sharply, and the blue-white fire blinked out in his eye, exited his withered lips, and flew into my open mouth. Suddenly, his corpse was just a corpse again, and released from the struggle, I fell backward onto the stone floor, choking and gagging on the Knife's essence.

I lost consciousness.

I didn't wake for a long, long time.

HOLGREN

My name is Holgren Angrado. I am a mage and the son of a mage and a bloodwitch. I am a thief, an inventor, and a scholar. I sold my soul to a demon, once, when I was young and foolish, in order to gain the power necessary slay the master I was apprenticed to. He deserved it.

Eventually, I died and went to one of the eleven hells. The third, if you must know. I can't say more about it other than the fact that it was very, very cold, vast, and strangely empty.

Amra Thetys brought me back from death and damnation.

I gave up my magic for the most part after I was forced to use it on her. I didn't miss it. Magic is a fading force in any case.

Except wherever Amra goes. Then, magic seems to fall like rain on parched earth. A deadly rain, granted, but nonetheless.

Now, she is gone.

She isn't dead; I would know if that were the case. Magic still has its uses, and when it comes to Amra's well-being, I take a very serious interest. That is what happens, I've discovered, when you love someone.

She isn't dead. But she is gone. She entered the skull-shaped door to the Telemarch's inner sanctum. I crouched in a corner and endured blows of magic and madness, poisoned by my own well, shielding the silently crying child, and watched her go, powerless to help her.

When it got close enough, I took Amra's knife and stabbed the creature in the heart. I did not really expect to affect it, given the immaterial nature it had shown to Amra, but the knife lodged itself satisfyingly between the thing's ribs. I smiled.

It screamed and took out my left eye with its ragged nails. Then, it beat me into unconsciousness.

Time passed. I slipped in and out of consciousness. I heard the muffled discharge of a pistol. More time passed.

When the door opened again, I expected Amra to emerge, but instead, a being of considerable power came and ripped the child and me free of the Telemarch's trap. He grappled our insane torturer, enduring blows that would have killed anyone mortal, and eventually got it in a headlock.

Then, he ripped the thing's head free of its body and howled.

Then, he sat down and stroked the girl's hair until he died. His corpse blew away in a sudden gust from a window, transformed somehow into a pile of dry, brown leaves. The girl cried harder, no longer silent now, not at all.

I tried to force the door. Impossible. Desperate, I summoned power from my well, though the last time I'd tried it, I'd almost died.

My well was no longer tainted, but my magic was not enough to force the door—not quickly. The wards on the Telemarch's sanctum were puissant.

The boy, Keel, and the Philosopher that had been assisting Amra arrived not long after we were freed. I told the boy to take the girl home and went back to battering down the wards that sealed the door. The Philosopher, Greytooth, gravely injured himself, threw his weight into the effort as well. We didn't speak.

At some point, the boy came back with the physicker. Greytooth and the boy held me down while the man inspected my eye socket. He shook his head, packed it lightly, and wrapped it up.

I went back to work on the door. After a moment, Greytooth rejoined me.

It took hours to force the door. Keel watched silently. When we finally did it, there was nothing behind it but empty air and the reeking residue of massive magics. No Amra, no Telemarch, no Knife.

"The rift disappeared hours ago as well," Greytooth said. It was the first thing he'd said since we'd met.

Amra was gone. Is gone. But she isn't dead.

I am going to find her, wherever she is, and bring her back.

May all the dead gods take pity on anything that stands in my way, for I will not.

Amra's World

or

A Very Brief Guide To The Known World, Inhabited By Countless Multitudes, Among Them Being One Particular Thief Known As Amra Thetys

by

Lhiewyn,

Sage of Lucernis, High Priest of Lagna the God of Knowledge (Deceased), Very Old Man

(Translated and edited by Michael McClung)

DEDICATIONS

Lhiewyn:

For Jessep, because everyone else I know well enough is dead. And stop "meditating" in the stacks, boy. I know what you're doing, and it will make you go blind.

Michael:

For all the readers over the years who have discovered Amra's world and come to love it as I do. Thank you.

THE WORLD: AN INCREDIBLY BRIEF OVERVIEW

The world is a big place. Really, really big. As far as we can tell, it is spherical, and it circles the sun, which is likely a big ball of fire hanging in the void. No, I don't know what it's hanging from. Don't be cheeky.

The stars are likely other balls of fire, either much smaller or much further away. Most are fixed, some move. Nobody knows why, and if anybody says they do they're lying. Oh, and astrologers, like children, should be beaten often on general principles.

There, wasn't that easy? You're welcome.

Oh, all right. So there's more to the world. The gods alone know why you'd want to know; probably to set out on some idiotic adventure far from home. I feel obliged to tell you that adventures are, on the whole, stunningly bad ideas, best avoided at all costs. Having spent thirty years wandering the world, I should know. I didn't get this useless leg from staying home and milking cows. Though, to be fair, cows can be bastards as well.

I'll tell you what I know. I very much doubt it will do you any good, but at least you won't be able to say I didn't warn you.

THE KNOWN WORLD: A SLIGHTLY LESS-BRIEF OVERVIEW & HISTORY

Virtually everyone who isn't a liar or a drunkard agrees the world boasts two large landmasses, or continents. There is some credible speculation that a third continent exists on the far side of the world, but no real proof. Those who have gone looking for it haven't come back. Now they certainly might have found some veritable paradise where they were treated like kings and queens, and sensibly gave up any interest in returning and letting the rest of plodding humanity know about it. Let's just say I'm not inclined to believe this is the case.

Of the two continents we are certain of, the northern one is home to virtually all of humanity, and stretches for thousands of leagues from east to west. Elamners call it "Sulamel" which means Landfall. No other culture calls it anything in particular as people are, by and large, ignorant twits.

The southern continent (named "Lubania" by the intrepid and very dead explorer Rafe Luban but universally known as "Deathland" to everyone else) is roughly half the size of Sulamel, and is longer than it is wide. Those who have explored some small portion of it and returned (yours truly) report that it is a barren place of rock and sand and ruined cities, hot as all the hells combined, and full to the brim with interestingly horrid ways to die. If you take only one piece of advice from this old scribe, let it be this: Don't go there. Just don't.

If you do go, please have this tombstone made up beforehand:

I Went To Deathland Even Though
Lhiewyn Of Lucernis Told Me Not To
And Now I'm Dead, Because I'm Stupid

And no, I'm not going to publish my maps and notes from that expedition, because I don't believe in encouraging stupidity. So stop asking.

Right then. As for Sulamel, read on. Anyplace that is especially deadly, I'll (thoughtfully) indicate by writing in big, bold letters: "**Stay the Hells Away**." You're welcome.

But first, a bit of history.

I can hear you whining from here. "History is useless. History is boring. Tell me about the exciting and exotic lands," you're saying. Stop it. You're saying this because you're an idiot. History is important and you don't need all that much of it to keep you healthy. Those who do not learn from it are doomed to repeat it, and even worse, the rest of us will probably suffer the consequences. So pay attention.

Prehistory

Nobody knows where humans come from. The furthest back we can trace our mutton-headed race is about five thousand years ago. We probably came from the southern continent after we mucked it up good and proper. After all, somebody lived in those shattered cities, and unless you count grohl, we're the only animal that makes human-sized dwellings.

The Age of Legend

It's said that, thousands of years ago, the gods walked the World and interacted with humans on a daily basis. It was, according to some accounts, a golden age of peace, an idyllic epoch. This is bullshit. The gods warred against each other and used humans as their pawns. They killed us and each other in many interesting and horrid ways. I'm the high priest of a dead god. He didn't cut himself shaving.

This went on for an unknown but very long time. War after war, Gods killing gods, demons killing gods, gods killing demons, demons killing demons and everybody killing humans until, very roughly, some twelve hundred years ago. The final War of the Gods was fought to a standstill. Those divine and infernal beings still alive agreed to an armistice and signed an accord. They marked out their metaphysical territories, so to speak, and all the powers more or less stuck to tending to their knitting after that.

For two centuries, near enough, humanity had a bit of breathing room. Civilization, highly advanced in some areas and unheard of in others, took off like a cur with its tail on fire. Huge leaps were made in every area of human endeavor, from the magical Art to the mundane sciences. Some of it was due to the fact that cities weren't in danger of being leveled as collateral damage in one divine skirmish or another. Some more of it was due to the fact that those gods whose aspects aligned with human endeavor began to do their jobs consistently.

It was a good couple of centuries for mortals. Then, of course, we fucked everything up.

The Cataclysm

There was a group of very clever, very wise men (why is it always men?) who called themselves Philosophers. Some considered them mystics, others thought them deluded fools, but their Philosophy afforded them undeniably real power. It is said they could disappear in one place and reappear instantly in another. It is said they were almost impossible to kill. They weren't mages; in fact they looked down on the Art as a false trail to what they called "liberation." Liberation from what? I'm not getting into that. Somebody might think it a good idea and revive the whole mad shambles.

So. The Philosophers, in pursuit of their "liberation," decided that reality itself needed to be adjusted, so that it better suited them. They started adjusting.

Think of it like this: You're sitting on a stool. You're not satisfied with your stool. Maybe it's too low. Maybe you want to rearrange the legs. So, *still sitting on your gods-damned stool*, you start hacking the legs off of it.

If the Philosophers had had some *other* reality to shift the world to while they made their "adjustments" then perhaps it might not have been so rats-in-a-bag insane. Alas, we have just the one.

Evidence suggests they did their tinkering on an island off the southwest coast of Sulamel (**Stay the Hells Away**), if you trace backwards the spread of the Cataclysm.

But what exactly was the Cataclysm? Put short, it was a loosening of the natural order. One witness's account should suffice to explain:

> *"The Cataclysm raced across the land, an unstoppable tide of unreason, first sickening and then severing every bond of nature and logic. Up became down, light became dark, the blood in your veins might turn to water or wine or molten lead. The very air might become poisonous vapor, or simply disappear, leaving countless thousands to suffocate like fish on land. You could not trust your senses. Silk could suddenly cut skin like razors. Between one moment and the next, your eyes might see something a thousand leagues or a thousand years removed. Reality itself was collapsing. Most living things died. Some became monsters. A few became dark powers, not far removed from gods."*

The Cataclysm emptied virtually the entire western portion of Sulamel. Those who fled before it mostly ended up settling around the Dragonsea, eventually giving rise to the cultures and countries we are familiar with today. This mass exodus came to be called the Diaspora.

As for those lands humanity fled: There have been several expeditions over the last hundred years or so into what most call the Empty Lands or the Silent Lands (**Stay the Hells Away**). No human civilization remains. No humans remain. Those pinnacles of civilization that still live on in legend and imagination, such as Thagoth, Hluria, and Trevell, are either gone without trace or are shattered ruins.

There has been one organized attempt to resettle the Silent Lands. Two centuries and more ago a Lucernan prince hacked out a portion of the wilderness and founded a colony. He named it Haspur. For more than a decade Haspur thrived, trading in natural resources and taming the countryside around it.

Then, overnight, every soul in Haspur disappeared. No one has the least clue what happened to them.

On those maps that bother to mark it at all, the notation reads "Ruined Haspur" (**Stay the Hells Away**).

You'd have to be mad, desperate, banished or hunted to call the Silent Lands home.

The Diaspora

The Diaspora is a nice, neat name for a very messy period in history. What records there are are generally fragmented. We know when it started, of course–the moment the Philosophers touched off the Cataclysm. But it's not as if everybody who was alive at the time just got up and headed out the door. Individuals, families, small groups, and entire nations fled at vastly different times, in every direction that was away from the danger that was engulfing the land in an unpredictable tide of chaos.

Survivors of the Cataclysm that fled eastward found accommodating lands to settle around the Dragonsea. They came in successive and overlapping waves, and by and large their strength at arms, technology and magic was far superior to the indigenous inhabitants. Those original peoples either assimilated, got pushed out, or expired. That's unpleasant, but then the truth usually is.

None of the old, pre-Cataclysm cultures survived unchanged either. Some morphed and became entirely new social constructs. Others blended and melded together, becoming hybrid cultures. A few kept the outward forms and observances that were their heritage, more or less. Generally less. Often you'll find they don't really understand the meanings or reasons for some of the more startlingly odd things they do, and if you ask them, they'll say that that's the way it's always been done. The real reason–obviously–is that people, by and large, are thought-challenged sheep.

Post-Diaspora

Right then. We've almost caught up to the present day, give or take eight centuries. If you want to delve into the minutiae of the history of every country on the Dragonsea, you've come to the wrong place. This person killed that person and became king. This country fought that country and won, then it fought another country and lost.... When you're my age, it all starts to sound like "blah blah blah people are bloodthirsty gits who never learn." If you really want to know more, say, about the Camlach occupation of the Low Countries, or the Helstrum-Elam wars, there are many thick, incredibly detailed, dusty volumes in the stacks of Lagna's temple in Lucernis. Just remember to drop a mark in the offering box. Silver is good, gold is better. And by all the dead gods, we do *not* lend out any materials. If you want a copy of something, you pay for Jessep to copy it out for you. And don't even think about trying to steal anything.

The Current Age

It's a little-known, rarely discussed, but undeniably true fact that the world is changing. The gods, rarely seen for centuries, seem to have disappeared entirely. Magic, the force that much of civilization once depended on, is increasingly being eschewed in favor of more mundane solutions to problems ranging from keeping rats out of the grain stores to killing lots of people quickly on the battlefield. Times are changing, even if people generally aren't.

Don't get me wrong. There are still lots of ghastly, dangerous beings of a supernatural bent roaming the world who would be more than happy to eat your face. Far, far too many deadly artifacts still litter the world, relics from the distant past waiting for the chance to wreak havoc once again. It's just that, for example, cities are more likely to fall from cannonade rather than the Art.

Why the change? Damned if I know. But the gods rarely get involved anymore and magic, from all indications, is on the way out. What this means for the future, I've no idea. But being a realist, I'd offer the caution that whatever comes next, it's probably not going to be rainbows and warm hugs. Good thing I'm as old as dirt and likely won't have to deal with whatever fuckery comes next.

And with that I end my incredibly brief yet inestimably useful treatise on the World and its history. You're welcome.

Oh, all right, there's a bit more I could say about the gods and religions and such. No idea why you'd want to know, but if you do, turn the page. Or don't. It's all the same to me.

THE GODS, GODDESSES, AND INFERNAL POWERS. ALSO MAGIC

There used to be so many divine and semi-divine beings running around loose you couldn't keep track of them, like cockroaches scattering in sudden light, if I'm honest. But over the millennia they did a damned fine job of thinning themselves out by making war on each other. They're just not the force that they once were. Sure, a few people still worship this or that god or goddess, but for the most part deities are only useful when you really need to let loose with some crude language. Religion, per se, isn't really a motivating force. There are exceptions, of course; adherents of the Keddy faith can be annoyingly dogmatic, and in Camlach, devotion to their Prophet of the Fields isn't just lip service. But on the whole, people lost a lot of faith in the gods when they did fuck-all, for the most part, to prevent or even moderate the effects of the Cataclysm. People *believe* in the gods, certainly, just as I believe in bedbugs. Belief doesn't automatically lead to worship.

So let's make this easy on everybody, shall we? I'll just jot down a few of those immortal beings who still have some hold on the popular imagination in one fashion or another and we can all call it a day.

Bath: God of secrets. Fate unknown. Common epithet being "tighter than Bath's arsehole."

Gorm: Peace-bringer. Got impaled for his trouble. Common epithet being "Gorm on a stick."

Isin: Goddess of love. Fate unknown. Common epithet being "Isin's (usually creamy) tits."

Kerf: Hero-maker. Fate unknown. Too many epithets to list, but balls, back, beard and staff are quite common.

Lagna: God of Knowledge. Got his head chopped off by a Low Duke of the eleven hells for knowing the solution to a supposedly impossible puzzle. Common epithet being "Lagna's reward."

Mour: Goddess of preservation. Destroyed in the Cataclysm, some say while preserving the city of Trevell. If so she did a rotten job, since Trevell is nowhere to be found. Younger sister of She who Casts Eight Shadows. No known epithets.

She Who Casts Eight Shadows: Just don't. You think you want to know, but that's because you're ignorant of the danger. Sometimes ignorance is a good thing, for example when you're eating meat from a street vendor. (Un)common epithet: "The Eightfold Bitch."

Vosto: God of fools and drunkards. Fate unknown. No common epithets; Vosto's one of the few gods that people still pray to with real devotion. Or desperation. Same difference.

As for the denizens of the lower planes, the less said the better. I'll just leave it at this: The gods and goddesses sometimes helped mortals, when it pleased or amused them to do so. The infernal powers treat mortals as food, which is what we are to them, when all is said and done. You might play with your food, but you certainly don't help it.

Other Miscellaneous Metaphysicalities

There are an unknown number of planes comprising reality. The one we inhabit is generally called the mortal plane. There is at least one and likely several planes that the gods inhabit(ed) and there are, as everyone generally knows, eleven lower planes, or hells.

The number of planes of existence could be infinite for all I know. I'm the high priest of the dead god of knowledge, but he's unavailable for questioning, being dead, and the office didn't come with any special pointy hat of omniscience.

Some gods have temples, some gods have worshipers. It doesn't seem to matter much to people whether the god is dead or not, or whether he or she answers prayers. Mostly it does no harm, I suppose. Keeps the disgruntled from rioting in the streets for the most part, and temples are good places to meet people and exchange recipes and the like. Or at least I've found them to be.

There is one kind of temple that holds no god as its patron. You can find it in most cities around the Dragonsea; the temple of the departed. The survivors of the Cataclysm needed a place to mourn all that was lost, and the temple of the departed was their answer. They're usually grim, gray places, staffed by volunteers. Generally speaking, they're one of the few religious houses that are respected. Even during times of extreme strife, they don't get violated. So if you find yourself in a city being invaded, my advice to you would be to head for one of those temples and don't come out until the smoke clears.

What else? Ah, yes. Souls. Yes, you have one. Yes, it can be destroyed. Yes, you can sell it if you're an idiot, and can find a buyer. No, I'm not going to tell you how to do that, because I'm extremely grumpy, not pathetically amoral.

Magic

And then there's magic. It comes, essentially, in three flavors. There's divine magic, which I know fuck-all about, not being a god. There's the Art, which mages employ. And then there's whatever unnatural or supernatural power bloodwitches, seers and necromancers call on to do what they do. First, let's discuss the Art.

A mage is a person, generally but not necessarily male, who is able to sense and tap into the magic that permeates the mundane world. He is a person able to use that power, generally called his well, to enforce his will upon reality and alter it. Maybe he turns a pink flower blue. Maybe he makes your head pop off and roll down the street. The only real limits to what a mage is capable of reside inside the mage himself, and boil down to three questions:

1. What change can he imagine with sufficient clarity to convince reality it should be as he wishes it?
2. How determined is he to effect that change? Put another way, is he himself utterly convinced that the change is unstoppable, inevitable, more real than the reality he wishes to replace?
3. How much power does he have to draw on, to transform that change from an imagining to an undisputed, objective fact?

If you think it's easy, give it a try. Even if you aren't a mage. Go pick a flower and try to convince yourself it's a color other than what your eyes tell you it is. Go on. This book will still be here when you return, head throbbing.

No two mages are alike, not in their will, their imagination, or the depth of their well. In a very real sense, each mage practices a completely different sort of magic from every other mage. And that, I suspect, is why they call it the Art rather than the Craft, or the Science.

As for bloodwitches, necromancers and seers, they seem to derive their uncanny powers from some source other than that which mages do. Or, if magic were a river, they dip their buckets in a different tributary. They seem to have much less control over their powers, especially seers. Necromancers tend to rely much more heavily on ritual, bric-a-brac and other external paraphernalia, though whether it's just for show is debatable.

Bloodwitches are generally but not exclusively female. Many are also necromancers and or seers, to a greater or lesser degree, but their primary power seems to involve the use and manipulation of blood, as their name would suggest. They might cleanse the poison from a dying man's blood. Or they might have put it there in the first place. They might be able to track down a missing child, say, were a drop of the child's blood kept for such an emergency (and it often is in the Low Countries). They also might make a man's blood boil in his body. Literally. Or dry it up in his veins. Or they might create a blood doll, a simulacrum of the person who had donated blood for the purpose.

There is some speculation that bloodwitches, seers and necromancers trace their lineage back to the original, indigenous people of the Dragonsea area, while those with magely power are the descendants of the people of the Diaspora. How much truth there is to such speculation, I honestly do not know, though I suspect there is something to to the notion. But one thing is certain: none of them make good enemies.

I think that about covers the metaphysical aspects of the World. What, you want to know more? At the risk of repeating myself, if you want to know more, there are may dusty tomes, etc. Temples don't keep themselves from falling down, you know. They require donations and offerings. And at Lagna's temple, you get access to the knowledge of the ages in return, rather than some feel-good singalong. Top that.

Right then. I'm old and it's time for my nap. If you want to know more and you can't find your answer in the stacks, you're perfectly welcome to write to the paunchy, middle-aged scribe who's translating this, Michael Something-foriegn-whatsit-lung, and he'll pass it along. If it's not an incredibly doltish question, I'll give you a reply. Eventually. If I don't die in my sleep between now and then.

-Lhiewyn

THE MAP

You can't navigate by it by land or sea, unless you want to end up getting very, very lost, but it gives you a good general idea of the geography of this part of the world.

If you want more accurate maps, we have a very nice collection in Lagna's temple in Lucernis. Looking is free, whatever the old man tells you. If you want a copy, however, that does cost money. He marks the ink bottles and inventories the parchment.

-Jessep

ABOUT THE AUTHOR

Michael McClung was born and raised in Texas, but now kicks around Southeast Asia. He's been a soldier, a cook, a book store manager, and a bowling alley pin boy. His first novel was published by Random House in 2003, and in 2016 he won Mark Lawrence's inaugural SPFBO contest with *The Thief Who Pulled on Trouble's Braids.*

In his spare time, he enjoys kickball, brooding and picking scabs. You cam email him at mcclungmike @ yahoo.com if you have any questions about his books. Or about kickball, brooding, or picking scabs.

Printed in Great Britain
by Amazon